THE DARKNESS THAT COMES BEFORE

The Darkness that Comes Before

The Prince of Nothing

Book One

R. Scott Bakker

PENGUIN
CANADA

PENGUIN CANADA

Published by the Penguin Group

Penguin Books, a division of Pearson Canada, 10 Alcorn Avenue, Toronto, Ontario,
   Canada M4V 3B2
Penguin Books Ltd, 80 Strand, London WC2R 0RL, England
Penguin Putnam Inc., 375 Hudson Street, New York, New York 10014, U.S.A.
Penguin Books Australia Ltd, 250 Camberwell Road, Camberwell, Victoria 3124, Australia
Penguin Books India (P) Ltd, 11, Community Centre, Panchsheel Park,
   New Delhi – 110 017, India
Penguin Books (NZ) Ltd, cnr Rosedale and Airborne Roads, Albany, Auckland 1310,
   New Zealand
Penguin Books (South Africa) (Pty) Ltd, 24 Sturdee Avenue, Rosebank 2196, South Africa

Penguin Books Ltd, Registered Offices: 80 Strand, London WC2R 0RL, England

First published 2003

10 9 8 7 6 5 4 3 2 1

Manufactured in Canada.

NATIONAL LIBRARY OF CANADA CATALOGUING IN PUBLICATION

Bakker, R. Scott (Richard Scott), 1967–
   The darkness that comes before / R. Scott Bakker.

Contents: bk. 1. The prince of nothing.
ISBN 0-14-301374-2 (bk. 1)

I. Title. II. Title: Prince of nothing.

PS8553.A3884D37   2003   C813'.6   C2003-900005-2
PR9199.4.B34D37 2003

Visit Penguin Books' website at **www.penguin.ca**

To Sharron

—◦◦◦—

before you, I never dared hope

Acknowledgments

A writer's work is solitary, which is, paradoxically, why we owe so much to others. When the threads are few, they must be strong. In light of this, I wish to thank:

My partner, Sharron O'Brien, for making this the best book it could be, and for making me a better man than I am.

My brother, Bryan Bakker, for believing in my work before there was any work to believe in.

My friend, Roger Eichorn, for his exhaustive critiques, his penetrating insights, and for his writing, which continually reminds me how it should be done.

My editor, Michael Schellenberg, for seeing possibility in disaster, for forgiving me my foul mouth, and for saying "fair enough" no matter how bad my arguments.

Everyone at Penguin Canada for being such a happy, welcoming family.

Nancy Proctor for her wonderful and indispensable diary of reader reactions.

Caitlin Sweet for her friendship and advice.

Nick Smith for opening the door, and Kyung Cho for guiding me through.

All my friends and family for their encouragement and support.

My cat, Scully, for her steadfast companionship, no matter how wee the hour.

I would also like to thank everyone who critiqued my chapters on the old DROWW, as well as the Social Sciences and Humanities Research Council of Canada for providing a working-class kid with an education he could never have afforded otherwise.

Speaking of which, I need to thank my grade seven teacher, Mr. Allen, for waking me up.

I haven't slept a wink since.

I shall never tire of underlining a concise little fact which these superstitious people are loath to admit—namely, that a thought comes when "it" wants, not when "I" want . . .

—FRIEDRICH NIETZSCHE, *BEYOND GOOD AND EVIL*

Contents

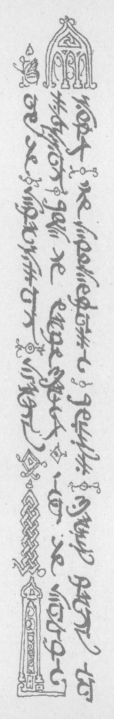

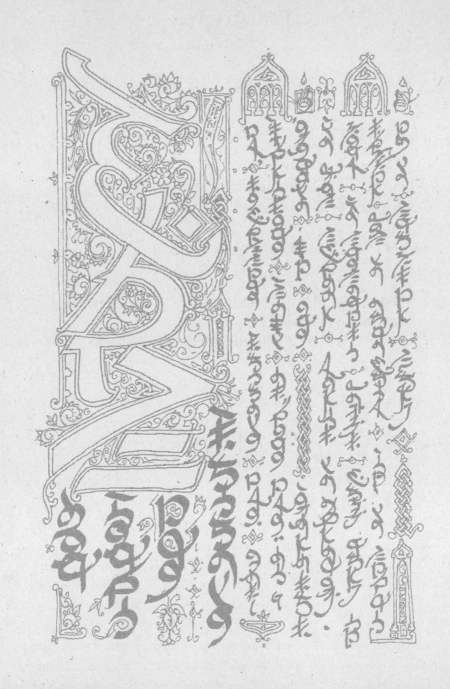

Prologue

The Wastes of Kûniüri

If it is only after that we understand what has come before, then we understand nothing. Thus we shall define the soul as follows: that which precedes everything.

—AJENCIS, *THE THIRD ANALYTIC OF MEN*

2147 Year-of-the-Tusk, the Mountains of Demua

One cannot raise walls against what has been forgotten.

The citadel of Ishuäl succumbed during the height of the Apocalypse. But no army of inhuman Sranc had scaled its ramparts. No furnace-hearted dragon had pulled down its mighty gates. Ishuäl was the secret refuge of the Kûniüric High Kings, and no one, not even the No-God, could besiege a secret.

Months earlier, Anasûrimbor Ganrelka II, High King of Kûniüri, had fled to Ishuäl with the remnants of his household. From the walls, his sentries stared pensively across the dark forests below, their thoughts stricken by memories of burning cities and wailing multitudes. When the wind moaned, they gripped Ishuäl's uncaring stone, reminded of Sranc horns. They traded breathless reassurances. Had they not eluded their pursuers? Were not the walls of

1

Ishuäl strong? Where else might a man survive the end of the world?

The plague claimed the High King first, as was perhaps fitting: Ganrelka had only wept at Ishuäl, raged the way only an Emperor of nothing could rage. The following night the members of his household carried his bier down into the forests. They glimpsed the eyes of wolves reflected in the light of his pyre. They sang no dirges, intoned only a few numb prayers.

Before the morning winds could sweep his ashes skyward, the plague had struck two others: Ganrelka's concubine and her daughter. As though pursuing his bloodline to its thinnest tincture, it assailed more and more members of his household. The sentries upon the walls became fewer, and though they still watched the mountainous horizon, they saw little. The cries of the dying crowded their thoughts with too much horror.

Soon even the sentries were no more. The five Knights of Trysë who'd rescued Ganrelka after the catastrophe on the Fields of Eleneöt lay motionless in their beds. The Grand Vizier, his golden robes stained bloody by his bowel, lay sprawled across his sorcerous texts. Ganrelka's uncle, who'd led the heartbreaking assault on Golgotterath's gates in the early days of the Apocalypse, hung from a rope in his chambers, slowly twisting in a draft. The Queen stared endlessly across festering sheets.

Of all those who had fled to Ishuäl, only Ganrelka's bastard son and the Bardic Priest survived.

Terrified by the Bard's strange manner and one white eye, the young boy hid, venturing out only when his hunger became unbearable. The old Bard continually searched for him, singing ancient songs of love and battle, but slurring the words in blasphemous ways. "Why won't you show yourself, child?" he would cry as he reeled through the galleries. "Let me sing to you. Woo you with secret songs. Let me share the glory of what once was!"

One night the Bard caught the boy. He caressed first his cheek and then his thigh. "Forgive me," he muttered over and over, but tears fell only from his blind eye. "There are no crimes," he mumbled afterward, "when no one is left alive."

But the boy lived. Five nights later, he lured the Bardic Priest onto Ishuäl's towering walls. When the man shambled by in a drunken stupor, he pushed him from the heights. He crouched for a long while at the fall's edge, staring down through the gloom at the Bard's broken corpse. It differed from the others, he decided, only in that it was still wet. Was it murder when no one was left alive?

Winter added its cold to the emptiness of Ishuäl. Propped on the battlements, the child would listen to the wolves sing and feud through the dark forests. He would pull his arms from his sleeves and hug his body against the chill, murmuring his dead mother's songs and savouring the wind's bite on his cheek. He would fly through the courtyards, answering the wolves with Kûniüric war cries, brandishing weapons that staggered him with their weight. And once in a while, his eyes wide with hope and superstitious dread, he would poke the dead with his father's sword.

When the snows broke, shouts brought him to Ishuäl's forward gate. Peering through dark embrasures, he saw a group of cadaverous men and women—refugees of the Apocalypse. Glimpsing his shadow, they cried out for food, shelter, anything, but the boy was too terrified to reply. Hardship had made them look fearsome—feral, like a wolf people.

When they began scaling the walls, he fled to the galleries. Like the Bardic Priest, they searched for him, calling out guarantees of his safety. Eventually, one of them found him cringing behind a barrel of sardines. With a voice neither tender nor harsh, he said: "We are Dûnyain, child. What reason could you have to fear us?"

But the boy clutched his father's sword, crying, "So long as men live, there are crimes!"

The man's eyes filled with wonder. "No, child," he said. "Only so long as men are deceived."

For a moment, the young Anasûrimbor could only stare at him. Then solemnly, he set aside his father's sword and took the stranger's hand. "I was a prince," he mumbled.

The stranger brought him to the others, and together they celebrated their strange fortune. They cried out—not to the Gods they had repudiated but to one another—that here was evident a great correspondence of cause. Here awareness most holy could be tended. In Ishuäl, they had found shelter against the end of the world.

Still emaciated but wearing the furs of kings, the Dûnyain chiselled the sorcerous runes from the walls and burned the Grand Vizier's books. The jewels, the chalcedony, the silk and cloth-of-gold, they buried with the corpses of a dynasty.

And the world forgot them for two thousand years.

Nonmen, Sranc, and Men:
The first forgets,
The third regrets,
And the second has all of the fun.

—ANCIENT KÛNIÜRI NURSERY RHYME

This is a history of a great and tragic holy war, of the mighty factions that sought to possess and pervert it, and of a son searching for his father. And as with all histories, it is we, the survivors, who will write its conclusion.

—DRUSAS ACHAMIAN, *COMPENDIUM OF THE FIRST HOLY WAR*

Late Autumn, 4109 Year-of-the-Tusk, the Mountains of Demua

Again the dreams had come.

Vast landscapes, histories, contests of faith and culture, all glimpsed in cataracts of detail. Horses skidding to earth. Fists clenching mud. Dead strewn on the shore of a warm sea. And as always, an ancient city, chalk dry in the sun, rising against dun hills. A holy city . . . *Shimeh*.

And then the voice, thin as though spoken through the reed throat of a serpent, saying, "*Send to me my son.*"

The dreamers awoke as one, gasping, struggling to wrest sense from impossibility. Following the protocol established after the first dreams, they found each other in the unlit depths of the Thousand Thousand Halls.

Such desecration, they determined, could no longer be tolerated.

Climbing pitted mountain trails, Anasûrimbor Kellhus leaned on his knee and turned to look at the monastic citadel. Ishuäl's ramparts towered above a screen of spruce and larches, only to be dwarfed by the rutted mountain slopes beyond.

Did you see it thus, Father? Did you turn and look for one last time?

Distant figures filed between the battlements before disappearing behind stone—the elder Dûnyain abandoning their vigil. They would wind down the mighty staircases, Kellhus knew, and one by one enter the darkness of the Thousand Thousand Halls, the great Labyrinth that wheeled through the depths beneath Ishuäl. There they would die, as had been decided. All those his father had polluted.

I'm alone. My mission is all that remains.

He turned from Ishuäl and continued climbing through the forest. The mountain breeze was bitter with the smell of bruised pine.

By late afternoon he passed the timberline, and after two days of scaling glacial slopes he crested the roof of the Demua Mountains. On the far side of the range, the forests of what once had been called Kûniüri extended beneath scudding clouds. How many vistas such as this, he wondered, must he cross before he found his father? How many ravine-creased horizons must he exchange before he arrived at Shimeh?

Shimeh will be my home. I shall dwell in my father's house.

Descending granite escarpments, he entered the wilderness.

He wandered through the gloom of the forest interior, through galleries pillared by mighty redwoods and hushed by the overlong absence of men. He tugged his cloak through thickets and negotiated the fierce rush of mountain streams.

Though the forests below Ishuäl had been much the same, Kellhus found himself unsettled for some reason. He paused in an attempt to regain his composure, using ancient techniques to impose discipline on his intellect. The forest was quiet, gentle with birdsong. And yet he could hear thunder . . .

Something is happening to me. Is this the first trial, Father?

He found a stream marbled by brilliant sunlight and knelt at its edge. The water he drew to his lips was more replenishing, more sweet, than any water he had tasted before. But how could water taste sweet? How could sunlight, broken across the back of rushing waters, be so *beautiful?*

What comes before determines what comes after. Dûnyain monks spent their lives immersed in the study of this principle, illuminating the intangible mesh of cause and effect that determined every happenstance and minimizing all that was wild and unpredictable. Because of this, events always unfolded with granitic certainty in Ishuäl. More often than not, one knew the skittering course a leaf would take through the terrace groves. More often than not, one knew what another would say before he spoke. To grasp what came before was to know what would come after. And to know what would come after was the beauty that stilled, the hallowed communion of intellect and circumstance—the gift of the Logos.

Kellhus's first true surprise, apart from the formative days of his childhood, had been this mission. Until then, his life had been a premeditated ritual of study, conditioning, and comprehension. Everything was grasped. Everything was understood. But now, walking through the forests of lost Kûniüri, it seemed that the world plunged and he stood still. Like earth in rushing waters, he was battered by an endless succession of surprises: the thin warble of an unknown bird; burrs in his cloak from an unknown weed; a snake winding through a sunlit clearing, searching for unknown prey.

The dry slap of wings would pass overhead and he would pause, taking a different step. A mosquito would land on his cheek, and he would slap at it, only to have his eyes drawn to a different configuration of tree. His surroundings inhabited him, possessed him, until he was moved by all things at once—the creak of limbs, the endless permutations of water over stones. These things wracked him with the strength of tides.

On the afternoon of the seventeenth day, a twig lodged itself between his sandal and his foot. He held it against storm-piled clouds and studied it, became lost in its shape, in the path it travelled through the open air—the thin, muscular branchings that seized so much emptiness from the sky. Had it simply fallen into this shape, or had it been cast, a mould drained of its wax? He looked up and saw one sky plied by the infinite forking of branches. Was there not one way to grasp one sky? He was unaware of how long he stood there, but it was dark before the twig slipped from his fingers.

On the morning of the twenty-ninth day, he crouched on rocks green with moss and watched salmon leap and pitch against a rushing river. The sun rose and set three times before his thoughts escaped this inexplicable war of fish and waters.

In the worst moments his arms would be vague as shadow against shadow, and the rhythm of his walk would climb far ahead of him. His mission became the last remnant of what he had once been. Otherwise he was devoid of intellect, oblivious to the principles of the Dûnyain. Like a sheet of parchment exposed to the elements, each day saw more words stolen from him—until only one imperative remained: *Shimeh . . . I must find my father in Shimeh.*

He continued wandering south, through the foothills of the Demua. His dispossession deepened, until he no longer oiled his sword after being wetted by the rain, until he no longer slept or ate. There was only wilderness, the walk, and the passing days. At night he would take animal comfort in the dark and cold.

Shimeh. Please, Father.

On the forty-third day, he waded across a shallow river and clambered onto banks black with ash. Weeds crowded the char blanketing the ground, but nothing else. Like blackened spears, dead trees spiked the sky. He picked his way through the debris, stung by weeds where they brushed his bare skin. Finally he gained the summit of a ridge.

The immensity of the valley below struck Kellhus breathless. Beyond the fire's desolation, where the forest was still dark and crowded, ancient fortifications loomed above the trees, forming a great ring across the autumnal distances. He watched birds wheel over and around the nearer ramparts, flash across stretches of mottled stone before dipping into the canopy. Ruined walls. So cold, and so forlorn, in a way the forest could never be.

The ruins were far too old to contradict the forest outright. They had been submerged, worn and unbalanced by ages of its weight. Sheltered in mossy hollows, walls breached earthen mounds, only to suddenly end, as though restrained by vines that wrapped them like great veins over bone.

But there was something in them, something not *now*, that bent Kellhus toward unfamiliar passions. When he brushed his hands across the stone, he knew he touched the breath and toil of Men—the mark of a destroyed people.

The ground wheeled. He leaned forward and pressed his cheek against the stone. Grit, and the cold of uncovered earth. Above, the sunlight was broken by a span of knotted branches. Men . . . here in the stone. Old and untouched by the rigour of the Dûnyain. Somehow they had resisted the sleep, had raised the work of hands against the wilderness.

Who built this place?

Kellhus wandered over the mounds, sensing the ruins buried beneath. He ate sparingly from his forgotten satchel—dried wafers and acorns. He peeled leaves from the surface of a small pool of rainwater, drank, then stared curiously at the dark reflection of his own face, at the growth of blond hair across his scalp and jaw.

Is this me?

He studied squirrels and those birds he could pick from the dim confusion of the trees. Once he glimpsed a fox slipping through the brush.

I am not one more animal.

His intellect flailed, found purchase, and grasped. He could sense wild cause sweep around him in statistical tides. Touch him and leave him untouched.

I am a man. I stand apart from these things.

As evening waxed, it began to rain. Through branches he watched the clouds build chill and grey. For the first time in weeks, he sought shelter.

He picked his way into a small gully where erosion had caused a sheaf of earth to fall away, revealing the stone facade of some structure. He climbed over the leafy clay into an opening, dark and deep. Inside he broke the neck of the wild dog that attacked him.

He was familiar with darkness. Light had been forbidden in the depths of the Labyrinth. But there was no mathematical insight in the cramped blackness he found, only a random jumble of earth-pinched walls. Anasûrimbor Kellhus stretched out and slept.

When he awoke the forest was quiet with snow.

The Dûnyain had no real knowledge of just how far Shimeh lay. They had merely provided him with as many provisions as he could efficiently carry. His satchel grew flimsier with the days. Kellhus could only passively observe as hunger and exposure wracked his body.

If the wilderness could not possess him, it would kill him.

His food ran out, and he continued to walk. Everything—experience, analysis—became mysteriously sharp. More snow came, and cold, harsh winds. He walked until he could no longer.

The way is too narrow, Father. Shimeh is too far.

———— ⬦ ————

The trapper's sled dogs yelped and nosed through the snow. He pulled them away and fastened their harness to the base of a stunted pine. Astonished, he brushed the snow away from the limbs curling beneath. His first thought was to feed the dead man to his dogs. The wolves would have him otherwise, and meat was scarce in the abandoned north.

He removed his mittens and placed his fingertips against the bearded cheek. The skin was grey, and he was certain the face would be as cold as the snow that half buried it. It was not. He cried out, and his dogs responded with a chorus of howls. He cursed, then countered with the sign of Husyelt, the Dark Hunter. The limbs were slack when he lifted the man from the snow. His wool and hair were stiff in the wind.

The world had always been strange with significance to the trapper, but now it had become terrifying. Running as the dogs pulled the sled, he fled before the wrath of the encroaching blizzard.

———— ⬦ ————

"Leweth," the man had said, placing a hand to his naked chest. His cropped hair was silver with a hint of bronze and far too fine to adequately frame his thick features. His eyebrows seemed perpetually arched in surprise, and his restless eyes were given to excuses, always feigning interest in trivial details to avoid his ward's watchful gaze.

Only later, after learning the rudiments of Leweth's language, did Kellhus discover how he'd come to be in the trapper's care. His first memories were of sweaty furs and smouldering fires. Animal pelts hung in sheaves from a low ceiling. Sacks and casks heaped the corners of a single room. The smell of smoke, grease, and rot crowded what little open space remained. As Kellhus would later learn, the chaotic interior of the cabin was actually an expression, and a painstaking one at that, of the trapper's many superstitious fears. Each thing had its place, he would tell Kellhus, and those things out of place portended disaster.

The hearth was large enough to hug all the interior, including Kellhus himself, in golden warmth. Beyond the walls, winter whistled through trackless leagues of forest, ignoring them for the most part, but periodically shaking the cabin hard enough to rock the furs on their hooks. The land was called Sobel, Leweth would tell him, the northernmost province of the ancient city of Atrithau—although it had been abandoned for generations. He preferred, he would say, to live far from the troubles of other men.

Though Leweth was a sturdy man of middle years, for Kellhus he was little more than a child. The fine musculature of his face was utterly untrained, bound as though by strings to his passions. Whatever moved Leweth's soul moved his expression as well, and after a short time Kellhus needed only to glance at his face to know his thoughts. The ability to anticipate his thoughts, to re-enact the movements of Leweth's soul as though they were his own, would come later.

In the meantime a routine developed. At dawn Leweth harnessed his dogs and left to check his runs. On the days he returned early, he enlisted Kellhus to mend snares, prepare skins, draw up a new pot of cony stew—to "earn his keep," as he put it. At night Kellhus worked, as the trapper had taught him, on stitching his own coat and leggings. Leweth would watch from across the fire, his hands living an arcane life of their own, carving, stitching, or simply straining against each other—small labours that paradoxically gifted him with patience, even grace.

Kellhus saw Leweth's hands at rest only when he slept or was extraordinarily drunk. Drink, more than anything else, defined the trapper.

Through the morning, Leweth never looked Kellhus in the eye, acknowledging him only at nervous angles. A curious halfness deadened the man, as though his thought lacked the momentum to become speech. If he spoke at all, his voice was tight, constricted by an ambient dread. By afternoon, a flush would have crept into his expression. His eyes would flare with brittle sunshine. He would smile, laugh. But by dark, his manner would be bloated, a distorted parody of what it had been just hours earlier. He would bludgeon his way through conversation, would be overcome by squalls of rage and bitter humour.

Kellhus learned much from Leweth's drink-exaggerated passions, but the time came when he could no longer allow his study to trade in caricatures. One night he rolled the casks of whisky out into the forest and drained them across the frozen ground. During the suffering that followed, he carried on with the chores.

They sat facing each other across the hearth, their backs against cozy heaps of animal pelts. His expression etched by firelight, Leweth talked, animated by the honest vanity of sharing his life with someone who was captive to the facts as he described them. Old pains returned in the telling.

"I had no choice but to leave Atrithau," Leweth admitted, speaking yet again of his dead wife.

Kellhus smiled sorrowfully. He gauged the subtle interplay of muscles beneath the man's expression. *He pretends to mourn in order to secure my pity.*

"Atrithau reminded you of her absence?" *This is the lie he tells himself.*

Leweth nodded, his eyes at once tear-filled and expectant. "Atrithau seemed a tomb after she died. One morning they called the muster for the militia to man the walls, and I remember staring off to the north. The forests seemed to . . . beckon me somehow. The terror of my childhood had become a sanctuary! Everyone in the city, even my brothers and my compatriots in the district cohort, seemed to secretly exult in her death—in my misery! I had to . . . I was *forced* to . . ."

Avenge yourself.

Leweth looked down to the fire. "Flee," he said.

Why does he deceive himself in this way?

"No soul moves alone through the world, Leweth. Our every thought stems from the thoughts of others. Our every word is but a repetition of words spoken before. Every time we listen, we allow the movements of another soul to carry our own." He paused, cutting short his reply in order to bewilder the man. Insight struck with so much more force when it clarified confusion. "This is truly why you fled to Sobel, Leweth."

For an instant Leweth's eyes slackened in horror. "But I don't understand . . ."

Of everything I might say, he fears most the truths he already knows and yet denies. Are all world-born men this weak?

"But you *do* understand. Think, Leweth. If we're nothing more than our thoughts and passions, and if our thoughts and passions are nothing more than movements of our souls, then we are nothing more than those who move us. Who you once were, Leweth, ceased to exist the moment your wife died."

"And that's why I fled!" Leweth cried, his eyes both beseeching and provoked. "I couldn't bear it. I fled to *forget!*"

Flare in his pulse rate. Hesitation in the flex of delicate muscles about his eyes. *He knows this is a lie.*

"No, Leweth. You fled to *remember*. You fled to conserve all the ways your wife had moved you, to shield the ache of her loss from the momentum of others. You fled to make a bulwark of your misery."

Tears spilled across the trapper's sagging cheeks. "Ah, cruel words, Kellhus! Why would you say such things?"

To better possess you.

"Because you've suffered long enough. You've spent years alone by this fire, wallowing in your loss, asking your dogs over and over whether they love you. You hoard your pain because the more you suffer, the more the world becomes an outrage. You weep because weeping has become evidence. 'See what you've done to me!' you cry. And you hold court night after night, condemning the circum-stances that have condemned you by reliving your anguish. You torment yourself, Leweth, in order to hold the world accountable for your torment."

Again he'll deny me—

"And what if I do? The world *is* an outrage, Kellhus. An *outrage!*"

"Perhaps it is," Kellhus replied, his tone one of pity and regret, "but the world has long ceased to be the author of your anguish. How many times have you cried out these very words? And each time they've been cramped by the same desperation, the despera-tion of one who needs to believe something he knows to be false. Only pause, Leweth, refuse to follow the grooves these thoughts have worn into you. *Pause*, and you'll see."

His thoughts forced inward, Leweth hesitated, his face stunned and slack.

He understands but lacks the courage to admit.

"Ask yourself," Kellhus pressed, "why this desperation?"

"There's no desperation," Leweth replied numbly.

He sees the place I've opened for him, realizes the futility of all lies in my presence, even those he tells himself.

"Why do you continue to lie?"

"Because . . . because . . ."

Through the wheeze of the fire, Kellhus could hear the pounding of Leweth's heart, fevered like that of a trapped animal. Sobs shud-dered through the man. He raised his hands to bury his face but then paused. He looked up to Kellhus and wept the way a child might before his mother. *It hurts!* his expression cried. *It hurts so much!*

"I know it hurts, Leweth. Release from anguish can be purchased only through more anguish." *So much like a child . . .*

"W-what should I do?" the trapper wept. "Kellhus . . . Please tell me!"

Thirty years, Father. What power you must wield over men such as this.

And Kellhus, his bearded face warm with firelight and compassion, answered: "No one's soul moves alone, Leweth. When one love dies, one must learn to love another."

———— ∽∽∽∽ ————

After a time the hearth fire burned low, and the two of them sat silently, listening to the gathering fury of yet another storm. The wind sounded like mighty blankets flapping against the walls. Outside the forest groaned and whistled beneath the dark belly of the blizzard.

"Weeping may muddy the face," Leweth said, broaching their silence with an old proverb, "but it does cleanse the heart."

Kellhus smiled in reply, his expression one of bemused recognition. Why, the ancient Dûnyain had asked, confine the passions to words when they spoke first in expression? A legion of faces lived within him, and he could slip through them with the same ease with which he crafted his words. At the heart of his jubilant smile, his compassionate laugh, flexed the cold of scrutiny.

"But you distrust it," Kellhus said.

Leweth shrugged. "Why, Kellhus? Why would the Gods send you to me?"

For Leweth, Kellhus knew, the world was fraught with gods, ghosts, even demons. It was steeped in their conspiracies, crowded with omens and portents of their capricious humours. Like a second horizon, their designs encompassed the struggles of men— shrouded, cruel, and in the end, always fatal.

For Leweth, discovering him beneath the snowdrifts of Sobel was no accident.

"You wish to know why I've come?"

"Why have you come?"

So far Kellhus had avoided any talk of his mission, and Leweth, terrified by the speed with which he had recovered and learned his language, had not asked. But the study had progressed.

"I search for my father, Moënghus," Kellhus said. "Anasûrimbor Moënghus."

"Is he lost?" Leweth asked, gratified beyond measure by this admission.

"No. He left my people long ago, while I was still a child."

"Then why do you search for him?"

"Because he sent for me. He asked that I journey to see him."

Leweth nodded, as though all sons must return to their fathers at some point. "Where is he?"

Kellhus paused for a heartbeat, his eyes apparently fixed upon Leweth, but actually focused on an empty point before him. As a cold man might curl into a ball, gather as much skin as possible into his arms and away from the world, Kellhus withdrew his surfaces from the room and sheltered within his intellect, unmoved by the press of outer events. The legions within were yoked, the variables isolated and extended, and the welter of possible consequences that might follow upon a truthful answer to Leweth's question bloomed through his soul. The probability trance.

He rose, blinked against the firelight. As with so many questions regarding his mission, the answer was incalculable.

"Shimeh," Kellhus said at length. "A city far to the south called Shimeh."

"He sent for you from *Shimeh?* But how's that possible?"

Kellhus adopted a faintly bewildered look that was not far from true. "Through dreams. He sent for me through dreams."

"Sorcery . . ."

Always the curious intermingling of awe and dread when Leweth uttered this word. There were witches, Leweth had told him, whose urgings could harness the wild agencies asleep in earth, animal, and tree. There were priests whose pleas could sound the Outside, move the Gods who moved the world to give men respite. And there were sorcerers whose assertions were decrees, whose words dictated rather than described how the world had to be.

Superstition. Everywhere and in everything, Leweth had confused that which came after with that which came before, confused the effect for the cause. Men came after, so he placed them before and called them "gods" or "demons." Words came after, so he placed them before and called them "scriptures" or "incantations." Confined to the aftermath of events and blind to the causes that preceded him, he merely fastened upon the ruin itself, men and the acts of men, as the model of what came before.

But what came before, the Dûnyain had learned, was inhuman. *There must be some other explanation. There is no sorcery.*

"What do you know of Shimeh?" Kellhus asked.

The walls shivered beneath a fierce succession of gusts, and the flame twirled with abrupt incandescence. The hanging pelts lightly rocked to and fro. Leweth looked about, his brow furrowed, as though he strained to hear someone.

"It's a long way off, Kellhus, through dangerous lands."

"Shimeh is not . . . holy for you?"

Leweth smiled. Like places too near, places too far could never be holy. "I've heard the name only a few times before," he said. "The Sranc own the North. The few Men who remain are endlessly besieged, bound to the cities of Atrithau and Sakarpus. We know little of the Three Seas."

"The Three Seas?"

"The nations of the South," Leweth replied, his eyes rounded in wonder. He found his ignorance, Kellhus knew, godlike. "You mean you've never heard of the Three Seas?"

"As isolated as your people are, mine are far more so."

Leweth nodded sagely. Finally, it was his turn to speak of profound things. "The Three Seas were young when the North was destroyed by the No-God and his Consult. Now that we're but a shadow, they're the seat of power for Men." He paused, disheartened by how quickly his knowledge had failed him. "I know little more than that—save a handful of names."

"Then how did you learn of Shimeh?"

"I once sold ermine to a man from the caravans. A dark-skinned man. A Ketyai. Never saw a dark-skinned man before."

"Caravans?" Kellhus had never heard the word before, but he spoke it as though he wanted to know which caravan the trapper referred to.

"Every year a caravan from the south arrives in Atrithau—if it survives the Sranc, that is. It travels from a land called Galeoth by way of Sakarpus, bringing spices, silks—wondrous things, Kellhus! Have you ever tasted pepper?"

"What did this dark-skinned man tell you of Shimeh?"

"Not much, really. He spoke mostly about his religion. Said he was Inrithi, a follower of the Latter Prophet, Inri"—his brows knotted for a moment—"something or another. Can you imagine? A *latter* prophet?" Leweth paused, eyes unfocused, struggling to render the episode in words. "He kept saying that I was damned unless I submit to his prophet and open my heart to the Thousand Temples—I'll never forget that name."

"So Shimeh was holy to this man?"

"The holiest of holies. It was the city of his prophet long ago. But there was some kind of problem, I think. Something about wars and about heathens having taken it from the Inrithi—" Leweth halted, as though struck by something of peculiar significance. "In the Three Seas *Men* war with *Men*, Kellhus, and care nothing for the Sranc. Can you imagine?"

"So Shimeh is a holy city in the hands of a heathen people?"

"All for the best, I think," Leweth replied, abruptly bitter. "The dog kept calling *me* a heathen as well."

They continued talking of distant lands far into the night. The wind howled and battered the sturdy walls of their cabin. And in the gloom of a faltering fire, Anasûrimbor Kellhus slowly drew Leweth into his own descending rhythms—slower breath, drowsy eyes. When the trapper was fully entranced, he peeled away his last secrets, hunted him until no refuge remained.

Alone, Kellhus snowshoed through frigid stands of spruce and toward the nearest of the heights that surrounded the trapper's cabin. Snowdrifts scrawled around the dark trunks. The air smelled of winter silence.

Kellhus had refashioned himself over the past several weeks. The forest was no longer the stupefying cacophony it had once been. Sobel was a land of winter caribou, sable, beaver, and marten. Amber slumbered in her ground. Bare stone lay clean beneath her sky, and her lakes were silver with fish. There was nothing more, nothing worthy of awe or dread.

Before him, the snow fell away from a shallow cliff. Kellhus stared up, searching for the path that would see the heights yield to him most readily. He climbed.

Except for a few stunted and leafless hawthorns, the summit was clear. At its centre stood an ancient stele—a stone shaft leaning against the distance. Runes and small graven figures pitted all four sides. What drew Kellhus here, time and again, was not merely the language of the graven text—aside from the idiom, it was indistinguishable from his own—but the *name* of its author.

It began,

And I, Anasûrimbor Celmomas II, look from this place and witness the glory worked by my hand . . .

and continued to catalogue a great battle between long-dead kings. According to Leweth, this land had once been the frontier of two nations: Kûniüri and Eämnor, both lost millennia ago in mythical wars against what Leweth called "the No-God." As with many of Leweth's stories, Kellhus dismissed his tales of the Apocalypse outright. But the name Anasûrimbor engraved in ancient diorite was something he could not dismiss. The world, he now understood, was far older than the Dûnyain. And if his bloodline extended as far as this dead High King, then so was he.

But such thoughts were irrelevant to his mission. His study of Leweth was drawing to conclusion. Soon he would have to continue south to Atrithau, where Leweth had insisted he could secure further means of travelling to Shimeh.

From the heights, Kellhus looked south across the winter forests. Ishuäl lay somewhere behind him, hidden in the glacial mountains. Before him lay a pilgrimage through a world of men bound by arbitrary custom, by the endless repetition of tribal lies. He would come to them as one *awake*. He would shelter in the hollows of their ignorance, and through truth he would make them his instruments. He was Dûnyain, one of the Conditioned, and he would possess all peoples, all circumstances. He would come before.

But another Dûnyain awaited him, one who had studied the wilderness far longer: Moënghus.

How great is your power, Father?

Turning from the panorama, he noticed something odd. On the far side of the stele he saw tracks in the snow. He studied them momentarily before resolving to ask the trapper about them. Their author had walked upright but had not been quite human.

———— ∞ ————

"They look like this," Kellhus said. With a bare finger he quickly pressed a replica of the track in the snow.

Leweth watched him, his manner stern. Kellhus needed only to glance at him to see the horror he tried to hide. In the background, the dogs yelped, trotted circles at the ends of their leather leashes.

"Where?" Leweth asked, staring intently at the strange track.

"The old Kûniüric stele. They move at a tangent to the cabin, to the northwest."

The bearded face turned to him. "And you don't know what these tracks are?"

The significance of the question was plain. *You're from the north, and you don't know these?* Then Kellhus understood.

"Sranc," he said.

The trapper looked beyond him, sifting through the surrounding wall of trees. The monk registered the flutter in the man's bowels, his quickening heartbeat and the litany of his thoughts, too quick to be a question: *What-do-we-do-what-do-we-do . . .*

"We should follow the tracks," Kellhus said. "Make sure they don't cross your runs. If they do . . ."

"It's been a hard winter for them," Leweth said. He needed to wring some significance from his terror. "They've come south for food . . . They hunt food. Yes, food."

"And if not?"

Leweth glanced at him, eyes wild. "For Sranc, Men are a sustenance of a different sort. They hunt us to calm the madness of their hearts." He stepped among his dogs, was distracted by their accumulation around his legs. "Quiet, shh, quiet." He slapped their ribs, pressed their chins to the snow by vigorously rubbing the backs of their heads. His arms swung wide and randomly, dispensing his affection among them equally.

"Could you bring me the muzzles, Kellhus?"

The trail was thin and grey through the drifts. The sky darkened. Winter evenings brought a strange hush to the interior of the forest, the sense that something greater than daylight was drawing to conclusion. They had run far in their snowshoes, and now they stopped.

They stood beneath the desolate limbs of an oak.

"We shouldn't return," Kellhus said.

"But we can't leave the dogs."

The monk watched Leweth for several breaths. Their exhalations fell on hard air. He could easily dissuade the trapper, he knew, from returning for anything. Whatever it was they followed knew of the runs, and perhaps even of the cabin itself. But tracks in the snow—empty marks—were far too little for him to use. For Kellhus the threat existed only in the fear manifested by the trapper. The forest was still his.

Kellhus turned and together they made for the cabin, running with the shambling grace of snowshoes. But after a short distance, Kellhus halted the man with a firm hand on his shoulder.

"What—" the trapper began to ask, but he was silenced by the sounds.

A chorus of muffled howls and shrieks perforated the quiet. A single yelp pierced the hollows, followed by dread, wintry silence.

Leweth stood as still as the dark trees. "Why, Kellhus?" His voice cracked.

"There's no time for why. We must flee."

--------⊗--------

Kellhus sat in ashen gloom, watching the dawn's rosy fingers poke through thickets of branch and dark pine. Leweth still slept.

We've run hard, Father, but have we run hard enough?

He saw something. A movement quickly obscured by the forest depths.

"Leweth," he said.

The trapper stirred. "What?" the man said, coughing. "It's still dark."

Another figure. Farther to the left. Closing.

Kellhus remained still, his eyes lost in explorations of the wooded recesses. "They come," he said.

Leweth bent forward from his frozen blankets. His face was ashen. Bewildered, he followed Kellhus's gaze into the surrounding gloom. "I see nothing."

"They move with stealth."

Leweth began shivering.

"Run," Kellhus said.

Leweth stared at him in astonishment. "Run? The Sranc run down everything, Kellhus. You don't flee them. They're too fast!"

"I know," Kellhus replied. "I'll remain here. Slow them."

--------⊗--------

Leweth could only stare at him. He could not move. The trees thundered about him. The sky tugged with its emptiness. Then an arrow jutted through his shoulder and he fell to his knees, stared at the red tip protruding from his breast. *"Kellllhuuss!"* he gasped.

But Kellhus was gone. Leweth rolled in the snow, searching for him, found him sprinting through the near trees, a sword in his hand. The first of the Sranc was beheaded, and the monk moved, moved like a pale wraith through the drifts. Another died, its knife sketching uselessly through open air. The others closed upon Kellhus like leathery shadows.

"Kellhus!" Leweth cried, perhaps out of anguish, perhaps hoping to draw them away, toward one who was already dead. *I would die for you.*

But the forms fell, clutching themselves in the snow, and a weird, inhuman howl rifled through the trees. More fell, until only the tall monk was left.

Far away, the trapper thought he heard his dogs barking.

⸻

Kellhus pulled him along. Points of snow winked in the rising sun as they crashed through the thickets. Leweth felt cramped around the agony in his shoulder, but the monk was relentless, yanked him to a pace he could scarcely have managed uninjured. They blundered through drifts, around trees, half tumbled into ravines and clawed their way out again. The monk and his arms were always there, a thin rack of iron that propped him again and again.

He still thought he could hear dogs.

My dogs . . .

At last he was thrown against a tree. The tree behind him felt a pillar of stone, a prop to die against. He could scarcely distinguish Kellhus, his beard and hood clotted with ice, from the canopy of bare branches.

"Leweth," Kellhus was saying, *"you must think!"*

Cruel words! They grasped him to clarity, thrust him against his anguish. "My dogs," he sobbed. "I hear . . . them."

The blue eyes acknowledged nothing.

"More Sranc come," Kellhus said between laboured breaths. "We need shelter. A place to hide."

Leweth rolled his head back, swallowed at the spike of pain in the back of his throat, tried to gather himself. "What . . . what direction have w-we c-come?"

"South. Always south."

Leweth pushed himself from the tree, hugged the monk's shoulders. He was seized by uncontrollable shivers. He coughed and peered through the trees. "How many st-streams"—he sucked air—"streams have we cr-crossed?"

He felt the heat of Kellhus's breath.

"Five."

"Wessst!" he gasped. He leaned back to look into the monk's face, still clutching him. He did not feel shame. There was no shame with this man. "W-we must g-go west," he continued, putting his forehead to the monk's lips. "Ruins. Ruins. N-Nonmen ruins. Many places to h-h-hide." He groaned. The world wheeled. "You c-can see it a sh-short distance fr-from here."

Leweth felt snowy ground slam into his body. Stunned, all he could do was curl into his knees. Through the trees he saw Kellhus's figure, distorted by tears, recede amidst the trees.

No-no-no.

He sobbed. "Kellhus? *Kelllhuuss!*"

What's happening?

"*Nooo!*" he shrieked.

The tall figure vanished.

The slope was treacherous. Kellhus hauled himself up by grasping limbs and securing his step in the deadfalls beneath the snow. The conifers begrudged any clear path across the pitched ground. Radial scaffolds of branches tore at him. A gloom unlike the pale of winter thatched his surroundings.

When he at last climbed free of the forest, the monk scowled at the sky and found himself stilled by the vista above him. Snow-covered, the ground rose with the hungry contours of a dog. The ruins of a gate and a wall towered over the nearer slopes. Beyond it, a dead oak of immense proportions bent against the sky.

Rain fell from dark clouds scrolling over the summit, froze against his coats.

Kellhus was astonished by the great stones of the gate. Many had a girth as huge as the oak they obscured. An uplifted face had been hewn from the lintel—blank eyes, as patient as sky. He passed beneath. The ground levelled somewhat. Behind him, the expanses of forest grew dim in the gathering rain. But the noise grew louder.

The tree had been long dead. Its colossal tendons were husked of their bark, and its limbs extended into the air like winding tusks. Stripped of its detail, the wind and rain sluiced through it with ease.

He turned as the Sranc broke from the bush, howling as they loped across the snow.

So clear, this place. Arrows hissed by him. He picked one from the air and studied it. Warm, as though it had been pressed against skin. Then his sword was in his hand, and it glittered through the space around him, seizing it like the branches of a tree. They came—a dark rush—and he was *there* before them, poised in the one moment they could not foresee. A calligraphy of cries. The thud of aston-ished flesh. He speared the ecstasy from their inhuman faces, stepped among them and snuffed out their beating hearts.

They could not see that circumstance was holy. They only hungered. He, on the other hand, was one of the Conditioned, Dûnyain, and all events yielded to him.

They fell back, and the howling subsided. They thronged for a moment around him—narrow shoulders and dog-shaped chests, stinking leather and necklaces of human teeth. He stood patient before their menace. Tranquil.

They fled.

He bent to one that still squirmed at his feet, lifting it by its throat. The beautiful face contorted with fury.

"*Kuz'inirishka dazu daka gurankas. . .*"

It spat at him. He nailed it to the tree with his sword. He stepped back. It shrieked, flailed.

What are these creatures?

A horse snorted behind him, stamped at the snow and ice. Kellhus retrieved his sword and whirled.

Through the sleet, the horse and rider were mere grey shapes. Kellhus watched their slow approach, standing his ground, his shaggy hair frozen into little tusks that clicked in the wind. The horse was large, some eighteen hands, and black. Its rider was draped in a long grey cloak stitched with faint patterns—abstracts of faces. He wore an uncrested helm that obscured his countenance. A powerful voice rang out, in Kûniüric:

"I can see that you're not to be killed."

Kellhus was silent. Watchful. The sound of rain like blowing sand.

The figure dismounted but maintained a wary distance. He studied the inert forms sprawled around them.

"Extraordinary," the stranger said, then looked to him. Kellhus could see the glitter of his eyes beneath the brow of his helm. "You must be a *name*."

"Anasûrimbor Kellhus," the monk replied.

Silence. Kellhus thought he could sense confusion, strange confusion.

"It speaks the language," the man muttered at length. He stepped closer, peering at Kellhus. "Yes," he said. "Yes . . . You do not merely mock me. I can see *his* blood in your face."

Kellhus again was silent.

"You have the patience of an Anasûrimbor as well."

Kellhus studied him, noting that his cloak was not stitched with stylized representations of faces but with actual faces, their features distorted by being stretched flat. Beneath the cloak, the man was powerfully built, heavily armoured, and from the way he comported himself, entirely unafraid.

"I see that you are a student. Knowledge is power, eh?"

This one was not like Leweth. Not at all.

Still the sound of sleet, patiently drawing the dead into the cold snow.

"Should you not fear me, mortal, knowing what I am? Fear too is power. The power to survive." The figure began to circle him, carefully stepping between Sranc limbs. "This is what separates your kind from mine. Fear. The clawing, grubbing, impulse to survive. For us life is always a . . . decision. For you . . . Well, let us just say *it* decides."

At last, Kellhus spoke. "The decision, then, would seem to be yours."

The figure paused. "Ah, mockery," he said sorrowfully. "That is one thing we share."

Kellhus's provocation had been deliberate but had yielded little— or so it seemed at first. The stranger abruptly lowered his obscured face, rolled his head back and forth on the pivot of his chin, muttering, "*It baits me! The mortal baits me . . . It reminds me, reminds . . .*" He began fumbling with his cloak, seized upon a misshapen face. "*Of this one! Oh, impertinent—what a joy this one was! Yes, I remember . . .*" He looked up at Kellhus and hissed, "I remember!"

And Kellhus grasped the first principles of this encounter. *A Nonman. Another of Leweth's myths come true.*

With solemn deliberation the figure drew his broadsword. It shined unnaturally in the gloom, as though reflecting some otherworldly sun. But he turned to one of the dead Sranc, rolled it onto its back with the flat of the blade. Its white skin was beginning to darken.

"This Sranc here—you could not pronounce its name—was our *elju* . . . our 'book,' you would say in your tongue. A most devoted animal. I'll be wrecked without it—for a time, anyway." He surveyed the other dead. "Nasty, vicious creatures, really." He looked back up to Kellhus. "But most . . . memorable."

An opening. Kellhus would explore. He said: "So reduced. You've become so pitiful."

"You pity me? A *dog* dares pity?" The Nonman laughed harshly. "The Anasûrimbor pities me! And so he should . . . *Ka'cûnuroi souk ki'elju, souk hus'jihla.*" He spat, then gestured with his sword to the surrounding dead. "These . . . these Sranc are our children now. But *before!* Before, you were our children. Our heart had been cut out and so we cradled yours. Companions to the 'great' Norsirai kings."

The Nonman stepped nearer.

"But no longer," he continued. "As the ages waxed, some of us needed more than your childish squabbles to remember. Some of us needed a more exquisite brutality than any of your feuds could render. The great curse of our kind—do you know it? Of course you know it! What slave fails to exult in his master's degradation, hmm?"

The wind wrapped his hoary cloak about him. He took another step.

"But I make excuses like a Man. Loss is written into the very earth. We are only its most dramatic reminder."

The Nonman had raised the point of his sword to Kellhus, who had fallen into stance, his own curved sword poised above his head.

Again silence, deadly this time.

"I am a warrior of ages, Anasûrimbor . . . *ages*. I have dipped my *nimil* in a thousand hearts. I have ridden both against and *for* the No-God in the great wars that authored this wilderness. I have scaled the ramparts of great Golgotterath, watched the hearts of High Kings break for fury."

"Then why," Kellhus asked, "raise arms now, against a lone man?"

Laughter. The free hand gestured to the dead Sranc. "A pittance, I agree, but still you would be *memorable*."

Kellhus struck first, but his blade recoiled from the mail beneath the Nonman's cloak. He crouched, deflected the powerful counter-stroke, swept the figure's legs out from beneath him. The Nonman toppled backward but managed to roll effortlessly back to his feet. Laughter rang from the helmed face.

"Most memorable!" he cried, falling upon the monk.

And Kellhus felt himself pressed. A rain of mighty blows, forcing him back, away from the dead tree. The ring of Dûnyain steel and Nonman *nimil* pealed across the windswept heights. But Kellhus could sense the moment—although it was far, far thinner than it had been with the Sranc.

He climbed into that narrow instant, and the unearthly blade fell farther and farther from its mark, bit deeper into empty air. Then Kellhus's own sword was scoring the dark figure, clipping and prodding the armour, tattering the grim cloak. But he could draw no blood.

"What are you?" the Nonman cried in fury.

There was one space between them, but the crossings were infinite . . .

Kellhus opened the Nonman's exposed chin. Blood, black in the gloom, spilled across his breast. A second stroke sent the uncanny blade skittering across snow and ice.

As Kellhus leapt, the Nonman scrambled backward, fell. The point of Kellhus's sword, poised above the opening of his helm, stilled him.

In the freezing rain, the monk breathed evenly, staring down at the fallen figure. Several instants passed. Now the interrogation could begin.

"You will answer my questions," Kellhus instructed, his tone devoid of passion.

The Nonman laughed darkly.

"But it is *you*, Anasûrimbor, who are the question."

And then came the *word*, the word that, on hearing, wrenched the intellect somehow.

A furious incandescence. Like a petal blown from a palm, Kellhus was thrown backward. He rolled through the snow and, stunned, struggled to his feet. He watched numbly as the Nonman was drawn upright as though by a wire. Pale watery light formed a sphere around him. The ice rain sputtered and hissed against it. Behind him rose the great tree.

Sorcery? But how could it be?

Kellhus fled, sprinted over the dead structures breaking the snow. He slipped on ice and skidded over the far side of the heights, toppled through the wicked branches of trees. He recovered his feet and tore himself through the harsh underbrush. Something like a thunderclap shivered through the air, and great, blinding fires rifled through the spruces behind him. The heat washed over him, and he ran harder, until the slopes were leaps and the dark forest a rush of confusion.

"ANASÛRIMBOR!" an unearthly voice called, cracking the winter silence.

"RUN, ANASÛRIMBOR!" it boomed. "I WILL *REMEMBER!*"

Laughter, like a storm, and the forest behind him was harrowed by more fierce lights. They fractured the surrounding gloom, and Kellhus could see his own fleeing shadow flickering before him.

The cold air wracked his lungs, but he ran—far harder than the Sranc had made him run.

Sorcery? Is this among the lessons I'm to learn, Father?

Cold night fell. Somewhere in the dark, wolves howled. Shimeh, they seemed to say, was too far.

PART I:
The Sorcerer

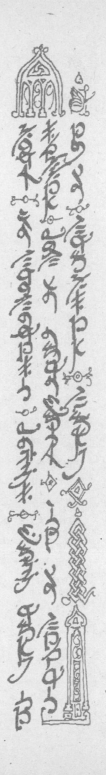

CHAPTER ONE

CARYTHUSAL

*There are three, and only three, kinds of men in the world:
cynics, fanatics, and Mandate Schoolmen.*

—ONTILLAS, ON THE FOLLY OF MEN

*The author has often observed that in the genesis of great events,
men generally possess no inkling of what their actions portend.
This problem is not, as one might suppose, a result of men's
blindness to the consequences of their actions. Rather it is a result
of the mad way the dreadful turns on the trivial when the ends of
one man cross the ends of another. The Schoolmen of the Scarlet
Spires have an old saying: "When one man chases a hare, he
finds a hare. But when many men chase a hare, they find a
dragon." In the prosecution of competing human interests, the
result is always unknown, and all too often terrifying.*

—DRUSAS ACHAMIAN, COMPENDIUM OF THE FIRST HOLY WAR

Midwinter, 4110 Year-of-the-Tusk, Carythusal

All spies obsessed over their informants. It was a game they played
in the moments before sleep or even during nervous gaps in

conversation. A spy would look at his informant, as Achamian looked at Geshrunni now, and ask himself, *How much does he know?*

Like many taverns found near the edge of the Worm, the great slums of Carythusal, the Holy Leper was at once luxurious and impoverished. The floor was tiled with ceramics as fine as any found in the palace of a Palatine-Governor, but the walls were of painted mud brick, and the ceiling was so low that taller men had to duck beneath the brass lamps, which were authentic imitations, Achamian had once heard the owner boast, of those found in the Temple of Exorietta. The place was invariably crowded, filled with shadowy, sometimes dangerous men, but the wine and hashish were just expensive enough to prevent those who could not afford to bathe from rubbing shoulders with those who could.

Until coming to the Holy Leper, Achamian had never liked the Ainoni—especially those from Carythusal. Like most in the Three Seas, he thought them vain and effeminate: too much oil in their beards, too fond of irony and cosmetics, too reckless in their sexual habits. But this estimation had changed after the endless hours he'd spent waiting for Geshrunni to arrive. The subtlety of character and taste that afflicted only the highest castes of other nations, he realized, was a rampant fever among these people, infecting even low-caste freemen and slaves. He had always thought High Ainon a nation of libertines and petty conspirators; that this made them a nation of kindred spirits was something he never had imagined.

Perhaps this was why he failed to immediately recognize his peril when Geshrunni said, "I know you."

Dark even in the lamplight, Geshrunni lowered his arms, which had been folded across his white silk vest, and leaned forward in his seat. He was an imposing figure, possessing a hawkish soldier's face, a beard pleated into what looked like black leather straps, and thick arms so deeply tanned that one could see, but never quite decipher, the line of Ainoni pictograms tattooed from shoulder to wrist.

Achamian tried to grin affably. "You and my wives," he said, tossing back yet another bowl of wine. He gasped and smacked his lips. Geshrunni had always been, or so Achamian had assumed, a narrow man, one for whom the grooves of thought and word were few and deep. Most warriors were such, particularly when they were slaves.

But there had been nothing narrow about his claim.

Geshrunni watched him carefully, the suspicion in his eyes rounded by a faint wonder. He shook his head in disgust. "I should've said, 'I know who you are.'"

The man leaned back in a contemplative way so foreign to a soldier's manner that Achamian's skin pimpled with dread. The rumbling tavern receded, became a frame of shadowy figures and points of golden lantern-light.

"Then write it down," Achamian replied, as though growing bored, "and give it to me when I'm sober." He looked away, as bored men often do, and noted that the entrance to the tavern was empty.

"I know you have no wives."

"You don't say. And how's that?" Achamian glanced quickly behind him, glimpsed a whore laughing as she pressed a shiny silver ensolarii onto her sweaty breasts. The vulgar crowd about her roared, "One!"

"She's quite good at that, you know. She uses honey."

Geshrunni was not distracted. "Your kind aren't allowed to have wives."

"My kind, eh? And just what is my kind?" Another glance at the entrance.

"You're a sorcerer. A Schoolman."

Achamian laughed, knowing his momentary hesitation had betrayed him. But there was motive enough to continue this pantomime. At the very least, it might buy him several more moments. Time to stay alive.

"By the Latter-fucking-Prophet, my friend," Achamian cried, glancing once again at the entrance, "I swear I could measure your accusations by the bowl. What was it you accused me of being last night? A whoreson?"

Amid chortling voices, a thunderous shout: *"Two!"*

The fact that Geshrunni grimaced told Achamian little—the man's every expression seemed some version of a grimace, particularly his smile. The hand that flashed out and clamped his wrist, however, told Achamian all he needed to know.

I'm doomed. They know.

Few things were more terrifying than "they," especially in Carythusal. "They" were the Scarlet Spires, the most powerful School in the Three Seas, and the hidden masters of High Ainon. Geshrunni was a Captain of the Javreh, the warrior-slaves of the Scarlet Spires, which is why Achamian had courted him over the past few weeks. This is what spies do: woo the slaves of their competitors.

Geshrunni stared fiercely into his eyes, twisted his hand palm outward. "There's a way for us to satisfy my suspicion," the man said softly.

"Three!" reverberated across mud brick and scuffed mahogany.

Achamian winced, both because of the man's powerful grip and because he knew the "way" Geshrunni referred to. *Not like this.*

"Geshrunni, please. You're drunk, my friend. What School would hazard the wrath of the Scarlet Spires?"

Geshrunni shrugged. "The Mysunsai, maybe. Or the Imperial Saik. The Cishaurim. There are so many of your accursed kind. But if I had to wager, I would say the *Mandate*. I would say you're a Mandate Schoolman."

Canny slave! How long had he known?

The impossible words were there, poised in Achamian's thought, words that could blind eyes and blister flesh. *He leaves me no choice.* There would be an uproar. Men would bellow, clutch their swords, but they would do nothing but scramble from his path. More than any people in the Three Seas, the Ainoni feared sorcery.

No choice.

But Geshrunni had already reached beneath his embroidered vest. His fist bunched beneath the fabric. He grimaced like a grinning jackal.

Too late . . .

"You look," Geshrunni said with menacing ease, "like you have something to say."

The man withdrew his hand and produced the Chorae. He winked, then with terrifying abruptness, snapped the golden chain holding it about his neck. Achamian had sensed it from their first encounter, had actually used its unnerving murmur to identify Geshrunni's vocation. Now Geshrunni would use it to identify him.

"What's this, now?" Achamian asked. A shudder of animal terror passed through his pinned arm.

"I think you know, Akka. I think you know far better than I."

Chorae. Schoolmen called them Trinkets. Small names are often given to horrifying things. But for other men, those who followed the Thousand Temples in condemning sorcery as blasphemy, they were called Tears of God. But the God had no hand in their manufacture. Chorae were relics of the Ancient North, so valuable that only the marriage of heirs, murder, or the tribute of entire nations could purchase them. They were worth the price: Chorae rendered their bearers immune to sorcery and killed any sorcerer unfortunate enough to touch them.

Effortlessly holding Achamian's hand immobile, Geshrunni raised the Chorae between thumb and forefinger. It looked plain enough: a small sphere of iron, about the size of an olive but encased in the cursive script of the Nonmen. Achamian could feel it tug at his bowels, as though Geshrunni held an *absence* rather than a thing, a small pit in the very fabric of the world. His heart hammered in his ears. He thought of the knife sheathed beneath his tunic.

"*Four!*" Raucous laughter.

He struggled to free his captive hand. Futile.

"Geshrunni . . ."

"Every Captain of the Javreh is given one of these," Geshrunni said, his tone at once reflective and proud. "But then, you already know this."

All this time, he's been playing me for a fool! How could I've missed it?

"Your masters are kind," Achamian said, rivetted by the horror suspended above his palm.

"Kind?" Geshrunni spat. "The Scarlet Spires are not *kind*. They're ruthless. Cruel to those who oppose them."

And for the first time, Achamian glimpsed the torment animating the man, the anguish in his bright eyes. *What's happening here?* He hazarded a question: "And to those who serve them?"

"They do not discriminate."

They don't know! Only Geshrunni . . .

"Five!" pealed beneath the low ceilings.

Achamian licked his lips. "What do you want, Geshrunni?"

The warrior-slave looked down at Achamian's trembling palm, then lowered the Trinket as though he were a child curious of what might happen. Simply staring at it made Achamian dizzy, jerked bile to the back of his throat. Chorae. A tear drawn from the God's own cheek. Death. Death to all blasphemers.

"What do you want?" Achamian hissed.

"What all men want, Akka. Truth."

All the things Achamian had seen, all the trials he'd survived, lay pinched in that narrow space between his shining palm and the oiled iron. Trinket. Death poised between the callused fingers of a slave. But Achamian was a Schoolman, and for Schoolmen nothing, not even life itself, was as precious as the Truth. They were its miserly keepers, and they warred for its possession across all the shadowy grottoes of the Three Seas. Better to die than to yield Mandate truth to the Scarlet Spires.

But there was more here. Geshrunni was alone—Achamian was certain of this. Sorcerers could see sorcerers, see the bruise of their crimes, and the Holy Leper hosted no sorcerers, no Scarlet Schoolmen, only drunks making wagers with whores. Geshrunni played this game on his own.

But for what mad reason?

Tell him what he wants. He already knows.

"I'm a Mandate Schoolman," Achamian whispered quickly. Then he added, "A spy."

Dangerous words. But what choice did he have?

Geshrunni studied him for a breathless moment, then slowly gathered the Chorae into his fist. He released Achamian's hand.

There was an odd moment of silence, interrupted only by the clatter of a silver ensolarii against wood. A roar of laughter, and a hoarse voice bellowed, *"You lose, whore!"*

But this, Achamian knew, was not so. Somehow he had won this night, and he had won the way whores always win—without understanding.

After all, spies were little different from whores. Sorcerers less so.

———— ❧ ————

Though he had dreamt of being a sorcerer as a child, the possibility of being a spy had never occurred to Drusas Achamian. "Spy" simply wasn't part of the vocabulary of children raised in Nroni fishing villages. For him the Three Seas had possessed only two dimensions in his childhood: there were places far and near and there were people high and low. He would listen to the old fish-wives tell their tales while he and the other children helped shuck oysters, and he learned very quickly that he was among the low, and that mighty people dwelt far away. Name after mysterious name would fall from those old lips—the Shriah of the Thousand Temples, the malevolent heathens of Kian, the all-conquering Scylvendi, the scheming sorcerers of the Scarlet Spires, and so on—names that sketched the dimensions of his world, infused it with terrifying majesty, transformed it into an arena of impossibly tragic and heroic deeds. He would fall asleep feeling very small.

One might think becoming a spy would add dimension to the simple world of a child, but precisely the opposite was the case. Certainly, as he matured, Achamian's world became more compli-cated. He learned that there were things holy and unholy, that the Gods and the Outside possessed their own dimensions, rather than being people very high and a place very far. He also learned that there were times recent and ancient, that "a long time ago" was not like another place but rather a queer kind of ghost that haunted every place.

But when one became a spy, the world had the curious habit of collapsing into a single dimension. High-born men, even Emperors and Kings, had the habit of seeming as base and as petty as the most vulgar fisherman. Far-away nations like Conriya, High Ainon, Ce Tydonn, or Kian no longer seemed exotic or enchanted but were as grubby and as weathered as a Nroni fishing village. Things holy, like the Tusk, the Thousand Temples, or even the Latter Prophet, became mere versions of things unholy, like the Fanim, the Cishaurim, or the sorcerous Schools, as though the words "holy" and "unholy" were as easily exchanged as seats at a gaming table. And the recent simply became a more tawdry repetition of the ancient.

As both a Schoolman and a spy, Achamian had crisscrossed the Three Seas, had seen many of those things that had once made his stomach flutter with supernatural dread, and he knew now that childhood stories were always better. Since being identified as one of the Few as a youth and taken to Atyersus to be trained by the School of Mandate, he had educated princes, insulted grandmasters, and infuriated Shrial priests. And he now knew with certainty that the world was hollowed of its wonder by knowledge and travel, that when one stripped away the mysteries, its dimensions collapsed rather than bloomed. Of course, the world was a much more sophisticated place to him now than it had been when he was a child, but it was also far simpler. Everywhere men grasped and grasped, as though the titles "king," "shriah," and "grandmaster" were simply masks worn by the same hungry animal. Avarice, it seemed to him, was the world's only dimension.

Achamian was a middle-aged sorcerer and spy, and he had grown weary of both vocations. And though he would be loath to admit it, he was heartsick. As the old fish-wives might say, he had dragged one empty net too many.

Perplexed and dismayed, Achamian left Geshrunni at the Holy Leper and hurried home—if it could be called that—through the shadowy ways of the Worm. Extending from the northern banks of the River Sayut to the famed Surmantic Gates, the Worm was a labyrinth of crumbling tenements, brothels, and impoverished Cultic temples. The place was aptly named, Achamian had always thought. Humid, riddled by cramped alleys, the Worm indeed resembled something found beneath a rock.

Given his mission, Achamian had no reason to be dismayed. Quite the opposite, if anything. After the mad moment with the Chorae, Geshrunni had told him secrets—potent secrets. Geshrunni, it turned out, was not a happy slave. He hated the Scarlet Magi with an intensity that was almost frightening once revealed.

"I didn't befriend you for the promise of your gold," the Javreh Captain had said. "For what? To buy my freedom from my masters? The Scarlet Spires relinquish nothing of value. No, I befriended you because I knew you would be useful."

"Useful? But for what end?"

"Vengeance. I would humble the Scarlet Spires."

"So you knew . . . All along you knew I was no merchant."

Sneering laughter. "Of course. You were too free with your ensolariis. Sit with a merchant or sit with a beggar, and it'll always be the beggar who buys your first drink."

What kind of spy are you?

Achamian had scowled at this, scowled at his own transparency. But as much as Geshrunni's penetration troubled him, he was terrified by the degree to which he'd misjudged the man. Geshrunni was a warrior and a slave—what surer formula could there be for stupidity? But slaves, Achamian supposed, had good reason to conceal their intelligence. A wise slave was something to be prized perhaps, like the slave-scholars of the old Ceneian Empire. A cunning slave, however, was something to be feared, to be eliminated.

But this thought held little consolation. *If he could fool me so easily . . .*

Achamian had plucked a great secret out of the obscurity of Carythusal and the Scarlet Spires—the greatest, perhaps, in many years. But he did not have his ability, which he'd rarely questioned over the years, to thank—only his incompetence. As a result, he'd learned *two* secrets—one dreadful enough, he supposed, in the greater scheme of the Three Seas; the other dreadful within the frame of his life.

I'm not, he realized, *the man I once was.*

Geshrunni's story had been alarming in its own right, if only because it demonstrated the ability of the Scarlet Spires to harbour secrets. The Scarlet Spires, Geshrunni said, was at war, had been for more than ten years, in fact. Achamian had been unimpressed—at first. The sorcerous Schools, like all the Great Factions, ceaselessly skirmished with spies, assassinations, trade sanctions, and delegations of outraged envoys. But this war, Geshrunni assured him, was far more momentous than any skirmish.

"Ten years ago," Geshrunni said, "our former Grandmaster, Sasheoka, was assassinated."

"Sasheoka?" Achamian was not inclined to ask stupid questions, but the idea that a Grandmaster of the Scarlet Spires could be assassinated was preposterous. How could such a thing happen? "Assassinated?"

"In the inner sanctums of the Spires themselves."

In other words, in the midst of the most formidable system of Wards in the Three Seas. Not only would the Mandate never dare such an act, but there was no way, even with the glittering Abstractions of the Gnosis, they could succeed. Who could do such a thing?

"By whom?" Achamian asked, almost breathless.

Geshrunni's eyes actually twinkled in the ruddy lamplight. "By the heathens," he said. "The Cishaurim."

Achamian was at once baffled and gratified by this revelation. The Cishaurim—the only heathen School. At least this explained Sasheoka's assassination.

There was a saying common to the Three Seas: "Only the Few can see the Few." Sorcery was violent. To speak it was to cut the world as surely as if with a knife. But only the Few—sorcerers— could see this mutilation, and only they could see, moreover, the blood on the hands of the mutilator—the "mark," as it was called. Only the Few could see one another and one another's crimes. And when they met, they recognized one another as surely as common men recognized criminals by their lack of a nose.

Not so with the Cishaurim. No one knew why or how, but they worked events as grand and as devastating as any sorcery without marking the world or bearing the mark of their crime. Only once had Achamian witnessed Cishaurim sorcery, what they called the Psûkhe—on a night long ago in distant Shimeh. With the Gnosis, the sorcery of the Ancient North, he'd destroyed his saffron-robed assailants, but as he sheltered behind his Wards, it had seemed as though he watched flashes of soundless lightning. No thunder. No mark.

Only the Few could see the Few, but no one—no Schoolman, at least—could distinguish the Cishaurim or their works from common men or the common world. And it was this, Achamian surmised, that had allowed them to assassinate Sasheoka. The Scarlet Spires possessed Wards for sorcerers, slave-soldiers like Geshrunni for men bearing Chorae, but they had nothing to protect them against sorcerers indistinguishable from common men, or against sorcery indistinguishable from the God's own world. Hounds, Geshrunni would tell him, now ran freely through the halls of the Scarlet Spires, trained to smell the saffron and henna the Cishaurim used to dye their robes.

But why? What could induce the Cishaurim to wage open war against the Scarlet Spires? As alien as their metaphysics were, they could have no hope of winning such a war. The Scarlet Spires was simply too powerful.

When Achamian had asked Geshrunni, the slave-soldier simply shrugged.

"It's been a decade, and still they don't know."

This, at least, was grounds for petty comfort. There was nothing the ignorant prized more than the ignorance of others.

Drusas Achamian walked ever deeper into the Worm, toward the squalid tenement where he'd taken a room, still more afraid of himself than his future.

———— ∞ ————

Geshrunni grimaced as he stumbled out of the tavern. He steadied himself on the packed dust of the alley.

"Done," he muttered, then cackled in a way he never dared show others. He looked up at a narrow slot of sky hemmed and obscured by mud-brick walls and ragged canvas awnings. He could see few stars.

Suddenly his betrayal struck him as a pathetic thing. He had told the only real secret he knew to an enemy of his masters. Now there was nothing left. No treason that might quiet the hatred in his heart.

And a bitter hatred it was. More than anything else, Geshrunni was a proud man. That someone such as he might be born a slave, be dogged by the desires of weak-hearted, womanish men . . . By sorcerers! In another life, he knew, he would have been a conqueror. He would have broken enemy after enemy with the might of his hand. But in this accursed life, all he could do was skulk about with other womanish men and gossip.

Where was the vengeance in gossip?

He'd staggered some way down the alley before realizing that someone followed him. The possibility that his masters had discovered his small treachery struck him momentarily, but he thought it unlikely. The Worm was filled with wolves, desperate men who followed mark after mark searching for those drunk enough to be safely plundered. Geshrunni had actually killed one once, several years before: some poor fool who had risked murder rather than sell himself, as Geshrunni's nameless father had, into slavery. He continued walking, his senses as keen as the wine would allow, his drunken thoughts reeling through scenario after bloody scenario. This would be a good night, he thought, to kill.

Only when he passed beneath the looming facade of the temple the Carythusali called the Mouth of the Worm did Geshrunni become alarmed. Men were quite often followed into the Worm, but rarely were they followed out. Above the welter of rooftops, Geshrunni could even glimpse the highest of the Spires, crimson against a field of stars. Who would dare follow him this far? If not . . .

He whirled and saw a balding, rotund man dressed, despite the heat, in an ornate silk overcoat that might have been any combination of colours but looked blue and black in the darkness.

"You were one of the fools with the whore," Geshrunni said, trying to shake away the confusion of drink.

"Yes," the man replied, his jowls grinning with his lips. "She was most . . . enticing. But truth be told, I was far more interested in what you had to say to the Mandate Schoolman."

Geshrunni squinted in drunken astonishment. *So they know.*

Danger always sobered him. Instinctively, he reached into his pocket, closed his fingers about his Chorae. He flung it violently at the Schoolman . . .

Or at who he thought was a Scarlet Schoolman. The stranger picked the Trinket from the air as though it had been tossed for his friendly perusal. He studied it momentarily, a dubious money-changer with a leaden coin. He looked up and smiled again, blinking his large bovine eyes. "A most precious gift," he said. "I thank you, but I'm afraid it's not quite a fair exchange for what I want."

Not a sorcerer! Geshrunni had seen a Chorae touch a sorcerer once, the incandescent unravelling of flesh and bone. But then what was this man?

"Who are you?" Geshrunni asked.

"Nothing you could understand, slave."

The Javreh Captain smiled. *Maybe he's just a fool.* A dangerous, drunken amiability seized his manner. He walked up to the man, placed a callused hand on his padded shoulder. He could smell jasmine. The cowlike eyes looked up at him.

"Oh my," the stranger whispered, "you are a daring fool, aren't you?"

Why isn't he afraid? Remembering the ease with which the man had snatched the Chorae, Geshrunni suddenly felt horribly exposed. But he was committed.

"Who are you?" Geshrunni grated. "How long have you been watching me?"

"Watching you?" The fat man almost giggled. "Such conceit is unbecoming of slaves."

He watches Achamian? What is this? Geshrunni was an officer, accustomed to cowing men in the menacing intimacy of a face-to-face confrontation. Not this man. Soft or not, he was at utter ease. Geshrunni could feel it. And if it weren't for the unwatered wine, he would have been terrified.

He dug his fingers deep into the fat of the man's shoulder.

"I said tell me, fat fool," he hissed between clenched teeth, "or I'll muck up the dust with your bowel." With his free hand, he brandished his knife. "Who are you?"

Unperturbed, the fat man grinned with sudden ferocity. "Few things are as distressing as a slave who refuses to acknowledge his place."

Stunned, Geshrunni looked down at his senseless hand, watched his knife flop onto the dust. All he'd heard was the snap of the stranger's sleeve.

"Heel, slave," the fat man said.

"What did you say?"

The slap stung him, brought tears to his eyes.

"I said *heel.*"

Another slap, hard enough to loosen teeth. Geshrunni stumbled back several steps, raising a clumsy hand. How could this be?

"What a task we've set for ourselves," the stranger said ruefully, following him, "when even their slaves possess such pride."

Panicked, Geshrunni fumbled for the hilt of his sword.

The fat man paused, his eyes flashing to the pommel.

"Draw it," he said, his voice impossibly cold—inhuman.

Wide-eyed, Geshrunni froze, transfixed by the silhouette that loomed before him.

"I said draw it!"

Geshrunni hesitated.

The next slap knocked him to his knees.

"What are you?" Geshrunni cried through bloodied lips.

As the shadow of the fat man encompassed him, Geshrunni watched his round face loosen, then flex as tight as a beggar's hand about copper. *Sorcery! But how could it be? He holds a Chorae—*

"Something impossibly ancient," the abomination said softly. "Inconceivably beautiful."

One man, a man long dead, looked out from behind the many eyes of Mandate Schoolmen: Seswatha, the great adversary of the No-God and founder of the last Gnostic School—their School. In daylight, he was vague, as uncertain as a childhood memory, but at night he possessed them, and the tragedy of his life tyrannized their dreams.

Smoky dreams. Dreams drawn from the sheath.

Achamian watched Anasûrimbor Celmomas, the last High King of Kûniüri, fall beneath the hammer of a baying Sranc chieftain. Even though Achamian cried out, he knew with the curious half-awareness belonging to dreams that the greatest king of the Anasûrimbor Dynasty was already dead—had been dead for more than two thousand years. And he knew, moreover, that it was not he himself who wailed, but a far greater man. Seswatha.

The words boiled to his lips. The Sranc chieftain flailed through blistering fire, collapsed into a bundle of rags and ash. More Sranc swept the summit of the hill and more died, struck down by the unearthly lights summoned by his song. Beyond, he glimpsed a distant dragon, like a figure of bronze in the setting sun, hanging above warring fields of Sranc and Men, and he thought: *The last Anasûrimbor King has fallen. Kûniüri is lost.*

Crying out the name of their king, the tall knights of Trysë surged about him, sprinting over the Sranc he had burned and falling like madmen upon the masses beyond. With a knight whom he did not know, Achamian dragged Anasûrimbor Celmomas through the frantic cries of his vassals and kinsmen, through the smell of blood, bowel, and charred flesh. In a small clearing, he pulled the King's broken body across his lap.

Celmomas's blue eyes, ordinarily so cold, beseeched him. "Leave me," the grey-bearded king gasped.

"No," Achamian replied. "If you die, Celmomas, all is lost."

The High King smiled despite his ruined lips. "Do you see the sun? Do you see it flare, Seswatha?"

"The sun sets," Achamian replied.

"Yes! Yes. The darkness of the No-God is not all-encompassing. The Gods see us yet, dear friend. They are distant, but I can hear them galloping across the skies. I can hear them cry out to me."

"You cannot die, Celmomas! You must not die!"

The High King shook his head, stilled him with tender eyes. "They call to me. They say that my end is not the world's end. That burden, they say, is *yours*. Yours, Seswatha."

"No," Achamian whispered.

"The sun! Can you see the sun? Feel it upon your cheek? Such revelations are hidden in such simple things. I see! I see so clearly what a bitter, stubborn fool I have been . . . And to you, you most of all, have I been unjust. Can you forgive an old man? Can you forgive a foolish old man?"

"There's nothing to forgive, Celmomas. You've lost much, suffered much."

"My son . . . Do you think he'll be there, Seswatha? Do you think he'll greet me as his father?"

"Yes . . . As his father, and as his king."

"Did I ever tell you," Celmomas said, his voice cracking with futile pride, "that my son once stole into the deepest pits of Golgotterath?"

"Yes." Achamian smiled through his tears. "Many times, old friend."

"How I miss him, Seswatha! How I yearn to stand at his side once again."

The old king wept for a moment. Then his eyes grew wide. "I see him so clearly. He's taken the sun as his charger, and he rides among us. I see him! Galloping through the hearts of my people, stirring them to wonder and fury!"

"Shush . . . Conserve your strength, my King. The surgeons are coming."

"He says . . . says such sweet things to give me comfort. He says that one of my seed will return, Seswatha—an Anasûrimbor *will return* . . ." A shudder wracked the old man, forcing breath and spittle through his teeth.

"At the end of the world."

The bright eyes of Anasûrimbor Celmomas II, White Lord of Trysë, High King of Kûniüri, went blank. And with them, the evening sun faltered, plunging the bronze-armoured glory of the Norsirai into twilight.

"Our King!" Achamian cried to the stricken men encircling him. "Our King is dead!"

But everything was darkness. No one stood around him, and no king lay propped against his thighs. Only sweaty blankets and a great buzzing absence where the clamour of war had once been. His room. He lay alone in his miserable room.

Achamian hugged his arms tight. Another dream drawn from the sheath.

He drew his hands to his face and wept, a short time for a long-dead Kûniüric King and longer for other, less certain things.

In the distance, he thought he heard howling. A dog or a man.

———— ∞∞ ————

Geshrunni was dragged through putrid alleys. He saw pitted wallscapes reel against black sky. His limbs thrashed of their own volition; his fingers clutched at greasy brick. Through bubbling blood, he could smell the river.

My face . . .

"What 'ore?" he tried to cry, but speaking was almost impossible without lips. *I've told you everything!*

The sound of boots tramping through watery muck. A giggle from somewhere above him.

"If the eye of your enemy offends you, slave, you pluck it out, no?"

"'lease . . . 'ercy. I 'eg you . . . 'erceeeee."

"Mercy?" the thing laughed. "Mercy is a luxury of the idle, fool. The Mandate has many eyes, and we have much plucking to do."

Where's my face?

Weightlessness, then the crash of cold, drowning water.

———— ∞∞ ————

Achamian awoke in pre-dawn light, his head buzzing with the memory of drink and of more nightmarish dreams. More dreams of the Apocalypse.

Coughing, he lurched from the straw bed to the room's only window. He drew the lacquered shutter aside, his hands trembling. Cool air. Grey light. The palaces and temples of Carythusal sprawled amid thickets of lesser structures. A dense fog covered the River Sayut, coursing through the alleys and avenues of the lower city like water through trenches. Isolated and as small as a fingernail, the Scarlet Spires loomed from the ethereal expanse, jutting like dead towers from white desert dunes.

Achamian's throat thickened. He blinked tears from his eyes. No fire. No chorus of wails. Everything still. Even the Spires affected a breathless, monumental repose.

This world, he thought, *must not end.*

He turned from the view to the room's single table and dropped onto the stool, or what passed for one—it looked like something salvaged from a wrecked ship. He wet his quill and unrolling a small scroll across scattered sheets of parchment, wrote:

Fords of Tywanrae. Same.
Burning of the Library of Sauglish. Different. See my face and
not S in mirror.

A curious discrepancy. What could it mean? For a moment, he pondered the sour futility of the question. Then he remembered awakening in the heart of night. After a pause, he added:

Death and Prophecy of Anasûrimbor Celmomas. Same.

But was it the same? In detail, certainly, but there had been a disturbing immediacy to the dream—enough to wake him. After scratching out "Same," he wrote:

Different. More powerful.

As he waited for the ink to dry, he reviewed his previous entries, following them up to the curl of the scroll. A cascade of image and passion accompanied each, transforming mute ink into fragmentary worlds. Bodies tumbling through the knotted waters of a river cataract. A lover grunting blood through clenched teeth. Fire wrapped like a wanton dancer about stone towers.

He pressed thumb and forefinger against his eyes. Why was he so fixated on this record? Other men, far greater than he, had gone mad trying to decipher the deranged sequence and permutations of Seswatha's Dreams. He knew well enough to realize he'd never find an answer. Was it some kind of perverse game, then? One like that his mother used to play when his father returned drunk from the boats, pecking and nettling, demanding *reason* where none was to be found, flinching each time his father raised his hand, shrieking when he inevitably struck?

Why peck and nettle when reliving Seswatha's life was battery enough?

Something cold reached through his breastbone and seized his heart. The old tremor rattled his hands, and the scroll rolled shut, wet ink and all. *Stop* . . . He clutched his hands together, but the shuddering simply migrated to his arms and shoulders. *Stop!* The howl of Sranc horns rifled through his window. He cringed beneath the concussion of dragon's wings. He rocked on the stool, his entire body shaking.

"Stop!"

For several moments, he struggled to breathe. He heard the distant ping of a coppersmith's hammer, the squabbling of crows on the rooftops.

Is this what you wanted, Seswatha? Is this the way it's supposed to be?

But like so many questions he asked himself, he already knew the answer.

Seswatha had survived the No-God and the Apocalypse, but he'd known the conflict was not over. The Scylvendi had returned to their pastures, the Sranc had scattered to feud over the spoils of a ruined world, but Golgotterath remained intact. From its black ramparts, the No-God's servants, the Consult, still kept watch, possessed of a patience that dwarfed the perseverance of Men, a patience no cycle of epic verses or scriptural admonition could match. Ink might be immortal, but meaning was not. With the passing of every genera-tion, Seswatha had known, the neck of his memory would be further broken—even the Apocalypse would be forgotten. So he passed not from but *into* his followers. By reincarnating his harrowing life in their dreams, he had made his legacy a never-ending call to arms.

I was meant to suffer, Achamian thought.

Forcing himself to confront the day ahead, he oiled his hair and brushed the flecks of muck from the white embroidery trimming his blue tunic. Standing at the window, he calmed his stomach with cheese and stale bread while watching sunlight burn the fog from the black back of the River Sayut. Then he prepared the Cants of Calling and informed his handlers in Atyersus, the citadel of the School of Mandate, of everything Geshrunni had told him the previous night.

He was not surprised by their relative disinterest. The secret war between the Scarlet Spires and the Cishaurim was, after all, not their war. But the summons to return home did surprise him. When he asked why, they said only that it involved the Thousand Temples—another faction, another war that was not their own.

Gathering his few possessions, he thought, *One more meaningless mission*.

How could he not be cynical?

In the Three Seas, all the Great Factions warred with tangible foes for tangible ends, while the Mandate warred against a foe no one could see for an end no one believed in. This made Mandate Schoolmen outcasts not only in the way of sorcerers, but also in the way of fools. Of course, the potentates of the Three Seas, Ketyai and Norsirai alike, knew of the Consult and the threat of the Second Apocalypse—how could they not, after centuries of harping Mandate emissaries?—but they did not believe.

After centuries of skirmishing with the Mandate, the Consult had simply disappeared. Vanished. No one knew why or how, though there had been endless speculation. Had they been destroyed by forces unknown? Had they annihilated themselves from within? Or had they simply found a way to elude the eyes of the Mandate? It had been three centuries since the Mandate had last encountered the Consult. For three centuries they had waged a war without a foe.

Mandate Schoolmen traversed the Three Seas hunting for an enemy they could not find and no one believed in. As much as they were envied their possession of the Gnosis, the sorcery of the Ancient North, they were a laughingstock, the charlatan in the courts of all the Great Factions. And yet every night Seswatha revisited them. Every morning they awoke from the horror and thought, *The Consult is among us*.

Had there ever been a time, Achamian wondered, when he hadn't felt this horror within him? The giddy hollow in the pit of his gut, as though catastrophe hinged upon something he'd forgotten? It came as a breathless whisper, *You must do something* . . . But no one in the Mandate knew what it was they should do, and until they did know, all their actions would be as empty as a mummer's play.

They would be sent to Carythusal to seduce high-placed slaves like Geshrunni. Or to the Thousand Temples, to do who knew what.

The Thousand Temples. What could the Mandate want with the Thousand Temples? Whatever it was, it warranted abandoning Geshrunni—their first real informant within the Scarlet Spires in a generation. The more Achamian pondered this, the more extraordinary it became.

Perhaps this mission will be different.

The thought of Geshrunni made him suddenly anxious. As mercenary as the man was, he had risked far more than his life to give the Mandate a great secret. Besides, he was at once intelligent and filled with hate—an ideal informant. It would not do to lose him.

After unpacking his ink and parchment, Achamian bent over the table and scratched a quick message:

I must leave. But know that your favours have not been forgotten, and that you have found friends who share your purpose. Speak to no one, and we will see you safe. A.

Achamian settled his room with the poxed keeper, then began rooting through the streets. He found Chiki, the orphan he'd employed to run errands, asleep in a nearby alley. The boy was curled in a hemp sack behind a buzzing heap of offal. Aside from the pomegranate-shaped birthmark that marred his face, he looked beautiful, his olive skin dolphin-smooth despite the filth, and his features as fine as any Palatine's daughter. Achamian shuddered to think how the boy made his living outside their paltry transactions. A week previous, Achamian had been accosted by a drunk, the aristocratic paint half smeared from his face, tugging on his crotch and asking if he'd seen his sweet "Pomegranate."

Achamian roused the sleeping child with the toe of his merchant's slipper. The boy fairly leapt to his feet.

"Do you remember what I taught you, Chiki?"

The boy stared at him with the shammed alertness of the just awakened. "Yes, Lord. I'm your runner."

"And what is it that runners do?"

"They deliver messages, Lord. Secret messages."

"Good," Achamian said, holding the folded parchment out to the boy. "I need you to deliver this to a man called Geshrunni. Remember that: *Geshrunni*. You can't miss him. He's a Captain of the Javreh, and he frequents the Holy Leper. Do you know where to find the Holy Leper?"

"Yes, Lord."

Achamian fetched a silver ensolarii from his purse, and could not help smiling at the boy's awestruck expression. Chiki snatched the coin from his palms as though from a trap. For some reason, the touch of his small hand moved the sorceror to melancholy.

CHAPTER TWO

ATYERSUS

*I write to inform you that during my most recent audience, the
Nansur Emperor, quite without provocation, publicly addressed
me as "fool." You are, no doubt, unmoved by this. It has become
a common occurrence. The Consult eludes us now more than
ever. We hear them only in the secrets of others. We glimpse them
only through the eyes of those who deny their very existence. Why
should we not be called fools? The deeper the Consult secretes
itself among the Great Factions, the madder our rantings sound to
their ears. We are, as the damned Nansur would say, "a hunter
in the thicket"—one who, by the very act of hunting, extinguishes
all hope of running down his prey.*

—ANONYMOUS MANDATE SCHOOLMAN, *LETTER TO ATYERSUS*

Late Winter, 4110 Year-of-the-Tusk, Atyersus

Summoned back home, Achamian thought, bruised by the irony of
that word, "home." He could think of few places in the world—
Golgotterath, certainly, the Scarlet Spires, maybe—more heartless
than Atyersus.

Small and alone in the centre of the audience hall, Achamian
struggled with his composure. The members of the Quorum, the

55

ruling council of the School of Mandate, stood in small knots dispersed throughout the shadows, scrutinizing him. They saw, he knew, a stocky man dressed in a plain brown travel smock, his square-cut beard streaked by fingers of silver. He would convey the sturdy sense of one who'd spent years on the road: the wide stance, the tanned leathery skin of a low-caste labourer. He would look nothing like a sorcerer.

But then no spy should.

Annoyed by their scrutiny, Achamian suppressed the urge to ask if they wanted, like any scrupulous slaver, to check his teeth.

Home at last.

Atyersus, the citadel of the School of Mandate, was home to him, would always be home, but the place dwarfed him in inexplicable ways. It was more than the ponderous architecture: Atyersus had been built in the manner of the Ancient North, whose architects had known nothing of arches or domes. Her inner galleries were forests of thick columns, their ceilings obscured by canopies of darkness and smoke. Stylized reliefs sheathed every pillar, providing the shining braziers with too much detail, or so Achamian thought. With every flicker the very ground seemed to shift.

Finally one of the Quorum addressed him: "The Thousand Temples is no longer to be ignored, Achamian, at least since this Maithanet has seized the Seat and declared himself Shriah." Inevitably, it had been Nautzera who'd broached the silence. The last man Achamian wanted to hear speak was always the first.

"I've only heard rumours," he replied in a measured tone—the tone one always took when addressed by Nautzera.

"Believe me," Nautzera said sourly, "the rumours scarce do the man justice."

"But how long can he survive?" A natural question. Many Shriahs had heaved at the rudder of the Thousand Temples, only to find that like any immense ship, it refused to turn.

"Oh, he survives," Nautzera said. "Flourishes, in fact. *All* the Cults have come to him in Sumna. *All* have kissed his knee. And with none of the political manoeuvring obligatory to such transitions of power. No petty boycotts. Not even a single abstention." He paused to allow Achamian time to appreciate the significance of this. "He has stirred something"—the grand old sorcerer pursed his lips, as though leashing his next word like a dangerous dog—"something *novel* . . . And not merely within the Thousand Temples."

"But surely we've seen his kind before," Achamian ventured. "Zealots holding out redemption in one hand to draw attention away from the whip in the other. Sooner or later, everyone sees the whip."

"No. We've not seen this 'kind' before. None has moved this fast, or with such cunning. Maithanet is no mere enthusiast. Within the first three weeks of his tenure two plots to poison him were uncovered—and here's the thing—*by Maithanet himself*. No fewer than seven of the Emperor's agents were exposed and executed in Sumna. This man is more than simply shrewd. Far more."

Achamian nodded and narrowed his eyes. Now he understood the urgency of his summons. Above all the mighty detest change. The Great Factions had prepared a place for the Thousand Temples and its Shriah. But this Maithanet, as the Nroni would say, had pissed in the whisky. More unsettling still, he had done so with intelligence.

"There is to be a *Holy War*, Achamian."

Stunned, Achamian searched the dark silhouettes of the other Quorum members for confirmation. "Surely you jest."

Nautzera strode from the shadows, pausing only when he stood close enough to tower over him. Achamian resisted the urge to step back. The ancient sorcerer had always possessed a disconcerting presence: intimidating because of his height and yet pathetic because of his great age. His skin seemed an insult to the silks that draped him.

"This is no jest, I assure you."

"Against whom, then? The Fanim?" Throughout its history, the Three Seas had witnessed only two prior Holy Wars, both waged against the Schools rather than the heathens. The last, the so-called Scholastic Wars, had been disastrous for both sides. Atyersus itself had been besieged for seven years.

"We don't know. So far Maithanet has declared only that there will be a Holy War. He has not deigned to tell anyone against whom. As I said, he's a fiendishly cunning man."

"So you fear another Scholastic War." Achamian could scarcely believe he was having this conversation. The possibility of another Scholastic War, he knew, *should* horrify him, but instead his heart pounded with exhilaration. Had it come to this? Had he grown so tired of the Mandate's futile mission that he now greeted the prospect of war against the Inrithi as a disfigured species of relief?

"This is precisely what we fear. Once again the Cultic Priests openly denounce us, refer to us as Unclean."

Unclean. *The Chronicle of the Tusk,* held by the Thousand Temples to be the very word of the God, had named them thus— those Few with the learning and the innate ability to work sorcery. "Cut from them their tongues," the holy words said, "for their blasphemy is an abomination like no other . . ." Achamian's father—who, like many Nroni, had despised the tyranny exercised by Atyersus over Nron—had beaten this belief into him. Faith may die, but her sentiments remain eternal.

"But I've heard nothing of this."

The old man leaned forward. His dyed beard was cut square like Achamian's own but meticulously braided in the fashion of the eastern Ketyai. Achamian was struck by the incongruity of old faces and dark hair.

"But you wouldn't have, would you now, Achamian? You've been in High Ainon. What priest would denounce sorcery in a nation ruled by the Scarlet Spires, hmm?"

Achamian glared at the old sorcerer.

"But this is to be expected, is it not?" He suddenly found the whole idea preposterous. *Things like this happen to other men, at other times*. "You say that this Maithanet is cunning. What better way to secure his power than by inciting hatred against those condemned by the Tusk?"

"You're right, of course." Nautzera had the most infuriating way of owning one's objections. "But there's a far more disturbing reason to believe that he'll declare against us rather than the Fanim . . ."

"And what reason is that?"

"Because, Achamian," a voice other than Nautzera's replied, "there's no way that a Holy War against the Fanim *could succeed*."

Achamian peered into the darkness between columns. It was Simas, a wry smile splitting his snow white beard. He wore a grey vestment over his blue silk gown. Even in appearance he was water to Nautzera's fire.

"How was your journey?" Simas asked.

"The Dreams were particularly bad," Achamian replied, somewhat bewildered by the shift between hard speculation and light pleasantries. In what now seemed a different lifetime, Simas had been his teacher, the one to bury the innocence of a Nroni fisherman's son in the mad revelations of the Mandate. They hadn't spoken directly in years—Achamian had been abroad for a long time—but the ease of manner, the ability to speak without the detours of jnan, remained. "What do you mean, Simas? Why couldn't a Holy War succeed against the Fanim?"

"Because of the Cishaurim."

Again the Cishaurim.

"I fear I don't follow you, old teacher. Surely it would be *easier* for the Inrithi to war against Kian, a nation with only one School— if the Cishaurim can be called such—than for them to war against all the Schools."

Simas nodded. "On the face of things, perhaps. But think on it, Achamian. We estimate that the Thousand Temples itself has some four to five thousand Chorae, which means it could field at least as many men immune to whatever sorceries we could muster. Add to that all of the Inrithi lords who also bear Trinkets, and Maithanet could field an army of perhaps ten thousand men who would be immune to us in every way."

In the Three Seas, Chorae were a crucial variable in the algebra of war. In so many ways the Few were like Gods compared with the masses. Only the Chorae prevented the Schools from utterly dominating the Three Seas.

"Certainly," Achamian replied, "but Maithanet could likewise field those men against the Cishaurim. However different the Cishaurim may be, they seem to share our vulnerabilities at least."

"Could he?"

"Why not?"

"Because between those men and the Cishaurim would stand all the armed might of Kian. The Cishaurim are not a School, old friend. They don't stand apart, as we do, from the faith and people of their nation. While the Holy War struggled to overcome the heathen Grandees of Kian, the Cishaurim would rain ruin upon them." Simas lowered his chin as though testing his beard against his breastbone. "Do you see?"

Achamian could see. He had dreamed of such a battle before— the Fords of Tywanrae, where the hosts of ancient Akssersia had burned in the fires of the Consult. At the mere thought of this tragic battle, images flashed before his eyes, shadowy men thrashing in waters, consumed in towering bonfires . . . How many had been lost at the fords?

"Like Tywanrae," Achamian whispered.

"Like Tywanrae," Simas replied, his voice both solemn and gentle. They had all shared this nightmare. The Schoolmen of the Mandate shared every nightmare.

Throughout this exchange, Nautzera had regarded them narrowly. Like a Prophet of the Tusk, his judgement was palpable—except where prophets saw sinners, Nautzera saw fools. "And as I said," the old man remarked, "this Maithanet is shrewd, a man of intellect. Surely he knows he cannot win a Holy War against the Fanim."

Achamian stared blankly at the sorcerer. His earlier exhilaration had fled, replaced by a cold and dank fear. Another Scholastic War . . . The thought of Tywanrae had shown him the terrifying dimensions of such a prospect.

"This is why I've been recalled from High Ainon? To prepare for this new Shriah's Holy War?"

"No," Nautzera replied decisively. "We've simply told you the reasons why we *fear* that Maithanet might call his Holy War against us. Ultimately, we don't know what he plans."

"Indeed," Simas added. "Between the Schools and the Fanim, the Fanim are undoubtedly the greatest threat to the Thousand Temples. Shimeh has been lost to the heathens for centuries, and the Empire is but a frail shadow of what it once was, while Kian has become the mightiest power in the Three Seas. No. It would be far more rational for the Shriah to declare the Fanim the object of his Holy War—"

"But," Nautzera interjected, "we all know that faith is no friend to reason. The distinction between the rational and the irrational means little when one speaks of the Thousand Temples."

"You're sending me to Sumna," Achamian said. "To discover Maithanet's true intent."

A wicked smile creased Nautzera's dyed beard. "Yes."

"But what good could I do? It's been years since I've been to Sumna. I've no more contacts there." This was true or untrue depending upon how one defined "contacts." There was a woman he knew in Sumna—Esmenet. But that had been a long time ago.

And there was also— Achamian was arrested by the thought. Could they know?

"But this isn't true," Nautzera replied. "In fact, *Simas* has informed us of that student of yours who"—he paused, as though searching for a term to deal with a matter too dreadful for polite conversation—"defected."

Simas? He looked to his old teacher. *Why would you tell them?*

Achamian spoke cautiously. "You refer to Inrau."

"Yes," Nautzera replied. "And this Inrau has become, or so I am told"—again a glance at Simas—"a Shrial *Priest*." His tone was thick with censure. *Your student, Achamian. Your betrayal.*

"You're too harsh, as always, Nautzera. Inrau was cursed: born with the sensitivities of the Few and yet with the sensibilities of a priest. Our ways would have killed him."

"Ah, yes . . . *sensibilities*," the old face replied. "But tell us, clearly if you could, your estimation of this former student. Has he crossed the pale, or might the Mandate retrieve him?"

"Could he be made our spy? Is this what you ask?"

Inrau a spy? Obviously Simas had compounded his betrayal by not telling them anything of Inrau.

"I thought it evident," Nautzera said.

Achamian paused, looked to Simas, whose face had become discouragingly serious.

"Answer him, Akka," his old teacher said.

"No," Achamian replied, turning back to Nautzera. Suddenly his heart felt a stone. "No. Inrau was born on the far side of the pale. He won't return."

Cold amusement—so bitter on such an old face. "Ah, Achamian, but he will."

Achamian knew what they demanded: the sorceries, and the betrayal they would entail. He had been close to Inrau, had promised to protect him. They had been . . . close.

"No," he replied, "I refuse. Inrau's spirit is frail. He doesn't have the mettle to do what you're asking. We need someone else."

"There is no one else."

"Nevertheless," he replied, only beginning to grasp the consequences of his rashness, "I refuse."

"You refuse?" Nautzera spat. "Because this priest is a weakling? Achamian, you must stifle the mother in—"

"Achamian acts out of loyalty, Nautzera," Simas interrupted. "Don't confuse the two."

"Loyalty?" Nautzera snapped. "But this is the very *heart* of the issue, Simas! What we share is incomprehensible to other men. As one we cry out in our sleep. With such a bond—like a vice!—how can loyalty to another be anything short of sedition?"

"Sedition?" Achamian exclaimed, knowing he had to proceed carefully. Such words were like casks of wine: once unstopped, things tended to deteriorate. "You mistake me—both of you. I refuse out of loyalty *to* the Mandate. Inrau is too frail. We risk alienating the Thousand—"

"Such a weak lie," Nautzera growled. He then laughed, as though realizing that he should have expected this impertinence all along. "Schools *spy*, Achamian. We are alienated in *advance*. But you know this." The old sorcerer turned away from him and warmed his fingers over the coals of a nearby brazier. Orange light trimmed his grand figure, sketched his narrow lines against colossal works of stone. "Tell me, Achamian, if this Maithanet and the threat of a Holy War against the Schools is the work of our—to put it mildly—elusive adversary, would not Inrau's delicate life, or for that matter the Mandate's fine reputation, be worth throwing into the balance?"

"*If*, Nautzera," he replied vaguely, "then certainly."

"Ah, yes. I'd forgotten that you numbered yourself among the sceptics. What is it you say? That we pursue *ghosts*." He held the word in his mouth, as though it were a morsel of questionable food. "I guess, then, you would say that a *possibility*, that we're witnessing the first signs of the No-God's return, is outweighed by an *actuality*, the life of a defector—that rolling the dice of apocalypse is worth the pulse of a fool."

Yes, that was precisely how he felt. But how could he admit as much?

"I'm prepared to be sanctioned," he tried to say evenly. But his voice! Churlish. Wounded. "*I'm* not frail."

Nautzera studied his face. "Sceptics," he snorted. "You all make the same error. You confuse us with the other Schools. But do we vie for power? Do we scurry around palaces, placing Wards and sniffing sorceries like dogs? Do we whine into the ears of Emperors or Kings? In the absence of the Consult, you confuse our actions with those who act for no purpose save that of power and its child-ish gratifications. You confuse us with the whores."

Could it be? No. He'd thought it through many times. Unlike the others, those like Nautzera, he could distinguish his age from the one he dreamt night after night. He could see the difference. The Mandate was not merely poised between epochs—it was poised between dreams and waking life. When the sceptics, those who thought the Consult had abandoned the Three Seas, looked at the Mandate, they saw not a School compromised by worldly ambition but the opposite: a School not in this world at all. The "mandate," which was the mandate of history after all, was not to wage a dead war, or to sanctify a long-dead sorcerer driven mad by that war's horrors, but to *learn*—to live *from* the past, not in it.

"Would you argue philosophy with me, then, Nautzera?" he asked, matching the man's fierce glare. "Before you were too harsh, but now you're simply too stupid."

Nautzera blinked in astonishment.

Simas hastily interceded: "I understand your reluctance, old friend. I too have my doubts—as you know." He looked pointedly at Nautzera, who continued to stare at Achamian in disbelief.

"There's *strength* in scepticism," Simas continued. "Those who believe thoughtlessly in dangerous times are the first to die. But these *are* dangerous times, Achamian. More so than in many, many years. Perhaps dangerous enough to be sceptical even of our scepti-cism, hmm?"

Achamian turned to him, caught by something in his tone.

Simas's gaze faltered. A small struggle darkened his face. He continued.

"You've noticed how intense the Dreams have become. I can see that much in your eyes. We've all become a little wild-eyed as of late . . . Something . . ." He paused, unfocused his eyes as though counting his own heartbeat. Achamian felt his hackles rise. He'd never seen Simas like this. Indecisive. Frightened, even.

"Ask yourself, Achamian," he said finally, "if our adversary, the Consult, were to seize power in the Three Seas, what vehicle would be more effective than *the Thousand Temples?* Where better to hide from us and yet wield incredible power? And what better way to destroy the Mandate, the last memory of the Apocalypse, than by declaring a Holy War against the Few? Imagine Men waging war against the No-God without us to guide and protect them."

Without Seswatha.

Achamian stared for a long moment at his old teacher. His doubt must have been plain for everyone to see. Nevertheless, images from the Dreams came to him—a trickle of small horrors. Seswatha's internment at Dagliash. The crucifixion. The glint of sunlight across the bronze nails through his forearms. Mekeritrig's lips reciting the Cants of Agony. His shrieks . . . His? But that was just it: these memories *weren't* his! They belonged to another, to Seswatha, whose suffering must be seen through if they were to have any hope of moving on.

And yet Simas watched him so strangely, his eyes curious with their own indecision. Something *had* changed. The Dreams had grown more intense. Relentless. So much so that any lapse in concentration saw the present swept away in some past trauma, at times horrific enough to make one's hands shake, one's mouth form around voiceless cries. The *chance* that such horror could return. Was it worth sacrificing Inrau, his love? The boy who had so eased his weary heart. Who had taught him to taste the air he breathed . . . *Curse!* The Mandate was a curse! Dispossessed of the God. Dispossessed even of the present. Only the clawing, choking fear that the future might resemble the past.

"Simas—" he began, but stumbled. He wanted to concede, but the mere fact that Nautzera stood in his periphery silenced him. *Have I grown so petty?*

Tumultuous times, certainly. A new Shriah, the Inrithi feverish with renewed faith, the possibility that the Scholastic Wars could be revived, the sudden violence of the Dreams . . .

These are the times I live in. All this happens now.

It seemed impossible.

"You understand our imperative as profoundly as any of us," Simas said quietly. "And the stakes. Inrau was with us for a short time. He might be made to understand—*without* Cants, perhaps."

"Besides," Nautzera added, "if you refuse to go, you merely force us to send someone—how should I put it?—less sentimental."

Achamian stood alone on the parapets. Even here, on the turrets overlooking the straits, he felt oppressed by the stonework of Atyersus, diminished by the cyclopean walls. The sea offered little compensation.

Things had happened so quickly, as though he'd been grasped by giant hands, rolled between palms, and then cast into a different direction. Different, but always the same. Drusas Achamian had worn many tracks across the Three Seas, had discarded many sandals, and never once had he even glimpsed that which he supposedly hunted. Absence—always the same absence.

The interview had gone on. It seemed obligatory that any audience with the Quorum be prolonged, weighted with ritual and insufferable seriousness. Perhaps such seriousness was appropriate to the Mandate, Achamian supposed, given the nature of the war—if groping in blackness could be called such.

Even after Achamian had capitulated, had agreed to recruit Inrau by means fair and foul, Nautzera had found it necessary to chastise him for his reluctance.

"How could you forget, Achamian?" the old sorcerer had implored, his expression at once sour and beseeching. "The Old Names still watch from the towers of Golgotterath—and where do they look? To the North? The North is wilderness, Achamian.

Sranc and ruin. No. They look south—to us!—and plot with a patience that beggars the intellect. Only the Mandate shares that patience. Only the Mandate remembers."

"Perhaps the Mandate," Achamian had replied, "remembers too much."

But now he could only think, *Have I forgotten?*

The Schoolmen of the Mandate could never forget what had happened—the violence of Seswatha's Dreams ensured that much. But if anything, the civilization of the Three Seas was insistent. The Thousand Temples, the Scarlet Spires, all the Great Factions warred interminably across the Three Seas. In the midst of such a labyrinth, the significance of the past might easily be forgotten. The more crowded the concerns of the present, the more difficult it became to see the ways in which the past portended the future.

Had his concern for Inrau, a student like a son, led him to forget this?

Achamian fully understood the geometry of Nautzera's world. It had once been his own. For Nautzera, there was no present, only the clamour of a harrowing past and the threat of a corresponding future. For Nautzera, the present had receded to a point, had become the precarious fulcrum whereby history leveraged destiny. A mere formality.

And why not? The anguish of the Old Wars was beyond description. Almost all the great cities of the Ancient North had fallen to the No-God and his Consult. The Great Library of Sauglish ransacked. Trysë, the holy Mother-of-Cities, plundered of life. The Towers of Myclai pulled down. Dagliash, Kelmeol . . . Entire nations put to the sword.

For Nautzera, this Maithanet was significant not because he was Shriah but because he might belong to this world without a present, this world whose only frame of reference was past tragedy. Because he might be an author of the Second Apocalypse.

A Holy War against the Schools? The Shriah an agent of the Consult?
How could he not tremble at these thoughts?

Despite the warm wind, Achamian shivered. Below him, the sea heaved through the straits. Dark rollers warred against one another, clashed with unearthly momentum, as though the very Gods warred beneath.

Inrau . . . For Achamian, to think this name was to know peace for a fleeting instant. He had known so little peace in his life. And now he was forced to throw that peace onto the scales with terror. He must sacrifice Inrau in order to answer these questions.

Inrau had been a coltish adolescent when he'd first come to Achamian, a boy still blinking in the daybreak of manhood. Though there had been nothing extraordinary about his appearance or his intellect, Achamian had immediately recognized something different about him—a memory, perhaps, of the first student he'd loved, Nersei Proyas. But where Proyas had grown proud, overfed on the knowledge that he would someday be King, Inrau had remained . . . Inrau.

Teachers found many self-serving reasons to love their students. More than anything, they loved them simply because they *listened*. But Achamian had not loved Inrau as a student. Inrau, he'd realized, was *good*. Not good in the jaded way of the Mandate, who trafficked in the mire as did all other men. No. The good he saw in Inrau had nothing to do with kind acts or praiseworthy purposes; it was something innate. Inrau harboured no secrets, no shadowy need to conceal faults or to write himself large in the estimation of other men. He was open in the way of children and fools, and he possessed the same blessed naïveté, an innocence that smacked of wisdom rather than ignorance.

Innocence. If there was anything Achamian had forgotten, it was innocence.

How could he not fall in love with such a boy? He could remember standing with him in this very place, watching silver sunlight roll across the back of swell after swell. "The sun!" Inrau had cried. And when Achamian had asked him what he meant, Inrau had merely laughed and said: "Can't you see? Can't you see the sun?"

And then Achamian had seen: lines of liquid sunlight, dazzling the watery distance—an inexhaustible glory.

Beauty. This was Inrau's gift. He never ceased to see beauty, and because of this, he always understood, always saw through and forgave the many blemishes that marred other men. With Inrau, forgiveness *preceded* rather than followed transgression. *Do what you will,* his eyes said, *for you are already forgiven.*

Inrau's decision to abandon the Mandate for the Thousand Temples had at once dismayed and relieved Achamian. He'd been dismayed because he knew he'd lost Inrau and the reprieve of his company. But he'd been relieved because he knew the Mandate would obliterate Inrau's innocence if the boy stayed. Achamian could never forget the night when he himself had first touched Seswatha's Heart. The fisherman's son had died that moment; his eyes had been doubled, and the world itself had been transformed, rendered cavernous by tragic history. Inrau would have likewise died. Touching Seswatha's Heart would have charred his own. How could such innocence, any innocence, survive the terror of Seswatha's Dreams? How could one find solace in mere sunlight, when the threat of the No-God loomed across every horizon? Beauty was denied victims of the Apocalypse.

But the Mandate did not tolerate defections. The Gnosis was far too precious to be trusted with malcontents. This had been Nautzera's unspoken threat throughout their exchange: *"The boy is a defector, Achamian. Either way, he should die."* How long had the Quorum known that his story of Inrau's drowning was a sham? From the very beginning? Or had Simas truly betrayed him?

Of the innumerable acts Achamian had committed in his life-time, securing Inrau's escape was the one he considered a genuine accomplishment, the one act good in and of itself, even if he'd forsaken his School in order to achieve it. Achamian had protected innocence, had allowed it to flee to a safer place. How could anyone condemn such a thing?

But every act could be condemned. The same as all bloodlines could be traced to some long-dead king, all deeds could be chased to some potential catastrophe. One need only follow the forks far enough. If Inrau were seized by another of the Schools and forced to yield those few secrets he knew, then the Gnosis would be eventually lost, and the Mandate would be condemned to the impotent obscurity of a Minor School. Perhaps even destroyed.

Had he done the right thing? Or had he simply made a wager?

Was the pulse of a good man worth rolling the dice of Apocalypse? Nautzera had argued no, and Achamian had agreed.

The Dreams. What had happened could not happen again. This world must not die. A thousand innocents—a thousand thousand!—were not worth the possibility of a Second Apocalypse. Achamian had agreed with Nautzera. He would betray Inrau for the reason innocents are always betrayed: fear.

He leaned against the stone and stared down and across the churning straits, struggling to remember what it had looked like that sunny day with Inrau. He could not.

Maithanet and holy war. Soon Achamian would leave Atyersus for the Nansur city of Sumna, the holiest of cities for the Inrithi, home of the Thousand Temples and the Tusk. Only Shimeh, the birthplace of the Latter Prophet, was as holy.

How many years had passed since he'd last visited Sumna? Five? Seven? He idly wondered if he would find Esmenet there, whether she still lived. She had always been able to ease his heart somehow.

And it would be good to see Inrau as well, despite the circumstances. At the very least the boy had to be warned. *They know, dear boy. I've failed you.*

So little comfort in the sea. Filled by a wan loneliness, Achamian looked beyond the straits in the direction of far-away Sumna. He yearned to once again see these two people, one whom he'd loved only to lose to the Thousand Temples, the other whom he thought he might love . . .

Were he a man and not a sorcerer and a spy.

After watching Achamian's lonely figure wind down into the cedar forests beneath Atyersus, Nautzera lingered on the parapets, savouring the odd flash of sunlight and studying the storm-heaped clouds that fissured the northern sky. This time of year, Achamian's voyage to Sumna was certain to be fraught with inclement weather. He would survive the voyage, Nautzera knew—through the Gnosis, if he had to—but would he survive the far greater storm that awaited him? Would he survive Maithanet?

Our task is so great, he thought, *and our tools so frail.*

Shaking himself from his reverie—a bad habit that had only worsened with age—he hastened into the ponderous galleries, ignoring the passage of peers and subordinates alike. After a time he found himself in the papyrus gloom of the library, his old bones aching from exertion. As expected, he found Simas hunched over an ancient manuscript. Lantern light glistened across a thin line of spilt ink, which Nautzera momentarily confused for blood. He watched the oblivious man for a moment, troubled by a flare of resentment. Why did he begrudge Simas so? Was it because the man's eyes had yet to fail, while Nautzera, like so many others, had to rely on his students to read to him?

"The light's better in the scriptorium," Nautzera said, startling the old sorcerer.

The friendly face jerked up, peered into the murk. "Is it, now? But not the company, I imagine."

Always some wry quip. Simas, in the end, was a predictable man. Or was that also part of the sham, like the faint air of doddering gentility he used to disarm his students?

"We should have told him, Simas."

The old man frowned and absently scratched his beard. "Told him what? That Maithanet has already called the faithful to declare the object of his Holy War? That half of his mission is mere pretext? Achamian will find out soon enough."

"No." They had needed that omission, at least, to make the prospect of betraying his student more palatable for the man.

Simas nodded and sighed deeply. "You're worried about the other thing, then. If there's one lesson we've learned from the Consult, old friend, it's that *ignorance* is a potent tool."

"As is *knowledge*. Would we deny him the tools he needs? What if he's careless? Men often grow careless in the absence of any real threat."

Simas shook his head with dismissive vigour. "But he travels to *Sumna*, Nautzera. Or have you forgotten? He'll take care. What sorcerer wouldn't in the den of the Thousand Temples, hmm? Especially in times such as these."

Nautzera pursed his lips and remained silent.

Simas leaned back from his manuscript, as if uncluttering his concentration. He studied Nautzera keenly. "You've heard new reports," he said at length. "Someone else is dead."

Simas had always possessed the uncanny ability to guess the cause of his many humours.

"Worse," Nautzera said. "Missing. This morning, Parthelsus reported that his primary informant in the Tydonni court has vanished without a trace. Our agents are being hunted, Simas."

"It must be them."

Them. Nautzera shrugged. "Or the Scarlet Spires. Or even the Thousand Temples. The Emperor's spies, remember, seem to be suffering a similar fate in Sumna . . . Either way, Achamian should have been told."

"Always so puritanical, Nautzera. No. Whoever assails us is either too timid or too canny to do so directly. Rather than strike at our sorcerers-of-rank, they strike at our informants, at our eyes and ears in the Three Seas. For whatever reason, they hope to render us deaf and dumb."

Though he appreciated the dreadful implications of this, Nautzera failed to see the connection. "So?"

"So Drusas Achamian was my student for many years. I know

him. He uses men, as a spy must, but he's never acquired a taste for it—the way a spy must. By nature, he's an uncharacteristically . . . open man. Weak."

Achamian *was* weak, or so Nautzera had always thought, but what bearing could this have on their obligations to him? "I'm too weary for your riddles, Simas. Speak plain."

Simas's eyes flashed in annoyance. "Riddles? I thought I was being quite clear."

At last we see the real you, "old friend."

"It comes to this," Simas continued. "Achamian *befriends* the people he uses, Nautzera. If he knew his contacts might be hunted, he would hesitate. And perhaps more important, if he knew that Atyersus itself had been *infiltrated*, he might censor the information he gave us in order to protect his contacts. Remember that he *lied*, Nautzera, *risked the Gnosis itself*, to protect that treacherous student of his."

Nautzera graced the man with a rare smile, and though it felt wicked upon his face, it seemed eminently justified. "I agree. Such a thing would be intolerable. But for a long time, Simas, our success has depended on granting autonomy to our agents in the field. We've always trusted those who know the situation best to make the best decisions. And now, at your insistence, we deny one of our brothers the knowledge he needs. Knowledge that could save his life."

Simas abruptly stood and approached him in the shadows. Despite the man's small stature and grandfatherly mien, Nautzera's skin prickled as he drew near.

"But it's never quite so simple, is it now, old friend? It's the concert of knowledge and ignorance that underwrites our decisions. Trust me when I tell you we've struck the proper proportion with Achamian. Was I wrong when I told you Inrau's defection would prove useful someday?"

"No," Nautzera admitted, remembering their heated arguments of two years past. He had worried that Simas was merely protecting a beloved student—then. But if the years had taught Nautzera one thing about Polchias Simas, it was that the man was as shrewd as he was devoid of sentiment.

"Then trust me in this," Simas urged, raising a friendly ink-stained hand to his shoulder. "Come, old friend. We have arduous tasks of our own."

Satisfied, Nautzera nodded. Arduous tasks, indeed. Whoever hunted their informants did so with galling ease, and that could mean only one thing: despite reliving Seswatha's anguish night after night, a Mandate Schoolman had turned traitor.

CHAPTER THREE

SUMNA

If the world is a game whose rules are written by the God, and sorcerers are those who cheat and cheat, then who has written the rules of sorcery?

—ZARATHINIUS, *A DEFENCE OF THE ARCANE ARTS*

Early Spring, 4110 Year-of-the-Tusk, En Route to Sumna

On the Sea of Meneanor, a storm touched them.

Achamian awoke from another of the dreams, hugging himself. The ancient wars of his sleep seemed tangled with the blackness of his cabin, the pitching floor, and the chorus of thundering water. He lay huddled, shivering as he fumbled to sort out the real from the dream. Faces haunted the blackness, cramped in astonishment and horror. Bronze-armoured forms struggled across the distance. Smoke smeared the horizon, and rising, knotted like branches of black iron, was a dragon. *Skafra . . .*

A thunderclap.

On the deck, braced against the sheets of rain, the Nroni sailors wailed, supplicated themselves to Momas, Aspect of storm and sea. And God of dice.

75

———— ⊶∞⊷ ————

The Nroni merchantman weighed anchor outside the harbour of Sumna, the ancient centre of the Inrithi faith. Leaning against a weathered rail, Achamian watched the pilot's boat row toward them through the swells. The great city was indistinct in the background, but he could discern the structures of the Hagerna, the vast compound of temples, granaries, and barracks that formed the administrative heart of the Thousand Temples. In its centre rose the legendary bastions of the Junriüma, the holy sanctum of the Tusk.

He could feel the tug of what should have been their grandeur, but they seemed mute in the distance, dumb. Just more stone. For the Inrithi, this was the place where the heavens inhabited the earth. Sumna, the Hagerna, and the Junriüma were far more than geographical sites; they were bound up in the very purpose of history. They were the hinges of destiny.

But they were eggshells of stone to Achamian. The Hagerna called to men unlike himself, men who could not, he supposed, escape the weight of their time. Men like his former student Inrau.

Whenever Inrau had discussed the Hagerna, he would speak as though the God himself had laid the keel of his words. Achamian had felt more than faintly alienated by this talk, as so often happened when confronted by another's excessive enthusiasm. There would be a momentum to Inrau's tone, a mad certainty that could put cities, even nations, to the sword, as though his righteous joy could be attached to any act of madness. Here again was reason why Maithanet should be so deeply feared: to possess this momentum was disease enough, but to be a carrier . . . There was pause for thought.

Maithanet carried a plague whose primary symptom was certainty. How the God could be equated with the absence of hesitation was something Achamian had never understood. After all, what was the God but the mystery that burdened them all? What was hesitation but a dwelling-within this mystery?

Perhaps, then, I am among the most pious of men, he thought, smiling inwardly. He was a man who lavished himself with false flattery. Too much brooding.

"Maithanet," he muttered under his breath, but the name was also empty. It could neither tether the grandiose rumours that fluttered about it nor provide motive enough for the crimes he was about to commit.

As though drawn by some half-understood sense of obligation to his sole passenger, the captain of the merchantman joined his meditative silence, standing somewhat nearer than prescribed by the dictates of jnan—a common low-caste error. He was a sturdy man, constructed, it seemed, of the same wood as his ship. Salt and sun on his forearms, the sea in his unkempt hair and beard.

"This city," he finally said, "is not such a good place for someone like you."

Someone like me . . . A sorcerer in a holy city. There was no indictment in the man's words or his tone. The Nroni had grown used to the Mandate, to Mandate gifts and Mandate demands. But they were still Inrithi, the faithful. A certain blankness of expression was their solution to this contradiction. They always spoke around the fact of their heresy, perhaps hoping that if they didn't touch it with words, they might somehow carry away their faith intact.

"They never know what we are," Achamian said. "That's the horrible fact of sinners. We're indistinguishable from the righteous."

"So I've been told," the man replied, avoiding his eyes. "The Few can see only each other." There was something disturbing about his tone, as though he probed for the details of some illicit sexual act.

Why speak of this? Was the fool trying to ingratiate himself?

An image struck Achamian: himself as a boy, climbing on the big rocks, the ones his father had used to dry the nets, pausing every few breathless instants simply to look around him. Something had happened. It was as though he'd opened different eyelids, ones beneath those he normally opened each morning. Everything was so agonizingly tight, as though the flesh of the world had been dried taut across the gaps between bone: the net against stone, the grid of shadows cast over the hollows, the watery beads cupped between the flex of tendons on his hands—so clear! And within this tightness, the sensation of inner blooming, of the collapse of seeing into *being*, as though his eyes had been wrung into the very heart of things. From the surface of the stone, he could see himself, a dark child towering across the disc of the sun.

The very fabric of existence. The onta. He had—and he could still never adequately express this—"experienced" it. Unlike most others, he'd known immediately he was one of the Few, known with a child's stubborn certainty. "Atyersus!" he could remember crying, feeling the vertigo of a life no longer to be determined by his caste, by his father, or by the past.

Those times when the Mandate had passed through his fishing village had profoundly marked him as a boy. First the clash of cymbals and then the cloaked figures, shielded by parasols and borne by slaves, steeped in the erotic aura of mystery. So remote! Faces impassive, touched only by the finest cosmetics, and by the proper jnanic contempt for low-caste fishermen and their sons. Only men of mythic stature could reside behind such faces—this he knew. Men braced by the glory of *The Sagas*. Dragon-slayers and assassins of kings. Prophets and abominations.

Mere months of training at Atyersus had seen that childishness wane. Jaded, pompous, and self-deceived—Atyersus differed only in scale.

Am I so different from this man? Achamian asked himself, watching the captain in his periphery. *Not really*, he thought, but he ignored the man nonetheless and turned back to stare at Sumna, hazy against the dark hills.

And yet he *was* different. So many cares, and the wages so slight. Different in that his tantrums could sweep away city gates, pulverize flesh, and snap bone. Such power, and yet the same vanities, the same fears, and far darker whims. He had expected the mythic to raise him up, to exalt his every act, and instead he was set adrift . . . Detachment enlightened no one. He could turn this ship into a shining inferno, then walk unscathed across the surface of the water, and yet he could never be . . . *certain.*

He had almost whispered this aloud.

The captain left momentarily, visibly relieved to be called away by his crew. The pilot had drawn up to the rolling ship.

Why are they so distant to me? Stung by this thought, he lowered his head, stared into the wine-dark depths. *Whom do I despise?*

To ask this question was to answer it. How could one not feel isolated, detached, when existence itself answered to their tongue? Where was the hard ground on which one might stand when mere words could sweep everything away? It had become a truism among scholars in the Three Seas to compare sorcerers to poets, a comparison Achamian had always thought absurd. He could scarcely imagine two vocations so tragically at odds. Save fear or political machination, no sorcerer had ever created with his words. The power, the brilliant flurries of light, possessed an irresistible direction, and it was the wrong one: the direction of destruction. It was as though men could only ape the language of God, could only debase and brutalize his song. When sorcerers sing, the saying went, men die.

When sorcerers sing. And yet even among his own, he was anathema. The other Schools could never forgive the Mandate their heritage, their possession of the Gnosis, the knowledge of the Ancient North. Before their extinction, the great Schools of the North had possessed benefactors, pilots to navigate them through shoals no human mind could conceive of. The Gnosis of the Nonmen Magi, the Quya, refined through another thousand years of human cunning.

In so many ways he was a god to these fools. He needed always to remember this—not merely because it was flattering, but because it was *they* who could not forget. They who feared, and thus they who inevitably hated—so much that they would risk all in a Holy

War against the Schools. A sorcerer who forgot this hatred forgot how to stay alive.

Standing before the blurred immensity of Sumna, Achamian listened to the seamen bicker in the background, and to the ship groan in rhythm with the swells. He thought of the burning of the White Ships in Neleost, thousands of years ago. He could still taste the musty smoke, see the glitter of doom across the evening waters, feel his other body shivering in the cold.

And Achamian wondered where it all went, the past, and why, if it were gone, it made his heart ache so.

In the choked streets beyond the quays, Achamian, who often became contemplative in the press of men, was once again struck by the absurdity of his presence here. It was a minor miracle that the Thousand Temples had ever allowed the Schools to maintain missions in Sumna. For the Inrithi, there was a sense that Sumna was not merely the heart of their faith and their priesthood, but the very heart of God. Literally.

The Chronicle of the Tusk was the most ancient and therefore the most thunderous voice of the past, so ancient that it was itself without any clear history—"innocent," as the great Ceneian commentator Gaeterius had written. Ribboned by characters, the Tusk recorded the great migratory invasions that marked the ascendancy of Men in Eärwa. For whatever reason, the Tusk had always been in the possession of one tribe, the Ketyai, and since the earliest days of Shigek, before even the rise of Kyraneas, it had been installed in Sumna—or so the surviving records suggested. As a result, Sumna and the Tusk had become inseparable in the thoughts of Men; pilgrimages to Sumna and to the Tusk were one and the same, as though the place had become an artifact and the artifact a place. To walk in Sumna was to walk through scripture.

Small wonder he felt out of place.

He found himself being jostled behind a small train of mules. Arms and shoulders, scowling faces and shouts. Movement through the small street came to a halt. Never had he seen the city so maddeningly crowded. He turned to one of the men pressing him, a Conriyan by appearance—solemn, broad-shouldered, with a heavy beard, a member of the warrior caste.

"Tell me," Achamian asked in Sheyic, "what's happening here?" He'd dispensed with jnan in his impatience: they were, after all, sharing sweat.

The man appraised him with dark eyes, a curious look on his face.

"You mean you don't know?" he asked, raising his voice above the din.

"Know what?" Achamian replied, feeling a small tickle in his spine.

"Maithanet has called the faithful to Sumna," he said, suspicious of Achamian's ignorance. "He's to reveal the object of the Holy War."

Achamian was stunned. He glanced at the faces packed around them, abruptly realizing how many of them had the hard-bitten look of war. Nearly all of them were openly armed. The first half of his mission, to discover the object of Maithanet's Holy War, was about to be accomplished for him.

Nautzera and the others must have known. But why didn't they tell me?

Because they needed him to come to Sumna. They knew he would resist recruiting Inrau, so they'd assembled everything they could to convince him that he must. A lie of omission—perhaps not so great a sin—but it had rendered him pliant to their purposes nonetheless.

Manipulation upon manipulation. Even the Quorum played games with their own pieces. It was an old outrage, but it never failed to sting.

The man had continued speaking, his eyes bright with sudden fervour: "Pray that it's the Schools we war against, my friend, rather than the Fanim. Sorcery is ever the greater cancer."

Achamian almost agreed.

Achamian reached out, planning to draw a finger through the groove down the centre of Esmenet's back, but he hesitated, clasping a handful of stained coverings instead. The room was dark, thick with the heat of their coupling. Through the shadows, he could see the scatter of crumbs and refuse across the floor. A blinding white crack in the shutters was the only source of light. The thunder of the street beyond had the rattle of thin walls.

"Nothing else?" he said, feeling remotely shocked by the unsteadiness in his own voice.

"What do you mean, 'nothing else?'" Her voice was marked by an old and patient bruise.

She had misunderstood, but before he could explain, a sudden sense of nausea and suffocating heat struck him. He pushed himself from the bed to his feet and immediately felt as though he might fall to his knees. His legs buckled, and he drunkenly braced himself against the sideboards. Chills skittered through his arm hairs and across his scalp and back.

"Akka?" she asked.

"Fine," he replied. "The heat." He drew himself up and rolled back onto the wheeling mattress. Her body felt like burning eels against his own. Such heat so early in spring! It was as though the very world had grown feverish at the prospect of Maithanet's Holy War.

"You've suffered the Fevers before," she said, her voice apprehensive. The Fevers were not contagious—everyone knew this.

"Yes," he said thickly, holding his forehead. *You're safe.* "They possessed me six years ago, while on mission in Cingulat . . . I almost died."

"Six years ago," she repeated. "My daughter died the same year." Bitterness.

He found himself resenting the ease with which his pain had become hers. An image of what her daughter might look like came to him: sturdy but fine-boned, dark languid hair chopped low-caste short, a cheek perfectly curved to the cup of a palm. But it was Esmi he actually envisaged. Her as a child.

They were silent a long time. His thoughts settled. The heat became embalming, lost the acrid edge of their exertions. She had mistaken what he'd said earlier, he realized, remembering the strange bruise in her tone. He had merely wanted to know if there was anything more to the rumours.

In a way, he'd always known he would return here, not only to Sumna, but to this place between the arms and legs of this tired woman. Esmenet. A strange, old-fashioned name for a woman of her character, but at the same time oddly appropriate for a prostitute.

Esmenet. How could a name affect him so?

She had dwindled in the four years since he had last come to Sumna. More haggard, her humour gouged by the accumulation of small wounds. Without hesitation, he'd searched for her after struggling through the packed harbour, struck by his own eagerness. Seeing her sitting in her window had been strange, an intermingling of loss and vanity, as though he'd recognized a childhood rival behind the bitten face of a leper or a beggar.

"Still fetching sticks, I see," she'd said, her eyes remarkably untouched by surprise.

The child-fat had also disappeared from her wit.

Gradually, she'd gathered him from his worries into her intricate world of anecdote and satire. Inexorably, the moments had led to this room, and Achamian had made love to her with an urgency that shocked him, as though he'd found an impossible reprieve in the animality of the act—a reprieve from the turmoil of his mission.

Achamian had come to Sumna for two reasons: to determine whether this new Shriah planned to wage his Holy War against the Schools, and to learn whether the Consult had any hand in these remarkable events. The first had been a tangible goal, something he could use to rationalize his betrayal of Inrau. The second . . . ghostly, possessing the feverish anemia of excuses that fall far short of absolution. How could he use the Mandate's war against the Consult to rationalize betrayal when the war itself had come to seem so irrational?

How else could one describe a war without a foe?

"Tomorrow I must find Inrau," he said, more to the darkness than to Esmenet.

"Do you still intend to . . . turn him?"

"I don't know. I know precious little any more."

"How can you say that, Akka? I sometimes wonder if there's anything you don't know."

She had always been the consummate whore, nursing first his loins and then his heart. *I don't know if I could bear this again.*

"I've spent my entire life among people who think me mad, Esmi."

She laughed at this. Though born a caste menial and never educated—formally anyway—Esmenet had always possessed a keen appreciation of irony. It was one of many things that so distinguished her from the other women, the other prostitutes.

"I've spent my entire life among people who think me a harlot, Akka."

Achamian smiled in the darkness. "But it's not the same. You *are* a harlot."

"So you're not mad, then?" She giggled at this, and Achamian felt himself sour. This girlishness was a charade—or so he'd always thought—something concocted for her men. It reminded him that he was a customer, that they weren't lovers after all.

"But that's just it, Esmi. Whether I'm mad or no depends on whether my enemy exists." He hesitated, as though these words had delivered him to a breathless precipice. "Esmenet . . . *You* believe me, don't you?"

"Believe an inveterate liar like you? Please don't insult me."

Flare of irritation, immediately regretted. "No. Seriously . . ."

She paused before answering. "Do I believe the Consult exists?"

She doesn't. People who repeated questions, Achamian knew, feared answering them.

Her beautiful brown eyes studied him in the gloom. "Let's just say, Akka, that I believe the *question* of the Consult exists."

There was something beseeching in her look. He felt more chills.

"Isn't that enough?" she asked.

Even for him, the Consult had withdrawn from the terror of fact to the rootless anxiety of questions. Had he, by mourning the absence of an answer, forgotten the importance of the question?

"I must find Inrau tomorrow," he said.

Her fingers burrowed through his beard, across his chin. He raised his head like a cat.

"We make a sad couple," she said, as though making a casual observation.

"Why would you say that?"

"A sorcerer and a harlot . . . There's something sad about that."

He grasped her hand and kissed the tips of her fingers.

"There's something sad about all couples," he said.

In his dream, Inrau walked through canyons of burnt brick, through faces and figures illuminated by rags of torchlight. And he heard a voice from nowhere, crying through his bones, across every finger's-breadth of his skin, speaking words like the shadows of fists striking just beyond the corner of his eyes. Words that battered whatever will remained to him. Words that walked with his limbs.

He glimpsed the sagging facade of a tavern, then a low, golden-dim enclosure of smoke, tables, and overhead beams. The entrance enveloped him. The rising ground tipped forward, directed him toward a malevolent blackness in the far corner of the room. It too enveloped him—another entrance. Everything rushed into the bearded man, his head slack against the chapped stucco, his face on a lazy, upward angle, but tight with some forbidden ecstasy—light spilling from his working mouth. Flakes of sun in his eyes.

Achamian . . .

Then the impossible mutter trailed into the rumble of patrons. The murky interior of the tavern became sturdy and mundane. The nightmarish angles squared. The play of light and shadow became crisp.

"What are you doing here?" Inrau sputtered, struggling to clear his thoughts. "Do you realize what's happening?" He scanned the interior of the tavern and through beams and haze saw a table of Shrial Knights in a far corner. So far they hadn't noticed him.

Achamian watched him sourly. "It's good to see you too, boy."

Inrau scowled. "Don't call me 'boy.'"

Achamian grinned. "But what else"—he winked—"is a beloved uncle supposed to call his nephew? Hmm, boy?"

Inrau exhaled a long breath and leaned back into his chair. "It is good to see you . . . Uncle Akka." No lie there. Despite the hurtful circumstances, it *was* good to see him. For some time he'd regretted leaving his old teacher's side. Sumna and the Thousand Temples were not the places, the sanctuaries, he'd imagined them to be—at least not until Maithanet had been elected to the Seat.

"I *have* missed you," Inrau continued, "but Sumna—"

"Is not such a good place for someone like me—I know."

"Then why have you come? Surely you've heard the rumours."

"I didn't simply 'come,' Inrau . . ." Achamian paused, his face abruptly troubled. "I was sent."

Inrau's scalp prickled. "Oh no, Achamian. Please tell me . . ."

"We need to know about this Maithanet," Achamian said in a forced tone. "About his Holy War. Surely you can see this."

Achamian downed his bowl of wine. For an instant, he looked broken. But the sudden pity Inrau felt for the man, the man who in so many ways had become his father, was dwarfed by a giddy sense of groundlessness. "But you promised, Akka. You *promised.*"

Tears glittered in the Schoolman's eyes. Wise tears, but filled with regret nonetheless.

"The world has had the habit," Achamian said, "of breaking the back of my promises."

Though Achamian had hoped to present Inrau the front of a teacher at last acknowledging a former student as his peer, an unvoiced question continued to rattle him: *What am I doing?*

Studying the young man, he felt a pang of affection. His face looked strangely aquiline, shaven as it was in the Nansur fashion. But the voice was familiar—the way it grew more and more tangled in competing ideas. And his eyes as well: exuberant, wide, and glassy brown, perpetually hinged on the cusp of honest self-doubt. Inrau had been cursed more than others, Achamian reflected, to be given the gift of the Few. In temperament, he was ideally suited to be a priest of the Thousand Temples. The touch of selfless candour, of forward passion—these were things the Mandate would have stripped from him.

"But Maithanet is more than you can understand," Inrau was saying. The young man's entire body seemed to flinch from the round-rushing air of the tavern. "Some almost worship him, though this angers him. He's to be obeyed, not worshipped. That's why he took his name—"

"His name?" It hadn't occurred to Achamian that his name might mean something. This in itself disturbed him. It was a Shrial tradition to take a new name. How could such simple things slip past him?

"Yes," Inrau replied. "From *mai'tathana*."

Achamian was unfamiliar with the word. But before he could ask, Inrau continued his explanation, his tone defiant, as though the former student could only now, finally beyond the reach of the Mandate, vent old resentments.

"Its meaning would be unknown to you. *Mai'tathana* is Thoti-Eännorean, the language of the Tusk. It means 'instruction.'"

So what's the lesson?

"And none of it troubles you?" Achamian asked.

"None of what troubles me?"

"The fact that Maithanet so effortlessly secured the Seat. That he was able, in a matter of *weeks*, to purge the Shrial Apparati of all the Emperor's spies."

"*Trouble* me?" Inrau cried incredulously. "My heart *exults* at these things. You have no inkling how deeply I despaired when I first came to Sumna. When I first realized how sordid and corrupt the Thousand Temples had become—realized that the *Shriah himself* was simply another of the Emperor's dogs. And then Maithanet arrived. Like a storm! One of those rare summer storms that sweep the earth clean. Troubled by the ease with which he cleansed Sumna? Akka, I *rejoiced*."

"Then what of this Holy War? Does your heart also rejoice at the thought of this? The thought of another Scholastic War?"

Inrau hesitated, as though shocked his earlier momentum had so quickly stalled.

"No one knows the object of his Holy War," he said numbly. As much as Inrau despised the Mandate, Achamian knew the thought of its destruction horrified him. *Part of him dwells with us still.*

"And if Maithanet does declare against the Schools, what will you think of him then?"

"He won't, Akka. I'm certain of this."

"But that wasn't my question, was it?" Achamian inwardly winced at the ruthlessness of his tone. "If Maithanet declares against the Schools, *what then?*"

Inrau drew his hands—delicate hands for a man, Achamian had always thought—across his face. "I don't know, Akka. I've asked this same question a thousand times, and still I don't know."

"But why is that? You're a Shrial Priest now, Inrau, an apostle of the God as revealed by the Latter Prophet and the Tusk. Doesn't the Tusk demand that all sorcerers be burned?"

"Yes, but . . ."

"But the Mandate is different? An exception?"

"Yes. It *is* different."

"Why? Because an old fool whom you once loved is one of them?"

"Keep your voice down," Inrau hissed, glancing apprehensively at the table of Shrial Knights. "You know full well why, Akka. Because I love you as a father and a friend, certainly, but because I also . . . respect the Mandate mission."

"So if Maithanet declares against the Schools, what would you think?"

"I would grieve."

"Grieve? I don't think so, Inrau. You'd think he's *mistaken*. As brilliant and as holy as Maithanet may be, you'd think, 'He hasn't seen what I've seen!'"

Inrau nodded vacantly.

"The Thousand Temples," Achamian continued, his tone more gentle, "has always been the most powerful of the Great Factions, but that power has often been blunted, if not broken, by corruption. Maithanet is the first Shriah in centuries to reclaim its pre-eminence. And now in the secret councils of every Faction, ruthless men ask, What will Maithanet do with this power? Who will he instruct with his Holy War? The Fanim and their Cishaurim priests? Or will he instruct those condemned by the Tusk, the Schools? Never has Sumna been filled with as many spies as now. They circle the Holy Precincts like vultures about the promise of a corpse. House Ikurei and the Scarlet Spires will try to devise ways to yoke Maithanet's agenda to their own. The Kianene and the Cishaurim will keep a wary eye on his every move, fearing that his lesson is for them. Minimize or exploit, Inrau—all of them are here for one of these two reasons. Only the Mandate stands outside this sordid circle."

An old tactic, made effective by desperate wit. When recruiting a spy one had to open a safe place with words, make it appear that what was at stake wasn't betrayal but a further, more demanding fidelity. Frames—give them greater frames with which to interpret the treachery out of their actions. Before all, a spy who recruits spies must be a master storyteller.

"I know this," Inrau said, staring at the palm of his right hand. "I do know this."

"And if there's anywhere," Achamian said, "that a hidden faction might be found, it's *here*. All the reasons you've given me for your devotion to Maithanet are reasons why the Mandate must have eyes in the Thousand Temples. If the Consult is to be found anywhere, Inrau, it will be found *here*."

In a sense, all Achamian had done was issue a string of non-contentious declarations, but the story he'd conjured for Inrau was clear, even if the young man could not recognize it as such. Of all the Shrial Priests in the Hagerna, Inrau alone would be the one who saw the greater frame, the one who acted on interests that were not provincial or self-deceived. The Thousand Temples was a good place, but it was hapless. It had to be protected from its own innocence.

"But the Consult," Inrau said, fixing Achamian with a pained look. "What if they *have* died out? If I do what you ask for *nothing*, Akka, then I'll be damned." As though fearing instant retribution, he anxiously peeked over his shoulder.

"But the question, Inrau, is what if they—"

Achamian paused, stilled by the young priest's horrified expression. "What is it?"

"They've seen me." Rigid swallow. "The Shrial Knights behind me . . . to your left."

Achamian had noticed the Knights enter shortly after his arrival, but aside from ensuring they weren't among the Few, he'd paid them scant attention. And why should he? With missions such as this, being conspicuous was typically an asset. Skulkers drew attention, not braggarts.

He hazarded a glance at the small grotto of lamplight where the three Knights sat. The one, a stocky man with woolly hair, still wore his hauberk, but the other two were attired in the gold-trimmed white of the Thousand Temples, the same as Inrau, though their dress consisted of the queer blend of martial uniform and priestly vestment unique to the Shrial Knights. The armoured man sketched loops in the air with a chicken bone, avidly describing something—a woman or a battle, perhaps—to his comrade across the table. The man between them, his face slack with upper-caste arrogance, met Achamian's eyes and nodded.

Without a word to his companions, the knight stood and began striding toward their table.

"One of them comes," Achamian said, pouring himself another bowl of wine. "Be afraid, calm, whatever, but let me talk. Understood?"

A breathless nod.

The Shrial Knight negotiated the intervening tables and patrons in a brusque manner, pausing once to firmly press a stumbling teamster from his path. He was lean and patrician tall, clean-shaven with short jet-black hair. The white of his elaborate tunic seemed to shrug off every shadow, but for some reason his face did not. He arrived bearing the scent of jasmine and myrrh.

Inrau looked up.

"I thought I recognized you," the Shrial Knight said. "Inrau, isn't it?"

"Y-yes, Lord Sarcellus."

Lord Sarcellus? The name was unfamiliar to Achamian, but Inrau's shock could only mean he was someone powerful—too powerful to ordinarily trouble himself with petty temple functionaries. A *Knight-Commander* . . . Achamian glanced past his torso and saw the other two Knights watching. The armoured one leaned sideways and muttered something that made the other laugh. *This is some kind of lark. Something to amuse his friends.*

"And who's this, now?" Sarcellus asked, turning to Achamian. "Is he giving you any trouble?"

Achamian quaffed his wine, and glared at a furious angle away from the Knight-Commander—a drunken elder who did not brook interruptions. "The boy is my sister-son," he grated, "and he's neck-deep in shit." Then, as though an afterthought, he added, "Lord."

"Is he, now? For what, pray tell?"

Groping through his pockets as though he looked for a misplaced coin, Achamian shook his head in mock disgust, still refusing to lay eyes on his inquisitor. "For acting a fool, what else? He may wear the gold-and-white, but he's a priggish idiot all the same."

"And who are you to upbraid a Shrial Priest, hmm?"

"What? Me chastise Inrau?" Achamian exclaimed, affecting a drunk's sarcastic fright. "As far as I'm concerned, the boy's a plum. I only bear my sister's message."

"Ah, I see. And who would she be, then?"

Achamian shrugged and grinned, momentarily regretting his full mouth of teeth. "My sister? My sister is a rutting sow."

Sarcellus blinked.

"Hmm. And what does that make you?"

"A sow's brother!" Achamian cried, at last looking the man full in the face. "Small wonder the boy's in shit, eh?"

Sarcellus smiled, but his large brown eyes remained curiously dead. He turned back to Inrau.

"The Shriah demands our industry, young apostle, more so now than any time previous. Soon he will declare the object of our Holy War. Are you sure that carousing with buffoons—even those bound to you by blood—is wise on the eve of something so momentous?"

"And what about *you*?" Achamian muttered, reaching for more wine. "Heed your uncle, boy. Puffed-up pompous curs like—"

Sarcellus's back hand snapped his head sideways, threw his chair on two teetering legs, then sent him crashing to the cobbled floor.

The tavern erupted in shouts and howls.

Sarcellus kicked the chair aside and, with the routine air of a tracker examining a trail, crouched over him. Achamian shielded his face behind convulsive arms. Somehow the mummer within him managed to squall, "Murder!"

An iron hand clamped about the nape of his neck and yanked him forward, lifting his ear to Sarcellus's lips.

"How I've longed to do that, pig," the man whispered.

Then he was gone. The bruising floor. A glimpse of his retreating back. Achamian tried pushing himself up. Fucking legs! Where were they? Head lolling back. A white teardrop of lantern light, shining across hanging brass, illuminating beams and ceiling, cobwebs and mummified flies. Then Inrau behind him, grunting as he pulled him to his feet, whispering something inaudible as he steered him to his seat.

Propped in his chair, he waved away Inrau's mothering hands. "I'm fine," he croaked. "Just need a moment. Catch my breath."

Achamian sucked air through his nostrils, pressed a hand against the side of his face, and drew hooked fingers through his beard. Inrau resumed his seat and apprehensively watched him reach for the wine.

"A b-bit more dramatic than I intended," Achamian said in an airy semblance of good humour. When his faltering hands spilled the first of the wine, Inrau reached out and gently tugged the decanter from him.

"Akka . . ."

Fucking hands! Always shaking.

Achamian watched him pour a bowl. Calm. How could the boy be so calm?

"A bit too dramatic, b-but effective . . . Effective all the same. And that's all that matters."

With thumb and forefinger he wiped the tears from his eyes. Where did they come from? *The sting. That's it, the sting.*

"I worked his levers, boy." A snort that was intended as a laugh. "Did you see how I did that?"

"I saw."

"Good," he declared, gulping down his bowl and gasping. "Watch and learn. Watch and learn."

Inrau silently poured him another. Achamian's cheek and jaw, once fiery and numb, began to ache.

An unaccountable rage seized him. "The furies I could have unleashed!" he spat, low enough to ensure he couldn't be overheard. *What if he comes back?* He glanced hurriedly over at Sarcellus and the other two Shrial Knights. They were laughing about something. Some joke or something. Something.

"The *words* I know!" he snarled. *"I could have boiled his heart in his chest!"*

Another bowl quaffed, like burning oil in his frigid gut.

"I've done it before." *Was that me?*

"Akka," Inrau said, "I'm afraid."

Never had Achamian seen so many gathered in one place. Not even in Seswatha's Dreams.

The great central square of the Hagerna was a wilderness of humanity. In the distance, bathed in sunlight, the sloped walls of the Junriüma towered over the masses. Of the surrounding structures, it alone seemed immune to the multitudes. The other buildings, engineered in the later and more graceful days of the Ceneian Empire, were overwhelmed by squirming thickets of warriors, wives, slaves, and tradesmen. Hanging arms and indistinct faces congested the balconies and long colonnades of the administrative compounds. Scores of youths were perched like pigeons across the curved horns and haunches of the three Agoglian Bulls that ordinarily dominated the heart of the plaza. Even the broad processional avenues, which wound down into the haze of greater Sumna, were thick and sluggish with people—latecomers who still hoped to press closer, closer to Maithanet and his revelation.

It hadn't taken Achamian long to regret pressing so close to the Junriüma. Sweat stung his eyes. From all sides limbs and bodies lurched against him. At long last Maithanet was to announce the object of his Holy War, and like water to a basin, the faithful had come in floods.

Achamian found himself periodically clamped by tides of movement. Standing still was impossible. The pressure behind him would swell, and he would find himself thrown against the backs of those before him. He could almost believe nothing moved at all save the ground at their feet, yanked by some hidden army of priests eager to see them suffocate.

At some point he cursed everything: the punishing sun, the Thousand Temples, the forearm between his shoulders, Maithanet. But his most savage moments he reserved for Nautzera and for his own damned curiosity. It seemed a combination of these two had placed him in this position.

Then he realized: *If Maithanet declares against the Schools . . .*

Among so many, what were the chances that he would be recognized as a sorcerer, as a spy? Already he'd encountered several men bearing the giddy aura of a Trinket. It was customary for members of the ruling castes to wear their Chorae openly about their necks. The mobs were pocked by tiny points that whispered death.

Me . . . the first casualty of the new Scholastic Wars.

The irony of this thought was enough to make him grimace. Images flitted before his soul's eye: of fanatics pointing at him and shrieking, *"Blasphemer! Blasphemer!"*; of his broken body tossed atop furious mobs.

How could I be such a fool?

Fear, heat, and stench buffeted him with nausea. His cheek and jaw throbbed anew. He'd seen others—their temples latticed by shining veins, their eyes drowsy with the confusion of near unconsciousness—lifted from the crowd and passed beneath the sun along a wave of uplifted hands. Watching them had stilled Achamian with both wonder and dismay, though he knew not why.

He looked toward the immensity of the Junriüma, the Vault-of-the-Tusk, rearing in stony silence above the multitudes. Clots of priests and other functionaries milled on the heights, leaning between the battlements. He saw a figure pour a basket of what looked like white-and-yellow flower petals. They fluttered down the granite slopes before whisking out and across the ranks of Shrial Knights who barricaded the landings below. As much fortress as temple enclosure, the Junriüma possessed the monolithic cast of a structure devoted to repulsing armies—as it had so many times in the past. Its only concession to faith was the great vaulted recess of its forward gate. Flanked by two Kyranean pillars, its dimensions were such that it could only dwarf any man standing beneath. Achamian hoped Maithanet would prove the exception.

Over the past days, especially after the unnerving encounter with the Knight-Commander, the new Shriah had burrowed a deep hole in his thoughts, a hole Achamian needed to fill with the force of the man's presence.

Is he worth your devotion, Inrau? Is Maithanet worth your life?

The Summoning Horns, whose bottomless timbre so resembled the ancient war-horns of the Sranc, sounded from behind him. Hundreds of them, reverberating across the great hollows of sky above. Everywhere around Achamian, men began crying out in rapture, producing a roar that gradually filled then eclipsed the oceanic moan of the Summoning Horns. The Horns trailed away and the roar grew, until it seemed even the walls of the Junriüma would crack and topple.

A parade of bald children dressed in scarlet spilled from the Vault's gate, leaping barefoot down the monumental stairs and terraces, waving palm fronds in the air. The roar subsided enough to distinguish individual shouts above the wash of murmuring men. Fragments of hymns were picked up, only to falter and fade. The masses had become an impatient ground, slowly quieted in anticipation of the footfalls about to tread upon them.

All of us for you, Maithanet. How that must feel . . .

Despite what Inrau had said, Achamian knew the young man did, in his manner, worship this new Shriah—a realization that had wounded his vanity. Achamian had always cherished his students' adoration, and none more so than Inrau's. Now the old master had been supplanted. How could he rival a man who could command events such as this?

But somehow he'd managed. Somehow he'd secured the Mandate eyes and ears in the heart of the Thousand Temples. Was it his cunning that had convinced Inrau, or was it his humiliation at the hands of Sarcellus? Was it pity?

Had he once again prevailed by failing?

An image of Geshrunni flashed through his thoughts.

The fact that he'd succeeded without Cants balmed his sense of shame—somewhat. He *would* have used them if Inrau had refused. Achamian was under no illusions. If he had failed his mission, the Quorum would kill Inrau. For men like Nautzera, Inrau was a defector, and all defectors died—as simple as that. The Gnosis, even the few rudiments known by Inrau, was more valuable than any single life.

But if he'd used the Cants of Compulsion, sooner or later the Luthymae, the College of monks and priests that managed the Thousand Temples' own vast network of spies, would have identified the mark of sorcery upon Inrau. Not all of the Few became sorcerers. Many used the "gift" to war against the Schools. And the College of Luthymae, Achamian had no doubt, would kill Inrau for bearing sorcery's mark. He had lost agents to them before.

The most the Compulsion could do was purchase time—that, and break his heart.

Perhaps this was why Inrau had agreed to become a spy. Perhaps he'd glimpsed the dimensions of the trap fate and Achamian had set for him. Perhaps what he'd feared was not the prospect of what would happen to him if he refused, but the prospect of what would happen to his old teacher. Achamian would have used the Cants, would have transformed Inrau into a sorcerous puppet, and he would have gone mad.

Priests draped in robes of gold-trimmed white and bearing golden replicas of the Tusk filed four abreast between the Kyranean pillars. The tusks gleamed in the sun. Hoarse shouts broke from the low thunder of the crowd, a few cascading into many. Like wet palms, the crowd closed tighter about Achamian. His back arched with the forward heave of the masses. His feet stumbled with them. He rolled his head back and gasped. The air had taste. The corners of the sky began to drift. Blinking sweat from his eyes, he held his mouth out to the promise of cooler air, as though somewhere just above him there was a surface where the breath of thousands ended and the sky began. Voices were thunder. He looked down, and the Junriüma filled his eyes. Through fields of upraised arms, he watched the emerging form of Maithanet.

The new Shriah was a powerful figure, as tall as any Norsirai, wearing a crisp white gown and sporting a thick black beard. He made the priests who flanked him seem womanish. Achamian had a sudden yearning to see his eyes, but from this distance, they were hidden in the shadow of his brows.

Maithanet came from the deep south, Inrau had told him, from Cingulat or Nilnamesh, where the hold of the Thousand Temples was uncertain. He had walked on foot, a lone Inrithi through the heathen lands of Kian. He had not so much come to Sumna as seized it. Among the jaded administrators of the Thousand Temples, his mysterious origins had been to his advantage. Simply to be an official of the Thousand Temples was to have the stink of corruption, a smell that no purity of conviction or greatness of spirit could ever scrub away.

The Thousand Temples had called out to Maithanet, and Maithanet had come.

Could the Consult have discovered this lack? Crafted you to fill it?

Simply thinking that name, Consult, stilled Achamian. Innumerable nightmares had riddled it with so much hatred, so much dread, that it had become as much an anchor of his being as his own name.

His thoughts were overwhelmed by the mouth-humid reverberations of the crowd. For several moments, the air shivered with their cries. He felt a blackening of his edges, a coldness in his chest and face. The noise of the crowd thinned and subsided. He heard something incoherent, but he was sure it was *Maithanet's* voice. More thunder. People straining to touch his distant image with their fingers. He reeled against the wet grip of the men surrounding him, felt the back of his throat hitching, the stinging vomit.

Fevers . . .

Then hands were all over him, and he was lifted by strangers onto the surface of the crowd. Palms and fingers, their touch so many and so light, there a moment and then gone. He could feel the sun burn against the black of his beard, against the wet salt on his cheeks. He glimpsed fumbling crevices of soaked cloth, of hair and skin—a ground of faces watching his shadow pass. Across the inner sky of half-closed eyes, the sun was spliced by tears, and he heard a voice, as clear and as warm as an autumn afternoon.

"By itself," the Shriah was crying, "Fanimry is an affront to the God. But the fact that the faithful, the Inrithi, tolerate this blasphemy is enough for the anger of the God to burn bright against us!"

His body prostrate across hands beneath the sun, Achamian found himself moved to delirious wonder by the sound of the man's voice. Such a voice! One that fell upon passions and thoughts rather than ears, with intonations exquisitely pitched to incite, to enrage.

"These people, these *Kianene*, are an obscene race, followers of a False Prophet. A *False* Prophet, my children! The Tusk tells us that there is no greater abomination than the False Prophet. No man is so vile, so wicked, as he who makes a mockery of the God's voice. And yet we sign treaties with the Fanim; we buy silk and turquoise that have passed through their unclean hands. We trade gold for horses and slaves bred in their venal stables. No more shall the faithful have intercourse with whorish nations! No more shall the faithful beat down their outrage in exchange for baubles from heathen lands! No, my children, we shall show them our *fury!* We shall loose upon them the *God's own vengeance!*"

Achamian floundered in the midst of the mob's thunder, tossed by palms that would sooner clench into fists, by hands that would rather strike down than lift up.

"No! We will trade with the heathen no longer. From this day forward we shall *seize!* Never again shall the Inrithi accommodate such obscenities! We shall curse that which is accursed! WE! SHALL! WAR!"

And the voice neared, as though the innumerable hands that bore Achamian could do nothing other than deliver him to the origin of such resounding words—words that had parted the shroud of the future with a terrible promise.

Holy War.

"*Shimeh!*" Maithanet cried, as though this name lay at the root of all sorrow. "The city of the Latter Prophet lies cupped in the heathen's palm. In unclean, blasphemous hands! The hallowed ground of Shimeh has become the very hearth of abominable evil. The *Cishaurim!* The Cishaurim have made the Juterum—the sacred heights!—the den of unspeakable ceremonies, a kennel of foul, iniquitous rites! Amoteu, the Holy Land of the Latter Prophet, Shimeh, the Holy City of Inri Sejenus, and the Juterum, the holy site of the Ascension, have all become home to outrage after outrage. Sin after loathsome sin! We shall reclaim these holy names! We shall cleanse these holy grounds! We shall turn our hands to the bloody work of war! We shall smite the heathen with the edge of the sharp sword. We shall pierce him with the point of the long spear. We shall scourge him with the agony of holy fire! *We shall war and we shall war until SHIMEH IS FREE!*"

The masses erupted, and through his nightmarish transit, Achamian wondered, with the strange lucidity of near unconsciousness, why the Fanim when the Schools were a cancer in their midst? Why murder another when one's own body needed to be healed? And why wage a Holy War that could not be won?

An impossibly distant surface of stone leaned across the sun—the Junriüma, stronghold of the Tusk—and men were lowering him

across the shaded steps. Water spilled across his face, fell between
his lips. He raised his head, saw a wall of shouts, flushed faces, and
raised arms.

They want Shimeh . . . Shimeh. The Schools were never threatened.

Every instant was taut with the exultant thunder of the assembly,
but for some reason, an intimacy existed between those on the
steps. Achamian glanced at the others—those who had been lifted
from the crowd like him, shivering and drenched in exhaustion—
but they were all transfixed by something on the steps above him.
He looked up, startled by a worn boot a hand's breadth from his
forehead. He looked into the limb-enclosed recesses of a man
kneeling against the knee of another. The man wept, blinked away
tears, then noticed him. In shock, Achamian watched the man's
face open in recognition and then tighten in monolithic fury—a
sorcerer . . . *here.*

Proyas.

It was Prince Nersei Proyas of Conriya . . . Another student
he had loved. For four years, Achamian had tutored him in the
non-sorcerous arts.

But before any word could be spoken, hands guided the Prince,
still staring, to one side, and Achamian found himself looking into
the serene and surprisingly youthful face of Maithanet.

The multitudes roared, but an uncanny hush had settled between
the two of them.

The Shriah's face darkened, but his blue eyes glittered with . . .
with . . .

He spoke softly, as though to an intimate: "Your kind are not
welcome here, friend. *Flee.*"

And Achamian fled. Would a crow wage war upon a lion? And
throughout the pinched madness of his struggle through the hosts
of Inrithi, he was transfixed by a single thought:

He can see the Few.

Only the Few could see the Few.

Maithanet grasped Proyas firmly by the arm, then loud enough to pierce the roaring adulation of the crowds, he whispered, "There are many things I need to discuss with you, my Prince."

His thoughts still buzzing with the fury and shock of seeing his old tutor, Proyas wiped at the tears that creased his cheeks and numbly nodded.

Maithanet bid him to follow Gotian, the illustrious Grandmaster of the Shrial Knights, who ushered him away from the glittering Shrial Procession and deep into the tomblike galleries of the Junriüma. Gotian hazarded several friendly comments, no doubt attempting to engage him in conversation, but Proyas could only think: *Achamian! Insolent wretch! How could you commit such an outrage?*

How many years had passed since he'd last seen him? Four? Five, even? All that time spent trying to cleanse his heart of the man's influence. All that time leading to this penultimate moment, kneeling at the feet of the Holy Father, feeling his glory wash over him in a golden rush, kissing his knee in an instant of pure, absolute submission to the God . . .

Only to see *Drusas Achamian* shivering on the step below him! An unrepentant blasphemer huddling in the shadow of the most glorious soul to walk the earth in a thousand years. Maithanet. The Great Shriah who would set Shimeh free, who would lift the yoke of emperors and heathens from the faith of the Latter Prophet.

Achamian. I loved you once, dear teacher, but this! This is beyond all tolerance!

"You seem troubled, my Prince," Gotian at last said, steering him through yet another corridor. Incense from a mélange of fragrant woods steamed through the open spaces, gifting the points of lantern light with haloes. Somewhere, a choir practised hymns.

"I apologize, Lord Gotian," he replied. "It's been a most remarkable day."

"That it has, my Prince," the silver-haired Grandmaster said, a wise smile creasing his face. "And it's about to become more remarkable still."

Before Proyas could ask him what he meant, the colonnaded hallway came to an end and opened onto a vast chamber flanked by colossal pillars . . . or what he had thought was a chamber, for he quickly realized that he stood within a courtyard. Sunlight poured through the distant ceiling, piercing the gloom with slanted beams and stretching fingers of light between the western columns. Proyas blinked and stared across the courtyard's sunken, mosaic floor—

Could it be?

He fell to his knees.

The Tusk.

A great winding horn of ivory, half in sunlight and half in shadow, suspended by chains that soared upward and were lost in the contrast of bright sky and pillared gloom.

The Tusk. Holiest of holies.

Shining with oils and ribbed by inscriptions, like the tattooed limbs of a Priestess of Gierra.

The first verses of the Gods. The first scripture. *Here*, before his eyes!

Here.

After several breathless moments, Proyas felt Gotian's consoling hand fall upon his shoulder. Blinking tears, he looked up at the Grandmaster.

"Thank you," he said, his voice hushed by the immensities that surrounded him. "Thank you for bringing me to this place."

Gotian nodded, then left him to his prayers.

Triumphs and regrets alike wheeled through his thoughts: his victory over the Tydonni at the Battle of Paremti; the words of hatred he'd uttered to his older brother the week before he died. It seemed that *here* the hidden nets were drawn to the surface at last, so that all these events could be gathered onto the deck of this moment. Even the years he'd spent under Achamian as a boy, chafing through drill after drill, laughing at his gentle jokes, had a place in preparation for this moment. Now. Before the Tusk.

I submit to your Word, God. I commend my soul to the fierce task that you have laid before me. I shall make a temple of the field of war.

The sound of birds frolicking among the high eaves. The smell of sandalwood rinsed by sky-clean air. Bands of streaming sunlight. And the Tusk, poised against the shadows of mighty Kyranean pillars. Motionless. Soundless.

"It's heartbreaking, is it not," a powerful voice said behind him, "to see the Tusk for the first time?"

Proyas turned, and though he'd long thought himself beyond adulation, he could not help staring at the man with adoring eyes. Maithanet. The new, incorruptible Shriah of the Thousand Temples. The man who would bring peace to the nations of the Three Seas by offering them Holy War.

A new teacher.

"Since the beginning, it's been with us," Maithanet continued, staring reverently at the Tusk, "our guide, our counsel, and our judge. It is the one thing that *witnesses* us, even as we behold it."

"Yes," Proyas said. "I can feel it."

"Cherish that feeling, Proyas. Grasp it tight to your breast and never forget. For in the days that follow, you will be besieged by many men who have forgotten."

"Your Grace?"

Maithanet walked to his side. He had exchanged his elaborate gold-chased robes for a plain white frock. His every movement, every pose, it seemed to Proyas, conveyed a sense of inevitability, as though the scripture of his acts had already been written.

"I speak of the Holy War, Proyas, the great hammer of the Latter Prophet. Many men will seek to pervert it."

"I have already heard rumours that the Emperor—"

"And there will be others as well," Maithanet said, his tone both sad and sharp. "Men from the Schools . . ."

Proyas felt chastened. Only his father, the King, ever dared interrupt him, and only when he'd uttered something foolish. "The Schools, your Grace?"

The Shriah turned his strong bearded profile to him, and Proyas was struck by the crisp blue of his eyes. "Tell me, Nersei Proyas," Maithanet said with the voice of edict. "Who was that man, that *sorcerer*, who dared pollute my presence?"

CHAPTER
FOUR

SUMNA

To be ignorant and to be deceived are two different things. To be ignorant is to be a slave of the world. To be deceived is to be the slave of another man. The question will always be: Why, when all men are ignorant, and therefore already slaves, does this latter slavery sting us so?

—AJENCIS, THE EPISTEMOLOGIES

But despite stories of Fanim atrocities, the fact of the matter is that the Kianene, heathen or no, were surprisingly tolerant of Inrithi pilgrimages to Shimeh—before the Holy War, that is. Why would a people devoted to the destruction of the Tusk extend this courtesy to "idolaters"? Perhaps they were partially motivated by the prospect of trade, as others have suggested. But the fundamental motive lies in their desert heritage. The Kianene word for a holy place is si'ihkhalis, which means, literally, "great oasis." On the open desert it is their strict custom to never begrudge travellers water, even if they be enemies.

—DRUSAS ACHAMIAN, COMPENDIUM OF THE FIRST HOLY WAR

The Holy War of the Inrithi against the Fanim was declared by Maithanet, the 116th Shriah of the Thousand Temples, on the Morn of Ascension in 4110 Year-of-the-Tusk. The day had been unseasonably hot, as though the God himself had blessed the Holy War with a premonition of summer. Indeed, the Three Seas buzzed with rumours of omens and visions, all of which attested to the sanctity of the task that lay before the Inrithi.

Word spread. In every nation, priests in the Shrial and Cultic temples railed against the atrocities and iniquities of the Fanim. How, they asked, could the Inrithi call themselves faithful when the city of the Latter Prophet had been enslaved? Through invective and passionate harangue, the abstract sins of a distant exotic people were brought close to the congregations of the Inrithi and transformed into their own. To tolerate iniquity, they were told, was to cultivate wickedness. When a man failed to weed his garden, did he not grow weeds? And it seemed to the Inrithi that they had been stirred from a mercantile inertia, that they had suffered from an unaccountable sloth of spirit. How long would the Gods endure a people who had made harlots of their hearts, who had allowed themselves to be numbed by venal ease? How long before the Gods abandoned them, or worse yet, turned against them in bright wrath?

In the streets of the great cities, vendors plied customers with rumours of this or that potentate declaring for the Tusk. And in the taverns, veterans argued over the comparative pieties of their lords. Called to the hearth, children listened wide-eyed, rapt with awe and dread, as their fathers described how the Fanim, a foul and wretched people, had despoiled the purity of an impossibly wondrous place, Shimeh. They would awaken shrieking in the middle of the night, blubbering about eyeless Cishaurim who saw through the heads of snakes. During the day, as they romped through the streets or the fields, little brothers would be forced to play the heathen so that their older siblings might trounce them with sword-like sticks. And in the dark, husbands would tell wives the latest news of the Holy War, and speak in solemn whispers about the glory of the task the Shriah had set before them. And the wives would weep—quietly, because faith made strong—knowing that very soon their husbands would leave them.

Shimeh. Men gnashed their teeth at the thought of this hallowed name. And it seemed to them that Shimeh had to be a hushed place, a ground that had held its breath for anguished centuries, waiting for the drowsy followers of the Latter Prophet at last to stir from their slumber and put right an ancient and heinous crime. They would come with sword and knife and cleanse that ground. And when the Fanim were dead, they would kneel and kiss the sweet earth that had begat the Latter Prophet.

They would join the Holy War.

The Thousand Temples issued edicts stating that those who profited from the absence of any great lord who had taken up the Tusk would be tried for heresy in the ecclesiastical courts and summarily executed. Thus assured of their birthrights, princes, earls, palatines, and lords of every nation declared themselves Men of the Tusk. Trivial wars were forgotten. Lands were mortgaged. Client knights were summoned by their thanes and barons. Indentured servants were provisioned with arms and housed in makeshift barracks. Great fleets of ships were contracted to make the journey by sea to Momemn, where the Shriah had announced the Holy War must gather.

Maithanet had called, and the entire Three Seas had answered. The back of the heathen would be broken. Holy Shimeh would be cleansed.

Mid-Spring, 4110 Year-of-the-Tusk, Sumna

Esmenet's daughter was never far from her thoughts. It was strange the way anything, even the most trivial happenstance, could summon memories of her. This time it was Achamian and his curious habit of sniffing each prune before taking it between his teeth.

Once her daughter had sniffed an apple at the market. It was a breathless memory, wan, as though rinsed of colour by the horrific fact of her death. An adorable little girl, bright beneath the shadows of passersby, with straight black hair, a chubby-tender face, and eyes like perpetual hope.

"Mama, it smells like . . ." she had said, hooking her voice as insight failed her, "it smells like *water and flowers*." She flashed her mother a triumphant smile.

Esmenet looked up at the sour vendor, who nodded at the entwined serpents tattooed on the back of her left hand. The message was clear: *I don't sell to your kind.*

"That's funny, my sweet. It smells overpriced to me."

"But, *Mama* . . ." her darling had said.

Esmenet blinked the tears from her eyes. Achamian was speaking to her.

"I find this difficult," he said with an air of confession.

I should've bought an apple somewhere else.

They both sat on low stools in her room, next to her beaten knee-high table. The shutters were open, and the chill spring air seemed to exaggerate the sounds of the street below. Achamian had draped a wool blanket over his shoulders, but Esmenet was content to shiver.

How long had Achamian stayed with her now? Long enough for them to feel safely bored with each other, she supposed. Almost as though they were married. A spy like Achamian, she had realized, one who recruited and directed those who actually had access to knowledge, spent most of his time simply waiting for something to happen. And Achamian had waited here, in her impoverished room in an ancient tenement that housed dozens of other whores such as herself.

It had been so strange at first. Many mornings she would lie awake, listening to the hideous sounds of him making mud in her pot. She would bury her head beneath sheets, insisting that he see a physician or a priest—only half joking, because it really was *hideous.* He started calling it his "morning apocalypse" after she once cried, more in exasperation than in good humour, "Just because you relive the Apocalypse every night, Akka, doesn't mean that you have to share it with me in the morning!" Achamian would chuckle ruefully while he cleaned himself, mutter something about the merits of heavy drinking and clean bowels. And Esmenet would find as much comfort as hilarity in the sight of a sorcerer splashing water on his ass.

She would get up, open the shutters, and sit half-naked on the sill as she always did, alternately gazing across the smoky clamour of Sumna and scanning the street below for possible custom. The two of them would eat a frugal breakfast of unleavened bread, sour cheese, and the like, while talking about any number of things: the latest rumours regarding Maithanet, the venal hypocrisy of priests, the way teamsters could make even soldiers blush with their curses, and so on. And it would seem to Esmenet that they were happy, that in some strange way they belonged in this place at this time.

Sooner or later, however, either someone would call up to her from the street or one of her regular patrons would knock at the door, and things would sour. Achamian would become grim, grab his cloak and satchel, and invariably go get drunk at some dingy tavern. Usually she would spy him from the sill when he returned, walking alone through the endless press of people, an aging, slightly rounded man who looked as though he'd lost his purse gambling. Every time, without exception, he would already be watching her when she saw him. He would wave hesitantly, try to smile, and a pang of sorrow would strike her, sometimes so hard she would gasp aloud.

What was it she felt? Many things, it seemed. Pity for him, certainly. In the midst of strangers, Achamian always looked so lonely, so misunderstood. *No one,* she would often think, *knows him the way I do.* There was also relief that he'd returned—returned to her, even though he had gold enough to buy far younger whores. A selfish sorrow, that one. And shame. Shame because she knew that he loved her, and that every time she took custom it bruised his heart.

But what choice did she have?

He would never come up to their room unless he saw her on the sill. One time, after being beaten by a particularly nasty fiend who claimed to be a coppersmith, she'd simply crawled into bed and wept herself to sleep. She awoke before dawn and hastened to the window when she realized Achamian hadn't returned. She huddled there for hours, waiting for him, watching the sun bronze the sea and then lance through the misty city. The first potters' wheels growled to life on the adjoining street, and the first trails of kiln and cooking smoke twined above rooftops into bluing sky. She cried softly. But even then she let one breast fall free from her blankets, as though she were a nursing mother, and allowed one long pale leg to hang down against the cold brick so that those looking up might glimpse the shadowy promise between her knees.

And then finally, as the sun began to warm her face and bare shoulder, she heard a tap at the door. She flew across the room and wrenched it open, and there was the dishevelled sorcerer. "Akka!" she cried, tears spilling from her eyes.

He glanced at her and then to the empty bed, told her he'd fallen asleep outside her door. And she had known then that she truly loved him.

Theirs was a strange marriage, if it could be called that. A marriage of outcasts sanctified by inarticulate vows. A sorcerer and a whore. Perhaps a certain desperation was to be expected of such unions, as though that strange word, "love," became profound in proportion to the degree one was scorned by others.

Esmenet wrapped her shoulders in her arms. She studied Achamian with an impatient sigh. "What?" she asked wearily. "What do you find difficult, Akka?"

Achamian turned his injured eyes away, said nothing.

When he had learned what the coppersmith had done, he'd been outraged. He fairly dragged her to several smithies, demanding she identify the man. And though she protested, claimed that such assaults were simply part of the custom she collected from the street, she was secretly thrilled, and part of her hoped that he would burn the man to cinders. For the first time, perhaps, she understood Achamian could *do that,* and had done it in the past.

But they had never found the man.

She suspected that Achamian had continued prowling the smithies, looking for someone who fit her description of the man. And she had no doubt that Achamian would have murdered him if he'd found him. He had continued talking about him long after the incident, pretending to be gallant when in fact, or so Esmenet had suspected, some small part of him wanted to murder all of her custom.

"Why do you stay here, Achamian?" she asked, a small hostility in her voice.

He looked at her angrily, and his question was plain: Why do you still sleep with them, Esmi? Why do you insist on remaining a whore while I stay with you?

Because sooner or later you'll leave me, Akka . . . And the men who feed me will have found different whores.

But before he could speak, there was a shy knock at her door.

"I'll leave," Achamian said, standing.

A bolt of terror passed through her. "When will you be back?" she asked, struggling not to sound desperate.

"After," he said. "After . . ."

He offered her the blanket, which she took in knotted hands. She had clenched everything with a strange fierceness lately, as though daring small things to be glass. She watched him answer the door.

"Inrau," Achamian said. "What are you doing here?"

"I've learned something important," the young man said breathlessly.

"Come in, come in," Achamian said, ushering the priest to his stool.

"I'm afraid I wasn't that careful," Inrau said, avoiding both of their looks. "I may have been followed."

Achamian studied him a moment, then shrugged. "Even if you've been followed, it's no matter. Priests have a penchant for prostitutes."

"Is this true, Esmenet?" Inrau said with a nervous smile. Her presence, Esmenet knew, made him uncomfortable. And like many kind men, he attempted to cover for his embarrassment with strained humour.

"They're much like sorcerers that way," she said wryly.

Achamian shot her a look of mock indignation, and Inrau laughed nervously.

"So tell us," Achamian said, his eyes betraying his smile. "What have you learned?"

A look of childlike concentration flashed across Inrau's face. He was dark-haired and slender, clean-shaven, with large brown eyes and feminine lips. He possessed, Esmenet thought, the attractive vulnerability of young men in the shadow of the world's bitter hammers. Such men were highly prized by whores, and not only because they tended to pay for damage done as much as for pleasure received. They offered compensation of a different sort. Such men might be safely loved—the way mothers love tender sons.

I can see why you fear for him so, Akka.

Gathering his breath, Inrau said, "The Scarlet Spires has agreed to join the Holy War."

Achamian knitted his brow. "This is a *rumour* you've heard?"

"I suppose." He paused. "But I was told by an Orate from the College of Luthymae. I guess Maithanet made his offer some time ago. In order to demonstrate that it wasn't frivolous, he actually sent six Trinkets to Carythusal—as a gesture of goodwill. Since the Luthymae have great powers over the dispensation of Chorae, Maithanet was compelled to give them an explanation."

"So it's true, then?"

"It's true." Inrau looked at him the way a hungry man who has found a foreign coin might look at a money-changer. *How much is this worth?*

"Excellent. Excellent. This is indeed important news."

Inrau's elation was contagious, and Esmenet found herself smiling with him.

"You've done good, Inrau," she said.

"Indeed," Achamian added. "The Scarlet Spires, Esmi, is the most powerful School in the Three Seas. Rulers of High Ainon since the last Scholastic War . . ." But too many questions seemed to crowd his thoughts for him to continue. Achamian had always been inclined to give fatuous explanations—he knew full well that she knew of the Scarlet Spires. But Esmenet forgave him this. In a sense, his explanations were a measure of his desire to include her in his life. In so many ways, Achamian was utterly unlike other men.

"*Six* Trinkets," he blurted. "A most extraordinary gift! Priceless!"

Is that why she loved him? The world seemed so small—so sordid—when she was alone. And when he returned it seemed as though he bore the entire Three Seas upon his back. She led a submerged life, a life catacombed by poverty and ignorance. Then this soft-hearted, portly man would arrive, a man who looked even less like a spy than he did a sorcerer, and for a time the roof of her life would be torn away, and sun and world would come pouring in.

I do love you, Drusas Achamian.

"Trinkets, Esmi! For the Thousand Temples they're the very Tears of God. To give six of them to a School of blasphemers! Remarkable." He combed his beard as he thought, his fingers tracing its five silver streaks and then tracing them again.

Trinkets. This reminded Esmenet that despite the wonder, Achamian's world was exceedingly deadly. Ecclesiastical law dictated that prostitutes, like adulteresses, be punished by stoning. The same, she reflected, was true of sorcerers, except there was just one kind of stone that could afflict them, and it need touch them only once. Thankfully, there were few Trinkets. The world, on the other hand, was filled with stones for harlots.

"Why, though?" Inrau asked, a measure of grief now in his voice. "Why would Maithanet pollute the Holy War by inviting a School?"

How difficult this must be for him, Esmenet thought, *to be pinned between men like Achamian and Maithanet.*

"Because he must," Achamian replied. "Otherwise the Holy War would be doomed. Remember that the Cishaurim reside in Shimeh."

"But Chorae are as lethal to them as they are to sorcerers."

"Perhaps . . . But that makes little difference in a war such as this. Before the Holy War could bring their Trinkets to bear on the Cishaurim, it would have to overcome the hosts of Kian. No, Maithanet *needs* a School."

Such a war! Esmenet thought. In her youth, her soul had quickened whenever she heard stories of war. And even now, she commonly plied the soldiers she pleasured for stories of battle. For a moment, she could almost see the tumult, see swords flash in the light of sorcerous fire.

"And the *Scarlet Spires*," Achamian continued. "There could be no better School for him to—"

"No School more hateful," Inrau protested.

The Mandate, Esmenet knew, reserved a special hatred for the Scarlet Spires. No School, Achamian had once told her, more begrudged the Mandate their possession of the Gnosis.

"The Tusk doesn't discriminate between abominations," Achamian replied. "Obviously Maithanet made his overture for strategic reasons. There's talk that the Emperor already moves to make the Holy War his instrument of reconquest. By allying himself with the Scarlet Spires, Maithanet need not depend on the Emperor's School, the Imperial Saik. Think of what the House Ikurei would make of his Holy War."

The Emperor. For some reason, his mention drew Esmenet's eyes to the two copper talents resting on her table, one askew upon the other, with their miniature profiles of Ikurei Xerius III, the Emperor of Nansur. *Her* Emperor. Like all the inhabitants of Sumna, she never really thought of him as her ruler, even though his soldiers provided her with almost as much custom as the

Shrial Priests. The Shriah was too near, she supposed. But then, not even the Shriah meant much to her. *I am too small*, she thought.

Then a question occurred to her.

"Shouldn't—" Esmenet began, but she paused when the two men looked at her strangely. "Shouldn't the question be, Why have the *Scarlet Spires* accepted Maithanet's offer? What could induce a *School* to join a Holy War? They make for odd bedfellows, don't you think? Not so long ago, Akka, you feared that the Holy War would be declared against the Schools."

There was a moment of silence. Inrau smiled as though amused by his own stupidity. From this moment on, Esmenet realized, Inrau would look upon her as an equal in these matters. Achamian, however, would remain aloof, the judge of all questions. As was proper, perhaps, given his calling.

"There are several reasons, actually," Achamian said at length. "Before leaving Carythusal, I learned that the Scarlet Spires has been warring—secretly—against the sorcerer-priests of the Fanim, the Cishaurim. Warring for ten bitter years." He momentarily bit his lip. "For some reason, the Cishaurim assassinated Sasheoka, who was then Grandmaster of the Scarlet Spires. Eleäzaras— Sasheoka's pupil—is Grandmaster now. He was rumoured to be close to Sasheoka, close in the manner of Ainoni men . . ."

Inrau said, "So the Scarlet Spires—"

"Hopes to avenge itself," Achamian said, completing his protege's thought, "to conclude their secret war. But there's more. None of the Schools understands the metaphysics of the Cishaurim, the Psûkhe. All of them, even the School of Mandate, are terrified by the fact that it cannot be seen as sorcery."

"Why does not seeing terrify you so much?" Esmenet asked. This was but one of many small questions she had never dared ask.

"Why?" Achamian repeated, suddenly very serious. "You ask this, Esmenet, because you've no idea of the power we wield. No inkling of how far out of proportion it is to the frailty of our bodies.

Sasheoka was slain precisely because he could not distinguish the work of the Cishaurim from the works of the God."

Esmenet scowled. She turned to Inrau. "Does he do this to you?"

"You mean fault the question rather than answer?" Inrau said wryly. "All the time."

But Achamian's expression darkened. "Listen. Listen to me carefully. This isn't a game we play. Any of us—but especially you, Inrau—could end up with our heads boiled in salt, tarred, and posted before the Vault-of-the-Tusk. And there's more at stake than even our lives. Far more."

Esmenet fell silent, faintly shocked by the reprimand. There were times, she realized, when she forgot the depths of Drusas Achamian. How many times had she held him after he'd awakened from one of his dreams? How many times had she heard him mutter strange tongues in his sleep? She glanced at him and saw that the anger in his eyes had been replaced by pain.

"I don't expect either of you to understand the stakes involved. I even grow tired of listening to myself prattle on about the Consult. But something is different this time. I know it pains you to consider this, Inrau, but your Maithanet—"

"He's not *my* Maithanet. He doesn't belong to anyone, and *that*"— Inrau hesitated, as though troubled by his own ardour—"that's what makes him worthy of my devotion. Perhaps I don't fully understand the stakes, as you say, but I know more than most. And I worry, Akka. I honestly worry that this is simply another fool's errand."

As Inrau said this, he glanced—involuntarily, Esmenet supposed—at the serpentine mark of the whore tattooed across the back of her hand. She bundled her fists under crossed arms.

Then, unaccountably, the real mystery behind these events struck her. She looked at each man in turn, her eyes wide. Inrau glanced down. Achamian, however, watched her keenly.

He knows, Esmenet thought. *He knows that I have a gift for these things.*

"What is it, Esmi?"

"You say that the Mandate only just learned of the Scarlet Spires' war against the Cishaurim?"

"Yes."

She found herself leaning forward, as though these words were something best whispered. "If the Scarlet Spires can keep such a thing secret from the Mandate for ten years, Akka, then how is it that *Maithanet*, a man who has only recently become Shriah, knows?"

"What do you mean?" Inrau asked with alarm.

"No," Achamian said thoughtfully. "She's right. There's no way Maithanet would even approach the Scarlet Spires unless he *knew* the School warred against the Cishaurim. It would be too absurd otherwise. The proudest School in the Three Seas joining a Holy War? Think about it. *How could he know?*"

"Perhaps," Inrau offered, "the Thousand Temples simply stumbled across the knowledge—like you did, only earlier."

"Perhaps," Achamian repeated. "But unlikely. At the very least this demands we watch him more closely."

Esmenet shivered yet again, but this time with exhilaration. *The world turns about people such as these, and I've just joined them.* The air, she thought, smelled of water and flowers.

Inrau looked momentarily at Esmenet before turning his plaintive eyes to his mentor. "I can't do what you ask . . . I can't."

"You must get closer to Maithanet, Inrau. Your Shriah is altogether too canny."

"What?" the young priest said with half-hearted sarcasm. "Too canny to be a man of faith?"

"Not at all, my friend. Too canny to be what he seems."

Late Spring, 4110 Year-of-the-Tusk, Sumna

Rain. If a city was old, really old, the gutters and pools would always glitter black, sodden by the detritus of ages. Sumna was ancient, her waters like pitch.

Hugging himself, Paro Inrau scanned the dark courtyard. He was alone. Everywhere he could hear the sound of water: the dull roar of rain, the gurgle of eaves, and the slap of gutters. Through the wash, he could hear the supplicants wail. Arched into shapes of pain and sorrow, their song rang across the wet stone and cupped his thoughts in stretched notes. Hymns of suffering. Two voices: one pitched high and plaintive, asking why we must suffer, always why; the other low, filled with the brooding grandeur of the Thousand Temples and bearing the gravity of truth—that Men were at one with suffering and ruin, that tears were the only holy waters.

My life, he thought. *My life.*

Inrau lowered his face, tried to grimace away his weeping. If only he could forget. If only . . .

The Shriah. But how could it be?

So lonely. Around him, Ceneian stoneworks loomed, piled away into the dark vastness of the Hagerna. He slid to a crouch and rocked against the wet stone. Fear this encompassing gave one no direction to run. He could only shrink inside, try to weep himself away into nothing.

Achamian, dear teacher . . . What have you done to me?

When Inrau thought of his years at Atyersus, studying under the watchful eyes of Drusas Achamian, he remembered those times he'd gone out with his father and uncle to cast nets far from the Nroni shore, those times when the clouds had grown dark and his father, heaving the silvery fish from the sea, had refused to return to the village.

"Look at this catch!" he would cry, his eyes frenzied by desperate good fortune. "Momas favours us, lads! The God favours us!"

Atyersus reminded Inrau of those perilous times not because Achamian resembled his father—no, his father had been strong, his legs bowed to the deck, his spirit indomitable before the pitching sea—but because like the fish, the riches he'd drawn from sorcery's bosom had been purchased against the threat of doom. To Inrau, Atyersus had seemed a violent storm frozen in soaring pillars and black curtains of stone, and Achamian had resembled his uncle, subdued before his father's wrath and yet striving ever harder to catch their fill so that he might save both his brother and his brother's son. He owed his life to Drusas Achamian—Inrau was certain of this. The Schoolmen of the Mandate never returned to the shore, and they killed those who abandoned their nets to do so.

How did men repay such debts? With monies owed, a man simply returned the money borrowed with the usurer's interest. What was given and what was returned were the same. But was the exchange this simple when a man owed his life to another? For returning him to shore, did Inrau owe Achamian one last voyage into stormy Mandate seas? To repay Achamian in the same coin he owed seemed wrong somehow, as though his old teacher had simply rescinded his gift rather than asking for a gift in return.

Inrau had made many exchanges in his life. By leaving the Mandate for the Thousand Temples, he'd traded the heartbreak of Seswatha for the tragic beauty of Inri Sejenus, the terror of the Consult for the hatred of the Cishaurim, and the condescending dismissal of faith for the pious condemnation of sorcery. And he had asked himself, in those early days, what it was that he'd gained by this exchange of callings.

Everything. He'd gained everything. Faith for knowledge, wisdom for cunning, heart for intellect—there were no scales for this, only men and their many-coloured inclinations. Inrau had been born for the Thousand Temples, and by allowing him to leave the School of Mandate, Achamian had given him everything. And because of this, the gratitude Inrau bore his old teacher was beyond measure or description. *Any price,* he would think as he wandered through the Hagerna, besotted by relief and joy. *Any price.*

And now the storm had come. He felt small, like a boy abandoned to dark, heaving seas.

Please! Let me forget this!

For an instant he thought he could hear the sound of boots echoing down one of the alleyways, but then the Summoning

Horns sounded—impossibly deep, like ocean surf heard through a stone wall. He hurried across the courtyard toward the immense temple doors, pulling his cloak against the downpour. The doors of the Irreüma grated open, throwing a broad lane of light across cobblestones sizzling with rain. Careful to avoid curious eyes, he shouldered through the sudden crowds of priests and monks who filed from the temple. He sprinted up the broad steps, between the bronze serpents that graced the entrance.

The doorkeepers scowled as he entered. At first he cringed, but then he realized he had tracked water and grit across their floor. He ignored them. Before him, two rows of columns formed a broad aisle haphazardly illuminated by hanging braziers. The columns soared up to support the clerestory, the raised central section of the roof, too high for the light to reach. To either side of the clerestory aisle were two more rows of lesser columns, flanking the small godhouses of various Cultic deities. Everything seemed to be reaching, reaching.

He placed an absent hand on the limestone. Cool. Impassive. No sign of the great load borne. Such was the strength of inanimate things. *Give me this strength, Goddess. Make me as a pillar.*

Inrau traced a circle around the column and walked into the shadow of her godhouse, felt soothed by her cool stone. *Onkis . . . beloved.*

"God has a thousand thousand faces," Sejenus had said, *"but men only one heart."* Every great faith was a labyrinth possessed of innumerable small grottoes, half-secret places where the abstractions fell away and where the objects of worship became small enough to comfort daily anxieties, familiar enough to weep openly about petty things. Inrau had found his grotto in the shrine of Onkis, the Singer-in-the-Dark, the Aspect who stood at the heart of all men, moving them to forever grasp far more than they could hold.

He knelt. Sobs wracked him.

If only he could have forgotten . . . forgotten what the Mandate had taught him. If he could've done that, then this last heartbreaking revelation would have been meaningless to him. If only Achamian had not come. The price was too high.

Onkis. Could she forgive him for returning to the Mandate?

The idol was worked in white marble, eyes closed with the sunken look of the dead. At first glance she appeared to be the severed head of a woman, beautiful yet vaguely common, mounted on a pole. Anything more than a glance, however, revealed the pole to be a miniature tree, like those cultivated by the ancient Norsirai, only worked in bronze. Branches poked through her parted lips and swept across her face—nature reborn through human lips. Other branches reached behind to break through her frozen hair. Her image never failed to stir something within him, and this is why he always returned to her: she *was* this stirring, the dark place where the flurries of his thought arose. She came before him.

He started at the sound of voices from the direction of the temple gate. *Doorkeepers. Must be.* Then he fumbled with his cloak and produced a small satchel of food: dried apricots, dates, almonds, and some salted fish. He came close enough that she might feel the warmth of his breath and, with trembling hands, placed the food in a small trough gouged from her pedestal. All food had its essence, its animas—what the blasphemers called the onta. Everything cast shadows across the Outside, where the Gods moved. With shaking hands he pulled out his humble ancestor lists and whispered the names, pausing to beg his great-grandfather to intercede on his behalf.

"Strength," he murmured. "Please, strength . . ."

The small scroll clattered to the floor. The silence was complete, oppressive. His heart ached, so much was at stake. These were the events upon which the world turned. Enough for a Goddess.

"Please . . . Speak to me."

Nothing.

Tears branched across his face. He raised his arms, held them open until his shoulders burned.

"Anything!" he cried.

Run, his thoughts whispered. *Run*.

Such a coward! How could he be such a coward?

Something behind him. The sound of flapping wings! Like the flutter of cloth among the towering pillars.

He turned his face to the shadowy ceiling, searching with his ears. Another flutter. Somewhere up in the clerestory. His skin prickled.

Is that you?

No.

Always doubting. Why was he always doubting?

Stumbling to his feet, he hastened from the godhouse. The temple gate had been closed, and the doorkeepers were nowhere to be seen. In a few moments he located the narrow stair that led up through the wall to the clerestory balconies. Midway up the stair the darkness became pitch. He paused for a moment and breathed deeply. The air smelled of dust.

The uncertainty, always so powerful in him, was snuffed out.

It's you!

His head was buzzing with rapture by the time he crested the stairs. The door to the balcony was ajar. Greyish light sifted through the opening. Finally—after all his love, all his time—Onkis would sing *to* him instead of through. Tentatively, he stepped out onto the balcony. He licked his lips, his stomach leaping.

He could hear the roar of the rainfall through the stone. The pillar capitals were the first things to resolve from the gloom, then the ceiling looming close above. It seemed unnatural for so much weight to be suspended so high. The trunks of the columns gradually grew brighter as they fell out of sight. The light from below was distant and diffuse, as soft as the worn edges of the stonework.

The balcony railing had an aura of dizziness, so he kept his back to the wall. The masonry seemed brittle, chapped ancient in the gloom. The wall frescoes had fallen off in sloughs. The ceiling was encrusted with hundreds of clay hornet's nests, and he was reminded of the barnacled hulls of warships hauled onto beach sand.

"Where are you?" he whispered.

Then he saw it, and horror throttled him.

It stood a short distance away, perched on the railing, watching him with shiny blue eyes. It had the body of a crow, but its head was small, bald, and human—about the size of a child's fist. Stretching thin lips over tiny, perfect teeth, it smiled.

Sweet-Sejenus-oh-God-it-can't-be-it-can't-be!

A parody of surprise flashed across the miniature face. "You know what I am," it said in a papery voice. "How?"

can't-be-cannot-be-Consult-here-no-no-no!

"Because," another voice replied, "he was once one of Achamian's students." The speaker had been concealed in the shadows farther down the clerestory. He now walked into the dim light.

Cutias Sarcellus smiled in greeting. "Weren't you, Inrau?"

A Knight-Commander consorting with a Consult Synthese?

Akka-akka-save-me!

Nightmarish terror and disbelief, stealing breath, panicking thought. Inrau staggered backward. The floor reeled. The sound of iron grating against stone behind him made him cry out. He whirled and saw another Shrial Knight stride from the darkness. He knew this one as well: Mujonish, who had accompanied him on tithe collections in the past. The man approached, his stance wary and his arms wide, as though he herded a dangerous bull.

What was happening? *Onkis?*

"As you can see," the crow-bodied Synthese said, "there's no place for you to go."

"Who?" Inrau managed to gasp. He could see the mark of sorcery now, the scar tissue of the Cants used to bind someone's soul to the abominable vessel before him. How had he missed it?

"He knows this form is but a shell," the Synthese said to Sarcellus, "but I don't see Chigra within him." The pea-sized eyes— little beads of sky blue glass—turned to Inrau. "Hmm, boy? You don't dream the Dream like the others, do you? If you did, you would recognize me. Chigra never failed to recognize me."

Onkis? Treacherous-god-bitch!

Through the terror an impossible certainty seized him. A revelation. Words of prayer had become tissue. Beneath he sensed other words, words of power.

"What do you want?" Inrau asked, his voice steadier this time. "What are you doing here?" He cared nothing for the answer, and everything for the time.

please-remember-please-remember . . .

"Doing? Why, what our kind always does: overseeing our stake in these affairs." It pursed its lips over its tiny teeth, but sourly, as though displeased by their taste. "No different, I suppose, from what you were doing in the Shriah's apartments, hmm?"

Breathing had become painful. He could not speak.

yes-yes-yes-that's-it-that's-it-but-what-comes-next? What-comes-after?

"Tsk, tsk," Sarcellus said, edging closer. "I'm afraid this is partially my fault, Old Father. Some weeks ago I bid the young apostle to be industrious."

"So it *is* your fault," the Synthese said with the miniature mockery of a scowl. It clicked several feet down the railing to follow Inrau's retreat. "Without direction, he simply threw his ardour into the wrong *vocation*. Spying on the God, rather than praying to Him." A small snort, like a cat's sneeze. "Ah, you see, Inrau? You've absolutely nothing to fear. The Knight-Commander bears the responsibility."

that's-it-that's-it-that's-it!

Inrau sensed Mujonish looming behind. Prayer seized his tongue. Blasphemy tumbled from his lips.

Turning with sorcerous speed, he punched two fingers through Mujonish's chain mail, cracked his breastbone, then seized his heart. He yanked his hand free, drawing a cord of glittering blood into the air. More impossible words. The blood burst into incandescent flame, followed his sweeping hand toward the Synthese. Shrieking, the creature dove from the railing into emptiness. Blinding beads of blood cracked bare stone.

He would have turned to Sarcellus, but the sight of Mujonish stilled him. The Shrial Knight had stumbled to his knees, wiping his bloody hands on his surcoat. Then, as though spilling from a bladder, his face simply fell apart, dropping outward, *unclutching* . . .

No mark. Not the faintest whisper of sorcery.

But how?

Something struck him hard about the head, and he toppled. Scrambling. A blow to his stomach sent him rolling. He glimpsed Sarcellus's shadowy form dancing about him. He gasped more words—words of shelter. Ghostly Wards leapt about him . . .

But they were useless. Reaching through the luminescent panes as though they were smoke, the Knight-Commander seized him about the throat and heaved him into the air. He raised a Chorae in his other hand, whisked it over Inrau's cheek.

Searing agony. The stone floor slammed into Inrau's face. He clutched at the pain. The skin flaked away beneath his fingers, transformed into salt by the Chorae's touch. The exposed flesh burned. He cried out again.

"You will *relent!*" he heard the Synthese cry.

Never.

Glaring at the hateful thing, Inrau resumed his blasphemous song. He saw the sun shining through the windows of its face. Too late.

Lights like a thousand hooks lanced from the Synthese's mouth. Inrau's Wards cracked and splintered in a blinding chatter. Then his song was choked from his lips. The air smothered him with the density of water. He floated off the clerestory floor. Streams of silvery bubbles were drawn from his gaping mouth to break against the ceiling. The weight of an ocean crushed him with an embalming fist.

At first he was calm. He watched the Synthese land on the Knight's shoulder and regard him with tiny blue button eyes. He admired the black of its feathers, shot through with glassy hints of purple. He thought of Achamian, hapless, oblivious to the peril.

Oh, Akka! It's worse than you dared imagine.

But there was nothing to be done.

His throat tightening, Inrau's thoughts turned to the Goddess, to her infidelities and to his. But his heart pounded more and more pressure into his skull until his lips curled and opened. Then he collapsed into thrashing madness, his idiot thoughts sure that somewhere there was some surface to break, some opening to air. A raw, irresistible reflex opened his lungs. Gagging convulsions, water like a sock in his throat, jerking in a haze of white beads . . .

Then hard floor, coughing, burning, choking air.

Sarcellus dragged him to his knees by his hair, wrenched his face toward the hazy blur of the Synthese. Inrau vomited, hacked more fire out of his lungs.

"I'm an Old Name," the tiny face said. "Even wearing this shell, I could show you the Agonies, Mandate fool."

"Wuh . . ." Inrau swallowed. Sobbed. *"Why?"*

Again the thin, tiny smile. "You worship suffering. Why do you *think?"*

Monumental rage filled him. It didn't understand! It didn't *understand.* With a coughing roar, he lurched forward, yanking his hair from his scalp. The Synthese seemed to flicker out of his path, but it wasn't its death he sought. *Any price, old teacher.* The stone rail slammed against his hips, broke like cake. Again he was floating, but it was so different—air whipping across his face, bathing his body. With a single outstretched hand, Paro Inrau followed a pillar to the earth.

PART II:
The Emperor

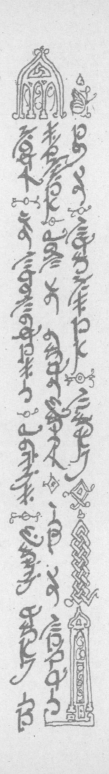

CHAPTER FIVE

MOMEMN

The difference between the strong emperor and the weak is simply this: the former makes the world his arena, while the latter makes it his harem.

—CASIDAS, THE ANNALS OF CENEI

What the Men of the Tusk never understood was that the Nansur and the Kianene were old enemies. When two civilized peoples find themselves at war for centuries, any number of common interests will arise in the midst of their greater antagonism. Ancestral foes share many things: mutual respect, a common history, triumph in stalemate, and a plethora of unspoken truces. The Men of the Tusk were interlopers, an impertinent flood that threatened to wash away the observed channels of a far older enmity.

—DRUSAS ACHAMIAN, COMPENDIUM OF THE FIRST HOLY WAR

Early Summer, 4110 Year-of-the-Tusk, Momemn

Designed to capture the setting sun, the Imperial Audience Hall possessed no walls behind the Emperor's raised dais. Sunlight streamed into the vaulted interior, shining across the marmoreal pillars of the concourse and gilding the tapestries suspended between them. A breeze tousled the smoke from censers arrayed about the dais, mingling the scent of fragrant oils with that of sky and sea.

"Any word of my nephew?" Ikurei Xerius III asked Skeaös, his Prime Counsel. "Anything from Conphas?"

"No, God-of-Men," the old man replied. "But all is well. I'm certain of it."

Xerius pursed his lips, doing his best to appear serene. "You may proceed, Skeaös."

With a swish of his silken robes, the wizened Counsel turned to the other functionaries assembled about the dais. For as long as Xerius could remember, he'd always been surrounded by soldiers, ambassadors, slaves, spies, and astrologers . . . For as long as he could remember, he'd been the centre of this scuttling herd, the peg from which the tattered mantle of Empire hung. Now it suddenly struck him that he'd never looked into any of their eyes—not once. Matching the Emperor's gaze was forbidden to those without Imperial Blood. The thought horrified him.

Save for Skeaös, I know none of these people.

The Prime Counsel addressed them. "This will be unlike any audience you've ever attended. As you know, the first of the great Inrithi lords has arrived. We are the portal through which he and his peers must pass before joining the Holy War. We cannot bar or tax their passage, but we can influence them, make them see that our interests coincide with what is right and what is true. As the audience proceeds, be silent. Do not fidget. Do not move. Cultivate a look of stern compassion. If the fool signs the Indenture, then and only then will we dispense with protocol. You may mingle with his entourage, share in whatever food or drink the slaves offer. But ration your words. Reveal nothing. *Nothing.* You may think you stand outside the circle of these events, but you do not. You *are* the circle. Make no mistake, my friends, the Empire itself lies in the balance."

The Prime Counsel looked to Xerius, who nodded.

"The time has come," Skeaös called, gesturing to the far side of the Imperial Audience Hall.

Great stone doors, Kyranean relics salvaged from the ruins of Mehtsonc, ponderously opened.

"His Eminence," a voice cried, "Lord Nersei Calmemunis, Palatine of Kanampurea."

Feeling curiously short of breath, Xerius watched his Imperial Ushers lead the Conriyan entourage down the concourse. Despite his earlier resolution to remain motionless—men who resembled statues, he was convinced, exhibited wisdom—he found himself tugging at the tassels of his linen kilt. He had received innumerable petitioners in his forty-five years, embassies of war and peace from across the Three Seas, but as Skeaös had said, he had never hosted an audience such as this.

The Empire itself . . .

Months had passed since Maithanet had declared Holy War against the heathens of Kian. Like naphtha, the fiend's summons had ignited the hearts of men in every Inrithi nation—pious, bloodthirsty, and covetous alike. Even now the groves and vineyards beyond Momemn's walls hosted thousands of these so-called Men of the Tusk. But until Calmemunis's arrival, they had consisted almost entirely of rabble: low-caste freemen, beggars, non-hereditary Cultic priests, and even, Xerius had been told, a band of lepers—men with little hope outside of Maithanet's promise, and even less understanding of the dreadful task their Shriah had set for them. Such men did not merit an emperor's spit, let alone his concern.

Nersei Calmemunis, however, was a far different matter. Of all the great Inrithi nobles rumoured to have mortgaged their birthrights for the Holy War, he was the first to reach the Empire's shores. His arrival had thrown Momemn's populace into an uproar. Clay blessing tablets, purchased from the temples at a copper talent apiece, had been strung across the streets. The fire-altars of Cmiral had burned an unending procession of victims donated in his name. Everyone understood that men such as Calmemunis, along with their client barons and knights, would be the keel and rudder of the Holy War.

But who would be its pilot?

Me.

Stung by a momentary panic, Xerius looked from the approaching Conriyans to the flutter of wings above. As always, sparrows wheeled and jousted beneath the dim vaults. As always, they calmed him. For a moment he wondered what an emperor was to a sparrow. Just another man?

He thought it unlikely.

When he lowered his gaze, the Conriyans were kneeling across the floor below him. Several of them, Xerius noticed with distaste, had tiny flower petals lodged in their hair and the oiled ringlets of their beards—marks of Momemn's adulation. They stood in unison, some blinking, others shielding their eyes against the sunlight.

For them, I'm darkness framed by sun and sky.

"It is always good," he said with surprising decisiveness, "to receive a cousin of our race from across the seas. How are things, Lord Calmemunis?"

The Palatine of Kanampurea stepped from his entourage and paused beneath the monumental steps, thoughtlessly choosing Xerius's long shadow to block the glare. Tall and broad of shoulder, the man cut an imposing figure. The small mouth pursed in his beard suggested some defect of breeding, but the rose-and-blue finery he wore was worth even an emperor's envy. The Conriyans might look brutish with their beards, especially amid the clean-shaven elegance of the Imperial Nansur Court, but their dress was impeccable.

"Good. How goes the war, Uncle?"

Xerius nearly bolted from his seat. Someone gasped.

"He means no offence, God-of-Men," Skeaös quickly murmured in his ear. "Conriyan nobles often refer to their betters as 'uncle.' It is their custom."

Yes, Xerius thought, *but why does he mention the war? Does he bait me?*

"What war do you refer to? The Holy War?"

Calmemunis looked narrowly at what must have been a wall of silhouettes above him. "I was told your nephew, Ikurei Conphas, marches against the Scylvendi in the north."

"Oh. That isn't a war. Simply a punitive expedition. A mere raid, in fact, if one compares it with the great war to come. The Scylvendi are nothing. It is the Fanim of Kian who are the sole object of my concern. After all, it is they, and not the Scylvendi, who desecrate Holy Shimeh."

Could they hear the hollow in his belly?

Calmemunis frowned. "But I've heard that the Scylvendi are a formidable people, that they've never been overcome in the field."

"You've been misled . . . So tell me, Lord Palatine, your journey from Conriya was without incident, I presume."

"None to speak of. Momas favoured us with kind seas."

"By his grace do we travel . . . Tell me, did you have occasion to confer with Proyas before you left Aöknyssus?" He could fairly hear Skeaös stiffen beside him. Not three hours earlier, the Prime Counsel had informed him of Calmemunis's feud with his illustrious kinsman. According to their sources in Conriya, Proyas had ordered Calmemunis whipped for impiety at the Battle of Paremti the previous year.

"Proyas?"

Xerius smiled. "Yes. Your cousin. The Crown Prince."

The small-mouthed face darkened. "No. We did not confer."

"But I thought Maithanet had charged him with marshalling all of Conriya for the Holy War."

"You were misled."

Xerius stifled a laugh. The man was stupid, he realized. He often wondered whether this was not the true function of jnan: the quick separation of wheat from chaff. The Palatine of Kanampurea, he now knew, was chaff.

"No," Xerius said. "I think not."

Several members of the Calmemunis's entourage scowled at this—the stocky officer to his right even opened his mouth in protest—but they held their tongues. They knew better, Xerius supposed, than to suggest their Palatine had actually *missed* something.

"Proyas and I do not . . ." Calmemunis paused, as though realizing mid-sentence that he had said too much. The small mouth gaped, baffled.

Oh, this one is art! *A real fool's fool.*

Xerius waved a dismissive hand, and watched its shadow flutter across the Palatine's men. The sun felt warm across his fingers. "But enough of Proyas."

"Indeed," Calmemunis snapped.

Afterward, Xerius had no doubt, Skeaös would find some slavish way to chastise him for mentioning Proyas. The fact that the Palatine had offended him first would count for nothing. As far as Skeaös was concerned, they were here to seduce, not to fence. The old ingrate, Xerius was convinced, was becoming as bad as his mother. No matter. *He* was Emperor.

"The provisions . . ." Skeaös whispered.

"You and your contingent will be provisioned, of course," Xerius continued. "And to ensure you're kept in a manner befitting your rank, I've appropriated a nearby villa for your comfort." He turned to the Prime Counsel. "Skeaös, will you please show the Palatine our Indenture."

Skeaös snapped his fingers, and an immense eunuch plodded from drapery to the far right of the dais, bearing a bronze lectern. A second followed, a long parchment scroll resting like a relic in his walrus arms. Calmemunis backed in astonishment from the steps as the first eunuch placed the stand before him. The second fumbled with the scroll for a moment—an indiscretion that would not go unpunished—then smoothly unrolled it across the sloped bronze. Both withdrew to a discreet distance.

The Conriyan Palatine squinted quizzically at Xerius, then bent to study the heavy document.

Several moments passed. Finally, Xerius asked, "Do you read Sheyic?"

Calmemunis glared at him.

I need to be more careful, Xerius realized. Few things were as incalculable as men who were at once stupid and thin-skinned.

"I read Sheyic. But I don't understand."

"That will not do," Xerius said, leaning forward on his bench. "You are the first man of true rank, Lord Calmemunis, to grace the gathering Holy War. It's crucial we understand each other implicitly, no?"

"Indeed," the Palatine replied, his tone and expression frigid in the manner of someone trying to maintain dignity in the midst of bewilderment.

Xerius smiled. "Good. The Nansur Empire, as you well know, has warred against the Fanim since the first Kiani tribesmen rode howling from the deserts. For generations we've battled them in the south, even as we've battled the Scylvendi in the north, losing province after province to their fanatic ardour. Eumarna, Xerash, even Shigek—losses purchased by the sacrifice of a thousand thousand Nansur sons. All of what is now called Kian once belonged to my Imperial ancestors, Palatine. Since who I am now, Ikurei Xerius III, is but the face of one divine Emperor, all of what is now called Kian once belonged to *me*."

Xerius paused, moved by his words and thrilled by the resonance of his voice across the distances of polished marble. How could they deny the force of his oratory?

"The Indenture before you, Lord Calmemunis, merely binds you, as all men must be bound, to the truth. And the truth—the undeniable truth—is that all the governorates of Kian are in fact provinces of the Nansur Empire. By marking this Indenture, you swear to undo an ancient wrong. You swear to return all lands liberated by the Holy War to their rightful possessor."

"What's this?" Calmemunis asked. He almost trembled with suspicion. Not good.

"As I said, it's an indenture whereby you swear to—"

"I heard you the first time," Calmemunis barked. "I was told nothing of this! This is sanctioned by the Shriah? Has Maithanet commanded this?"

The feeble-minded fool had the gall to interrupt *him?* Ikurei Xerius III, the Emperor who would see the Nansurium restored? Outrage!

"My generals tell me that you've brought some fifteen thousand men with you, Palatine. Surely you don't expect me to host and suckle so many for *nothing,* do you?" The world "suckle" caught his fancy, and he couldn't resist adding, "The Empire has only so many teats, my Conriyan friend."

"I-I've heard nothing of this," Calmemunis stammered. "I'm to swear that all heathen lands I conquer will be given away? Given to *you?*"

The stocky officer at his side could bear no more. "Sign nothing, Lord Palatine! The Shriah, I wager, has heard nothing of this either."

"And who would you be?" Xerius snapped.

"Krijates Xinemus," the man said briskly, "Lord Marshal of Attrempus."

"Attrempus . . . Attrempus. Skeaös, please tell me why that name sounds so familiar?"

"Certainly, God-of-Men. Attrempus is the sister of Atyersus, the fortress that the School of Mandate leases to House Nersei. Lord Xinemus, here, is a close friend of Nersei Proyas"—the old Counsel paused for the briefest of instants, no doubt to allow his Emperor time to digest the significance of this—"his childhood sword trainer, if I'm not mistaken."

Of course. Proyas wouldn't be so foolish as to allow an imbecile, especially one as powerful as Calmemunis, to parlay alone with the House Ikurei. He had sent a wet nurse. *Ah, Mother,* he thought, *the whole Three Seas knows our reputation.*

"Lord Marshal," Xerius said, "you forget your place. Didn't my Master of Protocol instruct you to remain silent?"

Xinemus laughed and ruefully shook his head. Turning to Calmemunis, he said, "We were warned this might happen, my Lord."

"Warned *what* might happen, Marshal?" Xerius cried. This was beyond all tolerance!

"That House Ikurei would play games with what is holy."

"Games?" Calmemunis exclaimed, whirling to confront Xerius. "Games with the *Holy War*? I came to you with an open heart, Emperor, as one Man of the Tusk to another, and you play games?"

Funereal silence. The Emperor of Nansur had just been *accused*.

"I have asked you—" Xerius stopped, struggling to purge the screech from his tone. "I've asked you—in all good courtesy, Palatine!—whether you'll sign my Indenture. Either you sign it, or you and your men starve. It is as simple as that."

Calmemunis had adopted the stance of one about to draw his weapon, and for a moment, Xerius grappled with the mad urge to flee, even though the man's weapons had been confiscated. The Palatine might be an idiot, but he was a frighteningly well-proportioned one. He looked as though he could leap the intervening steps seven at a time.

"So you would deny us provisions?" Calmemunis cried. "Starve *Men of the Tusk* in order to twist the Holy War to your ends?"

Men of the Tusk. The phrase made Xerius want to spit, and yet this prattling fool spoke it as though it were the God's secret name. More dull fanaticism. Skeaös had warned him of this as well.

"I speak only of what truth demands, Lord Palatine. If truth serves my ends, then it's because I serve the ends of truth." The Emperor of Nansur could not resist a wicked smile. "Whether your men starve or not is *your* decision, Lord Calmemunis. Your—"

Something warm and viscous struck his cheek. Stunned, he slapped at his face, then studied the muck on his fingers. A premonition of doom struck him, gouged his breast of all breath. What was this? Some kind of omen?

He looked up to the bickering sparrows. "Gaenkelti!" he shrieked.

The Captain of his Eothic Guard hastened to his side, bearing the odour of balsam and leather.

"Kill those birds!" Xerius hissed.

"Now, God-of-Men?"

Rather than reply, he snatched Gaenkelti's crimson cloak, which the man wore, according to Nansur custom, thrown forward over his left shoulder and hooked to his right hip. He used it to wipe the bird shit from his cheek and fingers.

One of his birds had defiled him . . . What could it mean? He had risked everything. Everything!

"Archers!" Gaenkelti cried to the upper galleries where the Eothic Bowmen were hidden. "Kill the sparrows!"

A short pause, then the twang of unseen bowstrings from above.

"Die!" Xerius roared. "Treacherous ingrates!"

Despite his wrath, he grinned at the sight of Calmemunis and his embassy scrambling to avoid the falling shafts. Arrows clattered to the floor throughout the Imperial Audience Hall. Most had missed their mark, but a few twirled to the ground like maple seeds, bearing small battling shadows. Soon the concourse was littered with felled sparrows, some flopping like speared fish, others lifeless.

The archers relented. Beating wings punctuated the silence.

An impaled sparrow had plopped onto the steps midway between him and the Palatine of Kanampurea. On a whim, Xerius pushed himself from his throne and trotted down the steps. He bent, scooped up the arrow and its thrashing message. He studied the bird for a moment, watched it convulse and shudder. *Was it you, little one? Who bid you do this? Who?*

A mere bird would never dare offend an emperor.

He looked up at Calmemunis and was seized by another whim, this one far darker. Holding shaft and sparrow before him, he approached the dumbstruck Palatine.

"Take this," Xerius said calmly, "as a token of my esteem."

Words of mutual outrage were exchanged, then Calmemunis, Xinemus, and their escort stormed from the Imperial Audience Hall, leaving Xerius alone with his thundering heart.

He scratched at the memory of bird shit upon his cheek. Squinting against the sun, he looked up to his throne, to the burnished silhouettes of his servants. He vaguely heard his Grand Seneschal, Ngarau, cry out for a basin of warm water. The Emperor had to be cleansed.

"What does it mean?" Xerius asked numbly.

"Nothing, God-of-Men," Skeaös replied. "We fully expected them to initially deny the Indenture. Like all fruits, our plan requires time to mature."

Our plan, Skeaös? You mean my plan.

He tried to stare down the insolent fool, but the sun confounded him. "I speak neither to you nor to the Indenture, you old ass." To accentuate his point he kicked over the bronze lectern. The Indenture swung like a pendulum in the air before skittering to the floor. Then he gestured to the skewered bird lying at his feet. "What does *this* mean?"

"Good fortune," Arithmeas, his favourite augur and astrologer, called out. "Among the lower castes, to be . . . ah, shat upon by a bird is the cause of great celebration."

Xerius wanted to laugh, but he could not. "But being shat upon is the only fortune they know, isn't it?"

"Nevertheless, there's great wisdom to this belief, God-of-Men. Small misfortunes such as this, they believe, portend good things. Some token blight must always accompany triumph, to remind us of our frailty."

His cheek tingled, as though it too recognized the truth of the augur's words. It was an omen! And a good one at that. He could *feel* it!

Again the Gods have touched me!

Suddenly revived, he climbed the steps, avidly listening as Arithmeas expanded on the way this event coincided with his star, which had just entered the horizon of Anagke, the Whore of Fate, and now stood upon two fortuitous axes with the Nail of Heaven. "An excellent conjunction," the portly augur exclaimed. "An excellent conjunction indeed!" Rather than resume his place on the high bench, Xerius strode passed it, bidding Arithmeas to accompany him. Trailing a small herd of functionaries, he walked between the great rose marble pillars that marked the missing wall and out onto the adjoining terrace.

Like a vast fresco chalked in smoky colours, Momemn spread out below him, stretching toward the setting sun. His palace, the Andiamine Heights, occupied the seaward quarter of the city, so that he could, if he wished, see Momemn in her labyrinthine entirety simply by turning his head from side to side: the square turrets of the Eothic Garrison to the north, the monumental prom-enades and structures of the temple-complex of Cmiral directly west, and the congested bedlam of the harbour along the banks of the River Phayus to the south.

Still listening to Arithmeas, he peered across the distant walls to where the groves and fields of the surrounding countryside were bleached by the belly of the sun. There, bunched and scattered across the landscape like mould on bread, he could see the tents and pavilions of the Holy War. Not many so far, but in a matter of months, Xerius knew, they could very well encircle the horizon.

"But the Holy War, Arithmeas . . . Does all this mean the Holy War will be mine?"

The Imperial Augur clasped his corpulent fingers and shook his jowls in affirmation. "But the ways of Fate are narrow, God-of-Men. There's much we must do."

So intent was Xerius on his augur's diagnoses and prescriptions, which included detailed instructions for the slaughter of ten bulls, that he initially failed to notice his mother's arrival. But there she was, a narrow shadow in his periphery, as unmistakable as death.

"Prepare the victims, then, Arithmeas," he said peremptorily. "That's enough for now."

As the augur departed, Xerius glimpsed slaves bearing the basin of water that had been summoned earlier.

"Arithmeas?"

"Yes, God-of-Men?"

"My cheek . . . Should I wash it?"

The man waved his hands in a comical fashion. "No! D-definitely not, God-of-Men. It's crucial that you wait at least three days. Crucial."

Several other questions assailed him, but his mother had approached, followed by the waddling bulk of her eunuch. She moved with the willowy grace of a fifteen-year-old virgin, despite her sixty whorish years. With a whisk of blue muslin and silk, she turned her profile to him, studying the city as he had moments earlier. Sunlight flashed along the scales of her jade headdress.

"A son," she said dryly, "hanging upon the words of a babbling, blubbery fool. How it warms a mother's heart."

He sensed something odd in her manner, something *bottled*. But then everyone had seemed peculiarly ill at ease in his presence of late—no doubt, Xerius supposed, because they had finally glimpsed the divinity that dwelt within him, now that the two great horns of his plan had been set in motion.

"These are trying times, Mother. Too perilous to ignore the future."

She turned and appraised him in a manner that was at once coquettish and masculine. The sun deepened her wrinkles and drew the shadow of her nose across her cheek. The old, Xerius had always thought, were *ugly*, both in flesh and spirit. Age forever transformed hope into resentment. What was virile and ambitious in young eyes became impotent and covetous in old.

I find you offensive, Mother. Both in appearance and in manner.

His mother's beauty had been legendary once. While his father yet lived, she'd been the Empire's most celebrated possession. Ikurei Istriya, the Empress of Nansur, whose dowry had been the burning of the Imperial Harem.

"I watched your audience with Calmemunis," she said mildly. "A disaster. Just as I told you, hmm, my godlike son?" Her smile riddled the cosmetics about her lips with small cracks. A longing to kiss those lips struck Xerius with bodily force.

"I suppose, Mother."

"Then why do you persist in this nonsense?"

And now this latest bizarre turn. His mother arguing against sweet reason.

"Nonsense, Mother? The Indenture will see the Empire *restored*."

"But if a fool such as Calmemunis can't be gulled into signing it, what hope does your Indenture have, hmm? No, Xerius, you serve the Empire best by serving the Holy War."

"Has Maithanet bewitched you as well, Mother? How does one bewitch a witch?"

Laughter. "By offering to destroy her enemies, how else?"

"But the whole world is your enemy, Mother. Or am I mistaken?"

"The whole world is every man's enemy, Xerius. You'd do well to remember that."

In his periphery, he glimpsed a guardsman approach Skeaös and whisper something in his ear. Harmony, his augurs had told him, was musical. It demanded that one be attuned to the nuances of every circumstance. Xerius was a man who needed not to look at things to see them. He possessed a refined sense of suspicion.

The old Counsel nodded, then momentarily glanced at his Emperor, his eyes troubled.

Do they plot? Is this treachery? But he shrugged these thoughts away; they occurred far too frequently to be trusted.

As though guessing the source of his distraction, Istriya turned to the old Counsel. "What say you, Skeaös, hmm? What say you of my son's infantile avarice?"

"Avarice?" Xerius cried. Why did she provoke him like this? "*Infantile?*"

"What else? You squander the gifts of the Whore. First Fate delivers you this Maithanet, and against my counsel you try to assassinate him. Why? Because you do not own him. Then she delivers you the Holy War, a hammer with which to crush our ancestral foe! And because you do not own it, you seek to destroy it as well! These are the tantrums of a child, not the ploys of a cunning Emperor."

"Trust me, Mother, I seek to procure, not destroy, the Holy War. The foreign dogs *will* sign my Indenture."

"With your blood! Have you forgotten what happens when one weds empty bellies to fanatic hearts? These are warlike men, Xerius. Men intoxicated by their faith. Men who *act* in the face of indignity! Do you truly expect them to endure your extortion? You risk the Empire, Xerius!"

Risk the Empire? No. To the northwest, few Nansur lived within sight of the mountains, such was their fear of the Scylvendi, and to the south, all the "old provinces," which had belonged to the Nansurium at the height of her power, lay in the thrall of heathen Kian. Now Fanim drums echoed across her old conquests, calling men to worship the False Prophet, Fane. Now the fortress of Asgilioch, which the ancient Kyraneans had raised to guard against Shigek, was again the frontier. He did not risk the Empire, only the pretence of one. Empire was the prize, not the wager.

"Fortunately your son is not quite so doltish as that, Mother. The Men of the Tusk won't starve. They'll eat from my bowl, but one day at a time. I don't intend to deny them the provisions they need to live, only the provisions they need to march."

"And what of Maithanet? What if he directs you to provision them?"

In matters of Holy War, an ancient constitution bound the Emperor to the Shriah. Xerius was obligated to supply the Holy War, on pain of Shrial Censure.

"Ah, but you see, Mother, that he cannot do. He knows as well as we that these Men of the Tusk are fools, that they think the God himself has ordained the overthrow of the heathen. If I provide Calmemunis with everything he requests, he'd march in a fortnight, certain that he could destroy the Fanim with his paltry household alone. Maithanet will mime outrage, of course, but he'll secretly applaud what I do, knowing it'll purchase the Holy War the time it needs to gather. Why else do you think he commanded it gather about Momemn rather than Sumna? Aside from taxing my purse, he *knew* I would do this."

She paused, her eyes abruptly narrow and appraising. No soul as serpentine as hers could fail to appreciate the subtlety of such a move.

"But does this mean that you play Maithanet, or that Maithanet plays you?"

Over the previous months Xerius had, he could now admit, underestimated this new Shriah. But he would not underestimate the fiend again. Not in this.

Maithanet, Xerius realized, understood that the Nansurium was doomed. For the past century and a half, those with knowledge or power in Nansur had awaited the catastrophe, the news that the Scylvendi tribes had united as of old and were rumbling toward the coasts. This had been how Kyraneas had fallen two thousand years ago, and how the Ceneian Empire had fallen more than a thousand years after. And this would be how, Xerius was certain, the Nansurium would fall as well. But it was the prospect of this inevitability conjoined with Kian, a heathen nation that waxed even as Nansur waned, that truly terrified him. After the Scylvendi left, and they always left, who would stop the Kianene heathens from snuffing out the muddied blood of Kyraneas, from cutting out the Three Hearts of God: Sumna, the Thousand Temples, and the Tusk?

Yes, this Shriah was shrewd. Xerius no longer regretted the failure of his assassins. Maithanet had given him a hammer like no other—a Holy War.

"Our new Shriah," he said, "is much overrated."

Let him think he plays me.

"But for what purpose, Xerius? Even if the great among the Holy War succumb to your demands, you don't truly think they'll spill their blood to hoist the Imperial Sun, do you? Even signed, your Indenture is worthless."

"Not worthless, Mother. Even if they break their oath, the Indenture is not worthless."

"Then *why*, Xerius? Why all these mad risks?"

"Come, Mother. Have you grown so old?" For a moment, he suffered an uncommon glimpse of how things must appear to her: the mercantile, and therefore extraordinary, demand that every high noble of the Holy War sign his Indenture; the dispatch of the greatest Nansur army assembled in a generation not against the heathens of Kian, but against their far more ancient and temperamental foe, the Scylvendi. How these two things alone must have taxed her! With plans as sublime as his, the logic was always hidden.

Xerius was not fool enough to think he was the equal of his ancestors in strength of arms or spirit. Ikurei Xerius III was no fool. The present age was different, and different strengths were called for. The great man of this day found his weapons in other men and in the shrewd calculation of events. Xerius now possessed both: his precocious nephew, Conphas, and this mad Shriah's Holy War. With these two instruments, he would win back the Empire.

"What is it you plan, Xerius? You must tell me!"

"Painful, isn't it, Mother? To stand at the heart of the Empire and yet be deaf to its beat—and after a lifetime of playing it like a drum!"

But instead of displaying outrage, her eyes opened in abrupt epiphany. "The Indenture is simply a *pretext*," she gasped. "Something to protect you from Shrial Censure when you . . ."

"When I *what*, Mother?" Xerius glanced nervously at the small crowd surrounding them. This was not the place for such a conversation.

"Is this why you've sent my grandson to his death?" she cried.

There it was finally, her true motive for this seditious interrogation. Her beloved grandson, poor sweet Conphas, who at this very moment marched somewhere on the Jiünati Steppe, searching for the dread Scylvendi. This was the Istriya that Xerius knew and despised: devoid of religious sentiment but obsessed with her progeny, with the fate of the House Ikurei.

Conphas was to be Restorer, wasn't he, Mother? You didn't think me capable of such glory, did you, you old bitch?

"You overreach, Xerius! You grasp for too much!"

"Ah, and for a moment I thought you understood." He had uttered this with offhand certainty, but much of him believed her, enough that sleep now required a full quart of unwatered wine. Even more this night, he imagined, after the incident with the birds . . .

"I understand well enough," Istriya snapped. "Your waters aren't so deep that this old woman can't wade in them, Xerius. You hope to extort signatures for your Indenture, not because you expect any Men of the Tusk to relinquish their conquests, but because you expect to *wage war against them afterward*. With your Indenture, you'll be immune to Shrial Censure when you subdue the petty, undermanned fiefdoms that are sure to arise in the Holy War's wake. And *that* is why you've sent Conphas on your so-called punitive expedition against the Scylvendi. Your plan requires manpower you do not have so long as the northern provinces must be guarded."

Dread churned his innards.

"Ah," she said wickedly, "it's one thing to rehearse your plans in the murk of your soul and quite another to hear them on the lips of another, isn't it, my foolish boy? Like listening to a mummer parrot your voice. Does it sound foolish to you now, Xerius? Does it sound *mad?*"

"No, Mother," he managed to say with some semblance of confidence. "Merely daring."

"Daring?" she cried, as though the word had unlatched something deranged within her. "By the Gods, how I wish I'd strangled you in your cradle! Such a foolish son! You've doomed us, Xerius. Can't you see? No one, no High King of Kyraneas, no Aspect-Emperor of Cenei, has ever defeated the Scylvendi on their ground.

They are the *People of War*, Xerius! Conphas is dead! The flower of your army is dead! Xerius! *Xerius!* You've brought catastrophe upon us all!"

"Mother, no! Conphas assured me he could do it! He's studied the Scylvendi as no other! He knows their *weaknesses!*"

"Xerius. Poor sweet fool, can't you see that Conphas is still a child? Brilliant, fearless, as beautiful as a God, but still a child . . ." She clutched at her cheeks and began clawing. "You've killed my child!" she wailed.

Her logic, or maybe it was her terror, swept through him with the force of a cataract. Panicked, Xerius looked to the others on the balcony, saw his mother's fear on all their faces, and realized that it had been there all along. It wasn't Ikurei Xerius III they feared, it was what he had done!

Have I destroyed everything?

He stumbled. Bony hands steadied him. Skeaös. Skeaös! He understood what he did. He had glimpsed the glory! The brilliance!

He whirled, gripped the old Counsel by his draped robe, and shook him so violently that his brooch, a golden eye with an onyx pupil, snapped and clinked across the ground.

"Tell me you see!" Xerius cried. "*Tell me!*"

Clutching his robe to prevent it from unravelling, the old man kept his eyes dutifully to the ground. "Y-you've made a wager, God-of-Men. Only after the number-sticks have been thrown can we know."

Yes! That was it!

Only after the number-sticks have been thrown . . .

Tears spilled from his eyes. He grasped the old Counsel by the cheeks and was shocked by the coarseness of his skin. His mother had told him nothing new. He'd always known that he'd wagered everything. How many hours had he plotted with Conphas? How many times had he been moved to wonder by his nephew's martial brilliance? Never had the Empire possessed an Exalt-General such as Ikurei Conphas. Never!

He will overcome the Scylvendi. He'll humble the People of War!
And it seemed to Xerius that he knew these things with impossible
certainty. *My star enters the Whore, bound by twin portents to the Nail
of Heaven . . .*

A bird shat upon me!

He dropped his hands to Skeaös's shoulders, and was struck by
the magnanimity of the act. *How he must love me.* He looked to
Gaenkelti, Ngarau, and the others, and suddenly the cause of their
doubt and fear seemed so very clear to him. He turned to his
mother, who had fallen to her knees.

"You—all of you—think you see a *man* who's made a mad wager.
But men are frail, Mother. Men are fallible."

She stared at him, the lampblack about her eyes muddied by
tears. "And are not emperors men, Xerius?"

"Priests, augurs, and philosophers all teach us that what we see is
smoke. The man I am is but smoke, Mother. The son you birthed is
but *my* mask, one more guise I've taken for this wearisome revel of
blood and semen you call life. I am what you told me I would be!
Emperor. Divine. Not smoke but *fire.*"

At these words, Gaenkelti fell to his knees. After a moment's
hesitation, the others followed.

But Istriya clutched her eunuch's arm and pulled herself to her
feet, all the while gaping at him. "And if Conphas should die in the
smoke, hmm, Xerius? If the Scylvendi should ride from the smoke
and put out your 'fire,' what then?"

He struggled to contain his outrage. "Your end approaches, and
you cling to the smoke because you fear that smoke is all there is.
You're afraid, Mother, because you're old, and nothing bewilders so
much as fear."

Istriya regarded him imperiously. "My age is my own affair. I've
no need of fools to remind me."

"No. I suppose your tits scarce let you forget."

Istriya screeched, flew at him as she had in his childhood. But
her giant eunuch, Pisathulas, restrained her, catching her with fists

that dwarfed her forearms. He bobbed his shaved head in terrified stupefaction.

"I should've killed you!" she shrieked. "Strangled you with your own cord!"

Unaccountably, Xerius began to laugh. Old and frightened! For the first time she looked pedestrian, far from the indomitable, all-knowing matriarch she had always seemed. His mother looked pathetic!

It was almost worth losing an Empire.

"Take her to her chambers," he said to the giant. "See that my physicians tend to her."

Sputtering and shrieking, she was carried bodily from the balcony. The immensity of the Andiamine Heights swallowed her murderous cries.

The rich colours of sunset had paled into those of dusk. The sun was half down, framed by a cloudy mantle of purple. For several moments Xerius simply stood, breathing deeply, wringing his hands to silence the tremors. His people watched him nervously from the corners of their eyes. The herd.

At last Gaenkelti, whose Norsirai heritage made him more outspoken than was seemly, broke the silence. "God-of-Men, may I speak?"

Xerius waved irritated assent.

"The Empress, God-of-Men . . . What she said—"

"Her fears are warranted, Gaenkelti. She simply spoke the truth dwelling in all our hearts."

"But she threatened to kill you!"

Xerius struck the Captain full on the face. The blond man's hands balled into fists for a moment, then unclenched. He glared fiercely at Xerius's feet. "I apologize, God-of-Men. I merely feared for—"

"For nothing," Xerius said sharply. "The Empress grows old, Gaenkelti. The tides have drawn her out of sight of shore. She's simply lost her bearings."

Gaenkelti fell to the ground, placed his lips firmly to Xerius's right knee. "Enough," Xerius said, drawing his Captain to his feet.

He let his fingertips linger on the gorgeous blue tattoos webbing the man's forearms. His eyes burned. His head ached. But he felt an extraordinary calm.

He turned to Skeaös. "Someone brought you a message, old friend. Was it news of Conphas?" A mad question, but strangely trivial when asked in the absence of breath.

When the Counsel hesitated, the tremors returned.

Please . . . Sejenus, please.

"No, God-of-Men."

Dizzying relief. Xerius almost staggered.

"Well, then? What was it?"

"The Fanim have sent an emissary in reply to your request to parlay."

"Good . . . good!"

"But not just any emissary, God-of-Men." Skeaös licked his thin, old-man lips. "A *Cishaurim*. The Fanim have sent a Cishaurim."

The sun went down, and so it seemed, all hope with it.

⁓⊷⊷⊶⁓

Like tattered cloth in the wind, the braziers fluttered in the small courtyard Gaenkelti had selected for the meeting. Surrounded by dwarf cherry trees and weeping hollies, Xerius squeezed his Chorae tight, until it felt his knuckles would burst. He probed the gloom of the adjoining porticoes, unconsciously counting his shadowy men. He turned to the lean sorcerer on his right: Cememketri, the Grandmaster of his Imperial Saik.

"Do you have enough?"

"More than enough," Cememketri replied, his voice indignant.

"Heed your tone, Grandmaster," Skeaös snapped from Xerius's left. "Our Emperor has asked you a question."

Cememketri bowed his head stiffly, as though against his will. Twin fires reflected in his large wet eyes. "There are three of us here, God-of-Men, and twelve crossbowmen, all bearing Chorae."

Xerius winced. "Three? Only you and two others remain?"

"It could not be helped, God-of-Men."

"Of course." Xerius thought of the Chorae in his right hand. He could humble the pompous mage with a touch, but then that would leave only two. How he despised sorcerers! Almost as much as he despised needing them.

"They come," Skeaös whispered. Xerius clenched his Chorae so tight the script engraved across it felt a brand in his palm.

Two Eothic Guardsmen entered the courtyard, bearing lamps rather than arms. They took positions on either side of the bronze doors, and Gaenkelti, still dressed in his ceremonial armour, filed between them, accompanied by a cowled figure draped in black-linen robes. The Captain led the emissary to the designated spot, where the spheres of light cast by the four braziers overlapped. Despite the illumination, Xerius could see only portions of the man's lips and left cheek beneath the cowl.

Cishaurim. For the Nansur the only name more hateful was Scylvendi. Nansur children—even the children of Emperors—were weaned on tales of the heathen sorcerer-priests, of their venereal rites and their unfathomable powers. To simply speak the name was to strike terror in the Nansur breast.

Xerius struggled to breathe. *Why send a Cishaurim? To kill me?*

The emissary drew back his cowl, pulling it wide over his shoulders. Then he lowered his arms so that the robe fell to the ground, revealing the long saffron cassock he wore beneath. His bald scalp was pale, shockingly so, and his face was dominated by the black sockets beneath his brow. Eyeless faces always unnerved Xerius, always reminded him of the dead skull beneath every man's expression, but the knowledge that this man could nevertheless *see* awakened a pang at the back of this throat, one that could not be silenced by swallowing. Just as his childhood tutors had claimed, a serpent coiled about the Cishaurim's neck—a Shigeki salt asp, black and shining as though oiled, its flickering tongue and surrogate eyes suspended next to the man's right ear. The sightless pits remained fixed upon Xerius, but the asp's head bobbed and turned, slowly scrutinizing the breadth of the courtyard, methodically tasting the air.

"Do you see it, Cememketri?" Xerius hissed under his breath. "Do you see the mark of sorcery?"

"None," the sorcerer said, his voice tight with the fear of being overheard.

The snake's eyes lingered for a moment on the dark porticoes that flanked the courtyard, as though assessing the threat posed by the shadows within. Then, like a tiller swinging on a greased hinge, it turned to Xerius.

"I am Mallahet," the Cishaurim said in flawless Sheyic, "adopted son of Kisma, of the tribe Indara-Kishauri."

"You're Mallahet?" Cememketri exclaimed. Another indiscretion: Xerius had not given him leave to speak.

"And you are Cememketri." The eyeless face bowed, but the snake's head remained rigid. "Honour, to an old foe."

Xerius sensed the Grandmaster stiffen next to him. "Emperor," the sorcerer murmured, "you must leave at once. If this is truly Mallahet, then you're in grave danger. We all are!"

Mallahet . . . He had heard that name before, in one of Skeaös's briefings. The one whose arms were scarred like a Scylvendi.

"So three are not enough," Xerius replied, inexplicably heartened by his Grandmaster's fear.

"Mallahet is second only to Seokti in the Cishaurim. And only then because their Prophetic Law bars non-Kianene from the position of Heresiarch. Even the Cishaurim are fearful of his power!"

"What the Grandmaster says is true, God-of-Men," Skeaös added in low tones. "You must leave at once. Let me negotiate in your stead . . ."

But Xerius ignored them. How could they be so hare-hearted when the Gods themselves had secured these proceedings? "Well met, Mallahet," he said, surprised by the steadiness of his voice.

After a brief pause, Gaenkelti barked: "You stand in the presence of Ikurei Xerius III, the Emperor of Nansur. You will kneel, Mallahet."

The Cishaurim wagged a finger, and the asp swayed with it as though in mockery. "Fanim kneel only before the One, before the God-that-is-Solitary."

Out of reflex or simple ignorance, Gaenkelti raised a fist to strike the man. Xerius stilled him with an outstretched palm.

"We shall rescind Protocol for this occasion, Captain," he said. "The heathens shall kneel before me soon enough." He cupped the fist holding the Chorae in his other hand, driven by an obscure impulse to conceal it from the serpent's eyes. "You've come to parlay?" he asked the Cishaurim.

"No."

Cememketri muttered a soldier's curse.

"Then why have you come?" Xerius asked.

"I have come, Emperor, so you might parlay with another."

Xerius blinked. "Who?"

For a moment, it seemed the Nail of Heaven flashed from the Cishaurim's brow. There was a shout from the blackness of the porticoes, and Xerius raised his hands before him.

Cememketri intoned something incomprehensible, dizzyingly so. A globe, composed only of ghostly trails of blue fire, leapt about them.

But nothing had happened. The Cishaurim stood, as motionless as before. The asp's eyes glowed like amber coals in the firelight.

Then Skeaös gasped, "His face!"

Superimposed like a transparent mask over Mallahet's skull-like visage was the face of another, a grizzled Kianene warrior who still bore the desert's mark on his hawkish features. Appraising eyes peered from the Cishaurim's empty sockets, and a phantom goatee hung from his chin, braided in the manner of a Kianene Grandee.

"Skauras," Xerius said. He had never seen the man before, but somehow he knew he looked upon the Sapatishah-Governor of Shigek, the heathen scoundrel whom the Southern Columns had fenced with for more than four decades.

The ghostly lips moved, but all Xerius heard was a far-off voice speaking in the lolling rhythms of Kiani. Then the real lips moved beneath, saying, "Excellent guess, Ikurei. You, I know by your coins."

"So what is this? The Padirajah sends one of his Sapatishah dogs to confer with me?"

Again the alarming lag of lips and voices. "You're not worthy of the Padirajah, Ikurei. I alone could break your Empire over my knee. Be thankful the Padirajah is a pious man, and abides by his treaties."

"All our treaties are moot, Skauras, now that Maithanet is Shriah."

"Even more reason for the Padirajah to spurn you. You too have become moot."

Skeaös leaned and whispered in his ear. "Ask him why the theatrics if you've become irrelevant. The heathen are afraid, God-of-Men. That's the only reason they come to you thus."

Xerius smiled, convinced his old Counsel had merely confirmed what he already knew. "If I've become moot, then why these extraordinary measures, hmm? Why make your better your messenger?"

"Because of the Holy War that you and your idolatrous brethren would wage against us. Why else?"

"And because you know the Holy War is my instrument."

The wraithlike expression smiled, and Xerius heard distant laughter. "You would wrest the Holy War from Maithanet, would you? Make it the great lever you'd use to undo centuries of defeat? We know of your petty schemes to bind the idolaters to your Indenture. And we know of the army you've sent against the Scylvendi. The ploys of a fool—all of them."

"Conphas has promised to pike a road of Scylvendi heads from the Steppe to my feet."

"Conphas is doomed. No one possesses cunning or might enough to overcome the Scylvendi. Not even your nephew. Your army and your heir are dead, Emperor. Carrion. If so many Inrithi did not muster on your shores, I would ride to you even now and bid you drink of my sword."

Xerius clutched his Chorae tighter to silence the tremors. An image of Conphas bleeding at the feet of some wild Scylvendi reaver flashed before his soul's eye, and he relished it, despite the horror of its implications. *Then Mother would have only me . . .*

Again Skeaös's voice in his ear. "He lies to frighten you. We heard from Conphas just this morn, and nothing was amiss. Remember, God-of-Men, the Scylvendi crushed the Kianene not eight years past. Skauras lost three sons in that expedition, including Hasjinnet, his eldest. *Goad* him, Xerius. Goad him! Angry men make mistakes."

But of course, he'd already considered this.

"You flatter yourself, Skauras, if you think Conphas is as foolish as Hasjinnet."

Ethereal eyes blinked over empty sockets. "The Battle of Zirkirta was a great woe for us, yes. But a woe you will share very shortly. You attempt to injure me, Ikurei, but you merely prophesy your own destruction."

"The Nansurium," Xerius said, "has endured far greater losses and survived."

But Conphas can't lose! The omens!

"Well enough, Ikurei. I'll grant you that trifle. The Solitary God knows you Nansur are a stubborn people. I'll even grant that Conphas may prosper where my own son faltered. I'll not underestimate that snake charmer. He was my hostage for four years, remember? But none of this makes Maithanet's Holy War your instrument. You hold no hammer above us."

"But I do, Skauras. The Men of the Tusk know nothing of your people—even less than Maithanet. Once they understand they war not only against you but against your Cishaurim, the leaders of the Holy War will sign my Indenture. The Holy War requires a School, and that School happens to be mine."

The disembodied lips grinned over the dour line of Mallahet's mouth.

Again, the uncanny, far-away voice. "*Hesha? Ejoru Saika? Matanati jeskuti kah—*"

"What? The Imperial Saik? You think your Shriah would cede you the Holy War for the Imperial Saik? Maithanet *has* plucked your eyes from the Thousand Temples, hasn't he? Do you see, Ikurei? Do you finally see how quick the sands run beneath your feet?"

"What do you mean?"

"Even we know more of your accursed Shriah's plans than you."

Xerius glanced at Skeaös's face, saw concern rather than calculation furrow his crinkled features. What was happening?

Skeaös . . . Tell me what to say! What does he mean?

"Speechless, Ikurei?" Mallahet's surrogate voice sneered. "Well, choke on this: Maithanet has sealed a pact with the *Scarlet Spires*. Even now, the Scarlet Magi prepare to join the Holy War. Maithanet already possesses his School, one that dwarfs your Imperial Saik in both numbers and power. As I said, you are moot."

"Impossible!" Skeaös spat.

Xerius whirled to face the old Counsel, stunned by his audacity.

"What's this now, Ikurei? You let your dogs howl at your table?"

Xerius knew he should be outraged, but such an outburst from *Skeaös* was . . . unprecedented.

"But he lies, God-of-Men!" Skeaös cried. "This is a heathen trick, meant to extort concessions—"

"Why would they lie?" Cememketri snapped, obviously eager to humiliate an old court foe. "Don't you think the heathen *want* us to possess the Holy War? Or do you think they'd rather treat with *Maithanet?*"

Had they forgotten the presence of their Emperor? They spoke as though he were a fiction whose usefulness had come to an end. *They think me irrelevant?*

"No," Skeaös retorted. "They know the Holy War's ours, but would have us think it's not!"

A cold fury uncoiled within Xerius. There would be much screaming tonight.

Either the two men remembered themselves or they sensed something of Xerius's humour, because they abruptly fell silent. Two years past, a Zeumi had entertained Xerius's court with trained tigers. Afterward, Xerius had asked him how he could command such fierce beasts with looks alone. "Because," the towering black-skinned man had said, "they see their future in my eyes."

"You must forgive my zealous servants," Xerius said to the wraith inhabiting the Cishaurim's face. "You can be assured that I will not."

Skauras's visage flickered then reappeared, as though nodding in and out of some unseen shaft of light. How the old wolf must be laughing. Xerius could almost see him regaling the Padirajah with descriptions of the disarray in the Imperial Court.

"I shall mourn them, then," the Sapatishah said.

"Save your dirges for your own folk, heathen. Regardless of who possesses the Holy War, you are doomed." The Fanim *were* doomed. Outrageous insolence aside, what Cememketri had said moments earlier was true. The Padirajah wanted him to possess the Holy War. One could not bargain with fanatics.

"Ah, strong words! At last I speak to an emperor of the Nansur. Tell me, then, Ikurei Xerius III, now that you understand we *both* bargain from a position of weakness, what do you propose?"

Xerius paused, possessed by a calculating cold. He had always been at his canny best when wroth. Alternatives tumbled through his soul, most of them foundering on the sharp fact of Maithanet and his demonic cunning. He thought of Calmemunis and his hatred of his cousin, Nersei Proyas, heir to the throne of Conriya . . .

And then he understood.

"To the Men of the Tusk you and your people are little more than sacrificial victims, Sapatishah. They speak and act as though their triumph is already inked in scripture. Perhaps the time will come when they respect you as we do."

"Shrai laksara kah."

"You mean fear."

Everything now hinged on his nephew, far to the north. More than ever. *The omens . . .*

"As I said—respect."

CHAPTER SIX

THE JIÜNATI STEPPE

It is said: a man is born of his mother and is fed of his mother. Then he is fed of the land, and the land passes through him, taking and giving a pinch of dust each time, until man is no longer of his mother, but of the land.

—SCYLVENDI PROVERB

. . . and in Old Sheyic, the language of the ruling and religious castes of the Nansurium, skilvenas means "catastrophe" or "apocalypse," as though the Scylvendi have somehow transcended the role of peoples in history and become a principle.

—DRUSAS ACHAMIAN, *COMPENDIUM OF THE FIRST HOLY WAR*

Early Summer, 4110 Year-of-the-Tusk, the Jiünati Steppe

Cnaiür urs Skiötha found the King-of-Tribes and the others crowded across a ridge that afforded them a panoramic view of the Hethanta Mountains and the Nansur army encamped below. Pulling his grey to a stop, he studied them from a distance, his heart hammering as though his blood had grown overthick. For a moment he felt like a boy excluded by his elder siblings and

159

their snide friends. He half-expected to hear taunts sailing on the wind.

Why would they disgrace me like this?

But he was not a child. He was the many-blooded chieftain of the Utemot, a seasoned Scylvendi warrior of more than forty-five summers. He owned eight wives, twenty-three slaves, and more than three hundred cattle. He had fathered thirty-seven sons, nineteen of the pure blood. His arms were ribbed with the swazond, ritual trophy scars, of more than two hundred dead foes. He was Cnaiür, breaker-of-horses-and-men.

I could kill any of them—pound them to bloody ruin!—and yet they affront me like this? What have I done?

But like any murderer, he knew the answer. The outrage lay not in the fact of his dishonour but in their presumption to know.

Flaring between snow-capped peaks, the sun bathed the assembled chieftains in pale morning gold. They looked like warriors from different nations and ages, despite the spiked Kianene battle-caps worn by the veterans of the Battle of Zirkirta. Some sported antique scale corselets, others mail hauberks and cuirasses of varying manufacture—the spoils of long-dead Inrithi princes and nobles. Only their scarred arms, stone faces, and long black hair marked them as the People—as Scylvendi.

Xunnurit, their King-of-Tribes by election, sat in their midst, his left arm braced imperiously on his thigh, his right raised to the distance. As though at his direction, the rider next to him raised the indented crescent of his bow. Cnaiür glimpsed a birch arrow sailing across the sky, saw it vanish in the grasses partway to the river. They measured distances, he realized, which could only mean they planned their assault.

Without me. Could they have simply forgotten?

Cursing, Cnaiür urged his mount toward them. He kept his face turned to the east, sparing himself the indignity of their smirking looks. The River Kiyuth wound across the valley floor, black save where frosted by shallow rapids. Even from this distance, he could see the Nansur army teeming along its banks, chopping down the remaining poplars, dragging them away with teams of horses. Fortified by earthworks and a palisade, the imperial encampment lay a mile or so beyond, a great oblong of innumerable tents and wains beneath the mountain the memorialists called Sakthuta, the "Two Bulls."

Three days ago he'd been astonished and appalled by this sight. For the Nansur to trespass was outrage enough, but to sink posts and raise walls as well?

Now, however, it filled him only with foreboding.

Baring his teeth, he barrelled into the midst of his brother chieftains.

"Xunnurit!" he bellowed. "Why wasn't I summoned?"

The King-of-Tribes cursed and yanked his roan about to face him. The morning breeze dimpled the fox-fur trim of his Kianene battlecap. Regarding Cnaiür with undisguised contempt, he said, "You were summoned like the rest, Utemot."

Cnaiür had met Xunnurit only five days earlier, shortly after arriving with his Utemot warriors. Their dislike had been mutual and immediate, like that of suitors for the same beauty. Xunnurit's contempt, Cnaiür had no doubt, was rooted in the scandalous rumours of his father's death long ago. The grounds of his own animosity, however, eluded him. Perhaps he'd simply matched disdain with disdain. Perhaps it was the silk trim of Xunnurit's fleece tunic or the ingrown vanity of his smile. Hatred needed no reasons, if only because they were so many and so easily had.

"We shouldn't attack," Cnaiür said bluntly. "This is juvenile foolishness."

Disapproval hung like musk in the morning air. The other chieftains scrutinized him, their faces guarded. Despite the rumours they had doubtless heard, Cnaiür's flayed arms demanded a grudging deference. Not a man among them, Cnaiür knew, had murdered half as many as he.

Xunnurit leaned forward and spat across the grasses—a gesture of disrespect. "Foolishness? The Nansur shit, piss, and poke asses on our hallowed land, Utemot. What would you have me do? Parlay? Capitulate and send Conphas tribute?"

Cnaiür debated whether to discredit the man or to discredit his scheme. "No," he replied, opting for wisdom instead of slander, "I would have us wait. We have Ikurei Conphas"—he raised a thick-fingered hand and clenched it into a fist—"trapped. His horses need rich fodder, ours do not. His men are accustomed to roofs, to pillows, to wine, and to the comforts of lax women, while ours sleep in their saddles and need only their horse's blood for sustenance. Mark me, as the days pass, the fawn will begin sprinting through their hearts and the jackal through their bellies. They will fear and they will hunger. Their fortifications of earth and timber will smack more of captivity than safety. And soon, desperation will drive them to a ground of our choosing!"

A low-throated rumble passed through the assembled chieftains, and Cnaiür glanced from face to weathered face. Some were young and eager to shed blood, but most possessed the sturdy wisdom of many campaigns—older faces, such as his own. They were men who had survived the many impatiences of youth and yet remained in the prime of their strength; they could see the wisdom of his words.

But Xunnurit looked unimpressed. "Always the tactician, eh, Utemot? Tell me, Cnaiür urs Skiötha, if you entered your yaksh and found men assaulting your wives, what tactics would you adopt? Would you wait in ambush outside, where you'd be most certain of success? Would you wait until *after* they'd desecrated both hearth and womb?"

Cnaiür sneered, noticing for the first time the two missing fingers on Xunnurit's left hand. Could the fool even draw a bow? "The foot of the Hethantas is a far different thing than my yaksh, Xunnurit."

"Is it? Is this what the memorialists tell us?"

It wasn't so much the man's cunning that shocked Cnaiür as the realization that he'd underestimated him.

Xunnurit's eyes flashed with triumph. "No. The memorialists say that battle is our hearth, earth our womb, and sky our yaksh. We've been violated, as surely as if Conphas had quickened our wives or cracked our hearthstone. Violated. Desecrated. Humiliated. We're beyond measuring tactical advantages, Utemot."

"And what of our victory over the Fanim at Zirkirta?" Cnaiür asked. Most of the men present had been at Zirkirta eight years before, where he himself had struck down Hasjinnet, the Kianene general.

"What of it?"

"How long did the tribes fall back before the Kianene? How long did we bleed them before we broke their back?" He graced Xunnurit with a macabre smile, the one that so often reduced his wives to tears. The King-of-Tribes stiffened.

"But that—"

"Is a different thing, Xunnurit? How can a battle be like a yaksh and yet not be like another battle? At Zirkirta, we practised patience. We waited, and by doing so, we utterly destroyed a powerful foe."

"But it's not simply a matter of waiting, Cnaiür," a third voice called out. It was Oknai One-Eye, the chieftain of the powerful Munuäti tribes from the interior. "The question is one of *how long* we must wait. Soon the droughts begin, and those of us from the Steppe's heart must drive our herds to summer pasture."

Numerous shouts followed the remark, as though this were the first sensible thing said.

"Indeed," Xunnurit added, rallied by this unsought support. "Conphas has come heavily laden, with a baggage train larger than his army. How long would you have us wait for the fawn and jackal to gnaw at their hearts and bellies? One month? Two? Even six?" He turned to the others and was rewarded by a swell of guttural assent.

Cnaiür ran a hand over his scalp, sorted through the hostile faces surrounding him. He understood their worries because they were also his. An overlong absence possessed many perils. Neglected herds meant wolves, pestilence, even famine. If one added to this the threat of slave revolts, wayward wives, and for tribes on the

Steppe's northern frontier such as his own, Sranc, then the incentive for a hasty return became irresistible.

He turned to Xunnurit, realizing the decision to attack was not something the man had foisted on the others. Even though they knew that haste was the curse of wisdom, they wanted to bring this war to a quick conclusion, far more so than they had at Zirkirta. But why?

All eyes were on him. "Well?" Xunnurit asked.

Had Ikurei Conphas intended this? It would be easy enough, he supposed, to learn the different demands the seasons placed on the People. Had Conphas deliberately chosen the weeks before the summer drought?

The thought dizzied Cnaiür with its implications. Suddenly, everything he had witnessed and heard since joining the horde possessed different meaning: the buggery of their Scylvendi captives, the mocking embassies, even the positioning of their privies—all calculated to gall the People into attacking.

"Why?" Cnaiür abruptly asked. "Why would Conphas bring so many supplies?"

Xunnurit snorted. "Because this is the Steppe. There's no forage."

"No. Because he expects a war of *patience*."

"Exactly!" Xunnurit exclaimed. "He intends to wait until hunger forces the tribes to disband. Which is why we must attack immediately!"

"Disband?" Cnaiür cried, dismayed that his insight could be so easily perverted. "No! He intends to wait until hunger or pride forces the tribes to *attack*."

The audacity of the claim provoked shouts from the onlookers. Xunnurit laughed in the rueful manner of one who'd mistaken naïveté for wisdom. "You Utemot dwell far from the Empire," he said, as though indulging a fool, "so perhaps ignorance of imperial politics is to be expected. How could you know that the stature of Ikurei Conphas grows while that of his uncle, the Emperor, falters?

You speak as though Ikurei Conphas were sent here to conquer, when he's been sent here to die!"

"Do you jest?" Cnaiür cried in exasperation. "Have you looked at his host? Their elite cavalry, their Norsirai auxiliaries, well nigh every column in the Imperial Army, even the Emperor's own Eothic Guard! They've stripped the Empire to assemble this expedition. Treaties must have been struck, fortunes of gold promised and spent. This is an army of *conquest*, not a funeral procession for—"

"Ask the memorialists!" Xunnurit snapped. "Other emperors have sacrificed as much, if not more. Xerius would have to fool Conphas, would he not?"

"Pfah! And you say the Utemot know nothing of the Empire! The Nansurium is a place besieged. She could ill afford to lose a fraction of such an army!"

Xunnurit leaned farther forward in his saddle, raised his fist in a threatening manner. His brows pinched over glaring eyes. His nostrils flared. "Then what better reason to smash it now! Afterward, we shall sweep to the Great Sea like our fathers of yore! We shall pull down their temples, impregnate their daughters, cut down their sons!"

To Cnaiür's alarm, shouts of agreement rifled the morning air. He silenced them with a killing look. "Are you all dog-eyed drunks? What better reason to let the Nansur languish! What do you think Conphas would do if he were in our midst? What—"

"Pick my sword from his ass!" someone cried out, prompting an explosion of hearty laughter.

Cnaiür could smell it then, the good-humoured camaraderie that amounted to little more than a conspiracy to mock one and the same man. His lips twisted into a grimace. Always the same, no matter what his claim to arms or intellect. They'd measured him many years ago—and had found him wanting.

But measure is unceasing . . .

"No!" Cnaiür roared. "He'd laugh at you as you laugh at me! He'd say a dog must be known to be broken, and I know these dogs!

Better than they know themselves!" A plaintive cast had crept into his tone and expression; he struggled to squelch it. "Listen. You must listen! Conphas has gambled on this very council—on our arrogance, on our . . . customary thoughts. He's done everything in his power to provoke us! Don't you see? *We* decide his genius on the field. Only we can make him a fool. And by doing the one thing that terrifies him, the one thing he's done everything to prevent. We must wait! Wait for him to come to us!"

Xunnurit had watched him intently, his eyes bright with gloating amusement. Now he smiled derisively. "Men call you Man-killing Cnaiür, speak of your prowess on the field, of your endless hunger for holy slaughter. But now"—he shook his head in a scolding manner—"where's that hunger gone, Utemot? Should we now call you Time-killing Cnaiür?"

More heart-gouging laughter, deep-throated and coarse, at once honest in the way of a simple people and yet bruised by an unsavoury glee, the sound of lesser men revelling in the degradation of one greater. Cnaiür's ears buzzed. Earth and sky shrank, until the whole world became laughing, yellow-toothed faces. He could feel it stir within him, his second soul, the one that blotted the sun and painted the earth with blood. Their laughter faltered before his menace. His glare struck even the smirks from their faces.

"Tomorrow," Xunnurit declared, nervously yanking his roan toward the distant Nansur encampment, "we shall sacrifice an entire nation to the Dead-God. Tomorrow we put an empire to the knife!"

⸻

Swaying silently upon wooden saddles, innumerable horsemen paced through grasses chill and grey with morning dew. Nearly eight years had passed since the Battle of Zirkirta, eight years since Cnaiür had last witnessed such a gathering of the People. Great congregations trailed their chieftains, enveloping slopes and heights nearly a mile distant. Screened by thickets of raised lances, hundreds of horsehide standards jutted from the masses, marking tribes and federations from across the Steppe.

So many!

Did Ikurei Conphas grasp what he'd done? The Scylvendi were fractious by nature, and aside from their ritual border raids on the Nansurium, they spent the majority of their time murdering one another. This penchant for feud and internecine warfare was the Empire's greatest bulwark against their race, greater even than the sky-gutting Hethantas. By invading the Steppe, Conphas had welded the People together, and so had delivered the Empire to its greatest peril in a generation.

What could prompt such a risk? For no apparent reason, Ikurei Xerius III had staked the Empire itself on his precocious nephew. What promises had Conphas made him? What circumstances had driven him?

All was not as it seemed; of this, Cnaiür was certain. And yet, as he stared across fields of armoured horsemen, he could not help repenting his earlier misgivings. Everywhere he looked, he saw grim, warlike riders, pelts nailed to their circular shields, their horses caparisoned in skirts stitched with plundered Nansur and Kianene coins. Countless thousands of Scylvendi, made terrible by cruel seasons and never-ending war, now united as in the days of legend. What hope could Conphas possibly have?

Nansur horns blared from beneath the mountains, startling man and horse alike. All eyes turned to the long ridge that obscured the valley. Cnaiür's grey snorted and pranced, swishing the scalps that adorned his bridle.

"Soon," he muttered, stilling his horse's romping head with a firm hand. "Soon the madness will break."

Cnaiür always remembered the hours before battle as unbearable, and because of this, he was always surprised whenever he actually endured them. There were moments when the enormity of what was about to happen seized him, left him stunned like one who'd just avoided a mortal fall. But such moments were fleeting. By and large the hours passed like any others, more anxious, perhaps, and punctuated by flashes of communal hate and awe, but otherwise as tedious as the rest. By and large he needed to remind himself of the insanity to come.

Cnaiür was the first of his tribesmen to gain the summit of the ridge. Smouldering between two incisor-shaped mountains, the rising sun blinded them, and several moments passed before Cnaiür could discern the far-away lines of the Imperial Army. Phalanxes of infantry formed a great segmented band across the open ground between the river and the fortified Nansur encampment. Mounted skirmishers ranged the broken slopes before them, poised to harass any Scylvendi attempting to cross the Kiyuth. As though greeting their ancient foe, the Nansur horns pealed once again, shivering through the raw morning air. A mighty shout rose from the ranks, followed by the hollow drum of swords pounding shields.

While the other tribes mustered along the ridge line, Cnaiür studied the Nansur, a hand raised against the sun. The fact that they occupied the middle ground rather than the east bank of the river did not surprise him, though he imagined Xunnurit and the others were now scrambling to alter their plans. He tried counting the ranks—the formations seemed extraordinarily deep—but had difficulty concentrating. The absurd magnitude of his circumstances weighed against him like something palpable. How could such things happen? How could whole nations—

He lowered his head, rubbed the back of his neck, rehearsing the litany of self-recriminations that always consummated such shameful thoughts. In his soul's eye, he saw his father, Skiötha, his face blackening as he suffocated in the muck.

When he looked up, his thoughts were as vacant as his expression. Conphas. Ikurei Conphas was the focus of what was about to unfold, not Cnaiür urs Skiötha.

A voice startled him: Bannut, his dead father's brother.

"Why are they deployed so close to their encampment?" The old warrior cleared his throat—a sound like a horse's low-chested nicker. "You'd think they'd use the river to deny us our charge."

Cnaiür resumed his appraisal of the Imperial Army. The giddiness of imminent bloodshed floated through his limbs. "Because Conphas needs a decisive battle. He wants us to draw our lines on his side of the river. Deny us room to manoeuvre and force an all-or-nothing confrontation."

"Is he mad?"

Bannut was right. Conphas was mad if he thought his men could prevail in a pitched battle. In desperation, the Kianene had made a similar bid at Zirkirta eight years before; they had purchased only disaster. The People did not break.

A laugh surfaced through the mutter of his surrounding kinsmen. Cnaiür jerked his head around. At him? Did someone laugh at him?

"No," he replied distantly, watching profiles over Bannut's shoulders. "Ikurei Conphas is not mad."

Bannut spat, a gesture meant, or so Cnaiür assumed, for the Nansur Exalt-General. "You speak as though you know him."

Cnaiür glared directly at the old man, trying to decipher the disgust in his tone. He *did* know Conphas, in a manner. While raiding the Empire the previous autumn, he'd captured several Nansur soldiers, men who prated about the Exalt-General with an adoration that had captured Cnaiür's interest. With hot coals and harsh questions, he'd learned much of Ikurei Conphas, of his brilliance in the Galeoth Wars, of his daring tactics and novel training regimens—enough to know he was different from any he'd ever met on the field. But this knowledge was wasted on old snakes such as Bannut, who had never forgiven him the murder of his father.

"Ride to Xunnurit," Cnaiür commanded, knowing full well the King-of-Tribes would have nothing to do with an Utemot messenger. "Find out what he intends."

Bannut was not fooled. "I'll take Yursalka with me," he said hoarsely. "He married one of Xunnurit's daughters, the deformed one, just last spring. Perhaps the King-of-Tribes will remember that generosity." Bannut spat one last time, as though to cement his meaning, and spurred into the surrounding Utemot.

For a long time, Cnaiür sat desolate upon his horse, numbly watching bumblebees dart between the bobbing heads of purple clover just below him. The Nansur continued pounding their distant shields. The sun slowly gathered the valley in its hot clasp. Horses stamped in impatience.

More horns rang across the interval, and the Nansur ceased their clamour. The rumble of his muttering kinsmen waxed, and a kindling rage crowded the grief from his breast. Always they spoke to one another and never to him; it was as though he were a dead man in their midst. He thought of all those he'd killed the first few years after his father's death, all those Utemot who'd sought to wrest the chieftain's White Yaksh from the dishonour of his name. Seven cousins, one uncle, and two brothers. Stubborn hate brimmed within him, a hate that ensured he would not yield, no matter how many indignities they heaped upon him, no matter how many whispers or guarded looks. He would murder all and any, foe and kinsmen alike, before he would yield.

He fixed his gaze on the bristling landscape of Conphas's army. *Will I kill you today, Exalt-General? I think so.*

Sudden shouts drew his attention to the left. Across the congestion of arms and horsemen, he saw Xunnurit's standard waving against the sky. Dyed horsetails whisked up and down, relaying the order for a slow advance. Far to the north, crowds of Scylvendi had already begun filing down the slopes. Crying out to his tribesmen, Cnaiür spurred his mount toward the river, trampling the clover and scattering the bees. The dew had burned off, and the grasses now rasped about his horse's shins. The air smelled of warming earth.

The Scylvendi horde gradually enveloped the eastern valley. Pressing through the scrub of the floodplain, Cnaiür glimpsed Bannut and Yursalka racing toward him across open ground, their leather bowcases swinging from their hips, their shields bouncing on their horses' rumps. They leapt some scrub, and Bannut was nearly unhorsed by a shallow ravine on the far side. Within moments they were reining their mounts parallel to Cnaiür.

For some reason, they seemed even more ill at ease than usual. After a conspiratorial glance at Bannut, Yursalka fixed Cnaiür with expressionless eyes. "We're to take the southernmost of the fords, then position ourselves opposite the Nasueret Column, on the enemy's left. If Conphas advances before we've reformed, we're to withdraw to the south and harass his flanks."

"Xunnurit himself told you this?"

Yursalka nodded carefully. Bannut glared, his old eyes bright with malicious self-satisfaction.

Rocking with his horse's gait, Cnaiür peered over the Kiyuth, sifting through the crimson banners of the Imperial Army's left. He found the standard of the Nasueret Column quickly: the Black Sun of Nansur halved by an eagle's wing, with the Sheyic symbol for nine embroidered in gold below.

Bannut cleared his throat again. "The Ninth Column," he said approvingly. "Our King-of-Tribes honours us." Though traditionally stationed on the Empire's Kianene frontier, the men of the Nasueret were rumoured to be among the Imperial Army's finest.

"Either that or he murders us," Cnaiür amended. Perhaps Xunnurit hoped hard consequences would follow from the hard words they'd traded the previous day.

They all want me dead.

Yursalka snorted something unintelligible, then spurred away, seeking, Cnaiür imagined, more honourable company. Bannut continued at Cnaiür's side, saying nothing.

When the Kiyuth grew near enough for them to smell its glacial ancestry, several detachments broke from the Scylvendi line and ploughed across the river's many fords. Cnaiür watched these cohorts apprehensively, knowing their immediate fortune would reveal much of Conphas's intentions. The Nansur skirmishers on the river's far side fell back before them, then broke and bolted, pelted by volleys of arrows. The Scylvendi pursued them toward the bulk of the Imperial Army, then hooked into a gallop parallel to the Nansur line, firing clouds of arrows from the backs of hard-running horses. More and more cohorts joined them, guiding their horses with only spur, cry, and knee. Soon, thousands were sweeping across the Imperial lines.

Cnaiür and his Utemot crossed the Kiyuth under cover of these marauders, trailing drapes of water as they climbed the far bank, then rode hard to their new position opposite the Nasueret. Cnaiür knew the river crossing and subsequent redeployment would be a critical time, and throughout he kept expecting to hear horns sound the Nansur advance. But the Exalt-General kept his columns leashed, allowing the Scylvendi to assemble in a vast crescent along the back of the river.

What was Conphas doing?

Across ground and grasses as uneven as a juvenile's beard, the Imperial Army awaited them. Cnaiür gazed across row after row of shield-bearing figures, heavy with armour and insignia, wearing red leather skirts and iron-banded harnesses trimmed by mail. Innumerable and nameless, soon to die for their trespasses.

Horns brayed. Thousands of swords beat as one. And yet it seemed an uncanny silence had settled upon the field, a collective intake of breath.

A breeze funnelled through the valley, tugging at the smell of horses, sweaty leather, and unwashed men. The chafe and clank of scabbards against harnesses reminded Cnaiür of his own armour. His hands as light as air-filled bladders, he checked the straps of his white-enamelled battlecap, a trophy of his victory over Hasjinnet at Zirkirta, then the lacings of his iron-ringed brigandine. He swung from his waist in his saddle, both to limber his muscles and to ease the tension. He whispered a memorial to the Dead-God.

Horsehair signals were traded between the massed tribes, and Cnaiür barked commands to his kinsmen. The first wave of lancers formed abreast of him. Shields were strung from necks.

Sensing Bannut's scrutiny, Cnaiür turned to him, found himself disquieted by his expression.

"You," the old warrior said, "shall be measured this day, Cnaiür urs Skiötha. Measure is unceasing."

Cnaiür gaped at the man, overcome by fury and astonishment. "This is not the place, Uncle, to revisit old wounds."

"I can think of no better place."

Concerns, suspicions, and premonitions beset him, but there was no time. The skirmishers were retiring. In the distance, lines of horsemen peeled away from the greater horde, pacing toward the phalanxes of the Imperial Army. The pilgrimage had ended; the worship was about to begin.

With a shout, he led the Utemot forward at a trot. Something akin to fear clutched him, a sense of falling, as though from a precipice. Within moments they found themselves within range of the Nansur bowmen. He cried out, and his lancers spurred to a gallop, bracing shields against shoulders and saddle horns. They crashed through a thicket of stunted sumacs. The first shafts whistled among them, tearing air like cloth, thudding into shield, ground, flesh. One clipped his shoulder, another punched a finger's length through the laminated leather of his shield.

They thundered across a stretch of level turf, gathering fatal momentum. More arrows descended upon them, and they were fewer. Horse shrieks, the clatter of shafts, then only the raw rumble of a thousand hoofs across the turf. His head low, Cnaiür watched the infantrymen of the Nasueret Column brace themselves. Pikes were lowered, pikes longer than any he'd ever seen. His breath caught in hesitation. But he spurred his horse faster, couching his lance, howling the Utemot battle cry. His kinsmen answered, and the air shivered, *"War and worship!"* Clumped grasses and wildflowers hurtled beneath him. The wall of pikes and shields and soldiers rushed closer. His tribe rode with him, outstretched like two great arms.

Taken in the chest, his horse toppled, gouged the steppe grass. He crashed against turf and shins, wrenched his shoulder and neck.

For an instant he was tangled in locked limbs. He winced beneath a great crushing shadow, but nothing came and he pushed free, tossing away his shield, drawing his sword, struggling to make sense of the confusion around him. Close enough to touch, a riderless horse stamped in wild circles, kicking into the Nansur. It was hacked to death by men packed so tight they seemed hammered together by nails.

The Nansur ranks were largely unbroken, and they fought with stubborn professionalism. The Utemot suddenly seemed wild and thin before them, impoverished in their undyed leather and looted armour. To either side his kinsmen were being cut down. He saw Okkiür, his cousin, pulled from his horse by hooks and cudgelled on the ground. He glimpsed his nephew Maluti thrash beneath falling swords, still shrieking the Utemot battle cry. Had so many already fallen?

He glanced at the expanse behind them, expecting to find the second wave of Utemot lancers. Save for a lone horse limping toward the river, the ground was empty. He saw his tribesmen in the distance, milling in their original positions, watching when they should have been riding. What was happening?

Treachery?

Treachery! He looked about for Bannut, found him curled in the grasses nearby, fumbling with his stomach as though he cradled a toy. A Nansur stumbled from the surrounding melee, drew his shortsword back to thrust into Bannut's throat. Cnaiür scooped a weighted javelin from the ground and flung it. The soldier saw him, foolishly drew up his shield. The javelin punched through the top corner, dragged the shield down with its weight. Cnaiür leapt toward him, seized the javelin, then violently heaved shield and man forward. The infantryman lurched to his hands and knees, scrambled beneath Cnaiür's raised broadsword, then slumped to the ground, headless.

Cnaiür grabbed Bannut by the harness and dragged him from the fracas. The old warrior cackled, blood bubbling between his lips. "Xunnurit remembered well the favour Yursalka did him!" he cried.

Cnaiür stared at him in horror. "What have you done?"

"Killed you! Killed the kin-slayer! The weeping faggot who'd be our chieftain!"

Horns blared through the uproar. Between heartbeats, Cnaiür saw his father in Bannut's grizzled face. But Skiötha had not died like this.

"I watched you that night!" Bannut wheezed, his voice growing more pinched with agony. "I saw the truth of what"—his body cramped and shook about a wracking cough—"what happened those thirty years past. I told all that truth! Now the Utemot will be delivered from the oppression of your disgrace!"

"You know nothing!" Cnaiür cried.

"I know all! I saw the way you looked at him. I know he was your lover!"

Lover?

Bannut's eyes were beginning to glass over, as though he looked into something bottomless. "Yours is the name of our shame," he gasped. "By the Dead-God I would see it blotted out!"

Cnaiür's blood felt like gravel. He turned away to blink back tears.

Weeper.

Through a screen of straining, hacking figures, he glimpsed Sakkeruth, a childhood friend, topple from his rearing mount. He remembered spearing fish with him beneath broad summer skies. Remembered . . .

No.

Faggot. Is this what they thought?

"No!" he snarled, turning back to Bannut. The old iron rage had at last found him. "I am Cnaiür urs Skiötha, breaker-of-horses-and-men." He speared the turf with his sword and seized the astonished man about the throat. "None have murdered so many! None bear as many holy scars! I'm the measure of disgrace and honour. Your measure!" His uncle gagged, flailed at him with blood-oily palms. Then he went slack. Strangled. The way the girl children of slaves were strangled.

Retrieving his broadsword, Cnaiür stumbled from his uncle's corpse, looked about vacantly. The carcasses of horses and men embroidered the ground before him. Reduced to clots of unhorsed warriors, his Utemot recoiled from the bristling wall of infantrymen. Several howled to their distant kinsmen, realizing they'd been stranded. A shameless handful broke and ran. Others gathered about Cnaiür.

Imperial officers bawled over the din. The Nansur ranks advanced. With his left hand outstretched before him, Cnaiür fell into stance, raising his broadsword high, until the sun flashed along its smeared length. The infantrymen picked their way over the fallen, their shields emblazoned with Black Suns, their faces masks of grim jubilation. Cnaiür saw one spear Bannut's body. More hollering broke out among the officers, hoarse over the braying of distant horns. Abruptly, the forward three ranks charged.

Cnaiür fell to a crouch, hacked at the greaved shin of the first man to rush him. The fool went down. He kicked his shield upwards, punched his blade through the bands of his armour just beneath the armpit. Exultation. He jerked his broadsword free, swept around and hacked at another, breaking his collarbone through his harness. Cnaiür cried out and raised his scarred arms, mighty tokens of his bloody past.

"Who?" he roared in their womanish tongue. "Who among you shall take the knife to my arms?"

A third fell, vomiting blood, but the rest closed on him in numbers, led by a stone-eyed officer who bellowed, "Die!" with every stroke of his sword. Cnaiür obliged him, shearing away part of his jaw with his lower teeth. Undeterred, the others crowded him with spears and shields, pressing him backward. Another officer rushed him, a young noble with the motif of House Biaxi across his shield. Cnaiür could see the terror in his eyes, the realization that the hulking Scylvendi before him was something more than human. Cnaiür swatted the shortsword from his feminine hands, savagely kicked him, struck. The boy fell backward, shrieking, slapping at the blood that jetted from his groin as though it were fire.

They jostled before him, now as eager to avoid as to close with him. *"Where are your mighty warriors?"* Cnaiür screamed. *"Show me your mighty warriors!"* His limbs fevered by all-conquering hatred, he cut them down, weak and strong alike, fighting like one mad with heartbreak, hacking shields until arms were broken, pounding figures until they stumbled and spouted plumes of blood.

The advancing ranks engulfed them, but still Cnaiür and his Utemot killed and killed, until the turf beneath their feet became bloody muck, treacherous with corpses. The Nansur relented, scrambled back several paces, gaping at the Utemot chieftain. Sheathing his broadsword, Cnaiür vaulted the bodies heaped before him. He caught a wounded straggler by the throat, crushed his windpipe. Roaring, he heaved the thrashing man above his head.

"I am the *reaver!*" he cried. "The measure of all men!" He sent the body crashing at their feet. "Is there no *cock* among you?" He spat, then laughed at their astonished silence. "All cunts, then." He shook the blood from his mane, raised his broadsword anew.

Panicked shouts erupted among the Nansur. Several threw themselves against the men packed behind, mad to escape his deranged aspect. Then rumbling hoofs breached the din of the greater battle, and all heads turned. More Utemot horsemen exploded into their midst, impaling some Nansur on long lances, trampling others. There was a brief moment of pitched melee, and Cnaiür hammered down two more, his sword now blunted to an edged iron pipe. Then the men of the Nasueret Column were fleeing, casting away weapons and shields as they ran.

Cnaiür and his kinsmen found themselves alone, chests heaving, blood streaming from unstaunched wounds. *"Ayaaah!"* they cried as cohort after wild cohort galloped by them. "War and worship!"

But Cnaiür ignored them, sprinting instead to the top of a low knoll. The valley opened before him, churning with dust, smoke, and countless thousands of warring men. For a moment the enormity of the spectacle struck him breathless. Far to the north, he saw divisions of Scylvendi horsemen, dark through skirts of dust, wheel and charge what looked to be a stranded Nansur column. Following the horsehide standard of the Munuäti, companies of horsemen streamed east between the isolated column and the centre, riding down fleeing men. At first he thought they raced toward the Nansur encampment, but a glance told him this was not so. The camp already burned, and Cnaiür could see Nansur slaves, priests, and craftsmen dangle and drop from the palisades. Someone had already raised the standard of the Pulit, the southernmost of the Scylvendi tribes, on the forward timber gate. So quickly . . .

He scrutinized the madness of the centre. Someone had set the intervening grasses aflame, and through the smoke he saw Xunnurit's Akkunihor pressed against the glittering black waters of the Kiyuth, assailed on all sides by the Eothic Guard and elements of a column he could not identify. Dead horses and men littered the great swath of land between his position and Xunnurit's desperate stand. Where were the Kuöti? The Alkussi? Cnaiür turned west, to the far side of the river—the wrong side—and saw a pitched battle along the wrinkled crest of the valley. He identified the Kidruhil, the elite Imperial Heavy Cavalry, overwhelming a shattered cohort of Scylvendi. He saw Nymbricani horsemen, the Emperor's Norsirai auxiliaries, disappear over a ridge farther north and the perfect phalanxes of what looked like two intact columns marching in their wake, one of them bearing *Nasueret* standards—

But how could that be? His Utemot had just annihilated the Nasueret. Hadn't they? And hadn't the Kidruhil been positioned on the Nansur's extreme right flank, the position of honour among the Ketyai? The position facing the Pulit . . .

He could hear his men call to him, but he ignored them. What was Conphas doing?

A hand clasped his shoulder. It was Balait, his second wife's eldest brother, someone he'd always respected. The man's corselet had been severed and now hung from one shoulder. He still wore his spiked battlecap, but blood coursed down his left temple, drawing a line through the spatter.

"Come, Cnaiür," he gasped. "Othkut has brought us horses. The field is confused; we must reassemble to strike."

"Something's wrong, Bala," Cnaiür replied.

"But the Nansur are doomed . . . Their camp already burns."

"Yet they own the centre."

"All the better! The flanks are ours, and what remains of their army has been drawn onto open ground. Even now, Oknai One-Eye leads his Munuäti to relieve Xunnurit! We shall close about them as a fist!"

"No," Cnaiür said blankly, watching the Kidruhil battle their way over the crest behind them. "Something's wrong! Conphas *gave* us the flanks so that he could seize the centre . . ." That would explain how the Pulit had taken the encampment so quickly. Conphas had withdrawn his Kidruhil at the battle's onset to throw them against the Scylvendi centre. And he'd given his Columns false standards in order to deceive them into thinking he'd deployed his main strength across his flanks. The Exalt-General *wanted* the centre.

"Maybe," Balait offered, "he thought taking the King-of-Tribes would throw us into disarray."

"No. He's not so foolish as that . . . Look. He's thrown all his horse into the centre . . . as though he *chases* something." Cnaiür worked his jaw, peering across the vista, his eyes sifting through scene after far-away scene of violence. The sharp threshing of swords. The murderous heave and hammer of war's bloody work. And beneath its beauty something unfathomable, as though the field itself had become a living sign, a pictogram like those the outlanders used to freeze breath onto stone and parchment.

What did it mean?

Balait had joined his meditation. "He's doomed," the man said, shaking his head. "Not even his Gods can save him!"

Then Cnaiür understood. His breath grew chill in his breast. The hot fury of bloodletting abandoned his limbs; he could feel only the ache of his injuries and the unspeakable hollow opened by Bannut's words.

"We must flee."

Balait stared at him in stunned contempt. "We must what?"

"The Chorae Bowmen—Conphas knows we position them behind the centre. Either they're destroyed or he's chased them from the field. Either way we—"

Then he glimpsed the first flashes of unholy light. Too late.

"A School, Bala! *Conphas has brought a School!*"

Near the heart of the valley, from infantry phalanxes hastily arrayed to meet Oknai One-Eye and his Munuäti, at least two dozen black-robed figures slowly climbed over the field and into the sky. Schoolmen. The sorcerers of the Imperial Saik. Several dispersed over the valley. Those remaining already sang their unearthly song, scorching earth and Scylvendi with shimmering flame. The Munuäti charge crumbled into an avalanche of burning horses and men.

For a long moment Cnaiür could not move. He watched mounted silhouettes topple in the heart of golden bonfires. He saw men thrown like chaff by incandescent blooms. He saw suns fall short of the horizon and come crashing to fiery earth. The air resounded with the concussions of sorcerous thunder.

"A trap," he murmured. "The entire battle was a bid to deny us our Chorae!"

But Cnaiür possessed his own Chorae—an inheritance from his dead father. Fingers numb, arms giddy with exhaustion, he pulled the iron sphere from beneath his brigandine and clutched it tight.

As though walking across the back of roiling smoke and dust, a Schoolman drifted toward them. He slowed, floating the height of a tree-top above them. His black silk robe boiled in the mountain wind, its gold trim undulating like snakes in water. White light flashed from his eyes and mouth. A barrage of arrows winked into cinders against his spherical Wards. The ghost of a dragon's head ponderously ascended from his hands. Cnaiür saw glassy scales and eyes like globes of bloody water.

The majestic head bowed.

He turned to Balait, crying, "Run!"

The horned maw opened and spewed blinding flame.

Teeth snapped. Skin blistered and sloughed. But Cnaiür felt nothing, only the warmth thrown by Balait's burning shadow. There was a momentary shriek, the sound of bones and bowels exploding.

Then the froth of sun-bright fire was gone. Bewildered, Cnaiür found himself in the centre of burnt ruin. Balait and the other Utemot still burned, sizzling like swine on the spit. The air smelt of ash and pork.

All dead . . .

A mighty shout braced the cacophony, and through screens of smoke and fleeing Scylvendi, he saw a bloodied tide of Nansur infantrymen rushing toward him across the slopes.

A stranger's voice whispered, *"Measure is unceasing . . ."*

Cnaiür fled, leaping over the slain, bounding like the others for the dark line of the river. He tripped over an arrow shaft embedded in the turf and slammed headlong into a dead horse. Bracing himself against sun-warmed flanks, he stumbled to his feet and lurched into a sprint. He swept past a young warrior limping with an arrow in his thigh, then another kneeling in the grasses, spitting blood. Then a band of his Utemot rumbled by on horses, led by Yursalka. Cnaiür cried out his name, and though the man momentarily looked at him, they continued riding. Cursing, he pressed harder. His ears roared. He blew spit after every sucking breath. Ahead he saw hundreds massed along the banks, some frantically tearing at their armour so they could swim, others dashing south toward a rapids that promised shallows. Yursalka and his Utemot cohort barrelled through the would-be swimmers and crashed into the waters. Many of their horses foundered in the swift current, but a few managed to drag their riders to the far banks. The ground steepened, and Cnaiür swallowed the distance with long loping strides. He leapt another dead horse, then crashed through a copse of goldenrods wagging in the wind. To his right he glimpsed a company of Imperial Kidruhil fanning across the slopes and galloping hard toward the fugitives. He staggered across the narrow floodplain, then finally blundered into the panicked midst of his countrymen. He yanked men aside, swatting his way to the muck and trampled brush of the riverbank.

He saw Yursalka press through the rushes and urge his sopping mount up the far side. A dozen other Utemot awaited him, their horses half-panicked and stamping.

"Utemot!" he roared, and somehow they heard him through the clamour. Two of them pointed in his direction.

But Yursalka was shouting at them, beating the air with an open hand. Their expressions blank, they jerked their horses about and hounded by Yursalka, galloped to the southwest.

Cnaiür spat at their retreating forms. He grabbed his knife and began sawing at his brigandine. Twice he was almost jostled into the water. Shouts of alarm rifled the air, made urgent by the swelling thunder of hoofs. He heard lances crack and horses shriek. He began stabbing at his brigandine's gut lacings. Bodies heaved against him, and he stumbled. He glimpsed a Kidruhil rider, towering black across the flare of the sun. He tore off his brigandine, whirled to the Kiyuth. Something exploded against his scalp. Hot blood choked his eyes. He fell to his knees. The rutted ground struck his face.

Screams, wails, and the sound of bodies plunging into rushing mountain water.

So like my father, he thought, then darkness came swirling down.

Hoarse, exhausted voices, framed by a more distant and more drunken chorus of singers. Pain, as though his head were nailed to the earth. His body leaden, as immovable as the river mud. Hard to think.

"What, do they bloat right after they die?"

Lurching horror. The voice had come from behind, very close. Looters?

"Another ring?" a second voice exclaimed. "Just saw off the fucking finger!"

Cnaiür heard approaching footsteps, sandalled feet barging through grasses. Slowly, because fast movements drew the eye, he tested his fingers and his wrist. They moved. He gently probed beneath his girdle, closed tingling fingers on his Chorae, withdrew it, then pressed it into the mud.

"He's squeamish," a third voice observed. "Always has been."

"Am not! It's just . . . just . . ."

"Just what?"

"Sacrilege, that's all. Robbing the dead is one thing. Desecrating them is quite another."

"Need I remind you," the third voice said, "that these here are what you call dead *Scylvendi*. Pretty hard to desecrate what's accursed in the first— Heyya! Another live one here."

The sound of a gritty blade scraping free of its scabbard, a thud, then a choking gasp. Despite his pounding head, Cnaiür smeared his face in the muck, scooped as much of it as he could bear into his mouth.

"Still can't get this blasted ring . . ."

"Just chop off the fucking finger, would you?" cried the second voice, now so close that it raised the hair on Cnaiür's neck. "By the Latter-fucking-Prophet! The only one lucky enough to find gold on these stinking savages, and he's paralyzed by scruples! Hello. What do we have here? Big brute. Sweet Sejenus, look at the scars on him!"

"They say Conphas wants us to collect all their heads anyway," the third voice said. "What does a finger matter?"

"There. A little spit. Do you think these could be rubies?"

A rough hand clasped Cnaiür's shoulder, peeled him from the muck. Eyes half-open to the setting sun. Limbs tensed in semblance of rigor. Soil-choked mouth drawn back in the sardonic grin. No breath.

"I'm serious," a looming shadow said. "Look at the scars on this bastard! He's killed hundreds!"

"They should offer bounties for ones like him. Imagine, one of our countrymen for every scar."

Hands rifled his body, patting, poking. No breath. Stiff motionlessness.

"Maybe we should take him to Gavarus," the first voice ventured. "They might want to string him up or something."

"Grand idea, that one," the shadow said scathingly. "How about you carry him?"

A laugh. "Not so grand any more, is it?" the second voice said. "Any luck there, Naff?"

"Not a single fucking thing," the shadow said, tossing Cnaiür back to the ground. "Next ring you find is mine, you little bastard. Otherwise I saw off *your* fingers!"

A kick from the blackness. Pain unlike any he'd ever experienced. The world roared. He struggled not to vomit.

"Sure," the first voice said amiably. "Who needs gold after a day like this? Imagine the triumph when we return! Imagine the songs! The Scylvendi destroyed on their own land. The *Scylvendi!* When we're old, we need only say that we served with Conphas at Kiyuth, and everyone will regard us with reverence and awe."

"Glory doesn't get you the good bird, boy. Glitter. It's all in the glitter."

———— ❧ ————

Morning. Cnaiür awoke shivering. He heard only the deep-running wash of the River Kiyuth.

A great iron ache radiated from the back of his head, and for a time he lay still, crushed by its weight. Convulsions wracked him, and he heaved bile into the footprints before his face. He coughed. With his tongue he probed a soft, salty gap between his teeth.

For some reason, the first clear thought to arise from his misery was of his Chorae. He scraped his fingers through vomit and gritty muck, found it quickly. He tucked it beneath his iron-plated girdle.

Mine. My prize.

The pain pressed like a shod hoof against the back of his skull, but he managed to push himself to his hands and knees. The grass was whitewashed with mud and sharp like small knives between his fingers. He dragged himself away from the rush of the river.

The turf of the embankment had been trampled into mud, now hardened into the brittle record of the earlier slaughter. The corpses seemed cemented to the ground, their flesh leathery beneath flies, their blood clotted like crushed cherries. He felt as though he crawled across one of those dizzying stone reliefs that panelled the temples of Nansur, where struggling men were frozen in unholy representation. But this was no representation.

Cresting the slope before him, a dead horse rose like a rounded mountain range, its belly in shadow, the bright point of the sun rising on the far side. Dead horses always looked the same, ridiculously stiff, as though they were carvings of wood simply tipped on their sides. He pushed himself onto it, rolled painfully over. Against his cheek, it was as cold as the river clay.

Save for jackdaws, vultures, and the dead, the battlefield was abandoned. He gazed across the gradual incline over which he'd fled.

Fled . . . He clamped shut his eyes. Again and again he was running, the blue sky shrunken by the roar behind him.

We were routed.

Defeated. Humiliated by their ancestral enemy.

For a long time he felt nothing. He remembered those mornings in his youth when, for whatever reason, he would awaken before dawn. He would creep from the yaksh and steal through the camp, searching for the higher ground where he could watch the sun embrace the land. The wind would hiss through the grasses. The squatting sun would rise, climb. And he would think, *I am the last. I am the only one.*

Like now.

For an absurd moment, he felt the queer exultation of one who'd prophesied his own destruction. He'd told Xunnurit, the eight-fingered fool. They'd thought him an old woman, a spinner of preposterous fears. Where was their laughter now?

Dead, he realized. All of them were dead. *All* of them! The horde had plumbed the horizon with its numbers, had shaken the Vault of Heaven with the thunder of its advance, and now it was gone, routed, dead. From where he lay, he could see great swaths of burned grassland, the burned husks of what had been arrogant thousands. More than routed—massacred.

And by the *Nansur!* Cnaiür had fought too many borderland skirmishes not to respect them as warriors, but in the end he despised the Nansur the way all Scylvendi despised them: as a mongrel race, a kind of human vermin, to be hunted to extinction if possible. For the Scylvendi, the mention of the Empire-behind-the-Mountains summoned innumerable images of degradation: leering priests grovelling before their unholy Tusk; sorcerers trussed in whorish gowns, uttering unearthly obscenities while painted courtiers, their soft bodies powdered and perfumed, committed earthly ones. These were the men who had conquered them. Tillers of earth and writers of words. Men who made sport with men.

His breath caught on a pain in the back of his throat.

He thought of Bannut, of the treachery of his kinsmen. He clutched the grass with aching hands—anchors—as though he were so weak, so empty, that he might be blown in an instant into the hollow sky. A forlorn cry uncoiled in his breast but was choked into a hiss by clenched teeth. He gasped air, moaned, rolled his head from side to side despite the agony. *No!*

Then he sobbed. Wept.

Weeper . . .

Bannut cackling, spitting up milky blood.

"I saw the way you looked at him! I know you were lovers!"

"No!" Cnaiür cried, but his hatred failed him.

All these years—pondering their silence, obsessing over the unspoken rebuke in their eyes, thinking himself mad for his suspicions, maligning himself for his fears, and still always pondering their hidden thoughts. How many slanders murmured in his absence? How many times, drawn by the sound of laughter, had he entered a yaksh only to find tight lips and insolent eyes? All this time they'd . . . He clutched his chest.

No!

He squeezed tears from his eyes, beat a scabbed fist against the turf harder and harder, as though he stoked a furnace. The face from thirty years ago floated before his soul's eye, possessed of a demonic calm.

"You task me!" he hissed under his breath. "Heap burden upon burd—"

A flare of sudden terror silenced him. The sound of voices, carried on the wind.

Lying still, with his eyes open only to where his lashes blurred his vision, he listened. They spoke Sheyic, but what they said was indecipherable.

Did looters still range the battlefield?

Fawn-hearted wretch! Get up and die!

The wind lulled and the sounds swelled. He could hear the step of horses and the periodic rustle of gear. At least two men, mounted. The aristocratic inflection in their speech suggested they were officers. They approached, but from what direction? He smothered the mad urge to sit up and look around.

"Since the days of Kyraneas, the Scylvendi have been here," the more refined voice was saying, "as relentless and as patient as the ocean. And unchanged! Peoples rise and peoples fall, whole races and nations are blotted out, yet the Scylvendi remain. And I've studied them, Martemus! I've plodded through every report of them I could find, ancient and recent. I even had my agents break into the Library of the Sareots! Yes, in Iothiah!—though they found nothing. The Fanim have let it crumble to ruin. But here's the thing: every account of the Scylvendi I read, no matter how ancient, could have been written yesterday. Thousands of years, Martemus, and the Scylvendi have remained unchanged. Take away their stirrups and their iron, and they would be indistinguishable from those who destroyed Mehtsonc two thousand years ago or those who sacked Cenei a thousand years later! The Scylvendi are just as the philosopher Ajencis claimed: a people without history."

"But so are all illiterate peoples, are they not?" the other man, Martemus, replied.

"Even illiterate peoples change over the centuries, Martemus. They migrate. They forget old gods and discover new ones. Even their tongues change. But not the Scylvendi. They're obsessed with custom. Where we raise vast edifices of stone to conquer the passage of years, they make monuments of their actions, temples of their wars."

The description made Cnaiür's heart itch. Who were these men? The one was definitely of the Houses.

"Interesting, I suppose," Martemus said, "but it doesn't explain how you *knew* you would defeat them."

"Don't be tedious. I despise tedium in my officers. First you ask impertinent questions, then you refuse to acknowledge my answers as answers."

"I apologize, Lord Exalt-General. I meant no offence. You yourself praise and castigate me for my forthright—"

"Ah, Martemus . . . always the same charade. The demure general from the provinces, without any ambition other than to serve. But I know you better than you think. I've seen your interest quicken when I mention matters of state. Just as I see the greed for glory in your eyes now."

It was as though a great stone had been dropped upon Cnaiür's chest. He could not breathe. It was him. *Him!* Ikurei Conphas!

"I'll not deny it. But I swear I didn't mean to question *you.* It's just that . . . that . . ."

These words brought the two men to a stop. Cnaiür could see them now, mounted shadows through the blur of eyelashes. He breathed shallow breaths.

"Just what, Martemus?"

"Through the entirety of this campaign, I've held my tongue. What we did seemed lunacy to me, so much so that . . ."

"That what?"

"That for a time my faith in you faltered."

"And yet you said nothing, asked nothing . . . Why?"

Cnaiür tried wrenching himself from the ground, but he could not. In his ears the disembodied voices had become mocking thunder. Murder him. He must!

"Fear, Lord Exalt-General. One does not rise from the bottom as I have without learning the lethality of questioning one's betters . . . especially when they're desperate."

Laughter. "So now, surrounded by this"—Conphas's shadow gestured to the fields of ruined dead—"you assume I'm no longer desperate; you think it's safe to ask these festering questions of yours."

A sudden awareness of himself and his environment struck Cnaiür. It was as though he saw himself from far away, a cringing man huddled next to the body of a horse, surrounded by ever-widening circles of dead. Even these images triggered recriminations. What kind of thoughts were these? Why must he always think one thought too many? Why must he always think?

Kill him!

"Exactly," Martemus replied.

Rush them. String their horses. Cut their throats in the confusion!

"Should I indulge you?" Conphas continued. "Should I allow you one more step toward the summit, Martemus?"

"My loyalty and discretion, Lord Exalt-General, are yours without reservation."

"I'd already assumed as much, but I thank you for the reassurance . . . What you would say if I told you the battle we've just fought, the glorious victory we've just won, is nothing more than the first engagement of the *Holy War?*"

"The Holy War? The *Shriah's* Holy War?"

"Whether the Holy War is the Shriah's or no is the very point at issue."

Move! Avenge yourself! Your people!

"But what about—"

"I'm afraid it would be irresponsible for me to disclose more, Martemus. Soon, perhaps, but not now. My triumph here, as magnificent, as *divine* as it is, will be sackcloth and ashes compared with what follows. Soon, all the Three Seas will celebrate my name, and then . . . Well, you're more soldier than officer. You understand that oftentimes commanders require their subordinates' ignorance as much as their knowledge."

"I see. I suppose I should have expected this."

"Expected what?"

"That your answers would stoke rather than sate my curiosity!"

Laughter. "Alas, Martemus, if I were to tell you all I know, you'd still suffer the same deficit. Answers are like opium: the more you imbibe, the more you need. Which is why the sober man finds solace in mystery."

"At the very least, you might explain to me—dullard that I am—how you could have known we'd win."

"As I said, the Scylvendi are obsessed with custom. That means they *repeat*, Martemus. They follow the same formula time and again. Do you see? They worship war, but they have no understanding of what it truly is."

"And what, then, is war truly?"

"Intellect, Martemus. War is *intellect*."

Conphas spurred his horse ahead, leaving his subordinate to wrestle with the import of what he'd just uttered. Cnaiür watched Martemus remove his plumed helmet, run a hand through his cropped hair. For a breathless moment he seemed to stare directly at him, as though he could hear the thrum of

Cnaiür's hammering heart. Then he abruptly spurred after his Exalt-General.

As Martemus closed on him, Conphas called out: "This afternoon, when our men have recovered from their revels, we start collecting Scylvendi heads. I'm going to build a road of trophies, Martemus, from here to our great diseased capital of Momemn. Think of the glory!"

Their voices faded, leaving only the rush of cold waters against buzzing silence and the pale smell of chopped turf.

So cold. The ground was so cold. Where should he go?

He had fled his childhood and had crawled into the honour of his father's name, Skiötha, Chieftain of the Utemot. With his father's shameful death, he'd fled and crawled into the name of his people, the Scylvendi, who were the wrath of Lokung, more vengeance than bone or flesh. Now they too had died shamefully. There was no ground left to him.

He lay nowhere, among the dead.

Some events mark us so deeply that they find more force of presence in their aftermath than in their occurrence. They are moments that rankle at becoming past, and so remain contemporaries of our beating hearts. Some events are not remembered—they are relived.

The death of Cnaiür's father, Skiötha, was such an event.

Cnaiür sits in the gloom of the Chieftain's great yaksh as it stood twenty-nine years ago. A fire waxes in its centre, bright to look at but illuminating little. Draped in furs, his father speaks to the other ranking tribesmen about the insolence of their Kuöti kinsmen to the south. In the shadows thrown by the hard men, slaves loiter nervously, bearing skins of *gishrut*, fermented mare's milk. When a horn is raised by a scarred arm, they refill it. The enclosure reeks of smoke and sour liquor.

The White Yaksh has seen many such scenes, but this time, one of the slaves, a Norsirai man, abandons the shadows and steps into firelight. He lifts his face and addresses the astonished tribesmen in perfect Scylvendi—as though he himself were of the land.

"I would make you a wager, Chieftain of the Utemot."

Cnaiür's father is dumbstruck, both by such insolence and by such a transformation. A man hitherto broken has become as august as any King. Only Cnaiür is not surprised.

The other men, who hedge the dark, fall silent.

From across the fire, his father replies: "You have already made your gambit, slave. And you have lost."

The slave smiles derisively, as though a sovereign among a callow people.

"But I would wager my life with *you*, Skiötha."

A slave *speaking a name*. How it overturns the ancient ways, upends the fundamental order!

Skiötha gropes through this absurdity and finally laughs. Laughter makes small, and this outrage must be made small. Fury would acknowledge the depth of this contest, would make one a contestant. And yet the slave *knows* this.

So the slave continues: "I have watched you, Skiötha, and I have wondered at the measure of your strength. Many here so wonder . . . Did you know this?"

His father's laughter trails. The fire wheezes softly.

Then Skiötha, fearing to look into the faces of his kinsmen, says, "I *have* been measured, slave."

As though fuelled by these words, the fire flutters bright, and presses farther into the pockets of darkness between the assembled men. Its renewed heat bites at Cnaiür's skin.

"But measure," the slave replies, "is not something accomplished and then forgotten, Skiötha. Old measure is merely grounds for the new. Measure is unceasing."

Complicity makes unforgettable, carves scenes with unbearable clarity, as though the extent of condemnation is to be found in the precision of detail. The fire so hot that it might be cradled in his lap. The cold of the earth beneath his thighs and buttocks. His teeth clenched, as though grinding sand. And the Norsirai slave's pale face turning to *him*, the blue eyes bright, more encompassing than any sky. Summoning eyes! Eyes that yoke, that speak:

Do you remember your part?

Cnaiür has been given a script for this moment.

From among the seated men, he says, "Are you *afraid*, Father?" Mad words! Treacherous and mad!

A stinging look from his father. Cnaiür lowers his eyes. Skiötha turns to the slave and asks with contrived indifference, "What, then, is your wager?"

And Cnaiür is gripped by the terror that he might die.

Fear that the *slave*, Anasûrimbor Moënghus, might die!

Not his father—Moënghus . . .

Afterward, when his father lay dead, he had wept before the eyes of his tribe. Wept with relief.

At last, Moënghus, the one who had called himself Dûnyain, was free.

Some names mark us so deeply. Thirty years, one hundred and twenty seasons—a long time in the life of one man.

And it meant nothing.

Some events mark us so deeply.

Cnaiür fled. After darkness fell, he skulked between the shining fires of the Nansur patrols. The vast, hollow bowl of night seemed something he might plummet into, so great was the land's rebuke.

With his own feet, the dead chased him.

CHAPTER SEVEN

MOMEMN

The world is a circle that possesses as many centres as it does men.
—AJENCIS, *THE THIRD ANALYTIC OF MEN*

Early Autumn, 4110 Year-of-the-Tusk, Momemn

All of Momemn had thundered.

Chilled by the shade, Ikurei Conphas dismounted beneath the immensity of the Xatantian Arch. His eyes lingered on its graven images for a moment, following panel after panel of captives and spoils. He turned to General Martemus, about to remind him that not even Xatantius had pacified the Scylvendi tribes. *I've wrought what no man has wrought. Doesn't that make me more than a man?*

Conphas could no longer count how many times this breathless thought had beset him, and though he was loath to admit it, he yearned to hear it echoed by others—especially Martemus. If only he could coax the words from him! Martemus possessed the unstudied candour of a lifelong field officer. Flattery was beneath his contempt. If the man said something, Conphas knew, it was true.

But now was not the time. Martemus stood dumbstruck, staring across the Scuäri Campus, the parade grounds of the Imperial

Precincts. Arrayed under the standards of every column in the Imperial Army, phalanxes of infantrymen in ceremonial dress filled the Scuäri's expanse. Hundreds of red-and-black streamers undulated in the breeze above the formations, painted with golden prayers. Between the phalanxes, a broad avenue ran toward the towering facade of the Allosian Forum. The gardens, compounds, and colonnades of the Andiamine Heights climbed high into the haze beyond.

Conphas saw his uncle awaiting them, a distant figure framed by the Forum's mighty columns. Despite the imperial pageantry, he looked small, like a hermit squinting from the entrance of his cave.

"Is this your first Imperial Audience-of-State?" Conphas asked Martemus.

The General nodded, turned to him with a faintly doddering air. "My first time in the Imperial Precincts."

Conphas grinned. "Welcome to the brothel."

Grooms took their horses. In accordance with custom, the hereditary priests of Gilgaöl brought basins of water. As Conphas expected, they smeared lion's blood on his limbs and, muttering prayers, cleansed his symbolic wounds. The Shrial Priests who arrived in their wake, however, surprised him. They anointed him with oils and murmurs, then finished by dipping their fingers in palm wine and tracing the Tusk across his forehead. Only when they closed the rite by crying out his new title, Shield-of-the-Tusk, did he understand why his uncle had incorporated them into the ceremony. The Scylvendi were as much heathen as the Kianene, so why not tap into the all-pervasive fervour of Holy War?

It was actually, Conphas realized with some distaste, a brilliant ploy, which probably meant that Skeaös was behind it. As far as Conphas could tell, his uncle had exhausted whatever brilliance he possessed—especially when it came to the Holy War.

The Holy War . . . The mere thought of it made Conphas want to spit like a Scylvendi, and he'd arrived at Momemn only the previous day.

Never in his life had Conphas felt anything approaching the elation he'd experienced at the Battle of Kiyuth. Surrounded by his half-panicked staff, he had looked across the undecided battlefield and somehow, unaccountably, had *known*—known with a certainly that had made his bones feel like iron. *I own this place. I am more . . .* The feeling had been akin to rapture or religious ecstasy. It had been, he later realized, a *revelation*, a moment of divine insight into the immeasurable might of *his* hand.

There could be no other explanation.

But who would have thought that revelations, like meat, could be poisoned by the passage of days?

At first things had gone exceedingly well. After the battle, the surviving Scylvendi had withdrawn into the deep Steppe. Some scattered bands continued to shadow the army, but they could do little more than maul the odd patrol. Unable to resist a final twist of the knife, Conphas arranged for a dozen captives to "overhear" his officers lauding those tribes who'd betrayed the horde—captives who, through daring and ingenuity not their own, later managed a miraculous escape. Not only would the Scylvendi, Conphas knew, believe their allegations of treachery, they would be gratified. Far better that the People defeat the People than the Nansur. Ah, sweet dissension. It would be a long time before the Scylvendi took to the field with one will.

If only dissension were as easily undone. Months earlier Conphas had promised his uncle he would mark his return march from the frontier with piked Scylvendi heads. To this end, he'd ordered the heads of every Scylvendi slain at Kiyuth collected, tarred, and heaped in wains. But as soon as the Imperial Army crossed the frontier, the cartographers and mathematicians began feuding over the proper spacing of their grisly trophies. When the dispute persisted, the sorcerers of the Imperial Saik, who like all sorcerers fancied themselves better cartographers than cartographers and better mathematicians than mathematicians, intervened. What followed was a bureaucratic war worthy of his uncle's court, one that somehow, following the mad alchemy of injured pride and spite, led to the murder of Erathius, the most outspoken of the imperial cartographers.

When the subsequent military inquest failed to resolve either the murder or the feud, Conphas summarily seized the most vocal partisan of each faction and, exploiting poorly worded articles of the Martial Code, had them publicly flayed. Not surprisingly, all differences were settled the following day.

But if this vexing affair had tainted his rapture, his return to Momemn had nearly spoiled it altogether. He found the capital encircled by the encamped Holy War, which had become a vast slum of tents and huts about the city's landward walls. As troubling as the sight was, Conphas still expected adoring masses to greet him. Instead, unkempt mobs of Inrithi howled insults, threw stones, and even, on one occasion, tossed burning sacks of human excrement. When he sent his Kidruhil ahead to clear a path, what could only be described as a pitched battle ensued. "They see only the Emperor's nephew," an officer sent by his uncle explained, "not the man who conquered the Scylvendi."

"They hate my uncle so much?"

The officer shrugged. "Until their lords acquiesce to his Indenture, he provides them only enough grain to survive."

The Holy War, the man told him, was growing by hundreds daily, even though, as rumour had it, the main contingents from Galeoth, Ce Tydonn, Conriya, and High Ainon were still months away. So far only three great lords had joined the Men of the Tusk: Calmemunis, the Palatine of the Conriyan province of Kanampurea; Tharschilka, an Earl from some obscure Galeoth march; and Kumrezzer, the Palatine-Governor of the Ainoni district of Kutapileth. Each of them had violently rebuffed the Emperor's demand to sign his Indenture. The negotiations had since deteriorated into a bitter contest of wills, with the Inrithi lords wreaking what havoc they could, short of incurring the Shriah's wrath, and with Ikurei Xerius III issuing proclamation after proclamation in an attempt to constrain and further coerce them.

"The Emperor," the officer concluded, "is most heartened by your arrival, Lord Exalt-General."

Conphas had nearly cackled aloud at that. The return of a rival heartened no emperor, but every emperor was heartened by the return of his army, particularly when he was besieged. Which was essentially the case. Conphas had been forced to enter Momemn by boat.

And now, the great triumph he'd so anticipated, the all-important *recognition* of what he'd wrought, had been overshadowed by greater events. The Holy War had dimmed his glory, had dwarfed even the destruction of the Scylvendi. Men would celebrate him, yes, but the way they celebrated religious festivals in times of famine: listlessly, too preoccupied by the press of events to truly understand what or whom they celebrated.

How could he not hate the Holy War?

Cymbals crashed. Horns sounded. Completing the ceremony, the Shrial Priests bowed and withdrew, leaving him doused in the pungent odour of palm wine. Ushers dressed in gold-chased kilts appeared, and Conphas, with Martemus at his side and with his retinue in tow, followed them at a slow march across the crowded silence of the Scuäri. Whole fields of red-skirted infantrymen fell to their knees as they passed, so that, like wind across wheat, they trailed a wake across the far reaches of the Campus. Conphas felt a momentary thrill. Had this not been his revelation? The source of his rapture on the banks of the River Kiyuth?

As far as my eye can see, they answer to me, to my hand. As far as my eye, and beyond . . .

Beyond. A breathless thought. Wanton.

A glance over his shoulder assured him that his earlier instructions were being observed. Two of his personal bodyguards followed close behind, dragging the captive between them, while a dozen more were busily marking their passage with the last of the severed

Scylvendi heads. Unlike past Exalt-Generals, he had no parade of slaves and plunder for his emperor, but the sight of tarred Scylvendi heads raised above the Campus, he thought, possessed a singular effect. Though he could not see his grandmother among the crowds flanking his uncle beneath the Forum, he knew she was there, and that she approved. "Give them spectacle," she was fond of saying, "and they will give you power."

Where power was perceived, power was given. For his entire life Conphas had been surrounded by tutors. But it had been his grandmother, fierce Istriya, who had done the most to prepare him for his birthright. Contrary to his father's wishes, she had insisted he spend his early childhood surrounded by the pomp and circumstance of the Imperial Court. And there she had reared him as if he were her own, teaching him the history of their dynasty and through it, all the unwritten secrets of statecraft. Conphas even suspected she had had a hand in the trumped-up charges that led to his father's execution, simply to guarantee the man would not interfere with the succession should her other son, Ikurei Xerius III, unexpectedly find himself upon the bier. But more than anything, she had ensured, even enforced, the perception that he, and he alone, was heir apparent. Even when he was a young boy, she had crafted him into a spectacle, as though his every breath were a triumph for the Empire. Now not even his uncle would dare contravene that perception, even if he did manage to produce a son who did not drool or require diapers into adulthood.

She had done so much that he could almost love her.

Conphas studied his uncle once again. He was nearer now, so much so that Conphas could make out details of his dress. The horn of white felt rising from his golden diadem surprised the Exalt-General. No Nansur Emperor had worn the crown of Shigek since the province's loss to the Fanim three centuries earlier. The presumption was outrageous! What could move him to such excess? Did he think heaping himself with empty ornaments could safeguard his glory?

He knows . . . He knows I've surpassed him!

Over the course of his return from the Jiünati Steppe, Conphas had pondered his uncle to the point of obsession. The real question, Conphas understood, was whether his uncle would be inclined to accommodate him as a tool with further uses or to dispose of him as a threat. The fact that Xerius had *sent* him to destroy the Scylvendi in no way diminished the possibility of disposal. The irony of murdering someone for successfully doing his bidding would mean nothing to Xerius. Such "injustices," as the philosophers would call them, were the bread and beer of imperial politics.

No. All things being equal, Conphas had realized, his uncle *would* try to kill him. The problem, quite simply, was that he had defeated the *Scylvendi*. Even if, as Conphas feared, his triumph did not translate into the power to overthrow his uncle, Xerius, who suspected conspiracy whenever two of his slaves farted, would simply assume he possessed that power. All things being equal, Conphas should have returned to Momemn with ultimatums and siege towers.

But all things were not equal. The Battle of Kiyuth had been but the first step in a larger scheme to wrest the Holy War from Maithanet, and the Holy War was key to his uncle's dream of a Restored Empire. If Kian could be crushed, and if all the old provinces could be reconquered, then Ikurei Xerius III would be remembered not as a warrior-emperor like Xatantius or Triamus but as a great statesman-emperor such as Caphrianas the Younger. This was his dream. So long as Xerius clung to this dream, Conphas realized, he would do everything in his power to accommodate his godlike nephew. By defeating the Scylvendi, Conphas had become more useful than dangerous.

Because of the Holy War. Everything came back to the accursed Holy War.

With Conphas's every step, the Forum encompassed more and more of the sky. His uncle, who looked even more ludicrous now that Conphas knew what he was wearing, grew still nearer. Though his painted face seemed impassive in the distance, Conphas saw, or thought he saw, his hands momentarily clutch the sides of his crimson gown. A nervous gesture? The Exalt-General nearly laughed. He found few things more amusing than his uncle's distress. Worms should wriggle.

He had always hated his uncle—even as a child. But for all the contempt he bore him, he'd learned long ago not to underestimate him. His uncle was like those uncommon drunks who slurred and staggered day after day yet became lethally alert when confronted by danger.

Did he sense danger now? Suddenly Ikurei Xerius III seemed a great riddle—inscrutable. *What are you thinking, Uncle?*

The question itched so much he felt compelled to scratch it with another's opinion.

"Tell me, Martemus," he said in a low voice, "if you had to guess, what would you say my uncle's thinking?"

Martemus was terse. Perhaps he thought conversing at such a time unseemly. "You know him far better than I, Lord Exalt-General."

"A most politic answer." Conphas paused, struck by a premonition that the cause of Martemus's anxiety went far deeper than the prospect of meeting his Emperor for the first time. When had the man ever been in awe of his betters?

Never.

"Should I be afraid, Martemus?"

The General's eyes remained riveted on the distant Emperor. He did not blink.

"You should be afraid, yes."

Not caring what his observers might think, Conphas studied the man's profile, noting yet again the classic Nansur cut of his jaw and his broken nose. "And why is that?"

Martemus marched in silence for what seemed a long while. For an exasperated moment, Conphas felt like striking him. Why deliberate so long over answers when the decision was always the same? Martemus spoke only the truth.

"I know only," the General finally replied, "that were I Emperor and you my Exalt-General, I would fear you."

Conphas snorted under his breath. "And what the Emperor fears, the Emperor kills. I see even you provincials have a sense of his true measure. And yet my uncle has feared me since the first evening I beat him at benjuka. I was eight. He would have had me strangled—had the entire matter blamed on an unfortunate grape—had it not been for my grandmother."

"I fail to see—"

"My uncle fears everybody and everything, Martemus. He's too well schooled in our dynasty's history not to. Because of this, only *new* fears incite him to murder. He scarcely notices old fears like me."

The General shrugged imperceptibly. "But didn't he . . ." He trailed off, as though shocked by his own gall.

"Have my father executed? Of course he did. But he never feared my father from the beginning. Only later, after . . . after the Biaxi faction had poisoned his heart with rumours."

Martemus glanced at him from the corner of his eye. "But what you've *accomplished*, Lord Exalt-General . . . Think on it! At your command every soldier here—to a man!—would lay down his life for you. Surely the Emperor knows this! Surely this is a *new* fear!"

Conphas had thought Martemus incapable of surprising him, but he was taken aback by both the import and the vehemence of his reply. Was he suggesting rebellion? Here? Now?

Suddenly he saw himself climbing the steps to the Forum, saluting his uncle, then wheeling to the thousands of soldiers assembled across the Scuäri Campus and crying out to them, imploring . . . no, *commanding* them to storm the Forum and the Andiamine Heights. He saw his uncle hacked to bloody rags.

The scene left him short of breath. Could it be a revelation of some sort? A glimpse of his future? Should he . . . ? But this was rank foolishness! Martemus simply did not see the greater scheme.

Even so, everything—the ranks falling to their knees in his

periphery, the oiled backs of the ushers before him, his uncle waiting as though at the terminus of some fatally steep chute—had become nightmarish. Suddenly he resented Martemus and his baseless fears. This was supposed to be his time! His moment of exultation.

"And what of the Holy War?" he snapped.

Martemus scowled but kept his face toward the looming Forum. "I don't understand."

Overcome by a sudden flash of impatience, Conphas glared at the man. Why was it so hard for them to see? Was this the way the Gods felt when plagued by the inability of men to grasp the grand portent of their designs? Did he expect too much of his followers? The Gods certainly did.

But perhaps that was the point. What better way to make them strive?

"You think," Martemus continued, "that the Emperor is more avaricious than fearful? That his hunger to restore the Empire eclipses his fear of you?"

Conphas smiled. The god had been appeased. "So I think. He *needs* me, Martemus."

"So you gamble."

The ushers had reached the monumental stair leading up to the Forum, and now they backed away to either side, bowing. The Emperor was nearly upon them.

"And where would you place your wager, Martemus?"

For the first time the General looked at him directly, his shining brown eyes filled with uncharacteristic adoration. "With you, Lord Exalt-General. And the Empire."

They had paused at the base of the monumental stair. After a sharp glance at Martemus, Conphas gestured for his bodyguards to follow with the captive, then began ascending the steps. His uncle awaited him on the highest landing. Skeaös, Conphas noted, stood at his side. Dozens of other court functionaries milled among the Forum's columns. Everyone watched with solemn faces.

Unbidden, Martemus's words returned to him.

"At your command every soldier here would lay down his life."

Conphas was a soldier, and as such he believed in training, provisions, planning—in short, preparation. But he also possessed, as all great leaders must, a keen eye for those fruit that ripen out of season. He knew full well the importance of timing. If he struck now, what would happen? What would—and here was the problem—all those assembled do? How many would throw their lot with him?

"With you . . . I would place my wager with you."

For all his failings, his uncle was a shrewd judge of character. It was as though the fool instinctively knew how to balance the staff against the plum, when to strike and when to soothe. Suddenly Conphas realized he had no inkling of which way many of those men who mattered most would turn. Of course Gaenkelti, the Exalt-Captain of the Eothic Guard, would stand by his Emperor—to the death, if need be. But Cememketri? Would the Imperial Saik prefer a strong emperor to a weak one? And what of Ngarau, who controlled the all-important coffers?

So many uncertainties!

A warm gust of wind sent leaves from some unseen grove skittering across his path. He paused on the landing immediately below his uncle, saluted him.

Ikurei Xerius III remained as still as a painted statue. Wizened Skeaös, however, gestured for him to approach. His ears buzzing, Conphas climbed the last remaining steps. Images of rioting soldiers flashed before his soul's eye. He thought of his ceremonial dagger, wondered whether its temper would be enough to puncture silk, damask, skin and bone.

It would do.

Then he stood before his uncle. His expression and his limbs stiffened in defiance. Though Skeaös stared at him with naked alarm, his uncle affected not to notice.

"Such a great victory, Nephew!" he abruptly exclaimed. "You've brought glory as no other to the House Ikurei!"

"You," Conphas said flatly, "are too gracious, Uncle." A momentary frown crossed his uncle's face. Conphas had failed to kneel and kiss his uncle's knee.

Their eyes locked, and for an instant Conphas was startled. He'd forgotten how much Xerius looked like his father.

All the better. He would grasp the back of his neck as though to place an intimate kiss, then punch his knife through his sternum. He would wrench the blade and halve his heart. The assassination would be quick and, Conphas realized, remarkably free of malice. Then he would cry out to his men below, command them to secure the Imperial Precincts. In the space of heartbeats the Empire would be his.

He raised his hand for the kiss, but his uncle waved it away and jostled by him, apparently captivated by something farther down the steps. "And what's this?" he cried, obviously speaking of the captive.

Conphas raked his gaze across the onlookers, saw Gaenkelti and several others scrutinizing him warily. Smiling falsely, he turned to join the Emperor. "Alas, Uncle, this is the only captive I have to offer you. Everyone knows Scylvendi make atrocious slaves."

"And who is he?"

The man had been thrust to his knees, and he now leaned over his nakedness, his scarred arms chained behind his back. One of the bodyguards grabbed his black mane and jerked his face to the Emperor. Though the memory of scorn haunted his expression, his grey eyes were vacant, fixed on things not of this world.

"Xunnurit," Conphas said, "their King-of-Tribes."

"I'd *heard* he'd been taken, but I dared not believe the rumours! Conphas! Conphas! A Scylvendi *King-of-Tribes* made captive! You've made our House immortal this day! I shall have him blinded, emasculated, and bound to the base of my throne, just like the ancient High Kings of Kyraneas."

"A splendid idea, Uncle." Conphas glanced to his right and finally saw his grandmother. She wore a green silk gown crisscrossed by a form-hugging sash of blue. As always, she looked an old whore playing the coquette. But there was something in her expression. She seemed different somehow.

"Conphas . . ." she gasped, her eyes rounded by wonder. "You left us as heir to the Empire, and you've returned to us as a *god!*"

A collective intake of breath followed these words. Treason—or at least something the Emperor was certain to interpret as such.

"You're too kind, Grandmother," Conphas said hastily. "I return as a humble slave who's simply done his master's bidding."

But she's right! Isn't she?

Somehow he'd slipped from the brink of striking his uncle down to covering for his grandmother's gaffes. Resolution. He had to stay focused!

"Of course, my dear boy. I spoke figuratively . . ." In a way curiously obscene for one so old, she sashayed to his side and hooked his knifing arm with her own. "Shame on you, Conphas. I can understand the *herd*"—she glanced wrathfully at her son's ministers—"reading scandal into my words, but you?"

"Must you always dote on him so, Mother?" Xerius said. He had begun prodding his trophy, as though testing for muscle tone.

By chance, Conphas caught Martemus's gaze from where the man patiently kneeled, so far entirely unacknowledged. The General nodded dangerously.

A familiar cool settled upon Conphas then, the one that allowed him to think and act with deliberation while other men scrambled. He looked across the seemingly endless ranks of infantrymen below. *"At your command every soldier . . ."*

He detached himself from his grandmother. "Listen," he said, "there are things I must know."

"Or what?" his uncle asked. Apparently he'd forgotten the King-of-Tribes. Or had his interest been a ruse?

Uncowed, Conphas stared hard into his uncle's painted eyes, smirked at the absurdity of his Shigeki crown. "Or we'll shortly find ourselves at war with the Men of the Tusk. Did you know they rioted when I attempted to enter Momemn? Killed twenty of my Kidruhil?" Conphas found his eyes straying to his uncle's soft, powdered neck. Perhaps that would be a better place to strike.

"Ah, yes," Xerius said in a dismissive manner. "A most unfortunate incident. Calmemunis and Tharschilka have been inciting more than just their own men. But I assure you, the matter has been concluded."

"What do you mean, 'concluded'?" For the first time in his life, Conphas cared nothing what his uncle thought of his tone.

"Tomorrow," Xerius declared with the voice of decree, "you and your grandmother will accompany me upriver to observe the transport of my latest monument. I know, Nephew, that you've a restless nature, that you're a student of decisive action, but you must be patient. This isn't Kiyuth, and we're not the Scylvendi . . . Things are not as they appear, Conphas."

Conphas was dumbstruck. *"This isn't Kiyuth, and we're not the Scylvendi."* What was that supposed to mean?

As though the matter were utterly closed, Xerius continued: "Is this the general you speak so highly of? Martemus, is it? I'm so very pleased he's here. I couldn't ferry enough of your men into the city to fill the Campus, so I was forced to use my Eothic Guard and several hundred of the City Watch."

Though stunned, Conphas replied without hesitation, "And dress them as my . . . as army regulars?"

"Of course. The ceremony is as much for them as for you, no?"

His heart thundering, Conphas knelt and kissed his uncle's knee.

Harmony . . . So sweet. This was what Ikurei Xerius III thought he groped for.

Cememketri, the Grandmaster of his Imperial Saik, had assured him that the circle was the purest of geometrical forms, the one most conducive to the mending of the spirit. One must not live one's life, he had said, in lines. But it was with circles of string that one made knots, and it was with circles of suspicion that one made intrigue. The very shape of harmony was cursed!

"How long must we wait, Xerius?" his mother asked from behind, her voice throaty with age and irritation.

The sun is hot, isn't it, bitch-mother?

"Soon," he said to the river.

From the prow of his great galley, Xerius stared across the brown waters of the River Phayus. Behind him sat his mother, the Empress Istriya, and his nephew, Conphas, flush from his astounding destruction of the Scylvendi tribes at Kiyuth. Ostensibly he had invited them to witness the transport of his latest monument from the basalt quarries of Osbeus downriver to Momemn. But as always there were further purposes behind any gathering of the Imperial Family. They would, he knew, scoff at his monument—his mother openly, his nephew silently. But they would not—*could not*—dismiss the announcement he would shortly make. The mere mention of the Holy War would be enough to command their respect.

For a time, anyway.

Ever since they'd left the stone quays in Momemn, his mother had been fawning over her grandson. "I burned over two hundred golden votives for you," she was saying, "one for each day you were in the field. And I offered thirty-eight dogs to the Gilgaöli priesthood, to be slaughtered in your—"

"She even furnished them with a lion," Xerius called over his shoulder. "The albino that Pisathulas purchased from that insufferable Kutnarmi trader, wasn't it, Mother?"

Though he could not see her, he could feel her eyes bore into his back. "That was to be a *surprise*, Xerius," she said with acidic sweetness. "Or did you forget?"

"I apologize, Mother. I quite—"

"I had the hide prepared," she said to Conphas, as though Xerius had not spoken. "A suitable gift for the Lion of Kiyuth, no?" She chuckled at her own conspiratorial wit.

Xerius clenched the mahogany rail tight.

"A *lion!*" Conphas exclaimed. "And an albino, no less! Small wonder the God favoured me, Grandmother."

"A bribe," she replied dismissively. "I was desperate to have you back in one piece. Mad with desperation. But now you've told me how you defeated the brutes, I feel foolish. Trying to bribe the Gods to look after one of their own! The Empire has never seen the likes of you, my dear, sweet Conphas. Never!"

"Whatever wisdom I possess, Grandmother, I owe to you."

Istriya nearly giggled. Flattery, especially from Conphas, had always been her favourite narcotic. "I was a rather harsh tutor, now that I recall."

"The harshest."

"But you were *tardy* all the time, Conphas. Waiting always brings out the worst in me. I could claw eyes out."

Xerius gritted his teeth. *She knows I listen! She baits me.*

Conphas was laughing. "I'm afraid I discovered the pleasures of women at an atrociously young age, Grandmother. I had other tutors to attend."

Istriya was sly—even flirtatious. The whorish crone. "Lessons drawn from the same book, I imagine."

"It all comes to fucking, doesn't it?"

Their laughter drowned out the whooshing chorus of the galley's oars. Xerius stifled a scream.

"And now with the *Holy War*, my dear Conphas! You'll be more, far more than the greatest Exalt-General in our history!"

What is she trying to do? Istriya had always goaded him, but never had she pressed her banter so close to sedition. She knew Conphas's victory over the Scylvendi had transformed him from a tool into a threat. Especially after the farce at the Forum the previous day. Xerius needed only to glimpse at his nephew's face to know that Skeaös had been right. There *had* been murder in Conphas's eyes. If not for the Holy War, Xerius would have ordered him cut down on the spot.

Istriya had been there. She knew all this, and yet she pushed further and further. Was she . . .

Was she trying to get Conphas killed?

Conphas was obviously discomfited. "My men would call that counting the dead before blood is drawn, Grandmother."

But was he *truly* uneasy? Could it be an act? Something concocted by the two of them to throw him off their scent? He peered down the length of the galley, searching for Skeaös. He found him with Arithmeas, summoned him with a look of fury but then cursed himself. What need had he of that old fool? His mother played games. She always played games.

Ignore them.

Skeaös scuttled to his side—the man walked like a crab—but Xerius ignored him. Drawing long, even breaths, he studied the river traffic instead. With sluggish grace, riverboats eased by one another, most of them heavy with wares. He saw the carcasses of swine and cattle, urns of oil and casks of wine; he saw wheat, corn, quarried stone, and even what he decided must be a troop of dancers, all ploughing across the river's broad back toward Momemn. It was good that he stood upon the Phayus. It was the great rope from which the vast nets of the Nansurium spread. Trade and the industry of men, all sanctioned by his image.

The gold they bear in their hands, he thought, *bears my face.*

He peered into the sky. His eyes settled upon a gull mysteriously suspended in the heart of a distant thunderhead. For a moment he thought he could feel harmony's brush, forget the nattering of his mother and nephew behind him.

Then the galley lurched and shuddered to a halt. Xerius teetered over the prow for a moment, caught himself. He pushed himself upright, looked wildly for the galley captain among the small herd of functionaries amidships. He heard shouts muffled by the timber, then the snapping of whips. Images came to him unbidden. Of cramped and wood-dark spaces. Rotten teeth clenched in agony. Sweat and stinging pain.

"What happened?" Xerius heard his mother ask.

"Sandbar, Grandmother," Conphas said in explanation. "Yet another delay, it would seem." His tone was clenched in impatience—a liberty of expression he would not have dared a few months earlier, but still minor compared with the previous day's outrage.

Cries resonated through the tiled deck. The oars made hash of the surrounding waters, but to no effect. With an expression that already begged for mercy, the captain approached and acknowledged that they'd run aground. Xerius berated the fool, all the while sensing his mother's scrutiny. When he glanced at her, he saw eyes far too shrewd to belong to a mother watching her son. At her side, Conphas lolled on his divan, smirking as though he watched a fixed cockfight.

Unnerved by their scrutiny, Xerius waved away the captain's plaintive explanations. "Why should the rowers reap what you've sown?" he cried. Disgusted by the man's infantile blubbering, he turned his back on him, ordered his bodyguards to drag him below. The man's subsequent howling simply fanned his anger. Why could so few men stomach the consequences of their actions?

"A judgement," his mother said dryly, "worthy of the Latter Prophet."

"We'll wait here," Xerius snapped to no one in particular.

After a moment, the whips and cries subsided. The oars fell silent. There was a rare moment of quiet on the deck. A dog's baying echoed across the waters. Children chased one another along the south bank, ducking between peppertrees, squealing. But there was another sound.

"Can you hear them?" Conphas asked.

"Yes, I can," Istriya replied, craning her neck to look upriver.

Xerius could also hear it: a faint chorus of shouts across the water. Squinting, he peered into the distance, where the Phayus bent and folded between dark slopes, searching for some visible sign of the barge bearing his new monument. He saw none.

"Perhaps," Skeaös whispered in his ear, "we should await your latest glory from the galley's aft, God-of-Men."

He started to rebuke the Prime Counsel for interrupting him with nonsense, then hesitated. "Continue," he muttered, studying the old man. Skeaös's face often reminded him of a shrivelled apple dimpled by two shiny black eyes. He looked like an ancient infant.

"From here, God-of-Men, your divine memorial will be revealed in increments, allowing your mother and nephew . . ." His expression was pained.

Xerius grimaced, looked askance at his mother. "No one dares taunt the Emperor, Skeaös."

"Of course, God-of-Men. Certainly. But if we wait aft, your obelisk will be exposed in one magnificent rush as the barge passes us."

"I *had* considered that . . ."

"But certainly."

Xerius turned to the Empress and the Exalt-General. "Come, Mother," he said, "let us retire from the sun. Some shade will flatter you."

Istriya scowled at the insult but seemed visibly relieved otherwise. The sun was high in the sky and hot for the season. She rose with stiff grace and reluctantly took her son's proffered hand. Conphas rolled to his feet after her, followed them. Formations of perfumed slaves and functionaries scattered from their path. With Skeaös waiting at a discreet distance, the three paused at tables bedecked with delicacies. Xerius was heartened when his mother complimented his kitchen slaves. Praising his servants had always been her way of repenting earlier indiscretions—her apology. Perhaps, Xerius thought, she would be indulgent with him today.

Finally they settled in the canopied rear of the galley, lounging on Nilnameshi settees. Skeaös stood on Xerius's right, his accustomed position. Xerius found his presence comforting: like over-strong wine, his family had to be watered down.

"And how is my half-sister?" Conphas asked him. Jnan had commenced.

"A satisfactory wife."

"And yet her womb remains closed," Istriya remarked.

"I have my heir," Xerius replied casually, knowing full well that the old crone celebrated his impotence. The strong seed forces the womb. She had called him weak.

Istriya's dark eyes flashed. "Yes . . . An heir without an inheritance."

Such directness! Perhaps age had at last caught up with immortal Istriya. Perhaps time was the only poison she could not avoid.

"Take care, Mother." Perhaps—and the thought filled Xerius with shrill glee—she would shortly die. Damnable old bitch.

Conphas interceded. "I think Grandmother refers to the Men of the Tusk, divine Uncle . . . I received word just this morning that they've raided and sacked Jarutha. We're past riots and Shrial petitions, Uncle. We're on the brink of open warfare."

To the heart of the matter so quickly. It was inelegant. Brutish.

"What do you intend to do, Xerius?" Istriya asked. "It's not merely your shrewish, sometimes impolitic mother who frets over these portentous events. Even the more dependable Houses of the Congregate are alarmed. One way or another, we must act."

"I've never known you to be impolitic, Mother . . . Only to appear so."

"Answer me, Xerius. What do you intend to do?"

Xerius sighed audibly. "It's no longer a question of intent, Mother. The deed has been accomplished. The Conriyan dog, Calmemunis, has sent envoys. He'll sign the Indenture tomorrow afternoon. He gives his personal assurance that the riots and raids end as of today."

"*Calmemunis!*" his mother hissed, as though surprised. In all likelihood, she'd known this before even Xerius himself. After all the years she'd spent plotting for and against husbands and sons, her network of spies plumbed the Nansurium to the pith. "What of the other Great Names? What of the Ainoni—what's his name?—Kumrezzer?"

"I know only that Calmemunis confers with him, Tharschilka, and some of the others today."

With the air of a bored oracle, Conphas said, "He'll sign as well."

"And what makes you so certain of that?" Istriya asked.

Conphas raised his bowl, and one of the ubiquitous slaves scurried forward to refill it. "All the early arrivals will sign. It should've occurred to me earlier, but now that I think about it, it seems plain that these fools fear the arrival of the *others* more than anything else. They think themselves invincible. Tell them the Fanim are as terrible in war as the Scylvendi and they laugh, remind you the God Himself rides at their side."

"So what are you saying?" Istriya asked.

Without thinking, Xerius had leaned forward in his settee. "Yes, Nephew. What are you saying?"

Conphas sipped from his bowl, shrugged. "They think triumph is assured them, so why share it? Or even worse, give it away altogether to their undeserving betters? Think. When Nersei Proyas arrives, Calmemunis will be little more than one of his lieutenants. The same applies to Tharschilka and Kumrezzer. When the main contingents from Galeoth and High Ainon arrive, they're sure to lose their pre-eminent positions. As of now, the Holy War's theirs, and they wish to wield—"

"You must delay the distribution of provisions, then, Xerius," Istriya interrupted. "Prevent them from marching."

"Perhaps," Skeaös added, "we can tell them we've found weevils in our granaries."

Xerius stared at his mother and nephew, trying to smooth the sneer from his expression. This was where their knowledge ended, and where his genius began. Not even Conphas, the cunning snake, could anticipate him on this. "No," he said. "They march."

Istriya stared at him, her face looking as astonished as her prunish skin would allow.

"Perhaps," Conphas said, "we should dismiss the slaves."

With a clap Xerius sent oiled bodies fleeing from the deck.

"What's the meaning of this, Xerius?" Istriya asked. Her voice quavered, as though robbed of breath by shock.

Conphas studied him, his lips hooked in a mild smile. "I think I know, Grandmother. Could it be, Uncle, that the Padirajah has asked for a . . . *gesture?*"

Struck mute by astonishment, Xerius gaped at his nephew. How could he have known? Too much penetration, and certainly too much ease of manner. At some level, Xerius had always been terrified of Conphas. It was more than just the man's wit. There was something dead inside his nephew. No, more than dead—something *smooth*. With others, even with his mother—although she too had seemed so remote lately—there was always the exchange of unspoken expectations, of the small, human needs that crotched and braced all conversation, even silences. But with Conphas there were only sheer surfaces. His nephew was never moved by another. Conphas was moved by Conphas, even if at times in mimicry of being moved by others. He was a man for whom everything was a whim. A perfect man.

But to master such a man! And master him he must.

"Flatter him," Skeaös had once told Xerius, "and be transformed into part of the glorious story that he sees as his life." But he could not. To flatter another was to humble oneself.

"How did you know this?" Xerius snapped. His fear added, "Need I send you to Ziek to find out?" *The Tower of Ziek*—who in Nansur failed to shudder when they glimpsed it rising from the congestion of Momemn? His nephew's eyes hardened for a moment. He had been moved—and why not? *Conphas* had been threatened.

Xerius laughed.

Istriya's sharp voice interrupted his mirth. "How could you joke about such things, Xerius?"

Had he been joking? Perhaps he had.

"Forgive my uncouth humour, Mother, but Conphas has guessed right, guessed a secret so deadly that it would destroy us, destroy us *all*, if . . ." He paused, turned back to Conphas. "This is why I must know *how* you anticipated this."

Conphas was wary now. "Because it's what I would do. Skauras . . . nay, *Kian* needs to understand that *we're* not fanatics."

Skauras. Hawk-faced Skauras. There was an old name. The shrewd Kianene Sapatishah-Governor of Shigek and the first leathery obstacle to be overcome by the Holy War. How little the Men of the Tusk understood the lay of the land between the Rivers Phayus and Sempis! Nansur and Kian had been at intermittent war for centuries. They knew each other intimately, had sealed countless truces with lesser daughters. How many spies, ransoms, even hostages—

Xerius shot forward, scrutinizing his nephew. An image of Skauras's ghostly face superimposed over that of the Cishaurim emissary floated before his soul's eye. "Who told you?" he asked with abrupt intensity. As a youth, Conphas had spent four years as a hostage of the Kianene. In Skauras's court no less!

Conphas looked at the floral mosaics beneath his sandalled feet. "Skauras himself," he finally said, looking directly at Xerius. There was a playfulness in his demeanour, but that of a game played by oneself. "I've never broken off communication with his court. But surely your spies have told you this."

And Xerius had worried about his mother's resources!

"You must be wary of such things, Conphas," Istriya said maternally. "Skauras is one of the old Kianene. A desert man. As ruthless as he's clever. He would use you to sow dissension among us if he could. Remember always, it's the *dynasty* that is important. House *Ikurei.*"

Those words! Tremors spilled into Xerius's hands. He clasped them together. Attempted to gather his thoughts. Looked away from their wolfish faces. All those years ago! Fumbling with a small black vial the size of a child's finger, pouring the poison into his father's ear. His *father!* And his mother's . . . no, *Istriya's* voice thundering in his thoughts: *The dynasty, Xerius! The dynasty!*

Her husband, she'd decided, had neither claw nor fang enough to keep the dynasty alive.

What was happening here? What were they doing? Plotting?

He glanced at the old, adulterate witch, wanting to *want* to have her killed. But for as long as he could remember, she had been the totem, the sacred fetish that held the mad machinery of power in place. The old, insatiable Empress alone was indispensable. Those times, in his youth, when she had awakened him in the heart of night, stroking his cock, tormenting him with pleasure, cooing into his tongue-wet ear: *"Emperor Xerius . . . Can you feel it, my lovely, godlike son?"* She had been so beautiful then.

It had been across her hand that he'd first come, and she'd taken his seed and bid him taste it. *"The future,"* she had said, *"tastes of salt . . . And it stings, Xerius, my lovely child . . ."* That warm laugh that had wrapped cold marble with comfort. *"Taste how it stings . . ."*

"Do you see?" Istriya was saying. "Do you see how it troubles him? This is what Skauras hopes for."

Conphas had been watching him carefully. "I'm not a fool, Grandmother. And no heathen living could make me a fool, either. *Especially* Skauras. Nevertheless, I do apologize, Uncle. I should've told you this earlier."

Xerius looked at both of them blankly. Outside the sun was fierce, bright enough to press the patterns stitched into the red canopy across the interior: animals entwined in circles around the Black Sun seal of Nansur. Everywhere—throughout the sanguine shade of the canopy, across furniture, floor, and limb—the Sun of the Empire ringed by incestuous beasts.

A thousand suns, he thought, feeling himself calm. *Across all the old provinces, a thousand suns! Our ancient strongholds will be retaken. The Empire will be restored!*

"Compose yourself, my son," Istriya was saying. "I know you're not so foolish as to suggest that Calmemunis and the others march against the Kianene, or that sacrificing all the Men of the Tusk gathered so far is the 'gesture' my grandson refers to. That would be madness, and the Emperor of Nansur is not mad. Is he, Xerius?"

During this time, the shouts they'd heard earlier had been growing nearer. Xerius stood and walked to the starboard rail. Leaning, he saw the first of the barge-towing longboats creep from behind the distant banks. He glimpsed the rowers, like the spine of a centipede. Their backs flashed in the sun.

Soon . . .

He turned to his mother and nephew, then glanced at Skeaös, who was wooden in the way of accidental interlopers. "The Empire covets what it has lost," Xerius said wearily. "Nothing more. And it will sacrifice anything, even a Holy War, to gain what it covets." So easily said! Such words were the world in small.

"You *are* mad!" Istriya cried. "So you'll send these first outlanders to their deaths, halve the Holy War, simply to show thrice-damned Skauras you're not a religious lunatic? You squander fortune, Xerius, and you tempt the endless wrath of the Gods!"

The violence of her response shocked him. But it mattered little what she thought of his plans. It was Conphas he needed . . . Xerius watched him.

After a stern moment of deliberation, Conphas slowly nodded and said, "I see."

"You see *reason* in this?" Istriya hissed.

Conphas shot Xerius an appraising look. "Think, Grandmother. Far more men are set to arrive than those who've gathered so far—true Great Names such as Saubon, Proyas, even Chepheramunni, King-Regent of High Ainon! But more important, it would seem the vulgar masses have been the first to answer Maithanet's call, those ill-prepared, stirred by sentiment more than the sober spirit of war. To lose this rabble would be to our advantage in innumerable ways: fewer stomachs to feed, a more cohesive army in the field . . ." He paused and turned to Xerius with what could only be described as wonder in his eyes—or something near to it. "And it would teach the Shriah, and those who follow, to *fear* the Fanim. Their dependence upon us, upon those who already respect the heathen, will grow with the measure of their fear."

"*Madness!*" Istriya spat, unmoved by her grandson's defection. "What? Do we then war against the Kianene under the conditions of some secret treaty? Why should we give them anything now, when we're at last in a position to seize? To break the back of a hated foe! And you would parlay with them? Say, 'I will lop off this and this limb but no other'? *Madness!*"

"But are 'we' in such a position, Grandmother?" Conphas replied, the filial deference now absent from his tone. "Think! Who's 'we' here? Certainly not the Ikurei. 'We' means the Thousand Temples. *Maithanet* swings this hammer—or have you forgotten?—while we merely scramble to pocket the pieces. Maithanet beggars us, Grandmother! So far he's done everything in his power to geld us. That's why he invited the Scarlet Spires, is it not? To avoid paying the price we'd demand for the Imperial Saik?"

"Spare me your picture-book explanations, Conphas. I'm not yet such an old, doddering fool." She turned to Xerius, glared at him with scathing eyes. His amusement must have been plain. "So, Calmemunis, Tharschilka, and countless thousands of others are destroyed. The herd is culled. What then, Xerius?"

Xerius could not help smiling. Such a plan! Even the great Ikurei Conphas was in awe! And Maithanet . . . The thought made Xerius want to chortle like a imbecile.

"What then? Our Shriah learns *fear*. Respect. All his mummery—all his sacrifices, hymns, and wheedling—will have been for naught. As you said earlier, Mother, the Gods cannot be bribed."

"But you can."

Xerius laughed. "Of course I can. If Maithanet commands the Great Names to sign my Indenture, to swear the return of all the old provinces to the Empire, then I will give them"—he turned to his nephew and lowered his head—"the Lion of Kiyuth."

"Splendid!" Conphas cried. "Why didn't I see it? Thrash them with one hand in order to soothe them with the other. Brilliant, Uncle! The Holy War *will* be ours. The Empire will be restored!"

The Empress stared at her progeny dubiously.

"What do you say, Mother?"

But Istriya's gaze had drifted to the Prime Counsel. "You've been awfully silent, Skeaös."

"It's not m-my place to speak, Empress."

"No? But this mad scheme is yours, isn't it?"

"It's *mine*, Mother," Xerius snapped, irked by her assumption. "The wretch has spent tedious weeks trying to talk me out of it." Even as he gave breath to these words, he knew he'd blundered.

"Is that so? And why's that, Skeaös? As much as I despise you and the inordinate influence you have over my son, I've always found your thinking sound. What insights have you to shed?"

Skeaös stared at her helplessly, said nothing.

"You fear for your life, don't you, Skeaös?" Istriya said mildly. "As you should. My son's justice is harsh and utterly devoid of consistency. But *I'm* not afraid, Skeaös. Old women are more reconciled to death than old men. By bringing life to the world, we come to see ourselves as debtors. What's given is taken." She turned to her son, her lips pursed in a predatory smile. "Which leads me to my point. From what Conphas says, Xerius, you give the Fanim little, if anything at all, by giving them the first half of the Holy War."

Biting back his fury, Xerius replied, "Surely a hundred thousand lives is more than a 'little,' Mother."

"Ah, but I speak of *practicalities*, Xerius. Conphas says these men are dross, more an impediment than an advantage. Since Skauras undoubtedly knows this as well, I ask you, my dear sweet son, what has he demanded in return? I know what you take, so tell me, *what have you given?*"

Xerius stared at her pensively. Memories of his meeting with the Cishaurim, Mallahet, and his arcane negotiations with Skauras flashed before his soul's eye. How cold that summer night now seemed! Cold and hellish . . .

The Empire will be restored . . . At all costs.

"Let me," Istriya continued, "make it simple for you, hmm? Tell me where the line falls, Xerius. Tell me where the *second*, useful half of the Holy War, of necessity falters."

Xerius locked eyes with Conphas. He saw the hated, knowing smirk that resided nowhere in his face but found agreement there—the only place he really needed it. What was Shimeh compared with the Empire? What was faith compared with imperial power? Conphas had sided with the Empire—with *him*. Suddenly the air seemed musky with his mother's humiliation. He relished it.

"This is war, Mother. As in a game of number-sticks, who can say what triumphs—or catastrophes—lie in the future?"

The grand Empress stared at him for a long while, her face disconcertingly blank beneath its skin of cosmetics.

"Shimeh," she said at last in a dead voice. "The Holy War is to perish before Shimeh."

Xerius smiled, then shrugged. He turned back to the river. By now the rowers' shouts were rifling the sky and the first of the longboats was passing by. Trailing long ropes of hemp, they towed a great, lumbering barge, so immense it seemed to bow the shining back of the river. He could see the black monument cradled in timbers, as long on its back as Momemn's gates were tall: a great obelisk for the temple-complex of Cmiral in Momemn. As it ploughed before him, it seemed he could feel the erotic warmth of basalt in the sun, radiating from the great planes and the massive profile of his face, the terrible visage of Ikurei Xerius III, at the pinnacle. He felt his heart overflow, and real tears spilled down his cheeks. He envisaged the monument being raised in the heart of Cmiral amid thousands of wondering eyes, its imperial countenance turned forever to the white sun. A shrine.

His thoughts leapt. *I will be immortal . . .*

He returned to his settee and reclined, consciously savouring the flares of hope and pride. Oh, sweet godlike vanity!

"Like an immense sarcophagus," his mother said. Always, the asp of truth.

CHAPTER EIGHT

MOMEMN

Kings never lie. They demand the world be mistaken.

—CONRIYAN PROVERB

When we truly apprehend the Gods, the Nilnameshi sages say, we recognize them not as kings but as thieves. This is among the wisest of blasphemies, for we always see the king who cheats us, never the thief.

—OLEKAROS, AVOWALS

Autumn, 4111 Year-of-the-Tusk, the Northern Jiünati Steppe

Yursalka of the Utemot awoke with a start.

A noise of some kind . . .

The fire was dead. Everything was blackness. Rain drummed against the hide walls of his yaksh. One of his wives groaned and fussed with her blankets.

Then he heard it again. A tap against the hide entrance. "Ogatha?" he whispered hoarsely. One of his younger sons had ambled off the previous afternoon and had failed to return. They'd assumed that the boy had been caught by the rain, that he would

223

return after it passed. Ogatha had done as much before. Nevertheless, Yursalka was worried.

Always wandering, that boy.

"Oggie?"

Nothing.

Another tap.

More curious than alarmed, he kicked his legs free, then crept nude to his broadsword. He was certain it was just Oggie playing games, but hard times had fallen upon the Utemot. One never knew.

He saw lightning flash through a seam in the conical ceiling. For an instant, the water dripping through seemed quicksilver. The subsequent thunder left his ears ringing.

Then another tap. He became tense. He carefully picked his way between his children and wives, paused before the entrance of his yaksh. The boy was mischievous, which was why Yursalka doted on him so, but throwing stones at his father's yaksh in the dead of night? Was that mischief?

Or malice?

He worked the pommel of his sword with his hand. He shivered. Outside chill autumn rain fell down, down. More soundless lightning, followed by air-hammering thunder.

He untied the flap, then slowly pulled it to one side with his broadsword. He could see nothing. The whole world seemed to hiss with the pasty sound of rain across mud and puddles. The roar reminded him of Kiyuth.

He ducked out into the sheeting water, clenched his teeth so they wouldn't chatter. His toes closed about one of the stones in the mud. He knelt, retrieved it, but could see next to nothing. It wasn't a stone, he realized, but a section of jerky, or maybe even a piece of wild asparagus—

Another flash of lightning.

For a moment, all he could do was blink away the brightness. Understanding rumbled in with the thunder.

A section of a child's finger . . . He held a child's severed finger.
Oggie?

Cursing, he threw the finger down and peered wildly through the
surrounding darkness. Rage, grief, and terror were all overwhelmed
by disbelief.

This isn't happening.

Incandescent white cracked the sky, and for an instant, he saw
the entire world: the desolate horizon, the sweep of distant pastures,
the surrounding yaksh of his kinsmen, and the lone figure standing
not more than a dozen yards away, watching . . .

"Murderer," Yursalka said numbly. "Murderer!"

He heard steps slosh through the mud.

"I found your son wandering the Steppe," the hated voice said.
"So I've returned him to you."

Something, a cabbage, hit him in the chest. Uncharacteristic
panic seized him.

"Y-you live," he sputtered. "I'm s-so relieved. All of us w-will be
so relieved!"

More lightning, and Yursalka saw him, like a hulking wraith, as
wild and as elemental as thunder and rain.

"Some things broken," the voice grated from the darkness, "are
never mended."

Yursalka howled and flew forward, sweeping his broadsword in a
great arc. But iron limbs caught him in the darkness. Something
exploded in his face. His sword fell from senseless fingers. A hand
throttled him, and he beat at a forearm made of stone. He felt his
toes drag grooves through the muck. He gagged, felt something
sharp arc above his groin. There was a steaming rush across his
thighs, the uncanny sensation of being gouged hollow.

He skidded and slapped into the mud, convulsed about his entrails.
I'm dead.

A brief flutter of white light, and Yursalka saw him crouching
above, saw deranged eyes and a famished grin. Then everything
went black.

"Who am I?" the blackness asked.

"Nnn-Cnaiür," he gasped. "M-man-killer . . . M-most v-violent of all men . . ."

A slap, open-handed as though he were a slave.

"No. I am your *end*. Before your eyes I will put your seed to the knife. I will quarter your carcass and feed it to the dogs. Your bones I will grind to dust and cast to the winds. I will strike down those who speak your name or the name of your fathers, until 'Yursalka' becomes as meaningless as infant babble. I will blot you out, hunt down your every trace! The track of your life has come to me, and it goes no further. I am your end, your utter obliteration!"

Then torchlight and commotion flooded the darkness. His earlier cries had been heard! He saw bare and booted feet stamp in the mud, heard men curse and grunt. He watched his younger brother do a bare-chested pirouette into the mud, saw his last surviving cousin stumble to his knees, then topple like a drunk into a puddle.

"I'm your *Chieftain!*" Cnaiür bellowed. "Challenge me or witness my justice! Either way, justice will be done!"

Curiously numb, Yursalka rolled his head through the muck, saw more and more Utemot gather about them. Torches sputtered and hissed in the rain, their orange light bleached white by sporadic flashes of lightning. He saw one of his wives, wrapped only in the bear pelt his father had given her, peering in horror at the spot where he lay. She stumbled toward him, her face vacant. Cnaiür struck her hard, as one might strike a man. She toppled from the pelt, fell motionless and naked at her chieftain's feet. She looked so cold.

"This man," Cnaiür thundered, "has betrayed his kinsmen on the field of battle!"

"To free us!" Yursalka managed to cry. "To release the Utemot from your yoke, your depravity!"

"You've heard his admission! His life and the lives of all his chattel are forfeit!"

"No . . ." Yursalka coughed, but the numbness was reclaiming him. Where was the justice in this? He'd betrayed his chieftain, yes, but for *honour*. Cnaiür had betrayed his chieftain, his father, for the love of another man! For an outlander who could speak killing words! Where was the justice in this?

Cnaiür extended his arms as though to grapple the thundering sky. "I am Cnaiür urs Skiötha, breaker-of-horses-and-men, Chieftain of the Utemot, and I have returned from the dead! Who dares dispute my judgement?"

The rain continued to spiral down. Save for looks of awe and terror, none dared dispute the madman. Then a woman, the half-Norsirai mongrel Cnaiür had taken wife, burst from the others and threw herself at him, weeping uncontrollably. She feebly beat at his chest, wailing something unintelligible. For a moment, Cnaiür held her tight, then he sternly pressed her back.

"It's me, Anissi," he said with shameful tenderness. "I am whole."

Then he turned from her toward Yursalka, a demon by torch-light, an apparition by lightning strike.

Yursalka's wives and children had gathered about their husband, wailing. Yursalka felt soft thighs beneath his head, the flutter of warm palms across his face and chest. But he could look only at the ravenous figure of his chieftain. He watched him catch his youngest daughter by the hair, snuff out her squeal with sharp iron. For a grisly moment, she remained fixed on his blade, and he shook her like a skewered doll. Yursalka's wives screamed and cowered. Looming above them, the chieftain of the Utemot hacked, again and again, until they groped and shuddered in the mud. Only Omiri, the lame daughter of Xunnurit whom Yursalka had married the previous spring, remained, weeping and clawing at her husband. Cnaiür seized her with his free hand, hoisted her by the back of the neck. Her mouth worked like a fish about a soundless shriek.

"Is this Xunnurit's misbegotten cunt?" he snarled.

"Yes," Yursalka gasped.

Cnaiür cast her like a rag to the mud. "She lives to watch our sport. Then she suffers the sins of her father."

Surrounded by his dead and dying family, Yursalka watched Cnaiür loop his bowel like rope about scarred arms. He glimpsed the callous eyes of his tribesman, knew they would do nothing.

Not because they feared their lunatic chieftain, but because it was the way.

Late Autumn, 4111 Year-of-the-Tusk, Momemn

Since Maithanet's declaration of Holy War a year and a half earlier, untold thousands had gathered about Momemn's walls. Among those well placed within the Thousand Temples, there were rumours of the Shriah's dismay. He had not, it was said, anticipated such an overwhelming response to his summons. In particular, he had not thought so many lower-caste men and women would take up the Tusk. Reports of freemen selling their wives and children into slavery so they might purchase passage to Momemn were common. A widowed fuller from the city of Meigeiri, it was said, actually drowned his two sons rather than sell them to the slavers. When dragged before the local ecclesiastical magistrate, he allegedly claimed he was "sending them ahead" to Shimeh.

Similar tales tarnished nearly every report sent to Sumna, so much so that they became more a matter of disgust than alarm for the Shrial Apparati. What disturbed them were the stories, rare at first, of atrocities committed either by or against the Men of the Tusk. Off the coast of Conriya a small squall killed more than nine hundred low-caste pilgrims who'd been promised passage on unseaworthy ships. To the north, a cohort of Galeoth freebooters wearing the Tusk destroyed no fewer than seventeen villages over the course of their southward march. They left no witnesses, and were discovered only when they attempted to sell the effects of Arnyalsa, a famed missionary priest, at market in Sumna. At Maithanet's direction, the Shrial Knights encircled their encampment and killed them all.

Then there was the story of Nrezza Barisullas, the King of Cironj and perhaps the wealthiest man in the Three Seas. When several thousand Tydonni who'd contracted his ships defaulted on their payment, he sent them to the island of Pharixas, an old pirate stronghold of King Rauschang of Thunyerus, demanding they storm the island in lieu of monies owed. They did, and with abandon. Thousands of innocents perished. *Inrithi* innocents.

Maithanet, it was said, wept at the news. He immediately placed all of House Nrezza under Shrial Censure, which voided all obligations, commercial or otherwise, to Barisullas, his sons, and his agents. The Censure was quickly rescinded, however, once it became clear that the Holy War would take months longer to assemble without Cironji ships. Before the fiasco was concluded, Barisullas would actually win reparations in the form of Shrial trade concessions from the Thousand Temples. Rumour had it that the Nansur Emperor sent his personal congratulations to the canny Cironji King.

But none of these incidents provoked anything approaching the uproar caused by the march of what came to be called the Vulgar Holy War. When word reached Sumna that the first Great Names to arrive had capitulated to Ikurei Xerius III and signed his Indenture, there was a great deal of concern that something untoward was about to happen. But without the luxury of sorcerers, Maithanet's entreaties, which extolled the virtues of patience and alluded darkly to the consequences of defiance, did not reach Momemn until Calmemunis, Tharschilka, Kumrezzer, and the vast mobs that followed them were days gone.

Maithanet was wroth. In ports around the Three Seas, the great state-sponsored contingents were finally preparing to embark. Gothyelk, the Earl of Agansanor, was already at sea with hundreds of Tydonni thanes and their households—more than fifty thousand trained and disciplined men. The gathering of the Holy War, the Shriah's advisers estimated, was mere months from completion. All told, they said, the Men of the Tusk would have numbered over three hundred thousand, just enough to ensure the heathens' utter destruction. The premature march of those already gathered was an unmitigated disaster, even if they were largely rabble.

Frantic messages were dispatched, imploring the lords to await the others, but Calmemunis in particular was a stubborn man. When Gotian, the Grandmaster of the Shrial Knights, intercepted him north of Gielgath with Maithanet's summons, the Palatine of Kanampurea allegedly said, "It's a sad thing when the Shriah himself doubts."

Confusion and tragedy, rather than fanfare, had characterized the departure of the Vulgar Holy War from Momemn. Since only a minority of those gathered were affiliated with one of the Great Names, the host possessed no clear leader—no organization at all, in effect. As a result, several riots broke out when the Nansur soldiery began distributing supplies, and anywhere from four to five hundred of the faithful were killed.

To his credit, Calmemunis acted quickly, and with the assistance of Tharschilka's Galeoth, his Conriyans were able to impose order on the mobs. The Emperor's provisions were distributed with a modicum of fairness. What disputes remained were settled at sword point, and the Vulgar Holy War soon found itself prepared to march.

The citizens of Momemn swamped the city walls to watch the Men of the Tusk depart. Many jeered at the pilgrims, who had long ago earned the contempt of their hosts. Most, however, remained silent, watching the endless fields of humanity trudge toward the southern horizon. They saw innumerable carts heaped with belongings, women and children walking dull-eyed through the dust, dogs prancing around countless feet, and endless thousands of impoverished low-caste men, hard-faced but carrying only hammers, picks, or hoes. The Emperor himself watched the spectacle from the enamelled heights of the southern gates. According to rumour, he was overheard remarking that the sight of so many hermits, beggars, and whores made him want to retch, but he'd "already given the vulgar filth his dinner."

Though the host could travel no more than ten miles a day, the Great Names were generally satisfied with their progress. By sheer numbers alone, the Vulgar Holy War created mayhem along the coasts. Field-slaves would notice strange men filing through the fields, an innocuous handful soon to be followed by thousands. Entire crops would be trampled, orchards and groves stripped. But with the Emperor's food in their bellies, the Men of the Tusk were as disciplined as could be expected. The incidences of rape, murder, and robbery were infrequent enough that the Great Names could still dispense justice—and more important, still pretend they led an army.

By the time they crossed into the frontier province of Anserca, however, the pilgrims had turned to outright banditry. Companies of fanatics ranged the Ansercan countryside, by and large restricting their depredations to harvests and livestock, but at times resorting to plunder and carnage. The town of Nabathra, famous for its wool markets, was sacked. When Nansur units under General Martemus, who had been instructed to shadow the Vulgar Holy War, attempted to restrain the Men of the Tusk, several pitched battles broke out. At first it seemed that the General, even though he had only two columns at his disposal, might bring the situation under control. But the weight of numbers and the ferocity of Tharschilka's Galeoth forced him to retire north and ultimately to shelter within Gielgath's walls.

Calmemunis issued a declaration blaming the Emperor, claiming Xerius III had issued edicts denying supplies to the Men of the Tusk, in direct contravention of his earlier oaths. In point of fact, however, the edicts had been issued by Maithanet, who had hoped this action might stall the horde's southward march and purchase enough time to convince them to return to Momemn.

With the Men of the Tusk slowed by the need to forage, Maithanet issued further edicts, one rescinding the Shrial Remission previously extended to all those who took up the Tusk, another punishing Calmemunis, Tharschilka, and Kumrezzer with

Shrial Censure, and a third threatening all those who continued under these Great Names with the same. This news, combined with the backlash against the bloodshed of the previous days, brought the Vulgar Holy War to a stop.

For a time even Tharschilka wavered in his resolve, and it seemed certain the core of the Vulgar Holy War at least would turn and begin marching back to Momemn. But then Calmemunis received news that an imperial supply train, apparently headed for the frontier fortress of Asgilioch, had miraculously fallen into the hands of his people. Convinced this was a sign from the God, he called together all the lords and impromptu leaders of the Vulgar Holy War and rallied them with inflammatory words. He asked them to pause and judge for themselves the righteousness of their endeavour. He reminded them that the Shriah was a man, who like all men made errors in judgement from time to time. "The ardour has been sapped from our blessed Shriah's heart," he said. "He's forgotten the sacred glory of what we do. But mark me, my brothers, when we storm the gates of Shimeh, when we deliver the Padirajah's head in a sack, he will remember! He will praise us for remaining resolute when his heart faltered!"

Though several thousand did defect and eventually filtered back to the imperial capital, the bulk of the Vulgar Holy War pressed on, now entirely immune to the exhortations of their Shriah. Bands of foragers scattered across the province, while the main body continued south, growing ever more fragmented. The villas of local caste nobles were looted. Numerous villages were put to the torch, the men massacred, the women raped. Walled towns that refused to open their gates were stormed.

Eventually, the Men of the Tusk found themselves beneath the Unaras Mountains, which for so long had been the southern bulwark for the cities of the Kyranae Plain. Somehow, they were able to rally and reorganize beneath the walls of Asgilioch, the ancient Kyranean fortress the Nansur called "the Breakers" for having stopped three previous Fanim invasions.

For two days the fortress gates remained shut against them. Then Prophilas, the commander of the imperial garrison, extended a dinner invitation to the Great Names and other caste nobles. Calmemunis demanded hostages, and when he received them, he accepted the invitation. With Tharschilka, Kumrezzer, and several lesser nobles, he entered Asgilioch and was promptly taken captive. Prophilas produced a Shrial Warrant and respectfully informed them that they would be held indefinitely unless they commanded the Vulgar Holy War to disband and return to Momemn. When they refused, he tried reasoning with them, assuring them they had no hope of prevailing against the Kianene, who were, he insisted, as wily and as ruthless as the Scylvendi on the field of battle. "Even if you marched at the head of a true army," he told them, "I would not throw the number-sticks for you. As it stands, you lead a migration of women, children, and slavish men. I beg of you, relent!"

Calmemunis, however, replied with laughter. He admitted that sinew for sinew, weapon for weapon, the Vulgar Holy War was likely no match for the Padirajah's armies. But this, he claimed, was of no consequence, for surely the Latter Prophet had shown that frailty, when suffused with righteousness, was unconquerable. "We have left Sumna and the Shriah behind us," he said. "With every step we draw nearer Holy Shimeh. With every step we draw closer to Paradise! Proceed with care, Prophilas, for as Inri Sejenus himself says, 'Woe to he who obstructs the Way!'"

Prophilas released Calmemunis and the other Great Names before sunset.

The following day, thousands upon thousands congregated in the valley beneath Asgilioch's turrets. A gentle rain washed over them. Hundreds of sacrificial fires were lit; the carcasses of the victims were piled high. Shakers covered their naked bodies in mud and howled their incomprehensible songs. Women sang gentle hymns while their husbands sharpened whatever weapons—picks, scythes, old swords and maces—they'd been able to scavenge. Children chased dogs through the crowds. Many of the warriors among them—the Conriyans, Galeoth, and Ainoni who'd marched with the Great Names—watched with dismay as a band of lepers climbed into the mountain passes, intent on being the first to set foot on heathen soil. The Unaras Mountains were not imposing, more a jumble of escarpments and bare stone slopes than a mountain range. But beyond them, drums called dusky, leopard-eyed men to worship Fane. Beyond them, Inrithi were gutted and hung from trees. For the faithful, the Unaras were the ends of the earth.

The rain stopped. Lances of sunlight pierced the clouds. Singing hymns, blinking tears of joy from their eyes, the first Men of the Tusk began filing into the mountains. Holy Shimeh, it seemed to them, must lie just beyond the horizon. Always just beyond.

When the news of the Vulgar Holy War's passage into heathen lands reached Sumna, Maithanet dismissed his court and retired to his chambers. His servants turned all petitioners away, informing them that the Holy Shriah prayed and fasted, and would do so until he learned the fate of the first wayward half of his Holy War.

———— ◆ ————

Bowing as low as jnan dictated, Skeaös said, "The Emperor has asked that I brief you on the way to the Privy Chamber, Lord Exalt-General. The Ainoni have arrived."

Conphas looked up from his handwriting, dropped his quill in his inkhorn. "Already? They said tomorrow."

"An old trick, my Lord. The Scarlet Spires is not above old tricks."

The Scarlet Spires. Conphas nearly whistled at the thought. The mightiest School in the Three Seas, about to take up residency in the Holy War . . . Conphas had always possessed a connoisseur's appreciation of life's larger inconsistencies. Absurdities such as this were like delicacies to him.

The previous morning had revealed hundreds of foreign galleys and carracks moored in the mouth of the River Phayus. The Scarlet Spires, the households of the King-Regent and more than a dozen

Palatine-Governors, as well as legions of low-caste infantry had been disembarking ever since. All High Ainon, it seemed, had come to join the Holy War.

The Emperor was jubilant. Since the departure of the Vulgar Holy War weeks earlier, more than ten thousand Thunyeri under Prince Skaiyelt, the son of the infamous King Rauschang, and at least four times as many Tydonni under Gothyelk, the bellicose Earl of Agansanor, had arrived. Unfortunately, both men had proven immune to his uncle's charms—violently so. When presented with the Indenture, Prince Skaiyelt had ransacked the imperial court with those unnerving blue eyes of his, then wordlessly marched from the palace. Old Gothyelk had kicked over the lectern, and called his uncle either a "gelded heathen" or a "depraved faggot"— depending on which translator one asked. The arrogance of barbarians, particularly Norsirai barbarians, was unfathomable.

But his uncle expected better of the Ainoni. They were Ketyai, like the Nansur, and they were an old and mercantile people, like the Nansur. The Ainoni were civilized, despite their archaic devotion to their beards.

Conphas studied Skeaös. "You think they do this intentionally? To catch us off balance?" He waved his parchment to dry in the air, then handed it to his dispatch—orders for Martemus to resume the patrols south of Momemn.

"It's what I would do," Skeaös replied frankly. "If one hoards enough petty advantages . . ."

Conphas nodded. The Prime Counsel had paraphrased a famous passage from *The Commerce of Souls*, Ajencis's classic philosophical treatise on politics. For a moment Conphas thought it strange that he and Skeaös should despise each other so. In the absence of his uncle, they shared a peculiar understanding, as though, like the competitive sons of an abusive father, they could from time to time set aside their rivalry and acknowledge their shared lot with simple talk.

He stood and looked down on the wizened man. "Lead on, old father."

Caring nothing for the fine points of bureaucratic prestige, Conphas had installed himself and his command on the lowest level of the Andiamine Heights, overlooking the Forum and the Scuäri Campus. The hike to the Privy Chamber on the summit was a long one, and he idly wondered whether the old Counsel was up to it. Over the years more than one Imperial Apparati had died of "the clutch," as the palace inhabitants called it. According to his grandmother, past emperors had actually used the climb to dispose of aging and quarrelsome functionaries, giving them messages allegedly too important to be trusted to slaves, then demanding their immediate return. The Andiamine Heights was no friend of soft hearts—literally or otherwise.

Prompted more by curiosity than malice, Conphas pressed the man to a brisk pace. He'd never seen anyone die of the clutch before. Remarkably, Skeaös did not complain, and aside from swinging his arms like an old monkey, he showed no signs of strain. With easy wind, he began briefing Conphas on the specifics of the treaty struck between the Scarlet Spires and the Thousand Temples—as far as they were known. When it seemed clear that Skeaös had not just the appearance but the stamina of an old monkey, Conphas grew bored.

After climbing several stairs, they passed through the Hapetine Gardens. As always, Conphas glanced at the spot where Ikurei Anphairas, his great-great-grandfather, had been assassinated more than a century before. The Andiamine Heights were filled with hundreds of such grottoes, places where long-dead potentates had committed or suffered this or that scandalous act. His uncle, Conphas knew, did his best to avoid such places—unless very drunk. For Xerius the palace fairly hummed with memory of dead emperors.

But for Conphas the Andiamine Heights was more a stage than a mausoleum. Even now hidden choirs filled the galleries with hymns. At times clouds of fragrant incense fogged the corridors and haloed the lanterns, so it seemed one climbed not to the summit of a hill but to the very gates of heaven. Had he been a visitor rather than a resident, Conphas knew, bare-chested slave girls would have served him heady wines laced with Nilnameshi narcotics. Pot-bellied eunuchs would have delivered gifts of scented oil and cere-monial weaponry. Everything would have been calculated to hoard petty advantages, as Skeaös might say, to distract, ingratiate, and overawe.

Still unwinded, Skeaös continued regurgitating an apparently endless train of facts and admonitions. Conphas listened with half an ear, waiting for the old fool to tell him something he didn't already know. Then the Prime Counsel turned to the topic of Eleäzaras, the Grandmaster of the Scarlet Spires.

"Our agents in Carythusal say his formidable reputation scarcely does him justice. He was little more than a Subdidact when his teacher, Sasheoka, died of unknown causes some ten years ago. Within two years, he was Grandmaster of the greatest School in the Three Seas. That speaks of daunting intelligence and ability. You must—"

"And hunger," Conphas interrupted. "No man achieves so much in so little time without hunger."

"I suppose you would know."

Conphas cackled. "Now that's the Skeaös I know and love! Surly. Seething with illicit pride. You had me worried, old man."

The Prime Counsel continued as though he'd said nothing. "You must exercise great caution when you speak to him. Initially, your uncle thought to exclude you from this meeting—that is, until Eleäzaras personally requested your presence."

"My uncle what?" Even when bored, Conphas possessed a keen ear for slights.

"Excluded you. He feared the Grandmaster would exploit your inexperience in these matters—"

"Exclude? *Me?*" Conphas looked askance at the old man, for some reason reluctant to believe him. Was he playing some kind of game? Fanning the fires of resentment?

Perhaps this was another one of his uncle's tests . . .

"But as I said," Skeaös continued, "that's all changed—which is why I'm briefing you now."

"I see," Conphas replied sceptically. What was the old fool up to? "Tell me, Skeaös, what's the point of this meeting?"

"Point? I fear I don't understand, Lord Exalt-General."

"The purpose. The intent. What does my uncle hope to secure from Eleäzaras and the Ainoni?"

Skeaös frowned, as though the answer were so obvious that the question simply had to be a prelude to mockery. "The point is to secure Ainoni support for the Indenture."

"And if Eleäzaras proves as intractable as, say, the Earl of Agansanor, what then?"

"With all due respect, my Lord, I sincerely doubt—"

"*If*, Skeaös, what then?" Conphas had been a field officer since the age of fifteen. If he wanted, he could make men jump with his tone.

The old Counsel cleared his throat. Skeaös, Conphas knew, possessed administrative courage in excess, but he had no pluck whatsoever when it came to face-to-face confrontations.

No wonder his uncle loved him so.

"If Eleäzaras spurns the Indenture?" the old man repeated. "Then the Emperor denies him provisions, like the rest."

"And if the Shriah demands my uncle supply them?"

"By then the Vulgar Holy War will have been destroyed—or so we . . . assume. Leadership, not provisions, will be Maithanet's primary concern."

"And who will that leader be?" Conphas had spat each question hard on the heels of each answer, as an interrogator might. The old man was beginning to look rattled.

"Y-you. The L-Lion of Kiyuth."

"And what will be my price?"

"Th-the Ind-denture, the s-signed oath that all the old provinces will be returned."

"So *I* am the linchpin of my uncle's plans, am I not?"

"Y-yes, Lord Exalt-General."

"So then tell me, dear old Skeaös, why would my uncle think to *exclude* me—*me!*—from his negotiations with the Scarlet Spires?"

The Prime Counsel's pace slackened. He looked to the florid whorls stitched across the rugs at their feet. Rather than speak, he wrung his hands.

Conphas grinned wolfishly. "You *lied* just now, didn't you, Skeaös? The question of whether I should attend his meeting with Eleäzaras never even arose, did it?"

When the man failed to respond, Conphas seized him by the shoulders, glared at him. "Need I ask my uncle?"

Skeaös matched his eyes for moment, then glanced down. "No," he said. "There's no need."

Conphas released his grip. With sweaty palms, he smoothed the front of the old man's silk robes.

"What kind of game are you playing, Skeaös? Did you think that by wounding my vanity, you could provoke me to act against my uncle? Against my Emperor? Are you trying to incite me to sedition?"

The man looked positively panicked. "No. No! I'm an old fool, I know, but my days on this earth are numbered. I rejoice at the life the gods have given me. I rejoice at the sweet fruits I've eaten, for the great men I've known. I even—and I know you'll find this difficult to believe—exult because I've lived long enough to witness *you* grow into your glory! But this plan of your uncle's—to deliver a Holy War to its destruction! A *Holy War!* I fear for my soul, Ikurei Conphas. My soul!"

Conphas was dumbstruck, so much so he utterly forgot his anger. He'd assumed Skeaös's insinuations to be yet another of his uncle's probes and had responded accordingly. The possibility that the fool acted on his own had never occurred to him. For so many years Skeaös and his uncle had seemed different incarnations of the same will.

"By the gods, Skeaös . . . Has Maithanet ensnared you as well?"

The Prime Counsel shook his head. "No. I care nothing for Maithanet—or Shimeh, for that matter . . . You're young. You wouldn't understand my motives. The young can never see life for what it is: a knife's edge, as thin as the breaths that measure it. What gives it depth isn't memory. I've memories enough for ten men, and yet my days are as thin and as shadowy as the greased linen the poor stretch over their windows. No, what gives life depth is the *future*. Without a future, without a horizon of promise or threat, our lives have no meaning. Only the *future is real*, Conphas, and unless I make amends to the gods, I've no future left."

Conphas snorted. "But I understand all too well, Skeaös. You've spoken like a true Ikurei. How does the poet Girgalla put it? 'All love begins with one's own skin'—or *soul*, as the case may be. But then, I've always thought the two interchangeable."

"Do you understand? *Can* you?"

He *did* understand, and better than Skeaös realized. His grandmother. Skeaös conspired with his grandmother. He could even hear her voice: "You must bait both of them, Skeaös. Poison them against one another. Conphas's infatuation with my son's madness will wane soon enough. Just you wait and see. He'll come running to us, and together we'll force Xerius to abandon his mad plan!"

He wondered whether the old drab had taken Skeaös as a lover. Likely, he concluded, and winced at the accompanying image. Like a prune fucking a twig, he thought.

"You and my grandmother," he said, "hope to save the Holy War from my uncle. A commendable undertaking, save that it verges on treachery. My grandmother I can understand—she has him bewitched—but you, Skeaös? You know, as few others do, what Ikurei Xerius III is capable of once his suspicions are roused. A bit reckless, don't you think, trying to me pit me against him like this?"

"But he listens to you! And more important, he *needs* you!"

"Perhaps he does . . . But either way, it's immaterial. Your ancient stomachs may find his fare too undercooked, but my uncle has laid out a feast, Skeaös, and I for one do not intend to gainsay it."

No matter how much he despised his uncle, Conphas had to admit that provisioning Calmemunis and the rabble that followed him was a move as brilliant as any he himself had made on the field of battle. The Vulgar Holy War would be annihilated by the heathen, and in a single stroke the Empire would cow this Shriah, perhaps compel him to demand that the remaining Men of the Tusk sign the Imperial Indenture and demonstrate to the Fanim that House Ikurei bargained in good faith. The Indenture would ensure the legality of any military action the Empire might take against the Men of the Tusk to retrieve her lost provinces, and the deal with the heathen would ensure that such military action would meet with little resistance—when the time came.

Such a plan! And devised not by Skeaös but by his *uncle*. As much as that fact galled Conphas, it must, he decided, gall the old Counsel more.

"It's not the feast we dispute," Skeaös replied, "it's the *price!* Surely you can see this!"

Conphas studied the Prime Counsel for several long moments. There was something curiously pathetic, he thought, about the notion of the man plotting with his grandmother, like two beggars sneering at those too poor to give more than coppers.

"The Empire? Restored?" he said coldly. "I should think your soul a bargain, Skeaös."

Skeaös opened his toothless mouth to retort but then closed it.

The Emperor's Privy Chamber was an austere room, circular, ringed by black marble columns, with a surrounding gallery for those rare occasions, mostly ritual, when the Houses of the Congregate were invited to observe the Emperor signing edicts into law. A small herd of ministers and slaves milled about the room's heart, clustered around the head of a mahogany table. Conphas glimpsed his uncle's reflection floating beneath the table's polish, like a corpse in brackish water. There was no sign of the Scarlet Schoolmen.

The Exalt-General loitered near the entrance for several moments, studying the ivory plaques set into the walls: renditions of the great lawmakers of antiquity and the Tusk, from the prophet Angeshraël to the philosopher Poripharus. He wondered inanely which of his dead relatives the artisan had used to model their faces.

The sound of his uncle's summons startled him.

"Come. We've only a few moments, Nephew."

The others had withdrawn, leaving only Skeaös and Cememketri at his uncle's side. The surrounding galleries, Conphas could not help noticing, were filled with Eothic Guardsmen and Imperial Saik.

Conphas took the seat his uncle indicated. "Both Skeaös and Cememketri agree," Xerius was saying, "that Eleäzaras is an infernally clever and dangerous man. How would you snare him, Nephew?" His uncle was trying to sound jocular, which meant he was afraid, as perhaps he should have been: no one yet knew *why* the Scarlet Spires had deigned to join the Holy War, and this meant no one knew the School's intent. For men like Skaiyelt and Gothyelk, the purpose was plain: redemption or conquest. But for Eleäzaras? Who could say what motivated any of the Schools?

Conphas shrugged. "Snaring him is out of the question. One must know *more* than one's opponent to trap him, and as it stands we know nothing. We know nothing of his deal with Maithanet. We don't even know *why* he would condescend to make such a deal—and to take such a risk! A School of its own volition joining a holy war . . . A *holy war!* In all honesty, Uncle, I'm not sure that securing his support for the Indenture should even be our priority at this point."

"So what are you saying? That we should simply probe for details? I pay my spies good gold for such trifles, Nephew."

Trifles? Conphas struggled with his composure. Though his uncle's heart was too whorish for religious faith, he was as jealous of his ignorance as any zealot. If the facts contradicted his aspirations, they did not exist.

"You once asked me how I prevailed at Kiyuth, Uncle. Do you remember what it was I told you?"

"Told me?" the Emperor nearly spat. "You're always 'telling' me things, Conphas. How do you expect me to sort one impertinence from the other?" This was perhaps the pettiest and most oft used weapon in his uncle's arsenal: the threat to read counsel as commandment. The threat loomed over all their exchanges: *You would presume to command the Emperor?*

Conphas graced his uncle with a conciliatory smile. "From what Skeaös says," he said smoothly, "I think we should simply bargain in good faith—as much as we can, anyway. We know too little to snare him." Stepping to the brink then stepping back by pretending no such step had been taken—this had always been his family's way, at least until his grandmother's recent antics.

"My thought precisely," Xerius said. At least he still remembered the rules.

Just then, a chamberlain announced the imminent arrival of Eleäzaras and his retinue. Xerius bid Skeaös to tie his Chorae about his hand, which the old Counsel did while Cememketri watched with distaste. This was something of a small dynastic tradition, adopted more than a century earlier, and observed whenever members of the Imperial Family conferred with outside sorcerers.

Chepheramunni, King-Regent and titular head of High Ainon, was announced first, but when the small Ainoni entourage filed into the chamber, he followed Eleäzaras like a dog. The Grandmaster's entrance was brisk and, Conphas thought, anti-climactic. His demeanour was more that of a banker than a sorcerer: impatient of spectacle, hungry for the ledgers. He bowed to Xerius, but no lower than would the Shriah. A slave drew his chair back for him, and he sat effortlessly, despite his trailing crimson gowns. With rouged cheeks and reeking of perfume,

Chepheramunni sat at his side, a chalky look of fear and resentment on his face.

The obligatory exchange of honorifics, introductions, and compliments was observed. When Cememketri, Eleäzaras's counterpart in the Imperial Saik, was introduced, the Grandmaster smiled disdainfully and shrugged, as though dubious of the man's station. Schoolmen, Conphas had been told, were often insufferably haughty when in the company of other Schoolmen. Cememketri flushed in anger, but to his credit did not respond in kind.

After these jnanic preliminaries, the Grandmaster turned to Conphas. "At long last," he said in fluent Sheyic, "I meet the famed Ikurei Conphas."

Conphas opened his mouth to reply, but his uncle spoke first.

"He's a rarity, isn't he? Few rulers possess such instruments to execute their will . . . But surely you haven't come all this way just to meet my nephew?"

Though Conphas could not be certain, Eleäzaras seemed to *wink* at him before turning to his uncle, as though to say, *"We must suffer these fools patiently, mustn't we?"*

"Of course not," Eleäzaras replied with damning brevity.

Xerius seemed oblivious. "Then might I ask *why* the Scarlet Spires has joined the Holy War?"

Eleäzaras studied his unpainted fingernails. "Quite simple, really. We were purchased."

"Purchased?"

"Indeed."

"A most extraordinary transaction! What are the details of your arrangement?"

The Grandmaster smiled. "Alas, I fear that secrecy is itself part of the arrangement. Unfortunately, I'm not able to divulge any of the details."

Conphas thought this an unlikely story. Not even the Thousand Temples was wealthy enough to "hire" the Scarlet Spires. They were here for reasons that transcended gold and Shrial trade concessions—of that much he was certain.

Changing directions as fluidly as a shark in water, the Grandmaster continued, "You worry, of course, about how our purposes bear upon your Indenture."

There was a sour pause. Then Xerius replied, "Of course." His uncle chafed more than most at being premeditated by another.

"The Scarlet Spires," Eleäzaras said demurely, "cares nothing about who possesses the land conquered by the Holy War. Accordingly, Chepheramunni will sign your Indenture—gladly. Will you not, Chepheramunni?"

The painted man nodded but said nothing. The dog had been trained well.

"But," Eleäzaras continued, "there are several conditions we would see met first."

Conphas had predicted this. Civilized men haggle.

Xerius protested. "Conditions? But for centuries the lands from here to Nenciphon have been—"

"I've heard all the arguments," Eleäzaras interrupted. "Dross. Pure dross. You and I both know what is truly at stake here, Emperor . . . Don't we?"

Xerius stared at him in dumb astonishment. He wasn't accustomed to interruptions, but then, he wasn't accustomed to parlaying with men who were more than his equals. High Ainon was a wealthy, densely populated nation. Of all the rulers and despots across the Three Seas, only the Padirajah of Kian possessed more commercial and military power than the Grandmaster of the Scarlet Spires.

"If you don't," Eleäzaras continued when Xerius failed to reply, "then I'm sure your precocious nephew does. Hmm, young Conphas? Do you know what's at stake here?"

Conphas thought it obvious. "Power," he said with a shrug. A strange fellowship, he realized, now existed between him and this sorcerer. From the outset, the Grandmaster had accorded him the status of kindred intellect.

Even the foreigners know you're a fool, Uncle.

"Precisely, Conphas. Precisely! History is only a pretext for power, no? What matters . . ." The white-haired sorcerer trailed with a small grin, as though he'd stumbled upon a more effective tack with which to make his point. "Tell me," he asked Xerius, "why did you provision Calmemunis, Kumrezzer, and the others? Why did you give them the means to march?"

His uncle opted for the rehearsed reply. "To put an end to their depredations. Why else?"

"Unlikely," Eleäzaras snapped. "I rather think that you provisioned the Vulgar Holy War in order to destroy it."

There was an uncomfortable pause.

"But this is madness," Xerius finally replied. "Damnation aside, what would we have to gain?"

"Gain?" Eleäzaras repeated with a wry grin. "Why the Holy War, of course . . . Our deal with Maithanet stripped you of whatever leverage you possessed with the Imperial Saik, so you needed something else to barter. If the Vulgar Holy War is destroyed, then it will be far easier for you to convince Maithanet that the Holy War needs you—or should I say, the now legendary military acumen of your nephew, here. Your Indenture will be his price, and the Indenture effectively cedes to you all the proceeds of the Holy War . . . I must admit, it's a splendid plan."

This small flattery was Xerius's undoing. For a brief instant his eyes flashed with jubilant conceit. Stupid men, Conphas had found, tended to be excessively proud of their few brilliant moments.

Eleäzaras smiled.

He plays you, Uncle, and you cannot even see.

The Grandmaster leaned forward as though aware of the discomfort generated by his proximity. Eleäzaras, Conphas realized, was a master practitioner of jnan.

"As of yet," he said coldly, "we don't know the specifics of the game you play, Emperor. But let me assure you of this: if it involves the betrayal of the Holy War, then it involves the betrayal of the *Scarlet Spires*. Do you know what this means? What it entails? If you betray us, Ikurei, then no one"—he glanced darkly at Cememketri—"not even your Imperial Saik, will be able to preserve you from our wrath. We are the Scarlet Spires, Emperor . . . Think on that."

"You threaten me?" Xerius fairly gasped.

"Assurances, Emperor. All arrangements require assurances."

Xerius yanked his face away, intent on Skeaös, who was fiercely whispering in his ear. Cememketri, however, could contain himself no longer.

"You overstep yourself, Eli. You act as though we sit in Carythusal when it's you who sit in Momemn. Two of the Three Seas lie between you and your home. Far too far to be uttering threats!"

Eleäzaras frowned then snorted, turning to Conphas as though the Grandmaster of the Imperial Saik did not exist. "In Carythusal they call you the Lion of Kiyuth," he said nonchalantly. His eyes were small, dark, and nimble. They scrutinized him from beneath bushy white brows.

"Do they?" Conphas asked, genuinely surprised that his grandmother's moniker had travelled so far so fast. Surprised and pleased—very pleased.

"My archivists tell me you're the first to defeat the Scylvendi in pitched battle. My spies, on the other hand, tell me your soldiers worship you as a god. Is this so?"

Conphas smiled, deciding the Grandmaster would lick his ass as clean as a cat's if given the opportunity. For all his penetration, Eleäzaras had misjudged him.

It was time to set him straight. "What Cememketri said just now is true, you know. No matter what your deal with Maithanet, you've delivered your School to its greatest peril since the Scholastic Wars. And not just because of the Cishaurim. You'll be a small enclave of profanity within a great tribe of fanatics. You'll need every friend you can get."

For the first time something like real anger surfaced in Eleäzaras's eyes, like a glimpse of coals through a smoky fire. "We can make the world burn with our song, young Conphas. We need no one."

———— ✦ ————

Despite his uncle's gaffes, Conphas left the negotiations confident that the House Ikurei had secured far more than it had surrendered. For one, he was almost certain he knew why the Scarlet Spires had accepted Maithanet's offer to join the Holy War.

Few things reveal a competitor's agenda more thoroughly than the process of negotiating a deal. Over the course of their haggling, it became obvious that the heart of Eleäzaras's concern lay with the Cishaurim. In exchange for Chepheramunni's signature on the Indenture, he demanded that Cememketri and the Imperial Saik surrender all the intelligence they'd amassed on the Fanim sorcerer-priests over centuries of warring against them. Of course, this was to be expected: the Scarlet Spires had gambled its very existence on its ability to overcome the Cishaurim. But there was an undeniable intensity in the way the Grandmaster uttered their name. Eleäzaras said "Cishaurim" in the same manner a Nansur would say "Scylvendi"—the way one names an old and hated foe.

For Conphas, this could mean only one thing: the Scarlet Spires had been at war with the Cishaurim long before Maithanet had declared the Holy War. Like House Ikurei, the Scarlet Spires had embroiled itself in the Holy War in order to *use* it. For the Scarlet Spires the Holy War was an instrument of revenge.

When Conphas mentioned his suspicions, his uncle sneered— initially at least. Eleäzaras, he insisted, was too mercantile to risk so much for a trifle like vengeance. When Cememketri and Skeaös also endorsed the theory, however, the Emperor realized he'd harboured the same suspicions all along. It was official: the Scarlet Spires had joined the Holy War to bring some pre-existing war with the Cishaurim to conclusion.

In itself, the conjecture was comforting. It meant the Scarlet Spires' agenda would not cross their own until the end—when it no longer mattered. It would be difficult for Eleäzaras to make good on his threat once he and his School were dead. But what bothered Conphas was the question of what had motivated Maithanet to call on the Scarlet Spires at all. Certainly, of all the Schools, it was the most apt to destroy the Cishaurim in an open confrontation. But on the face of it, Conphas could think of no School more unlikely to join a Holy War. And as far as Conphas knew, the Shriah had approached no other School—not even the Imperial Saik, which had been the traditional bulwark against the Cishaurim through the Jihads. Only the Scarlet Spires.

Why?

Unless Maithanet had somehow learned of their war. But this answer was even more troubling than the question. With nearly every imperial spy in Sumna now dead, they had plenty of reasons to be wary of Maithanet's cunning as it was. But this! A Shriah who had penetrated the Schools? And the *Scarlet Spires*, no less.

For not the first time, Conphas suspected that Maithanet, and not House Ikurei, occupied the centre of the Holy War's web. But he dared not share his misgivings with his uncle, who tended to be even more stupid when afraid. Instead, he explored this fear on his own. No longer did he gloat over future glories in the dark hours before sleep. Rather, he fretted over implications that he could neither stomach nor verify.

Maithanet. What game did he play? For that matter, who was he?

The news arrived days afterward. The Vulgar Holy War had been annihilated.

The reports were sketchy at first. Urgent messages from Asgilioch related the terrifying accounts of some dozen or so Galeoth who had managed to escape across the Unaras Spur. The Vulgar Holy War had been utterly overcome on the Plains of

Mengedda. Shortly afterward, two couriers arrived from Kian, the one bearing the severed heads of Calmemunis, Tharschilka, and a man who may or may not have been Kumrezzer, the other bearing a secret message from Skauras himself, and delivered, as per the Sapatishah's instructions, to his former hostage and ward, Ikurei Conphas. It simply read:

> *We cannot count the carcasses of your idolatrous kin, so many have been felled by the fury of our righteous hand. Praise be the Solitary God. Know that House Ikurei has been heard.*

After dismissing the courier, Conphas spent several hours brooding over the message in his quarters. Again and again, the words rose of their own volition.

. . . so many have been felled . . .

We cannot count . . .

Even though he was only twenty-seven years of age, Ikurei Conphas had seen the carnage of many fields of war—enough that he could almost see the masses of Inrithi sprawled and tangled across the Plains of Mengedda, their dead-fish eyes staring into earth or across endless sky. But it wasn't guilt that moved his soul to ponder—and perhaps in a strange way even to grieve—it was the sheer scale of this first accomplished act. It was as though until now, the dimensions of his uncle's plan had been too abstract for him to truly comprehend. Ikurei Conphas was in awe of what he and his uncle had done.

. . . House Ikurei has been heard.

The sacrifice of an entire army of men. Only the Gods dared such acts.

We have been heard.

Many, Conphas realized, would suspect it had been House Ikurei that had spoken, but no one would know. A strange pride settled through him then, a secret pride disconnected from the estimations of other men. In the annals of great events, there would be many accounts of this first tragic event of the Holy War. Responsibility for this catastrophe would be heaped upon Calmemunis and the other Great Names. In the ancestor lists of their descendants, they would be names of shame and scorn.

There would be no mention of Ikurei Conphas.

For an instant, Conphas felt like a thief, the hidden author of a great loss. And the exhilaration he felt almost possessed a sexual intensity. He saw clearly now why he so loved this species of war. On the field of battle, his every act was open to the scrutiny of others. Here, however, he stood outside scrutiny, enacted destiny from a place that transcended judgement or recrimination. He lay hidden in the womb of events.

Like a God.

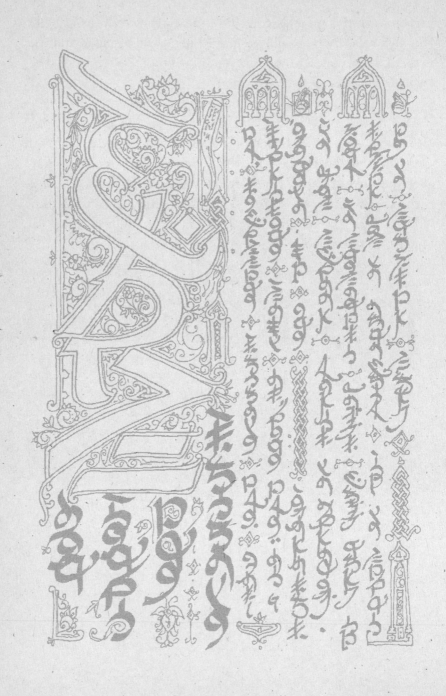

PART III:
The Harlot

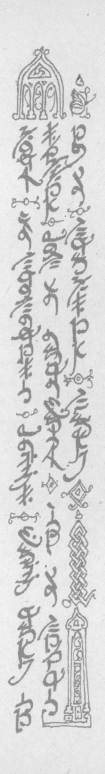

HAPTER NINE

SUMNA

And the Nonman King cried words that sting:
"Now to me you must confess,
For death above you hovers!"
And the Emissary answered ever wary:
"We are the race of flesh,
We are the race of lovers."

—"BALLAD OF THE INCHOROI," ANCIENT KÛNIÜRI FOLK SONG

Early Winter, 4110 Year-of-the-Tusk, Sumna

"Will you come next week?" Esmenet asked Psammatus, watching him pull his white silk tunic over his head then down across his stomach and his still-shining phallus. She sat naked in her bed, sheets bundled about her knees.

Psammatus paused, absently smoothing away wrinkles. He looked at her with pity. "I fear this is my last visit, Esmi."

Esmenet nodded. "You've found someone else. Someone younger."

"I'm sorry, Esmi."

"No. Don't be sorry. Whores know better than to pout like wives."

Psammatus smiled but did not reply. Esmenet watched him retrieve his gown and his lavish gold-and-white vestments. There was something touching and reverent in the way he dressed. He even paused to kiss the golden tusks embroidered across each of his flowing sleeves. She would miss Psammatus, miss his willowy silver hair and his fatherly face. She would even miss the gentle way he coupled. *I'm becoming an old whore*, she thought. *One more reason for Akka to abandon me.*

Inrau was dead, and Achamian had left Sumna a broken man. After all these days, she still caught her breath at the memory of his departure. She'd begged him to take her with him. In the end she'd even wept and fallen to her knees: "Please, Akka! I *need* you!" But this was a lie, she knew, and the bewildered resentment in his eyes meant he knew as well. She was a prostitute, and prostitutes hardened themselves to men, all men, out of necessity. No. As much as she feared losing Achamian, what she feared more was the prospect of returning to her old life, to the endless succession of hunger, anguished glares, and spilt seed. She wanted the Schools! The Great Factions! She wanted Achamian, yes, but she wanted his *life* more.

And this was the irony that held her breathless. For even in the midst of enjoying that new life through Achamian, she'd been unable to relinquish the old. "You say you love me," Achamian had cried, "and yet you still take custom. Tell me why, Esmi! Why?"

Because I knew you would leave me. All of you leave me . . . all the ones I love.

"Esmi," Psammatus was saying. "Esmi. Please don't cry, my sweet. I'll return next week. I promise."

She shook her head and wiped the tears from her eyes. Said nothing.

Weeping for a man! I'm stronger than this!

Psammatus sat beside her to bind his sandals. He looked pensive, even scared. Men such as Psammatus, she knew, came to whores to escape uncomfortable passions as much as to glut them.

"Have you heard of a young priest named Inrau?" she asked, hoping to at once set him at ease and carry on a pathetic remnant of her life with Achamian.

"Yes, I have, in fact," Psammatus replied, his profile both puzzled and relieved. "He's the one they say committed suicide."

The same thing the others said. News of Inrau's death had caused a great scandal in the Hagerna. "Suicide. You're certain of this?" *What if it's true? What will you do then, Akka?*

"I'm certain that's what they *say*." He turned and looked at her sombrely, running a finger down her cheek. Then he stood and hooked his blue cloak—the one he used to conceal his vestments—on his arm.

"Leave the door open, would you?" Esmenet asked.

He nodded. "Well met, Esmi."

"Well met."

In the gathering shadows of evening, Esmenet stretched naked across the sheets and drowsed for a short time, her thoughts wheeling through regret after regret. Inrau's death. Achamian's flight. And as always, her daughter . . . When her eyes fluttered open, a figure darkened her door. Someone waiting.

"Who are you?" she asked wearily. She cleared her throat. Without a word, the man walked to the side of her bed. He was tall, even statuesque, wearing a coal black coat over a silvered brigandine and a black tunic of crushed damask. A *new customer*, she thought, looking into his face with the innocence of the recently awakened. *A beautiful one.*

"Twelve talents," she said, leaning up from the covers. "Or a half-silver if you—"

He slapped her—*hard*. Esmenet's head snapped back and to the side. She fell face first from her bed.

The man cackled. "You're *not* a twelve-talent whore. Decidedly not."

Her ears ringing, Esmenet scrambled on all fours and threw her back against the wall.

The man sat on the end of her crude bed and began pulling off his leather gloves finger by finger. "As a matter of etiquette, one should never begin a relationship with lies, whore. It sets a unfortunate precedent."

"We have a relationship?" she asked breathlessly. The entire left side of her face was numb.

"Through a mutual acquaintance, yes." His eyes lingered on her breasts for a moment before flickering between her thighs. Esmenet allowed her knees to part a bit more, as though an accident of exhaustion.

"And who would that be?" she asked, heart hammering in her chest.

The man gazed below her navel with the shamelessness of a slave-owner. "A certain Mandate Schoolman"—he drew his eyes up as though from a reverie—"named Drusas Achamian."

Akka. You knew this would happen.

"I know him," she said cautiously, resisting the urge to once again ask the man who he was.

Don't ask questions. Ignorance is life.

Instead she said, "What do you want to know?" She let her knees drift farther apart.

Be the whore . . .

"Everything," the man replied with a heavy-lidded smirk. "I want to know everything, and everyone, he has known."

"It'll cost," she said, trying to steady her voice. "*Both* will cost."

You must sell him.

"Why am I not surprised? Ah, business. It makes everything so straightforward, does it not?" He hummed under his breath as he rooted through his purse. "Here . . . *Eleven* copper talents. Six to betray your body, and five to betray the Schoolman." A savage grin. "A fair estimation of their relative worth, don't you think?"

"A half-silver, at least," she said. "For each."

Barter . . . Be the whore.

"Such conceit!" he replied, nevertheless dipping two pale fingers back into his purse. "How about one of *these?*"

She looked at the shining gold with frank hunger.

"It'll do," she said, her mouth dry.

The man grinned. "I imagined as much."

The coin disappeared and he began undressing, watching her with feral honesty as she hastened to light candles against the evening gloom.

When the time came, there was something animal in his proximity, a smell or heat that spoke directly to her body. He cupped her left breast in a heavy, callused hand, and any illusion she had had of using his lust as a weapon evaporated. His presence was overwhelming. As he lowered her to the bed, she feared she might swoon.

Be compliant . . .

He knelt before her and effortlessly pulled her raised hips and spread legs across his thighs. And she found herself aching for the moment she had feared. Then he was inside. She cried out. *What's he doing to me? What's he doing—*

He began moving. His mastery of her body was inhuman. Soon one gasping moment slurred into another. When he caressed her, her skin was like water, alive with shivers that rippled across her, through her. She began writhing, grinding against him with desperation, moaning through clenched teeth, drunk with nightmarish ecstasy. Through her pained eyes he seemed her burning centre, blurring into her, flooding her with rapture after rapture, thrust after thrust. Time and again, he would bring her to the ringing brink of climax, only to pause, and ask questions, endless questions . . .

"And what precisely did Inrau say about Maithanet?"

"Don't stop . . . *Pleaase.*"

"What did he say?"

Tell the truth.

She remembered trying to pull his face down to her own, gasping, "*Kiss me . . . Kiss me.*"

She remembered his thick chest pressing against her breasts, and shuddering, crumbling beneath him as though made of sand.

She remembered lying still and sweaty with him, panting for air, feeling the thick throb of his heart through his member, his slight-est movement like lightning between her thighs, an agonizing bliss that made her weep and groan with wild abandon.

And she remembered answering his questions with the urgency of pounding hips. *Anything! I would give you anything!*

When she climaxed for the final time, she felt as though she'd been pitched from a precipice, and she heard her own husky shrieks as though from afar, shrill against the thunder of his dragon roar.

Then he withdrew and she felt ransacked, her limbs trembling, her skin numb and cold with sweat. Two of the candles were gutted, but the room was illuminated in grey light. *How long?*

He was standing above her, his godlike frame shining in the glow of the remaining candle. "Morning comes," he said.

The golden coin fluttered in his hand, bewitching her with its glitter. He held it above her and let it slip between his fingers. It plopped onto the sticky pools across her belly. She glanced down and gasped in horror.

His seed was black.

"Shush," he said, gathering his finery. "Say a word of this to no one. Do you understand, whore?"

"I understand," she managed, tears now streaming. *What have I done?*

She stared at the coin and the Emperor's profile across it, remote and golden against downy pubic hair and slopes of bare skin—skin threaded and smeared by glistening pitch. Bile flooded the back of her throat. The room became brighter. *He's opening the shutters.* But when she looked up, he was gone. She heard the arid slap of wings receding into the dawn.

Cool morning air rushed through the room, rinsing away the stench of inhuman rutting. *But he smelled of myrrh.*

Esmenet rolled over and vomited across the floor.

———— ◦≈◦ ————

Some time passed before she managed to wash, dress, and leave her room. When she stumbled into the street, she knew she could never return. She weathered the pungent crush of others—the custom district was adjacent to the ever-packed Ecosium Market—feeling curiously alive to the sights and sounds of her city: coppersmiths hammering; the cry of a one-eyed man proclaiming the curative power of his sulphur products; barking dogs; the insistent begging of a man without legs; another man calling out the names of his meats; the harsh shouts of mule drivers beating their teams until they screamed. Unending sounds. And a welter of smells: dry summer stone, incense, the tug of roasting meat, feces, and smoke—everywhere the smell of smoke.

A brisk morning vigour animated the market, and she passed through the crowds like a weary shadow. To its pith, her body ached, and she found walking painful. She clutched the gold coin tightly, periodically exchanging hands to wipe her palms of sweat. She stared numbly at things and people: at a cracked amphora bleeding oil across a vendor's mat; at young Galeoth slave girls negotiating the masses with downcast eyes and woven baskets of grain perched upon their heads; at a haggard dog, alert and peering through thickets of scissoring legs; at the hazy profile of the Junriüma rising in the distance. She stared and she thought, *Sumna.*

She loved her city, but she had to escape.

Achamian had told her that this might happen, that if Inrau had in fact been murdered, then men might come to her, looking for him.

"If that happens, Esmi, then whatever you do, don't ask questions. You don't want to know anything about them, understand? Ignorance is life . . . Be compliant. Be the whore all the way down. Barter, as a whore barters. And above all, you must sell me, Esmi. You must tell them everything you know. And tell them the truth, for they likely know much of it already. Do these things, and you'll survive."

"But why?"

"Because spies prize a weak and mercantile soul above all other things, Esmi. They'll spare you on the chance you might prove valuable. Hide your strength, and you will survive."

"But what about you, Akka? What if they learn something they can use to injure you?"

"I'm a Schoolman, Esmi," he had replied. "A Mandate Schoolman."

At last, through a screen of passing people, she saw a little girl standing barefoot in dusty sunlight. She would do. With large brown eyes the girl watched Esmenet approach, too wary to return her smile. She clutched a stick to the breast of her threadbare shift.

I survived, Akka. And I did not survive.

Esmenet stooped before the child and astounded her with the gold talent.

"Here," she said, pressing it into small palms.

So like my daughter.

———◦∞◦———

Alone and on muleback, Achamian descended into the valley of Sudica. He had taken this route south from Sumna to Momemn on a whim, or so he had thought, hoping only to avoid the heavily cultivated lands nearer the coast. Sudica had not been peopled for a very long time. It was home only to shepherds, their flocks of sheep, and ruins.

The day was clear and surprisingly warm. Nansur was not a dry country, but its character was such that it always reminded Achamian of one. Its people were densely clustered around the rivers and the coasts, leaving large expanses of land that were inhospitable only because of their vulnerability to the Scylvendi.

Sudica was such a place. In the days of Kyraneas, Achamian had read, it had been one of the great provinces, the birthplace of generals and of ruling dynasties. Now there were only sheep and half-buried stone. Whatever country Achamian found himself in, it seemed he would search out places like these, places that slumbered, that dreamed of ancient times. This was a habit shared by a great many of the Mandate, a deep obsession with blasted monuments of word or stone—so deep they would often find themselves walking through ruined temples or wandering into the library of a learned host without recalling why. It had made them the chroniclers of the Three Seas. For them to wander among half-walls and fallen pillars, or through the words of an ancient treatise, was in a way to travel in peace with their other memories, to be one man instead of two.

The most famous landmark of Sudica was the ruined fortress-temple of Batathent. It required some time negotiating hillsides and crossing scrubland before Achamian could ride up into its shadow. The immense truncated walls spilled into gravel. Obviously the site had been raided over the years for its granite and bright limestone. All that remained of the temple within were rows of massive columns, far too imposing, Achamian supposed, to be pulled down and dragged to the coast. Batathent had been one of the few strongholds to survive the collapse of Kyraneas during the First Apocalypse, a sanctuary for those fleeing the hunting parties of Scylvendi and Sranc. A protective hand cupped about the frail light of civilization.

Achamian wandered across the site, awed by the conjunction of old stone and his own learning. He returned to his mule only when the growing dark made him worry of finding his way.

That night he laid out his mat and slept beneath the pillars, finding sad comfort in the way the sun's heat lingered in the winter-cold stone.

In his sleep, he dreamed of that day when every child was stillborn, that day when the Consult, beaten back to the black ramparts of Golgotterath by the Nonmen and the ancient Norsirai, brought emptiness, absolute and terrible, into the world: Mog-Pharau, the No-God. In his sleep, Achamian watched glory after glory flicker out through Seswatha's anguished eyes. And he awoke, as he always awoke, a witness to the end of the world.

He washed his hair and beard in a nearby stream, oiled them, and then returned to his humble camp. He mourned, he realized, not only for Inrau but for the loss of his old confidence. Numerous inquiries had led him through the labyrinthine offices of the Thousand Temples—nowhere. His discussions with various Shrial Apparati often loomed large in his thoughts, and in those memories the priests seemed even taller and wicker-thin. Many of the men had been disconcertingly sharp as well as stubbornly committed to the official explanation of Inrau's death: suicide. His own final foolishness, Achamian knew, had been offering them gold for truth. What had he been thinking? There had been more gold in the bowls from which they sipped anpoi than he could possibly muster. He was a beggar before the wealth of the Thousand Temples. Before the power of Maithanet.

Since learning of Inrau's death, Achamian had moved as though in a fog, possessed of that same inner shrinking he'd felt as a child when his father had bidden him to find the old rope he used for whippings. *"Find the rope,"* the voice would grate, and the ceremony would begin: lips trembling, hands shaking as they clasped the cruel hemp . . .

If Inrau had in fact committed suicide, then Achamian would be his murderer.

Find the rope, Akka. Find it now.

He was relieved when the Mandate instructed him to travel to Momemn and join the Holy War. With the loss of Inrau, Nautzera and other members of the Quorum had abandoned their obscure hopes of penetrating the Thousand Temples. Now they wanted him to watch the Scarlet Spires—again. As much as the irony of this stung him, he had not argued. The time had come to move on. Sumna merely confirmed a conclusion he could not bear. Even Esmenet began to irritate him. Mocking eyes and cheap cosmetics. The endless wait while she pleasured other men. As easily as it stirred his flesh, her tongue left his thoughts cold with uncertain spit. And yet he ached at the thought of her—the taste of her skin, bitter with perfume.

Sorcerers were not accustomed to women. Their mysteries were of a lesser kind, to be held in contempt by men of learning. But the mystery of this one woman, this Sumni harlot, stirred fear rather than disdain within him. Fear and longing. But why? After Inrau's death, distraction was what he had needed most of all, and she had stubbornly refused to be that distraction. Quite the opposite. She pried him for the nuances of his day, debating— more with herself than with him—the meanings of each meaningless thing he learned. Her conspiracies were as impertinent as they were absurd.

One night he told her as much, hoping only to silence her for a short time. She had paused, but when she spoke, it was with a weariness that far surpassed his own, the tone of one injured to honesty by the pettiness of another. "This is only a game I play, Achamian . . . There is truth inside a game." He'd lain in the darkness, consumed by inner turmoil, feeling that if he could unravel his hurts the way she could, he would crumble, collapse into dust. *This isn't a game. Inrau is dead. Dead!*

Why couldn't she . . . be what he needed her to be? Why couldn't she stop lying with other men? Didn't he have gold enough to keep her?

"Not you too, Drusas Achamian," she had once cried when he'd offered her money. "I'll not play whore with you!" Words that had at once elated and devastated him.

One time, when he'd returned to the tenement and hadn't found her sitting in her window, he had dared come up to her door, moved by some shameful curiosity. *What's she like with the others? Is she the same as she's with me?* He could hear her gasp beneath some grunting body, hear her bed creak to the rhythm of thrusting groins. And it seemed his heart stopped. Clammy skin and ringing ears.

He'd placed numb fingertips against the door. There, on the other side . . . There she was, his Esmi, her legs wrapped around another man, her breasts shining with his sweat. He remembered flinching when she climaxed and thinking: *That cry is mine! Mine!*

But he owned nothing of her. Perhaps for the first time he had understood that. And yet he thought: *Inrau is dead, Esmi. You're all I have left.*

He heard the man crawl off her. "Mmmmmm," Esmi moaned. "Ah, Callustras, you're dreadfully gifted for an old soldier. What would I do without that thick cock of yours, hmm?"

A masculine voice replied, "I'm sure you find plenty to feed your cunny, dear."

"Morsels only. You, you're my banquet."

"Tell me, Esmi, who's that man who was here the last time I came? Another morsel?"

Achamian placed a wet cheek against the door. Cold, breathless anguish.

She laughed. "Here when you *came*? By the Gods, I hope not."

Achamian could almost hear the man smile and shake his head.

"Silly whore," he said. "I'm serious. The look he gave me as he passed through the door . . . I half expected he'd ambush me on the way back to the barracks."

"I'll speak to him about that. He gets . . . jealous."

"Jealous of a whore?"

"Callustras, that purse of yours is so full . . . Are you sure you don't want to spend more?"

"I'm afraid I've spent everything otherwise . . . But perhaps if you rattle my purse a little something'll fall out."

A moment of breathless silence. The faint sound of slapping.

Esmi whispered something barely audible, but Achamian was sure he heard: "Don't worry about your purse, Callustras. *Just do that to me again . . .*"

He had fled into the street then, her empty window oppressing him from above, his thoughts buzzing with images of sorcerous murder, of Esmi writhing in rapture beneath a soldier's chest. *"Do that to me again . . ."* He felt polluted, as though witnessing something obscene had made him obscene.

She's just playing the whore, he had tried to remind himself, *just like I play the spy*. The only difference was that she was far better at it. Coy humour, venal honesty, naked appetite—all those things that deadened a man's shame at spilling seed for coin. She was gifted.

"I couple with them in every way," she had once admitted. "I'm growing old, Akka, and there's nothing as pathetic as an old, starving whore." There had been real dread in her voice.

Achamian had lain with many whores in many cities through the years, so why was Esmenet so different? He'd first come to her because of her beautiful boyish thighs and seal-smooth skin. He'd returned because she was so good, because she joked and lusted the way she had with Callustras—whoever he was. But at some point, he'd come to know the woman apart from her spread legs. What was it he'd learned? With whom had he fallen in love?

Esmenet, the Whore of Sumna.

Often, in his soul's eye, she was inexplicably thin and wild, buffeted by rain and winds, obscured by the swaying of forest branches. This woman who had once lifted her hand to the sun, holding it so that for him its light lay cupped in her palm, and telling him that truth was air, was sky, and could only be claimed, never touched by the limbs and fingers of a man. He couldn't tell her how profoundly her musings affected him, that they thrashed like living things in the wells of his soul and gathered stones about them.

Sparrows erupted from an old oak in the nearby ravine, startling him.

Regret, he thought, remembering an old Shiradi proverb, *makes a leper of the heart*.

With a sorcerous word he ignited his fire and prepared water for his morning tea. While waiting for the water to boil, he studied his surroundings: the nearby pillars of Batathent soaring into the morning sky; the lonely trees, dark above rambling scrub and dead grasses. He listened to the muffled hiss and pop of his small fire.

When he reached out to retrieve the boiling water, he noticed that his hands were shaking as though palsied. Was it because of the cold?

What's happened to me?

Circumstances, he told himself. He had been overwhelmed by circumstances. With sudden resolution, he set the water aside and began rooting through his meagre baggage. He withdrew his ink, his quill, and a single sheet of parchment. Sitting cross-legged on his mat, he wet his quill.

In the centre of the left margin, he scratched,

MAITHANET

Without a doubt, the heart of the mystery. The Shriah who could see the Few. Inrau's murderer—perhaps. To the right of this, he wrote,

HOLY WAR

Maithanet's hammer, and Achamian's next destination. Below this, near the bottom of the sheet, he wrote,

SHIMEH

The object of Maithanet's Holy War. Could it be as simple as this? Free the city of the Latter Prophet from the yoke of the Fanim? The aims declared by cunning men were rarely their true aims.

He drew a line from "Shimeh" to the right, and wrote,

THE CISHAURIM

Hapless victims of Maithanet's Holy War? Or were they complicit somehow?

He scratched another line from this toward "Holy War" in the centre, stopping short to write,

THE SCARLET SPIRES

At least the School's motive was clear: the destruction of the Cishaurim. But as Esmenet had pointed out, how did Maithanet know of its secret war against the Cishaurim?

He pondered his handwriting for a moment, watching the ink flatten as it dried. For good measure, he added,

THE EMPEROR

adjacent to "Holy War." In Sumna, the air was rife with rumours of the Emperor's bid to compromise the Holy War, to transform it into an instrument of imperial reconquest. Although Achamian cared little whether the Ikurei Dynasty succeeded or failed, it would doubtless be an important variable in the algebra of these events.

And then, alone in the top right corner, he scratched,

THE CONSULT

A name like a pinch of salt in pure water. It meant so many things: the Apocalypse, the hilarity and contempt with which the Great Factions regarded the Mandate. Where were they? Did they even have a place on this page?

He studied the map for a moment, testing his tea through rolling steam. It felt warm in his stomach, braced him against the morning chill. He was missing something, he realized. Forgetting . . .

His hand trembled as he wrote,

INRAU

below "Maithanet." *Did he kill you, dear boy? Or did I?*

Achamian shook away these thoughts. He paid Inrau no respect by grieving for him, and even less by wallowing in self-pity. He avenged nothing. If any redress were to be found, it lay somewhere *here*, on this page. *I'm not his father. I must be what I am: a spy.*

Achamian often made such maps—not because he worried he might forget something, but because he worried he might overlook something. Visualizing the connections, he found, always suggested further possible connections. Moreover, this simple exercise had often proved a valuable guide for his inquiries in the past. The crucial difference this time, however, was that instead of naming individuals and their connections to some petty agenda, this map named Great Factions and their connections to a Holy War. The scale of this mystery, the stakes, far exceeded anything he had encountered before . . . aside from his dreams.

His breath caught.

A prelude to the Second Apocalypse? Could it be?

Achamian's eyes returned to "The Consult" isolated in its corner, realizing his map had already yielded its first dividend. If the Consult still plied the Three Seas, then they *had* to be connected somehow. There was no way they could remain aloof in such epic times. Where, then, would they hide?

Inexorably, his eyes were drawn back to

MAITHANET

Achamian took another sip of his tea. *Who are you, my friend? How can I discover who you are?*

Perhaps he should return to Sumna. Perhaps he could mend things with Esmenet, see if she'd absolve a fool of his frail pride. At the very least he could make sure she—

Achamian hastily set down his beaten cup, clutched his quill, and scribbled,

PROYAS

between "Maithanet" and "Holy War." Why hadn't he thought of this sooner?

After encountering Proyas on the steps beneath the Shriah, Achamian had learned the Prince had become one of Maithanet's few confidants. This didn't surprise him. In the years following Achamian's tutelage, Proyas had become obstinate with piety. Unlike Inrau, who'd committed himself to the Thousand Temples so that he might better serve, Proyas had embraced the Tusk and the Latter Prophet so that he might better judge—or so Achamian thought. The memory of Proyas's last letter, the one that had thrown even their terse correspondence on the pyre, still stung.

"Do you know what pains me most when I look upon you, old teacher? Not the fact that you're a blasphemer, but the thought I once loved a blasphemer."

How does one work his way back from such harsh words? But he had to, Achamian knew, and for reasons that were at once the best and the worst. He had to bridge the gulf between them, not because he loved Proyas still—remarkable men often compelled such love—but because he needed some path to Maithanet. He needed answers, both to quiet his heart and, perhaps, to save the world.

How Proyas would laugh if he told him that . . . No wonder the Three Seas thought the Mandate mad!

Achamian stood and poured the remainder of his tea upon the hissing fire. He looked at his map of connections one last time and considered the broad, blank spaces across the parchment, idly wondering how they might be filled.

He broke camp, packed his mule, and continued his lonely journey. Sudica passed without demarcation—more hills, more stony earth.

———⌾———

Esmenet walked through the gloom with the others, her heart thundering. She could feel the teetering immensity of the Gate of Pelts above her, as though it were a hammer Fate had held poised for a thousand years in anticipation of her escape. She glanced at the surrounding faces but saw only weariness and boredom. For them, passage from the city seemed uneventful. These people, she imagined, escaped Sumna every day.

For an absurd moment, she found herself fearing for her fear. If escaping Sumna meant nothing, did that mean the whole world was a prison?

Then suddenly she found herself blinking tears in the sunlight. She paused, glancing at the tan towers hulking above. Then she looked around, breathing deeply, ignoring the curses of those behind her. Soldiers lounged on either side of the gate's dark maw, eyeing those who entered the city but asking no questions. People on foot, on wains, and on horseback bustled about her. To either side of the road, a thin colonnade of mongers hawked their wares, hoping to profit from vagrant hungers.

Then she saw what before had been only a hazy band on the horizon, surfacing here and there from the crowded circuit of Sumna's walls: the countryside, winter pale and piling endlessly away into the distance. And she saw the sun, late-afternoon sun, spread across the land as though it were water.

A teamster cracked his whip next to her ear, and she scrambled to the side. A wain groaned by her, pulled by flabby oxen. Its driver flashed her a toothless grin.

She glanced at the greening tattoo across the back of her left hand. The mark of her tribe. The Sign of Gierra, though she was no priestess. The Shrial Apparati insisted all harlots be tattooed with parodies of the sacred tattoos borne by the temple-prostitutes. No one knew why. To better fool themselves into thinking the Gods were fooled, Esmenet supposed. It seemed a different thing here, without walls, without the threat of Shrial Law.

She considered calling after the teamster, but as he trundled away her eyes were drawn to the road, which struck a perfect line across the broken landscape, like mortar between chapped bricks.

Sweet Gierra, what am I doing?

The open road. Achamian had once told her it was like a string tied about his neck, choking him if he did not follow. She almost wished it felt that way now. She could understand being dragged to some destination. Instead, it felt like a long fall, and a sheer one at that. Simply staring down it made her feel dizzy.

Such a fool! It's just a road!

She had rehearsed her plan a thousand times. Why fear now?

She was not a wife. Her purse she carried between her legs. She would, as the soldiers said, sell peaches on the way to Momemn. Men might stand midway between women and the Gods, but they hungered like beasts.

The road would be kind. Eventually, she would find the Holy War. And in the Holy War she would find Achamian. She would clutch his cheek and kiss him, at long last a fellow traveller.

Then she would tell him what had happened, of the danger.

Deep breath. She tasted dust and cold.

She began walking, her limbs so light they might have danced.

It would be dark soon.

CHAPTER
TEN

SUMNA

How should one describe the terrible majesty of the Holy War?
Even then, still unblooded, it was both frightening and wondrous
to behold, a great beast whose limbs were composed of entire
nations—Galeoth, Thunyerus, Ce Tydonn, Conriya, High
Ainon, and the Nansurium—and with the Scarlet Spires as the
dragon's maw, no less. Not since the days of the Ceneian Empire
or the Ancient North has the world witnessed such an assembly.
Even diseased by politics, it was a thing of awe.

—DRUSAS ACHAMIAN, *COMPENDIUM OF THE FIRST HOLY WAR*

Midwinter, 4111 Year-of-the-Tusk, Sumna

Even after night fell, Esmenet continued walking, intoxicated by
the sheer impossibility of it. Several times she even raced into the
dark fields, her feet whisking through frosted grass, her arms
outstretched as she twirled beneath the Nail of Heaven.

The cold was iron hard, the spaces endless. The darkness was
crisp, as though scraped of sight and smell by winter's razor. So
different from the humid murk of Sumna, where inky sensations
stained everything. Here, in the cold and dark, the parchment of

the world was blank. Here, it seemed, was where it all started.

She at once savoured and shuddered at the thought. The Consult, Achamian had once told her, believed much the same thing.

Eventually, as the night waxed, she sobered. She reminded herself of the arduous days ahead, of the dread purpose that drove her.

Achamian was being watched.

She could not think this without remembering that night with the stranger. Sometimes she felt nauseated, glimpsing the pitch that was his seed everytime she blinked. Other times she grew very cold, reviewing and assessing every spoken word, every stinging climax with the dispassion of a tax-farmer. She found it difficult to believe she had been that whorish woman, treacherous, adulterate . . .

But she had been.

It was not her betrayal that shamed her. Achamian, she knew, would not fault her. No, what shamed her was what she had *felt*, not what she had done.

Some prostitutes so despised what they did they sought pain and punishment whenever they coupled. Esmenet, however, counted herself among those who could laugh, from time to time, about being paid for being pleasured. Her pleasure was her own, no matter who fondled her.

But not that night. The pleasure had been more intense than any she'd ever experienced. She had felt it. Gasped it. Shuddered it. But she had not owned it. Her body had been notched that night. And it shamed her to fury.

She often grew wet at the thought of his abdomen against her belly. Sometimes she flushed and tensed at the memory of her climaxes. Whoever he was, whatever he was, he had taken her body captive, had seized what was hers and remade it not in his own image, but in the image of what he needed her to be. Infinitely receptive. Infinitely docile. Infinitely gratified.

But where her body groped, her intellect grasped. She quickly realized that if the stranger knew about her, he knew about Inrau.

And if he knew about Inrau, there was simply no way his death could have been a suicide. This was why she had to find Achamian. The possibility that Inrau had committed suicide had almost broken him.

"What if it's true, Esmi? What if he did kill himself?"

"He didn't. Enough, Akka. Please."

"He did! . . . Oh, sweet Gods, I can feel it! I forced him into a position where all he could do was betray. Me or Maithanet. Don't you see, Esmi? I forced him to pit love against love!"

"You're drunk, Akka. Your fears always get the best of you when you're drunk."

"Sweet Gods . . . I killed him."

How empty her reassurances had been: wooden recitations born of flagging patience born of the unaccountable suspicion that he punished himself simply to secure her pity. Why had she been so cold? So selfish? At one point, she had even caught herself resenting Inrau, blaming him for Achamian's departure. How could she think such things?

But that was going to change. Many things were going to change.

Somehow, impossibly, she had a part in whatever it was that was happening. She would be its equal.

You did not kill him, my love. I know this!

And she also knew *who* the killer was. The stranger, she supposed, could have hailed from any of the Schools, but somehow she knew he did not. What she had suffered was beyond the Three Seas.

The Consult. They had murdered Inrau, and they had ravished her.

The *Consult*.

As terrifying as this intuition was, it was also exhilarating. No one, not even Achamian, had seen the Consult in centuries. And yet she . . . But she did not ponder this overmuch, because when she did, she began to feel . . . fortunate. That she could not bear.

So she told herself she travelled for Achamian. And in unguarded moments, she styled herself a character from *The Sagas*, like Ginsil or Ysilka, a wife mortally ensnared in her husband's machinations. The road before her, it seemed, would sing with a furtive glamour, as though hidden witnesses to her heroism watched her every step.

She shivered in her cloak. Her breath piled before her. She walked, pondering the sense of chill expectancy that accompanied so many winter mornings. Dawn's light was slow in coming.

By mid-morning, she came across a roadside hostel, where she loitered in hopes of joining the small group of wayfarers who assembled in its yards. Two old men, their backs stooped beneath great bushels of dried fruits, waited with her. From their scowls Esmenet supposed they had glimpsed the tattoo on the back of her left hand. Everyone, it seemed, knew that Sumna branded her whores.

When the group at last took to the road, she followed it as unobtrusively as possible. A small cadre of blue-skinned priests, devotees of Jukan, led them, singing soft hymns and clinking finger cymbals. A handful of the others joined them in singing, but most kept to themselves, trudging, muttering in low voices. Esmenet saw one of the old men speaking to the driver of a wain. The teamster turned and looked at her in the blank way she had seen so often: the look of one who yearns for what must be loathed. He glanced away when she smiled. Sooner or later, she knew, he would manufacture some accidental way to speak to her.

Then she would have to make a decision.

But then a band on her left sandal snapped. She was able to knot the ends back into usable shape, but they pinched and chafed the skin beneath her woollen socks. Blisters broke, and soon she was limping. She cursed the teamster for not hurrying. She heartily cursed the canon that made it illegal for women to wear boots in the Nansurium. Then the knot gave way, and try as she might, she could not repair it.

The group dwindled farther and farther down the road.

She thrust the sandal into her satchel and began walking without it. Her foot went almost immediately numb. After twenty steps, the first hole opened in her sock. A short time after, her sock was little more than a ragged skirt about her ankle. She hopped as much as she walked, frequently pausing to rub warmth into the sole of her foot. She could see no sign of the others. Behind her, she glimpsed a distant band of men. They seemed to be walking pack animals . . . or warhorses.

She prayed it was the former.

The road she followed was the Karian Way—a relic of the Ceneian Empire, though kept in good repair by the Emperor. It ran straight through the province of Massentia, which in summer people called the Golden because of its endless fields of grain. The problem with the Karian Way was that it struck deep into the Kyranae Plains rather than heading directly toward Momemn. More than a thousand years before, it had linked Holy Sumna to ancient Cenei. Now it was maintained only so far as it serviced Massentia; it trailed into pasture, Esmenet had been told, after intersecting the far more important Pon Way, which did lead to Momemn.

Despite this detour through the interior, Esmenet had chosen the Karian Way after much careful deliberation. Even though she could neither afford nor read maps, and even though she had never before set foot outside of Sumna, she possessed intimate knowledge of this and many other roads.

All prostitutes ranked their custom according to their tastes. Some liked large men, others small. Some favoured priests with their hesitant, uncallused hands, while others favoured soldiers and their rough confidence. But Esmenet had always prized experience. Those who had suffered, who had overcome, who had seen far-away or astounding things—these were the men she prized.

When she was younger, she had coupled with such men and thought: *Now I'm part of what they've seen. Now I'm more than what I was.* When she pestered them with questions afterward, she did so as much to learn the details of her enrichment as out of curiosity. They left lightened of both silver and seed, but she had convinced herself that they took some part of her with them, that she had expanded somehow, that she, Esmenet, haunted eyes that watched and warred with the world.

Several people had cured her of this belief. There was the old whore, Pirasha, who would have starved had it not been for Esmenet's generosity. "No, sweetling," she once told her. "When women dip their cups in men, they draw only what's been stolen." Then there was the dashing Kidruhil cavalryman, the one she had thought she loved, who came to her a second time without any recollection of the first. "You must be mistaken," he had exclaimed. "I'd remember a beauty such as you!"

Then she had given birth to her daughter.

She could remember thinking, not long after her daughter was born, that childbirth had signalled the end of her delusions. She knew now, however, that it had simply marked the transition from one set of self-deceptions to another. The death of a child: that marked the end of delusions. Gathering little clothing into a bundle, giving it to the expectant mother the floor below, saying kind words to ease her—*her!*—of her embarrassment . . .

Much foolishness had died with her daughter, and much bitterness had been born. But Esmenet was not, like some, inclined to spite. Even though she knew it belittled her, she continued to indulge her hunger for stories of the world, and she continued to prize the best storytellers. She wrapped her legs around them—gladly. She pretended to rise to their ardour, and sometimes, given the curious way pretence so often blurred into actuality, she did rise. Afterward, as their interests receded into the dark world they had come from, they became impenetrable. Even her kinder patrons seemed danger-ous. So many men, she'd found, harboured a void of some kind, a place accountable only to other men.

Then the real seduction would begin. "Tell me," she sometimes purred, "what have you seen that makes you more . . . more than other men?" Most found the question amusing. Others were perplexed, annoyed, indifferent, or even outraged. A rare handful, Achamian among them, found it fascinating. But every one of them answered. Men needed to be more. This was why, she had decided, so many of them gambled: they sought coin, certainly, but they also yearned for a demonstration, a sign that the world, the Gods, the future—*someone*—had somehow set them apart.

So they told her stories—thousands of them over the years. They smiled at their accounts, thinking they thrilled her, as they had when she was young, with knowledge of just *who* had bedded her. And with one exception, none of them guessed that she cared nothing for what their stories said about them, and everything for what their stories said about the world.

Achamian had understood.

"You do this with all your custom?" he once asked without warning.

She wasn't shocked. Others had asked as much. "It comforts me to know my men are more than cocks."

A half-truth. But true to form, Achamian was sceptical. He frowned, saying, "It's a pity."

This had stung, even though she had no idea what he meant. "What's a pity?"

"That you're not a man," he replied. "If you were a man, you wouldn't need to make teachers of everyone who used you."

She had wept in his arms that night.

But she had continued her studies, ranging far through the eyes of others.

This was why she knew that Massentia was safe, that despite the longer distance, the Karian and Pon Ways were a far better route for a lone woman to take than the more direct routes along the coast. And this was also why she knew enough to walk with other travellers, so those passing by would simply assume she belonged.

And this was why her broken sandal frightened her so. Before, intoxicated by openness and sheer daring, she had felt unburdened by her solitude. Now it weighed against her. She felt exposed, as though archers lay hidden behind every clutch of trees, waiting for a glimpse of her tattooed hand, for a whispered word, or for some other inevitable cue.

The road climbed, and she hobbled on as best she could. A welling sense of despair only made her bare foot seem more painful. How could she walk all the way to Momemn like this? How many times had she been told that safe travel was always a matter of preparation? Each painful step seemed a rebuke.

The Karian Way gradually dropped before her, levelling over a shallow floodplain, then crossing what looked to be a minor river before spearing into the dark hills that ringed the horizon. Jutting from thickets of leafless trees, a ruined Ceneian aqueduct parsed the near distances, crumbling into small fields of debris where the locals had pillaged its stone. Mud tracks wound into the farther heights, skirting fallow fields, disappearing into climbing tracts of forest. But what held Esmenet's hope and attention were the rustic buildings clustered about the bridge: a village of some kind, trailing thin lines of smoke into the grey sky.

She had some money. More than enough to repair her sandal.

She chided herself for her misgivings as she neared the village. One of the things that characterized Massentia, she had heard, was the fact that it possessed few of the great plantations that dominated so much of the Empire. Massentia was a land of free yeomen and craftsmen. Forthright. Honest. Proud. Or so she had heard.

But then she remembered the way such men scowled when they saw her hanging from her window in Sumna. "Men who own their drudgery," old Pirasha had once told her, "think they own the Truth as well." And the Truth was not kind to whores.

Esmenet cursed herself for worrying. Everyone said Massentia was safe.

She hobbled onto the packed earth of what passed for a humble market square, searching the surrounding shanties and facades for a cobbler. When she found none, she smelled the air for some sign of the fish oil that tanners hammered into their hides. A strip of leather was all she really needed. She passed thawing heaps of clay, then four interconnected potters' sheds. In one, an old man worked his wheel despite the cold, coaxing curves from the clay with his thumbs. The mouth of an oven glowed behind him. His cough, which sounded like gurgling mud, startled her.

She idly wondered if the village was poxed.

A group of five boys mooned about the entrance to a stable, staring. The oldest, or at least the tallest, watched her with frank admiration. He would have been handsome had his eyes been even. She remembered one of her patrons telling her it was rare to find beautiful children in villages such as these, because they were so often sold to wealthy travellers. Esmenet found herself wondering whether a bid had ever been made on this boy.

She smiled as he sauntered toward her. *Perhaps he—*

"Are you a *whore?*" he asked baldly.

Esmenet could only stare in shock and fury.

"She is! She is!" another boy cried. "From Sumna! That's why she hides her hand!"

A number of soldier's curses came to her. "Go finger your chimney," she snapped, "you little fucking pissant."

The boy grinned, and Esmenet immediately realized he was one of *them:* men who think more of a dog's bark than a woman's words.

"Let me see your hand."

Something in his voice unsettled her.

"Don't you have stalls to muck?" *Slave,* her tone sneered.

The casual viciousness of his look hardened into something else. When he grabbed for her hand, she struck him on the cheek. He stumbled back, shocked.

Recovering himself, he stooped to the ground. "She's a whore," he told his compatriots, his tone grim, as though unfortunate truths entailed unfortunate consequences. He stood, rolling a dirty stone between his fingers. "An adulterate whore."

A nervous moment passed. The four hesitated. They stood on a threshold of some kind, and they knew it, even if they understood nothing of its significance. Rather than rallying them with words, the handsome one whipped his stone.

Esmenet ducked, dodged it. But the others were crouching, gathering missiles of their own.

They began pelting her. She cursed, drawing up her arms. The thick wool of her cloak saved her from any real harm.

"Bastards!" she cried. They paused, at once cowed and amused by her ferocity. One of the boys, the fat one, guffawed when she bent to scoop up her own stones. She hit him first, just above his left eyebrow, splitting skin and sending him wailing to his knees. The others simply stared, dumbstruck. Blood had been drawn.

She raised another stone in her right hand, hoping they would duck and run. As a child, before her body bid her to other vocations, she had worked the wharves, earning bread or quartercoppers by throwing stones at scavenging gulls. She had been very good.

But the tall one struck first, throwing a fistful of dirt at her face. Most of it missed—the fool threw as though his arm were made of rope—but some grit momentarily blinded her. She frantically rubbed at her eyes. Then an explosion in her ear sent her staggering. Another stone bruised off her fingers . . .

What was happening?

"Enough! Enough!" a hoarse voice boomed. "What are you boys doing?"

The fat boy still wailed. Esmenet blinked at the sting, saw an old man wearing stained Shrial vestments in the boys' midst, brandishing a fist like the knob of a leg bone.

"Stoning her!" the half-handsome instigator called out. "She's a whore!" The others eagerly seconded him.

The old priest scowled at them for a moment, then turned to her. She could see him clearly now, the liver spots, the miserly hunch of someone who had screeched in innumerable faces. His lips were purple in the chill.

"Is this true?"

He snatched her hand in his own, which was shockingly strong, and studied the tattoo. He peered into her face.

"Are you a priestess?" he barked. "A servant of Gierra?"

She could tell that he knew the answer, that he asked only out of some perverse urge to humiliate and instruct. Staring into his bleary eyes, she suddenly understood her peril.

Sweet Sejenus . . .

"Y-yes," she stammered.

"Liar! This is a whore's mark," he cried, twisting her hand to her face as though trying to shove food into her mouth. "A *whore's* mark!"

"I'm a whore no more," she protested.

"Liar! Liar!"

A sudden coldness descended on Esmenet. She graced him with a false smile, then wrested back possession of her hand. The sputtering old fool stumbled backward. She looked briefly at the crowd that had gathered, glanced scathingly at the boys, then turned back to the road.

"Do not walk away from me!" the old priest howled. "Do not walk away from me!"

She continued walking with what dignity she could muster.

"Suffer not a whore to live," the old priest recited, "for she maketh a pit of her womb!"

Esmenet halted.

"Suffer not a whore to *breathe*," the priest continued, his tone now gleeful, "for she mocks the seed of the righteous! Stone her so that thy hand shall not be tempt—"

Esmenet whirled. *"Enough!"* she exploded.

Stunned silence.

"I am *damned!*" she cried. "Don't you see? I'm already dead! Isn't that enough?"

Too many eyes watched her. She turned away, continued limping toward the Karian Way.

"Whore!" someone shouted.

Something cracked against the back of her skull. She fell to her knees. Another stone bruised off her shoulder. She raised warding hands, stumbled to her feet, tried walking quickly forward. But the youths were capering around her again, bombarding her with small, river-round stones. Then she glimpsed the tall one in her periphery, hefting something as big as his hand. She cringed. The concussion snapped her teeth together, sent her teetering, toppling. She rolled in cold muck, pulled herself to all fours, raised one knee from the ground. A small stone slapped into her cheek, brought stinging tears to her left eye, then she was up, walking as best as she could manage.

This entire time everything had seemed nightmarishly practical. She needed to leave as quickly as she could. The stones were no more than gusts of rain and wind, impersonal obstacles.

Now she was weeping uncontrollably. "Stop!" she shrieked. "Leave me alone!"

"*Whore!*" the priest roared.

A much larger crowd had gathered about her now, jeering, reaching to the gravelly mud at their feet.

A numbing thump near her spine. Shoulders jerking backward. An involuntary hand reaching. An explosion in her temple. Then the ground again. Spitting grit.

Stop! Pleassse!

Was that her voice?

Small, sharp, against her forehead. Arms up. Curling like a dog.

Please. Someone.

The sound of thunder. Then a great shadow blotting the sky. Through tears and fingers, she looked up, saw the veined belly of a horse and above, a rider peering down at her. Handsome, full-lipped face. Large brown eyes at once furious and concerned.

A Shrial Knight.

The stones had stopped. Esmenet wailed into her muddy hands.

"Who started this?" a voice boomed.

"See here!" the priest roared. "These matt—"

The Shrial Knight leaned forward and struck him with a mailed fist.

"Pick him up!" he commanded the others. "*Now.*"

Three men scrambled to pull the priest to his feet. Spit and blood trailed from his trembling lips. He loosed a single, coughing sob, looked about in dazed horror.

"Y-you haven't the authority!" he cried.

"Authority?" he laughed. "You would like to debate authority?"

While the Shrial Knight bullied the priest, Esmenet struggled to her feet. She wiped the blood and tears from her face, then brushed at the mud caked to her woollen robe. Her heart hammered in her ears, and twice she feared she would swoon for lack of breath. The urge to scream almost overcame her, not in terror or in pain, but in disbelief and naked outrage. How had this happened? What had happened?

She glimpsed the Shrial Knight striking the priest again, and cursed herself for flinching. Why should she pity that obscene ingrate? She breathed deeply. Wiped at more burning tears. Calmed.

Her hands cupped before her, she turned to the youth who had started it all. She glared at him with all the hate she could muster, then slipped her pinky finger from the others so that it wagged like a tiny phallus. She glanced down, to be sure he noticed, then smiled at him wickedly. The boy paled.

He looked to the Shrial Knight, all fright and apprehension, then to his friends, who had also noticed Esmenet's derisive attention. Two of them grinned despite themselves, and one, possessed of that uncanny and unsettling ability of the young to conspire with those they had tormented only moments earlier, cried out, "It's true!"

"Come," the Shrial Knight said to her, holding down a hand. "I've had my fill of these provincial fools."

"Who are you?" she croaked, once again overwhelmed by tears.

"Cutias Sarcellus," the man said warmly, "First Knight-Commander of the Shrial Knights."

She reached up, and he took her tattooed hand.

———— ✿ ————

Men of the Tusk hastened throughout the darkness—tall figures, mostly in shadow save for the rare glimmer of iron. Leading his mule, Achamian hurried among them. Their bright eyes afforded him only passing interest. They had, Achamian supposed, grown accustomed to strangers.

The journey troubled Achamian. Never before had he threaded his way through such an encampment. Each firelight he skirted seemed a world filled with its own amusement or desperation. He heard drifting fragments of conversation, glimpsed combative faces over fire. He moved between these pockets, part of a shadowy procession. Twice, he climbed hills that rose high enough to reveal the River Phayus and its congested alluvial plains. Each time he was stilled by awe. Shining fires peppered the distance—those near pocking the darkness with glimpses of canvas and warlike men, those far forming constellations that glittered across the slopes. Years ago he'd watched an Ainoni drama held in an amphitheatre near Carythusal, and he'd been struck by the contrast of the dark onlookers and the illuminated performers on the floor. Here, it seemed, were a thousand such dramas. So many men, so far from home. Here, he could sound the true measure of Maithanet's strength.

Such numbers. How can we fail?

He pondered this thought, "we," for some time.

To the west, he could discern the winding circuit of Momemn's walls, her monstrous towers capped by the glow of torches. He veered toward them, the ground becoming more bald and packed the closer they loomed. Daring the light of several Conriyan fires, he asked where he might find the contingent from Attrempus. He crossed a creaking footbridge over the stagnant waters of a canal. Finally he found the camp of his old friend Krijates Xinemus, the Marshal of Attrempus.

Though Achamian immediately recognized Xinemus, he paused in the darkness beyond the firelight, watching him. Proyas had once told him that he and Xinemus looked remarkably similar, like, as he put it, "strong and weak brothers." Of course it had never occurred to Proyas that this comparison might offend his old teacher. Like many arrogant men, Proyas thought his insults an extension of his honesty.

Cradling a bowl of wine, Xinemus sat before a small fire, discussing something in low tones with three of his senior officers. Even in the ruddy firelight, he looked tired, as though he spoke of some issue far beyond their ability to redress. He scratched absently at the dead skin that, Achamian knew, perpetually bedevilled his ears, then unaccountably turned and peered into the darkness—at Achamian.

The Marshal of Attrempus scowled. "Show yourself, friend," he called.

For some reason, Achamian found himself speechless.

Now the others were staring at him also. He heard one of them, Dinchases, mutter something about wraiths. The man to his right, Zenkappa, made the sign of the Tusk.

"That's no wraith," Xinemus said, coming to his feet. He ducked his head as though peering through fog. "Achamian?"

"If you weren't here," the third officer, Iryssas, said to Xinemus, "I'd swear it was you . . ."

Glancing at Iryssas, Xinemus suddenly strode out toward Achamian, his expression one of baffled joy. "Drusas Achamian? Akka?"

Breath finally came to Achamian's lips. "Hello, Zin."

"Akka!" the Marshal cried, catching him like a sack in his arms.

"Lord Marshal."

"You smell like an ass's ass, my friend," Xinemus laughed, pushing him back. "Like the stink of stink!"

"The days have been hard," the sorcerer said.

"Fear not. They'll grow harder still."

Claiming he'd sent his slaves to bed, Xinemus assisted him with his baggage, saw to the care of his mule, then helped him pitch his battered tent. Years had passed since Achamian had last seen the Marshal of Attrempus, and though he'd thought their friendship immune to the passage of time, their talk was awkward at first. By and large they discussed trivialities: the weather, the temperament of his mule. Whenever one of them mentioned something more substantial, an inexplicable shyness forced the other to give a noncommittal reply.

"So how have you been?" Xinemus eventually asked.

"As well as one could expect."

For Achamian, everything seemed horribly unreal, so much so that he half-expected Xinemus to call him Seswatha. His friendship with Xinemus was one born of the far-away Conriyan court. To meet the man here while on mission embarrassed him in the manner of someone caught, not in a lie, but in circumstances that, given enough time, were certain to make a liar of him. Achamian found himself racking his soul, wondering what he'd told Xinemus of his previous missions. Had he been honest? Or had he succumbed to the juvenile urge to appear to be more than he was?

Did I tell him I was a broken-down fool?

"Ah, with you Akka, one never knows what to expect."

"So the others are with you?" he asked, even though he knew the answer. "Zenkappa? Dinchases?"

Another fear had assailed him. Xinemus was a pious man, among the most pious Achamian had ever known. In Conriya, Achamian had been a tutor who also happened to be a Schoolman. But here he was a Schoolman through and through. There would be no overlooking his sacrilege here—in the midst of the Holy War, no less! How much would Xinemus tolerate? Perhaps, Achamian thought, this was a mistake. Perhaps he should camp elsewhere—alone.

"Not for long," Xinemus replied. "I'll send them off."

"There's no need . . ."

Xinemus held a knot up to the dim firelight. "And the Dreams?"

"What of them?"

"You told me once that they waxed and waned, that sometimes details in them changed, and that you'd decided to record them in the hope of deciphering them."

The fact that Xinemus remembered this unsettled him.

"Tell me," he said in a clumsy attempt to switch topics, "where are the Scarlet Spires?"

Xinemus grinned. "I was wondering when you were going to ask . . . Somewhere south of here, at one of the Emperor's villas— or so I've been told." He hammered at a wooden stake, cursed when he smashed his thumb. "Are you worried about them?"

"I'd be a fool not to be."

"They covet your learning that much?"

"Yes. The Gnosis is iron to their bronze . . . Though I doubt they'd try anything in the midst of the Holy War." For a School of blasphemers to be part of the Holy War already beggared the understanding of the Inrithi. For them to actually speak their blasphemy in pursuit of their own arcane ends would be beyond all toleration.

"Is that why . . . they sent you?"

Xinemus rarely referred to the Mandate by name. They were always "they."

"To watch the Scarlet Spires? In part, I suppose. But of course there's"—an image of Inrau flashed across his soul's eye—"more . . . There's always more."

Who killed you?

Somehow Xinemus had secured his gaze in the darkness. "What's wrong, Akka? What's happened?"

Achamian looked to his hands. He wanted to tell Xinemus, to recount his absurd suspicions regarding the Shriah, to explain the deranged circumstances surrounding Inrau's death. He certainly trusted the man as he trusted no other, inside or outside of the Mandate. But the story just seemed too long, too tortuous, and too polluted by his own failings and frailties to be shared. Esmenet he could tell, but then she was a whore. Shameless.

"Well enough, I suppose," Achamian said breezily, tugging on the ropes. "It'll keep the rain off me at least."

Xinemus studied him for a wordless moment. Thankfully, he did not press the issue.

They joined the other three men about Xinemus's fire. Two were captains of the Attrempus garrison, leather-faced contemporaries of their Marshal. The senior officer, Dinchases—or Bloody Dench, as he was called—had been with Xinemus for as long as Achamian had known the Marshal. The junior, Zenkappa, was a Nilnameshi slave Xinemus had inherited from his father and later freed for valour on the field. Both, as far as Achamian could tell, were good men. The third man, Iryssas, was the youngest son of Xinemus's only surviving uncle and, if Achamian remembered correctly, Majordomo of House Krijates.

But none of the men acknowledged their arrival. They were either too drunk or too engrossed in discussion. Dinchases, it seemed, was telling a story.

". . . then the big one, the Thunyeri—"

"Do you blasted idiots even remember Achamian?" Xinemus cried. "Drusas Achamian?"

Wiping eyes and stifling laughs, the three men turned to appraise him. Zenkappa smiled and raised his bowl. Dinchases, however, regarded him narrowly, and Iryssas with outright hostility.

Dinchases glanced at Xinemus's scowl, then reluctantly raised his bowl as well. Both he and Zenkappa inclined their heads, then poured a libation. "Well met, Achamian," Zenkappa said with genuine warmth. As a freed slave, Achamian imagined, he perhaps had less difficulty with pariahs. Dinchases and Iryssas, on the other hand, were caste nobles—Iryssas one of true rank.

"I see you pitched your tent," Iryssas remarked casually. He possessed the guarded, probing look of a dangerous drunk.

Achamian said nothing.

"So I suppose I should resign myself to your presence then, eh, Achamian?"

Achamian met his gaze directly, cursed himself for swallowing. "I suppose you should."

Xinemus glared at his young cousin. "The Scarlet Spires are actually part of this Holy War, Iryssas. You should welcome Achamian's presence. I know I do."

Achamian had witnessed countless exchanges such as these. The faithful trying to rationalize their fraternization with sorcerers. The rationale was always the same: *They are useful . . .*

"Perhaps you're right, Cousin. Enemies of our enemies, eh?" Conriyans were jealous of their hatreds. After centuries of skirmishing with High Ainon and the Scarlet Spires, they had come, however grudgingly, to appreciate the Mandate. Overmuch, the priests would say. But of all the Schools only the Mandate, steeped in the Gnosis of the Ancient North, was a match for the Scarlet Spires.

Iryssas raised his cup, then emptied it across the dust at his feet. "May the gods drink deep, Drusas Achamian. May they celebrate one who is damned—"

Cursing, Xinemus kicked the fire. A cloud of sparks and ash engulfed Iryssas. He fell backward, crying out, instinctively beating at his hair and beard. Xinemus leapt after him, roaring: *"What did you say? What did you say?"*

Though of slighter build than Iryssas, Xinemus pulled him to his knees as if he were a child, berating him with curses and open-handed cuffs. Dinchases looked to Achamian apologetically. "We're not with him," he said slyly. "We're just piss drunk." Zenkappa found this too hilarious to remain seated. He rolled on the ground in the shadows beyond his log, howling with laughter.

Even Iryssas was laughing, though in the hounded way of a henpecked spouse. "Enough!" he cried to Xinemus. "I'll apologize! *I'll apologize!*"

Shocked both by Iryssas's insolence and by the violence of Xinemus's response, Achamian watched, his mouth agape. Then he realized he'd never really seen Xinemus in the company of his soldiers before.

Iryssas scrambled back to his seat, his hair askew and his black beard streaked with ash. At once smiling and frowning, he leaned forward on his camp stool toward Achamian. He was bowing, Achamian realized, but was too lazy to lift his ass from his seat. "I *do* apologize," he said, looking to Achamian with bemused sincerity. "And I do like you, Achamian, even though you *are*"—he shot a ducking look at his lord and cousin—"a damned sorcerer."

Zenkappa began howling anew. Despite himself, Achamian smiled and bowed in return. Iryssas, he realized, was one of those men whose hatreds were far too whimsical to become the fixed point of an obsession. He could despise and embrace by guileless turns. Such men, Achamian had learned, inevitably mirrored the integrity or depravity of their lords.

"Besotted fool!" Xinemus cried at Iryssas. "Look at your eyes! More squint than a monkey's asshole!"

Further paroxysms of laughter followed. This time Achamian found their hilarity irresistible.

But he laughed far longer than the others, wailing as though possessed by some demon. Tears of relief creased his cheeks. How long had it been?

The others grew quiet, watched as he struggled with his composure.

"It's been too long," Achamian at last managed. His breath shuddered as he exhaled. His tears suddenly stung.

"Far too long, Akka," Xinemus said, placing a friendly hand on his shoulder. "But you're back and for a time free from the wiles of conniving men. Tonight, you can drink in peace."

He slept fitfully that night. For whatever reason, heavy drinking at once intensified and deadened the Dreams. The way they slurred into one another made them seem less immediate, more dreamlike, but the passions that accompanied them . . . They were unbearable at the best of times. With drink they became lunatic with misery.

He already lay awake by time Paäta, one of Xinemus's body-slaves, arrived with a basin of fresh water. While he washed, Xinemus pressed his grinning face through the flaps and challenged him to a game of benjuka.

Soon afterward, Achamian found himself sitting cross-legged on a thatched mat opposite Xinemus, studying the gilded benjuka plate between them. A sagging canopy sheltered them from the sun, which burned so bright that the surrounding encampment seemed a desert bazaar despite the chill. All that was missing, Achamian mused, were camels. Though most of the passersby were Conriyans from Xinemus's own household, he saw all manner of Inrithi: Galeoth, stripped to the waist and painted for some festival that apparently confused winter for summer; Thunyeri, sporting the black-iron hauberks they never seemed to shed; and even an Ainoni nobleman, whose elaborate gowns looked positively ludicrous amid the welter of larded canvas, wains, and haphazard stalls.

"Hard to believe, isn't it?" Xinemus said, apparently referring to the sheer numbers of Inrithi.

Achamian shrugged. "Yes and no . . . I was at the Hagerna when Maithanet declared the Holy War. Sometimes I wonder whether Maithanet called the Three Seas or the Three Seas called Maithanet."

"You were at the *Hagerna?*" Xinemus asked. His expression had darkened.

"Yes." *I even met your Shriah . . .*

Xinemus snorted in the bullish way he often used to express disapproval. "Your move, Akka."

Achamian searched Xinemus's face, but the Marshal seemed thoroughly absorbed by the geometries of piece and possibility across the plate. Achamian had agreed to the game knowing it would drive the others away, and so allow him to tell Xinemus about what had happened in Sumna. But he'd forgotten how benjuka tended to bring out the worst in them. Every time they played benjuka, they bickered like harem eunuchs.

Benjuka was a relic, a survivor of the end of the world. It had been played in the courts of Trysë, Atrithau, and Mehtsonc before the Apocalypse, much as it was studied in the gardens of Carythusal, Nenciphon, and Momemn now. But what distinguished benjuka was not its age. In general, there was a troubling affinity between games and life, and nowhere was this affinity more striking, or more disturbing, than in benjuka.

Like life, games were governed by rules. But unlike life, games were utterly defined by those rules. The rules *were* the game, and if one played by different rules, then one simply played a different game. Since a fixed framework of rules determined the meaning of every move as a move, games possessed a clarity that made life seem a drunken brawl by comparison. The proprieties were indubitable, the permutations secure; only the outcome was shrouded.

The cunning of benjuka lay in the absence of this fixed framework. Rather than providing an immutable ground, the rules of benjuka were yet another move *within* the game, yet another piece to be played. And this made benjuka the very image of life, a game of baffling complexities and near poetic subtleties. Other games could be chronicled as shifting patterns of pieces and number-stick results, but benjuka gave rise to *histories*, and whatever possessed history possessed the very structure of the world. Some, it was said, had bent themselves to the benjuka plate and lifted their heads as prophets.

Achamian was not among them.

He pondered the plate, rubbing his hands together for warmth. Xinemus taunted him with a nasty chuckle.

"Always so dour when you play benjuka."

"It's a wretched game."

"You say that only because you try too hard."

"No. I say that because I lose."

But Xinemus was right. The *Abenjukala,* a classic text on benjuka from Ceneian times, began, "Where games measure the limits of intellect, benjuka measures the limits of soul." The complexities of benjuka were such that a player could never intellectually master the plate and so *force* another to yield. Benjuka, as the anonymous author put it, was like love. One could never force another to love. The more one grasped for it, the more elusive it became. Benjuka likewise punished a grasping heart. Where other games required industrious cunning, benjuka demanded something more. Wisdom, perhaps.

With an air of chagrin, Achamian moved the only stone among his silver pieces—a replacement for a piece stolen, or so Xinemus claimed, by one of his slaves. Another aggravation. Though pieces were nothing more than how they were used, the stone impoverished his play somehow, broke the miserly spell of a complete set.

Why do I get the stone?

"If you were drunk," Xinemus said, answering his move decisively, "I might understand why you did that."

How could he make jokes? Achamian stared at the patterns across the plate, realizing that the rules had shifted yet again—this time disastrously. He searched for options but saw none.

Xinemus smiled winningly and began paring his nails with a knife. "Proyas will feel the same way," he said, "when he finally arrives." Something in his tone made Achamian look up.

"Why's that?"

"You've heard of the recent disaster."

"What disaster?"

"The Vulgar Holy War has been destroyed."

"What?" Achamian had heard talk of the Vulgar Holy War before leaving Sumna. Weeks ago, before the arrival of the bulk of the Holy War, a number of great lords from Galeoth, Conriya, and High Ainon had decided to march against the heathen on their own. The moniker "vulgar" had been given to them because of the hosts of lordless rabble that followed. It had never occurred to Achamian to ask how it fared. *It's started. The bloodshed has started.*

"On the Plains of Mengedda," Xinemus continued. "The heathen Sapatishah, Skaurus, sent the tarred heads of Tharschilka, Kumrezzer, and Calmemunis to the Emperor as a warning."

"Calmemunis? You mean Proyas's cousin?"

"Arrogant, headstrong fool! I begged him not to march, Akka. I reasoned, I shouted, I even grovelled—*abased* myself like a fool!—but the dog wouldn't listen."

Achamian had met Calmemunis once, in the court of Proyas's father. Outrageous conceit coupled with stupidity—enough to make Achamian wince. "Aside from thinking the God Himself stirred him, why do you think he marched?"

"Because he knew once Proyas arrived, he'd be little more than a fawning lapdog. He's never forgiven Proyas for the incident at Paremti."

"The Battle of Paremti? What happened?"

"You don't know? I've forgotten how long it's been, old friend. I've much gossip to share."

"Later," Achamian said. "Tell me what happened at Paremti."

"Proyas had Calmemunis whipped."

"Whipped?" This concerned Achamian deeply. Had his old student changed so much? "For cowardice?"

As though he shared Achamian's concern, Xinemus's face darkened. "No. For impiety."

"You jest. Proyas had a peer whipped for *impiety*? How far has his fanaticism gone, Zin?"

"Too far," Xinemus said quickly, as though ashamed for his lord. "But for a brief time only. I was sorely disappointed in him, Akka. Heartbroken that the godlike child you and I had taught had grown to be a man of such . . . extremes."

Proyas had been a godlike child. Over the four years he had spent as court tutor in the Conriyan capital of Aöknyssus, Achamian had fallen in love with the boy—even more than with his legendary mother. Sweet memories. Strolling through sunlit foyers and along murky garden paths, discussing history, logic, and mathematics, and answering a never-ending cataract of questions . . .

"Master Achamian? Where have all the dragons gone?"

"The dragons are within us, young Proyas. Within *you*."

The knitted brow. The hands clenched in frustration. Yet another indirect answer from his tutor.

"So there are no more dragons in the world, Master Achamian?"

"You're in the world, Proyas, are you not?"

Xinemus had been Proyas's sword trainer at the same time, and it was through their periodic squabbles over the boy that they had come to respect each other. As much as Achamian loved the Prince, Xinemus—who nurtured the devotion he would need to serve the child as king—loved Proyas more. So much so that when Xinemus glimpsed the strength of the teacher in the pupil, he invited Achamian to his villa on the Meneanor Sea.

"You've made a child wise," Xinemus had said, attempting to explain the extraordinary offer. Very rarely did caste nobles host sorcerers.

"And you've made him dangerous," Achamian had replied.

They had found their friendship somewhere in the laughter that had followed.

"Fanatic for a time?" Achamian now asked. "Does that mean he's regained his senses?"

Xinemus grimaced, absently scratched the side of his nose. "Somewhat. The Holy War and his acquaintance with Maithanet have rekindled his zeal, but he's wiser now. More patient. More tolerant of weakness."

"Your lessons, I imagine. What did you do?"

"I beat him until he was bloody."

Achamian laughed.

"I'm quite serious, Akka. After Paremti I left the court in disgust. Wintered in Attrempus. He came to me, alone—"

"To beg forgiveness?"

Xinemus grimaced. "One would hope so, but no. He travelled all that way to upbraid me." The Marshal shook his head and smiled. Achamian knew why: even as a child Proyas had been given to endearing excesses. Travelling alone two hundred miles simply to deliver a rebuke was something only Proyas would do.

"He accused me of abandoning him in his hour of need. Calmemunis and his crew had brought charges against him, both to the ecclesiastical courts and to the King, and for a while things went sour, though he was never in any real danger."

"Of course you know he was only seeking your approval, Zin," Achamian said, suppressing a twinge of envy. "He's always worshipped you, you know—in his way . . . So what did you do?"

"I listened to him rant with what patience I could muster. Then I led him into the postern bailey and threw him a training sword. 'You wish to punish me,' I said, 'so *punish* me.'" Xinemus smiled as Achamian roared with laughter.

"He was tenacious as a whelp, Akka, but he's absolutely relentless now. He refused to yield. I'd knock him senseless, and he'd drag himself back up, soaked by blood and snow. Each time I'd say: 'I've trained you as best as I know how, my Prince. Yet still you lose.' Then he'd rush me again, yelling like a madman.

"The following morning he said nothing, avoided me like pestilence. But come afternoon he sought me out, his face bruised like apples. 'I understand,' he said. I asked him, 'Understand what?' 'Your lesson,' he replied. 'I understand your lesson.' I said, 'Oh, and what lesson was that?' And he said: 'That I've forgotten how to learn. That life is the God's lesson, and that even if we undertake to teach impious men, we must be ready to learn from them as well.'"

Achamian stared at his friend with candid awe. "Is that what you'd intended to teach him?"

Xinemus frowned and shook his head. "No. I just wanted to pound the arrogant piss out of him. But it sounded good to me, so I simply said, 'Indeed, my Lord Prince, indeed,' then nodded the sage way you do when you agree with someone you think isn't as clever as you."

Achamian smiled and nodded sagely.

Xinemus growled with laughter. "Either way, Proyas has refrained from repeating Paremti ever since. And when he returned to Aöknyssus, he offered to compensate Calmemunis lash for lash, in his father's court."

"And Calmemunis actually accepted? Surely the man's not that foolish."

"Oh, the oaf accepted, *whipped* Nersei Proyas before the eyes of King and court. And that's the *real* reason why Calmemunis never forgave Proyas. He lashed away his last shreds of honour. When he realized this, he claimed that Proyas had tricked him."

"So you think that's why Calmemunis insisted on leading the Vulgar Holy War?"

Xinemus nodded sadly. "That's why he, and a hundred thousand others, are dead."

Great catastrophes were often wrought by such small things. The intolerance of a prince and the stupidity of an arrogant lord. But where were these facts? Did they lie somewhere across those distant fields of dead?

One hundred thousand dead . . .

Achamian glanced down at the benjuka plate. For some reason he saw it instantly—his move. As though surprised that Achamian still wanted to play, Xinemus watched as he repositioned an apparently irrelevant piece.

One hundred thousand dead—was this also a move of some kind?

"Cunning devil," Xinemus hissed, studying the plate. After a moment's hesitation, he made his countermove.

A mistake, Achamian realized. In one thoughtless instant, Xinemus had utterly undone his earlier advantage. *Why do I see it so clearly now?*

Benjuka. Two men. Two different ends. One outcome. Who determined that outcome? The victor? But true victories were so rare—as rare across the benjuka plate as they were in life. More often the result would be uneasy compromise. But a compromise shaped by whom? By no one?

Soon enough, Achamian realized, the Holy War proper would march from Momemn, cross the fertile province of Anserca, and then pass into hostile lands. All this time the prospect of the campaign had seemed an abstraction, a mere move that could not, as yet, be countered. *But this isn't a game. The Holy War will march, and no matter what, thousands upon thousands will die.*

So many men. So many competing ends. And only one outcome. What would that outcome be? And who would shape it?

No one?

The thought terrified Achamian. The Holy War suddenly seemed a mad wager, a casting of number-sticks against an utterly black future. The lives of innumerable thousands—including Achamian—for distant Shimeh. How could any prize be worth such a wager?

"A hundred thousand dead," Xinemus continued, apparently unaware of the seriousness of his position on the plate. "A handful of them men I knew. And to make matters worse, the Emperor has been quick to exploit our dismay. He bids us to learn from the Vulgar Holy War's mistake."

"Which was?" Achamian asked, still distracted by the plate.

"The folly of marching without Ikurei Conphas."

Achamian looked up. "But I thought the Emperor provisioned Calmemunis and the others, made it possible for them to march in the first place."

"Indeed. But then he's promised to provision any who sign his accursed Indenture."

"So Calmemunis and the others *did* sign . . ." There had been uncertainty about this in Sumna.

"Why not? Men like him care nothing for their word. Why not promise to return all conquered lands to the Empire when your promise means nothing?"

"But certainly," Achamian pressed, "Calmemunis and the others must have seen the Emperor's plan. Ikurei Xerius knows full well that the Great Names will yield nothing to him. The Indenture is simply a pretext, something to prevent Shrial Censure when he orders Conphas to retake the Holy War's conquests."

"Ah, but you forget why Calmemunis marched in the first place, Akka. He didn't march for Shrial Remission or for the glory of the Latter Prophet—or even to carve out a kingdom of his own, for that matter. No. Calmemunis possessed the heart of a thief. He marched to deny Proyas any glory."

Arrested by a sudden thought, Achamian paused to study his friend. "But you, Zin . . . You *do* march for the Latter Prophet. How do all these vendettas and agendas make you feel?"

For a moment, Xinemus seemed taken aback. "You're right, of course," he said slowly. "I *should* be outraged. But I guess I expected this to happen. To be honest, I worry more about what *Proyas* will think."

"And why's that?"

"Certainly the news of the disaster will appall him. But all this score-settling and politicking . . ." Xinemus hesitated, as though silently rehearsing something long thought but never spoken. "I was among the first to arrive here, Akka, sent by Proyas to coordinate all those Conriyans who followed. I've been part of the Holy War since the first of the pavilions were pitched beneath Momemn's walls. I know that the bulk of those who rumble around us are pious men. Good men—no matter what nation they hail from. And all of them have heard of Nersei Proyas and the respect Maithanet bears him. All of them, even other Great Names such as Gothyelk or Saubon, are prepared to follow his lead. So much of what happens in this game with the Emperor will depend on how Proyas responds . . ."

"And Proyas is often impractical," Achamian concluded. "You fear that this game with the Emperor will provoke Proyas the Judge, rather than Proyas the Tactician."

"Precisely. As it stands the Emperor holds the Holy War hostage. He refuses to provision us beyond our daily needs unless we condescend to sign his Indenture. Of course, Maithanet can command him to provision the Holy War on pain of Shrial Censure, but now it seems that even *he* hesitates. The destruction of the Vulgar Holy War has convinced him that we're doomed unless we march with Ikurei Conphas. The Kianene have bared their teeth, and faith alone, it seems, won't be enough to overcome them. Who better to pilot us through those shoals than the great Exalt-General who has crushed the *Scylvendi?* But not even a Shriah as powerful as Maithanet can force an Emperor to send his only heir against the heathen. And of course, once again, the Emperor will not send Conphas unless the Great Names sign his Indenture."

"Remind me," Achamian said wryly, "never to cross paths with the Emperor."

"He's a fiend," Xinemus spat. "A cunning fiend. And unless Proyas is able to outmanoeuvre him, all of us will be spilling blood for Ikurei Xerius III rather than Inri Sejenus."

For some reason, the Latter Prophet's name reminded Achamian of the chill. He stared numbly at the silver-and-onyx geometries of the benjuka plate. He leaned forward, clutched the small sea-rounded stone he'd used to replace the missing piece, then tossed it across the glaring dust beyond their canopy. The game suddenly seemed childish.

"So you concede?" Xinemus asked. He sounded disappointed; he still thought he would win.

"I've no hope," Achamian replied, thinking not of benjuka but of Proyas. The Prince would arrive a man besieged, and Achamian had to further harass him, tell him even his gilded Shriah played some dark game.

Despite the winter gloom, it was warm in the pavilion. Esmenet sat up, hugging her knees in her arms. Who would have thought riding could make legs so sore?

"You think of someone else," Sarcellus said.

His voice was so different, she thought. So confident.

"Yes," she said.

"The Mandate Schoolman, I suppose."

Shock. But then she remembered telling him . . .

"What of it?" she asked.

He smiled, and as always she found herself at once thrilled and unsettled. Something about his teeth maybe? Or his lips?

"Exactly," he said. "Mandate Schoolmen are fools. Everyone in the Three Seas knows this . . . Do you know what the Nilnameshi say of women who love fools?"

She turned her face to him, fixed him with a languid look. "No. What do the Nilnameshi say?"

"That when they sleep, they do not dream."

He pressed her gently to his pillow.

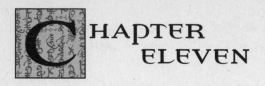

CHAPTER ELEVEN

MOMEMN

Reason, Ajencis writes, is the capacity to overcome unprece-dented obstacles in the gratification of desire. What distinguishes man from beasts is man's capacity to overcome infinite obstacles through reason.

But Ajencis has confused the accidental for the essential. Prior to the capacity to overcome infinite obstacles is the capacity to confront them. What defines man is not that he reasons, but that he prays.

—EKYANNUS I, 44 EPISTLES

Late Winter, 4111 Year-of-the-Tusk, Momemn

Prince Nersei Proyas of Conriya stumbled then steadied himself as his men rowed the boat through the breakers. He'd resolved to come to the beaches of Nansurium standing, but the Meneanor, which had resolved to pound the coasts until all the world was sea, was making things difficult. Twice now, frothing walls of surf had almost tossed him overboard, and he found himself debating the wisdom of his resolution. He scanned the sand-barren shoreline, saw that only the standard of Attrempus occupied the immediate beach, and decided that arriving dry and sitting was far better than arriving half-drowned.

The Holy War at last!

But as profoundly as this thought moved him, it was accompanied by a certain apprehension. He'd been the first to kiss Maithanet's knee at Sumna, and now, he was certain, he would be the last of the Great Names to join the Holy War.

Politics, he thought sourly. It was not, as the philosopher Ajencis had written, the negotiation of advantage within communities of men; it was more an absurd auction than an exercise in oratory. One bartered principle and piety to accomplish what principle and piety demanded. One sullied himself in order to be cleansed.

Proyas had kissed Maithanet's knee, had committed himself to the course that faith and principle demanded of him. The God himself had sanctioned this course! But from the outset it had been mired in politics: the endless wrangling with the King, his father; the infuriating delays involved in assembling the fleet; the innumerable concessions, contracts, pre-emptive strikes, retaliatory strikes, flatteries, and threats. A soul sold, it seemed, in order to be saved.

Has this been your test? Have you found me wanting?

Even the voyage at sea had been a trial. Always fickle, the Meneanor was especially tempestuous in winter. Struck by a storm off the coasts of Cironj and driven out of the Meneanor altogether. Forced by unfavourable winds to venture dangerously close to heathen coasts—at one point they had been mere days from *Shimeh* itself, or so his fool navigator had told him, as though the irony would thrill rather than gall him. Then the second storm as they laboriously tacked north, the one that had scattered the fleet and robbed more than five hundred men of their lives. At every turn it seemed something must conspire against him. If not men then the elements, and if not the elements then men. Even his dreams had tormented him: that the Holy War had already marched; that he would arrive, share a bowl of wine with the Emperor, then be told to go home.

Perhaps he should have expected this. Perhaps meeting Achamian in Sumna—while kneeling before Maithanet, no less!—had been more than an outrageous coincidence. Perhaps it had been an omen, a reminder that the gods often laughed where men gnashed their teeth.

Just then an immense roller tipped the boat forward and doused its occupants with foaming, sun-flashing water. Like an acorn across silk, the keel slid sideways along the back of a wave. Several of the rowers cried out. For a moment it seemed certain they would founder. One of the oars was lost. Then the boat scraped up and across immovable sand, and they found themselves stranded in the midst of several tidal pools. Proyas leapt out with his men and against their protests, helped them drag the launch farther up onto the bone-white beach. He glimpsed his fleet scattered across the bright sea. It seemed impossible. They were here. They had arrived.

As the others began retrieving the gear, Proyas walked several paces inland and fell to his knees. The sand burned his skin. The wind rifled his short, jet hair. The air smelled of salt, fish, and burning stone—not so different, he thought, from the smell of Conriya's distant coast.

It's begun, sweet Prophet . . . The Holy War has begun. Let me be the font of your righteous fury. Let my hand be the hand that delivers your hearth from wickedness. Let me be your hammer!

Sheltered by the ambient thunder of the breakers, it seemed safe to weep. He blinked tears from his eyes.

In his periphery, he could see the men who had awaited him approach across the white slopes. He cleared his throat, stood as they neared, absently brushing the sand from his tunic. Beneath the flapping standard of Attrempus, they fell to their knees and, with their hands turned inward upon their thighs, bowed their heads before him. A low escarpment framed them, and beyond that a great grey smear across the sky—Momemn, Proyas supposed, and her innumerable fires.

"I actually *missed* you, Xinemus," Proyas said. "What do you make of that?"

The burly, thick-bearded man at the forefront stood. Not for the first time, Proyas was struck by how much he resembled Achamian.

"I'm afraid, my Lord Prince," Xinemus replied, "that your kind sentiment will be short-lived . . ." He hesitated. "That is, once you hear the news I bear you."

Already it begins.

Months ago, before he'd returned to Conriya to raise his army, Maithanet had warned him that House Ikurei would likely cause the Holy War grief. But Xinemus's demeanour told him that something far more dramatic than mere politicking had transpired in his absence.

"I've never been one to begrudge the messenger, Xinemus. You know that." He momentarily studied the faces of the Marshal's retinue. "Where's that ass Calmemunis?"

The dread in Xinemus's eyes could scarcely be concealed. "Dead, my Lord Prince."

"Dead?" he asked sharply. *Please don't let it begin like this!* He pursed his lips and asked more evenly, "What has happened?"

"Calmemunis marched—"

"*Marched?* But the last I heard, he lacked the provisions. I sent a letter to the Emperor himself, asking him to deny Calmemunis anything he might need to march."

Please! Not like this!

"When the Emperor denied him provisions, Calmemunis and the others rioted, even sacked several villages. They hoped to march against the heathen on their own so they might garner all the glory. I very nearly came to blows with the damned—"

"Calmemunis *marched?*" Proyas felt numb. "The Emperor provisioned him?"

"As I see it, my Lord Prince, Calmemunis gave the Emperor precious little choice. He's always known how to incite men, Calmemunis. It was either provision and be rid of him or risk open war."

"The Holy Shriah would have interceded before then," Proyas snapped, unwilling to acquit anyone of this crime. "Calmemunis marched, and now he's dead? Do you mean to say—"

"Yes, my Lord Prince," Xinemus said solemnly. He'd already digested these facts. "The first battle of the Holy War has ended in catastrophe. They're all dead—Istratmenni, Gedapharus—all the pilgrim barons of Kanampurea, along with countless thousands of others, have been destroyed by the heathen at a place called the Plains of Mengedda. As far as I know, only some thirty or so Galeoth from Tharschilka's contingent survived."

But how could this be? The Holy War *overcome* in battle?

"Only thirty? How many marched?"

"More than a hundred thousand—the first of the Galeoth to arrive and the first Ainoni, along with the hosts of rabble that descended on Momemn shortly after the Shriah's call."

The rumbling crash and hiss of surf filled the silence. The Holy War, or a sizable fraction of it, had been slaughtered. *Are we doomed? Can the heathen be that strong?*

"What does the Shriah say?" he asked, hoping to silence these dread premonitions.

"The Shriah has fallen silent. Gotian says that he's gone into mourning for the souls lost at Mengedda. But there's rumour that he's become frightened the Holy War will be unable to overcome the heathen, that he waits for a sign from the God and the sign does not come."

"And the Emperor? What does he say?"

"The Emperor has claimed all along that the Men of the Tusk underestimate the ferocity of the heathen. He mourns the loss of the Vulgar Holy War—"

"Of the what?"

"That's what it's come to be called . . . Because of the rabble."

A shameful relief accompanied this explanation. When it became evident that the dregs—old men, women, even orphaned children—would answer the Shriah's call, Proyas had actually worried that the campaign would be more a migration than an army.

"The Emperor publicly mourns," Xinemus continued, "but privately insists that no war against the heathen, holy or otherwise, can succeed without the leadership of his nephew, Conphas. Emperor or not, the man is a mercenary dog."

Proyas nodded, finally grasping the outline of the events confronting him. "And I suppose the price he demands for the great Ikurei Conphas is nothing other than his Indenture, hmm? That wretch Calmemunis has sold us all."

"I tried, my Lord . . . I tried to restrain the Palatine. But I'd neither the rank nor the wit to stay him!"

"No man has wit enough to reason with a fool, Zin. And you're not to blame for your rank. Calmemunis was an arrogant, impetuous man. In the absence of his betters, he no doubt became drunk with conceit. He doomed himself, Zin. It's as simple as that."

But it was not, Proyas knew, quite that simple. The Emperor had a hand in this. Of that much he was certain.

"But still," Xinemus said, "I cannot help feeling there's more I could've done."

Proyas shrugged. "Saying 'I could have done more,' Zin, is what marks a man as a man and not a God." He snorted ruefully. "Actually, it was Achamian who told me that."

Xinemus smiled wanly. "And me as well . . . A most wise fool, that Achamian."

And wicked . . . a blasphemer. How I wish you'd remember that, Zin.

"A wise fool, indeed."

Seeing their prince safely arrived, the rest of the Conriyan host had begun to disembark from the fleet. Looking out to the Meneanor, Proyas saw more launches swept ashore by the rough surf. Soon these beaches would be choked with men, *his* men, and they could very well be doomed. *Why, God? Why beleaguer us when it's Your will we seek to accomplish?*

He spent some time grilling Xinemus on the particulars of Calmemunis's defeat. Yes, Calmemunis was most certainly dead: the Fanim had sent his severed head as a message. No, no one knew for sure how the heathens had destroyed them. The survivors, Xinemus said, had reported that the heathen were beyond numbering, that they possessed at least two men for every Inrithi. But the survivors of a great defeat, Proyas knew, were prone to say such things. Proyas felt afflicted by endless questions, each so desperate to be uttered that he often interrupted Xinemus mid-reply. And he felt afflicted, moreover, with a curious sense of having been deceived, as though his time in Conriya and at sea had been the result of another's machinations.

He was unaware of the approaching imperial retinue until it was nearly upon him.

"Conphas himself," Xinemus said grimly, nodding across the beach, "has come to woo you, my Prince."

Though he'd never met him, Proyas recognized Ikurei Conphas immediately. The man's bearing conveyed a palpable sense of the Nansur imperial tradition: the godlike equanimity of his expression, the martial familiarity of the way he held his silvered helmet under his right arm. The man was even able to walk through sand with catlike grace.

Conphas smiled when their eyes met: the smile of heroes who'd hitherto encountered each other only in rumour and reputation. Then he stood before him, the near mythic man who had mastered the Scylvendi. Proyas found it difficult not to be impressed, even faintly awed, by his presence.

Bowing slightly at the waist and holding out his hand for a soldier's shake, Conphas said, "In the name of Ikurei Xerius III, the Emperor of Nansur, I welcome you, Prince Nersei Proyas, to our shores, and to the Holy War."

Your shores . . . Would that it were your Holy War as well.

Proyas neither bowed nor took the proffered hand.

Rather than displaying shock or insult, Conphas's eyes became at once ironic and appraising.

"I fear," he continued easily, "that recent events have made it difficult for us to trust each other."

"Where is Gotian?" Proyas asked.

"The Grandmaster of the Shrial Knights awaits you on the escarpment. He does not like sand in his boots."

"And you?"

"I was wise enough to wear sandals."

There was laughter at this—enough to make Proyas grind his teeth.

When Proyas said nothing, Conphas continued: "Calmemunis, I understand, was your man. It isn't surprising that you should seek to blame others rather than your own. But let me assure you, the Palatine of Kanampurea perished of his own folly."

"Of that, Exalt-General, I have no doubt."

"Then you will accept the Emperor's invitation to join him on the Andiamine Heights?"

"To speak of his Indenture, no doubt."

"Among other matters."

"I would speak with Gotian first."

"So be it, my Prince. But perhaps I might save you some wasted breath and tell you what the Grandmaster will say. Gotian will tell you that the Most Holy Shriah holds *your* man, Calmemunis, solely responsible for the disaster on the Plains of Mengedda. And he'll tell you that the Shriah has been deeply moved by this disaster, and that he now seriously ponders the Emperor's single, and eminently justified, demand. And it is, I assure you, *justified*. On the ancestor lists of every family of means in the Empire, you'll find the names of dozens who have died warring for the very lands that the Holy War would reconquer."

"That may be, Ikurei, but it is we who lay down our lives this time."

"The Emperor understands and appreciates this, which is why he has offered to grant *title* to the lost provinces—under the auspices of the Empire, of course."

"It is not enough."

"No, I suppose it's never enough, is it? I admit, my Prince, that we find ourselves in a most curious predicament. Unlike you, the House Ikurei is not known for its piety, and now that we're at last defending a just cause, we find ourselves impugned for our past deeds. But the scandal of the arguer has no bearing on the truth or falsehood of his arguments. Is this not what Ajencis himself tells us? I urge you, Prince, to see past our flaws and scrutinize our demand in the sweet light of reason."

"And if reason tells me otherwise?"

"Why then you have the example of Calmemunis to live by, don't you? As much as it might pain you to admit, the Holy War *needs* us."

Once again, Proyas made no reply.

Conphas continued with a heavy-lidded smile: "So you see, Nersei Proyas, both reason and circumstance are on our side."

When Proyas still refused to reply, the Exalt-General bowed, then turned with casual disdain. Followed by his shimmering retinue, he receded across the beach. The breakers clamoured with renewed fury, and the wind whipped a fine spray across Proyas and his men. It was chill.

Proyas did his best to conceal his shaking hands. In the battle *for* the Holy War, a skirmish had just been fought, and Ikurei Conphas had bested him before his own—with ease, no less! All his troubles so far, Proyas knew, would be but gnats compared with the Exalt-General and his thrice-damned uncle.

"Come, Xinemus," he said absently, "we must ensure the fleet disembarks in good order."

"There's one other thing, my Prince . . . Something I forgot to mention."

Proyas sighed deeply, was troubled by the audible tremor that passed through it. "What is it now, Zin?"

"Drusas Achamian is here."

———— ⊶≫⊷ ————

Achamian sat alone by the fire, waiting for Xinemus's return. Save for a handful of slaves and passing Men of the Tusk, the camp about him was abandoned. The Marshal's men were still on the beaches, Achamian knew, helping their Prince and their kinsmen disembark. The sense of surrounding canvas hollows troubled him. Dark and empty tents. Cold firepits.

This was what it would be like, he realized, if the Marshal and his men were destroyed on the battlefield. Abandoned belongings. Places where words and looks had once warmed the air. Absence.

Achamian shuddered.

The first few days after joining Xinemus and the Holy War, Achamian had busied himself with matters concerning the Scarlet Spires. He placed a series of Wards about his tent, discreetly, so as not to offend Inrithi sensibilities. He found a local man to show him the way to the villa where the Scarlet Schoolmen were sequestered. He made maps, lists of names. He even hired three adolescent brothers, the children of a non-hereditary Shigeki slave owned by a Tydonni thane, to watch the track leading to the villa to report on significant comings and goings. There was little else for him to do. His single attempt to ingratiate himself with the local magnate the Spires had contracted to provision them had been a disaster. When Achamian persisted, the man had literally tried to stab him with a spoon—not out of any sense of loyalty to the Spires, but out of terror.

The Nansur, it seemed, were learning quickly: for the Scarlet Schoolmen, any cause for suspicion, be it a bead of sweat or familiarity with a stranger, was tantamount to betrayal. And no one betrayed the Scarlet Spires.

But all these tasks were little more than routine. The entire time, Achamian would think, *After this, Inrau. I'll tend to you after this . . .*

Then "after" came. There was no one to question. No one to watch. No one, save Maithanet, to even suspect.

There was nothing to do but wait.

Of course, according to the reports he sent his Mandate handlers in Atyersus, he was aggressively pursuing this hint or that innuendo. But that was simply part of the pantomime all of them, even zealots like Nautzera, played. They were like starving men dining on grass. When one starved, why not cultivate the illusion of digestion?

But this time the illusion sickened rather than soothed. The reason seemed obvious enough: Inrau. By falling into the hole that was the Consult, Inrau had made it too deep to be papered over.

So Achamian began hunting for ways to deaden his heart or at the very least to crowd some of the recriminations from his thoughts. *When Proyas comes*, he would tell his dead student. *I'll tend to you when Proyas comes.*

He took to heavy drink: unwatered wine mostly; some anpoi when Xinemus was in a particularly good mood; and *yursa*, a dreadful liquor the Galeoth made from rotten potatoes. He smoked poppy oil and hashish, but he abandoned the former after the boundary between the trances and the Dreams collapsed.

He began rereading the few classics Xinemus had brought with him. He laughed over Ajencis's Third and Fourth *Analytics*, realizing for the first time the subtlety of the philosopher's sense of humour. He frowned at the lyrics of Protathis, finding them overwrought even though they had seemed to speak his soul's own tongue twenty years earlier. And he started, as he had many times, *The Sagas*, only to set them aside after a few hours. Either their florid inaccuracies made him furious to the point of huffing breath and shaking hands, or their truths made him weep. It was a lesson, it seemed, that he must relearn every few years: seeing the Apocalypse made it impossible to read accounts of it.

Some days, when he was too restless to read, he ranged through the encampment, into warrens and down byways so segregated from the greater Holy War that Norsirai openly called him a "pick" because of his skin. Once five Tydonni chased him from their petty fief with knives, hollering slurs and accusations. Other days he wandered through Momemn's mud-brick canyons, to different agoras, to the ancient temple-complex of Cmiral, and once, to the gates of the Imperial Precincts. Inevitably he found himself in the company of whores, even though he never remembered setting out to find them. He forgot faces, ignored names. He revelled in the heave of grunting bodies, in the greasiness of skin wiping unwashed skin. Then he wandered home, emptied of everything but his seed.

He would try very hard not to think of Esmi.

Ordinarily, Xinemus returned in the evening, and they made time for a few moves in their running game of benjuka. Then they sat by the Marshal's fire, passed a sharp bowl of a drink that the Conriyans called *perrapta* and insisted cleansed the palate for dinner, but that Achamian thought made everything taste like fish. Then they dined on whatever Xinemus's slaves could scrounge. Some nights they would be joined by the Marshal's officers, usually Dinchases, Zenkappa, and Iryssas, and their time would consist of ribald jokes and irreverent gossip. Other nights, it would be just the two of them, and they would speak of deeper and more painful things. Occasionally, like this night, Achamian found himself alone.

Word of the Conriyan fleet had arrived before dawn. Xinemus had left shortly after to prepare for the Crown Prince's arrival. His temper had been short because he dreaded, Achamian had no doubt, informing Proyas of Calmemunis and the Vulgar Holy War. When Achamian had suggested the possibility of accompanying him to meet Proyas, Xinemus had simply stared at him incredulously and barked, "He's going to hang me as it is!"

Before departing, however, he rode up to the morning fire and promised Achamian he would let Proyas know of his presence and of his need.

The day had been long with hope and dread.

Proyas was Maithanet's friend and confidant. If anyone could coax information from the Holy Shriah, it would be him. And why shouldn't he? So much of what he was, of what made others refer to him as the Sun Prince, was due to his old tutor—to Drusas Achamian.

Don't worry, Inrau . . . He owes me.

Then the sun fell without word from Xinemus. Doubt took hold, as did drink. Fear hollowed his unspoken declarations, so he filled them with anger and spite.

I made him! Made him what he is! He wouldn't dare!

He repented these harsh thoughts and began to reminisce. He remembered Proyas as a boy, weeping, cradling his arm, running through the gloom of the walnut grove, through lances of sunlight. "Climb into books, you fool!" he had shouted. "Their branches never break." He remembered coming upon Inrau unawares in the scriptorium, watching him draw, in the bored fashion of juvenile boys, a row of phalluses across an unspoiled sheet. "Practising your letters, hmm?"

"My sons," he muttered to the fire. "My beautiful sons."

Finally he heard horsemen filing down the dark lanes. He saw Xinemus heading a small party of Conriyan knights. The Marshal dismounted in the shadows then strode to the firelight, rubbing the back of his neck. His eyes had the weary look of a man with one last difficult task.

"He'll not see you."

"He must be incredibly busy," Achamian blurted, "and exhausted! What a fool I was. Perhaps tomorrow . . ."

Xinemus sighed heavily. "No, Akka. He will not see you."

———— ⌘ ————

Near the heart of Momemn's famed Kamposea Agora, Achamian paused at a stall of bronze wares. Ignoring the proprietor's scowl, he lifted a large polished plate, pretended to look for imperfections. He turned it from side to side, peering into the smeared reflection of the throngs passing behind him. Then he saw the man again, apparently haggling with a sausage-seller. Clean-shaven. Black hair chopped in the haphazard way of slaves.

Wearing a blue linen tunic beneath a robe striped in the Nilnameshi fashion. Achamian glimpsed an exchange of coppers in the stall's shadow. The man's reflection turned into sunlight, holding a sausage pinched in bread. His bored eyes sifted through the teeming market, settling on this or that. He took a small bite, then glanced at Achamian's back.

Who are you?

"What's this?" the bronze-peddler cried. "You checking teeth for pepper?"

"For pox," Achamian said darkly. "I fear I might have the pox." He did not need to look at the man to know the horror those words would evoke. A woman lingering over the wine bowls quickly scuttled into the crowd.

Achamian watched the reflected figure saunter from the stall. Though he doubted he was in any immediate danger, being followed was not something to be ignored. Odds were the man belonged to the Scarlet Spires, which would be interested in him for the obvious reasons, or perhaps even the Emperor, who spied on everyone for the sake of spying on everyone. But there was always the chance the man belonged to the College of Luthymae. If the Thousand Temples had killed Inrau, then they probably knew he was here. And if this was the case, Achamian needed to know what this man knew.

Smiling, Achamian offered the plate to the bronze-peddler, who flinched as though it were a burning coal. Achamian tossed it onto the gleaming stacks instead, drawing passing stares with the racket. *Let him think I argue.*

But if he were to confront the man, the question was more one of where than of how. The Kamposea was definitely not the place. *Some alley, perhaps.*

Beyond the agora, Achamian saw a cohort of birds wheeling above the great domes of the Temple Xothei, whose silhouette loomed above the tenements hedging the north end of the market. East of the temple stood a towering scaffold strung by a web of ropes to a leaning obelisk—the Emperor's latest gift to the temple-complex of Cmiral. It was somewhat smaller, Achamian noted, than the obelisks rising in the smoke beyond.

He jostled his way north through rumbling crowds and shouting vendors, looking for breaks between the buildings that might mark some rarely used exit from the market. The man, he trusted, still followed. He almost stumbled across a peacock, its broad fan of angry red eyes in full display. The Nansur thought the bird holy and allowed them to roam free in their cities. Then he glimpsed a woman sitting in the window of one of the nearer tenements and was momentarily reminded of Esmenet.

If they know about me, then they know about her . . .

All the more reason to seize the fool who followed him.

At the north end of the market, he passed among paddocks cramped with sheep and pigs. He even saw an immense snorting bull. Sacrificial victims to sell to the Cultic priests of Cmiral, Achamian supposed. Then he found his alley: a narrow slot between mud-brick walls. He passed a blind man sitting before a trinket-cluttered mat and hastened into the humid dark.

The whine of flies filled his ears. He saw piles of ash and greasy entrails amid dried bones and dead fish. The stench was guttural with rot, but he retreated to a point where he was sure the man would not immediately see him.

And waited.

The smell extorted a cough from him.

He struggled to concentrate, rehearsing the contorted words of the Cant he would use to snare his hunter. The difficulty of the thoughts behind them unnerved him, as they often did. He was always faintly incredulous of his ability to work sorcery, more so when days would pass without his uttering a significant Cant—as in this case. But in his thirty-nine years with the Mandate, his abilities—at least in this regard—had never failed him.

I'm a Schoolman.

He watched sun-bright figures flit to and fro across the opening. Still no man.

The muck had crept above the lip of his sandals and now slithered between his toes. The fish between his feet, he noted, trembled. He saw a maggot roll from an empty eye socket.

This is madness! No fool is fool enough to follow someone here.

He rushed from the alley, held his hand against the bleary sun in order to scan his corner of the market.

The man was nowhere to be seen.

I'm the fool . . . Was he even following me?

Fuming, Achamian abandoned his search and hastened to purchase those things that had brought him into Momemn in the first place.

He had learned nothing of the Scarlet Spires, even less of Maithanet and the Thousand Temples, and Proyas still refused to meet with him. Since he could find no new books to read, and Xinemus had taken to upbraiding him for his drunkenness, Achamian had decided to revisit an old passion of his. He would cook. All sorcerers had studied alchemy to some extent, and all alchemists, at least those worth their salt, knew how to cook.

Xinemus thought that he degraded himself, that cooking was for women and slaves, but Achamian knew different. Xinemus and his officers would scoff until they tasted, and then they would accord him a quiet honour, as they would any other skilled practitioner of an ancient art. Finally Achamian would be more than the blasphemous beggar at their table. Their souls might be imperilled, but at least their appetites would be gratified.

But the duck, the leeks, curry, and chives were all forgotten when he glimpsed the man again, this time beneath the ramparts of the Gilgallic Gate in the crush to leave the city. He caught only a momentary glimpse of his profile, but it was the same man. Same ragged hair. Same threadbare robe.

Without thinking, Achamian dropped his purchases.

Now it's my turn to follow.

He thought of Esmi. Did they know he'd stayed with her in Sumna? *I can't risk losing him, witnesses or no witnesses.*

This was the kind of hasty action that Achamian ordinarily despised. But over the years he'd found that circumstances were unkind to elaborate plans, and that most everything deteriorated into such rash acts anyway.

"You!" he shouted over the roar, then once again cursed himself for his stupidity. What if he fled? Obviously he knew that Achamian had spotted him. Otherwise why wouldn't he have followed him into the alley?

But luckily the man hadn't heard. Achamian doggedly worked his way toward him, glaring all the while at the back of his head. He was cursed, even viciously elbowed a couple of times, as he shoved through the sweaty slots between people. But he remained intent on the man. The back of his head grew nearer.

"Sweet Sejenus, man!" a perfumed Ainoni cried in Achamian's periphery. "Do that again and I'll fucking knife you!"

Nearer. The Cants of Compulsion boiled through his thoughts. The others would hear, he knew. They would know. Blasphemy.

What happens, happens. I need to take this man!

Closer. Close enough . . .

He reached out, grabbed his shoulder, and yanked him around. For a heartbeat, he could only stare at him speechlessly. The stranger scowled, shrugged Achamian's hand away.

"What's the meaning of this?" he spat.

"I-I apologize," Achamian said hastily, unable to look away from his face. "I thought you were someone else." *But it was him, wasn't it?*

Had he seen the bruise of sorcery, he would have thought it a trick, but there was nothing, only a quarrelsome face. He had simply made a mistake.

But how?

The man appraised him for a contemptuous moment, then shook his head. "Drunken fool."

For a nightmarish moment Achamian could only stumble along with the crowd. He cursed himself for dropping his food.

No matter. Cooking was for slaves anyway.

Esmenet sat alone by Sarcellus's fire, shivering.

Once again she felt as though she'd been thrown beyond the circuit of what was possible. She had journeyed to find a sorcerer, only to be rescued by a knight. And now she found herself staring across the innumerable campfires of a holy war. When she squinted, peered over Momemn, she could even see the Emperor's palace, the Andiamine Heights, rising against the murky sea. The sight made her cry, not only because she finally witnessed the world she had yearned to see for so long, but also because it reminded her of the tales she used to tell her daughter, the ones Esmenet would continue telling long after she had fallen asleep.

She had always been a bad one for that. Giving selfish gifts.

The camp of the Shrial Knights occupied the heights to the north of Momemn and above the Holy War, along terraced slopes that had once been cultivated. Because Sarcellus was First Knight-Commander, second only to Incheiri Gotian, his pavilion dwarfed those of his men. It had been pitched, as per his order, at the edge of the terrace so that Esmenet might marvel over the sights to which he'd delivered her.

Two blonde slave girls sat on a reed mat nearby, quietly eating rice and muttering to one another in their mother tongue. Esmenet had already caught them nervously glancing in her direction, as though fearful she concealed some hunger they had not gratified. They had bathed her, rubbed fine oils into her skin, and dressed her in blue muslin and silk gowns.

She found herself hating them for fearing her, and yet loving them too.

She could still taste the peppered pheasant they had prepared for her dinner.

Do I dream?

She felt a fraud, a whore who was also a mummer, and so twice damned, twice degraded, but she felt an overweening pride as well, terrifying because of its deranged conceit. *This is me!* something within her cried. *Me as I truly am!*

Sarcellus had told her it would be like this. How many times had he apologized for the discomforts of the road? He travelled frugally, bearing crucial correspondence for Incheiri Gotian, the Grandmaster of the Shrial Knights. But he insisted this would change when they reached the Holy War, where he promised to keep her in a fashion befitting her beauty and her wit.

"It'll be like the light after a long darkness," he had said. "It will illuminate, and it will blind."

She ran a trembling palm along the brocaded silk that spilled across her lap. In the firelight, she could not see the tattoo on the back of her left hand.

I like this dream.

Breathless, she brought her wrist to her lips, tasted the bitterness of perfumed oil.

Fickle whore! Remember why you're here!

She turned her left hand to the fire, slowly, as though to dry it of sweat or dew, and watched the tattoo surface from the shadows between her tendons.

This . . . this is what I am.

An aging whore.

And everybody knew what happened to old whores.

Without warning, Sarcellus stepped from the darkness. He possessed, Esmenet had decided, a disturbing affinity to the night, as though he walked *with* rather than through it. And this despite his white Shrial vestments.

He paused, stared at her wordlessly.

"He doesn't love you, you know. Not really."

She held his eyes across the firelight, breathed heavily. "Did you find him?"

"Yes. He's made camp with Conriyans . . . as you said."

Part of her found his reluctance endearing. "But *where*, Sarcellus?"

"Near the Ancilline Gate."

She nodded, looked away nervously.

"Have you asked yourself *why*, Esmi? If you owe me anything at all, you owe me this question . . ."

Why him? Why Achamian?

She had told him much about Akka, she realized. Too much.

No man she'd ever met had been as inquisitive as Cutias Sarcellus—not even Achamian. His interest in her was nothing short of ravenous, as though he found her tawdry life as exotic as she found his. And why not? House Cutias was one of the greater Houses of the Congregate. For someone like Sarcellus, suckled on honey and meat, coddled by slaves, experiences such as hers were as distant as far-away Zeum.

"Ever since I can remember," he had confided to her, "I've been drawn to the vulgar, to the poor—to those who provide the fat upon which my kind lives." He chuckled. "My father used to cane me for playing number-sticks with the field-slaves or for hiding in the scullery, trying to sneak peaks up skirts . . ."

She smacked him playfully. "Men are dogs. The only difference is they sniff asses with their eyes."

He had laughed, exclaiming, "*This!* This is why I cherish your company so! To live a life like yours is one thing, but to be able to *speak* it, to share it, is another thing altogether. This is why I'm your devotee, Esmi. Your pupil."

How could she not be swept away? When she stared into his gorgeous eyes, with irises the brown of giving earth and whites like wetted pearls, she saw herself mirrored in a way she'd never dared imagine. She saw someone extraordinary, someone exalted rather than demeaned by her suffering.

But now, watching him clench his fists in the firelight, she saw herself as cruel.

"I told you," she said carefully. "I love him."

Not you . . . Him.

Esmenet could think of no two men more dissimilar than Achamian and Sarcellus. In some respects, the differences were obvious. The Knight-Commander was ruthless, impatient, intolerant. His judgements were instant and irrevocable, as though he made things right simply by declaring them right. His regrets were few, and never catastrophic.

In other respects, however, the differences were more subtle—and more telling.

Those first days after her rescue, Sarcellus had seemed utterly unfathomable to her. Though his anger was violent, expressed with the ardour of a child's tantrum and the conviction of a prophet's condemnation, he never begrudged those who angered him. Though he approached every obstacle as something to be crushed, even the inconsequential snags that filled his day-to-day administrative life, he was graceful rather than crude in his methods. Though his arrogance was feckless, he was never threatened by criticism and more able than most to laugh at his own folly.

The man had seemed a paradox, at once reprehensible and beguiling. But then she realized: he was *kjineta*, a caste noble. Where *suthenti*, caste menials like herself and Achamian, feared others, themselves, seasons, famines, and so on, Sarcellus feared only particulars: that so-and-so might say such-and-such, that the rain might postpone the hunt. And this, she understood, changed everything. Achamian was perhaps every bit as temperamental as Sarcellus, but fear made his anger bitter, liable to spite and resentment. He could also be arrogant, but because of fear, it seemed shrill instead of reassuring, and it certainly did not brook contradiction.

Sheltered by his caste, Sarcellus had not, as the impoverished must, made fear the pivot of his passions. As a result he possessed an immovable self-assurance. He felt. He acted. He judged. The fear of being wrong that so characterized Achamian simply did not exist for Cutias Sarcellus. Where Achamian was ignorant of the answers, Sarcellus was ignorant of the questions. No certitude, she thought, could be greater.

But Esmenet had not reckoned the consequences of her scrutiny. A troubling sense of intimacy followed upon her understanding. When his questions, his banter, even his lovemaking had made it clear he wanted more than peaches to sweeten the road to Momemn, she found herself secretly watching him with his men, daydreaming, wondering . . .

Of course, she found many things about him intolerable. His dismissiveness. His capacity for cruelty. Despite his gallantry, he often spoke to her the way a herdsman would use his crook, continually correcting her when her thoughts strayed. But once she understood the origin of these tendencies, she began to see them more as traits belonging to his kind than as failings. What lions kill, she had thought, they do not murder. And what nobles take, they do not steal.

She found herself feeling something she could not describe—at least not at first. Something she had never felt before. And she felt it more in his arms than anywhere else.

Days passed before she understood.

She felt safe.

This had been no small revelation. Before realizing this, she had feared she was falling in love with Sarcellus. And for a short time, the love she bore Achamian had actually seemed a lie, the infatuation of a cloistered girl for a worldly man. While she marvelled at the comfort she felt in Sarcellus's embrace, she found herself pondering the desperation of her feelings for Achamian. The one seemed right and the other wrong. Should not love feel right?

No, she had realized. The Gods punished such love with horrors. With dead daughters.

But she could not tell Sarcellus this. He would never understand—unlike Achamian.

"You love him," the Knight-Commander repeated dully. "That I believe, Esmi. That I accept . . . But does he love you? *Can* he love you?"

She frowned. "Why couldn't he?"

"Because he's a *sorcerer*. A *Schoolman*, for Sejenus's sake!"

"You think I care that he's damned?"

"No. Of course not," he replied, softly, as though trying to be gentle with hard truths. "I say this, Esmi, because Schoolmen cannot love—Mandate Schoolmen least of all."

"Enough, Sarcellus. You know nothing of what you speak."

"Really?" he said, a pained sneer in his voice. "Tell me, what part do you play in his delusions, hmm?"

"What do you mean?"

"You're his tether, Esmi. He's fastened on you because you bind him to what's real. But if you go to him, cast away your life and go to him, you'll simply be one of two ships at sea. Soon, very soon, you'll lose sight of shore. His madness will engulf you. You'll awaken to find his fingers about your throat, the name of someone long, long dead ringing in your—"

"I said *enough*, Sarcellus!"

He stared at her. "You *believe* him, don't you?"

"Believe what?"

"All that madness they prattle about. The Consult. The Second Apocalypse."

Esmenet pursed her lips, said nothing. Where did this shame come from?

He nodded slowly. "I see . . . No matter. I'll not fault you for it. You've spent much time with him. But there's one last thing I would have you consider."

Her eyes burned when she blinked. "What?"

"You do know that wives, even mistresses, are forbidden Mandate Schoolmen."

She felt cold, ached as though someone had pressed freezing iron against her heart. She cleared her throat. "Yes."

"So you know"—he licked his lips—"know the most you could ever be . . ."

She looked at him with hate. "Is his whore, Sarcellus?"

And what am I to you?

He knelt before her, scooped her hands into his own. He tugged on them gently. "Sooner or later, he *will* be recalled, Esmi. He'll be forced to leave you behind."

She looked to the fire. Tears traced burning lines across her cheeks.

"I know."

On his knees, the Knight-Commander saw a tear lingering on her upper lip. A miniature replica of the fire glittered within it.

He blinked, glimpsed himself fucking the mouth of her severed head.

The thing called Sarcellus smiled.

"But I press you," he said. "I apologize, Esmi. I just want you to . . . to see. Not to suffer."

"No matter," she said softly, avoiding his look. But her hands tightened about his own.

He freed his fingers and gently clutched her knees. He thought of her cunny, pressed tight and greasy between her legs, and shivered with hunger. To simply be where the Architect had been! To thrust where he had thrusted. It at once humbled and engorged. To plunge into a furnace stoked by the Old Father!

He pressed himself to his feet. "Come," he said, turning to the pavilion.

He saw blood and grunting rapture.

"No, Sarcellus," she said. "I must think."

He shrugged, smiled wanly. "When you can, then."

He looked to Eritga and Hansa, his two slave girls, and with a gesture bid them to keep watch. Then he left Esmenet and strode through the flaps of the Knight-Commander's pavilion. He cackled under his breath, thinking of the things he would do to her. He hardened against his breeches; the limbs of his face shuddered in delectation. Such poetry he would cut into her!

The lanterns burned low, cast an orange gloom through the pavilion's study. He reclined on cushions set before a low table covered in scrolls. He ran his wrist down his flat stomach, clasped his cock's aching length . . . Soon. Soon.

"Ah, yes," a small voice said. "The promise of release." A breath, as though drawn through a reed. "I stand among your makers, and yet the genius of your manufacture still moves me to incredulity."

"Architect?" the thing called Sarcellus gasped. "Father? You would risk this? What if someone sees your mark?"

"One bruise does not show among many." There was a flutter of wings and a dry click as a crow alighted on the table. A bald human head rolled on its neck, as though working out kinks. "Any who sense me," the palm-sized face explained, "will dismiss my mark. The Scarlet Schoolmen are everywhere."

"Is it time?" the thing called Sarcellus asked. "Has the time come?"

A smile, no bigger than the curl of a toenail. "Soon, Maëngi. Soon."

A wing unfolded and reached out, drawing a line across Sarcellus's chest. Sarcellus's head snapped to the side; his limbs popped rigid. From his crotch to his extremities, rapture galloped across his skin. Searing rapture.

"So she stays?" the Synthese asked. "She does not run to him?" The wingtip continued its lazy caresses.

The thing called Sarcellus gasped. "For now . . ."

"Has she mentioned her night with me? Told you anything?"

"No. Nothing."

"And yet she acts . . . open, as though she shares everything?"

"Yesss, Old Father."

"As I suspected . . ." Tiny scowl. "She's far more than the simple whore I took her to be, Maëngi. She's a student of the game." The scowl became a smile. "A twelve-talent whore after all . . ."

"Should I—" Maëngi felt a deep pulse between his rectum and the root of his phallus. So close. "Sh-should I kill her?" He arched against the agonizing wingtip. *Please! Father please!*

"No. She does not run to Drusas Achamian, which means something . . . Her life's been too hard for her not to weigh loyalties
against advantages. She may yet prove useful."

The wingtip withdrew, was folded into glossy black. Tiny lids
closed then opened over glass-bead eyes.

Maëngi drew a shuddering breath. Without thinking he cupped
his phallus in his right hand, began rubbing its head with his
thumb. "What of Atyersus," he asked breathlessly. "Do they suspect
anything?"

"The Mandate know nothing. They merely send a fool on a fool's
errand."

He relaxed his grip, swallowed. "I'm no longer so sure Drusas
Achamian is a fool, Old Father."

"Why?"

"After delivering the Shriah's message to Gotian, I met with
Gaörtha—"

The small face grimaced. "You met with him? Did I sanction this?"

"N-no. But the whore asked me to find Achamian for her, and I
knew Gaörtha had been assigned to watch him."

The small head bent from side to side.

"I fear my patience fails me, Maëngi."

The thing called Sarcellus pressed sweaty palms down his vestments. "Drusas Achamian spotted Gaörtha following him."

"He *what?*"

"In the Kamposea market . . . But the fool knows nothing, Old
Father! Nothing. Gaörtha was able to shift skins."

The Synthese hopped to the mahogany lip of the table.
Though it seemed as light as hollow bones and bundled papyrus,
it bore the intimation of something immense, as if a leviathan
rolled through waters at right angles to everywhere. Light bled
from its eyes.

HOW

Roared through what passed for Maëngi's soul.

I HATE

Shattering whatever thoughts, whatever passions he might call
his own.

THIS WORLD.

Crushing even the unquenchable hunger, the all-encompassing
ache . . .

Eyes like twin Nails of Heaven. Laughter, wild with a thousand
years of madness.

SHOW ME, MAËNGI . . .

Wings fanned before him, blotting the lanterns, leaving only a
small white face against black, a frail mouthpiece for something
terrible, mountainous.

SHOW ME YOUR TRUE FACE.

The thing called Sarcellus sensed the fist of his expression
slacken then part . . .

Like Esmenet's legs.

———⚬∞⚬———

It was spring, and once again the networks of fields and groves
surrounding Momemn were crowded by Inrithi, far better armed,
and far more dangerous, than those who had perished in Gedea.
Tidings of the slaughter on the Plains of Mengedda had hung like a
pall for many days over the Holy War. "How could it be?" they
asked. But the apprehension was quickly stifled by rumours of
Calmemunis's arrogance, by reports of his refusal to obey
Maithanet's summons. Defy Maithanet! They wondered at such
folly, and the priests reminded them of the difficulty of the path, of
the trials that would break them if they strayed.

And there was much talk of the Emperor's impious contest with
the Great Names as well. With the exception of the Ainoni, all the
Great Names had refused to sign the Indenture, and about the
evening fires, there were many drunken debates as to what their
leaders should do. Far and away most cursed the Emperor, and some
few even suggested that the Holy War should storm Momemn and
seize the supplies that would be needed to march. But some others

took the Emperor's side. What was the Indenture, they asked, but a mere scrap of paper? And look, they said, at the dividends of signing. Not only would the Men of the Tusk find themselves pain-lessly provisioned, they would be ensured the guidance of Ikurei Conphas as well, the greatest military intellect in generations. And if the destruction of the Vulgar Holy War was not evidence enough, what of the Shriah, who would neither force the Emperor to provi-sion the Holy War nor force the Great Names to sign his Indenture? Why would Maithanet hesitate so, if he too did not fear the might of the heathen?

But how could one fret when the very heavens shivered with their might? Such a congregation! Who could imagine that such potentates would take up the Tusk? And far more, besides. Priests, not merely of the Thousand Temples but from every Cult, repre-senting every Aspect of God, had clambered from the beaches or wound down from the hills to take their place in the Holy War, singing hymns, clashing cymbals, making the air bitter with incense and the noise of adulation. Idols were anointed with oils and attar of rose, and the priestesses of Gierra made love to calloused warriors. Narcotics were reverently circulated and sipped, and the Shakers cried rapturously from the dust. Demons were cast out. The purification of the Holy War began.

The Men of the Tusk would gather after the ceremonies, swap wild rumours or speculate about the degeneracy of the heathen. They would joke that Skaiyelt's wife had to be more mannish than Chepheramunni, or that the Nansur were given to receiving one another up the ass, which was why they always marched in such tight formations. They would bully malingering slaves or howl at women carrying baskets of laundry up from the River Phayus. And out of habit, they would scowl at the strange groups of foreigners who endlessly prowled the encampment.

So many . . . Such glory.

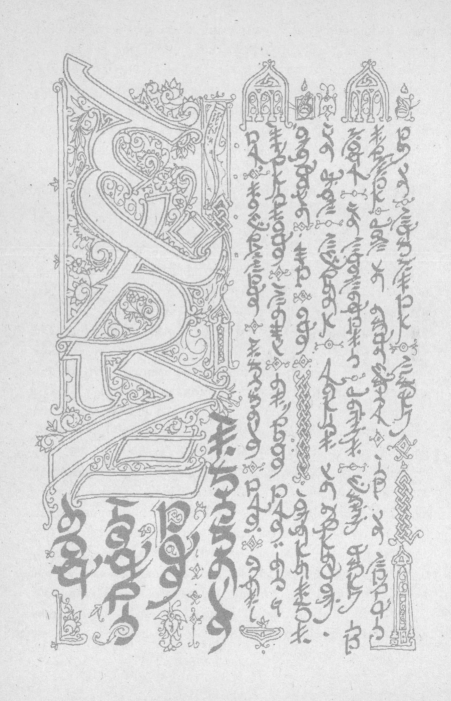

PART IV:
The Warrior

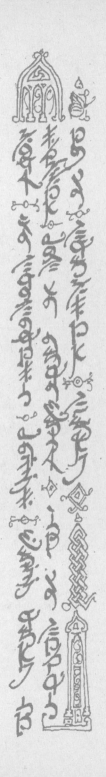

CHAPTER TWELVE

THE JIÜNATI STEPPE

*I have explained how Maithanet yoked the vast resources of the
Thousand Temples to ensure the viability of the Holy War. I have
described, in outline, the first steps taken by the Emperor to bind
the Holy War to his imperial ambitions. I have attempted to
reconstruct the initial reaction of the Cishaurim in Shimeh from
their correspondence with the Padirajah in Nenciphon. And I
have even mentioned the hated Consult, of whom I can at long
last speak without fear of ridicule. I have spoken, in other words,
almost exclusively of powerful factions and their impersonal ends.
What of vengeance? What of hope? Against the frame of competing
nations and warring faiths, how did these small passions come to
rule the Holy War?*

—DRUSAS ACHAMIAN, COMPENDIUM OF THE FIRST HOLY WAR

*. . . though he consorts with man, woman, and child, though
he lays with beasts and makes a mockery of his seed, never
shall he be as licentious as the philosopher, who lays with all
things imaginable.*

—INRI SEJENUS, SCHOLARS, 36, 21, THE TRACTATE

Early Spring, 4111 Year-of-the-Tusk, the Northern Jiünati Steppe

Leaving the Utemot encampment behind him, Cnaiür rode north across barren grasslands. He passed the herds of cattle, waving reluctantly at the distant horsemen—no more than armed children—who guarded them. The Utemot had become a thin people, not so different from the wandering tribes to the northeast that they drove away time and again. The disaster at Kiyuth had exacted a heavier toll on them than on many other tribes, and now their cousins to the south, the Kuöti and the Ennutil, raided their pastures at will. Even though Cnaiür had accomplished much with little in the ways of small tribal war, the Utemot, he knew, were very near extinction. Something as simple as another summer drought could doom them.

He crested balding hillocks, urged his mount through scrub and spring-swollen streams. The sun was white and distant and seemed to throw no shadows. The air smelled of winter's retreat, of damp earth beneath thatched grasses. The Steppe spread before him, swept by silvery wind-chased waves. Halfway to the horizon, the barrows of his ancestors swelled from the turf. Cnaiür's father was buried there, as were all the fathers of his line, back to the beginning.

Why had he come here? What purpose could such a solitary pilgrimage serve? No wonder his tribe thought him mad. He was a man who took counsel with the dead rather than the wise.

The unkempt silhouette of a vulture rose from the burial mounds, floated like a kite, then dipped back out of view. Several moments passed before the peculiarity of this struck Cnaiür. Something had died here—recently. Something unburied or unburned.

He urged his mount to a cautious trot, peering between the barrows. The wind numbed his face and tossed his hair into ribbons.

He found the first dead man a short distance from the nearest mound. Two black arrows, fired close enough to punch through the wire-knitted plates of his brigandine, jutted from his back. Cnaiür dismounted and scrutinized the surrounding turf, parting the grasses with palm and finger. He found tracks.

Sranc. Sranc had killed this man. He studied the barrows once again, searching the grasses. Listened. He could hear only wind and, periodically, the squabbling cries of distant vultures.

The dead man was unmutilated. The Sranc had not finished.

He rolled the corpse over with his boot; the arrows snapped with two dry cracks. The grey face gaped skyward, arched back in rigor, but the blue eyes had not sunken. The man was Norsirai—the blond hair told him that much. But who was he? Part of a band of raiders, outnumbered and pursued south by the Sranc? It had happened before.

Cnaiür grabbed his horse's bridle, pulled it down to the grasses. He drew his sword, then keeping low, sprinted across the turf. Shortly, he found himself among the barrows . . .

Where he found the second dead man. This one had died facing his foe. A broken arrow protruded from the back of his left thigh. Wounded, forced to abandon the flight, then murdered in a manner common to the Sranc: gutted, then strangled with his own bowel. But aside from his gaping belly, Cnaiür could see no other wounds. He knelt and grabbed one of the corpse's cold hands. He pinched the calluses. Too soft. Not raiders after all. At least not all of them. Who were these men? What outland fools— and from some *city*, no less—would risk the Sranc to travel to *Scylvendi* land?

A change in the wind revealed how close he'd drawn to the vultures. He dashed quickly to the left so that he might approach what had to be the greatest concentration of dead from behind one of the larger barrows. Halfway to the summit, he came across the first of the Sranc bodies, its neck partially severed. Like all dead Sranc, it was as rigid as stone, its skin chapped and purple-black. It lay curled like a dog, still clutching its bone bow. From its position and the bruised grasses, Cnaiür knew it had been struck on the summit of the barrow, hard enough to very nearly roll to the bottom.

He found the weapon that had killed it a short distance above. An iron axe, black, with a ring of human teeth set into a handle of leathered human skin. A Sranc killed by a Sranc weapon . . .

What had happened here?

Cnaiür suddenly found himself keenly aware that he crouched on the side of a *barrow,* in the midst of his dead forefathers. In part, he was outraged at the sacrilege, but he was more frightened by far. What could this mean?

His breath sharp beneath his breastbone, he crept to the summit.

The vultures were congregated around the base of the adjacent barrow, hunched over their spoils, their backs rifled by the wind. A handful of jackdaws squabbled among them, skipping from face to face. Their scavenge matted the ground: the corpses of Sranc sprawled or huddled against one another, matting the circumference of the barrow, heaped in places, heads lolling from broken necks, faces nestled in the crotches of inert arms and legs. So many! Only the barrow's apex was bald.

The last stand of a single man. An impossible stand.

The survivor sat cross-legged on the barrow summit, his forearms resting against his knees, his head bowed beneath the shining disc of the sun. The Steppe's pale lines framed him.

No animal possesses senses as keen as those of vultures; within moments they began croaking in alarm, scooping the wind in great ragged wings. The survivor lifted his head, watching them take flight. Then, as though his senses were every bit as keen as a vulture's, he turned to Cnaiür.

Cnaiür could discern very little of his face. Long, heavy-featured but aquiline. Blue eyes, perhaps, but that simply followed from his blond hair.

Yet with horror Cnaiür thought, *I know this man . . .*

He stood, walked toward the carnage, his limbs buoyant with disbelief. The figure regarded him impassively.

I know this man!

He picked his way through the dead Sranc, numbly realized that each of them had perished as a result of a single, unerring strike.

No . . . It can't be. This can't be.

The pitch of the ground seemed far steeper than it was. The Sranc at his feet seemed to howl soundlessly, warning him, beseeching him, as though the horror of the man on the summit above was enough to transcend the abyss between their races.

He paused several paces below the outlander. Warily, he raised his father's sword before him, his scarred arms outstretched. At last, he dared look at the sitting man directly, his heart thundering with something beyond fear or rage . . .

It was him.

Bloodied, pale, but it *was* him. A nightmare made flesh.

"You . . ." Cnaiür whispered.

The man did not move but studied him passionlessly. Cnaiür saw blood welling like pitch from a hidden wound, blackening his grey tunic.

With the deranged certainty of one who's dreamed a moment a thousand times, Cnaiür climbed five more steps, then placed the polished tip of his blade beneath the man's chin. With it, he raised the impassive face to the sun. The lips . . .

Not him! Almost him . . .

"You are Dûnyain," he said, his voice deep and cold.

The bright eyes regarded him, but there was absolutely nothing in the expression—no fear, no relief, neither recognition nor the lack of it. Then, like a flower sinking on a bruised stalk, the man slumped back against the turf.

Cnaiür's heart hammered.

What does this mean?

Bewildered, the Chieftain of the Utemot looked across the thatched carcasses of the Sranc to the burial mounds of his line, the ancient earthen record of his blood. Then, returning his eyes to the unconscious figure before him, he suddenly felt the bones in the mound beneath his feet—curled in a fetal position, buried deep. And he realized . . .

He stood atop the summit of his father's barrow.

———— ⊗◦⊗ ————

Anissi. The first wife of his heart. In the darkness, she was a shadow, willowy and cool against his sunburned frame. Her hair curled across his chest in patterns reminiscent of the strange writings he'd seen so many times in Nansur. Through the hide of the yaksh, the night rain sounded like an endless breath.

She shifted, drew her face from his shoulder to his arm. He was surprised. He'd thought her asleep. *Anissi . . . How I love this peace between us.*

Her voice was drowsy and young. "I asked him . . ."

Him. It troubled Cnaiür, hearing his wives refer to the outlander in this way—*his* way—as if they'd somehow penetrated his skull and practised thievery. Him. The son of Moënghus. The Dûnyain. Through rain and hide walls, Cnaiür could feel the itch of the man's presence across the dark encampment—a terror from beyond the horizon.

"And what did he say?"

"He said the dead men you found were from Atrithau."

Cnaiür had already determined as much. Aside from Sakarpus, Atrithau was the only city north of the Steppe—the only city of Men, anyway.

"Yes, but who were they?"

"He called them his followers."

A pang of apprehension clutched his heart. Followers. *He is the same . . . He possesses men the way his father once possessed—*

"What does it matter," Anissi asked, "the identity of dead men?"

"It matters." Everything mattered when it came to the Dûnyain. Since his discovery of Anasûrimbor Kellhus, one thought had tyrannized the movements of Cnaiür's soul, *Use the son to find the father*. If this man followed Moënghus, then he knew where to find him.

Even now Cnaiür could see his own father, Skiötha, thrashing and kicking in icy mud at the feet of Moënghus. His throat crushed. A chieftain slain by an unarmed slave. The years had turned this image into a narcotic, into something Cnaiür obsessively revisited. But for some reason it was never quite the same. Details changed. Sometimes, rather than spitting at his father's blackening face, Cnaiür would cradle it. Sometimes, rather than Skiötha dying at the feet of Moënghus, Moënghus would die at the feet of Cnaiür, son of Skiötha.

A life for a life. A father for a father. Vengeance. Wouldn't this remedy the imbalance that had unhinged his heart?

Use the son to find the father. But could he risk such a thing? What if it happened again?

For an instant Cnaiür forgot how to breathe.

He'd counted only sixteen summers the year his cousin Okyati had ridden into camp with Anasûrimbor Moënghus. Okyati and his war party had taken the man from a band of Sranc travelling across Suskara. This in itself was enough to make the outlander an item of interest: few men survived such captivity. Okyati dragged the man to Skiötha's yaksh and laughing harshly, said, "He's fallen into kinder hands."

Skiötha claimed Moënghus as his tribute and gave him to his first wife, Cnaiür's birth mother, as a gift. "For the sons you have borne me," Skiötha said. And Cnaiür thought, *For me*.

Throughout the transaction, Moënghus had simply watched, blue eyes glittering from a battered face. When his gaze momentarily settled on Skiötha's son, Cnaiür sneered at him with adolescent contempt. The man was little more than a bundle of rags, pale skin, mud, and clotted blood—another broken outlander, less than an animal.

But this, Cnaiür now knew, was precisely what the man had wanted his captors to think. For a Dûnyain, even degradation was a potent tool—perhaps the most potent.

Afterward, Cnaiür would see the new slave from time to time, twisting tendon into string, curing hides, bearing sacks of dung for their fires, and the like. The man scurried the same as the others, moved with the same hollow-limbed haste. If Cnaiür noticed him at all it was because of the man's provenance. *There . . . there's the one who survived the Sranc.* Cnaiür would glare at him for a heart-beat before moving on. But how long had those dark eyes studied him afterward?

Several weeks passed before Moënghus actually spoke to him. The man chose his moment well: the night of Cnaiür's return from the Rite-of-the-Spring-Wolves. Reeling from loss of blood, Cnaiür had staggered home through the darkness, the wolf's head bound to his girdle. He collapsed before the entrance of his mother's yaksh, heaving sputum against the bare earth. Moënghus was the first to find him, the first to staunch his pulsing wounds.

"You've killed the wolf," the slave said, drawing him up from the dust. The shadowy encampment swam about Moënghus's face, and yet his glistening eyes seemed as fixed and immovable as the Nail of Heaven. In his anguish, Cnaiür found a shameful reprieve in those outland eyes—sanctuary.

Thrusting aside the man's hands, he croaked, "But it didn't happen as it should."

Moënghus nodded. "You have killed the wolf."

You have killed the wolf.

Those words. Those capturing words! Moënghus had seen his anguish, had uttered the only words that might balm his heart. Nothing had happened as it should have, and yet the outcome was proper. He *had* killed the wolf.

The following day, as Cnaiür recovered in the leathery gloom of his mother's yaksh, Moënghus brought him a stew of wild onion and rabbit. After the steaming bowl had exchanged hands, the broken man looked up, raised his face from hunched shoulders. All the marks of his slavery—the timid stoop, the shallow breath, the fear-quickened eyes—fell away. The transformation was so abrupt, so complete, that for several moments Cnaiür could only stare at him in startled wonder.

But it was an outrage for a slave to look a warrior in the eye, so Cnaiür took up the slave-stick and beat him. The blue eyes were unsurprised and remained fixed on him the whole time, tugging at his own with their disturbing calm, as if forgiving him his . . . ignorance. Cnaiür fell short of truly punishing him, just as he fell short of the indignation that should have driven his stick.

The second time Moënghus dared look at him, Cnaiür beat him viciously—so viciously his mother chastised him afterward, accused him of wilfully damaging her property. The man was insolent, Cnaiür told her, but his heart was crimped by shame. Even then he had known that desperation rather than pious fury had fuelled his arm. Even then he'd known that Moënghus had stolen his heart.

Only years afterward would he understand how those beatings had bound him to the outlander. Violence between men fostered an unaccountable intimacy—Cnaiür had survived enough battlefields to understand that. By punishing Moënghus out of desperation, Cnaiür had demonstrated need. *You must be my slave. You must belong to me!* And by demonstrating need, he'd opened his heart, had allowed the serpent to enter.

The third time Moënghus matched his gaze, Cnaiür did not reach for his stick. Instead he asked: "Why? Why do you provoke me?"

"Because you, Cnaiür urs Skiötha, are more than your kinsmen. Because you alone can understand what I've to say."

You alone.

More capturing words. What young man does not chafe in the shadow of his elders? What young man does not harbour secret resentments, pompous hopes?

"Speak."

Moënghus spoke about many things over the months that followed, about how Men slumbered, about how the Logos, the way of intellect, was the only thing that could awaken them. But all of it was a blur to Cnaiür now. Of all their secret transactions, he remembered only the first with any clarity. But then inaugural sins always burned the brightest. Like beacons.

"When the warriors raid the Empire across the mountains," Moënghus said, "they always use the same trails, do they not?"

"Yes. Of course."

"But why?"

Cnaiür shrugged. "Because the trails are mountain passes. There's no other way to cross into the Empire."

"And when the warriors gather to raid their neighbours' pastures, they always use the same trails, do they not?"

"No."

"Why not?"

"Because they ride across open ground. The ways of crossing the Steppe are without number."

"Exactly!" Moënghus exclaimed. "And is not every task like a journey? Every accomplishment a destination? Every hunger a point of departure?"

"I suppose . . . The memorialists say as much."

"Then the memorialists are wise."

"Make your point, slave."

Laughter, flawless in its coarse Scylvendi cadences—the laugh of a great warrior. Even then Moënghus had known what poses to strike. "Do you see? You grow impatient because you think the path I take too convoluted. Even words are like journeys!"

"So?"

"So if all things men do are journeys, I ask you, why are the ways of the Scylvendi, the customs that bind what men do, like mountain passes? Why do they ride the same trails, over and over again, when the ways to their destination are without number?"

For some reason, this question thrilled Cnaiür. The words were so audacious he felt bold for simply hearing them, and so compelling he felt at once exhilarated and aghast, as though they had touched a place that ached to be touched all the more because it was forbidden.

The ways of the People, he'd been told, were as immutable and as sacred as the ways of the outlanders were fickle and degenerate. But why? Weren't these ways simply different trails used to reach similar destinations? What made the Scylvendi way the *only* way, the only track an upright man might follow? And how could this be when the trackless Steppe dwelt, as the memorialists said, in all things Scylvendi?

For the first time Cnaiür saw his people through the eyes of an outsider. How strange it all seemed! The hilarity of skin dyes made from menstrual blood. The uselessness of the prohibitions against bedding virgins unwitnessed, against the right-handed butchering of cattle, against defecating in the presence of horses. Even the ritual scars on their arms, their swazond, seemed flimsy and peculiar, more a mad vanity than a hallowed sign.

For the first time he had truly asked *why*. As a child he'd been prone to question, so much so that any question he asked his mother, no matter how practical, had occasioned complaints and reproofs—expressions, he knew, of an old maternal grudge against a gallingly precocious child. But the questions of children were only accidentally profound. Children questioned as much to be rebuffed as to be answered, as they must in order to learn which questions were permissible and which were not. To truly ask why, however, was to move beyond all permission.

To question everything. To ride the trackless Steppe.

"Where no paths exist," Moënghus had continued, "a man strays only when he misses his destination. There is no crime, no transgression, no sin save foolishness or incompetence, and no obscenity save the tyranny of custom. But you already know this . . . You stand apart from your tribe."

Moënghus's hand had drifted out to clasp his own. There was something lethargic, something thick and swollen, in his tone. His eyes were soft, plaintive, wet like his lips.

"Is it a sin for me to touch you thus? Why? What mountain pass have we strayed from?"

"None . . ." Breathless.

"Why?"

"Because we ride the Steppe." *And there is nothing more holy.*

A smile, like a father or a lover suddenly struck by the violence of his adoration. "We Dûnyain, Cnaiür, are guides and trackers, students of the Logos, the Shortest Way. Of all the world, we alone have awakened from the dread slumber of custom. We alone."

He drew Cnaiür's young hand to his lap. Thumbs probed the spaces between his calluses.

How could bliss ache so?

"Tell me, Chieftain-son, what do you desire before all things? What circumstance? Tell *me*, one who is awake, and I'll show you the trail you must follow."

Cnaiür wet his lips and lied, "To become a great chieftain of the People."

Those words! Those heartbreaking words!

Moënghus had nodded in the weighty manner of a memorialist satisfied by powerful omens. "Good. We shall ride together, you and I, across the open Steppe. I shall show you a track like no other."

Months later, Skiötha was dead and Cnaiür had become Chieftain of the Utemot. He had attained what he had pretended to covet, the White Yaksh—his destination.

Though his tribesmen begrudged him the path he had travelled, custom bound them to him. He had walked forbidden trails, and his kinsmen, constrained by the deep tracks of stupidity and blind habit, could only scowl and mutter behind his back. What pride he had felt! But it was a strange pride, wan, like the lonely sense of exemption and impunity he'd experienced as a young boy watching his brothers and sisters sleep by firelight, thinking, *I could do anything.*

Anything. And they would not know.

Then, two seasons later, the other women strangled his mother for giving birth to a blonde girl. As they raised her corpse on the vulture poles, he began to understand what had actually happened.

His mother's death, he knew, was a destination, the outcome of a journey. And Moënghus was the traveller.

At first, he was baffled. The Dûnyain had seduced and impregnated his mother, that much was clear. But to what end? What further destination?

And then he understood: to secure access to her son—to Cnaiür urs Skiötha.

Thus began his obsessive rehearsal of the events that had brought him to the White Yaksh. Step by step, he recounted the skid of small, juvenile treasons into patricide. Soon the reedy sense of gratification at having outwitted his betters evaporated. Soon the jaw-tight jubilation at having destroyed someone hapless changed into stunned incredulity, desolate disbelief. He had taken pride in transcending his kinsmen, in being more, and he'd exulted in the demonstration of that transcendence. He had found the shortest way. He had seized the White Yaksh. Was this not proof of his superiority? So Moënghus had told him before leaving the Utemot. So he had thought.

Now he understood: he had done nothing except betray his father. Like his mother, he had been seduced.

My father is dead. I was the knife.

And Anasûrimbor Moënghus had wielded him.

The revelation was as breathtaking as it was heartbreaking. Once, when Cnaiür was a child, a whirlwind had roared through the Utemot encampment, its shoulders in the clouds, yaksh, cattle, and lives swirling like skirts about its feet. He had watched it from a distance, wailing, clutching his father's rigid waist. Then it had vanished, like sand settling in water. He could remember his father running through the hail to assist his kinsmen. He could remember beginning to follow, then stumbling to a halt, transfixed by the vista before him as though the scale of the transformation had dwarfed his eyes' ability to believe. The great rambling web of tracks, pens, and yaksh had been utterly rewritten, as though some mountain-tall child had drawn sweeping circles with a stick. Horror had replaced familiarity, but order had replaced order.

Like the whirlwind, his revelation regarding Moënghus had blasted a different, far more horrifying order from what he had known. Triumph became degradation. Pride became remorse. Moënghus was no longer the greater father of his heart. Instead he was an impossible tyrant, a slaver masquerading as a slave. The words that had elevated him, that had revealed truth and rapture, became words that had abased him, that had forced obscene advantages. The expressions that had comforted him became chits in some mad game. Everything—the look, the touch, the endearing mannerism—had been taken up by the whirlwind and violently rewritten.

For a time, he'd truly thought himself awake, the only one who did not stumble and grope through the dreams foisted on the Scylvendi by the customs of their forefathers. For them, the Steppe was ground not just to their feet and their bellies but to their souls as well. And yet he, Cnaiür urs Skiötha, knew and lived the truth of the Steppe. He alone was *awake*. Where others filed through illusory canyons, his soul ranged the trackless plains. He alone was truly of the land.

He alone. Why was there such terrible power in standing not apart from but *before* one's tribe?

But the whirlwind had seized this as well. He could remember his mother weeping after his father's death, but did she weep for Skiötha, whom she had lost to death, or, as Cnaiür himself had done, for Moënghus, whom she had lost to the horizon? For Moënghus, Cnaiür knew, the seduction of Skiötha's first wife was but a waystation, a point of departure for the seduction of Skiötha's first-born son. What lies had he whispered as he speared her in the dark? That he did lie Cnaiür was certain, since he neither spoke nor loved *for her*. And if he lied to her, then . . .

Everything that happened was a quest, as Moënghus had said. Even the movements of one's soul—thought, desire, love—were journeys across something trackless. Cnaiür had thought himself a point of departure, the origin of all his far-travelling thoughts. But he was nothing more than a muddied track, a trail used by another to reach his destination. The thoughts he had called his own had all along belonged to another. His wakefulness was but one more dream in a deeper slumber. By some unearthly cunning, he had been tricked into obscenity after obscenity, degradation after degradation, and *he had wept with gratitude*.

And his tribesmen, he realized, knew this, if only in the dim way that wolves smell frailty. The scorn and laughter of fools meant nothing when one dwelt in the truth. But when one was deceived . . .

Weeper.

Such torment!

For thirty years Cnaiür had lived with this whirlwind, intensifying its thunder with further insight and endless recriminations. Seasons of anguish had been heaped upon it.

Awake, it moved through him without breath, with the curious flatness of performing a task with empty lungs.

But asleep . . . He had suffered many dreams.

Moënghus's face rises from the depths of a pool, pale through the greenish cast of the water. Throughout the surrounding darkness, caverns intertwine, like the thin tunnels one finds beneath large stones pulled from the grass. Just beneath the surface, the pale Dûnyain pauses as though tugged by some deep restraint, smiles, and raises his mouth. With horror, Cnaiür watches as an earthworm presses through the smiling lips and pierces the water. It feels the air like a blind finger. Watery and obscene, the bland pink of hidden places. And always, his own inarticulate hand drifts over the pool and, in a quiet moment of insanity, touches it.

But now Cnaiür was awake, and the face had returned. He'd found it on his pilgrimage to the barrows of his ancestors. It had come from the northern wastes, wracked by exposure, riddled by Sranc wounds.

Anasûrimbor Kellhus, son of Anasûrimbor Moënghus. But what did this second coming mean? Would it provide an answer to the whirlwind, or would it merely redouble its fury?

Dare he use the son to find the father? Dare he cross the trackless Steppe?

Anissi raised her head from his chest and studied his face. Her breasts skimmed the hollow of his belly. Her eyes glistened in the dark. She was, Cnaiür thought, far too beautiful to belong to him.

"You still haven't spoken to him," she said, dipping her head to the fall of her hair, then lowering her lips to kiss his arm. "Why?"

"I told you . . . He has great power."

He could feel her think. Perhaps it was the closeness of her lips to his skin. "I share your . . . misgivings," she said. "But sometimes I don't know who's more frightening, you or him."

Anger stirred in him, the slow, dangerous anger of one whose authority is unquestioned and absolute. "Frightened of me? Why?"

"I fear *him* because already he speaks our tongue as well as any slave of ten years. I fear him because his eyes . . . do not seem to blink. He has already made me laugh, made me cry."

Silence. Scenes flashed through his thoughts, a string of broken and breaking images. He stiffened against the mat, tensed his limbs against her softness.

"I fear you," she continued, "because you've told me this would happen. Each of these things you knew would happen. You know this man, and yet you've never spoken to him."

His throat ached. *You've cried only when I've hit you.*

She kissed his arm and touched his lips with a finger. "Yesterday he said to me, 'Why does he wait?'"

Since he'd found the man, events had moved with such certainty, as though the smallest happening was soaked in waters of fate and portent. There could be no greater intimacy between him and this man. With his bare hands he had choked him to death in dream after dream.

"You never mentioned me?" he asked—and commanded.

"No. I didn't. Again you know him. And he knows you."

"Through you. He sees me through you." For a moment he wondered what it was the outlander saw, what image of him would leak from the beautiful expressions of Anissi. Much of the truth, he decided.

Of all his wives, only Anissi had the courage to hold him when he cried out in his sleep. Only she whispered to him when he awoke weeping. The others were stiff, dead in the pretence of sleep. Which was good. The others he would have beaten, beaten for daring witness such weakness.

In the dark, Anissi grabbed his shoulder and tugged as though to pull him from some great danger. "Lord, this is sacrilege. He's a *witch*. A sorcerer."

"No. He is less. And he's more."

"How? How do you know?" The caution was gone from her voice. She was insistent.

He closed his eyes. Bannut's grizzled face flashed from the darkness, surrounded by the furore of Kiyuth.

Weeping faggot . . .

"Sleep, Anissi."

Dare he use the son to find the father?

———— ❧ ————

The day was sunny, with a warmth that spoke of summer's inevitability. Cnaiür paused before the broad cone of the yaksh, following the patterns of stitching across its hide faces. This was the type of day when the last of the winter would be dried from the leather and wood crevices of the yaksh, when the smell of rot would be replaced with that of dust.

He squatted before the entrance flap and touched two fingers to the ground, bringing them to his lips as was custom. He took comfort in this act, though the reasons for it were long dead. He hooked the flap and slipped into the dim interior, where he sat cross-legged with his back to the opening.

He struggled to sort the chained figure from the dark. His heart thundered.

"My wives tell me you've learned our language with a swiftness that's . . . mad."

Pallid light filtered from behind him. He saw naked limbs, grey like dead branches. The smell of urine and bowel crowded the air. The man looked and reeked of frailty and sickness. This, Cnaiür knew, was no accident.

"I learn quickly, yes." The shadowy head lowered, as though dipping to . . .

Cnaiür suppressed a shiver. So much alike.

"My wives tell me you're a witch."

"I'm not." Prolonged breath. "But you already know this."

"I think I know." He pulled his Chorae from a small pouch fixed to his girdle, then tossed it in a low arc. Fetters clattered. The outlander snapped the sphere from the air as though it were a fly.

Nothing happened.

"What's this?"

"A gift to my people from very ancient times. A gift from our God. It kills witches."

"The runes across it?"

"Mean nothing. Not now."

"You don't trust me. You fear me."

"I fear nothing."

No response. A pause to reconsider ill-chosen words.

"No," the Dûnyain finally said. "You fear many things."

Cnaiür clamped his teeth. Again. It was happening again! Words like levers, shoving him backward over a trail of precipices. Rage fell through him like fire through choked halls. A scourge.

"You," he grated, "know I'm different from the others. You felt my presence through my wives because of my knowledge. Know that I will do the contrary of many things you say, simply because it is you who say it. Know that each night I will use the entrails of a hare to decide whether I shall let you live.

"I know who you are, Anasûrimbor. I know that you're Dûnyain."

If the man was taken aback, there was no indication. He simply said, "I'll answer your questions."

"You will relate everything you've concluded about your present circumstance. You will explain your purpose in coming here. If you don't do so to my satisfaction, I'll have you put to death—immediately."

The threat was powerful, the words thick with certainty. Other men would brood over them, weigh them in silence in order to gauge their reply. But the Dûnyain did not. He answered immediately, as if there could be no surprise in anything Cnaiür might say or do.

"I still live because my father passed through your lands in your youth and committed some crime for which you seek redress. I don't think it possible for you to kill me, though this is your desire. You're too intelligent to find satisfaction in substitutes. You understand the danger I represent, and yet you still hope to use me as the instrument of your greater desire. My circumstances, then, are of a piece with your purpose."

Momentary silence. Cnaiür's thoughts tumbled both in shock and in affirmation, then he recoiled in sudden suspicion. *This man is intellect . . . War.*

"You're troubled," the voice said. "You'd anticipated this appraisal, but not that I would speak it, and because I've spoken it, you fear that I merely cater to your expectations in order to mislead you in some deeper way." A pause. "Like my father, Moënghus."

Cnaiür spat. "Words for your kind are knives! But they don't always cut, do they? Crossing Suskara nearly killed you. Perhaps I should think as a Sranc."

The outlander began to reply, but Cnaiür had already rolled to his feet and bowed out into the clear Steppe air, crying out for assistance. He watched impassively as his people dragged the Norsirai from the yaksh, then bound his naked form to a pole near the centre of the camp. For hours the man sobbed and howled, shrieked for mercy as they plied him in the old ways. His bowels even relaxed, such was the agony.

Cnaiür struck Anissi when she began weeping. He believed none of it.

That night Cnaiür returned, knowing, or hoping, that the darkness would protect him.

The air still reeked beneath the skins. The outlander was as silent as moonlight.

"Now," Cnaiür said, "your purpose . . . And don't think I'm deluded into believing I've broken you. Your kind is not to be broken."

There was a rustle in the blackness. "You're right." The voice was warm in the dark. "For my kind there's only mission. I've come for my father, Anasûrimbor Moënghus. I've come to kill him."

Silence, save for a gentle southern wind.

The outlander continued: "Now the dilemma is wholly yours, Scylvendi. Our missions would seem to be the same. I know where and, more important, how to find Anasûrimbor Moënghus. I offer you the very cup you desire. Is it poison or no?"

Dare he use the son?

"It's always poison," Cnaiür grated, "when you thirst."

The wives of the chieftain ministered to Kellhus, rinsed his broken skin with ointments made by the old women of the tribe. Sometimes he spoke to them as they did so, calmed their frightened eyes with tender words, made them smile.

When the time came for their husband and the Norsirai to depart, they congregated on the chill ground outside the White Yaksh and solemnly watched as the men prepared their horses. They sensed the monolithic hatred of the one and the godlike indifference of the other. And when the two figures were encompassed by distant grasses, they did not know for whom they wept—for the man who had mastered them or the man who had known them.

Only Anissi knew the source of her tears.

∞∞

Cnaiür and Kellhus rode southeast, crossing from Utemot lands into those of the Kuöti. Near the southern limit of the Kuöti pastures, they were overtaken by several horsemen with polished wolf-skull pommels and plumed cantles. Cnaiür spoke with them briefly, reminded them of the Ways, and they rode away—eager, he imagined, to tell their chieftain that at last the Utemot were without Cnaiür urs Skiötha, breaker-of-horses and most violent of men.

Once they were alone, the Dûnyain again tried to engage him in conversation.

"You cannot maintain this silence forever," he said.

Cnaiür studied the man. His blond-bearded face was grey against the overcast distances. He wore the sleeveless harness common to the Scylvendi, and his pale forearms extended from the pelt cloak draping from his shoulders. The marmot tails trimming the cloak swayed with his horse's gait. He might have been Scylvendi were it not for his pale hair and unscarred arms—both of which made him look a woman.

"What do you want to know?" Cnaiür asked with suspicious reluctance. He thought it a good thing he was disturbed by the northerner's flawless Scylvendi. It was his reminder. As soon as the northerner no longer disturbed him, he knew, he would be lost. This was why he so often refused to speak to the abomination, why they'd ridden these past days in silence. Habit was the peril here as much as the cunning of the man. As soon as the presence of the man failed to sting, as soon as he fell flush with circumstance, he would, Cnaiür knew, somehow stand before him in the passage of events, would steer him in ways that could not be seen.

Back at the camp Cnaiür had used his wives as intermediaries in order to insulate himself from Kellhus. This was but one of many precautions he'd taken. He'd even slept with a knife in hand, knowing the man need not break his chains to visit him. He could come as another—even as Anissi—the way Moënghus had come to Cnaiür's father those many years ago, wearing the face of his eldest son.

But now Cnaiür had no brokers to preserve him. He could not even depend upon silence, as he'd initially hoped. As they neared the Nansurium, they would be forced to discuss plans. Even wolves needed plots to preserve them in a land of dogs.

Now he was alone with a Dûnyain, and he could imagine no greater peril.

"Those men," Kellhus said. "Why did they grant you passage?"

Cnaiür shot him a wary glance. *He begins with small things so that he may slip unnoticed into my heart.*

"It's our custom. All the tribes make seasonal raids on the Empire."

"Why?"

"For many reasons. For slaves. For plunder. But for worship, most of all."

"For worship?"

"We are the People of War. Our God is dead, murdered by the peoples of the Three Seas. It's our place to avenge him." Cnaiür found himself regretting this reply. On the surface it seemed innocuous enough, but for the first time he realized just how much this fact said about the People, and by extension, about him. *There are no small things for this man.* Every detail, every word, was a knife in the hands of this outlander.

"But how," the Dûnyain pressed, "can one worship what is dead?"

Say nothing, he thought, but he was already speaking.

"Death is greater than man. It should be worshipped."

"But death is—"

"I'll ask the questions," Cnaiür snapped. "Why were you sent to murder your father?"

"This," Kellhus said wryly, "is something you should've asked before accepting my bargain."

Cnaiür quashed the impulse to smile, knowing that this was the reaction the Dûnyain sought.

"Why so?" he countered. "Without me there's no way you could cross the Steppe alive. Until the Hethanta Mountains, you're mine. I have until then to make my judgement."

"But if it's impossible for outlanders to cross the Steppe alone, how did my father make his escape?"

The hairs raised along Cnaiür's arms, but he thought: *Good question. One that reminds me of your kind's treachery.*

"Moënghus was cunning. In secret he'd scarred his arms and concealed them. After he'd murdered my father and the Utemot were bound by honour not to molest him, he shaved his face and dyed his hair black. Since he could speak as though he were one of the People, he simply crossed the land as we do, as an Utemot riding to worship. His eyes were nearly pale enough . . ." Then Cnaiür added, "Why do you think I forbade you clothing in your captivity?"

"Who gave him the dye?"

Cnaiür's heart almost stopped. "I did."

The Dûnyain merely nodded and looked away to the dreary horizon. Cnaiür found himself following his eyes.

"I was possessed!" he snarled. "Possessed by a demon!"

"Indeed," Kellhus replied, turning back to him. There was compassion in his eyes, but his voice was stern, like that of a Scylvendi. "My father inhabited you."

And Cnaiür found himself *wanting* to hear what the man would say. *You can help me. You are wise . . .*

Again! The witch was doing it again! Redirecting his discourse. Conquering the movements of his soul. He was like a snake probing for opening after opening. Weakness after weakness. *Begone from my heart!*

"Why were you sent to murder your father?" Cnaiür demanded, seizing on this unanswered question as evidence of the inhuman depths of this contest. And it was a contest, Cnaiür realized. He did not speak with this man; he warred against him. *I will trade knives.*

The Dûnyain looked at him curiously, as though wearied by his senseless suspicion. Another ploy.

"Because my father summoned me," he replied cryptically.

"And this is grounds for murder?"

"The Dûnyain have hidden from the world for two millennia, and they would remain hidden, if they could, for all eternity. Yet thirty-one years ago, while I was still but a child, we were discovered by a band of Sranc. The Sranc were easily destroyed, but as a precaution, my father was sent into the wilderness to ascertain the extent of our exposure. When he returned some months later, it was decided that he must be exiled. He'd been contaminated, had become a threat to our mission. Three decades passed, and it was assumed he'd perished."

The Dûnyain frowned. "But then he returned to us, returned in a way that was unprecedented. He sent us dreams."

"Sorcery," Cnaiür said.

The Dûnyain nodded. "Yes. Although we didn't know this at the time. We knew only that the purity of our isolation had been polluted, that its source had to be found and eliminated."

Cnaiür studied the man's profile, which gently rocked to his horse's canter. "So you're an assassin."

"Yes."

When Cnaiür was silent, Kellhus continued, "You don't believe me."

How could he? How could he believe one who never truly *spoke* but steered and manoeuvred, manoeuvred and steered, endlessly?

"I don't believe you."

Kellhus turned to the surrounding expanses of grey-green plain. They had passed beyond the rolling pastures of the Kuöti and now crossed the great tablelands of the Jiünati interior. Aside from a small stream ahead and the thin palisade of brush and poplars along its sunken banks, the distances were as bland as an ocean's. Only the sky, filled with clouds like sailing mountains, possessed depth.

"The Dûnyain," Kellhus said after a time, "have surrendered themselves to the Logos, to what you would call reason and intellect. We seek absolute awareness, the self-moving thought. The thoughts of all men arise from the darkness. If you *are* the movement of your soul, and the *cause* of that movement precedes you, then how could you ever call your thoughts your own? How could you *be* anything other than a slave to the darkness that comes before? Only the Logos allows one to mitigate that slavery. Only knowing the sources of thought and action allows us to own our thoughts and our actions, to throw off the yoke of circumstance. And only the Dûnyain possess this knowledge, plainsman. The world slumbers, enslaved by its ignorance. Only the Dûnyain are *awake*. Moënghus, my father, threatens this."

Thoughts arising from darkness? Perhaps more than most, Cnaiür knew this to be true. He was plagued by thoughts that could not be his own. How many times, after striking one of his wives, had he looked to his stinging palm and thought: *Who moved me to do this? Who?*

But this was irrelevant.

"That isn't why I don't believe you," Cnaiür said, thinking, *He already knows this.* The Dûnyain could read him, he knew, as easily as a tribesman could read the temper of his herds.

As though he could see this thought, Kellhus said, "You don't believe that a son could be his father's assassin."

"Yes."

The man nodded. "Sentiments, like a son's love for his father, simply deliver us to the darkness, make us slaves of custom and appetite . . ." The shining blue eyes held Cnaiür's own, impossibly calm. "I don't love my father, plainsman. I do not love. If his murder will allow my brethren to pursue their mission, then I *will* murder him."

Cnaiür stared at the man, his head buzzing with exhaustion. Could he believe this? What the man said made undeniable sense, but then Cnaiür suspected that he could make anything sound believable.

"Besides," Anasûrimbor Kellhus continued, "certainly you know something of these matters."

"What matters?"

"Sons murdering fathers."

<hr />

Rather than reply, the Scylvendi shot him a momentary, damaged glare, then spat.

Maintaining an expression of bland expectancy, Kellhus cupped him in the palm of his senses. The Steppe, the nearing stream, everything in his periphery receded. Cnaiür urs Skiötha became all. The quick rhythm of his breath. The pose of muscle around his eyes. His pulse, like an earthworm twitching between the sinews of his neck. He became a chorus of signs, a living text, and Kellhus would read him. If these circumstances were to be owned, then everything had to be measured.

Since abandoning the trapper and fleeing south through the northern wastes, Kellhus had encountered many men, especially in the city of Atrithau. There he discovered that Leweth, the trapper who had saved him, was not an exception. World-born men were every bit as simple-minded and as deluded as the trapper had been. Kellhus needed only to utter a few rudimentary truths and they would be moved to wonder. He needed only to assemble these truths into coarse sermons, and they would surrender possessions, lovers, even children. Forty-seven men had accompanied him when he rode from Atrithau's southern gates, calling themselves the *adûnyani*, the "little Dûnyain." Not one survived the trek across Suskara. Out of love they had sacrificed everything, asking only for words in return. For the semblance of meaning.

But this Scylvendi was different.

Kellhus had confronted suspicion and distrust before, and he'd discovered that it could be turned to his advantage. Suspicious men, he'd found, yielded more than most when they finally gave their trust. Believing nothing at first, they suddenly believed everything, either to do penance for their initial misgivings or simply to avoid making the same "mistake." Many of his most fanatical followers had been doubters—in the beginning.

But the distrust harboured by Cnaiür urs Skiötha differed from anything he'd so far encountered, both in proportion and in kind. Unlike the others, this man *knew* him.

When the Scylvendi, his expression at once slack with shock and tight with hatred, had found him atop the barrow, Kellhus had thought, *Father . . . at last I've found you . . .* Each of them had seen Anasûrimbor Moënghus in the face of the other. They had never met, yet they knew each other with intimacy.

At first this bond had proven remarkably advantageous to Kellhus's mission. It had preserved his life, and it promised safe passage across the Steppe. But it had also rendered his circumstances incalculable.

The Scylvendi continued to deny his every attempt to possess him. He was not awed by the insights Kellhus offered. He was neither soothed by his rationalizations nor flattered by his oblique praise. And when his thoughts quickened in interest at what Kellhus said, he immediately recanted, remembering events decades dead. So far the man had yielded only grudging words and spit.

Somehow, after thirty years of obsessing over Moënghus, the man had happened upon several key truths regarding the Dûnyain. He knew of their ability to read thoughts through faces. He knew of their intellect. He knew of their absolute commitment to mission. And he knew they spoke not to share perspectives or to communicate truths but to come before—to dominate souls and circumstances.

He knew too much.

Kellhus studied him from his periphery, watched him lean back as the ground dipped toward the stream, his scarred shoulders immobile, his hips swaying to his horse's gait.

Was this what you intended, Father? Is he an obstacle you've placed in my path? Or is he an accident?

Likely the latter, Kellhus decided. Despite the crude lore of his people, the man was uncommonly intelligent. The thoughts of the truly intelligent rarely followed the same paths. They forked, and the thoughts of Cnaiür urs Skiötha had branched far, tracking Moënghus into places no world-born man had ventured.

Somehow he saw through you, Father, and now he sees through me. What was your mistake? Can it be undone?

Kellhus blinked and, in that instant, plunged away from slopes, sky, and wind, and dreamed a hundred parallel dreams of act and consequence, chasing threads of probability. Then he saw.

So far he'd tried to circumvent the Scylvendi's suspicion, when what he needed was to make it work *for* him. He looked at the plainsman anew, immediately saw the grief and fury fuelling his relentless distrust, then grasped the path of word, tone, and expression that would press the man to a place where he could not escape, where his suspicion would force dawning trust upon him.

Kellhus saw the Shortest Way. The Logos.

"I apologize," he said hesitantly. "What I said was inappropriate."

The Scylvendi snorted.

He knows that I speak false . . . Good.

Cnaiür looked him full in the face, his deep-set eyes wild with defiance.

"Tell me, Dûnyain, how does one steer thoughts the way others steer horses?"

"What do you mean?" Kellhus asked sharply, as though he were deciding whether to be offended. The tonal cues of the Scylvendi tongue were numerous, subtle, and differed drastically between men and women. Though the plainsman did not realize it, he'd denied Kellhus important tools by restricting him to his wives.

"Even now," Cnaiür barked, "you seek to steer the movements of my soul!"

The faint thrum of his heartbeat. The density of blood in his weathered skin. *He's still uncertain.*

"You think this is what my father did to you."

"That *is* what your father—" Cnaiür paused, his eyes dilating in alarm. "But you say this to misdirect me! To avoid my question!"

So far Kellhus had successfully anticipated each fork of the Scylvendi's thought. Cnaiür's responses followed a clear pattern: he would lunge down the tracks Kellhus opened for him then recoil. So long as their discourse approximated this pattern, Kellhus knew, the Scylvendi would think himself secure.

But how to proceed?

Nothing deceived so well as the truth.

"Every man I've met," he finally said, "I understand better than he understands himself."

The flinching look of a fear confirmed. "But how is that possible?"

"Because I have been bred. Because I have been trained. Because I am one of the Conditioned. I am Dûnyain."

Their horses romped through and across the shallow stream. Cnaiür leaned sideways and spat into the water. "Another answer that's not an answer," he snapped.

Could he tell him the truth? Not all of it, certainly.

Kellhus began with the semblance of hesitation: "All of you— your kinsmen, your wives, your children, even your foes beyond the mountains—cannot see the true sources of their thoughts and deeds. Either they assume they're the origin or they think it lies somewhere beyond the world—in the Outside, as I've heard it called. What comes before you, what truly determines your thoughts and deeds, is either missed altogether or attributed to demons and gods."

The flat eyes and tight teeth of unwanted recollections. *My father has already told him this* . . .

"What comes before determines what comes after," Kellhus continued. "For the Dûnyain, there's no higher principle."

"And just what comes before?" Cnaiür asked, trying to force a sneer.

"For Men? History. Language. Passion. Custom. All these things determine what men say, think, and do. These are the hidden puppet-strings from which all men hang."

Shallow breath. A face freighted by unwanted insights. "And when the strings are seen . . ."

"They may be seized."

In isolation this admission was harmless: in some respect all men sought mastery over their fellows. Only when combined with knowledge of his abilities could it prove threatening.

If he knew how deep I see . . .

How it would terrify them, world-born men, to see themselves through Dûnyain eyes. The delusions and the follies. The deformities.

Kellhus did not see faces, he saw forty-four muscles across bone and the thousands of expressive permutations that might leap from them—a second mouth as raucous as the first, and far more truthful. He did not hear men speaking, he heard the howl of the animal within, the whimper of the beaten child, the chorus of preceding generations. He did not see men, he saw example and effect, the deluded issue of fathers, tribes, and civilizations.

He did not see what came after. He saw what came before.

They rode through the saplings on the stream's far bank, ducking branches hazed by early spring green.

"Madness," Cnaiür said. "I don't believe you . . ."

Kellhus said nothing, steered his horse between trees and slapping limbs. He knew the paths of the Scylvendi's thoughts, the inferences he would make—if he could forget his fury.

"If all men are ignorant of the origins of their thoughts . . ." Cnaiür said.

Anxious to clear the brush, their horses galloped the last few lengths to open, endless ground.

"Then all men are deceived."

Kellhus secured his gaze for a crucial instant. "They act for reasons that are not their own."

Will he see?

"Like slaves . . ." Cnaiür began, a stunned scowl on his face. Then he recalled at whom he looked. "But you say this simply to exonerate yourself! What does it matter enslaving slaves, eh, Dûnyain?"

"So long as what comes before remains shrouded, so long as men are already deceived, what does it matter?"

"Because it's *deceit*. Womanish deception. An outrage against honour!"

"And you've never deceived your foes on the field of battle? You've never enslaved another?"

Cnaiür spat. "My enemies. My foes. Those who'd do the same to me if they could. That's the bargain all warriors strike, and it *is* an honourable one. But what you do, Dûnyain, makes all men your foe."

Such penetration!

"Does it? Or does it make them my children? What father does not rule his yaksh?"

At first Kellhus feared he'd been too oblique, then Cnaiür said: "So that's what we are to you? Children?"

"Didn't my father wield you as his instrument?"

"Answer my question!"

"Children to us? Of course you are. How else could my father have used you so effortlessly?"

"Deceit! Deceit!"

"Then why do you fear me so, Scylvendi?"

"Enough!"

"You were a weak child, were you not? You wept easily. You flinched each time your father raised his hand . . . Tell me, Scylvendi, how is it I know this?"

"Because it describes every child!"

"You prize Anissi above your other wives, not because of her greater beauty but because she alone weathers your torment and still loves. Because she alone—"

"She told you this! The whore told you this!"

"You hunger for illicit congress, for—"

"I said *enough!*"

For thousands of years the Dûnyain had been bred to the limits of their senses, trained to lay bare what came before. There were no secrets in their presence. No lies.

How many frailties of spirit did the Scylvendi suffer? How many trespasses of heart and flesh had he committed? All unspeakable. All gagged by fury and endless recrimination, hidden even from himself.

If Cnaiür urs Skiötha suspected Kellhus, then Kellhus would pay the wages of his suspicion. Truth. Unspeakable truth. Either the Scylvendi preserved his self-deception by abandoning his suspicion, thinking Kellhus a mere charlatan whom he need not fear, or he embraced the truth and shared the unspeakable with Moënghus's son. Either way Kellhus's mission would be served. Either way Cnaiür's trust would eventually be secured, be it the trust of contempt or the trust of love.

The Scylvendi nearly gaped at him, his eyes pinned wide by bewildered horror. Kellhus looked through this expression, saw the inflections of face, timbre, and word that would calm him, return him to inscrutability, or extinguish whatever self-possession remained.

"Is it this way with all many-blooded warriors? Do they all flinch from the truth?"

But something went wrong. For some reason the word "truth" struck the violence from Cnaiür's passion, and he went drowsy-calm, like a foal during bloodletting.

"Truth? You need only speak something to make it a lie, Dûnyain. You do not speak as other men speak."

Again his knowledge . . . But it was not too late.

"And how is it that other men speak?"

"The words men utter do not . . . belong to them. They do not follow tracks of their making."

Show him the folly. He'll see.

"The ground upon which men speak is trackless, Scylvendi . . . Like the Steppe."

Kellhus instantly recognized his error. Fury sparked in the man's eyes, and there could be no mistaking its source.

"The Steppe," Cnaiür grated, "is trackless, eh, Dûnyain?"

Is this the path you took, Father?

There could be no question. Moënghus had used the Steppe, the central figure of Scylvendi belief, as his primary vehicle. By exploiting the metaphoric inconsistency between the trackless Steppe and the deep tracks of Scylvendi custom, he'd been able to steer Cnaiür toward acts that would have otherwise been unimaginable to him. To be faithful to the Steppe, one must repudiate custom. And in the absence of customary prohibitions, any act, even the murder of one's father, became conceivable.

A simple and effective stratagem. But in the end, it had been too simple, too easily deciphered in his absence. It had allowed Cnaiür far too much insight into the Dûnyain.

"Again the whirlwind!" the man cried inexplicably.

He's mad.

"All of this!" he ranted. "Every word a whip!"

Kellhus saw only murder and riot in his face. Shining vengeance in his eyes.

By the end of the Steppe. I need him to cross Scylvendi lands, nothing more. If he hasn't succumbed by the time we reach the mountains, I will kill him.

That night they gathered dead grasses and wove them into rough sheaves. After they'd accumulated a small stack, Cnaiür set them alight. They sat close to the small fire, gnawing their provisions in silence.

"Why do you think Moënghus summoned you?" Cnaiür asked, struck by the peculiarity of speaking that name. *Moënghus* . . .

The Dûnyain chewed, his gaze lost in the fire's golden folds. "I don't know."

"You must know something. He sent you dreams."

Glittering in the firelight, the implacable blue eyes searched his own. *The scrutiny begins*, Cnaiür thought, but then he realized the scrutiny had begun long before, with his wives in the yaksh, and it had never ended.

Measure is unceasing.

"The dreams were of images only," Kellhus said. "Images of Shimeh. And of a violent contest between peoples. Dreams of history—the very thing that is anathema to the Dûnyain."

The man continually did this, Cnaiür understood, continually seeded his replies with comments that begged for retort or interrogation in their own right. History an anathema to the Dûnyain? But this was the man's purpose: to deflect the movements of Cnaiür's soul away from the more important questions. Such maddeningly subtlety!

"Yet he summoned you," Cnaiür pressed. "Who summons another without giving reasons?" *Unless he knows that the summoned will be compelled to come.*

"My father needs me. That's all I know."

"Needs you? For what?" *This. This is the question.*

"My father is at war, plainsman. What father fails to call on his son in times of war?"

"One who numbers his son among his enemies." *There's something more here . . . something I'm missing.*

He looked to the Norsirai across the fire and somehow knew the man had seen this revelation within him. How could he prevail in a war such as this? How could he overcome someone who could smell his thoughts from the subtleties of his expression? *My face . . . I must hide my face.*

"At war against whom?" Cnaiür asked.

"I don't know," Kellhus replied, and for instant he almost looked forlorn, like a man who'd wagered all in the shadow of disaster.

Pity? He seeks to elicit pity from a Scylvendi? For a moment Cnaiür almost laughed. *Perhaps I have overestimated—* But again his instincts saved him.

With his shining knife, Cnaiür sawed off another chunk of *amicut*, the strips of dried beef, wild herbs, and berries that were the mainstay of their provisions. He stared impassively at the Dûnyain as he chewed.

He wants me to think he's weak.

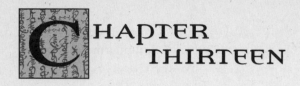

Chapter Thirteen

The Hethanta Mountains

Even the hard-hearted avoid the heat of desperate men. For the bonfires of the weak crack the most stone.

—CONRIYAN PROVERB

So who were the heroes and the cravens of the Holy War? There are already songs enough to answer that question. Needless to say, the Holy War provided further violent proof of Ajencis's old proverb, "Though all men be equally frail before the world, the differences between them are terrifying."

—DRUSAS ACHAMIAN, COMPENDIUM OF THE FIRST HOLY WAR

Spring, 4111 Year-of-the-Tusk, the Central Jiünati Steppe

Never before had Cnaiür endured such a trial.

They travelled southeast, by and large unseen and unmolested. Before the catastrophe at Kiyuth, Cnaiür and his kinsmen had not been able to travel more than a day without encountering parties of Munuäti, Akkunihor, or other Scylvendi tribes. Now three or four days typically passed before he and Kellhus were intercepted. They crossed some tribal lands without any challenge at all.

At first Cnaiür had dreaded the sight of galloping horsemen. Custom protected any Scylvendi warrior on pilgrimage to the Empire, and in better days such encounters were occasions for gossip, exchanges of information, and familial greetings. A time to set aside the knife. But it was uncommon for a lone Scylvendi warrior to be accompanied by a slave, and these were not better days. In desperate times, Cnaiür knew, men rationed nothing so jealously as tolerance. They were more strict in their interpretation of custom and less forgiving of uncommon things.

But most of the bands they encountered consisted of boys with girlish faces and sapling limbs. If the sight of Cnaiür's scarred arms did not awe them into stammering deference, they would posture the way juveniles do, taking pride in aping the words and manner of their dead fathers. They would nod sagely at Cnaiür's explanation and scowl at those who asked childish questions. Few of them had seen the Empire, so it remained a place of wonder. All of them, at some point, bid him to avenge their dead kin.

Soon Cnaiür found himself yearning for these encounters—for the escape they offered.

The Steppe unfolded before Cnaiür and Kellhus, featureless for the most part. Indifferent to the desolation between them, the pastures grew thicker and green. Purple blossoms no bigger than Cnaiür's fingernail bobbed in the wind, which combed the grasses into sweeping waves across the distance. His hatred dulled by boredom, Cnaiür would watch cloud shadows sail ponderously toward the horizon. And even though he knew they rode through the heart of the Jiünati Steppe, it seemed he travelled through a stranger's land.

On the ninth day of their journey, they awoke to woollen skies. It began to rain.

On the Steppe the rain seemed endless. Grey encompassed every distance until it seemed they travelled through a void. The northerner turned to him, his eyes lost in the hollows beneath his brows. Tails of wet hair curled into his beard, framing his narrow face.

"Tell me," Kellhus said, "about Shimeh."

Pressing, always pressing.

Shimeh . . . Does Moënghus truly dwell there?

"It's holy to the Inrithi," Cnaiür replied, keeping his head bowed against the rain, "but possessed by the Fanim." He did not bother to raise his voice over the dreary roar: he knew the man would hear him.

"How did this happen?"

Cnaiür weighed these words carefully, as though tasting them for poison. He'd resolved to ration what he would and would not say about the Three Seas to the Dûnyain. Who knew what weapons the man might fashion?

"The Fanim," he replied warily, "have made it their mission to destroy the Tusk in Sumna. They've warred for many years against the Empire. Shimeh is but one of many prizes."

"Do you know these Fanim well?"

"Well enough. Eight years ago I led the Utemot against them at Zirkirta, far to the south of here."

The Dûnyain nodded. "Your wives told me you were unconquered on the field of battle."

Anissi? Did you tell him this? He could see her betraying him in innumerable ways, thinking she spoke in his interest. Cnaiür turned his face away, watched the grasses resolve from the grey. Such comments, he knew, were simply plays on his vanity. He no longer responded to anything remotely intimate.

Kellhus returned to his earlier tack. "You said the Fanim seek to destroy the Tusk. What is the Tusk?"

The question shocked Cnaiür. Even the most ignorant of his cousins knew of the Tusk. Perhaps he simply tested his answers against those of others.

"The first scripture of Men," he said to the rain. "There was a time, before the birth of Lokung, when even the People were bound by the Tusk."

"Your God was born?"

"Yes. A long time ago. It was our God who laid waste to the northern lands and gave them to the Sranc." He tipped his head back and, for a moment, savoured the break of cold water across his forehead and face. It tasted sweet on his lips. He could feel the Dûnyain watching, scrutinizing his profile. *What do you see?*

"What of the Fanim?" Kellhus asked.

"What of them?"

"Will they hinder our passage through their land?"

Cnaiür suppressed the urge to look at the man. Either intentionally or inadvertently, Kellhus had struck upon an issue that had troubled him ever since he'd resolved to undertake this quest. That day—so long ago, it now seemed—hiding among the dead at Kiyuth, Cnaiür had heard Ikurei Conphas speak of an Inrithi Holy War. But a Holy War against whom? The Schools or the Fanim?

Cnaiür had chosen their path carefully. He intended to cross the Hethanta Mountains into the Empire, even though a lone Scylvendi could not expect to live long among the Nansur. It would have been better to avoid the Empire altogether, to travel due south to the headwaters of the River Sempis, which they could have followed directly into Shigek, the northernmost governorate of Kian. From there they simply could have followed the traditional pilgrimage routes to Shimeh. The Fanim were rumoured to be surprisingly tolerant of pilgrims. But if the Inrithi were in fact mounting a Holy War against Kian, this route would have proven disastrous. For Kellhus especially, with his fair hair and pale skin . . .

No. He needed, somehow, to learn more about this Holy War before striking true south, and the nearer they travelled to the Empire, the greater the probability of happening across that intelligence became. If the Inrithi didn't wage Holy War against the Fanim, they could skirt the edges of the Empire and reach Fanim lands unscathed. If they did wage Holy War, however, they would likely be forced to cross the Nansurium—a prospect that Cnaiür dreaded.

"The Fanim are a warlike people," Cnaiür finally replied, using the rain as a weak excuse not to look at the man. "But I'm told that they're tolerant of pilgrims."

He took care not to glance or to speak to Kellhus for some time after, though something inner grimaced all the while. The more he avoided looking at the man, the more dreadful he seemed to become. The more godlike.

What do you see?

Cnaiür pinched images of Bannut from his eyes.

The rain lasted another day before trailing into a drizzle that veiled far-away slopes with sheets of mist. Another day passed before their wool and leather dried.

Not long after, Cnaiür became obsessed with the thought of murdering the Dûnyain in his sleep. They'd been discussing sorcery, far and away the most frequent theme of their rare discussions. The Dûnyain continually returned to the subject, even telling Cnaiür of a defeat he'd suffered at the hands of a Nonman warrior-magi far to the north. At first Cnaiür assumed this preoccupation stemmed from some fear on the man's part, as though sorcery were the one thing his dogma could not digest. But then it occurred to him that Kellhus *knew* he thought talk of sorcery harmless and so used it to broach the silence in the hope of steering him toward more useful topics. Even the story of the Nonman, Cnaiür realized, was likely another lie—a false confession meant to draw him into an exchange of confessions.

After recognizing this latest treachery, he unaccountably thought: *When he falls asleep . . . I'll kill him tonight when he falls asleep.*

And he continued to think this, even though he knew he could not murder the man. He knew only that Moënghus had summoned Kellhus to Shimeh—nothing more. It was unlikely he would ever find him without Kellhus.

Regardless, the following night he slipped from his blankets and crept across the cold turf with his broadsword. He paused next to the embers of their fire, staring at the man's inert form. Even breaths. His face as calm at night as it was impassive by day. Was he awake?

What manner of man are you?

Like a bored child, Cnaiür combed the tips of the surrounding grass with his sword's edge, watching the stalks bend then spring upright in the moonlight.

Scenarios flashed through his soul's eye: his strike stilled by Kellhus's bare palms; his strike stilled by the treachery of his own hand, Kellhus's eyes popping open, and a voice from nowhere saying, *"I know you, Scylvendi . . . better than any lover, any God."*

He crouched, poised over the man for what seemed a long while. Then, seized by paroxysms of self-doubt and fury, he crawled back to his blankets. He shivered for a long time, as though cold.

Over the next two weeks the great tablelands of the Jiünati interior gradually transformed into a jumble of broken inclines. The ground became loamy, and the grasses surged to sweep the flanks of their horses. Bees scribbled across the near distances, and great clouds of gnats assailed them when they splattered across stagnant waters. With each day, however, the season seemed to retreat. The ground became more stony, the grasses shorter and paler, and the insects more lethargic.

"We're climbing," Kellhus noted.

Even though the terrain had alerted Cnaiür to their approach, Kellhus glimpsed the Hethanta Mountains across the horizon first. As always when sighting the mountains, Cnaiür could feel the Empire on the far side, a labyrinth of luxuriant gardens, sprawling fields, and ancient, hoary cities. In the past, the Nansurium had been the destination of his tribe's seasonal pilgrimages, a place of shouting men, burning villas, and shrieking women. A place of retribution and worship. But this time, Cnaiür realized, the Empire would be an obstacle—perhaps an insurmountable one. They had encountered no one who knew of the Holy War, and it looked as though they would be forced to cross the Hethantas and enter the Empire.

When he sighted the first yaksh in the distance, he was heartened far more than was manly. As far as he could tell, they rode through Akkunihor land. If anyone knew whether the Empire waged holy war against Kian, it would be the Akkunihor, who were the sieve through which a great many pilgrimages passed. Without a word he yanked his horse toward the encampment.

Kellhus was the first to see that something was amiss.

"This camp," he said tonelessly, "is dead."

The Dûnyain was right, Cnaiür realized. He could see several dozen yaksh, but no people and, more significantly, no livestock. The pasture they rode over was uncropped. And the encampment itself had the empty, dried-out look of abandoned things.

His elation faded into disgust. No plain men. No plain talk. No escape.

"What happened?" Kellhus asked.

Cnaiür spat across the grasses. He knew what had happened. After the disaster at Kiyuth, the Nansur had ranged all across this land. Some detachment had come across this camp and butchered or enslaved everyone. Akkunihor. Xunnurit had been Akkunihor. Perhaps his whole tribe had been obliterated.

"Ikurei Conphas," Cnaiür said, faintly shocked by how unimportant that name had become to him. "The Emperor's nephew did this."

"How can you be sure?" Kellhus asked. "Perhaps the inhabitants no longer needed this place."

Cnaiür shrugged, knowing this was not the case. Though places on the Steppe could be discarded, things could not be—not by the People, at least. Everything was needed.

Then, with unaccountable certainty, he realized that Kellhus would kill him.

The mountains were looming, and the Steppe swept out behind them. *Behind* them. The son of Moënghus no longer needed him.

He'll kill me while I sleep.

No. Such a thing could not happen. Not after travelling so far, after enduring so much! He must use the son to find the father. It was the only way!

"We must cross the Hethantas," he declared, pretending to survey the desolate yaksh.

"They look formidable," Kellhus replied.

"They are . . . But I know the shortest way."

That night they camped among the abandoned yaksh. Cnaiür rebuffed Kellhus's every attempt to draw him into conversation, listening instead to the howl of mountain wolves on the wind and jerking his head to the click and creak of the empty yaksh about them.

He had struck a bargain with the Dûnyain: freedom and safe passage across the Steppe in return for his father's life. Now, with the Steppe almost behind them, it seemed he had always known the bargain was a sham. How could he *not?* Was not Kellhus the son of Moënghus?

And why had he decided to cross the mountains? Was it truly to discover whether the Empire was embroiled in a holy war, or was it to draw out the lie he had been chasing?

Use the son. Use a *Dûnyain* . . .

Such a fool!

He did not sleep that night. Neither did the wolves. Before dawn he crept into the pitch black of a yaksh and huddled among weeds. He found an infant's skull and wept, screamed at the bindings, at the wood, at the hide surfaces; he beat his fists against the treacherous earth beneath.

The wolves laughed and wailed despicable names. Hateful names.

Afterward, he put his lips to the earth and breathed. He could feel *him* listening from somewhere out there. He could feel him knowing.

What did he see?

It did not matter. The fire burned and it had to be fed.

On lies if need be.

Because the fire burned true. The fire alone.

So cold against swollen eyes. The Steppe. The trackless Steppe.

They left the deserted camp at dawn, their horses trotting through grasses pocked here and there by patches of rotten leather and bone. Neither man spoke.

The Hethantas climbed into the eastern sky. The slopes grew steeper, and they followed winding ridge lines in order to conserve their horses. By midday they found themselves deep in the foothills. As always, Cnaiür found the change in terrain unsettling, as though the years had tattooed linear horizons and vast bowl skies onto his heart. In the hills, anything or anyone might be concealed. In the hills, one must find summits to see.

Dûnyain country, he thought.

As though to confirm these ruminations, the heights of the next crest revealed some twenty or so riders in the distance, filing down the same trail they followed into the mountains.

"More Scylvendi," Kellhus remarked.

"Yes. Returning from a pilgrimage." Would they know about the Holy War?

"What tribe?" Kellhus asked.

The question provoked Cnaiür's suspicion. It was too . . . Scylvendi for an outlander.

"We shall see."

Whoever the riders were, they were as concerned as he was at the sudden appearance of strangers. A handful broke into a gallop toward them, while the rest herded together what appeared to be a group of captives. He studied them as they neared, looking for the telltale signs that would identify their tribe. He realized quite quickly that they were men rather than boys, but none of them wore Kianene battlecaps, which meant they were too young to have fought the Fanim at Zirkirta. Then he saw the white paint streaking their hair. They were Munuäti.

Images from Kiyuth assailed him: thousands of Munuäti racing across smoking plains into the sorcerous fires of the Imperial Saik. Somehow these men had survived.

Cnaiür needed only a glimpse of their leader to know he would not like the man. Even from a distance, he projected a restless arrogance.

Of course the Dûnyain saw as much and more. "The one in the lead," he warned, "sees us as an opportunity to prove himself."

"I know. Say nothing."

The strangers reined to a raucous halt before them. Cnaiür noticed the several fresh-cut swazond on their arms.

"I am Panteruth urs Mutkius of the Munuäti," the leader declared. "Who are you?" His six kinsmen jostled behind him, watching with an air of scarcely bridled banditry.

"Cnaiür urs Skiötha—"

"Of the Utemot?" Panteruth studied them, dubiously eyeing the swazond bridling Cnaiür's arms, then glaring at Kellhus. He spat in Scylvendi fashion. "Who's this? Your slave?"

"He's my slave, yes."

"You allow him weapons?"

"He was born to my tribe. I thought it prudent. The Steppe has grown desperate."

"That it has," Panteruth snapped. "What say you, slave? Were you born to the Utemot?"

The presumption stunned Cnaiür. "You doubt my word?"

"The Steppe has grown desperate, as you say, Utemot. And there's been talk of *spies* . . ."

Cnaiür snorted. "Spies?"

"How else could the Nansur overcome us?"

"By wits. By strength of arms. By guile. I was at Kiyuth, stripling. What happened had nothing to do wi—"

"I too was at Kiyuth! What I saw could be explained only by treachery!"

There was no mistaking the tone: the wilful affront-taking of someone who wanted to spill blood. Cnaiür's limbs began to tingle. He glanced at Kellhus, knowing the Dûnyain would take everything he needed from his expression. Then he turned back to the Munuäti.

"Do you know who I am?" he said, not just to Panteruth but to his men as well.

This seemed to shock the young warrior. But he recovered quickly. "We've heard the stories. There's not a man on the Steppe who hasn't laughed at the name of Cnaiür urs Skiötha."

Cnaiür cuffed him hard about the side of his head.

A mad instant, then scrambling violence.

Cnaiür spurred into Panteruth, struck him a second time with his fist, knocking him from his saddle. Then he yanked his horse to the right, away from the man's stunned compatriots, drawing his broadsword. When the others spurred after him, reaching for their own weapons, he jerked his horse back into their midst and cut two down before they'd cleared their blades. He ducked a sweeping cut from the third, then thrust, punched through his brigandine, his breastbone, and halved his heart.

He whirled, looking for the Dûnyain. Kellhus stood a short distance from him, a horse stamping behind, three inert forms at his feet. For an instant their eyes locked.

"The others come," Kellhus said. Cnaiür turned, saw the rest of Panteruth's band fanning across the slope, riding hard toward them. Munuäti war cries rifled the air.

Sheathing his sword and retrieving his bow, Cnaiür dismounted. Sheltering behind the bulk of his mount, he nocked a shaft, drew the gut back, and sent one of the riders toppling with an arrow in the eye. Another shaft, and a second horseman crumpled in his saddle, clutching a bloody arm. Arrows, sounding like knives shearing linen, hissed through the air around him. Abruptly his horse screamed, cantered, and kicked; Cnaiür stumbled back, tripping over the fallen. Then, through the legs of his dancing horse, he glimpsed the Dûnyain.

Beyond Kellhus, the approaching riders had opened like a hand, eight of them in the palm, close abreast, intent on riding the Dûnyain down, while five others played the fingers, galloping around his flank and firing arrows at short range. The shafts flickered across the grasses. Those off target thudded into the turf, while the others were simply swatted from their trajectories—by the Dûnyain.

Kellhus crouched, hefted a small hatchet from the saddle of a dead horse, threw it in a perfect arc across the incline. As though drawn by a string, it chopped into the face of the nearest galloping archer. The man fell, his corpse rolling like a bundle of heavy rope between the legs of the following bowman's mount. The second horse stumbled, gouged the turf, and went down thrashing.

The fingers scattered, but the palm thundered up the slope. For an instant, the Dûnyain stood motionless, his curved sword extended, the rush of pounding horses looming ever closer before him . . .

He's dead, Cnaiür thought, rolling to his feet. The horsemen were almost upon him as well.

The Dûnyain vanished, swallowed by the shadowy gaps between riders. Cnaiür glimpsed flashes of steel.

The three horses directly before Cnaiür faltered mid-gallop, kicked air, and then careered into the turf. Cnaiür leapt, glimpsed roiling torsos and crushed men. A flailing hoof bucked his thigh, and he fell headlong onto the grasses on the far side. He grimaced, clutched his bruised leg while kicking himself to his side with the other. *Thwack.* An arrow pocked the turf next to him. *Thwack.* Another.

The other Munuäti chargers had thundered past, veering away from their fallen kinsmen. Now they hooked across the slope for another assault.

Cursing, Cnaiür stumbled to his feet—*thwack*—seized a round shield from the ground, and broke into a run toward the Munuäti archer. Sprinting, he drew his broadsword. Snapping concussion. An iron arrowhead punched through the laminated leather of the shield. A second caught his hip, ringing off the iron plates of his girdle. Cnaiür dashed right, using the first archer as cover from the second. Where was the third? He heard the fierce cries of the Munuäti chargers behind him.

Spit thick and sour in his mouth. Legs pounding. The bowman growing closer, jerking his mount around to face him, nocking another shaft, realizing the futility, frantically reaching over his shoulder for his broadsword . . . Cnaiür leapt, crying savagely, driving his sword into the hairy smear of the man's armpit. The Munuäti grunted and fell forward, hugging himself. Seizing his matted hair, Cnaiür yanked him from the saddle. The other mounted bowman pounded toward him, his sword now drawn.

Cnaiür hooked a foot in the stirrup, kicked himself up, then vaulted off the saddle into the air. He hurtled into the astonished Munuäti and bore him to the ground. Though winded, the man grappled with him, fumbled for his knife. Cnaiür butted him in the face, felt his scalp open on the rim of the man's helm. Somehow he'd lost his battlecap. He butted him again, felt the nose crack beneath his forehead. The Munuäti pulled his knife clear, and Cnaiür caught his wrist. Hissing breath. Hard eyes and clenched teeth. The creak of leather and armour.

"*I'm stronger,*" Cnaiür grated, butting the man's face again.

No fear in the man's eyes—only stubborn hate.

"*Stronger!*"

He pressed the shaking arm to the turf, squeezed the wrist until the knife slipped from senseless fingers. Butted him yet again. Jerked a leg up.

Thwack! The third bowman.

The Munuäti beneath him gurgled then went limp. A shaft had nailed his throat to the turf. Cnaiür heard galloping hoofs, glimpsed a towering shadow.

He dove, heard the swoop of a broadsword.

He rolled to a crouch, saw the Munuäti rein to a turf-chopping stop then spur his mount for another pass. Blinking blood from his eyes, Cnaiür searched the ground. Where was his sword? Horse and rider leapt toward him.

Without thinking, Cnaiür caught the bobbing reins. With sheer might he wrenched the horse off-stride then shrieking to the ground. The astounded Munuäti rolled clear. Cnaiür kicked through the grasses methodically, at last finding his sword in a pocket of weeds. He scooped it up, arrested the Munuäti's initial strike with a ringing clang.

The man's sword flashed shining arcs across the sky. The assault was furious, but within heartbeats, Cnaiür was hammering him back, throwing him off balance with pure ferocity. The man stumbled.

And it was over. The Munuäti stared at Cnaiür stupidly, bent over to pick up his arm.

And lost his head as well.

I am stronger.

His chest heaving, Cnaiür scanned the small battlefield, afflicted by a sudden worry that Kellhus was dead. But he found the Dûnyain almost immediately: he stood alone amidst a knot of dead, sword poised as earlier, awaiting the galloping rush of a single Munuäti lancer.

Leaning into his lance, the horseman howled, giving voice to the Steppe's fury through the thud of galloping hoofs. *He knows*, Cnaiür thought. *Knows he's about to die.*

As he watched, the Dûnyain *caught* the iron tip of the man's lance with his sword, guiding it to turf. The lance snapped, jerking the Munuäti back against his high cantle, and the Dûnyain leapt, impossibly throwing a sandalled foot over the horse's head and kicking the rider square in the face. The man plummeted to the grasses, where his leathery tumble was stilled by the Dûnyain's sword.

What manner of man . . . ?

Anasûrimbor Kellhus paused over the corpse, as though committing it to memory. Then he turned to Cnaiür. Beneath wind-tossed hair, streaks of blood scored his face, so that for a moment he possessed the semblance of expression. Beyond him, the dark escarpments of the Hethantas piled into the sky.

Striding through the carnage, Cnaiür silenced the wounded.

Eventually he came to Panteruth, who crawled toward the crest. He sent the man's desperate sword singing across the grasses, then buried his own in the turf. He kicked the man savagely, then yanked him to his feet as though he were a doll. He spit into the broken face, stared into the bleary, bloodied eyes.

"*See, Munuäti?*" he cried. "See how easily the People of War are undone? *Spies!*" he spat. "A *woman's* excuse!" With an open palm he swatted him to ground. Kicked him again, beat him from the dark fury that deafened his heart. Beat him until the man shrieked, wept.

"What? Weep?" Cnaiür screamed. "You who'd call me a traitor to the land!" He clamped a powerful hand about the man's throat. "Choke!" he cried. "*Choke!*" The man gagged and flailed. The ground itself thundered with Cnaiür's fury. The very sky flinched.

He dropped the broken man to the ground.

A shameful death. A fitting death. Panteruth urs Mutkius would not return to the land.

From a distance, Kellhus watched Cnaiür retrieve his sword. The plainsman walked toward him, picking his way with strange care among the bodies. His eyes were wild, bright beneath an overcast sky.

He's mad.

"There are others," Kellhus said. "Chained together on the path below. Women."

"Our prize," Cnaiür said, avoiding the monk's scrutiny. He walked past Kellhus toward the sound of wailing.

Standing with her chained wrists before her, Serwë cried out as the figure neared them. *"Pleease!"*

The others shrieked when they realized it was a Scylvendi who walked toward them, a *different* Scylvendi—more brutal, dark through tear-lashed eyes. They huddled behind Serwë, as far away as the chains would allow them.

"Pleeaase!" Serwë cried again as the great towering figure approached, drenched in the blood of his kinsmen. *"You must save us!"*

But then she glimpsed the man's merciless eyes.

The Scylvendi slapped her to the ground.

"What will you do with her?" Kellhus asked, staring at the woman who huddled across the fire.

"Keep her," Cnaiür said, tearing off another mouthful of horse flesh from the rib he held in his hands. "We've done bloody work," he continued, chewing. "Now she's my prize."

There's more. He fears . . . Fears to travel alone with me.

Abruptly, the plainsman stood, tossed the shining rib into the fire, then came to a crouch next to the woman. "Such a beauty," he said almost absently. The woman shrank from his outstretched hand. Her chains rattled. He caught her, smearing grease on her cheek.

She reminds him of someone. One of his wives . . .

Anissi, the only one he dares love.

Kellhus watched while the Scylvendi took her again. With her whimpers, her suffocated cries, it seemed the ground beneath slowly spun, as though stars had stopped their cycle and the earth had begun to wheel instead. There was something . . . something *here*, he could sense. Something outraged.

From what darkness had this come?

Something is happening to me, Father.

Afterward, the Scylvendi pulled her to her knees before him. He cupped her lovely face in his palm, turned it in the firelight. He ran thick fingers through her golden hair. He muttered to her in an incomprehensible language. Kellhus watched the swollen eyes lift to the Scylvendi, terrified that she had comprehended. He growled something else, and she winced beneath the hand that held her. *"Kufa . . . Kufa,"* she gasped. She began to cry again.

More harsh questions, to which she replied with the shyness of the beaten, glancing up to the cruel face and down again. Kellhus looked through her expression and into her soul.

She had suffered much, he realized, so much that she'd long ago learned to hide hatred and resolution beneath abject terror. Her eyes found his, momentarily, then flashed to the darkness around him. *She wants to be certain we are only two.*

The Scylvendi clamped her head between two scarred hands. More incomprehensible words in a guttural voice thick with threat. He let her go, and she nodded. Her blue eyes glittered in the shining fire. The Scylvendi withdrew a small knife from his leggings and began prying at the soft iron of her manacles. After several moments, the chains clattered to the earth. She rubbed her bruised wrists. Glanced at Kellhus again.

Does she have the courage?

The Scylvendi left her and returned to his place before the fire— next to Kellhus. He'd stopped sitting across from him some time ago: to prevent him, Kellhus knew, from reading his face.

"You've freed her, then?" Kellhus asked, knowing this was not the case.

"No. She bears different chains now." After a moment he added, "Women are easy to break."

He does not believe this.

"What language did you speak?" A genuine question.

"Sheyic. The language of the Empire. She was a Nansur concubine until the Munuäti took her."

"What did you ask her?"

The Scylvendi looked at him sharply. Kellhus watched the small drama of his expression—a squall of significances. Remembered hatred, but a previous resolution remembered as well. Cnaiür had already decided how to handle this moment.

"I asked her about the Nansurium," he said finally. "There's a great movement in the Empire—in the whole Three Seas. A new Shriah rules the Thousand Temples. There's to be a Holy War."

She did not tell him this; she confirmed it. He knew this before.

"A Holy War . . . Waged against whom?"

The Scylvendi attempted to gauge him, to sound the quizzical mask he wore as a face. Kellhus had grown increasingly troubled by the shrewdness of the Scylvendi's unspoken guesses. The man even knew he intended to kill him . . .

Then something strange came across Cnaiür's expression. A realization of some sort, followed by a look of supernatural dread, the sources of which eluded Kellhus.

"The Inrithi gather to punish the Fanim," Cnaiür said. "To retake their lost holy lands." Faint disgust coloured his tone. As though a *place* could be holy. "To retake Shimeh."

Shimeh . . . My father's house.

Another groove. Another correspondence of cause. The implications for the mission bloomed through his intellect. *Is this why you've summoned me, Father? For holy war?*

The Scylvendi had turned, turned to look at the woman across the fire.

"What's her name?" Kellhus asked.

"I didn't ask," Cnaiür replied, reaching for more horsemeat.

Her limbs sketched by a glowing bed of coals, Serwë clasped the knife the men had used to butcher the horse. Quietly, she clambered over to the sleeping form of the Scylvendi. The man slumbered, breathing evenly. She raised the knife to the moon, her fists shaking. She hesitated . . . remembering his grip, his look.

Those insane eyes had stared through her as though she were glass, transparent to his hunger.

And his voice! Grating, elemental words: "*If you leave, I will hunt you, girl. As sure as the earth, I will find you . . . Hurt you as you have never been hurt.*"

Serwë clamped shut her eyes. *Strike-strike-strike-strike!*

The steel dipped . . .

Was stilled by a callused hand.

A second hand clamped across her mouth, stifled the scream.

Through her tears she saw the silhouette of the second, bearded man. The Norsirai. The head slowly shook from side to side.

There was a pinch, and the knife fell from her senseless fingers, was caught before it fell upon the Scylvendi. She felt herself lifted, pulled back to the far side of the smouldering firepit.

In the light, she could discern his features. Sad, tender even. He shook his head once again, his dark eyes brimming with concern . . . even vulnerability. He lifted his hand from her lips slowly, then brought it to his chest.

"*Kellhus,*" he whispered, then nodded.

She gathered her hands, stared at him wordlessly. "*Serwë,*" she replied at last, in a tone as hushed as his own. Burning tears streamed down her cheeks.

"*Serwë,*" he repeated—gently. He reached out a hand to touch her but hesitated, drew it back to his lap. For a moment he fumbled in the dark behind him, eventually producing a blanket of wool still warm from the fire.

Dumbstruck, she took it from him, held by the faint glitter of the moon in his eyes. He turned away and stretched back out across his mat.

In the midst of quiet, anguished sobs, she fell asleep.

Dread.

Tyrannizing her days. Stalking her sleep. Dread that made her thoughts skitter, flit from terror to terror, that made her bowels quail, her hands perpetually shake, her face utterly slack for fear that one crimped muscle might cause the whole to collapse.

First with the Munuäti and now with this far darker, far more threatening Scylvendi, with limbs like roots cramped about stone, with words like rolling thunder, with eyes like glacial murder. Instant obedience, even to those whims he did not speak. Stinging retribution, even for those things she did not do. Punishment for her breathing, for her blood, for her beauty, for nothing.

Punishment for punishment.

She was helpless. Utterly alone. Even the Gods had forsaken her.

Dread.

Serwë stood in the morning chill, numb, exhausted in ways she would never understand. The Scylvendi and his strange Norsirai companion had packed the last of the looted supplies on the surviving Munuäti horses. She watched the Scylvendi stride to where he had staked the other twelve captive women of the Gaunum household. They clutched their chains for comfort and huddled in abject terror. She saw them, knew them, but found them unrecognizable.

There, the wife of Barastas, who had hated her almost as much as the wife of Peristus. And there, Ysanna, who had helped in the gardens until the Patridomos had deemed her too beautiful. Serwë knew all of them. But who were they?

She could hear them weeping, pleading, not for mercy—they had crossed the mountains, and they knew they were far beyond mercy's reach—but for sanity. What sane man destroys useful tools? This one could cook, that one could couple, and this one could fetch a thousand slaves in ransom, if he would just let her live . . .

Young Ysanna, her left eye swollen shut from a Munuäti blow, was crying out to her.

"Serwë, Serwë! Tell him I don't look like this! Tell him I'm beautiful! Serwë, pleeease!"

Serwë looked away. Pretended not to hear.

Too much dread.

She couldn't remember when she'd ceased feeling her tears. Now, for some reason, she had to taste them before realizing she wept.

Deaf to their cries, the Scylvendi stomped into their midst, clubbed those that clutched at him, and unlocked the two curved prongs of the ingenious stake the Scylvendi used to anchor their captives to the ground. He heaved first one stake then the other from the earth, dropped them with a clank. The women wailed and cringed around him. When he drew his knife, some of them began to shriek.

He grabbed the chain of one shrieker, Orra, a plump scullery slave, and yanked her toward him. The shrieking stopped. But then, rather than killing her, he began prying at the soft iron of her manacles, as he had done for Serwë the previous night.

Bewildered, Serwë glanced at the Norsirai—what was his name? Kellhus? He regarded her for a grave yet somehow heartening moment, then looked away.

Orra was free, just sitting, rubbing her wrists, dumbfounded. The Scylvendi began freeing another.

Suddenly Orra began running up the slope, absurd with pounding girth and desperation. When no one pursued her, she stopped, her face anguished. She crouched, wildly looking around, and Serwë was reminded of the Patridomos's cat, who was always too fearful to stray far from its dinner bowl no matter how the children tormented it. Eight others joined Orra in her wary vigil, including Ysanna and Barastas's wife. Only four continued running.

Something about this made it difficult to breathe.

The Scylvendi left the chains and stakes where they lay, walked back to Serwë and Kellhus.

The Norsirai asked him something unintelligible. The Scylvendi shrugged and looked at Serwë.

"Others will find them, use them," he said casually. He had said this to her, Serwë knew, because the one called Kellhus did not speak Sheyic. He leapt onto his horse and studied the eight remaining women. "Follow," he shouted in a matter-of-fact tone, "and I will put out your eyes with arrows."

Then, madly, they began wailing again, begging him *not* to leave. Barastas's wife even sobbed for her chains. But the Scylvendi seemed not to hear them. He bid Serwë to mount her horse.

And she was glad. Glad of heart! And the others were envious.

"Here, Serwë!" she heard Barastas's wife shriek. "Come back here, you filthy, rutting sow! I own you! *Own!* Fucking peach! *Come back here!*"

Each word both struck Serwë like a fist and passed right through her, leaving her untouched. She saw Barastas's wife marching toward their train of horses, her hands sweeping in deranged gestures. The Scylvendi yanked his mount about, pulled his bow from its case. He nocked and loosed an arrow in one effortless motion.

The shaft caught the noblewoman in the mouth, shattering teeth and embedding itself in the moist hollows of her throat. She fell forward like a doll, thrashed amid grasses and goldenrods. The Scylvendi grunted with approval, then continued leading them into the mountains.

Serwë tasted tears.

None of this is happening, she thought. No one suffered like this. Not really.

She feared she might vomit for dread.

The Hethantas massed above them. They negotiated steep granite slopes, picked their way through narrow ravines, beneath cliffs of sedimentary rock pocked with strange fossils. For the most part, the trail followed a thin river hedged by spruce and stunted screw pine. Always they climbed higher, into colder air, until even the mosses were left behind. Fuel for their fires grew scarce. The nights became viciously cold. Twice they awoke covered by snow.

By day the Scylvendi walked ahead with his pony, alone, rarely speaking. Kellhus followed Serwë. She found herself talking to him, compelled by something in his demeanour. It was as if the man's mere presence betokened intimacy, trust. His eyes encompassed her, as though his look somehow mended the broken ground beneath her feet. She told him about her life as a concubine in Nansur, about her father, a Nymbricani, who had sold her to House Gaunum when she turned fourteen. She described the jealousy of the Gaunum wives, how they had lied to her about her first child, saying that it had been stillborn when Griasa, an old Shigeki slave woman, had watched them strangle it in the kitchens. "Blue babies," the old woman had whispered in her ear, her voice cracked by an outrage almost too weary to be spoken. "That's all you'll ever bear, child." This, Serwë explained to Kellhus, became the morbid joke shared by all the members of the household, especially among those concubines or slaves proper fortunate enough to be visited by their masters. *We bear them blue babies . . . Blue like the priests of Jukan.*

At first she spoke to him in the way she'd spoken to her father's horses as a child—the thoughtless talk of one heard but not understood. But she soon discovered that he *did* understand. After three days, he began asking her questions in Sheyic—a difficult language, one that she had mastered only after years of captivity in Nansur. The questions thrilled her somehow, filled her with a longing to do them proper service. And his voice! Deep, wine-dark like the sea. And the way he spoke her name. As though jealous of its sound. *Serwë*—like an incantation. In mere days, her wary affection became awe.

By night, however, she belonged to the Scylvendi.

She could not fathom the relationship between these two men, though she pondered it often, understanding that her fate somehow lay between them. Initially, she'd assumed that Kellhus was the Scylvendi's slave, but this was not the case. The Scylvendi, she eventually realized, hated the Norsirai, even *feared* him. He acted like someone trying to preserve himself from ritual pollution.

At first this insight thrilled her. *You fear!* she would silently howl at the Scylvendi's back. *You're no different from me! No more than I am!*

But then it began to trouble her—deeply. Feared by a *Scylvendi?* What kind of man is feared by a Scylvendi?

She dared ask the man himself.

"Because I've come," Kellhus had replied, "to do dreadful work."

She believed him. How could she not believe such a man? But there were other, more painful questions. Questions she dare not speak, though she asked him with her eyes each night.

Why don't you take me? Make me your prize? He fears you!

But she knew the answer. She was Serwë. She was nothing.

The fact of her nothingness was a lesson hard learned. Her childhood had been happy—so happy that she now wept whenever she thought of it. Picking wildflowers on the prairies of Cepalor. Thrashing like an otter in the river with her brothers. Romping around the midnight fires. Her father had been indulgent, if not kind; her mother had showered her with adoration. "Serchaa, sweet Serchaa," she would say, "you're my beautiful charm, my bulwark against heartbreak." Serwë had thought herself something then. Loved. Prized above her brothers. Happy in the immeasurable way of children who have no real suffering to throw upon the balance.

She had heard many tales of suffering, to be sure, but then the hardships related had always been ennobling, encased in morals, and containing lessons she had already learned. Besides, even if fate did betray her, and she was certain it would not, she would be steadfast and heroic, a beacon of strength for the flagging souls about her.

Then her father sold her to the Patridomos of House Gaunum.

Her first night as the property of House Gaunum had seen much foolishness knocked from her. She understood quite quickly that there was nothing—no viciousness, no depravity—she would not commit to stay men and their heavy hands. As a Gaunum concubine, she lived in perpetual anxiety, pinned between the hatred of the Gaunum wives and the capricious appetites of the Gaunum men. She was nothing, they told her. Nothing. Just another worth-less Norsirai peach. She almost believed them.

Soon she began praying for this or that son of the Patridomos to come visit her—even those who were cruel. She flirted with them. Seduced them. She was the delight of their guests. Other than pride in their ardour, pleasure in their gratification, what else did she have?

In the great villa of House Gaunum, there had been a shrine filled with small idols to the ancestors of the House. She had knelt and prayed in that shrine more times than she could count, and every time she had begged for mercy. She could feel the dead Gaunum in every corner of that place, whispering hateful things, moving her with dreadful premonitions. And she had begged and begged for mercy.

Then, as though in answer to her prayers, the Patridomos himself, who had always seemed a distant, silver-haired god to her, accosted her in the gardens. He grasped her chin and exclaimed: "By the Gods! You're worthy of the Emperor himself, girl . . . Tonight. Expect me tonight." How her soul had danced that day! *Worthy of the Emperor!* How carefully she'd shaved herself and mingled the finest perfumes in anticipation of his visit. *Worthy of the Emperor!* How she had wept when he failed to arrive. "Don't weep, Serchaa," the other girls had said. "He prefers little boys."

For several days afterward, she had despised little boys.

And she continued praying to the idols, even though their squat little faces now seemed to laugh at her. She, Serwë, had to mean something, hadn't she? All she wanted was some sign, something, anything . . . She grovelled before them.

Then one of the Patridomos's sons, Peristus, took her to bed with his wife. Serwë had pitied the wife at first, a girl with the face of a man who'd been married to Gaunum Peristus to secure an alliance between Houses. But as Peristus used her to build up the seed he would plant in his wife's womb, Serwë could feel the woman's hatred, as though they shared the bed with a small fire. Just to spite the prig, she had cried out, had fanned Peristus's lust with whorish words and deeds, and had stolen his seed for herself.

The ugly little wife had wept, ranted like a madwoman, and no matter how many times Peristus struck her, she would not stop. Though troubled by the glee this occasioned, Serwë had rushed to the shrine to thank the Gaunum ancestors. And shortly after, when she realized she carried Peristus's child, she stole one of the hostler's pigeons and sacrificed it to them.

During the sixth month of her pregnancy, Peristus's wife whispered, "Three months till the funeral, hmm, Serchaa."

Terrified, Serwë had gone to Peristus himself, only to be slapped and dismissed. She was nothing to him. So she returned to the Gaunum idols. She offered anything, everything. But her child was born blue, so they said. Blue like the priests of Jukan.

Even still, Serwë continued to pray—this time for vengeance. She prayed to the Gaunum for the destruction of the Gaunum.

A year later, the Patridomos rode from the villa with all his men. The gathering Holy War had grown unruly, and the Emperor had need of his generals. Then the Scylvendi arrived. Panteruth and his Munuäti.

The barbarians found her in the shrine, shrieking, smashing stone idols against the floor.

The villa burned, and almost all the ugly Gaunum wives and their ugly Gaunum children were put to the sword. Barastas's wife, the younger concubines, and the more beautiful female slaves were herded through the gates. Serwë screamed like the others, wailed for her burning home. The home she had hated.

Nightmarish misery. Brutality. Unlike anything she had hitherto suffered. Each of them was bound to the saddle of a Munuäti warrior who made them run and run, all the way to the Hethantas. At night they huddled and wept and screamed when the Munuäti came for them, their phalluses greased with animal fat. And Serwë thought of a word, a Sheyic word that did not exist in her native Nymbricani . . . A word of outrage.

Justice.

Despite all her vanities and all her peevish sins, she meant something. She was something. She was Serwë, daughter of Ingaera, and she deserved far more than what had been given. She would have dignity, or she would die hating.

But her courage had come at a horrible time. She had tried not to weep. She had tried to be strong. She had even spit in the face of Panteruth, the Scylvendi who claimed her as his prize. But Scylvendi were not quite human. They looked down on all outlanders as though from the summit of some godless mountain, more remote than the most brutal of the Patridomos's sons. They were Scylvendi, the breakers-of-horses-and-men, and she was Serwë.

But she had clung to the word—somehow. And watching the Munuäti die at the hands of these two men, she had dared rejoice, had dared believe she would be delivered. At last, *justice!*

"Please!" she had cried at Cnaiür's approaching figure. *"You must save us!"*

Worthless, the Gaunum had told her. Just another worthless Norsirai peach. She had believed them, but she had continued praying. Begging. *Show them! Please! Show them I mean something . . .*

And then, begging mercy from an insane Scylvendi. Demanding justice.

Worthless fool! Ever since Cnaiür had thrust his blood-spattered frame against her, she had understood. There was only whim. There was only submission. There was only pain, death, and dread.

Justice was but another treacherous Gaunum idol.

Her father, pulling her half-naked from her blankets, thrusting her into the callous arms of a stranger. "You belong to these men now, Serwë. May our Gods watch over you."

Peristus, looking up from his scrolls, frowning with amused incredulity. "Perhaps, Serwë, you've forgotten what you are. Give me your hand, child."

The Gaunum idols, leering at her with faces of stone. Sneering silence.

Panteruth, wiping her spit from his face, drawing his knife. "The track you follow is narrow, bitch, and you know it not . . . I will show you."

Cnaiür, clenching her wrists tighter than any manacles. "Mend yourself to my will, girl. Utterly. I will tolerate no remainder. I will stamp out all that does not submit."

Why were they so mean to her? Why did everyone hate her? Punish her? Hurt her? Why?

Because she was Serwë, and she was nothing. She would always be nothing.

That was why Kellhus abandoned her every evening.

At some point, they crossed the spine of the Hethantas, and the trail began to fall. The Scylvendi forbade them from making fires, but the nights began to warm. Before them spread the Kyranae Plain, dark in the waxy distance, like the skin of an overripe plum.

Kellhus paused at the promontory's lip and looked over jumbled ravines and ancient forests. Kûniüri had looked much the same from the roof of the Demua, he supposed, but while Kûniüri was dead, this land was alive. The Three Seas. The last great civilization of Men. At long last he had arrived.

I draw near, Father.

"We cannot continue like this," the Scylvendi called out from behind him.

He's decided it must be now. Kellhus had been anticipating this moment ever since they'd broken camp hours before.

"What do you mean, Scylvendi?"

"There's no way two men such as us could cross Fanim lands during a Holy War. We would be gutted as spies long before reaching Shimeh."

"But this is why we've crossed the mountains, isn't it? To travel through the Empire instead . . ."

"No," the Scylvendi said sullenly. "*We* cannot travel through the Empire . . . I brought you here to kill you."

"Or," Kellhus replied, still speaking to the vista before him, "to be killed by me."

Kellhus turned his back to the Empire, toward Cnaiür. Surfaces of rock, sunbathed and soaring, framed the man. Serwë stood nearby. There was blood, he noted, on her fingernails.

"That is what you've been thinking, isn't it?"

The Scylvendi wet his lips. "You tell me."

Kellhus cupped the barbarian within his scrutiny the way a child might imprison a bird within tingling palms—alive to every tremor, to the pulse of a pea-sized heart, to the small heat of panicked respiration.

Should he give the man a glimpse, show him just how transparent he was? For days now, ever since Cnaiür had learned the truth of the Holy War from Serwë, he had refused to discuss anything regarding it or his plans. But his intentions had been clear: he had led them into the Hethantas to play for time, the way Kellhus had witnessed others do when they were too weak to surrender their obsessions. Cnaiür needed to continue hunting Moënghus, even when he knew the hunt to be a farce.

But now they were about to enter the Empire, a land where Scylvendi were flayed alive. Before, as they neared the Hethantas, Cnaiür had simply feared that Kellhus would kill him. Now, sure that his mere presence was about to become a mortal threat, he was certain. Kellhus had glimpsed the resolution over the course of the morning, in the man's words and his wary glances. If he could not use the son to kill the father, Cnaiür urs Skiötha would kill the son.

Even though he knew this to be impossible.

So much torment.

Hatred, tidal in its scope and strength, enough to murder endless thousands, enough to murder self or even truth. A most potent tool.

"What would you have me say?" Kellhus asked. "That now we've reached the Empire, I no longer need you? That now I no longer need you, I intend to kill you? After all, one does not cross the Empire in the company of a Scylvendi."

"You said it yourself, Dûnyain. Back when you were chained in my yaksh. For your kind there is only mission."

Such penetration. Hatred, but pleated by an almost preternatural cunning. Cnaiür urs Skiötha was dangerous . . . Why should he suffer his company?

Because Cnaiür still knew this world better than he. And more important, he knew *war*. He was bred to it.

I have use for him still.

If the pilgrim routes to Shimeh were closed, Kellhus had no alternative but to join the gathering Holy War. Yet the prospect of war presented a near insuperable dilemma. He'd spent hours in the probability trance, trying to draft models of war, but he lacked the principles he needed. The variables were too many and too fickle. War . . . Could any circumstance be more capricious? More perilous?

Is this the path you've chosen for me, Father? Is this your test?

"And what is my mission, Scylvendi?"

"Assassination. Patricide."

"And after thirty years among world-born men, what kind of power do you think my father, a Dûnyain possessing all the gifts I possess, wields?"

The Scylvendi looked stunned. "I had not thought—"

"I have. You think that I have no need of you? That I have no need of Cnaiür urs Skiötha the many-blooded? The breaker-of-horses-and-men? A man who can strike down three in the space of as many heartbeats? A man who is immune to my methods, and therefore to those of my father as well? Whoever my father is, Scylvendi, he will be powerful. Far too powerful for any one man to kill."

Kellhus could hear Cnaiür's heart thunder beneath his breast, see his thoughts roil through his eyes, and smell the numbness that spread through his limbs. Oddly, the man glanced for a beseeching moment at Serwë, who had started trembling in terror.

"You say this to deceive me," Cnaiür murmured. "To lull me . . ."

Again the wall of his distrust, blunt and stubborn.

He must be shown.

Kellhus drew his blade and lunged forward.

The Scylvendi reacted instantly, though in the wooden manner of reflexes dulled by disbelief. He parried the first sweep easily but fell back before the ringing combination that followed. With each impact, Kellhus could see his anger brighten, feel it awaken and grab hold his limbs. Soon the Scylvendi was countering with blinding speed and bone-jarring power. Only once had Kellhus seen Scylvendi children practising the *bagaratta*, the "sweeping way" of Scylvendi sword fighting. At the time it had seemed excessively ornate, freighted with dubious flourishes.

Not so when combined with strength. Twice Cnaiür's great sweeps almost struck him to his heels. Kellhus retreated, affecting fatigue, planting the false scent of an impending kill.

He could hear Serwë screaming.

"Kill him, Kellhus! Kill him!"

Grunting, the barbarian redoubled his fury. Kellhus parted a hammering rain of blows, feigning desperation. He reached out and clamped Cnaiür's right wrist, yanked him forward. Somehow, impossibly, Cnaiür managed to bring his free hand up, seemingly through Kellhus's sword arm. He pound his palm into Kellhus's face.

Kellhus fell backward, kicking Cnaiür twice in the ribs. He rolled into a handstand, effortlessly vaulted back into stance.

He tasted his own blood. *How?*

The Scylvendi stumbled, clutching his side.

He'd misjudged the man's reflexes, Kellhus realized, as he had so many other things.

Kellhus cast his sword aside and strode toward the man. Cnaiür howled, lunged, struck. Kellhus watched the sword-point arc through flashing sunlight, across hanging escarpments and scudding clouds. He caught it in his palms, as one might a lover's face or a fly. He twisted the blade about, wrenching the pommel from Cnaiür's hand. He stepped within his reach and struck him in the face. As the man pedalled backward, he bounced low and swept his legs from beneath him.

Rather than scramble out of reach, Cnaiür rolled to his feet and leapt at him. Kellhus leaned back, caught the Scylvendi by the back of his girdle and his neck, then heaved him back the way he came, closer to the ledge. When Cnaiür tried to stand, Kellhus struck him backward even farther.

Further blows, until the Scylvendi was more a rabid beast than a man, sucking shuddering breaths, swinging arms that were punished with senselessness. Kellhus struck him hard, and he fell slack, cracking his skull on the edge of the promontory.

Heaving him up, Kellhus thrust the barbarian out over the precipice and, with one arm, held him dangling over the distant Empire. The wind swept his jet hair across the abyss.

"*Do it!*" Cnaiür gasped through snot and spittle. His feet swayed over nothingness.

So much hatred.

"But I spoke true, Cnaiür. I do need you."

The Scylvendi's eyes rounded in horror. *Let go,* his expression said. *For that way lies peace.*

And Kellhus realized he'd misjudged the Scylvendi yet again. He'd thought him immune to the trauma of physical violence when he was not. Kellhus had beaten him the way a husband beats his wife or a father his child. This moment would dwell within him forever, in the way of both memories and involuntary cringes. Yet more degradation for him to heap on the fire.

Kellhus hoisted him to safety and let him drop. Another trespass.

Serwë crouched beneath her horse, weeping—not because he had saved the Scylvendi but because he had not killed him. "*Iglitha sun tamatha!*" she wailed in her father's tongue. "*Iglitha sun tamatheaaa!*"

If you loved me.

"Do you believe me?" he demanded of the Scylvendi.

The Scylvendi stared at him with dull shock, as though bewildered by the absence of his wrath. He pushed himself to unsteady feet.

"Shut up," he said to Serwë, though he could not look away from Kellhus.

Serwë continued wailing, crying out to Kellhus.

Cnaiür's eyes clicked from Kellhus to his prize. He strode toward her, struck her silent with an open palm. "I said *shut up!*"

"Do you believe me?" Kellhus asked again.

Serwë whimpered, struggled to swallow her sobs.

So much sorrow.

"I believe you," Cnaiür said, momentarily unable to match his gaze. He stared at Serwë instead.

Kellhus had already known this would be his answer, but there was a great difference between knowing an admission and exacting it.

Yet when the Scylvendi at last looked at him, the old fury animated his eyes, burning with almost carnal intensity. If Kellhus had assumed as much earlier, he now knew with utter certainty: the Scylvendi was insane.

"I believe you *think* you need me, Dûnyain. For now."

"What do you mean?" Kellhus asked, genuinely perplexed. *He's becoming more erratic.*

"You plan on joining this Holy War. On using it to travel to Shimeh."

"I see no other way."

"But for all your talk of needing, you forget I'm a heathen to the Inrithi," Cnaiür said, "little removed from the Fanim they hope to slaughter."

"Then you're a heathen no more."

"A convert?" Cnaiür snorted incredulously.

"No. A man who's awakened from his barbarity. A survivor of Kiyuth who's lost faith in the ways of his kinsmen. Remember, like all peoples, the Inrithi think *they* are the chosen ones, the pinnacle of what it means to be upright men. Lies that flatter are rarely disbelieved."

The extent of his knowledge, Kellhus could see, alarmed the Scylvendi. The man had tried to secure his position by keeping him ignorant of the Three Seas. Kellhus tracked the inferences that animated his scowl, watched him glance at Serwë . . . But there were more pressing matters.

"The Nansur will care nothing for such stories," Cnaiür said. "They'll see only the scars upon my arms."

The sources of this resistance eluded Kellhus. Did the man *not* want to find and kill Moënghus?

How can he still be a mystery to me?

Kellhus nodded, but in a shrugging manner that dismissed even as it acknowledged objections. "Serwë says peoples from across the Three Seas gather in the Empire. We'll join them and avoid the Nansur."

"Perhaps . . ." Cnaiür said slowly. "If we can make it to Momemn without being challenged." But then he shook his head. "No. Scylvendi don't wander. The sight of me will provoke too many questions, too much outrage. You have no inkling of how much they despise us, Dûnyain."

There was no mistaking the despair. Some part of the man, Kellhus realized, had abandoned hope of finding Moënghus. How could he have missed this?

But the more important question was whether the Scylvendi spoke true. Would it be impossible to cross the Empire with Cnaiür? If so, he would have to—

No. Everything depended on the domination of circumstance. He would not join the Holy War, he would seize it, wield it as his instrument. But as with any new weapon, he needed instruction, training. And the chances of finding another with as much experience and insight as Cnaiür urs Skiötha were negligible. *They call him the most violent of all men.*

If the man knew too much, Kellhus did not know enough—at least not yet. Whatever the dangers of crossing the Empire, it was worth the attempt. If the difficulties proved insurmountable, then he would reassess.

"When they ask," Kellhus replied, "the disaster at Kiyuth will be your explanation. Those few Utemot who survived Ikurei Conphas were overcome by their neighbours. You'll be the last of your tribe. A dispossessed man, driven from his country by woe and misfortune."

"And who will you be, Dûnyain?"

Kellhus had spent many hours wrestling with this question.

"I'll be your reason for joining the Holy War. I'll be a prince you encountered travelling south over your lost lands. A prince who's dreamed of Shimeh from the far side of the world. The men of the Three Seas know little of Atrithau, save that it survived their mythic Apocalypse. We shall come to them out of the darkness, Scylvendi. We'll be whoever we say we are."

"A prince . . ." Cnaiür repeated dubiously. "From where?"

"A prince of Atrithau, whom you found travelling the northern wastes."

Though Cnaiür now understood, even appreciated, the path laid for him, Kellhus knew that the debate raged within him still. How much would the man bear to see his father's death avenged?

The Utemot chieftain wiped a bare forearm across his mouth and nose. He spat blood. "A prince of nothing," he said.

<hr />

In the morning light, Kellhus watched the Scylvendi ride up to the pole. Perched high on it was a skull, still leathered by skin and framed by a shock of dark, woolly hair. Scylvendi hair. Some distance away to either side rose further poles—further Scylvendi heads, planted the distance prescribed by Conphas's mathematicians. So many miles, so many Scylvendi heads.

Kellhus turned in his saddle to Serwë, who stared at him searchingly.

"They will kill him if we're found," she said. "Doesn't he know this?" Her tone said: *We don't need him, my love. You can kill him.* Kellhus could see the scenarios brimming behind her eyes. The shrill cry she had crafted over the days, poised for their first encounter with Nansur pickets.

"You mustn't betray us, Serwë," Kellhus replied sternly, like a Nymbricani father to his daughter.

The beautiful face slackened, shocked. "I would never betray *you*, Kellhus," she blurted. "You must know—"

"I know that you wonder what binds me to this Scylvendi, Serwë. This isn't for you to understand. Know only that if you betray him, you betray *me*."

"Kellhus, I . . ." The shock had transformed to hurt, to tears.

"You *must* suffer him, Serwë."

She turned away from his terrible eyes, began weeping. "For *you*?" she spat bitterly.

"I am only the promise."

"Promise?" she cried. "*Whose* promise?"

But Cnaiür had returned, riding around them to their small train of horses. He smiled wryly when he noticed Serwë crying.

"Hold tight this moment, woman," he said in Sheyic. "It will be your only measure of this man." His laughter was harsh.

He leaned from his pony and began rooting through one of the packs. He withdrew a stained woollen shirt and stripped to the waist. The shirt did little to conceal his brutal heritage, but at least it covered the scars. The Nansur would not take kindly to such records.

The plainsman gestured to the thin file of poles. They followed the contour of the land, some leaning, others straight, lowering into the horizon and leading away from the Hethantas. Their grim burdens were turned away from them, toward the distant sea. The endless scrutiny of the dead.

"This is the way to Momemn," he said and spat across trampled grasses.

CHAPTER FOURTEEN

THE KYRANAE PLAIN

Some say men continually war against circumstances, but I say they perpetually flee. What are the works of men if not a momentary respite, a hiding place soon to be discovered by catastrophe? Life is endless flight before the hunter we call the world.

—EKYANNUS VIII, *111 APHORISMS*

Spring, 4111 Year-of-the-Tusk, the Nansur Empire

The warbling of a lone woodlark, like an aria against the rush of wind through the forest canopy. *Afternoon,* she thought. *The birds always snooze in the afternoon.*

Serwë's eyes fluttered open, and for the first time in a long while, she felt at peace.

Beneath her cheek, Kellhus's chest rose and fell to the rhythm of his sleep. She had tried to join him on his mat before, but he'd always resisted—to appease the Scylvendi, she had thought. But this morning, after a dark night of travel, he had relented. And now she savoured the press of his strong body against hers, the drowsy sense of sanctuary afforded by his sheltering arm. *Kellhus, do you know how much I love you?*

Never had she known such a man. A man who *knew* her, and yet still loved.

For an idle moment, her eyes followed the rafters of the immense willow they slept beneath. Limbs arched against the depths of further limbs, parted like a woman's legs, and then parted again, winding away into great skirts of leaves that bobbed and dipped beneath the sunlit wind. She could feel the soul of the great tree, brooding, sorrowful, and infinitely wise, the rooted witness of innumerable suns.

Serwë heard splashing.

Shirtless, the Scylvendi squatted at the river's edge, cupping water in his left hand and gingerly rinsing the wound on his forearm. She watched him through the blur of lashes, feigning sleep. Scars hooked and creased his broad back, a second record to match the scars banding his arms.

As though aware of her scrutiny, the forest grew hushed, its silence coloured by the stern grandeur of trees. Even the solitary bird fell quiet, yielding to the slurp and trickle of Cnaiür's bathing.

For perhaps the first time, she felt no fear of the Scylvendi. He looked lonely, she thought, even gentle. He lowered his head to the water and began rinsing his long black hair. The filmy surface of the river slowly passed before him, bearing twigs and bits of fluff. Near the far bank, she glimpsed the ripples of a water-bug skimming across the river's glassy back.

Then she saw the boy on the far side.

At first she glimpsed only his face, half-hidden in the crook of a mossy deadfall. Then she saw slender limbs, as still as the branches screening them.

Do you have a mother? she thought, but when she realized he watched the Scylvendi, a sudden terror struck her.

Go away! Run!

"Plainsman," Kellhus said softly. Startled, the Scylvendi turned to him.

"*Tus'afaro to gringmut t'yagga,*" Kellhus said. Serwë felt his nod brush the top of her head.

The Scylvendi followed his gaze and peered into the shadowy recesses of the far bank. For a breathless moment, the boy stared back at the plainsman.

"Come here, child," Cnaiür said over the hushed water. "I've something to show you."

The boy hesitated, both wary and curious.

No! You must run . . . Run!

"Come," Cnaiür said, lifting his hand and motioning with his fingers. "You're safe."

The boy stood from behind his shield of fallen branches, tense, uncertain—

"Run!" Serwë cried.

The boy flickered into the wood, flashing between white sun and deep green shadow.

"Fucking wench!" Cnaiür snarled. He exploded across the waters, knife drawn. At the same instant, Kellhus was gone as well, rolling to his feet and ploughing through the Scylvendi's wake.

"Kellhus!" she cried, watching him sprint beneath the far canopy. "Don't let him kill him!"

But a sudden horror struck her breathless, an unaccountable certainty that Kellhus *also* meant the child harm.

You must suffer him, Serwë.

Her body still groggy, she stumbled to her feet and plunged into the dark water. Her bare feet skidded across the slick rocks, but she hurled herself forward, falling just short of the far bank. Then she was up, soaked in cold, running across gravel, lunging through brush into the sun-dappled gloom.

She ran like something wild, bounding over the matted leaves, leaping ferns and fallen branches, following their fleet shadows deeper through the screen of dark trees. Her feet felt weightless, her lungs bottomless. She was breath and vaulting speed—nothing more.

"*Bas'tushri!*" echoed through the hollows of the wood. "*Bas'tushri!*" The Scylvendi, calling to Kellhus. But from where?

She caught herself on the trunk of a young ash. She looked around, heard the distant crash of someone barrelling through underbrush, but saw nothing. For the first time in weeks, she was alone.

They would kill the boy if they caught him, she knew, to prevent him from telling anyone what he had seen. They travelled through the Empire secretly, made fugitives by the scars that striped the Scylvendi's arms. But she wasn't a fugitive, she realized. The Empire was her land—or at least the land her father had sold her to . . .

I'm home. There's no need to suffer him.

She pressed herself away from the tree and with blank eyes and an itching heart, began walking at right angles to her previous path. She walked for some time, once hearing faint shouts through the ambient rush of leaves in the wind. *I'm home*, she would think. But then thoughts of Kellhus would assail her, curiously smeared into images of the Scylvendi's brutality. Kellhus's eyes as she spoke, pinched by concerns or suppressed smiles. The thrill of his hand encompassing her own, as though this modest intimacy bespoke an impossible promise. And the things he said, words that had sounded her to the pith, had rendered her squalid life a portrait of heart-breaking beauty.

Kellhus loves me. He's the first to love me.

Then, with a shaking hand, she felt her belly through her soaked shift.

She began shivering. The others—the women originally taken with her by the Munuäti—were dead, she imagined. She did not mourn them. A small, peevish part of her had actually celebrated the death of the Gaunum wives, the ones who had strangled her baby—her blue baby. But wherever she went in the Empire, she knew there would be other Gaunum wives.

Serwë had always been keenly aware of her beauty, and for a time among her Nymbricani kinsmen, she had thought it a great gift of the Gods, an assurance that her future husband would be a man of many cattle. But here, in the Empire, it ensured only that she would be a pampered concubine, despised by some Patridomos's wives and doomed to give birth to blue babies.

Her stomach was flat, but she could feel it. Feel the baby.

Images of the Scylvendi's urgent fury assaulted her; still she thought: *Kellhus's child. Our baby.*

She turned and began to retrace her steps.

<hr>

After a short time, Serwë realized she was lost and was once again terrified. She looked to the white glare of the sun through the shroud of vaulting branches and distant leaves, trying to determine north. But she couldn't remember which direction she'd initially come.

Where are you? she thought, too afraid to call out.

Kellhus . . . Find me, please.

A sudden wail pealed beneath the canopies. The boy? Had they found the boy? But she realized this couldn't be: the cry had belonged to a man.

What's happening?

The thud of hoofs from across a low rise to her right heartened her.

He comes! When he realized I was lost, he fetched the horses to better—

But when the two horsemen broke the crest, her skin pimpled with dread. They galloped down the shallow slope, kicking up leaves and humus, and then, astonished by her apparition, reined their chargers to a rebellious stop.

She recognized them immediately by their armour and insignia: common officers of the Kidruhil, the elite cavalry of the Imperial Army. Two of the Gaunum sons had belonged to the Kidruhil.

The younger, handsome one looked almost as frightened as she was; he sketched an old-wives' ward against ghosts above his horse's mane. But the older one grinned like a spiteful drunk. A scythe-shaped scar hooked across his forehead, around a deep socket, then parsed his left cheek.

The Kidruhil here? Does that mean they're dead? In her soul's eye, she saw the little boy, peering from behind black branches. *Did he live? Did he warn . . . ? Is this my fault?*

This thought, more than any fear of the men, paralyzed her. She hissed in terror, her chin lifting of its own volition, as though she were baring her throat to their sheathed weapons. Tears sketched her cheeks. *Run!* she frantically thought, but she couldn't move.

"She's with them," the scarred man said, still struggling with his lathered horse.

"Who knows?" the other nervously replied.

"She's with them. Peaches like this don't wander the woods alone. She don't belong to us, and she sure as hell ain't no goatherd's daughter. *Look* at her!"

But the other had been gawking the entire time. At her bare legs, at the swell of her breasts beneath her shift, but especially at her face, as though afraid it would disappear if he glanced away. "But we haven't the time," he said unconvincingly.

"Fuck that," the first spat. "We always have time to bugger something like this." He dismounted with odd grace, staring at his comrade as though daring him to play a malicious trick. *Just follow me*, his eyes said, *and you'll see.*

Cowed by something incomprehensible, the younger one followed his harsh companion's lead. He still stared at Serwë, his eyes somehow both shy and vicious.

They were both fumbling with their iron-and-leather skirts, the one with the scar approaching her, the younger one hanging back with the horses. He was already desperately tugging at his flaccid member. "Maybe," he said in a curious voice, "I'll just *watch*, then . . ."

They're dead, she thought. *I killed them.*

"Just watch where you blow your snot," the other said, laughing, his eyes at once hungry and humourless.

You deserve this.

With thoughtless economy, the older man bared his dagger, clenched her woollen shift, and slit it open from neck to belly. Avoiding her eyes, he used the point to draw aside the cloth, revealing her right breast.

"My," he said, exhaling a thick breath. He reeked of onions, rotten teeth, and bitter wine. At last he met her terrified gaze. He raised a hand to her cheek. The nail of his thumb was bruised purple.

"Leave me alone," she whispered, her voice pinched by burning eyes and trembling lips. The impotent demand of a child tormented by other children.

"Shush," he said softly. He gently pressed her to her knees.

"Don't be mean to me," she murmured through tears.

"Never," he said, his voice stricken, as though with reverence.

With a creak of leather, he fell to one knee and buried his dagger in the forest floor. He was breathing heavily. "Sweet Sejenus," he hissed. He looked terrified.

She flinched from the shaking hand he slid beneath her breast. The first sobs wracked her.

please-please-please-please . . .

One of the horses spooked. There was a sound, like an axe striking sodden deadwood. She glimpsed the younger horseman, saw his head lolling from a shank of neck, his falling torso spouting blood. Then she saw the Scylvendi, his chest heaving, his limbs greasy with sweat.

The scarred man cried out, scrambling to his feet and scraping his longsword clear. But the Scylvendi seemed unconcerned by him. His murderous look sought her instead.

"Has the dog hurt you?" he barked as much as asked.

Serwë shook her head, numbly straightening her clothes. She glimpsed the knife pommel embedded in a whorl of leaves.

"Listen to me, barbarian," the Kidruhil said hastily. Tremors passed through his sword. "I had no idea she was *yours* . . . No idea."

Cnaiür fixed him with glacial eyes, a strange humour in the set of his thick jaw. He spat on the corpse of his comrade, grinned wolfishly.

The officer moved away from Serwë, as though to disassociate himself from his crime. "C-come now, *friend*. Hmm? T-take the horses. All y-yours—"

To Serwë it seemed that she'd *floated* to her feet, that she'd flown at the scarred man, and that the knife had simply appeared in the side of his neck. Only his frantic backhand knocked her back to earth.

She watched him fall to his knees, his bewildered hands fumbling at his neck. He threw an arm backward, as though to ease his descent, but he toppled, lifting his back and hips from the ground, kicking up leaves with one foot. He turned to her, retching blood, his eyes round and shining. Begging her . . .

"*Guh . . . g-guh . . .*"

The Scylvendi crouched above him and casually jerked the knife from his neck. Then he stood, apparently oblivious to the blood jetting—like the final squirts of a little boy's piss, she thought inanely—first across his stomach and waist, and then across his tanned knees and shins. Through the Scylvendi's legs, the dying man still watched her, his eyes becoming glassy with lethargic panic.

Cnaiür loomed above her. Broad shoulders and narrow hips. Long chiselled arms banded by scars and veins. Wolf-skin hanging between his sweaty thighs. For a moment her terror and hatred deserted her. He'd saved her from humiliation, perhaps even death.

But the memory of his brutalities could not be silenced. The feral splendour of his frame became something famished, preternaturally deranged.

And he would not let her forget.

Clamping his left hand about her throat, he yanked her gagging from the ground and threw her against a tree. With his right he brandished the knife, raising it menacingly before her face, holding it still just long enough for her to glimpse her reflection distorted across its blood-smeared length. Then he pressed the tip against her temple. It was still warm. She winced at its prick, felt blood pool in her ear.

He glared at her with an intensity that made her sob. His eyes! White-blue in white, cold with the utter absence of mercy, bright with the ancient hatreds of his race . . .

"P-please . . . Don't kill me, pleeaase!"

"That whelp you warned nearly cost us our lives, wench," he snarled. "Do anything like that again and I *will* kill you. Try to flee again and I promise, I'll murder the world to find you!"

Never again! Never . . . I promise. I'll suffer you! I will!

He released her throat and seized her right arm, and for a moment, she cringed as she wept, expecting a blow. When it did not come, she wailed aloud, choking on her own shuddering breaths. The very forest, the spears of sunlight through forking limbs, the trees like temple pillars, thundered with his anger. *I promise.*

The Scylvendi turned to the scarred man, who still writhed sluggishly against the forest floor.

"You have killed him," he said, his accent thick. "You know this?"

"Y-yes," she said numbly, trying to compose herself. *God, what now?*

With the knife, he cut a lateral line across her forearm. The pain was sharp and quick, but she bit her lip rather than cry out. "*Swazond,*" he said in harsh Scylvendi tones. "The man you have killed is gone from the world, Serwë. He exists only here, a scar upon your arm. It is the mark of his *absence*, of all the ways his soul will not move, and of all the acts he will not commit. A mark of the weight you now bear." He smeared the wound with his palm, then clutched her hand.

"I don't understand," Serwë whimpered, as bewildered as she was terrified. Why was he doing this? Was this his punishment? Why had he called her *by name?*

You must suffer him . . .

"You are *my* prize, Serwë. My tribe."

✷

When they found Kellhus at the camp, Serwë leapt from the scarred man's horse, which had shied from crossing the river, and bound through the waters toward him. And then she was in his arms, clutching him fiercely.

Strong fingers combed through her hair. The hammer of his heart murmured in her ears. He smelled of sun-dried leaves and sturdy earth. Through her tears she heard: "Shush, child. You're safe now. Safe with me." So like her father's voice!

The Scylvendi rode across the river, leading her horse. He snorted aloud as he neared them.

Serwë said nothing, but she stared at him with baleful eyes. Kellhus was here. It was safe to hate him once again.

Kellhus said, *"Breng'ato gingis, kutmulta tos phuira."* Though she knew nothing of Scylvendi, she was certain he had said, "She's yours no longer, so leave her alone."

Cnaiür simply laughed then replied in Sheyic: "We have no time for this. Kidruhil patrols usually number more than fifty. We have killed only a dozen."

Kellhus pressed Serwë away and held her shoulders firmly in his hands. For the first time, she noticed the arcs of blood speckled across his tunic and beard. "He's right, Serwë. We're in great danger. They'll hunt us now."

Serwë nodded, more tears flooding her eyes. "It's all my fault, Kellhus!" she hissed. "I'm so sorry . . . But he was just a *child*. I couldn't let him die!"

Cnaiür snorted once again. "The whelp warned no one, girl. What mere boy could escape a *Dûnyain?*"

A bolt of terror struck her.

"What does he mean?" she asked Kellhus, but now his own eyes brimmed with tears. *No!* In her soul's eye, she glimpsed the child, small limbs askew somewhere deep in the forest, sightless eyes searching for sky. *I did this . . .* Another absence where a soul should have moved. What acts would the nameless boy have accomplished? What kind of hero might he have been?

Kellhus turned away from her, overcome by grief. As though finding solace in urgent action, he began rolling his sleeping mat beneath the grand willow. He paused and without looking at her said in a pained voice: "You must forget this, Serwë. We haven't the time."

Shame, as though her innards had become cold water.

I forced this crime upon him, she thought, staring at Kellhus as he bound their gear to his saddle. Once again her hand found her belly. *My first sin against your father.*

"The Kidruhil horses," the Scylvendi said. "We shall ride them to death first."

———— ∞ ————

For the first two days, they eluded their pursuers with relative ease, relying on the primeval forests that blanketed the headwaters of the River Phayus and the Scylvendi's martial acumen to preserve them. Nevertheless, the flight took a heavy toll on Serwë. Day and night on horseback, negotiating steep gullies, galloping across stony slopes, and hazarding the innumerable tributaries of the Phayus, was nearly more than she could handle. By the first night, she was swaying on the back of her horse, struggling with both numb limbs and eyes that refused to stay open, while Cnaiür and Kellhus led the way on foot. They seemed unconquerable, and it galled her that she was so weak.

By the end of the second day, Cnaiür allowed them to make camp, suggesting that they had lost whatever pursuers they might have had. Two things, he said, were in their favour: the fact that they travelled east, when any Scylvendi raiding party would surely withdraw to the Hethantas after meeting the Kidruhil, and the fact that he and Kellhus had been able to kill so many after the colossal misfortune of encountering them in their hunt for the boy. Serwë was far too exhausted to mention the one she'd killed, so she rubbed the clotted blood on her forearm instead, surprised by the feeling of pride that flared through her.

"The Kidruhil are arrogant fools," Cnaiür continued. "Eleven dead will convince them that the raiding party must be large. This means that they will be cautious in their pursuit and send out for reinforcements. It also means that if they encounter our eastward trail, they will think it a ruse and follow it west toward the mountains, hoping to pick up the trail of the main party."

That night they ate raw fish he speared from a nearby stream, and despite her hate, Serwë found herself admiring the affinity between this man and the open wilds. For him it seemed a place of innumerable clues and small tasks. He could guess approaching terrain from the sight and song of certain birds, and he could ease the strain on their horses by feeding them cakes of fungus scratched from the humus. There was far more to him than abuse and murder, she realized.

As Serwë marvelled over her ability to savour food that would have made her vomit in her previous life, Cnaiür told them episodes from his many forays into the Empire. The westward provinces of the Empire, he said, offered them their only hope of throwing off their pursuers: they had been long abandoned because of the depredations of his kinsmen. Their peril would be far greater once they crossed into the great tracts of cultivated land along the lower Phayus.

And not for the first time, Serwë wondered why these men would risk such a journey.

They resumed their trek in daylight, intending to travel into the following night. In early morning, Cnaiür felled a young doe, and Serwë took it to be a good omen, though the prospect of eating venison raw did not appeal to her. She found herself to be continuously hungry but had ceased speaking of it because of the Scylvendi's scowl. At midday, however, Kellhus urged his mount even to hers and said, "You're hungry again, aren't you, Serwë?"

"How do you know these things?" she asked. It never ceased to thrill her each time Kellhus guessed her thoughts, and the part of her that held him in reverent awe would find further confirmation.

"How long has it been, Serwë?"

"How long has what been?" she asked, suddenly fearful.

"Since you've been with child."

But it's your child, Kellhus! Yours!

"But we've not yet coupled," he said gently.

Serwë suddenly felt bewildered, unsure as to what he meant, and more unsure still whether she had spoken aloud. But *of course* they had coupled. She was with child, wasn't she? Who *else* could be his father?

Tears swelled in her eyes. *Kellhus . . . Are you trying to hurt me?*

"No, no," he replied. "I'm sorry, sweet Serwë. We'll stop to eat very soon."

She stared at his broad back as he rode ahead to join Cnaiür. She was accustomed to watching their brief exchanges, and drew petty satisfaction from the moments of hesitation, even anguish, that would crack Cnaiür's weather-beaten expression.

But this time she felt compelled to watch Kellhus, to note the way the sun flashed through his blond hair, to study the sumptuous line of his lips and the glitter of his all-knowing eyes. And he seemed almost *painfully* beautiful, like something too bright for cold rivers, bare rock, and knotted trees. He seemed—

Serwë held her breath. Feared for a moment that she might swoon. *I didn't speak and yet still he knew.*

"I am the promise," Kellhus had said above the long road of Scylvendi skulls.

Our promise, she whispered to the child within her. *Our God.*

But could it be? Serwë had heard innumerable stories of the Gods communing with Men as Men long ago in the days of the Tusk. This was scripture. This was true! What was impossible was that a God might walk *now*, that a God might fall in love with *her*, with Serwë, the daughter sold to House Gaunum. But perhaps this was the *meaning* of her beauty, the reason she had suffered the venal covetousness of man after man. She was also something too beautiful for the world, something awaiting the arrival of her betrothed.

Anasûrimbor Kellhus.

She smiled tears of rapturous joy. She could see him as he truly was now, radiant with otherworldly light, haloes like golden discs shining about his hands. She could *see* him!

Later, as they chewed strips of raw venison in a breezy stand of poplars, he turned to her and in her native tongue of Nymbricani said, "You understand."

She smiled but was not surprised that he knew her father's language. He'd bid her speak it to him many times—not to learn, she now knew, but to listen to her secret voice, the one sheltered from the wrath of the Scylvendi.

"Yes . . . I understand. I'm to be your wife." She blinked the tears from her eyes.

He smiled with godlike compassion and tenderly stroked her cheek. "Soon, Serwë. Very soon."

That afternoon they crossed a broad valley, and as they crested the summit of the far slopes, they caught their first glimpse of their pursuers. Serwë could not see them at first, only the outer skirt of sunlit trees along a distant stony defilade. Then she glimpsed the shadows of horses behind, their thin legs scissoring through the gloom, their riders hunched to avoid unseen branches. Abruptly, one appeared at the brink, the sun smearing his helm and armour bright white. Serwë shrank into the shadows.

"They seem confused," she said.

"They lost our trail along the stony ground," Cnaiür said grimly. "They're searching for the route we took down."

Afterward, Cnaiür increased their pace. With their train of horses in tow, they thundered through the wood, the Scylvendi guiding them down rolling slopes until they came to a shallow, gravelly stream. They then changed direction, riding downstream along the muddy banks, at times splashing through the stream itself, until it joined a much larger river. The air was beginning to cool, and grey evening shadows had all but swallowed the open spaces.

Several times Serwë had thought she could hear the Kidruhil shouting through the forests behind them, but the ever-present sound of rushing waters made it difficult to be certain. Yet curiously, she felt unafraid. Though the elation she'd felt for the greater part of the day had vanished, the sense of inevitability had not. Kellhus rode beside her, and his reassuring eyes never failed to find her the moment her heart weakened.

You have nothing to fear, she would think. *Your father rides with us.*

"These forests," the Scylvendi said, pitching his voice to be heard over the river, "continue for a short time before thinning into pastures. We ride for as long as we can into dark without risking our horses or our necks. These men who follow us are not like the others. They are determined. They live their lives hunting and battling my people through these forests. They will not stop until they run us down. But once we clear the forest, our advantage lies in our extra horses. We will run them until they are dead. Our only hope is to race along the Phayus far ahead of any word of our coming and reach the Holy War."

Following his lead, they rode along the river until the moonlight transformed it into a ribbon of quicksilver through bluebacked stone and the looming dark of the surrounding forest. After a time the moon lowered, and the horses began stumbling and shying from the path. With a curse, the Scylvendi bid them stop. Wordlessly, he began stripping the horses of their gear and tossing it into the river.

Too weary for words, Serwë dismounted, stretched against the evening chill, and stared for a moment at the Nail of Heaven glittering amid clouds of paler stars. She glanced back the way they had come and was arrested by a far different glitter: a watery string of lights slowly crawling along the river.

"Kellhus?" she said, her voice croaking from disuse.

"I've already seen them," Cnaiür replied, heaving a saddle far out into the rushing water. "The advantage of the pursuer: torches at night." There was a difference in his tone, Serwë realized, an ease she'd never heard before. The ease of a workman in his element.

"They've been gaining ground," Kellhus noted, "moving too quickly to be picking out our trail. They just follow the river. Perhaps we can use this to our advantage."

"You have no experience in these matters, Dûnyain."

"You should listen to him," Serwë said, more hotly than she intended.

Cnaiür turned to her, and though his expression was lost in the darkness, she could sense his outrage. Scylvendi tribesmen did not brook shrewish women.

"The only way we could use this to our advantage," he replied, his fury scarcely bridled, "is by striking through the forest. They would continue ahead, perhaps lose our trail altogether, but by sunrise they would realize their mistake. Then they would be forced to backtrack—but not *all of them* would do so. They know we are bent on travelling east, and they would know they were now ahead of us. They would send word ahead of our coming, and we would be doomed. Our only hope is to outrun them, understand?"

"She understands, plainsman," Kellhus replied.

Leading their horses on foot, they continued. Kellhus guided them now, unerringly taking advantage of every stretch of open ground, so that at times Serwë found herself running. Several times she fell, tripping over something unseen, yet she always managed to recover herself before the Scylvendi could upbraid her. She was perpetually winded, her lungs burning, a cramp periodically knifing into her side. She was bruised, scraped, and so exhausted that her legs wobbled whenever she stood still. But there was no question of stopping, not so long as the string of torches prickled in the distance.

Eventually the river turned, cascading over a series of stone shelves. Under the starlight, Serwë glimpsed a great body of water ahead of them.

"The River Phayus," Cnaiür said. "Very soon, we will ride, Serwë."

Rather than follow the tributary to the Phayus, they veered to the right and plunged into the blackness of the forest interior.

For the first while, Serwë could see almost nothing, and she felt as though she followed a train of sounds through a nightmarish tunnel of blackness jostling with blackness. Cracking twigs. Snorting horses. The periodic stamping of hoofs. But gradually, a pallid twilight began etching details from the gloom: slender trunks, deadfalls, the mosaic of leaves across the forest floor. The Scylvendi had spoken true, she realized. The wood was growing thinner.

As dawn gathered on the eastern horizon, Cnaiür called them to a halt. Clutched in the roots of an upturned tree, a great disc of earth reared above him. "Now we ride," he said. "We ride hard."

At last she was off her feet, but her relief was short-lived. With Cnaiür ahead and Kellhus in the rear, they barrelled through the brush. As the forest thinned, the latticed confusion of the canopy descended, until it seemed they raced through it, lashed by innumerable branches. Through the staccato thud of hoofs, she heard the swell of morning birdsong.

They broke from the oppressive brush and across the pastures at a gallop. Serwë cried out and laughed aloud, exhilarated by the sudden rush over open ground. Cool air numbed her stinging face and combed her hair into streaming tails. Before them, the red orb of the sun crested the horizon, burnishing the purple distance with orange and magenta.

The pastures gradually gave way to cultivated land, until the distances were thatched with young wheat, barley, and millet fields. They skirted small agrarian villages and the vast plantations that belonged to the Houses of the Congregate. As a concubine indentured to House Gaunum, Serwë had been sequestered in similar villas, and as she stared at the rambling compounds, the roofs tiled in red clay, and the rows of spearlike junipers, she was troubled that something once so familiar could become so threatening and strange.

The slaves lifted their heads from the fields and watched them gallop along the dusty byways. Teamsters cursed them as they thundered past. Women dropped their burdens and yanked astonished children out of harm's way. What did these people think? Serwë wondered, her thoughts drunk with fatigue. What did they see?

Daring fugitives, she decided. A man whose harsh face reminded them of Scylvendi terror. Another man, whose blue eyes plumbed them in the haste of a single glance. And a beautiful woman, her long blonde hair askew—the prize these men would deny their unseen pursuers.

By late afternoon, they urged their lathered horses to the summit of a stony hill, where the Scylvendi at last allowed them a momentary respite. Serwë nearly toppled from her saddle. She fell to the turf and stretched through the grasses, her ears ringing, the ground slowly wheeling beneath her. For a time, all she could do was breathe. Then she heard the Scylvendi curse.

"Tenacious bastards," he spat. "Whoever leads those men is as canny as he is stubborn."

"What should we do?" Kellhus asked, and the question somehow disappointed her.

You know. You always know. Why do you cater to him?

She struggled to her feet, amazed that her limbs could so quickly stiffen, and then followed their gazes to the horizon. Beneath the rose sun she glimpsed a small veil of dust trailing toward the river, but little more.

"How many?" Cnaiür asked Kellhus.

"The same as before . . . sixty-eight. Although they now ride different horses."

"Different horses," Cnaiür repeated dryly, as though as disgusted by what this meant as by Kellhus's ability to draw such conclusions. "They must have seized them somewhere on the way."

"You failed to anticipate this?"

"Sixty-eight," Cnaiür said, ignoring his question. "Too many?" he asked, staring hard at Kellhus.

"Too many."

"Even if we attack at night?"

Kellhus nodded, his eyes strangely unfocused. "Perhaps," he replied at length, "but only if all other alternatives have been exhausted."

"What alternatives?" Cnaiür asked. "What . . . should we do?"

Serwë glimpsed a curious anguish in his expression. *Why does it trouble him so? Can't he see we're meant to follow?*

"We've gained some ground on them," Kellhus said firmly. "We continue riding."

With Kellhus in the lead, they wound into the shadow of the hill, slowly gathering speed. They scattered a small herd of sheep, then pressed their long-suffering horses harder than ever before.

Hurtling across the pasture, Serwë felt the ache seep from her jerking limbs. They outran the hill's shadow, and the evening sun fell warm upon her back. She urged her horse faster and pulled even with Kellhus, flashing him a fierce grin. He made her laugh with a funny face: eyes shocked at her audacity, brows pinched in indignant outrage. With the Scylvendi behind them, they galloped side by side, laughing at their hapless pursuers, until the evening passed into twilight and the distant fields were rinsed of all colour save grey. They had, she thought, outdistanced the very sun.

Abruptly her horse—her prize for having killed the scarred man—faltered mid-stride, throwing its head back with a grunting shriek. She could almost feel its heart burst . . . Then exploding ground, grass and dirt between her teeth, and throbbing silence.

The sound of approaching hoofs.

"Leave her!" she heard the Scylvendi bark. "They want us, not her. She's stolen property to them, a pretty bauble."

"I will not."

"This is not like you, Dûnyain . . . Not like you at all."

"Perhaps," she heard Kellhus say, his voice now very close and very gentle. Hands cupped her cheeks.

Kellhus . . . No blue babies.

No blue babies, Serwë. Our child will be pink and alive.

"But she'll be safer—"

Darkness, and dreams of a great, shadowy race across heathen lands.

Floating. *Where's the knife?*

Serwë awoke gasping for breath, the whole world rushing and bucking beneath her. Hair whisked and fluttered in her face, stinging her eyes. She smelled vomit.

"This way!" she heard the Scylvendi shout over chopping hoofs, his voice impatient, even urgent. "The crest of that hill!"

A man's strong back and shoulders were crushed against her breasts and cheek. Her arms were wrapped impossibly tight around his torso, and her hands . . . She couldn't feel her hands! But she could feel rope chafing at her wrists. She was tied! Trussed to the back of a man. To Kellhus.

What was happening?

She lifted her head, felt knives probe the back of her eyes. Headless pillars flashed by, and the dancing line of an amputated wall. Ruins of some kind, and beyond, the dark avenues of an olive grove. Olive groves? Had they come so far already?

She looked back and was surprised by the absence of their riderless horses. Then, through thin skirts of dust, she saw a large cohort of horsemen darkening the near distance. The Kidruhil, hard faces intent on the chase, longswords waving and flashing beneath the sun.

They spilled around and through the ruined temple.

She felt a giddy sense of weightlessness, then slammed into Kellhus's back. The horse began kicking upward across a steep incline. She glimpsed the chalky remnants of a wall behind them.

"Fuck!" she heard the Scylvendi roar. Then: "Kellhus! You see them?"

Kellhus said nothing, but his back arched and his right arm jerked up as he heaved the horse in a different direction. She glimpsed his bearded profile as he glanced to his left.

"Who are they?" he called.

And Serwë saw another surge of horsemen, more distant but sweeping toward them across the same slope. Kellhus's horse yanked them at a tangent up the incline, kicking up gravel and dust.

She looked back to the Kidruhil below and watched them leap the ruined wall in staggered ranks. Then she saw another party, three horsemen, erupt from a stand of trees then veer to intercept them on their way up the hill.

"Kellllhuuss!" she cried, struggling against the ropes to secure his attention.

"Still, Serwë! Sit still!"

One of the Kidruhil toppled from his mount, clutching an arrow shaft in his chest. The Scylvendi, Serwë realized, remembering the doe he'd killed. Without pause, however, the other two galloped passed their fallen comrade.

The first reined parallel to them, raised a javelin. The slope levelled and the horses gathered speed. The Kidruhil hurled the shaft across the mottled blur of ground and grasses.

Serwë winced.

But somehow Kellhus reached out and seized it from the air—as though it were a plum hanging from a tree. In a single motion, he twirled the javelin and flung it back, where it punctured the man's astonished face. For a grisly moment Serwë watched the man teeter in his saddle, then slump to the rushing ground.

The other simply took his place, reining closer as though intending to ram them, his longsword raised to strike. For an instant, Serwë met his eyes, bright against his dusty face, mad with murderous determination. Baring clenched teeth, he struck—

Kellhus's blow snapped through his body like the bowstring of some great siege engine. His sword flickered across the intervening space. Dropping his weapon, the Kidruhil glanced down. Bowel and bloody slop gushed across his pommel and thighs. His horse shied away and cantered to a halt.

Then they were pounding down the far side of the summit, and the ground disappeared.

Their horse shrieked and stumbled to a gravelly stop behind Cnaiür's mount. Before them yawned a steep drop, nearly three times the height of the trees that crowded its base. Not sheer, but far too steep for horses. A patchwork of dark groves and fields stretched into the hazy distance beyond.

"Along the crest," the Scylvendi spat, yanking his horse about. But he paused when Kellhus's mount screamed once again. Before Serwë knew what was happening, her arms had been cut free and Kellhus had vaulted to the ground. He hoisted her from the saddle and steadied her as she struggled to find her legs. "We're going to slide down, Serwë. Can you do that?"

She thought she would vomit. "But I can't feel my han—"

Just then the first of the Kidruhil leapt over the summit.

"Go!" Kellhus shouted, almost shoving her over the rounded edge. The dusty earth broke beneath her feet and she began skidding down, but her screams were drowned by shrieks. A horse tumbled and thrashed in an avalanche of dust beside her. Clawing, scraping with fingers she could barely feel, she brought herself to a stop. The horse continued falling.

"Move, wench, move!" the Scylvendi cried from above. She watched him half pedal, half skid past her, trailing a streamer of dust into the giddy emptiness below. She risked a hesitant step, then she was falling again. She struggled, trying to keep her feet braced below her and her back to the slope, but she hit something *hard* and bounced outward in an explosion of sand, flailing at open air. Somehow she landed on her hands and knees, and for a moment, it seemed she might brake her descent, but another rock caught her left foot, jerked her knee to her chest, and she plummeted, battered and scraped, rolling headlong through a cloud.

Amid the rattle of falling stones, she stopped, and the Scylvendi was cradling her head. The concern in his look bewildered her. "Can you stand?" he asked.

"Don't know," she gasped.

Where's Kellhus?

He eased her to a seated position, but his concern was already elsewhere.

"Stay," he said brusquely. "Don't move." He was drawing his sword even as he stood.

She looked up the slope and immediately became dizzy. She saw a cloud of dust toppling down and realized that it was Kellhus hastening his descent by making leap after sliding leap. Then the pain in her side struck her, something *sharp* agonizing her every breath.

"How many?" Cnaiür asked Kellhus as he skidded to a halt.

"Enough," he said, seemingly unwinded. "They won't follow us down this way. They'll go around."

"Like the others."

"What others?"

"The dogs that surprised us when we first broke for the summit. They must have started down the moment we veered away from them, because I glimpsed only the stragglers—over there, to the right . . ."

Even as Cnaiür said this, Serwë heard the rumble of hooves through the screen of hardwoods.

But we have no horses! No way to flee!

"What does this mean?" she cried, gasping at the flare of pain that punished her.

Kellhus knelt before her, his heavenly face blotting out the sun. Once again she could see his halo, the shimmering gold that marked him apart from all other men. *He'll save us! Don't worry, my sweet, I know He will!*

But he said, "Serwë, when they come, I want you to close your eyes."

"But you're the *promise*," she said, sobbing.

Kellhus brushed her cheek, then wordlessly withdrew to take his place at the Scylvendi's side. She glimpsed flashes of movement beyond them, heard the neigh and snort of fierce warhorses.

Then the first stallions, caparisoned in mail skirts, stamped from shade into sunlight, bearing riders in white-and-blue surcoats and heavy hauberks. As the horsemen closed in a ragged semicircle, Serwë realized they possessed silver faces, as passionless as those of the Gods. And she knew they had been sent—sent to protect him! To shelter the promise.

One drew closer than the others and pulled his helm from a shock of thick black hair. He tugged at two straps, then pulled the silver war mask from his stocky face. He was surprisingly young, and he sported the square-cut beard so common to the men of the Eastern Three Seas. Ainoni maybe, or Conriyan.

"I'm Krijates Iryssas," the young man said in heavily accented Sheyic. "These pious but dour fellows are Knights of Attrempus and Men of the Tusk . . . Have you seen any fugitive criminals about?"

Stunned silence. At last Cnaiür said, "Why do you ask?"

The knight looked askance at his comrades then leaned forward in his saddle. His eyes twinkled. "Because I'm dying for the lack of honest conversation."

The Scylvendi smiled.

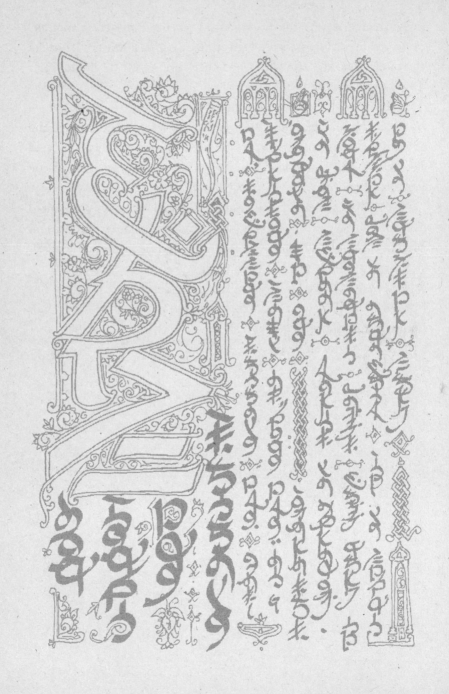

PART V:
The Holy War

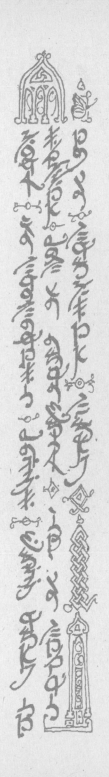

CHAPTER FIFTEEN

MOMEMN

Many have condemned those who joined the Holy War for mercenary reasons, and doubtless, should this humble history find its way into their idle libraries, they will blast me as well. Admittedly, my reasons for joining the Holy War were "mercenary," if by that one means I joined it in order to procure ends outside of the destruction of the heathen and the reconquest of Shimeh. But there were a great many mercenaries such as myself, and like myself, they inadvertently furthered the Holy War by killing their fair share of heathen. The failure of the Holy War had nothing to do with us.

Did I say failure? Perhaps "transformation" would be a better word.

—DRUSAS ACHAMIAN, COMPENDIUM OF THE FIRST HOLY WAR

Faith is the truth of passion. Since no passion is more true than another, faith is the truth of nothing.

—AJENCIS, THE FOURTH ANALYTIC OF MAN

"Remember what I said," Xinemus muttered to Achamian as an aging slave led them into Proyas's immense pavilion. "Be formal. Be cautious . . . He's seeing you only to shut me up, nothing more."

Achamian frowned. "How times have changed, eh, Zin?"

"You wielded too much influence over him as a child, Akka, left too deep a mark. Zealous men often confuse purity with intolerance, particularly when they're young."

Though Achamian suspected matters were a great deal more complicated, he said only, "You've been reading again, haven't you?"

They followed the slave through a succession of embroidered flaps, turning left, then right, then left again. Though Proyas had arrived several weeks earlier, the administrative chambers they passed through seemed haphazardly arranged and, in some cases, only half unpacked. Achamian found this troubling. Normally, Proyas was fastidious to a fault.

"Turmoil and crisis," Xinemus said by way of explanation. "Ever since his arrival . . . He has more than half his staff out in the field, counting chickens."

Counting chickens, Achamian recalled, was a Conriyan turn of phrase for futile endeavours.

"Things are that bad?"

"Worse. He's losing this game the Emperor plays, Akka. You'd do well to remember that too."

"Perhaps I should wait, wait until—" Achamian began saying, but it was too late.

The old slave halted at an entrance to a much larger enclosure, swept his hand in a flourish that revealed a darkened armpit. Enter at your peril, his expression said.

The room was cooler, more dim. Censers hazed the interior with the scent of aromatic woods. Carpets lay scattered about a central fire, making the ground a cozy jumble of Ainoni pictograms and

stylized scenes drawn from Conriyan legend. Reclined among cushions, the Prince watched from the far side of the shining hearth.
Achamian immediately fell to his knees, bowing. He glimpsed a
filament of smoke spiralling from a tiny coal thrown by the fire.

"Rise, Schoolman," Proyas said. "Take a cushion by my hearth. I
won't ask you to kiss my knee."

The Crown Prince of Conriya wore only a linen kilt embroidered
with the insignia of his dynasty and nation. A close-cropped beard,
now the fashion of young nobles in Conriya, outlined his face. His
expression was blank, as though he struggled to suspend judgement.
His large eyes were hostile, but not hateful.

I won't ask you to kiss my knee . . . Not a very promising beginning.

Achamian took a deep breath.

"You have honoured me beyond estimation, my Prince, by granting me this audience."

"Perhaps more than you know, Achamian. Never in my life have
so many men clamoured for my ear."

"Regarding the Holy War?"

"What else?"

Achamian winced inwardly. For an instant he found himself at a
loss for words. "Is it true you raid the valley?"

"And farther . . . If you think to upbraid me for my tactics,
Achamian, think again."

"What do sorcerers know of tactics, my Prince?"

"Far too much, if you ask me. But then everyone and his cousin
is an authority on tactics of late, eh, Marshal?"

Xinemus glanced apologetically at Achamian. "Your tactics are
impeccable, Proyas. It's the proprieties I worry about."

"And what would you have us eat? Our prayer mats?"

"The Emperor closed his granaries only when you and the other
Great Names started looting."

"But what he gave us was a pittance, Zin! Enough to prevent
riots. Enough to control us! Not a grain more."

"Even still, raiding *Inrithi*—"

Proyas scowled and waved his hands. "Enough! You say this, while I say that, over and over again. For once I'd rather hear Achamian speak! Did you hear that, Zin? You've irritated me that much . . ."

From Xinemus's grave look, Achamian gathered Proyas was not joking.

So changed . . . What's happened to him? But even as he asked this, Achamian recognized the answer. Proyas suffered, as all men of high purpose must, the endless exchange of principles for advantages. No triumph without remorse. No respite without siege. Compromise after anxious compromise, until one's entire life felt a defeat. It was a malady Mandate Schoolmen knew well.

"Achamian . . ." Proyas said when he did not immediately speak, "I have a nation of migrants to feed, an army of bandits to restrain, and an Emperor to outwit. So let's dispense with the niceties of jnan. Just tell me what you want."

Proyas's face was a battleground of expectancy and impatience. He *wanted* to see his old tutor, Achamian guessed, but he did not want to want this. *This was a mistake.*

Involuntary intake of breath. "I wonder whether my Prince still recalls what it was I taught him those many years ago."

"Those recollections, I fear, are the only reason you're here."

Achamian nodded. "Does he recall what it means to think in terms of possibilities?"

Impatience regained the heights of Proyas's expression. "You mean to think 'as if'?"

"Yes, my Prince."

"As a child I tired of your games, Achamian. As a man I simply have no time for them."

"This is no game."

"Isn't it? Then why are you *here*, of all places, Achamian? What business could the Mandate have with the Holy War?"

This was the question. When one warred with the intangible, convolutions were certain to abound. Any mission without purpose, or with a purpose that had evaporated into abstraction, inevitably confused its own means as its end, took its own striving as the very thing striven for. The Mandate was here, Achamian had realized, to determine whether it *should* be here. And this was as significant as any Mandate mission could be, since it had become every Mandate mission. But he could not tell Proyas this. No, he had to do what every Mandate agent did: populate the unknown with ancient threats and seed the future with past catastrophes. In a world that was already terrifying, the Mandate had become a School of fear-mongers.

"Our business? To discover the truth."

"So you would lecture me on truth rather than possibilities . . . I'm afraid those days have passed, Drusas Achamian."

You called me Akka, once.

"No. My lecturing days are over. The best I can manage now, it seems, is to remind people of what they once knew."

"There are many things I once claimed to know but no longer care to. You must be specific."

"I would merely remind you, my Prince, that when we're most certain, we're most certain to be deceived."

Proyas smiled menacingly. "Ah . . . you would challenge my faith."

"Not challenge—merely temper."

"Temper, then. You'd have me ask new questions, consider troubling 'possibilities.' And what, pray tell, are these troubling possibilities?" The sarcasm was naked now, and it stung. "Tell me, Achamian, how great a fool have I become?"

In that instant, Achamian understood the depth to which the Mandate had been crippled. Not only had they become preposterous, they had become stale, a matter of rote. How does one recover credibility from such an abyss?

"The Holy War," Achamian said, "might not be what it seems."

"Not what it seems?" Proyas cried with mock astonishment—a rebuke for a teacher who had fatally stumbled. "For the Emperor the Holy War is a lecherous means to restore his Empire. For so many of my peers, it's simply a venal instrument of conquest and glory. For Eleäzaras and the Scarlet Spires, it's a vehicle for some arcane who-knows-what. And for so many others it's merely a cheap way to redeem a squandered life. The Holy War not what it seems? There hasn't been a night, Achamian, when I haven't prayed you're *right!*"

The Crown Prince leaned forward and poured himself a bowl of wine. He offered none to Achamian or Xinemus.

"But prayers," Proyas continued, "are never enough, are they? Something will happen, some treachery or small atrocity, and my heart will cry, 'Fie on this! Damn them all!' And do you know what, Achamian? It's a *possibility* that saves me, that drives me to continue. What if? I ask myself. What *if* this Holy War is in fact divine, a good *in and of itself?*"

His breath hung on these last words, as though no breath could follow them.

What if . . .

"Is that so hard to believe? Is that so impossible—that despite men and their rutting ambitions, this one thing, this Holy War, could be good for its own sake? If it is impossible, Achamian, then my life has as little meaning as yours . . ."

"No," Achamian said, unable to muzzle his anger, "it's not impossible."

The plaintive fury in Proyas's eyes dulled, became waxy with regret. "I apologize, old tutor. I didn't mean to . . ." He interrupted himself with another draught of wine. "Perhaps now is not such a good time to peddle your possibilities, Achamian. I fear the God tests me."

"Why? What's happened?"

Proyas glanced at Xinemus. A worried look.

"There's been a massacre of innocents," he said. "Galeoth troops under Coithus Saubon cut down the inhabitants of an entire village near Pasna."

Pasna, Achamian recalled, was a town some forty miles up the River Phayus, famed for its olive groves.

"Does Maithanet know?"

Proyas grimaced. "He will."

Suddenly Achamian understood.

"You defy him," he said. "Maithanet has forbidden these raids!" Achamian could scarce conceal his jubilation. If Proyas had defied his Shriah . . .

"I like not your manner," Proyas snapped. "What care you—" He stopped, as though struck by a realization of his own. "Is this the possibility you wish me to consider?" he asked, wonder and fury in his tone. "That Maithanet . . ." A sudden gallows laugh. "That Maithanet conspires with the *Consult?*"

"As I said," Achamian replied evenly, "a possibility."

"Achamian, I'll not insult you. I know the Mandate mission. I know the solitary horror of your nights. You and your kind *live* the myths we put aside with childhood. How can one not respect that? But don't confuse whatever disagreements I may have regarding Maithanet with the reverence and devotion I bear the Holy Shriah. What you're saying—the 'possibility' you're asking me to entertain—is blasphemous. Do you understand?"

"Yes. All too well."

"Do you have *more,* then? More than your nightmares?"

Achamian did have more, more because he had so much less. He had Inrau. He wet his lips. "In Sumna, an agent of ours"—he swallowed—"of mine, has been murdered."

"An agent assigned, no doubt, to spy on Maithanet . . ." Proyas sighed, then shook his head ruefully, as though resigning himself to blunt and perhaps hurtful words. "Tell me, Achamian, what's the penalty for spying in the Thousand Temples?"

The sorcerer blinked. "Death."

"*This?*" Proyas exploded. "This is what you bring to me? One of your spies is executed—for *spying!*—and you suspect that *Maithanet*—the greatest Shriah in generations!—conspires with the Consult? These are your grounds? Trust me, Schoolman, when ill fortune befalls a Mandate agent, it need not—"

"There's more!" Achamian protested.

"Oh, we must hear this! What? Did some drunk whisper some lurid tale?"

"That day in Sumna, when I saw you kiss Maithanet's knee—"

"Oh yes, by all means, let us speak of *that!* Do you realize the *outrage*—"

"He *saw* me, Proyas! He knew I was a sorcerer!"

This forced a pause, but little else. "And you think I don't know this? I was *there*, Akka! So he, like other great Shriahs before him, has the gift of seeing the Few. What of it?"

Achamian was dumbstruck.

"What of it?" Proyas repeated. "What does it mean other than that he, unlike *you*, chose the path of righteousness?"

"But—"

"But *what?*"

"The dreams . . . They've been so forceful of late."

"Ah, back to the nightmares again . . ."

"Something is happening, Proyas. I know it. I *feel* it!"

Proyas snorted. "And this brings us to the rub now, doesn't it Achamian?"

Achamian could only stare in bewilderment. There was something more, something he was forgetting . . . When did he become such an old fool?

"Rub?" he managed to ask. "What rub?"

"The difference between knowing and feeling. Between knowledge and faith." Proyas caught his bowl and downed it as though punishing the wine. "You know, I remember asking you about the God once, many years ago. Do you remember what you said?"

Achamian shook his head.

"'I've heard many rumours,' you said, 'but I've never met the man.' Do you remember? Do you remember how I capered and laughed?"

Achamian nodded, smiled wanly. "You repeated it incessantly for weeks. Your mother was furious. I would've been dismissed had not Zin—"

"Always your accursed advocate, that Xinemus," Proyas said, grinning at the Marshal. "You do know you'd be friendless without him?"

A sudden pang in Achamian's throat made it impossible to reply. He blinked at burning eyes.

No . . . Please, not here.

The Marshal and the Prince both stared at him, their expressions at once embarrassed and concerned.

"Anyway," Proyas continued hesitantly, "my point is this: What you said of my God, you must say of your Consult as well. All you have are rumours, Achamian. Faith. You know nothing of what you speak."

"What are you saying?"

His voice hardened. "Faith is the truth of passion, Achamian, and no passion is more true than another. And that means there's no possibility you could speak that I could consider, no fear you could summon that could be more true than my adoration. There can be no discourse between us."

"Then I apologize . . . We'll speak of this no more! I didn't mean to offend—"

"I knew this would pain you," Proyas interrupted, "but it must be said. You're a *blasphemer*, Achamian. Unclean. Your very presence is a trespass against *Him*. An outrage. And as much as I once loved you, I love my God more. Far more."

Xinemus could bear no more. "But surely—"

Proyas silenced the Marshal with an upraised hand. His eyes reflected fervour and fire. "Zin's soul is his own. He can do with it what he will. But, Achamian, you must respect me on this: I don't want to see you again. Ever. Do you understand?"

No.

Achamian looked first to Xinemus, then back to Nersei Proyas.

It doesn't need to be like this . . .

"So be it," he said.

He stood abruptly, straining to stiffen the hurt from his face. The fire-warm folds of his robe burned where they pressed against his skin. "I ask only one thing," he said brusquely. "You know Maithanet. Perhaps you alone he trusts. Simply ask him about a young priest, Paro Inrau, who plunged to his death in the Hagerna several weeks ago. Ask him if his people had him killed. Ask him if they knew the boy was a spy."

Proyas stared at him with the vacancy of one preparing to hate. "Why would I do such a thing, Achamian?"

"Because you loved me once."

Without a word, Drusas Achamian turned and left the two Inrithi noblemen sitting mute by the fire.

Outside, the night air was humid with unwashed thousands. The Holy War.

Dead, Achamian thought. *My students are all dead.*

———◁≫◁≫———

"You disapprove," Proyas said to the Marshal. "What is it this time? The tactics or the proprieties?"

"Both," Xinemus coolly replied.

"I see."

"Ask yourself, Proyas—for once set scripture aside and truly *ask* yourself—whether the feeling within your breast—now, at this very moment—is wicked or righteous."

Earnest pause.

"But I feel nothing."

———◁≫◁≫———

That night Achamian dreamed of Esmenet, lithe and wild upon him, and then of Inrau crying out from the Great Black: *"They're here, old teacher! In ways you cannot see!"*

But inevitably, the other dreams stirred beneath, the hoary nightmare that always reared its dreadful frame, shrugging away the tissue of lesser, more recent longings. And then Achamian found himself on the Fields of Eleneöt, dragging the broken body of a great High King from the clamour of war.

Celmomas's blue eyes beseeched him. "Leave me," the grey-bearded king gasped.

"No . . . If you die, Celmomas, all is lost."

But the High King smiled through ruined lips. "Do you see the sun? Do you see it flare, Seswatha?"

"The sun sets," Achamian replied, tears now spilling across his cheeks.

"Yes! Yes . . . The darkness of the No-God is not all-encompassing. The Gods see us yet, dear friend. They are distant, but I can hear them galloping across the skies. I can hear them cry out to me."

"You cannot die, Celmomas! You must not die!"

The High King shook his head, tears streaming from curiously tender eyes. "They call to me. They say my end is not the world's end. That burden, they say, is yours . . . Yours, Seswatha."

"No," Achamian whispered.

"The sun! Can you see the sun? Feel it upon your cheek? Such revelations are hidden in such simple things. I see! I see so clearly what a bitter, stubborn fool I have been . . . And to you, you most of all, have I been unjust. Can you forgive an old man? Can you forgive a foolish old man?"

"There is nothing to forgive, Celmomas. You've lost much, suffered much."

"My son . . . Do you think he'll be there, Seswatha? Do you think he'll greet me as his father?"

"Yes. As his father and as his king."

"Did I ever tell you," Celmomas said, his voice cracking with heartbroken pride, "that my son once stole into the deepest pits of Golgotterath?"

"Yes." Achamian smiled through his tears. "Many times, old friend."

"How I miss him, Seswatha! How I yearn to stand at his side once again."

The old king wept for a moment, then his eyes grew wide. "I *see* him so clearly. He's taken the sun as his charger, and he rides among us. I see him! Galloping through the hearts of my people, stirring them to wonder and fury!"

"Shush . . . Conserve your strength, my King. The surgeons are coming."

"He says . . . says such sweet things to give me comfort . . . He says that one of my seed will return, Seswatha. An *Anasûrimbor* will return—" The High King winced and shuddered. Spittle hissed through clenched teeth.

"—at the end of the world."

Then the shining eyes of Anasûrimbor Celmomas II, White Lord of Trysë, High King of Kûniüri, grew slack and dull. The evening sun flashed then flickered out, and the gleaming bronze of the Norsirai host paled in the No-God's twilight.

"Our King!" Achamian cried to the grim knights about him. "Our King is dead!"

━━━━◦❈◦━━━━

She found herself wondering whether such games were common to the Kamposea Agora.

Her back was turned to him, but Esmenet could feel his appraising look. She ran fingers across a hanging sheaf of oregano, as though to see whether it had been properly dried. She leaned forward, knowing that her white linen gown, a traditional *hasas*, would crease along her buttocks and open along her side, gracing the stranger with a glimpse of her bare hip and her right breast. A hasas was little more than a long bolt of linen cut with an intricately embroidered collar and joined at the waist by a leather girdle. Though it was the garment of choice for free-wives on hot days, it was also popular among prostitutes—for the obvious reasons.

But she was no longer a prostitute. She was . . .

She no longer knew what she was.

Sarcellus's Cepaloran body-slaves, Eritga and Hansa, had spotted the man as well. They giggled over the cinnamon, pretending to fuss over the length of the sticks. For not the first time this day,

Esmenet found herself despising them, the way she had often found herself despising her competing neighbours in Sumna—particularly the young ones.

He watches me! Me!

He was an extraordinarily beautiful man: blond but clean-shaven, square-chested, and wearing only a blue linen kilt with gold tassels that stuck to his sweaty thighs. The network of blue tattoos along his arms meant he was an officer of some kind in the Emperor's Eothic Guard. Other than that, Esmenet knew him not at all.

They had encountered one another only a short time earlier—she with Eritga and Hansa, he with three of his comrades. The crush had shoved her against him. He smelled of orange peels and salty skin. He was tall: her eyes scarcely reached his collarbone. Something about him made her think of strapping health. She looked up and, without knowing why, smiled at him in the shy yet knowing way that simultaneously protested modesty and promised abandon.

Afterward, flustered, excited, and dismayed, she had pulled Eritga and Hansa down a quiet byway peopled by strolling browsers and lined by spice stalls with their heaped flat baskets and curtains of drying herbs. Compared with the reeking crowds, the fragrances should have proven a welcome relief, but Esmenet had found herself mourning the stranger's scent.

Now, his friends mysteriously absent, he loitered in the sun a short distance from them, watching them with unsettling candour.

Ignore him, she thought, unable to shake the image of his hard stomach pressing against her.

"What are you doing?" she snapped at the two girls.

"Nothing," Eritga said petulantly, her Sheyic heavily accented.

The sound of a stick snapping a trestle made all three of them jump. The old spice-monger, whose skin seemed stained the colour of his wares, stared at Eritga with outraged eyes. He brandished his stick, raising it to the flax awning.

"She is your mistress!" he cried.

The sunburned girl cringed. Hansa clutched her shoulders.

The spice-monger turned to Esmenet, raised a palm to his neck and lowered his right cheek—a caste merchant's gesture of deference. He smiled at her approvingly.

Never in her life had she been so clean, so well-fed, or so well-dressed. Aside from her eyes and her hands, she looked, Esmenet knew, like the wife of some humble caste noble. Sarcellus had given her innumerable gifts: clothing, unguents, perfumes—but no jewellery.

Avoiding her eyes, Eritga stamped from the awning, confirming what Esmenet had known all along: the girl did not think herself Esmenet's servant. Neither did Hansa, for that matter. At first Esmenet had thought it mere jealousy: the girls loved Sarcellus, she'd assumed, and dreamed, as enslaved girls do, of being more than simply bedded by their master. But Esmenet had begun to suspect that Sarcellus himself had a hand in their attitude. Whatever doubt she might have harboured had been dismissed this morning, when the two girls refused to allow her to leave the encampment on her own.

"Eritga!" Esmenet called. "Eritga!"

The girl glared at her, her hate naked now. She was so fair-haired she seemed browless in the sunlight.

"Go home!" Esmenet commanded. "Both of you!"

The girl sneered and spit onto the packed dust.

Esmenet took a threatening step forward. "Beat your freckled ass home, *slave*, before I—"

Another snap of the stick across the trestle. The spice-monger scurried from his stall and struck Eritga across the face. The girl fell, shrieking, while the vendor struck her again and again, crying curses in an unfamiliar tongue. Hansa pulled Eritga clear, then with the spice-monger still shouting and waving his stick, they fled down the alley.

"They go home now," the man said to Esmenet, beaming with pride and pressing a pink tongue against the gaps in his teeth. "Fucking slaves," he added, spitting over his left shoulder.

But Esmenet could only think, *I'm alone.*

She blinked at the tears threatening her eyes. "Thank you," she said to the old man.

The gnarled face softened. "What you buy?" he asked gently. "Pepper? Garlic? I have very good garlic. I winter it very special way."

How long had it been since she was last alone? Since that village months ago, she realized, where Sarcellus had rescued her from being stoned. She shuddered, suddenly feeling horribly on her own. She hid her tattoo in the palm of her right hand.

From the day Sarcellus had saved her, she had not once been alone. Not truly. Since she'd arrived in the Holy War, Eritga and Hansa had been ever-present. And Sarcellus himself had somehow managed to spend a great deal of his time with her. In fact, he'd been remarkably attentive, given the selfishness that seemed to characterize so much of his life otherwise. He'd indulged her on many occasions, taking her here, to the Kamposea Agora, several times, bringing her to worship at the Cmiral, spending an entire afternoon with her in the Temple of Xothei, laughing as she marvelled at its great dome and listening as she explained how the Ceneians had built it in near antiquity.

He had even toured the Imperial Precincts with her, teasing her for gawking as they walked in the cool shadow of the Andiamine Heights.

But he had never left her alone. Why?

Was he afraid she'd seek out Achamian? It struck her as a silly fear.

She went cold.

They were watching Akka. *They!* He had to be told!

But then why did she hide from him? Why did she dread the thought of bumping into him each time she left the encampment? Whenever she glimpsed someone who resembled him, she would instantly look away, afraid that if she did not, she might *make* whoever it was into Achamian. That he would see her, punish her with a questioning frown. Stop her heart with an anguished look . . .

"What you buy?" the spice-monger was repeating, his face now troubled.

She looked at him blankly, thinking, *I have no money.* But then why had she come to the agora?

Then she remembered the man, the Eothic Guardsman watching her. She glanced across the alley and saw him waiting, staring at her keenly. *So beautiful . . .*

Her breath tightened. She felt heat flush her thighs.

This time she did not look away.

What do you want?

He looked at her intently, lingering for that heartbeat that sealed all unspoken assignations. He tilted his head slightly, looked to the far end of the market then back.

She looked away, nervous, a fluttering in her chest.

"Thank you," she mumbled to the spice-monger. He flapped his arms in disgust as she turned away. Numb, she began walking in the direction the stranger had indicated.

She could see him in her periphery, following her through a shadowy screen of people. He kept his distance, but it seemed he already pressed his sweaty chest against her back, his narrow hips against her buttocks, moving, whispering in her ear. She struggled for breath, walked faster, as though pursued.

I want this!

They found themselves among emptied paddocks, surrounded by the smell of sacrificial livestock. The outer compounds of the temple-complex loomed above them. Somehow, without speaking, they closed upon one another in the gloom of an adjacent alley.

This time he smelled of sunburned skin. His kiss was crushing, vicious even. She sobbed, pressed her tongue deep into his mouth, felt the knife's edge of his teeth.

"Ah, yes," he nearly cried. "So sweet!" He clutched her left breast. His other hand jostled with her gown, skidded up along the inside of her thighs.

"No!" she exclaimed, pushing him back.

"What?" He leaned against her elbows, searching for her mouth.

She turned her face away. "Coin," she breathed. False laugh. "No one eats for free."

"Ah, Sejenus! How much?"

"Twelve talents," she gasped. "*Silver* talents."

"A whore," he hissed. "You're a *whore!*"

"I'm twelve silver talents . . ."

The man hesitated. "Done."

He began digging through his purse, glanced at her as she nervously adjusted her gown.

"What's this?" he asked sharply. She followed his eyes to the back of her left hand.

"Nothing."

"Really? I'm afraid I've seen this 'nothing' before. It's a mockery of the tattoos borne by Gierric Priestesses, no? What they use in Sumna to brand their whores."

"So. What of it?"

The man grinned. "I'll give you twelve talents. Copper."

"Silver," she said. Her voice sounded uncertain.

"A bruised peach is a bruised peach, no matter how you dress it."

"Yes," she whispered, feeling tears brim in her eyes.

"What was that?"

"Yes! Just hurry!"

He fumbled coins from his purse. Esmenet glimpsed a halved silver slip through his fingers. She snatched the sweaty coppers. He hiked the front of her hasas and knifed into her. She climaxed almost immediately, blowing air through clenched teeth. She beat feebly at his shoulders with her monied fists. He continued to thrust, slow yet hard. Again and again, grunting a little louder each time.

"Sweet Sejenus!" he hissed, his breath hot in her ear.

She climaxed again, this time crying out. She could feel him shudder, feel the telltale thrust, deep, as though he hunted for her very centre.

"By the God," he gasped.

He withdrew, pressed himself from her arms. He seemed to look through her. "By the God . . ." he repeated, differently this time. "What have I done?"

Panting, she raised a hand to his cheek, but he stumbled backward, trying to smooth his kilt. She glimpsed a trail of wet stains, the shadow of his softening phallus.

He could not look at her, so he looked away, toward the bright entrance of the alley. He began walking toward it, as though stunned.

Leaning against the wall, she watched him find his composure, or a blank-faced version of it, in the sunlight. He disappeared, and she leaned her head back, breathing heavily, smoothing her hasas with clumsy hands. She swallowed. She could feel him run down her inner thigh, first hot, then cold, like a tear that runs to the chin.

For the first time, it seemed, she could smell the stink of the alley. She saw the glint of his half-silver among withered, eyeless fish.

She rolled her shoulder against the mud brick, looked to the bright agora. She dropped the coppers.

She pinched shut her eyes, saw black seed smeared across her belly.

Then she fled, truly alone.

Hansa, Esmenet realized, had been crying. Her left eye looked as though it might soon swell shut. Eritga looked up from tending the fire. A red welt marred her face—from the spice-monger, Esmenet imagined—but she seemed unscathed otherwise. She grinned like a freckled jackal, lifting her invisible eyebrows and looking to the pavilion.

Sarcellus was waiting for her inside, sitting in the gloom.

"I missed you," Sarcellus said.

Despite his strange tone, Esmenet smiled. "And I you."

"Where have you been?"

"Walking."

"Walking . . ." He snorted air through his nostrils. "Walking where?"

"In the city. In the markets. What's it to you?"

He looked at her curiously. He seemed to be . . . smelling her.

He jumped up, seized her wrist, and yanked her close—so fast that Esmenet gasped aloud.

Staring at her, he reached down and grabbed the hem of her gown, began pulling it up. She stopped him just above her knee.

"What are you doing, Sarcellus?"

"I missed you. As I said."

"No. Not now. I have the stink of—"

"Yes," he said, prying her hands away. "*Now.*"

He raised the linen folds, making an awning. He crouched, knees out like an ape.

A shudder passed through her, but from terror or fury, she did not know. He lowered her hasas. Stood. Stared at her without expression. Then he smiled.

Something about him reminded her of a scythe, as though his smile could cut wheat.

"Who?" he asked.

"Who what?"

He slapped her. Not hard, but it seemed to sting all the more for it. "*Who?*"

She said nothing, turned to the bedchamber.

He grabbed her arm, yanked her violently around, raised his hand for another strike . . .

Hesitated.

"Was it Achamian?" he asked.

Never, it seemed to Esmenet, had she hated a face more. She felt the spit gather between her lips and teeth.

"*Yes!*" she hissed.

Sarcellus lowered his hand, released her. For a moment he looked broken.

"Forgive me, Esmi," he said thickly.

But for what, Sarcellus? For what?

He embraced her—desperately. At first she remained stiff, but when he began sobbing, something within her broke. She relented, relaxed against the press of his arms, breathed deep his smell— myrrh, sweat, and leather. How could this man, so stern, more self-assured than any she had known, weep at striking someone like her? Treacherous. Adulterate. How could he—

"I know you love him," she heard him whisper. "I know . . ."

But Esmenet was not so sure.

The sorcerer joined Proyas at the appointed hour on a knoll overlooking the vast, squalid expanse of the Holy War. To the east, cupped within the far-flung walls and turrets of Momemn, the sun smouldered like a great coal, rising.

Proyas closed his eyes, savoured the sun's faint morning heat. *On this day*, he at once thought and prayed, *everything changes*. If the reports were true, then at long last the interminable debate of dogs and crows, crows and dogs, would be over. He would have his lion.

He turned to Achamian. "Remarkable, isn't it?"

"What? The Holy War? Or this summons?"

Proyas felt chastised by his tone and annoyed by his lack of deference. He had realized he needed Achamian while tossing on his cot hours earlier. At first, his pride had argued against it: his words of the previous week had been as final as words could be— "*I do not want to see you again. Ever.*" To repent them now that he needed the man seemed base, mercenary. But must he repent his words in order to break them?

"Why the Holy War, of course," he replied nonchalantly. "My scribes tell me that more than—"

"I have an army of rumours to chase, Proyas," the Schoolman said. "So please, dispense with the jnanic pleasantries and just tell me what you want."

Achamian was typically curt in the mornings. An effect of the Dreams, Proyas had always supposed. But there was something more in his tone, something too close to hatred.

"The bitterness I can understand, Akka, but you *will* defer to my station. A covenant binds the School of Mandate to House Nersei, and if need be, I will invoke it."

Achamian looked at him searchingly. "Why, Prosha?" he asked, using the diminutive form of his name, as he had as his tutor. "Why are you doing this?"

What could he tell him that he did not already know or could bear to hear? "It's not your place to question me, Schoolman."

"All men, even princes, must answer to reason. One night you ban me from your presence forever, then scarcely a week afterward, you summon me, and I'm not to ask questions?"

"I didn't summon *you!*" Proyas cried. "I summoned a Mandate Schoolman under the auspices of the treaty my father signed with your handlers. Either you abide by that treaty or you breach it. The choice is yours, Drusas Achamian."

Not today. He would not be drawn into the morass today! Not when everything was about to change . . . Maybe.

But obviously Achamian had his own agenda. "You know," he said, "I've thought over what you said that night. I've done little else."

"What of it?"

Please, old tutor, leave this for another day!

"There's faith that knows itself as faith, Proyas, and there's faith that confuses itself for knowledge. The first embraces uncertainty, acknowledges the mysteriousness of the God. It begets compassion and tolerance. Who can entirely condemn when they're not entirely certain they're in the right? But the second, Proyas, the second embraces certainty and only pays lip service to the God's mystery. It begets intolerance, hatred, violence . . ."

Proyas scowled. Why wouldn't he relent? "And it begets, I imagine, students who repudiate their old teachers, hmm, Achamian?"

The sorcerer nodded. "And Holy Wars . . ."

Something in this reply unsettled Proyas, threatened to foment already restless fears. Only his years of study saved him from speechlessness.

"Dwell in me," he quoted, "and thou shalt find reprieve from uncertainty." He fixed Achamian with a scornful look. "Submit, as the child submits to his father, and all doubts shall be conquered."

The Schoolman stared back for a sour moment. Then he nodded with the wry disgust of one who'd known all along the mawkish manner of his undoing. Even Proyas could feel it: the sense that by quoting scripture, he'd resorted to little more than a shoddy trick. But why? How could the Latter Prophet's own voice, the First and Final Word, sound so . . . so . . .

He found the pity he saw in his old teacher's eyes unbearable.

"Do not dare judge me," Proyas grated.

"Why have you summoned me, Proyas?" Achamian asked wearily. "What do you want?"

The Conriyan Prince gathered his thoughts with a deep breath. Despite his efforts to the contrary, he'd allowed Achamian to distract him with the muck of petty matters. No more.

Today would be the day. It had to be.

"Last night I received word from Zin's nephew, Iryssas. He's found someone of interest."

"Who?"

"A Scylvendi."

Now there was a name that gnawed children's hearts.

Achamian looked at him narrowly but otherwise seemed unimpressed. "Iryssas left only a week or so ago. How could he find a Scylvendi so near Momemn?"

"It seems this Scylvendi was on his way to join the Holy War."

Achamian looked perplexed. Proyas remembered the first time he ever saw that look: as a youth, playing benjuka with him beneath the temple elms in his father's garden. How he had exulted.

This time the expression was fleeting. "Some kind of hoax?" Achamian asked.

"I don't know what to think, old tutor, which is why I've summoned you."

"It must be a lie," Achamian declared. "Scylvendi don't join Inrithi Holy Wars. We're little more than—" He halted. "But why would you summon me *here*?" he asked with an air of pondering aloud. "Unless . . ."

Proyas smiled. "I expect Iryssas shortly. His courier thought he could be at most only a few hours ahead of the Majordomo's party. I sent Xinemus out to bring them here."

The Schoolman glanced at the dawn in their periphery—a great crimson sclera about a golden iris. "He travels through the night?"

"When they found the man and his companions, they were being pursued by the Emperor's Kidruhil. Apparently Iryssas thought it prudent to return as quickly as possible. It seems the Scylvendi has made some rather provocative claims."

Achamian held out his hand, as though to ward away excessive details. "Companions?"

"A man and a woman. I know nothing more, save that neither is Scylvendi and the man says he's a prince."

"And just what claims has this Scylvendi made?"

Proyas paused to swallow away the tremors that threatened his voice. "He claims to know the Fanim manner of war. He claims to have defeated them on the field of battle. And he offers his wisdom to the Holy War."

At last Achamian understood. The agitation. The impatience for his own concerns. Proyas had seen what benjuka players called the *kut'ma*, or the "hidden move." He hoped to use this Scylvendi, whoever he was, both to gall and to defeat the Emperor. Despite himself, Achamian smiled. Even after so many hard words, he could not help sharing something of his old student's excitement.

"So he claims to be your kut'ma," he said.

"Is what he says possible, Akka? Have the Scylvendi warred against the Fanim?"

"The southern tribes commonly raid Gedea and Shigek. When I was stationed in Shimeh, there was—"

"You've been to *Shimeh?*" Proyas blurted.

Achamian scowled. Like most teachers, he despised interruptions. "I've been many places, Proyas."

Because of the Consult. When one did not know where to look, one had to look everywhere.

"I apologize, Akka. It's just that . . ." Proyas trailed, as though mystified.

The Prince, Achamian knew, had transformed Shimeh into the summit of a holy mountain, a destination that required warring thousands to achieve. The idea that a blasphemer might just step from a boat . . .

"At the time," Achamian continued, "there was a great uproar about the Scylvendi. The Cishaurim had sent twenty of their own to Shigek to join a punitive expedition the Padirajah was preparing to send into the Steppe. Neither the Padirajah's army nor the Cishaurim were ever heard from again."

"The Scylvendi massacred them."

Achamian nodded. "So, yes, it's quite possible your Scylvendi has warred against and overcome the Fanim. It's even possible he has wisdom to share. But why would he share it with us? With Inrithi? That's the question."

"Their hatred of us runs that deep?"

Achamian glimpsed a howling rush of Scylvendi lancers galloping into the fire and thunder of Seswatha's voice. An image from the Dreams.

He blinked. "Does a Momic Priest hate the bull whose throat he cuts? No. For the Scylvendi, remember, the whole world is a sacrificial altar, and we're simply the ritual victims. We're beneath their contempt, which is what makes this so extraordinary. A *Scylvendi* joining the Holy War? It's like . . . like—"

"Like entering the sacrificial pens," Proyas finished in a dismayed tone, "and striking bargains with the beasts."

"Exactly."

The Crown Prince pursed his lips, looked out over the encampment, searching, Achamian supposed, for a sign of his dashed hopes. Never before had he seen Proyas like this—even as a child. He looked so . . . fragile.

Are things so desperate? What are you afraid you'll lose?

"But of course," Achamian added in a conciliatory manner, "after Conphas's victory at Kiyuth, things might have changed on the Steppe. Drastically, perhaps." Why did he always cater to him so?

Proyas glanced at him sidelong, hooked his lips in a sardonic grin. He returned his gaze to the tangled sweep of tents, pavilions, and alleyways before them, then said, "I'm not so wretched yet, old—" He paused, squinting. "There!" he exclaimed, pointing to nothing obvious that Achamian could see. "Zin comes. We'll see whether this Scylvendi is my kut'ma or no soon enough."

From despair to eagerness in the bat of an eye. *He'll make a dangerous king,* Achamian involuntarily thought. That is, if he survived the Holy War.

Achamian swallowed, tasted dust on his teeth. Habit, especially when combined with dread, made it easy to ignore the future. But this was something he could not do. With so many warlike men gathered in one place, something catastrophic simply had to follow. This was a law as inexorable as any in Ajencis's logic. The more he remembered it, the more prepared he would be when the time came.

Somewhere, someday, thousands of the thousands about me will lie dead.

The nagging question, the one he found morbid to the point of sickness and yet felt compelled to ask, was, Who? *Who* will die? Someone must.

Me?

Finally his eyes sorted Xinemus and his mounted party from the encampment's confusion. The man looked haggard, as could be expected, given that his Prince had sent him out in the dead of night. His square-bearded face was turned toward them. Achamian was certain that he stared at him rather than Proyas.

Will you die, old friend?

"Do you see him?" Proyas asked.

At first Achamian thought he referred to Xinemus, but then he saw the Scylvendi, also on horseback, speaking to a wild-haired Iryssas. The sight chilled him.

Proyas had been watching him, as though keen to gauge his reaction. "What's wrong?" he asked.

"It's just been—" Achamian caught his breath.

"Been what?"

So long . . . Two thousand years, in fact, since he'd last seen a Scylvendi.

"During the Apocalypse . . ." he began, then trailed in hesitation. Why did he always grow so shy when he spoke of these things, these *real* things? "During the Apocalypse, the Scylvendi joined the No-God. They brought down Kyraneas, sacked Mehtsonc, and laid siege to Sumna shortly after Seswatha had fled there—"

"You mean 'here,'" Proyas said.

Achamian looked at the man quizzically.

"After Seswatha fled *here,*" Proyas explained, "where ancient Kyraneas once stood."

"Y-yes . . . Here." This *was* ancient Kyranean soil upon which he stood. Here—only buried as though beneath layers. Seswatha had even passed through Momemn once, though it was called Monemora then and was little more than a town. And that, Achamian realized, was the source of his disquiet. Ordinarily, he had little trouble keeping the two ages, the present and the apocalyptic, apart. But this Scylvendi . . . It was as though he bore ancient calamities upon his brow.

Achamian studied the nearing figure, the thick arms, banded by scars, the brutal face with eyes that saw only dead foes. Another man, as filthy and as travel-worn as the Scylvendi but with the blond hair and beard of a Norsirai, rode close behind. He spoke to a woman, also flaxen-haired, who swayed precariously in her saddle. Achamian pondered them for a moment—the woman looked injured—but found his attention inexorably drawn back to the Scylvendi.

A Scylvendi. It seemed too bizarre to believe. Was there a greater significance to this? He'd suffered so many dreams of Anasûrimbor Celmomas of late, and now this, a waking vision of the world's ancient end. A Scylvendi!

"Don't trust him, Proyas. They're cruel, utterly merciless. As savage as Sranc, and far more cunning."

Proyas laughed. "Did you know the Nansur begin every toast and every prayer with a curse against the Scylvendi?"

"So I've heard."

"Well, where you see a wraith from your nightmares, Schoolman, I see the enemy of my enemy."

The sight of the barbarian, Achamian realized, had reignited Proyas's hopes.

"No. You see an enemy, plain and simple. He's a heathen, Proyas. Anathema."

The Crown Prince looked at him sharply. "As are you."

Such a blunder! How could he make him understand?

"Proyas, you must—"

"No, Achamian!" the Prince cried. "I 'must' nothing! Just this once, spare me your murky forebodings! Please!"

"You summoned me for my counsel," Achamian snapped.

Proyas whirled. "Petulance, old tutor, does not become you. What's happened to you? I summoned you for your counsel, yes, but instead you give me prattle. A counsellor, as you seem to have forgotten, provides his Prince with the facts necessary for sober judgements. He does not make his own judgements, then upbraid his Prince for not sharing them." He turned away with a sneer. "Now I know why the Marshal frets about you so."

The words stung. Achamian could see from his expression that Proyas had meant to injure, had intended to strike as near a mortal wound as possible. Nersei Proyas was a commander, one struggling against an emperor for the soul of a holy war. He needed resolution, the appearance of unanimity, and above all, obedience. The Scylvendi was nearly upon them.

Achamian knew this, and yet still the words stung.

What's happened to me?

Xinemus had reined his black to a halt at the base of the knoll. He hailed them as he dismounted. Achamian had not the heart to respond in kind. *What do you say about me, Zin? What do you see?*

Taking their cue from Xinemus, the party milled about their horses for a moment. Achamian heard Iryssas chiding the Norsirai about his appearance, as though the man were a bond brother rather than a foreigner about to meet his prince. With murmurs and weary steps, they began climbing the slope. Dismounted, the Scylvendi towered over Xinemus, loomed over everyone, in fact, with the exception of the Norsirai. He was lean-waisted, and his broad shoulders possessed the faintest of stoops. He looked hungry, not in the way of beggars but in the way of wolves.

Proyas afforded Achamian a final glance before greeting his guests. *Be what I need you to be,* his eyes warned.

"So rarely is the look of a man a match for the rumour," the Prince said in Sheyic. His eyes lingered on the barbarian's sinew-strapped arms. "But you look every bit as fierce as your people's reputation, Scylvendi."

Achamian found himself resenting Proyas's congenial tone. His ability to effortlessly swap quarrels for greetings, to be embittered one moment and affable the next, had always troubled Achamian. He certainly did not share it. Such mobility of passion, he'd always thought, demonstrated a worrisome capacity for deceit.

The Scylvendi glowered at Proyas, said nothing. Achamian's skin prickled. The man, he realized, bore a Chorae tucked behind his girdle. He could hear its abyssal whisper.

Proyas frowned. "I know you speak Sheyic, friend."

"If I remember aright," Achamian said in Conriyan, "the Scylvendi have little patience for wry compliments, my Prince. They think them unmanly."

The barbarian's ice blue eyes flashed to him. Something within Achamian, something wise in the estimation of bodily threat, quailed.

"Who is this?" the man asked, his accent thick.

"Drusas Achamian," Proyas said, his tone far stiffer now. "A sorcerer."

The Scylvendi spat, whether in contempt or as a folk-ward against sorcery, Achamian did not know.

"But it's not your place to question," Proyas continued. "My men delivered you and your companions from the Nansur, and I can just as easily have them deliver you back. Do you understand?"

The barbarian shrugged. "Ask what you will."

"Who are you?"

"I am Cnaiür urs Skiötha, Chieftain of the Utemot."

As limited as his knowledge of the Scylvendi was, Achamian had heard of the Utemot, as had every other Mandate Schoolman. According to the Dreams, Sathgai, the King-of-Tribes who had led the Scylvendi under the No-God, was Utemot. Could this be another coincidence?

"The Utemot, my Prince," Achamian murmured to Proyas, "are a tribe from the northern extremes of the Steppe."

Once again, the barbarian raked him with an icy stare.

Proyas nodded. "So tell me, Cnaiür urs Skiötha, why would a Scylvendi wolf travel so far to confer with Inrithi dogs?"

The Scylvendi as much sneered as smiled. He possessed, Achamian realized, that arrogance peculiar to barbarians, the thoughtless certitude that the hard ways of his land made him harder by far than other, more civilized men. *We are*, Achamian thought, *silly women to him.*

"I have come," the man said bluntly, "to sell my wisdom and my sword."

"As a mercenary?" Proyas asked. "I think not, my friend. Achamian tells me there's no such thing as Scylvendi mercenaries."

Achamian tried to match Cnaiür's glare. He could not.

"Things went hard for my tribe at Kiyuth," the barbarian explained. "And harder still when we returned to our pastures. Those few of my kinsmen who survived the Nansur were destroyed by our neighbours to the south. Our herds were stolen. Our wives and children were led away in captivity. The Utemot are no more."

"So what?" Proyas snapped. "You hope to make the Inrithi your tribe? You expect me to believe this?"

Silence. A hard moment between two indomitable men.

"My land has repudiated me. It has stripped me of my hearth and my chattel. So I renounce my land in return. Is this so difficult to believe?"

"But then why—" Achamian began in Conriyan, only to be hushed by Proyas's hand. The Conriyan Prince studied the barbarian in silence, appraising him in the unnerving manner Achamian had seen him appraise others before: as though he were the absolute centre of all judgement. If Cnaiür urs Skiötha was discomfited, however, he did not show it.

Proyas exhaled heavily, as though coming to a risky, and therefore weighty, resolution. "Tell me, Scylvendi, what do you know of Kian?"

Achamian opened his mouth to protest, but hesitated when he glimpsed Xinemus's scowl. *Don't forget your place!* the Marshal's expression shouted.

"Much and little," Cnaiür replied.

These were the kind of responses, Achamian knew, that Proyas despised. But then the Scylvendi simply played the same game the Prince did. Proyas wanted to know what the Scylvendi knew about the Fanim before revealing just how much he *needed* him to know. Otherwise the man might just tell him what he wanted to hear. The evasive reply, however, meant the Scylvendi had sensed this. And this meant he was uncommonly shrewd. Achamian ran his eyes along the scarred length of the barbarian's arms, trying to count his swazond in a glance. He could not.

Very many, he thought, *have underestimated this man.*

"How about war?" Proyas asked. "What do you know of the Kianene manner of war?"

"Much."

"How so?"

"Eight years ago, the Kianene invaded the Steppe much as the Nansur did, hoping to put an end to our raids on Gedea. We met them at a place called Zirkirta. Crushed them. These here"—he ran a thick finger across several scars low on his right wrist—"are that battle. This one is their general, Hasjinnet, son of Skauras, the Sapatishah of Shigek."

There was no pride in his voice. For him war was simply a fact to be described—little different, Achamian imagined, from describing the birth of a foal on his pastures.

"You killed the Sapatishah's son?"

"Eventually," the Scylvendi said. "First I made him sing."

Several of the watching Conriyans laughed aloud, and though Proyas conceded only an aloof smile, Achamian could tell he exulted. Despite his coarse manners, this Scylvendi was saying exactly what Proyas had hoped to hear.

But Achamian remained unconvinced. How did they know the Utemot had been annihilated? And more important, what did this have to do with risking life, limb, and skin crossing the Nansurium to join the Holy War? Achamian found himself looking over the Scylvendi's left shoulder at the Norsirai man who had accompanied him. For an instant, their eyes locked, and Achamian was struck by an intimation of wisdom and sorrow. Unaccountably, he thought: *Him . . . The answer lies with him.*

But would Proyas realize this before he brought them under his protection? Conriyans regarded issues of hospitality with absurd seriousness.

"So you know Kianene tactics?" Proyas was asking.

"I know them. Even then, I had been a chieftain of many years. I advised the King-of-Tribes."

"Could you describe them to me?"

"I could . . ."

The Crown Prince grinned, as though he had at last recognized a kindred spark in the man. Achamian could only watch with numb concern. Any interruption, he knew, would be dismissed out of hand.

"You're cautious," Proyas said, "which is good. A heathen in a Holy War should be cautious. But you've little need to be wary of me, my friend."

The Scylvendi snorted. "Why is that?"

Proyas opened his arms, gesturing to the great whorl and scatter of tents that plumbed the distances. "Have you ever witnessed such a gathering? The glory of the Inrithi has assembled across these fields, Scylvendi. The Three Seas have never been so peaceful. All their violence has gathered *here*. And when it marches against the Fanim, I assure you, your battle at Kiyuth will seem a mere skirmish in comparison."

"And when will it march?"

Proyas paused. "That might very well depend upon you."

The barbarian stared at him, dumbstruck.

"The Holy War is paralyzed, Scylvendi. A host, especially a host as great as this, marches on its belly. But Ikurei Xerius III, despite agreements forged more than a year ago, denies us the provisions we need. By ecclesiastical law the Shriah can demand that the Emperor provision us, but he cannot demand that the Nansur march *with* us."

"So march without them."

"And so we would, but the Shriah hesitates. Months ago, some Men of the Tusk secured the provisions they needed by yielding to the Emperor's demands—"

"Which are?"

"To sign an indenture ceding to the Empire all lands conquered."

"Unacceptable."

"Not to the Great Names at issue. They thought that they were invincible, that waiting for the rest to gather would simply rob them of glory. What is a mark on parchment in exchange for glory? So they marched, crossed into Fanim lands, and were utterly destroyed."

The Scylvendi had raised a contemplative hand to his chin—an oddly disarming gesture, Achamian thought, for a man of such savage aspect. "Ikurei Conphas," he said decisively.

Proyas raised his brows in appreciation. Even Achamian found himself impressed.

"Go on," the Prince said.

"Without Conphas, your Shriah fears the Holy War will be entirely destroyed. So he refuses to demand the Emperor provision you, dreading a repeat of what happened earlier."

Proyas smiled bitterly. "Indeed. And the Emperor, of course, has made his Indenture Conphas's price. The only way for Maithanet to wield his instrument, it seems, is to sell it."

"To sell you."

Proyas released a heavy breath. "Make no mistake, Scylvendi, I'm a devout man. I don't doubt my Shriah, only his appraisal of these recent events. I'm convinced that the Emperor bluffs, that even if we march without signing his accursed Indenture, he'll send Conphas and his Columns to eke whatever advantage he can from the Holy War . . ."

For the first time, Achamian realized that Proyas actually feared Maithanet would capitulate. And why not? If the Holy Shriah could stomach the Scarlet Spires, could he not stomach the Emperor's Indenture as well?

"My hope," Proyas continued, "and it's just a hope, is that Maithanet might accept you as a surrogate for Conphas. With you as our adviser, the Emperor can no longer argue that our ignorance will doom us."

"The Exalt-General's surrogate?" the Scylvendi chieftain repeated. He shuddered with what, Achamian realized a heartbeat later, was laughter.

"You find this amusing, Scylvendi?" Proyas asked, his expression baffled.

Achamian seized the opportunity. "Because of Kiyuth," he murmured in quick Conriyan. "Think of the hatred he must bear Conphas because of Kiyuth."

"Revenge?" Proyas snapped back, also in Conriyan. "You think that's his real reason for travelling here? To wreak his revenge on Ikurei Conphas?"

"Ask him! Why has he come here, and *who are the others?*"

Proyas glanced at Achamian, the chagrin in his eyes overmatched by the admission. His ardour had almost duped him, and he knew it. He had almost brought a Scylvendi to his hearth—a Scylvendi!—without any hard questions.

"You know not the Nansur," the barbarian was saying. "The great Ikurei Conphas replaced by a Scylvendi? There will be more than wailing and gnashing of teeth."

Proyas ignored the remark. "One thing still troubles me, Scylvendi . . . I understand that your tribe was destroyed, that your land turned against you, but why would you come *here?* Why would a Scylvendi cross the Empire, of all places? Why would a heathen join a Holy War?"

The words swatted the humour from Cnaiür urs Skiötha's face, leaving only wariness. Achamian watched him tense. It seemed a door to something dreadful had been unlatched.

Then from behind the barbarian, a resonant voice declared, "I am the reason Cnaiür has travelled here."

All eyes turned to the nameless Norsirai. The man's bearing was imperious despite the rags clothing him, the mien of one steeped in a life of absolute authority. But it was moderated somehow, as though seasoned by hardship and sorrow. The woman clutching his waist glared from face to face, seemingly both outraged and mystified by their scrutiny. *How,* her eyes cried, *could you not know?*

"And just who are you?" Proyas asked of the man.

The clear blue eyes blinked. The serene face dipped only enough to acknowledge an equal. "I am Anasûrimbor Kellhus, son of Moënghus," the man said in heavily accented Sheyic. "A prince of the north. Of Atrithau."

Achamian gaped, uncomprehending. Then the name, Anasûrimbor, struck him like a sudden blow to the stomach. Winded him. He found himself reaching out, clutching Proyas's arm.

This can't be.

Proyas glanced at him sharply, warning him to hold his tongue. *There'll be time for you to pry later, Schoolman.* His eyes clicked back to the stranger.

"A powerful name."

"I cannot speak for my blood," the Norsirai replied.

"One of my seed will return, Seswatha—"

"You don't look a Prince. Am I to believe you're my equal?"

"Nor can I speak for what you do or do not believe. As for my appearance, all I can say is that my pilgrimage was hard."

"An Anasûrimbor will return—"

"Pilgrimage?"

"Yes. To Shimeh . . . We have come to die for the Tusk."

". . . at the end of the world."

"But Atrithau lies far beyond the pale of the Three Seas. How could you have *known* of the Holy War?"

Hesitation, as though he were both frightened and unconvinced by what he was about to say. "Dreams. Someone sent me dreams."

This cannot be!

"Someone? Who?"

The man could not answer.

CHAPTER SIXTEEN

MOMEMN

Those of us who survived will always be bewildered when we recall his arrival. And not just because he was so different then. In a strange sense he never changed. We changed. If he seems so different to us now, it is because he was the figure that transformed the ground.

—DRUSAS ACHAMIAN, COMPENDIUM OF THE FIRST HOLY WAR

Late Spring, 4111 Year-of-the-Tusk, Momemn

The sun had just set. The man who called himself Anasûrimbor Kellhus sat cross-legged in the light of his fire, outside a pavilion whose canvas slopes had been stitched with black embroidered eagles—a gift from Proyas, Achamian supposed. In appearance there was nothing immediately impressive about the man, save perhaps for his long straw-coloured hair, which was as fine as ermine and seemed curiously out of place in the firelight. Hair meant for the sun, Achamian thought. The young injured woman who had clutched his side so fiercely the previous day sat next to him, her dress simple yet elegant. The two of them had bathed and exchanged their rags for clothes drawn from the Prince's own finery.

465

As he neared, Achamian was struck by the woman's beauty. She had looked little more than a beaten waif earlier.

They both watched him approach, their faces vivid in the firelight.

"You must be Drusas Achamian," the Prince of Atrithau said.

"Proyas has warned you about me, I see."

The man smiled understandingly—much more than understandingly. It was unlike any smile Achamian had ever seen. It seemed to understand him much more than he wanted to be understood.

Then the realization struck.

I know this man.

But how does one recognize a man never met? Unless through a son or other kin . . . Images of his recent dream, of holding the dead face of Anasûrimbor Celmomas in his lap, flickered through his soul's eye. The resemblance was unmistakable: the furrow between the brows, the long hollow of the cheeks, the deep-set eyes.

He is an Anasûrimbor! But that's impossible . . .

And yet the times seemed rife with impossible things.

Gathered around Momemn's grim walls, the Holy War was a sight as astonishing as anything from Achamian's nightmares of the Old Wars—save, perhaps, for the heartbreaking Battles of Agongorea and the hopeless Siege of Golgotterath. The arrival of the Scylvendi and the Atrithau Prince had merely confirmed the absurd scale of the Holy War, as though the ancient histories had themselves come to anoint it.

One of my seed will return, Seswatha—an Anasûrimbor will return . . .

As remarkable as the Scylvendi's arrival had been, it smacked of happenstance. But Prince Anasûrimbor Kellhus of Atrithau was a different story. Anasûrimbor! Now there was a name. The Anasûrimbor Dynasty had been the third and most magnificent dynasty to rule Kûniüri—the bloodline the Mandate had thought snuffed out thousands of years before, if not with the death of Celmomas II on the fields of Eleneöt, then certainly with the sack of great Trysë shortly afterward. But not so. The blood of the first great rival of the No-God had somehow been preserved. Impossible.

    . . . *at the end of the world.*

"Proyas has warned me," Kellhus said. "He told me that your kind suffers nightmares of my ancestors."

Achamian felt a pang of betrayal at this. He could almost hear the Prince: *"He'll suspect you of being an agent of the Consult . . . And failing that, he'll hope that Atrithau still wars against the Consult, and that you bear news of his elusive enemy. Humour him, if you wish. But don't try to convince him that the Consult doesn't exist. He will never listen."*

"But I've always believed," Kellhus continued, "that one must ride another man's horse for a day before criticizing."

"To better understand him?"

"No," the man replied with an eye-twinkling shrug. "Because then you're a day away and you have his horse . . ."

Achamian ruefully shook his head and grinned, and after a moment, all three of them burst out laughing.

I like this man. What if he is who he claims to be?

As their laughter trailed, Kellhus introduced him to the woman, Serwë, and bid him welcome. Achamian sat cross-legged on the far side of the fire.

Achamian rarely entered situations like this with a definite plan. He usually came with a handful of curiosities and little more. In the process of giving breath to these curiosities he would ask questions, and in the answers he received he would find himself looking for certain cues, certain telltale signs of word and expression. He would never know exactly what he was looking for, only that he was looking. When he found whatever it was, he trusted that he would know. A good spy always knew.

The inadequacy of this method, however, became apparent from the outset. Never before had he met a man quite like Anasûrimbor Kellhus.

There was his voice, which always seemed pitched to the timbre of a promise. At times, Achamian actually found himself straining to listen, not because the man murmured, or because his accent was prohibitive—he displayed a remarkable fluency given his recent arrival—but because his voice had dimension. It seemed to whisper: *There's more that I'm telling you . . . Only listen and see.*

And there was his face, the frank drama of its expression. There was an innocence about it, a brevity of display possessed only by the young—though in no way did it strike Achamian as naive. The man appeared wise, amused, and sorrowful by guileless turns, as though he experienced his passions and the passions of others with a startling immediacy.

And then there were his eyes, shining soft in the firelight, blue like water that makes one thirst. They were eyes that followed Achamian's every word, as though no amount of attentiveness could do justice to the importance of what he said. And yet, at the same time they were haunted by a strange reserve—not the reserve of men who make judgements they dare not speak, like Proyas, but the reserve of a man who dwells in the certainty that it's not his place to judge.

More than anything, though, it was what the man said that stirred Achamian to awe.

"And why have you joined the Holy War?" Achamian asked, trying to convince himself he still thought the man's answer to Proyas fraudulent.

"You're referring to the dreams," Kellhus replied.

"I suppose I am."

For a brief moment, the Prince of Atrithau regarded him paternally, almost sorrowfully, as though Achamian had yet to understand the rules of this encounter.

"Life had been an endless reverie for me before the dreams," he explained. "Itself a dream, perhaps . . . The dream you ask about—the dream of the Holy War—was a dream that *awakens*. A dream that *makes* a dream of one's prior life. What does one do when he has such dreams?" he asked. "Go back to sleep?"

Achamian shared his smile. "Could you?"

"Go back to sleep? No. Never. Not even if I wanted to. Sleep is never had through wanting. It can't be grasped like an apple to sate one's hunger. Sleep is like ignorance or forgetfulness . . . The harder one strives for such things, the further they recede from one's grasp."

"Like love," Achamian added.

"Yes, like love," Kellhus said softly, glancing at Serwë for a brief instant. "And why have you, a sorcerer, joined the Holy War?"

This question caught Achamian off guard. He found himself answering more openly than he'd intended.

"I don't know why . . . Because I've been directed by my School, I suppose."

Kellhus smiled gently, as though recognizing a shared pain. "But what's your purpose here?"

Achamian bit his lip but did not flinch from the humiliating truth otherwise. "We search for an ancient and implacable evil," he said slowly, with the resentment of men who are often ridiculed. "An evil that we haven't been able to find for more than three hundred years. And yet night after night we're afflicted by dreams of the horrors that evil once wrought."

Kellhus nodded, as though even this mad admission found some precedent in his own life. "It's difficult, is it not, to search for those things we cannot see?"

These words filled Achamian with an unaccountable sorrow.

"Yes . . . Very difficult."

"Perhaps, Achamian, we're not so different, you and I."

"How do you mean?"

But Kellhus did not answer. He did not need to. The man had sensed his earlier incredulity, Achamian realized, and had answered it by showing him the irony of one man anguished by dreams denying another man the rapture of his. Suddenly, Achamian found himself believing the man's story. How could he believe in himself otherwise?

Despite these moments of subtle instruction, Achamian realized the man's discourse and manner knew absolutely nothing of edict.

Their conversation was devoid of the intangible rivalries that hung like an odour, sometimes sweet but mostly sour, about the exchanges of other men. Because of this, their talk possessed the character of a voyage. At times they laughed, and other times they fell silent, stilled by the gravity of their themes. And these moments were like waystations, small shrines by which to orient a greater pilgrimage.

This man, Achamian realized, was not interested in convincing him of anything. Certainly, there were things he wished to show him, things he hoped to share, but each was offered within the frame of a common understanding: *Let us be moved, you and I, by the things themselves. Let us discover each other.*

Before coming to their fire, Achamian had been prepared to be very suspicious, even bitterly critical, of anything the man might say. The Ancient North was now home to countless tribes of Sranc, its great cities—Trysë, Sauglish, Myclai, Kelmeöl, and the others— all gutted ruin, two thousand years dead. And where Sranc ranged, no Men could go. The Ancient North was dark to the Mandate. Inscrutable. And Atrithau was a lone beacon in that darkness, frail before the long, hoary shadow of Golgotterath. A single light held against the black heart of the Consult.

Centuries past, when the Consult still skirmished openly with the Mandate, Atyersus had maintained a mission in Atrithau. But the mission had gone silent centuries ago, shortly before the Consult itself withdrew into obscurity. Periodically, they'd sent expeditions north to investigate, but they invariably failed, either turned back by the Galeoth, who were exceedingly jealous of the northern caravan route, or vanishing into the vast Istyuli Plains, never to be seen again.

As a result, the Mandate knew very little of Atrithau, only what could be gleaned from the traders who managed to survive the great circuit from Atrithau to Galeoth. And hence Achamian knew he would be utterly captive to the facts as Kellhus portrayed them. He would have no way of knowing whether he spoke truthfully— no way of knowing whether he was a prince of anything at all.

And yet, Anasûrimbor Kellhus was a man who moved the souls of those around him. Speaking with him, Achamian found himself arriving at insights he would scarcely have had otherwise, finding answers to curiosities he'd never before dared admit—as though his very soul had been at once quickened and opened. According to the commentaries, the philosopher Ajencis had been such a man. And how could a man like Ajencis lie? It was as though Kellhus were himself a living revelation. An exemplar of Truth.

Achamian found himself trusting him—trusting, despite a thousand years of suspicion.

The night waxed, and the fire burned perilously low. Serwë, who had said very little, lay asleep with her head upon Kellhus's lap. Her sleeping face stirred a wan loneliness within Achamian.

"Do you love her?" Achamian asked.

Kellhus smiled ruefully. "Yes . . . I need her."

"She worships you, you know. I can tell by the way she watches you."

But this seemed to sadden Kellhus. His face darkened. "I know," he said at length. "For some reason, she makes more of me than I am . . . Others do this as well."

"Perhaps," Achamian said with a smile that felt curiously false, "they know something you don't."

Kellhus shrugged. "Perhaps." He looked at Achamian earnestly. Then, with a pained voice, he added, "Ironic, isn't it?"

"And what's that?"

"Here you possess privileged knowledge, and yet no one believes you, while I possess nothing, and everyone insists that I have privileged knowledge."

And Achamian could only think, *But do you believe me?*

"How do you mean?" he asked.

Kellhus looked at him pensively. "This afternoon a man fell to his knees before me and *kissed* the hem of my robe." He laughed then, as though still astonished by the sad absurdity of the act.

"Your dream," Achamian said matter-of-factly. "He thinks that the Gods move you."

"I assure you, they haven't moved me otherwise."

Achamian doubted this and for a moment found himself frightened. *Who is this man?*

They sat silently for a while. Distant shouts sounded from somewhere in the surrounding encampment. Drunks.

"Dog!" someone bellowed. *"Dog!"*

"I do believe you, you know," Kellhus said at last.

Achamian's heart fluttered, but he said nothing.

"I believe in your School's mission."

It was Achamian's turn to shrug. "That makes two of you."

Kellhus chuckled. "And who, may I ask, is my gullible companion?"

"A woman. Esmenet. A prostitute whom I've known from time to time." Achamian could not help glancing at Serwë as he said this. *Not as beautiful as this woman, but beautiful nonetheless.*

Kellhus had been watching him closely. "She's a beautiful woman, I imagine."

"She's a prostitute," Achamian replied, yet again unnerved by his ability to speak his thoughts.

Achamian blamed the silence that followed on these sour words. He repented them but could not take them back. He looked to Kellhus, his eyes apologetic.

But the matter had already been forgiven and forgotten. The silences between men are always fraught with uncomfortable significance—accusations, hesitations, judgements of who is weak and who is strong—but silences with this man undid rather than sealed these things. The silence of Anasûrimbor Kellhus said, *Let us move on, you and I, and recall these things at a better time.*

"There's something," Kellhus said at length, "I would ask of you, Achamian, but I fear that our acquaintance is too slight."

Such honesty. If only I could follow.

"All one can do, Kellhus, is ask."

The man smiled and nodded. "You're a teacher, and I'm an ignorant stranger in a bewildering land . . . Would you consent to teach me?"

With these words, a hundred questions assailed Achamian, but he found himself saying, "I would consider myself fortunate, Kellhus, to count an Anasûrimbor among my students."

Kellhus grinned. "It's agreed, then. I count you, Drusas Achamian, my first friend amid this wonder."

These words aroused an odd shyness in Achamian, and he found himself relieved when Kellhus stirred Serwë and told her they were about to retire.

Afterward, negotiating the dark canvas alleys leading to his own tent, Achamian experienced a strange euphoria. Though the increments of such things have no measure, he felt subtly transformed by his encounter with Kellhus, as though he'd been shown a much-needed example of something profoundly human. An example of life's own proper pose.

Lying awake in his humble tent, he dreaded sleep. The prospect of suffering the nightmares yet again seemed unbearable. Insight, he knew, was as often snuffed as kindled by trauma.

When slumber at last overcame him, he dreamed anew of the disaster on the Fields of Eleneöt, of the death of Anasûrimbor Celmomas II beneath Sranc hammers. And when he awoke gasping for sober air, the voice of the dying High King—so similar to Kellhus's own!—resounded through his soul, overwhelmed his heart's rhythm with its prophetic cadences.

One of my seed will return, Seswatha—an Anasûrimbor will return . . .

. . . at the end of the world.

But what did this mean? Was Anasûrimbor Kellhus in fact a *sign*, as Proyas hoped? A sign not of the God's divine sanction of the Holy War, as Proyas assumed, but of the No-God's imminent return?

. . . the end of the world.

Achamian began trembling, shaking with a horror he'd never before experienced while awake.

The No-God returning? Please, sweet Sejenus, let me die before—

It was unthinkable! He hugged his shoulders and rocked in the blackness of his tent, whispering, "No!" Over and over again, *"No!"*

Please . . . This can't be happening—not to me! I'm too weak. I'm just a fool . . .

Beyond the canvas of his tent, all seemed airy silence. Innumerable men slumbered, dreaming of terror and glory against the heathen, and they knew nothing of what Achamian feared. They were innocents, like Proyas, filled by the heedless momentum of their faith, thinking that a place, a city called Shimeh, was the very nail about which the fate of the world spun. But the nail, Achamian knew, was to be found in a far darker place, a place far to the north where the earth wept pitch. A place called Golgotterath.

For the first time in many, many years, Achamian prayed.

Reason returned afterward, and he felt slightly foolish. As extraordinary as Kellhus had been, there was really nothing other than the dreams of Celmomas and the coincidence of a name to warrant such a terrifying conclusion. Achamian was a sceptic, and he prided himself on the fact. He was a student of the ancients, of Ajencis, and a practitioner of logic. The Second Apocalypse was but the most dramatic of a hundred banal conclusions. And if anything defined his waking life, it was banality.

Nevertheless, he lit his candle with a sorcerous word and rummaged through his pouch, retrieving the map he had made shortly before joining the Holy War. He glanced at the names scattered across the parchment, pausing at

MAITHANET

So long as the old antagonism between him and Proyas persisted, he realized, he would have little hope of learning more about Maithanet or of forwarding his investigation of Inrau's death.

I'm sorry, Inrau, he thought, forcing his eyes away from his beloved student.

Then he studied

THE CONSULT

scratched—far more hastily, it now seemed to him—all alone in the top right corner, and still isolated from the thin web of connections that joined the others. In the candlelight, it seemed to waver against the pale, mottled sheet, as though it were something too deranged to be captured in ink.

He dipped his quill in the horn, then carefully scrawled

ANASÛRIMBOR KELLHUS

below the hated name.

———⊗⊗⊗———

With the reluctant gait of a man unsure of his destination, Cnaiür walked through the encampment. The lane he followed wound between a jumble of slumbering camps. Here and there, a fire still burned, tended by muttering men, mostly drunk. Odours assailed him, bearing the sharpness of foul smells in cool dry air: livestock, rancid meat, and oily smoke—some fool was burning wet wood.

Memories of his recent meeting with Proyas dominated his thoughts. To cement his plan to outmanoeuvre the Emperor, the Conriyan Prince had sought counsel from the five Conriyan Palatines who had taken up the Tusk. Proud men wagging proud tongues. Even the more bellicose Palatines, such as Gaidekki or Ingiaban, spoke more to score than to solve. Watching them, Cnaiür had realized they all played an infantile version of the same game the Dûnyain played. Words, Moënghus and Kellhus had taught him, could be used hand open or fist closed—as a way to embrace or a way to enslave. For some reason these Inrithi, who had nothing tangible to gain or to lose from one another, all spoke with their fists closed—fatuous claims, false concessions, mocking praise, flattering insults, and an endless train of satiric innuendoes.

Jnan, they called it. A mark of caste and cultivation.

Cnaiür had weathered the farce as best he could, but—inevitably, it now seemed—they soon cast their nets about him as well.

"Tell me, Scylvendi," Lord Gaidekki had asked, flushed with drink and daring, "those scars of yours, do they reflect the man or the man's measure?"

"How do you mean?"

The Palatine of Anplei grinned. "Well, I should think that if you, say, killed Lord Ganyama here, he would deserve two scars at the most. But if you were to kill *me*?" He looked to the others, his eyebrows raised and his lips drawn down, as though speaking in deference to their learned opinions. "What? Twenty scars? Thirty?"

"I suspect," Proyas said, "that Scylvendi swords are great levellers."

Lord Imrotha laughed too hard at this.

"Swazond," Cnaiür said to Gaidekki, "measure foes, not fools." He stared impassively at the startled Palatine, then spat into the fire.

But Gaidekki was not easily intimidated. "So what am I?" he asked dangerously. "Fool or foe?"

In that moment, Cnaiür recognized yet another hardship he would have to suffer in the months to come. The perils and deprivations of war were nothing; he had shouldered them his entire life. The disgrace of consorting with Kellhus was a hardship of a different order, but something he could endure in the name of hate. But the degradation of participating day after day in the peevish unmanly ways of the Inrithi was something he had not considered. How much must he suffer to see vengeance done?

Thankfully, Proyas deftly pre-empted his reply to Gaidekki, declaring the council at an end. Too disgusted to bear their farewell fencing, Cnaiür had simply marched from the pavilion into the night.

He let his gaze wander as he walked. The moon was full and bright, smudging silver across the back of charging clouds. Moved by a peculiar melancholy, he looked to the stars. Scylvendi children were told that the sky was a yaksh, impossibly vast and pricked by innumerable holes. He remembered his father pointing skyward once. "See, Nayu?" he had said, "see the thousand thousand lights peeking through the leather of night? This is how we know that a greater sun burns beyond this world. This is how we know that when it's night, it is truly day, and that when it's day, it is truly night. This is how we know, Nayu, that the World is a lie."

For Scylvendi, the stars were a reminder: only the People were true.

Cnaiür paused. The dust beneath his sandals still shed the sun's heat. Throughout the immediate darkness, the silence seemed to hiss.

What was he doing here? Among Inrithi dogs. Among men who scratched breath upon parchment and sustenance from dirt. Among men who had sold their souls into bondage.

Among the cattle.

What was he doing?

He raised his hands to his brows, drew his thumbs across his eyes. Squeezed.

Then he heard the Dûnyain's voice drifting through the dark.

With his eyes pinched shut, he felt a youth once again, standing in the heart of the Utemot encampment, overhearing Moënghus talk to his mother.

He saw Bannut's bloodied face, grinning rather than grimacing as he strangled him.

Weeper.

Running fingernails across his scalp, he continued walking. Through a screen of dark camps, he glimpsed the Dûnyain's firelight. He saw the bearded Schoolman, Drusas Achamian, sitting, leaning forward as though straining to listen. Then he saw Kellhus and Serwë, fire-bright against the surrounding murk. Serwë slept, her head upon the Dûnyain's lap.

He found a place beside a wain where he could watch. He crouched.

Cnaiür had intended to scrutinize what the Dûnyain said, hoping to confirm any one of his innumerable suspicions. But he quickly realized that Kellhus was playing this sorcerer the way he played all the others, battering him with closed fists, beating his soul down paths of his manufacture. Certainly it did not sound like this. Compared with the banter of Proyas and his Palatines, what Kellhus said to the Schoolman possessed a heartbreaking gravity. But it was all a game, one where truths had become chits, where every open hand concealed a fist.

How could one determine the true intent of such a man?

The thought struck Cnaiür that Dûnyain monks might be even more inhuman than he had thought. What if things such as truth and meaning had no meaning for them? What if all they did was move and move, like something reptilian, snaking through circumstance after circumstance, consuming soul after soul for the sake of consumption alone? The thought made his scalp prickle.

They called themselves students of the Logos, the Shortest Way. But the shortest way to what?

Cnaiür cared nothing for the Schoolman, but the sight of Serwë asleep with her head upon Kellhus's thighs filled him with uncharacteristic fear, as though she lay within the coils of some malevolent serpent. Scenarios flashed through his soul: of stealing away with her in the dead of night; of grabbing her, peering so hard into her eyes that her centre would be touched, then telling her the truth of Kellhus . . .

But these glimpses gave way to fury.

What kind of fawn-hearted thoughts were these? Always straying, always wandering across the trackless and the weak. Always betraying!

Serwë frowned and fidgeted, as though troubled by a dream. Kellhus absently stroked her cheek. Unable to look away, Cnaiür beat his fists against the dust.

She is nothing.

The Schoolman departed a short time after. Cnaiür watched Kellhus steer Serwë to their pavilion. She was so like a little girl when roused from sleep: body swaying, head bowed, watching her feet through pouting lashes. So innocent.

And pregnant, Cnaiür now suspected.

Several moments passed before the Dûnyain reappeared. He walked to the fire, began dousing it by prodding the pit with a stick. The last licks of flame winked out, and Kellhus became an eerie apparition etched by the orange pool of coals at his feet. Without warning, he looked up.

"How long were you intending to wait?" he asked in Scylvendi.

Cnaiür pulled himself to his feet, beat the dust from his breeches. "Until the sorcerer was gone."

Kellhus nodded. "Yes. The People despise witches."

Despite the Dûnyain's proximity, Cnaiür stood near enough the coals to feel their arid heat. Ever since Kellhus had swung him over the precipice that day in the mountains, he'd found himself battling a strange bodily shyness whenever the man loomed next to him.

No man cows me.

"What do you want from the man?" he asked, spitting into the coals.

"You heard. Instruction."

"I heard. What do you want from him?"

Kellhus shrugged. "Have you even asked yourself why my father has summoned me to Shimeh?"

"You said you didn't know." *So you said.*

"But to *Shimeh* . . ." Kellhus looked at him sharply. "Why Shimeh?"

"Because that's where he dwells."

The Dûnyain nodded. "Indeed."

Cnaiür could only stare. There was something Proyas had said to him earlier this night . . . He had asked the man about the Scarlet Spires, about the School's reasons for joining the Holy War, and Proyas had replied as though startled by his ignorance. Shimeh, he had said, was the home of the Cishaurim.

The words were pasty in his mouth. "You think Moënghus is Cishaurim?"

"He summoned me by sending dreams . . ."

Of course. Moënghus had summoned him using sorcery. Sorcery! He'd said as much himself when Kellhus first mentioned the dreams. But then why had the connection escaped him? Only the Cishaurim practised sorcery among the Fanim. Moënghus simply *had* to be Cishaurim. He knew this, but—

Cnaiür scowled. "You said nothing to me! Why?"

"You didn't want to know."

Was that it? Had he hidden from this knowledge? All this time Moënghus had been little more than a shadowy destination, at once elusive and compelling, like the object of some obscene carnal urge. And yet he had never truly asked Kellhus anything about him. Why?

I need know only the place.

But such thoughts were foolishness. Juvenile. Great hunger yielded no feasts. So the memorialists admonished headstrong Scylvendi youths. So Cnaiür himself had admonished Xunnurit and the other chieftains before Kiyuth. And yet here, on the deadliest pilgrimage of his entire life . . .

The Dûnyain watched him, his expression expectant, even sorrowful. But Cnaiür knew better, knew something not quite human studied him from behind his all-too-human face.

Scrutiny, so utter, so exacting, it was palpable.

You can see me, can't you? See me looking back at you . . .

Then he understood: he hadn't asked Kellhus about Moënghus because asking betokened ignorance and need. He might as well bare his throat to a wolf as display such deficits to a Dûnyain. He hadn't asked about Moënghus, he knew, because Moënghus was *here,* in his son.

He could not say this, of course.

Cnaiür spat. "I know little of the Schools," he said, "but I do know this: Mandate Schoolmen do not reveal the secrets of their practice—to anyone. If you wish to learn sorcery, you're wasting your time with that sorcerer."

He'd spoken as though Moënghus had not been mentioned. The Dûnyain, however, did not bother feigning puzzlement. They both stood, he realized, in the same dark place, the same shadowy nowhere beyond the benjuka plate.

"I know," Kellhus replied. "He told me of the Gnosis."

Cnaiür kicked dust across the coals, studied the scatter of black over the pitted glow. He began walking to the pavilion.

"Thirty years," Kellhus called from behind. "Moënghus has dwelt among these men for thirty years. He'll have great power—more than either of us could hope to overcome. I need more than sorcery, Cnaiür. I need a nation. A nation."

Cnaiür paused, looked skyward once again. "So it's to be this Holy War, then, is it?"

"With your help, Scylvendi. With your help."

Day for night. Night for day. Lies. All lies.

Cnaiür continued walking, striding between barely visible guy ropes to the canvas flaps.

To Serwë.

For several moments the Emperor stared at his old Counsel in stunned silence. Despite the late hour, the man still wore the charcoal silk robes of his station. He'd breathlessly entered Xerius's private apartment only moments earlier, as his body-slaves were preparing him for bed.

"Could you kindly repeat what you just said, dear Skeaös. I fear I misheard you."

His eyes downcast, the old man said, "Proyas has apparently found a Scylvendi who's warred against the heathen before—inflicted a crushing defeat upon them, actually—and has now proposed to Maithanet that he'll be a suitable replacement for Conphas."

"Outrage! Impertinent, overweening Conriyan dog!" Xerius swung his palms through the scrambling crowd of prepubescent slaves. A young boy skidded prostrate across the marble floor, wailing and shielding his face. There was the clash of spilled decanters. Xerius stepped over him, confronting old Skeaös. "Proyas! Was there ever a more grasping man alive? Thieving, black-hearted wretch!"

Skeaös stuttered a hasty reply. "Never, God-of-Men. B-but this is unlikely to interfere with our divine purpose." The old Counsel was careful to keep his gaze firmly fixed on the floor. No one may look the Emperor in the eye. This, Xerius thought, was why he truly seemed a God to these fools. What was God but a tyrannical shadow in one's periphery, the voice that could never fall within one's field of vision? The voice from nowhere.

"*Our* purpose, Skeaös?"

Dreadful silence, broken only by the child's whimper.

"Y-yes, God-of-Men. The man is a *Scylvendi* . . . A Scylvendi leading the Holy War? Surely this is little more than a joke."

Xerius breathed deeply. The man was right, wasn't he? This was but one more way for the Conriyan Prince to gall him—like the raids down the River Phayus. And yet he still found himself troubled . . . Something odd about his Prime Counsel's manner.

Xerius valued Skeaös far above any other of his preening, lapdog advisers. In Skeaös he found the perfect marriage of subservience and intellect, of deference and insight. But lately he had sensed a pride, an illicit identification of counsel and edict.

Studying the frail form, Xerius felt himself calm—the calm of suspicion. "Have you heard the saying, Skeaös? 'Cats look down upon Man, and dogs look up, but only pigs dare look Man straight in the eye.'"

"Y-yes, God-of-Men."

"Pretend that you are a pig, Skeaös."

What would be in a man's face when he looked into the counte-nance of God? Defiance? Terror? What *should* be in a man's face? The aged, clean-shaven face slowly turned and lifted, glimpsed the Emperor's eyes before turning back to the floor.

"You tremble, Skeaös," Xerius muttered. "*That* is good."

<hr>

Achamian sat patiently before a small breakfast fire, sipping the last of his tea, listening absently as Xinemus briefed Iryssas and Dinchases on the morning agenda. The words meant little to him.

Since meeting Anasûrimbor Kellhus, Achamian had fallen into a funk of obsessive brooding. No matter how hard he tried, he could not fit the Prince of Atrithau into anything that resembled sense. No less than seven times had he prepared the Cants of Calling to inform Atyersus of his "discovery." No less than seven times had he faltered mid-verse, trailing into murmurs.

Of course the Mandate had to be told. News that an Anasûrimbor had arrived would send Nautzera, Simas, and the others into an uproar. Nautzera in particular, Achamian knew, would be convinced that Kellhus marked the fulfilment of the Celmomian Prophecy—that the Second Apocalypse was about to begin. Though every man occupied the centre of whatever place he found himself, men such as Nautzera believed they occupied the centre of their time as well. *I live now*, they would think without thinking, *therefore something momentous must happen.*

But Achamian was not such a man. He was rational and as such, compelled to be sceptical. The libraries of Atyersus were littered with proclamations of impending doom, every generation just as convinced as the last that the end was nigh. Achamian could think of no delusion more dogged and few conceits more worthy of scorn.

The arrival of Anasûrimbor Kellhus simply *had* to be a coinci-dence. In the absence of any supporting evidence, he decided, reason compelled him to adopt this conclusion.

The missing thumb of the matter, as the Ainoni say, was that he could not trust the Mandate to likewise withhold judgement. After centuries of starving for crumbs, they would, Achamian knew, fall into a frenzy over a scrap such as this. So the questions cycled through his soul, and more and more, he began to fear the answers. How would Nautzera and others interpret his tidings? What would they do? How ruthless would they be in the prosecution of their fears?

I gave them Inrau . . . Must I give them Kellhus too?

No. He had told them what would happen to Inrau. He had told them, and they had refused to listen. Even his old teacher, Simas, had betrayed him. Achamian was a Mandate Schoolman as they were. He dreamed the Dream of Seswatha as they did. But unlike Nautzera and Simas, he had not been gouged of his compassion. He knew better. And more important, he knew Anasûrimbor Kellhus.

Or at least something of him. Enough, perhaps.

Achamian set down his bowl of tea then leaned forward, elbows on knees. "What do you make of the newcomer, Zin?"

"The Scylvendi? Quick-witted. Bloodthirsty. And catastrophically loutish. No slight goes unpunished with that one, if only because he bristles at everything . . ." He cocked his head, adding, "Don't tell him I said that."

Achamian grinned. "I mean the other one. The Prince of Atrithau."

The Marshal became uncharacteristically solemn. "Truthfully?" he asked after a moment's hesitation.

Achamian frowned. "Of course."

"I think there's something"—he shrugged—"something about him."

"How so?"

"Well, there's the name, which made me suspicious at first. Actually, I've been meaning to ask you—"

Achamian raised a hand. "After."

Xinemus breathed deeply, shook his head. Something about his manner made Achamian's skin tingle. "I don't know what to think," he said finally.

"Either that or you're afraid to say what you think."

Xinemus glared at him. "You spent an entire evening with him. You tell me: have you ever met a man like him?"

"No," Achamian admitted.

"So what makes him different?"

"He's . . . better. Better than most men."

"Most men? Or do you mean *all* men?"

Achamian regarded Xinemus narrowly. "He frightens you."

"Sure. So does the Scylvendi, for that matter."

"But in a different way . . . Tell me, Zin, just what do you think Anasûrimbor Kellhus is?"

Prophet or prophecy?

"More," Xinemus said decisively. "More than a man."

A long silence ensued, filled only by the shouts of some distant commotion.

"The fact is," Achamian finally ventured, "neither of us knows anything—"

"What's this now?" Xinemus exclaimed, staring over Achamian's shoulder.

The Schoolman craned his neck. "What's what?"

At first glance, it appeared that a mob approached. Crowds jostled through the narrow lane while clots of men filtered through the surrounding camps. Men trudged through firepits, pulled down laundry lines, knocked ad hoc chairs and grills aside. Achamian even saw a pavilion half-collapse as the men streaming around it barged through its guy ropes.

But then he glimpsed a disciplined formation of crimson-clad soldiers filing through the heart of the multitude and in their midst a rectangle of bare-backed slaves carrying a mahogany palanquin.

"A procession of some kind," Xinemus said. "But who would . . ."

His voice trailed. They had both glimpsed it at the same time: a long crimson banner capped by the Ainoni pictogram for Truth and bearing a coiled, three-headed serpent. The symbol of the Scarlet Spires.

The gold stitching shimmered in the sun.

"Why would they fly their standard like that?" Xinemus asked.

Good question. For many Men of the Tusk, all that separated sorcerers from heathens was that sorcerers were even more fit to burn. Striking their mark in the heart of the encampment was nothing short of foolhardy.

Unless . . .

"Do you have your Chorae?" Achamian asked.

"You know I don't wear it when—"

"Do you have it?"

"With my things."

"Fetch it . . . Quickly!"

They flew their standard, Achamian realized, for *his* benefit. They had a choice: either risk inciting a mob or risk startling a Mandate Schoolman. The fact that they thought the latter a greater threat testified to the wretched relations between their two Schools.

Obviously the Scarlet Spires wanted to make his acquaintance. But why?

Sure enough, the riotous throngs grew closer as the procession stubbornly battled its way forward. Achamian saw clods of dirt explode into dust against the palanquin. Cries of *"Gurwikka!"*, a common pejorative for "sorcerer" among the Norsirai, soon rifled the sky.

Xinemus hastened from his pavilion, bawling orders to his slaves as he did so. His brigandine swung from his shoulders, unfastened, and he clutched his scabbard in his left hand. Many of his men were already gathering about him. Achamian saw dozens of others scrambling from all corners of their immediate vicinity, but their numbers seemed no match for the brawling hundreds, perhaps even thousands, who approached.

With characteristic brusqueness, Xinemus swatted a path through his men to Achamian's side.

"Are you sure they're coming for you?" he shouted over the growing roar.

"Why else would they strike their Mark? By making this public, they guarantee witnesses. As strange as it sounds, I think they do this to reassure me."

Xinemus nodded thoughtfully. "They forget how much they're hated."

"Who doesn't?"

The Marshal glanced at him strangely, then looked to the nearing mob, scratching his beard. "I'm going to set up a perimeter. Or try to, anyway. You stay here. Stay visible. When whoever the fool is meets with you, you tell him to lower his Mark and skulk away immediately. *Immediately*. Do you understand?"

The words stung. In all the years Achamian had known Krijates Xinemus, the man had never barked commands at him. The ever-amiable Xinemus had abruptly become the Marshal of Attrempus, a man with a task and numerous men at his disposal. But this, Achamian realized, wasn't what hurt. The situation, after all, called for decisiveness. What stung was the undertone of anger, the sense that his friend somehow blamed him.

Achamian watched as Xinemus harassed his men into a line, then, with the help of Dinchases, positioned them in a thin semicircle through the surrounding camps, using the stagnant canal that curled behind them to protect their flanks. There was a bustling moment as the slaves hastened to put out the fire they had been poking just moments earlier. Others rushed off into the slots between tents to smother whatever open flame they could find.

The mob, and the Scarlet Spires, was nearly upon them.

Xinemus's soldiers had linked arms, and the first of the rioters began gathering before them, flushed and in no mood for constraint. At first they simply milled in confusion, hollering insults in a variety of different tongues. But as the procession neared, their numbers grew. They became bolder. Achamian saw a wild-haired Thunyeri throwing punches, only to be dragged down by his own comrades. Other bands linked arms as well and tried to force their way through the line. Xinemus threw what few spare men he had into these shoving matches and, for the time being at least, managed to forestall any breaks.

The standard of the Scarlet Spires trundled nearer, pausing, then advancing, then pausing again. Over heads, Achamian glimpsed polished black staffs rising and falling as though a great centipede had been upended. Then he glimpsed the Javreh, the slave-soldiers of the Scarlet Spires, beating their way forward with grim determination. The enigmatic palanquin moved forward with them.

Who could it be? Who would be fool enough—

Suddenly a wedge of Javreh broke clear and came face to face with Xinemus's men. There was a moment of confusion. Xinemus rushed to clarify matters, coming within reaching distance as he did so. Beyond, the palanquin swayed as its bearers struggled against the heave of massed bodies. The Three-Headed Serpent tipped in the breeze but otherwise stood still. Then exhausted Javreh were spilling through the line, bruised, bloody. Some even needed to be carried bodily. The palanquin followed, like a boat popping through a broken dyke. Xinemus watched as though thunderstruck.

Then everything, it seemed, came raining down upon them: looted plates, wine bowls, chicken bones, stones, and even the corpse of a cat, which Achamian was forced to duck.

Apparently unaffected, the slaves gently lowered their burden by kneeling until their foreheads touched dust and the palanquin rested across their tanned backs.

The downpour ceased, and the shouts grew more and more sporadic. Achamian found himself holding his breath. A Javreh Captain drew aside a wicker screen, then immediately fell to his knees. A crimson-slippered foot appeared, followed by the embroidered folds of a magnificent gown.

There was an instant of utter silence.

It was Eleäzaras himself. The Grandmaster of the Scarlet Spires and de facto ruler of High Ainon.

Achamian found himself struck dumb by disbelief. The Grandmaster? Here?

Some few among the mob, it seemed, knew what he looked like. A great murmur passed through them, swelling for several moments, then fading as the import of what they witnessed struck them. They stood in the presence of one of the most powerful men in the Three Seas. Only the Shriah or the Padirajah could claim more power than the Grandmaster of the Scarlet Spires. Blasphemer or not, a man of such power commanded respect, and respect commanded silence.

Eleäzaras raked his onlookers with amused eyes, then turned to Achamian. He was tall, statuesque in the manner of thin, gracile men. He walked as though along a balance, one foot before another. He kept his hands folded in his sleeves, as was the formal custom of eastern magi. Halting at the distance prescribed by jnan, he graced Achamian with a shallow bow. Achamian glimpsed tanned scalp beneath thinning grey hair, which was braided into an elaborate bun at the back of his neck.

"You must excuse the company I happen to be keeping," he said, waving a dismissive, long-fingered hand at the gawking throngs. "Spectacle is ever the narcotic, I'm afraid."

"As are contradictions," Achamian replied blandly. As astonishing as this impromptu audience might be, the Scarlet Spires was no friend of Mandate Schoolmen. He saw no reason to pretend otherwise.

"Indeed. I was told you were a student of Ajencis's logic. You make quite irresistible morsels, you Mandate Schoolmen, did you know?"

Ainoni, Achamian thought sourly.

"We're always fighting off the scavengers, if that's what you mean."

Eleäzaras shook his head. "Don't flatter yourself. Conceit does not sit well with martyrdom. Never has. Never will."

"I always thought them the same." The surrounding mob had grown more unruly, forcing him to raise his voice.

The Grandmaster's lips tightened into a sour line. "Clever man. Clever little man. Tell me, Drusas Achamian, how is it that after all these years you still find yourself in the field, hmm? Did you offend someone? Nautzera, perhaps? Or did you bugger Proyas as a boy? Is that why House Nersei sent you packing those years ago?"

Achamian was speechless. They had researched him, armed themselves with as many painful facts and innuendoes as they could find. And here he'd thought he was watching them!

"Ah . . ." Eleäzaras said. "You didn't expect me to be quite so tactless, did you? The blunt knife, I assure you, has its—"

"*Unclean wretches!*" someone howled with alarming ferocity. More shouts followed. Achamian glanced around, saw that Xinemus's men were once again scuffling to hold their position. Many Inrithi leaned over their linked arms, screaming obscenities.

"Perhaps we should retire to the Marshal's pavilion," Eleäzaras said.

Achamian glimpsed Xinemus's furious face behind the Grandmaster.

"That's not possible."

"I see."

"What do you want, Eleäzaras?" Xinemus had bid Achamian to end this meeting before it started, but this he could not do. Not only did he speak to Eleäzaras, the mightiest Anagogic Sorcerer in the Three Seas, he also spoke to the man who had negotiated his School's treaty with Maithanet. Perhaps Eleäzaras knew how Maithanet had learned of their war with the Cishaurim. Perhaps he would trade that knowledge for whatever it was he wanted.

"Want?" the Grandmaster repeated. "Why, merely to make your acquaintance. The Few, if you haven't already noticed, are somewhat"—his eyes darted to and from the rumbling mass of Inrithi—"*out of place* here . . . Jnan demands our affiliation."

"As well as tedious obscurity, it seems."

The Grandmaster smiled. "But not mockery. Never mockery. That is a mistake only half-tutored prigs make. The true practitioner of jnan never laughs at another more than he laughs at himself."

Fucking Ainoni.

"What do you want, Eleäzaras?"

"To make your acquaintance, as I said. I needed to meet the man who has utterly overturned my impression of the Mandate . . . To think that I once thought yours the gentlest of Schools!"

Now Achamian was genuinely perplexed. "What are you talking about?"

"I'm told you were recently a resident of Carythusal."

Geshrunni. They had discovered Geshrunni.

Did I kill you too?

Achamian shrugged. "So your secret is out. You war against the Cishaurim." How could they begrudge him this when they had made it plain to all by joining the Holy War? There had to be more.

The Gnosis? Did Eleäzaras merely distract him while others probed his Wards? Was this simply a bold prelude to abduction? It had happened before.

"Our secret is out," Eleäzaras agreed. "But then so is yours."

Achamian fixed him with quizzical look. The man spoke as though to goad him with knowledge of some obscene secret, one so shameful that any allusion, no matter how indirect, simply could not *not* be understood. And yet he had no idea what the man was talking about.

"It was sheer coincidence," Eleäzaras continued, "that we found his body. It was brought to us by a fisherman who works the mouth of the River Sayut. But it wasn't so much the fact that you killed him that troubled us. After all, in the greater game of benjuka, one often gains pieces by disposing of them. No, what troubled us was the *manner*."

"Me?" He laughed incredulously. "You think I killed Geshrunni?"

The shock had been so total he'd simply blurted these words. Now it was Eleäzaras who was startled.

"You do have a facility for lies," the Grandmaster said after a moment.

"And you for delusion! Geshrunni was the best-placed informant the Mandate has had in a generation. Why would we kill him?"

The clamour had swelled. Riotous figures heaved in Achamian's periphery, shaking fists, bellowing insults and accusations. But they seemed curiously trivial, as though rendered smoke by the absurdity of this, his first meeting with the Grandmaster of the Scarlet Spires.

Eleäzaras studied him for a pensive moment, then shook his head ruefully, as though saddened the persistence of hardened liars. "Why is any informant murdered, hmm? In so many ways so many men are more useful dead. But as I mentioned, it was the manner that sparked my admittedly morbid curiosity."

Scowling, Achamian hunched his shoulders in disbelief. "Someone plays you for a fool, Grandmaster."

Someone plays both of us . . . But who?

Eleäzaras glared, pursing his lips as though holding a bitter segment of lime against his teeth. "My Master of Spies warned me of this," he said tightly. "I'd assumed you had some obscure reason for what you did, something belonging to your accursed Gnosis. But he insisted that you were simply mad. And he told me I'd know by the way you lied. Only madmen and historians, he said, believe their lies."

"First I'm a murderer, and now I'm a madman?"

"Indeed," Eleäzaras spat in a tone of condemnation and disgust. "Who else collects human faces?"

Just then, more stones sailed over their heads.

Suppressing the urge to wring his hands, Eleäzaras blinked away images of his near disastrous encounter with the Mandate Schoolman the previous day. The face of one nameless man haunted him in particular: a strapping Tydonni thane, his left eye snow blue in the wake of an old scar. Some faces were more suited to expressions of malice than others, certainly. But this man . . . At the time he'd seemed the very incarnation of hatred, an infernal deity in the guise of callused flesh and fevered blood.

They despise us so. And well they should.

Rather than bear the indignity of camping outside Momemn's walls, the Scarlet Spires had leased, at an exorbitant price, a nearby villa from one of the Nansur Houses. By Ainoni standards it was rather severe, more of a fortress than a villa, but then, Eleäzaras supposed, the Ainoni never had to build with the Scylvendi in mind. And at least it allowed him a certain measure of tranquil luxury. The encamped Holy War had become an intolerable slum, as his recent expedition to meet that thrice-damned Mandate Schoolman had reminded him.

Eleäzaras had dismissed his slaves and now sat alone in a shaded portico overlooking the villa's single courtyard. He studied Iyokus, his Master of Spies and closest adviser, as he made his pale way through the sunlit gardens. The man hurried, as though chased by the surrounding brilliance. Watching him move from sun to shadow was like witnessing dust blink into stone. Iyokus nodded as he approached his chair. His very presence often touched Eleäzaras with menace—something like glimpsing the first flush of plague in a man's face. The smell of his old-fashioned perfumes, however, carried a strange sense of comfort.

"I have news from Sumna," Iyokus said, pouring himself a silver bowl of wine from the table, "about Kutigha."

Until recently, Kutigha had been their last surviving spy in the Thousand Temples—all the others had been executed. His handler had not heard from him in weeks.

"So you think he's dead?" Eleäzaras asked sourly.

"Yes," Iyokus replied.

After all these years, Eleäzaras had grown accustomed to Iyokus, but somewhere in his own body lurked a small memory of his initial revulsion. Iyokus was addicted to *chanv*, the drug that held a greater part of the Ainoni ruling castes within its clasp—except, and this thought often surprised Eleäzaras, for Chepheramunni, the latest puppet they had installed on the Ainoni throne. For those who could afford her sweet bite, chanv sharpened the mind and extended one's life for periods greater than a hundred years, but it also sapped the body of its pigment and, some said, the soul of its will. Iyokus looked the same now as the day Eleäzaras had joined the School as a boy many, many years before. Unlike other addicts, Iyokus refused to use cosmetics to compensate for the deficits of his skin, which was more translucent than the greased linen that the poor used in their windows. Like dark, arthritic worms, veins branched across his features. One could even see the dark in the centre of his red eyes when he closed his lids. His fingernails were waxy black from bruising.

As Iyokus drew his chair to the table, a tiny sweat touched Eleäzaras, and he found himself glancing at the length of his own tanned arms. As thin as they were, they possessed wiry strength, vitality. Despite the disturbing aesthetics of addiction, Eleäzaras himself might have succumbed to the drug's lure, particularly because of the way it reputedly sharpened the intellect. Perhaps the only aspect of chanv that had prevented him from slipping into that wan and strangely narcissistic love affair—addicts rarely married or produced live children—was the unsettling fact that no one knew its source. For Eleäzaras, this was intolerable. Throughout his vicious, steep climb to the pinnacle he'd now reached, he had always refused to act in ignorance of crucial facts.

Until this day.

"So we have no more sources in the Thousand Temples?" Eleäzaras asked, though he already knew the answer.

"None worth listening to . . . A shroud has fallen across Sumna."

Eleäzaras glanced across the bright grounds—cobbled paths lined by spearlike junipers, a gigantic willow draped about a pool of glassy green, guards with falcon faces.

"What does this mean, Iyokus?" he asked. *I've delivered the greatest School in the Three Seas to its greatest peril.*

"It means we must have *faith*," Iyokus said with an air of shoulder-shrugging fatalism. "Faith in this Maithanet."

"Faith? In someone we know nothing of?"

"That's why it's faith."

The decision to join the Holy War had been the most difficult of Eleäzaras's life. At first, upon receiving Maithanet's invitation, he had wanted to laugh. The Scarlet Spires? Joining a Holy War? The prospect was too absurd to warrant even momentary consideration. Perhaps this is why Maithanet had included a gift of six Trinkets with his invitation. Trinkets were the one thing that a sorcerer could not laugh away. *This offer*, the Trinkets said, *demands serious consideration.*

Then Eleäzaras had realized what it was that Maithanet truly offered them.

Vengeance.

"Then we must double our expenditures in Sumna, Iyokus. This is intolerable."

"I agree. Faith *is* intolerable."

A ten-year-old image of the man assailed Eleäzaras, sent faint tremors through his fingertips: Iyokus falling against him in the aftermath of the assassination, his skin blistered, streaked by blood, his mouth croaking the very words that had lashed through Eleäzaras's soul ever since: *"How could they do this?"*

It was uncanny the way certain days defied the passage of years, became virulent, and plagued the present as an undying yesterday. Even here, far from the Scarlet Spires and ten years on, Eleäzaras could still smell sweet roasted flesh—so much like swine left overlong on the spit. How long had it been since he'd last been able to stomach pork? How many times had he dreamt of that day?

Sasheoka had been Grandmaster then. They'd been meeting in the council chambers deep in the galleries beneath the Scarlet Spires, discussing the possible defection of one of their number to the Mysunsai School. The most sacrosanct chambers of the Scarlet Spires were nested in Wards. One could not step or lean against bare stone without feeling the indent of inscription or the aura of incantations. And yet the assassins had simply flickered into existence.

A strange noise, like the humming flutter of netted birds, and a light, as though a door had been thrown open across the surface of the sun, framing three figures. Three hellish silhouettes.

Shock, chilling bone and paralyzing thought, and then furniture and bodies were blown against the walls. Blinding ribbons of the purest white lashed across the corners of the room. Shrieks. Terror clawing through his bowels.

Sheltered by a hollow between the wall and an overturned table, Eleäzaras had crawled through his own blood to die—or so he thought. Some of his peers still survived. He glimpsed the instant that Sasheoka, his predecessor and teacher, crumpled beneath the blinding touch of the assassins. And Iyokus, on his knees, his pale head blackened by blood, swaying behind the shimmering of his Wards, struggling to reinforce them. Cataracts of light obscured him, and Eleäzaras, somehow unnoticed by the intruders, felt the words boil to his lips. He could see *them*—three men in saffron robes, two crouching, one erect, bathed in the incandescence of their exertions. He saw serene faces with the deep sockets of the blind, and energies wheeling from their foreheads as though through a window to the Outside. A golden phantom reared from Eleäzaras's outstretched hands—a scaled neck, a mighty crest, jaws scissoring open. With a queen's deliberate grace, the dragon's head dipped and scourged the Cishaurim with fire. Eleäzaras had wept with rage. Their Wards collapsed. Stone cracked. The flesh was swept from their bones. Their agony had been too brief.

Then quiet. Strewn bodies. Sasheoka a sizzling ruin. Iyokus gasping on the floor. Nothing. They had sensed nothing. The onta had only been bruised by their own sorceries. It was as if the Cishaurim had never been. Iyokus stumbling toward him . . . *How could they do this?*

The Cishaurim had started their long and secret war. Eleäzaras would end it.

Vengeance. This was the gift the Shriah of the Thousand Temples had offered them. The gift of their ancient enemy. A Holy War.

A perilous gift. It had occurred to Eleäzaras that the Holy War was in fact what the six Trinkets were symbolically. To give Chorae to a sorcerer was to give something that could not be taken, to make a gift of his death and impotence. By taking the vengeance proffered by Maithanet, Eleäzaras and the Scarlet Spires had given themselves to the Holy War. By seizing, Eleäzaras realized, he had surrendered. And now the Scarlet Spires, for the first time in its glorious history, found itself dependent upon the whims of other men.

"And what of our spies in the Imperial Precincts?" Eleäzaras asked. He loathed fear, so he would avoid discussing Maithanet if he could. "Have they discovered anything more of the Emperor's plan?"

"Nothing . . . so far," Iyokus replied dryly. "There's a rumour, however, that Ikurei Conphas received a message from the Fanim shortly after the destruction of the Vulgar Holy War."

"A message? Regarding what?"

"The Vulgar Holy War, presumably."

"But what was its import? Was it an acknowledgement, a receipt for an agreed-upon transaction? Was it an admonition, a warning against any further action by the Holy War? Or a premature peace overture? *What was it?*"

"Any of those things," Iyokus replied, "or perhaps all. We've no way of knowing."

"Why send it to Ikurei Conphas?"

"For any number of reasons . . . He was, recall, the Sapatishah's hostage for a time."

"That boy, Conphas, he's the one we must worry about." Ikurei Conphas was intelligent, excessively so, which inevitably meant that he was unscrupulous as well. Another frightening thought: *He will be our general.*

Holding the silver bowl in steepled fingers, Iyokus seemed to gaze at the small coin of wine in its bottom. "May I speak frankly, Grandmaster?" he asked at length.

"By all means."

Emotion pooled in Iyokus's face as readily as water in a sackcloth, but his apprehension was now plain. "The Scarlet Spires is degraded by all this . . ." he began uncomfortably. "We've become subordinates when our destiny is to rule. Abandon this Holy War, Eli. There's too much uncertainty. Too many unknowns. We play number-sticks with our very lives."

You too, Iyokus?

Eleäzaras felt coils of rage flex about his heart. The Cishaurim had planted a serpent within him those ten years ago, and it had grown fat on fear. He could feel it writhe within him, animate his hands with the womanish desire to scratch out Iyokus's disconcerting eyes.

But he said only: "Patience, Iyokus. Knowing is always a matter of patience."

"Yesterday, Grandmaster, you were almost killed by the very men we're to march with . . . If that doesn't demonstrate the absurdity of our position, then nothing does."

He referred to the riot. What a fool he'd been to corner Drusas Achamian in such a place! All of it could have ended there— hundreds of pilgrims dead at the hands of a Grandmaster, the Scarlet Spires at open war with the Men of the Tusk—if it hadn't been for the level head of the Mandate Schoolman. "Don't do it, Eleäzaras!" the man had cried as the mobs surged toward them. "Think of your war against the Cishaurim!"

But there had been a threat in the slovenly man's voice as well: *I won't let you do it. I'll stop you, and you know I can . . .*

What perverse irony! For the threat—not the reason—had stayed his hand. The threat of the Gnosis! His designs had been saved by the lack of the very thing his School had coveted for generations.

How he despised the Mandate! All the Schools, even the Imperial Saik, recognized the ascendancy of the Scarlet Spires— save for the Mandate. And why should they when a mere field spy could cow their Grandmaster?

"The incident," Eleäzaras replied, "merely demonstrates some- thing we've always known, Iyokus. Our position in the Holy War is precarious, true, but all great designs require great sacrifices. When all this comes to fruition, when Shimeh is smoking ruin and the Cishaurim are extinct, the Mandate will be the only School left that can humble us." An arcane empire—that would be the wages of his desperate labour.

"Which reminds me," Iyokus said, "I received a missive from the Minister of Records in Carythusal. He went through all reports of the dead, as you directed. There *was* another, from years back."

Another faceless corpse.

"Do we know who he was? What were the circumstances?"

"Half-rotted. Found in the delta. The man was unknown. Because five years have passed, we have little hope of determining his identity."

The Mandate. Who would have guessed that they played such dark games? But what game? Yet another unknown.

"Perhaps," Iyokus continued, "the Mandate has at long last put aside all that tripe about the Consult and the No-God."

Eleäzaras nodded. "I agree. The Mandate now plays as we play, Iyokus. That man, Drusas Achamian, left little doubt of that . . ." Such a gifted liar! Eleäzaras had almost believed he knew nothing of Geshrunni's death.

"If the Mandate is part of the game," Iyokus said, "everything changes. Do you realize that? We can no longer count ourselves the first School of the Three Seas."

"First we crush the Cishaurim, Iyokus. In the meantime, make certain that Drusas Achamian is watched."

CHAPTER SEVENTEEN

THE ANDIAMINE HEIGHTS

The event itself was unprecedented: not since the fall of Cenei to the Scylvendi hordes had so many potentates gathered in one place. But few knew Mankind itself lay upon the balance. And who could guess that a brief exchange of glances, not the Shriah's edict, would tip that balance?

But is this not the very enigma of history? When one peers deep enough, one always finds that catastrophe and triumph, the proper objects of the historian's scrutiny, inevitably turn upon the small, the trivial, the nightmarishly accidental. When I reflect overmuch on this fact, I do not fear that we are "drunks at the sacred dance," as Protathis writes, but that there is no dance at all.

—DRUSAS ACHAMIAN, *COMPENDIUM OF THE FIRST HOLY WAR*

Late Spring, 4111 Year-of-the-Tusk, Momemn

With Cnaiür, Xinemus, and the five Conriyan Palatines who had taken up the Tusk, Kellhus followed Nersei Proyas through the galleries of the Andiamine Heights. One of the Emperor's eunuchs led them, trailing the oily scent of musk and balsam.

Turning from a discussion with Xinemus, Proyas summoned Cnaiür to his side. Kellhus had closely mapped the capricious swings of Proyas's humour over the course of their journey to the Imperial Precincts. The man had been elated and anxious by turns. Now he was clearly elated. The thought nearly leapt from the man's profile: *This will work!*

"Though it galls the rest of us," Proyas said, trying to sound offhand, "in many ways the Nansur are the most ancient people of the Three Seas, descendants of the Ceneians of near antiquity and the Kyraneans of far antiquity. They live their lives in the shadow of monumental works and so feel compelled to erect monuments"—he opened his hands to the soaring marmoreal vaults—"such as this."

He explains away the strength of his enemy's house, Kellhus realized. *He fears this place may overawe the Scylvendi.*

Cnaiür grimaced and spat on the gloomy pastorals passing beneath their feet. Over a fat shoulder, the eunuch glared at him then nervously quickened his pace.

Proyas glanced at the Scylvendi, his disapproving eyes belied by a smirk. "Ordinarily, Cnaiür, I would not presume to amend your manners, but things may go better for us if you avoid spitting."

At this, one of the more hard-humoured Palatines, Lord Ingiaban, laughed aloud. The Scylvendi squared his jaw but said nothing otherwise.

A week had passed since they had joined the Holy War and secured the hospitality of Nersei Proyas. In that time, Kellhus had spent long hours in the probability trance, assessing, extrapolating, and reassessing this extraordinary twist of circumstance. But the Holy War had proven incalculable. Nothing he'd thus far encountered could compare with the sheer number of variables it presented. Of course the nameless thousands who constituted its bulk were largely irrelevant, significant only in their sum, but the handful of men who were relevant, who would ultimately determine the Holy War's fate, had remained inaccessible to him.

That would change in a matter of moments.

The great contest between the Emperor and the Great Names of the Holy War had come to a head. Offering Cnaiür as a substitute for Ikurei Conphas, Proyas had petitioned Maithanet to settle the dispute of the Emperor's Indenture, and Ikurei Xerius III had accordingly invited all the Great Names to plead their case and hear the Shriah's judgement. They were to meet in his Privy Gardens, sequestered somewhere within the gilded compounds of the Andiamine Heights.

One way or another, the Holy War was about to march on distant Shimeh.

Whether the Shriah sided with the Great Names and ordered the Emperor to provision the Holy War or with the Ikurei Dynasty and ordered the Great Names to sign the Imperial Indenture meant little to Kellhus. Either way it seemed the leaders of the Holy War would have competent counsel. The brilliance of Ikurei Conphas, the Nansur Exalt-General, was grudgingly acknowledged even by Proyas. And the intelligence of Cnaiür, as Kellhus knew first-hand, was beyond question. What mattered was that the Holy War eventually prevail against the Fanim, and bear him to Shimeh.

To his father. His mission.

Is this what you wanted, Father? Is this war to be my lesson?

"I wonder," Xinemus said wryly, "what the Emperor will make of a Scylvendi drinking his wine and pinching his servants' bums?"

The Prince and his fellow potentates rumbled with laughter.

"He'll be too busy snapping his teeth in fury," Proyas replied.

"I have little patience for these games," Cnaiür said, and although the others heard this as a curious admission, Kellhus knew it to be a warning. *This will be his trial, and I'll be tried through him.*

"The games," another Palatine, Lord Gaidekki, replied, "are about to end, my savage friend."

As always, Cnaiür bristled at their patronizing tone. His nostrils even flared.

How much degradation will he bear to see my father dead?

"The game is never over," Proyas asserted. "The game is without beginning or end."

Without beginning or end . . .

❰∘❱

Kellhus had been a boy of eleven the first time he heard this phrase. He'd been summoned from his training to a small shrine on the first terrace, where he was to meet Kessriga Jeükal. Even though Kellhus had already spent years minimizing his passions, the prospect of meeting Jeükal frightened him: he was one of the Pragma, the senior brethren of the Dûnyain, and meetings between such men and young boys usually resulted in anguish for the latter. The anguish of trial and revelation.

Sunlight fell in shafts between the shrine's pillars, making the stone pleasantly warm beneath his small feet. Outside, under the ramparts of the first terrace, the poplars were combed by the mountain wind. Kellhus lingered in the light, feeling the bland warmth of the sun soak his gown and bare scalp.

"You have drunk your fill, as they directed you?" the Pragma asked. He was an old man, his face as empty of expression as the architecture of the shrine was devoid of flourish. One might have thought he stared at a stone rather than a boy, so blank was his expression.

"Yes, Pragma."

"The Logos is without beginning or end, young Kellhus. Do you understand this?"

The instruction had begun.

"No, Pragma," Kellhus replied. Though he still suffered fear and hope, he had long before overcome his compulsion to misrepresent the extent of his knowledge. A child had little choice when his teachers could see through faces.

"Thousands of years ago, when the Dûnyain first found—"

"After the ancient wars?" Kellhus eagerly interrupted. "When we were still refugees?"

The Pragma struck him, fiercely enough to send him rolling across the hard stone. Kellhus scrambled back to position and wiped the blood from his nose. But he felt little fear and even less regret. The blow was a lesson, nothing more. Among the Dûnyain, everything was a lesson.

The Pragma regarded him with utter dispassion. "Interruption is weakness, young Kellhus. It arises from the passions and not from the intellect. From the darkness that comes before."

"I understand, Pragma."

The cold eyes peered through him and saw this was true. "When the Dûnyain first found Ishuäl in these mountains, they knew only one principle of the Logos. What was that principle, young Kellhus?"

"That which comes before determines that which comes after."

The Pragma nodded. "Two thousand years have passed, young Kellhus, and we still hold that principle true. Does that mean the principle of before and after, of cause and effect, has grown old?"

"No, Pragma."

"And why is that? Do men not grow old and die? Do not even mountains age and crumble with time?"

"Yes, Pragma."

"Then how can this principle not be old?"

"Because," Kellhus answered, struggling to snuff a flare of pride, "the principle of before and after is nowhere to be found within the circuit of before and after. It is the *ground* of what is 'young' and what is 'old,' and so cannot itself be young or old."

"Yes. The Logos is without beginning or end. And yet Man, young Kellhus, does possess a beginning and end—like all beasts. Why is Man distinct from other beasts?"

"Because like beasts, Man stands within the circuit of before and after, and yet he apprehends the Logos. He possesses intellect."

"Indeed. And why, Kellhus, do the Dûnyain breed for intellect? Why do we so assiduously train young children such as you in the ways of thought, limb, and face?"

"Because of the Quandary of Man."

"And what is the Quandary of Man?"

A bee had droned into the shrine, and now it etched drowsy, random circles beneath the vaults.

"That he is a beast, that his appetites arise from the darkness of his soul, that his world assails him with arbitrary circumstance, and yet he apprehends the Logos."

"Precisely. And what is the solution to the Quandary of Man?"

"To be utterly free of bestial appetite. To utterly command the unfolding of circumstance. To be the perfect instrument of Logos and so attain the Absolute."

"Yes, young Kellhus. And are you a perfect instrument of Logos?"

"No, Pragma."

"And why is that?"

"Because I am afflicted by passions. I am my thoughts, but the sources of my thoughts exceed me. I do not own myself, because the darkness comes before me."

"Indeed it does, child. What is the name we give to the dark sources of thought?"

"Legion. We call them the legion."

The Pragma raised a palsied hand, as though to mark a crucial waystation in their pilgrimage. "Yes. You are about to embark, young Kellhus, on the most difficult stage of your Conditioning: the mastery of the legion within. Only by doing this will you be able to survive the Labyrinth."

"This will answer the question of the Thousand Thousand Halls?"

"No. But it will enable you to ask properly."

Somewhere near the summit of the Andiamine Heights, they passed through an ivory-panelled corridor then found themselves blinking in the Emperor's Privy Garden.

Between paved lanes, the grass was soft and immaculate, dark beneath the shade of different trees, which formed spokes about a circular pool in the garden's heart: a watery rendition of the Imperial Sun. Hibiscus, standing lotus, and aromatic shrubs thronged from plots adjacent to the lanes. Kellhus glimpsed hummingbirds sorting between blooms in the sunlight.

Where the public areas of the Imperial Precincts had been constructed to overawe guests with dimension and ostentation, the Privy Garden had been designed, Kellhus understood, to foster intimacy, to move visiting dignitaries with the gift of the Emperor's confidence. This was a place of simplicity and elegance, the humble heart of the Emperor made earth and stone.

Gathered beneath cypress and tamarisk trees, the Inrithi lords— Galeoth, Tydonni, Ainoni, Thunyeri, and even some Nansur—stood in clots around what must have been the Emperor's bench. Though decked in finery and lacking arms, they looked more like soldiers than courtiers. Pubescent slaves floated among them, their swelling breasts bare and their coltish legs glistening with oils, trays of wine and various delicacies swaying from their hips. Bowls were tipped back in toasts; greasy fingers were wiped on fine muslins and silks.

The Lords of the Holy War. All gathered in one place.

The study deepens, Father.

Faces turned and voices fell silent as they approached. Several hailed Proyas, but most stared at Cnaiür, emboldened by the open scrutiny of numbers.

Proyas, Kellhus knew, had purposefully prevented any of the Great Names from meeting Cnaiür in order to better control this moment. Their expressions attested to the wisdom of his decision. Even dressed as an Inrithi—a white linen tunic under a knee-length, grey silk coat—Cnaiür radiated feral strength. His embattled face. His powerful frame, iron limbs, and neck-breaking hands. His swazond. His eyes like cold topaz. Everything about him either spoke of murderous deeds or suggested murderous intent.

Most of the Inrithi were impressed. Kellhus saw awe, envy, even lust. Here at last was a *Scylvendi*, and the aspect of the man, it seemed, was more than a match for the rumours they had heard.

Cnaiür weathered their scrutiny with disdain, looking from man to man as though appraising cattle. Proyas murmured several words to Xinemus, then hastened to draw both Cnaiür and Kellhus aside.

Suddenly the lords erupted in solicitations. Xinemus deflected them, crying, "You'll hear what the man has to say soon enough."

Proyas grimaced, muttered, "That went as well as could be expected, I suppose."

The Conriyan Prince, Kellhus had discovered, was a pious yet quietly tempestuous man. He possessed a strength, a moral certainty that somehow compelled others to seek his sanction. But he was also keen to unearth impieties, dubious of the very men drawn to his certainty.

Kellhus had found this combination of doubt and certitude perplexing at first. But after his evening with Drusas Achamian, he realized the Crown Prince had been trained to be suspicious. Proyas was wary out of habit. As with the Scylvendi, Kellhus had been forced to move at tangents when dealing with him. Even after several days of discussion and probing questions, the man still harboured reservations.

"They seem anxious," Kellhus said.

"And why not?" Proyas replied. "I bring them a Prince who claims to dream of Shimeh and a Scylvendi heathen who could be their general." He glanced pensively at his fellow Men of the Tusk. "These men will be your peers," he said. "Heed them. Learn them. To a man they're exceedingly proud, and proud men, I've found, aren't inclined to make wise decisions . . ."

The implication was clear: soon their lives would depend upon the wise decisions of these men.

The Prince gestured to a tall Galeoth standing beneath the hanging rose and green of a tamarisk tree. "That's Prince Coithus Saubon, seventh son of King Eryeat and leader of the Galeoth contingent. The man he argues with is his nephew, Athjeäri, Earl of Gaenri. Coithus Saubon has quite a reputation in these parts: he commanded the army his father sent against the Nansurium several years ago. He managed several successes, or so I'm told, but was humiliated by Conphas after the Emperor made him Exalt-General. Perhaps no man living hates the Ikureis as much as he. But he cares nothing for the Tusk or the Latter Prophet."

Again, Proyas left the implications unspoken. The Galeoth Prince was a mercenary who would support them only where their ends coincided with his own.

Kellhus appraised the man's face, which was strong-jawed and bard-handsome beneath a shock of reddish-blond hair. Their eyes met. Saubon nodded in guarded courtesy.

A barely perceptible quickening of his heartbeat. A faint flush rising to his cheeks. Eyes vaguely narrowing, as though half-squinted against an unseen blow.

He fears nothing more than the estimation of other men.

Kellhus nodded in return, his expression frank, guileless. Saubon had been raised, he realized, under the harsh gaze of another—a cruel father, perhaps, or mother.

He would make a demonstration of his life, shame the eyes that measure.

"Nothing impoverishes," Kellhus said to Proyas, "more than ambition."

"Indeed," Proyas replied in approval, also nodding to the Galeoth Prince.

"That man there," the Prince continued, gesturing to a thick-waisted Tydonni beyond the Galeoth, "is Hoga Gothyelk, Earl of Agansanor and elected leader of the contingent from Ce Tydonn. Before I was born, my father was bested by him at the Battle of Maän. He calls his limp 'Gothyelk's gift.'" Proyas smiled, a devoted son who took much heart in his father's humour. "According to rumour, Hoga Gothyelk is as pious in the temple as he's indomitable on the field."

And again the implication: *He's one of us.*

Unlike Saubon, the Earl of Agansanor was unaware of their momentary scrutiny: he was busy berating three younger men in what must have been his native tongue. His beard, a long pelt of iron grey, swung and shivered as he hollered. His broad nose flared. His eyes flashed beneath overgrown brows.

"Those men he upbraids?" Kellhus asked.

"His sons—three of them, anyway. In Conriya we call them the Hoga Brood. He scolds them for drinking too heavily. The Emperor, he says, wants them drunk."

But far more than their drinking, Kellhus knew, had incited the old Earl's fury. Something weary haunted his expression, something whose momentum had faltered over the course of a long and turbulent life. Hoga Gothyelk no longer felt anger, not truly—only varieties of sorrow. But for what reason?

He's done something . . . He thinks himself damned.

Yes, there it was: the hidden resolution, like slack threads in the taut creases of his face, around the eyes.

He's come to die. Die cleansed.

"And that man," Proyas continued, daring to point, "in the centre of that group wearing masks . . . Do you see him?"

Proyas had gestured to their extreme left, where far and away the largest party had gathered: the Palatine-Governors of High Ainon. To a man they were dressed in spectacular gowns. Beneath their plaited wigs they wore masks of white porcelain across their eyes and cheeks. They looked like bearded statues.

"The one whose hair is wired like a fan across his back?" Kellhus asked.

Proyas graced him with a sour smile. "Indeed. That's none other than Chepheramunni himself, the King-Regent of High Ainon and lapdog of the Scarlet Spires . . . Do you see how he spurns all offers of food and drink? He fears the Emperor will try to drug him."

"Why do they wear masks?"

"The Ainoni are a debauched people," Proyas replied, casting a wary glance at their immediate vicinity. "A race of mummers. They're overly concerned with the subtleties of human intercourse. They regard a concealed face a potent weapon in all matters concerning jnan."

"Jnan," Cnaiür muttered, "is a disease you *all* suffer."

Proyas smiled, amused by the relentlessness of the plainsman's contempt. "Doubtless we do. But the Ainoni suffer it mortally."

"Forgive me," Kellhus said, "but just what is 'jnan'?"

Proyas shot him a puzzled look. "I've never pondered it much before," he admitted. "Byantas, I recall, defines it as 'the war of word and sentiment.' But it's far more. The subtleties that guide the conduct between men, you might say. It's"—he shrugged—"simply something we do."

Kellhus nodded. *They know so little of themselves, Father.*

Troubled by the inadequacy of his reply, Proyas redirected their attention to a small group of men standing about the garden's pool, all wearing the same white tusk-emblazoned vestments over their tunics.

"There. The one with silver hair. That's Incheiri Gotian, Grandmaster of the Shrial Knights. He's a good man—the Shriah's own envoy. Maithanet has directed him to judge our suit against the Emperor."

Gotian awaited the Emperor in silence, clutching in his hands a small ivory canister—a missive, Kellhus assumed, from Maithanet himself. Though Gotian presented the look of self-assurance, Kellhus saw instantly that he was anxious: the rapid pulse of his juggler beneath the dark skin of his neck, the flexing of tendons along the back of his hand, the taut pose of the musculature about his lips . . .

He does not feel equal to his burden.

But more than anxiety simmered beneath his expression: his eyes also betrayed a curious longing, one that Kellhus had witnessed many times in many faces.

He yearns to be moved . . . Moved by someone more holy than he.

"A good man," Kellhus repeated. *I need only convince him I'm more holy.*

"And that there," Proyas said, nodding to his right, "is Prince Skaiyelt of Thunyerus, standing in the shadow of that giant—the one they call Yalgrota."

Whether by design or otherwise, the small Thunyeri contingent occupied the periphery of the gathered Inrithi lords. Of all the nobility gathered in the garden, they alone were geared for battle, wearing hauberks of black chain under sleeved surcoats embroidered with stylized animals. To a man they sported wiry beards and long corn-silk hair. Skaiyelt's face was uniformly scarred, as though by pox, and he muttered sombrely to hard-eyed Yalgrota, who hulked above him, glaring across heads at Cnaiür.

"Have you ever seen such a man?" Proyas hissed, staring at the giant with frank admiration. "Let's pray his interest in you is academic, Scylvendi."

Cnaiür matched Yalgrota's gaze without blinking. "Yes," he said evenly, "for his sake. A man is measured by more than his frame."

Proyas arched his brows, grinned sidelong at Kellhus.

"You think," Kellhus asked the Scylvendi, "that he's not as long as he's tall?"

Proyas laughed aloud, but Cnaiür's ferocious eyes seized Kellhus. *Play these fools if you must, Dûnyain, but do not play me!*

"You're beginning," Proyas said, "to remind me of Xinemus, my Prince."

Of the man he esteems above all others.

An angry cry surfaced from the background bustle of voices: *"Gi'irga fi hierst! Gi'irga fi hierstas da moia!"* Gothyelk, once again chastising one of his sons, this time from across the garden.

"What are those pendants the Thunyeri wear between their thighs?" Kellhus asked Proyas. "They look like shrivelled apples."

"The shrunken heads of Sranc . . . They make fetishes of their enemies, and we can expect"—his distaste soured into a grimace—"that they'll sport *human* heads soon enough, once the Holy War begins its march. As I was about to say, the Thunyeri are young to the Three Seas. They embraced the Thousand Temples and the Latter Prophet only in my grandfather's time, so they're zealous in the way of converted peoples. But interminable war with the Sranc has rendered them morbid, melancholy . . . deranged, even.

Skaiyelt is no exception in this regard, as far as I can tell—the man can't speak a word of Sheyic. He'll need to be . . . managed, I imagine, but not taken seriously otherwise."

There's a great game here, Kellhus thought, *and there's no place for those who don't know the rules*. Nevertheless, he asked, "Why's that?"

"Because he's uncouth, an illiterate barbarian."

The answer he expected: the one certain to alienate the Scylvendi.

As though on cue, Cnaiür snorted. "And just what," he asked scathingly, "do you think the others say of me?"

The Prince shrugged. "Much the same, I imagine. But that'll quickly change, Scylvendi. I've—"

Proyas stopped mid-reply, his attention stolen by the sudden hush that had fallen upon the Inrithi nobles. Three figures approached through the shade of the surrounding colonnades. Two men, Eothic Guardsmen by the look of their armour and insignia, pulled a shambling third between them. The man was naked, emaciated, and freighted by heavy shackles about his neck, wrists, and ankles. From the scars that latticed his arms, it was obvious he was Scylvendi.

"Cunning fiends," Proyas muttered under his breath.

The Guardsmen yanked the man into sunlight. He wobbled drunkenly, heedless of his exposed phallus. He raised a piteous face to the warmth of the sun. His eyes had been gouged out.

"Who is he?" Kellhus asked.

Cnaiür spat, watched the Guardsman chain the man to the base of the Emperor's bench.

"Xunnurit," he said after a moment. "Our King-of-Tribes at the Battle of Kiyuth."

"A token of Scylvendi weakness, no doubt," Proyas said tightly. "Of Cnaiür urs Skiötha's weakness . . . Evidence in what will be your trial."

"You will sit here in posture," the Pragma said, neither stern nor gentle, "and repeat this proposition: 'The Logos is without beginning or end.' You will repeat this without cessation, until you are directed otherwise. Do you understand?"

"Yes, Pragma," Kellhus replied.

He lowered himself onto a small mat of woven reeds in the centre of the shrine. The Pragma sat opposite him on a similar mat, his back to the sunlit poplars and the scowling precipices of the mountains beyond.

"Begin," the Pragma said, becoming motionless.

"The Logos is without beginning or end. The Logos is without beginning or end. The Logos is without . . ."

At first he puzzled over the ease of the exercise. But the words quickly lost their meaning and became a repetitive string of unfamiliar sounds, more a pasty exercise of tongue, teeth, and lips than speaking.

"Cease saying this aloud," the Pragma said. "Speak it only within."

The Logos is without beginning or end. The Logos is without beginning or end. The Logos is without . . .

This was far different and, as he quickly discovered, far more difficult. Speaking the proposition aloud had braced the repetition somehow, as though propping thought against his organs of speech. Now it stood alone, suspended in the nowhere of his soul, repeated and repeated and repeated, contrary to all the habits of inference and drifting association.

The Logos is without beginning or end. The Logos is without beginning or end. The Logos is without . . .

The first thing he noted was the curious slackness of his face, as though the exercise had somehow severed the links shackling expression to passion. His body grew very still, far more so than he'd ever experienced before. At the same time, however, curious waves of tension assailed him from within, as though something deep balked, refusing inner breath to his inner voice. And the repetition was muted to a whisper, became a thin thread undulating through violent eddies of inarticulate, unformed thought.

The Logos is without beginning or end. The Logos is without beginning or end. The Logos is without beginning or end. The Logos is without . . .

The sun waxed across the dishevelled mountainsides, mottling his periphery with the contrast of dark plummets and bright bald faces. Kellhus found himself at war. Inchoate urges reared from nothingness, demanding thought. Unuttered voices untwined from darkness, demanding thought. Hissing images railed, pleaded, threatened—all demanding thought. And through it all:

The Logos is without beginning or end. The Logos is without beginning or end. The Logos is without . . .

Long afterward, he would realize this exercise had demarcated his soul. The incessant repetition of the Pragma's proposition had pitted him against himself, had shown him the extent to which he was other to himself. For the first time he could truly see the darkness that had preceded him, and he knew that before this day, he had never truly been awake.

When the sun at last set, the Pragma broke his fast of silence.

"You have completed your first day, young Kellhus, and now you will continue through the night. When the dawn sun broaches the eastern glacier, you will cease repeating the *last* word of the proposition but otherwise continue. Each time the sun breaks from the glacier, you will cease repeating the last word. Do you understand?"

"Yes, Pragma." Words spoken, it seemed, by someone else.

"Then continue."

As darkness entombed the shrine, the struggle intensified. By turns, his body became remote to the point of giddiness and near to the point of suffocation. One moment he would be an apparition, an accident of coiling smoke, so insubstantial it seemed the night breeze might smear him into nothingness. In another, he would be a bundle of cramped flesh, every sensation sharpened until even the night chill chattered like knives across his skin. And the proposition became something drunken, something that stumbled and staggered through a nightmarish chorus of agitations, distractions, and frenzied passions. They howled within him—like something dying.

Then the sun broke from the glacier, and he was dumbstruck by its beauty. Smouldering orange cresting cold planes of shining snow and ice. And for a heartbeat the proposition escaped him, and he thought only of the way the glacier reared, curved like the back of a beautiful woman . . .

The Pragma leapt forward and struck him, his face a rictus of counterfeit rage. "Repeat the proposition!" he screamed.

           ⤜⤛

For Kellhus, each of the Great Names represented a question, a juncture of innumerable permutations. In their faces, he saw fragments of other faces surfacing as though all men were but moments of one man. An instant of Leweth passing like a squall through Athjeäri's scowl as he argued with Saubon. A glimpse of Serwë in the way Gothyelk looked upon his youngest son. The same passions, but each cast in a drastically different balance. Any one of these people, he concluded, might be as easily possessed as Leweth had been—despite their fierce pride. But in their sum, they were incalculable.

They were a labyrinth, a thousand thousand halls, and he had to pass through them. He had to own them.

What if this Holy War exceeds my abilities? What then, Father?

"Do you feast, Dûnyain?" Cnaiür asked in bitter Scylvendi. "Grow fat on faces?" Proyas had left them to confer with Gotian, and for the moment, the two of them were alone.

"We share the same mission, Scylvendi."

So far, events had exceeded his most optimistic forecasts. His claim to royal blood had secured him, almost effortlessly, a position among the Inrithi ruling castes. Not only had Proyas supplied him with the "necessities of his princely rank," he had accorded him a place of honour at his council fire. So long as one possessed the bearing of a prince, Kellhus discovered, one was treated as a prince. Acting became being.

His other claim, however—his claim to have dreamt of Shimeh and the Holy War—had secured him a far different position, one more fraught with peril and possibility. Some openly scoffed at the claim. Others, like Proyas and Achamian, viewed it as a possible warning, like the first flush of disease. Many, searching for whatever scrap of divine sanction they could find, simply accepted it. But all of them conceded Kellhus the same position.

For the peoples of the Three Seas, dreams, no matter how trivial, were a serious matter. Dreams were not, as the Dûnyain had thought before Moënghus's summons, mere rehearsals, ways for the soul to train itself for different eventualities. Dreams were the portal, the place where the Outside infiltrated the World, where what transcended men—be it the future, the distant, the demonic, or the divine—found imperfect expression in the here and now.

But it was not enough to simply assert that one had dreamed. If dreams were powerful, they were also cheap. Everyone dreamed. After patiently listening to descriptions of his visions, Proyas had explained to Kellhus that literally thousands claimed to dream of the Holy War, some of its triumph, others of its destruction. One could not walk ten yards along the Phayus, he said, without seeing some hermit screech and gesticulate about his dreams.

"Why," he asked with characteristic honesty, "should I regard your dreams as any different?"

Dreams were a serious matter, and serious matters demanded hard questions.

"Perhaps you shouldn't," Kellhus had replied. "I'm not sure I do."

And it was this, his reluctance to believe his own prophetic claims, that had secured his perilous position. When anonymous Inrithi, having heard rumours of him, fell to their knees before him, he would be cross the way a compassionate father would be cross. When they begged to be touched, as though grace could be communicated across skin, he would touch them, but only to raise them up, to chide them for abasing themselves before another. By claiming to be less than what he seemed to be, he moved men, even learned men such as Proyas and Achamian, to hope or fear that he might be *more*.

He would never utter it, never claim it, but he would manufacture the circumstances that would make it seem true. Then all those who counted themselves secret watchers, all those who breathlessly asked *"Who is this man?"* would be gratified like never before. He would be *their* insight.

They would be unable to doubt him then. To doubt him would be to think their own insights empty. To disown him would be to disown themselves.

Kellhus would step onto conditioned ground.

So many permutations . . . But I see the path, Father.

Laughter pealed across the garden. Some young Galeoth thane, weary of standing, had thought the Emperor's stool a good place to rest. He sat for several moments, oblivious to the surrounding mirth, alternately studying the glazed pork *jumyan* he'd pilfered from a slave and the naked man chained at his feet. When he finally realized that everyone laughed at him, he decided he rather liked the attention and began striking a series of mock imperial poses. The Men of the Tusk roared. Eventually, Saubon collected the youth and led him back to his applauding kinsmen.

Moments afterward, a file of Imperial Apparati, all dressed in the voluminous robes of their station, announced the arrival of the Emperor. With Conphas at his side, Ikurei Xerius III appeared just as the hilarity subsided, his expression a mixture of benevolence and distaste. He sat upon his stool and rekindled his guests' mirth when he adopted the very pose—his left palm facing up upon his lap, his right curled down before him—that the young Galeoth had aped just moments before. Kellhus watched his face grow pale with rage as one of his eunuchs explained the laughter. There was murder in his eyes when he dismissed the man, and he struggled with his posture for a moment. To be premeditated, he knew, was the most galling of insults. In this way even an Emperor might be made a slave—though, Kellhus realized, he did not know why. Finally Xerius settled on the Norsirai posture: hands braced on his knees.

Several long moments of silence passed as he mastered his rage. During this time, Kellhus studied the faces of the imperial retinue: the seamless arrogance of the Emperor's nephew, Conphas; the panic of the slaves, so attuned to their master's tumultuous passions; the tight-lipped disapproval of the Imperial Counsels, arrayed in a semicircle behind their Emperor—their centre. And . . .

A *different* face, among the Counsels . . . a troubling face.

It was the subtlest of incongruities, a vague wrongness, that drew his attention at first. An old man dressed in fine charcoal silk robes, a man obviously deferred to and respected by the others. One of his companions leaned to him and muttered something inaudible through the rumble of voices. But Kellhus could see his lips:

Skeaös . . .

The Counsel's name.

Drawing a deep breath, Kellhus allowed the momentum of his own thought to slow and still. Who he was in his everyday concourse with other men ceased to exist, peeled away like petals in bloom. The tempo of events slowed. He became a *place*, a blank field for a single figure: the weathered landscape of an old man's face.

No perceptible blush reflex. Disconnect between heart rate and apparent expression—

But the drone of surrounding voices trailed into silence, and he withdrew, reassembled. The Emperor was about to speak. Words that could seal the fate of the Holy War.

Five heartbeats had passed.

What could this mean? A single, indecipherable face among a welter of transparent expressions.

Skeaös . . . Are you my father's work?

The Logos is without beginning or. The Logos is without beginning or. The Logos is without beginning or. The Logos is without . . .

For a moment, he could taste blood on his split lips, but the sensation was slowly rinsed away by the ruthless litany. The inner cacophony faltered, trailed into deathlike silence. His body became an utter stranger, a disposable frame. And the movement of time itself, the pace of the before and after, transformed.

The shadows of the shrine's pillars swept across the bare floor. Sunlight fell upon, then flickered from, his face. He wet and soiled himself, but there was no discomfort, no smell. And when the old Pragma stood and poured water across his lips, he was merely a smooth rock embedded in moss and gravel beneath a waterfall.

The sun skirted the pillars before him then lowered behind him, drawing his shadow across the lap of the Pragma and then amid the burnished trees, where it congregated with its kinsmen and bloated into night. Again and again, he witnessed the sun rise and topple, the momentary respite of night, and with each dawning the proposition was further dismembered. While the world quickened, the movement of his soul slowed.

Until he whispered only:

The Logos. The Logos. The Logos . . .

He was a hollow filled by echoes bereft of any authoring voice, each phrase a flawless reiteration of the preceding. He was a wayfarer through the abyssal gallery of mirror set against mirror, his every step as illusory as the last. Only sun and night marked his passage, and only then by narrowing the gap between mirrors to the impossible place where vanishing point threatened to kiss vanishing point—to the place where the soul fell utterly still.

When the sun reared yet again, his thoughts receded to a single word:

The. The. The. The . . .

And it seemed at once an absurd stutter and the most profound of thoughts, as though only in the absence of "Logos" could it settle into the rhythm of his heart muscling through moment after moment. Thought thinned and daylight swept through, over, and behind the shrine, until night pierced the shroud of the sky, until the heavens revolved like an infinite chariot wheel.

The. The . . .

A moving soul chained to the brink, to the exquisite moment before *something,* anything. *The* tree, *the* heart, *the* everything transformed into nothing by repetition, by the endless accumulation of the same refusal to *name.*

A corona of gold across the high slopes of the glacier.

. . . and then nothing.

No thought.

"The Empire welcomes you," Xerius announced, his voice straining to be mild. He drew his gaze across the Great Names of the Men of the Tusk, lingering for a moment on the Scylvendi at Kellhus's side. He smiled.

"Ah, yes," he said, "our most extraordinary addition. The Scylvendi. They tell me that you're a Chieftain of the Utemot. Is this so, Scylvendi?"

"It is so," Cnaiür answered.

The Emperor measured this reply. He was in no mood, Kellhus could see, for the niceties of jnan. "I, too, have a Scylvendi," he said. He bared his forearm from intricate sleeves and grasped the chain between his feet. He yanked it savagely, and the huddled Xunnurit raised his blinded, broken face to the onlookers. His naked body was skeletal, malnourished, and his limbs seemed to hang from different hinges, hinges that all turned in, away from the world. The long strips of swazond along his arms now seemed a measure more of the bones beneath than of his bloody past.

"Tell me," the Emperor said, finding comfort in this petty brutality. "Of what tribe is this one?"

Cnaiür seemed unaffected. "This one was of the Akkunihor."

"'Was,' you say? He's dead to you, I suppose."

"No. Not dead. He is nothing to me."

The Emperor smiled as though warming to a small mystery, a suitable distraction from weightier matters. But Kellhus could see the machinations beneath, the confidence that he would show this savage to be an ignorant fool. The need.

"Because we've broken him? Hmm?" the Emperor pressed.

"Broken whom?"

Ikurei Xerius paused. "This dog *here*. Xunnurit, King-of-Tribes. *Your* King . . ."

Cnaiür shrugged, as though puzzled by a child's petty caprice. "You have broken nothing."

There was some laughter at this.

The Emperor soured. Kellhus could see an appreciation of Cnaiür's intellect stumble to the forefront of his thoughts. There was reassessment, a revision of strategies.

He's accustomed, Kellhus thought, *to recovering from blunders*.

"Yes," Xerius said. "To break one man is to break nothing, I suppose. It's too easy to break a man. But to break a *people* . . . Surely this is *something*, no?"

The imperial expression became jubilant when Cnaiür failed to reply.

The Emperor continued: "My nephew here, Conphas, has broken a people. Perhaps you've heard of them. The People of War."

Again, Cnaiür refused to answer. His look, however, was murderous.

"*Your* people, Scylvendi. Broken at Kiyuth. Were you at Kiyuth, I wonder?"

"I was at Kiyuth," Cnaiür grated.

"Were you broken?"

Silence.

"Were you *broken*?"

All eyes were now on the Scylvendi.

"I was"—he searched for the proper Sheyic term—"*schooled* at Kiyuth."

"Were you now!" the Emperor cried. "I should imagine. Conphas is a most demanding instructor. So tell me, what lesson did you learn?"

"Conphas was my lesson."

"Conphas?" the Emperor repeated. "You must forgive me, Scylvendi, but I'm puzzled."

Cnaiür continued, his tone deliberate. "At Kiyuth, I learned what Conphas has learned. He is a general bred on many battle-fields. From the Galeoth he learned the effectiveness of disciplined pike formations against mounted charges. From the Kianene he learned the effectiveness of channelling his opponent, of the false flight, and of the wisdom of hoarding his horsemen in reserve. And from the Scylvendi he learned the importance of the *gobokzoy*, the 'moment'—that one must read his enemy from afar and strike at the instant of their unbalance.

"At Kiyuth, I learned," he continued, turning his hard eyes upon Conphas, "that war is *intellect*."

The shock was plain on the Imperial Nephew's face, and Kellhus wondered at the force of these words. But too much happened for him to focus on this problem. The air was taut with this contest of Emperor and barbarian.

Now it was the Emperor's turn to remain silent.

Kellhus understood the stakes of this exchange. The Emperor needed to show the incompetence of the Scylvendi. Xerius had made his Indenture the price of Ikurei Conphas. Like any merchant, Xerius could justify this price only by maligning the wares of his competitors.

"Enough of this prattle!" Coithus Saubon cried. "The Great Names have heard enough—"

"But it is not for the Great Names to decide!" the Emperor snapped.

"Nor is it for Ikurei Xerius to decide," Proyas added, his eyes bright with zeal.

Grizzled Gothyelk cried: "Gotian! What says the Shriah? What says *Maithanet* of our Emperor's Indenture?"

"But it's *too soon!*" the Emperor sputtered. "We haven't sounded this man—this *heathen!*"

But others clamoured, "Gotian!"

"Then what say *you*, Gotian?" the Emperor cried. "Would you have a *heathen* lead you against the heathen? Would you be punished as the Vulgar Holy War was punished on the Plains of Mengedda? How many dead? How many enslaved by Calmemunis's rash humour?"

"The *Great Names* lead!" Proyas shouted. "The Scylvendi will be our adviser—"

"*An outrage still!*" the Emperor roared. "An army with ten generals? When you founder, and you will, for you know not the cunning of the Kianene, then to *whom* will you turn? A Scylvendi? In your moment of crisis? Of all the absurdities! It *will* be a heathen's Holy War then! Sweet Sejenus, this man's a *Scylvendi*," he cried plaintively, as though to a loved one gone mad. "Does this mean nothing to you fools? He is a blight upon the very earth! His very name is blasphemy! An abomination before the God!"

"You'd speak of *outrage* to us?" Proyas cried in reply. "You'd school in piety those who'd sacrifice their very lives for the Tusk? What of your iniquities, Ikurei? What of you, who'd make a tool of the Holy War?"

"I would *preserve* the Holy War, Proyas! Save the God's instrument from your ignorance!"

"But we're ignorant no longer, Ikurei," Saubon answered. "You've heard the Scylvendi speak. *We've* heard him speak."

"But this man would sell you! He's *Scylvendi*! Haven't you *heard* me?"

"How could we not?" Saubon spat. "You screech louder than my wife."

Rumbling laughter.

"My uncle speaks the truth," Conphas called out, and a hush fell across the noblemen. The great Conphas had finally spoken. He would be the more sober voice.

"You know nothing of the Scylvendi," he continued matter-of-factly. "They're not heathens like the Fanim. Their wickedness isn't

one of distortion, of twisting the true faith into an abomination.
They're a people *without* gods."

Conphas strode down to the King-of-Tribes at the Emperor's feet,
yanked the blinded face back for all to see. He grabbed one of the
emaciated arms.

"They call these scars swazond," he said, as though a patient
tutor, "a word that means 'dyings.' To us, they are little more than
savage trophies, not unlike the shrunken Sranc heads that the
Thunyeri stitch onto their shields. But they're far more to the
Scylvendi. Those dyings are their *only purpose*. The very meaning of
their lives is written into those scars. *Our* dyings . . . Do you understand this?"

He looked into the faces of the assembled Inrithi, was satisfied by
the apprehension he saw there. It was one thing to admit a heathen
into their midst; it was quite another to have the details of his
wickedness enumerated.

"What the savage said earlier is not true," Conphas resumed.
"This man isn't 'nothing.' He's far, far more. He's a token of their
humiliation. The humiliation of the Scylvendi." He stared hard at
Xunnurit's impassive face, the sunken, weeping sockets. Then he
looked to Cnaiür where he stood at Proyas's side.

"Look at him," he said casually. "Look at the one you'd make
your general. Don't you think he thirsts for vengeance? Don't you
think that even now he struggles to beat down the fury in his heart?
Are you so naive as to believe that he doesn't plot our destruction?
That his soul does not twist, as men's souls do, with scenarios, with
images—his vengeance glutted and our ruin complete?"

Conphas looked to Proyas.

"Ask him, Proyas. Ask him what moves his soul."

There was a pause filled by the ambient murmur of muttering
noblemen. Kellhus turned to the enigmatic face hovering above the
Emperor.

As a child, he'd seen expressions in the same manner as world-
born men, as something understood without understanding. But

now he could see the joists beneath the planks of a man's expression, and because of this, he could calculate, with terrifying exactitude, the distribution of forces down to a man's foundation.

But this Skeaös baffled him. Where he saw through others, he saw only the mimicry of depth in the old man's face. The nuanced musculature that produced his expression was unrecognizable—as though moored to different bones.

This man had not been trained in the manner of the Dûnyain. Rather, his face was not a face.

Moments passed, incongruities accumulated, were classified, cobbled into hypothetical alternatives . . .

Limbs. Slender limbs folded and pressed into the simulacrum of a face.

Kellhus blinked, and his senses leapt back into their proper proportion. How was this possible? Sorcery? If so, it possessed nothing of the strange torsion he'd experienced with the Nonman he'd battled so long ago. Sorcery, Kellhus had realized, was inexplicably grotesque—like the scribblings of a child across a work of art—though he did not know why. All he knew was that he could distinguish sorcery from the world and sorcerers from common men. This was among the many mysteries that had motivated his study of Drusas Achamian.

This face, he was relatively certain, had nothing to do with sorcery. But then how?

What is this man?

Abruptly, Skeaös's eyes flashed to his own. The rutted brow clenched into a false frown.

Kellhus nodded in the amicable and embarrassed way of one caught staring at another. But in his periphery he glimpsed the Emperor looking toward him in alarm, then whirling to scrutinize his Counsel.

Ikurei Xerius had not known this face differed, Kellhus realized. None of them knew.

The study deepens, Father. Always it deepens.

"As a youth," Proyas was saying, "I was tutored by a Mandate Schoolman, Conphas. He'd say you're rather optimistic about the Scylvendi."

Several laughed openly at this—relieved.

"Mandate stories," Conphas said evenly, "are worthless."

"Perhaps," Proyas replied, "but of a par with *Nansur* stories."

"But that's not the question, Proyas," old Gothyelk said, his accent so thick that his Sheyic was barely comprehensible. "The question is, how can we trust this heathen?"

Proyas turned to the Scylvendi at his side, suddenly hesitant.

"Then what of it, Cnaiür?" he asked.

Throughout the exchange, Cnaiür had remained silent, doing little to conceal his contempt. Now he spat in Conphas's direction.

No thought.

The boy extinguished. Only a *place*.

This place.

Motionless, the Pragma sat facing him, the bare soles of his feet flat against each other, his dark frock scored by the shadows of deep folds, his eyes as empty as the child they watched.

A place without breath or sound. A place of sight alone. A place without before or after . . . almost.

For the first lances of sunlight careered over the glacier, as ponderous as great tree limbs in the wind. Shadows hardened and light gleamed across the Pragma's ancient skull.

The old man's left hand forsook his right sleeve, bearing a watery knife. And like a rope in water, his arm pitched outward, fingertips trailing across the blade as the knife swung languidly into the air, the sun skating and the dark shrine plunging across its mirror back . . .

And the place where Kellhus had once existed extended an open hand—the blond hairs like luminous filaments against tanned skin—and grasped the knife from stunned space.

The slap of pommel against palm triggered the collapse of place into little boy. The pale stench of his body. Breath, sound, and lurching thoughts.

I have been legion . . .

In his periphery, he could see the spike of the sun ease from the mountain. He felt drunk with exhaustion. In the recoil of his trance, it seemed all he could hear were the twigs arching and bobbing in the wind, pulled by leaves like a million sails no bigger than his hand. Cause everywhere, but amid countless minute happenings—diffuse, useless.

Now I understand.

"You would sound me," Cnaiür said at length. "Make clear the riddle of the Scylvendi heart. But you use your own hearts to map mine. You see a man abased before you, Xunnurit. A man bound to me by kinship of blood. What an offence this must be, you say. His heart *must* cry for vengeance. And you say this because *your* heart would so cry. But my heart is not your heart. This is why it is a riddle to you.

"Xunnurit is not a name of shame to the People. It is not even a name. He who does not ride among us is not us. He is other. But you, who mistake your heart for mine—who see only two Scylvendi, one broken, one erect—think he must still belong to me. You think his degradation is my own, and that I would avenge this. Conphas would have you think this. Why else would Xunnurit be among us? What better way to discredit the strong man than by making a broken man his double? Perhaps it is the Nansur heart that should be sounded."

"But *our* heart is Inrithi," Conphas said scathingly. "It's already known."

"Yes it is," Saubon said fiercely. "It would seize the Holy War from the God and make it its own."

"No!" Conphas spat. "My heart would save the Holy War *for* the God. Save it from this abominable dog, and save you from your folly. The Scylvendi are anathema!"

"As are the Scarlet Spires!" Saubon retorted, advancing toward Conphas. "Would you have us cast *them* out as well?"

"That's different," Conphas snapped. "The Men of the Tusk need the Scarlet Spires . . . Without them, the Cishaurim would destroy us."

Saubon paused a few paces away from the High General. He looked lean, wolfish. "The Inrithi *need* this Scylvendi as well. This is what you tell us, Conphas. We must be saved from our own folly on the field of battle."

"*Calmemunis* and your kinsman Tharschilka have told you that, fool. With their death on the Plains of Mengedda."

"Calmemunis," Saubon spat. "Tharschilka . . . Rabble marching with rabble."

"Tell me, Conphas," Proyas asked. "Did you not know that Calmemunis was doomed beforehand? If so, why did the Emperor provision him?"

"None of this is to the point!" Conphas cried.

He lies, Kellhus realized. *They knew the Vulgar Holy War would be destroyed. They wanted it to be destroyed* . . . Suddenly Kellhus understood that the outcome of this debate was in fact paramount to his mission. The Ikureis had sacrificed an entire host in order to strengthen their claim over the Holy War. What further disaster would they manufacture once it became an inconvenience?

"The question," Conphas ardently continued, "is whether you can trust a *Scylvendi* to lead you against the Kianene!"

"But that isn't the question," Proyas countered. "The question is whether we can trust a Scylvendi over *you*."

"But how could this even be an issue?" Conphas implored. "Trust a Scylvendi over *me*?" He laughed harshly. "This is madness!"

"*Your* madness, Conphas," Saubon grated, "and your uncle's . . . If it weren't for your fucking forecasts of doom and your thrice-damned Indenture, none of this would be an issue!"

"But it's *our* land you would seize! The blood of *our* ancestors smeared across every plain, every hillock, and you would *begrudge* us our claim?"

"It's the *God's* land, Ikurei," Proyas said cuttingly. "The very land of the Latter Prophet. Or would you put the pathetic annals of Nansur before the *Tractate?* Before our Lord, Inri Sejenus?"

Conphas remained silent for a moment, gauging these words. One did not, Kellhus realized, lightly enter a contest of piety with Nersei Proyas.

"And who are *you*, Proyas, to ask this question?" Conphas returned, rallying his earlier calm. "Hmm? You who would put a heathen—a Scylvendi, no less!—before Sejenus."

"We are all instruments of the Gods, Ikurei. Even a heathen— a Scylvendi, no less—can be an instrument, if such is the God's will."

"Would we guess at God's will, then? Eh, Proyas?"

"That, Ikurei, is Maithanet's task." Proyas turned to Gotian, who had been watching them keenly all this time. "What does Maithanet say, Gotian? Tell us. What says the Shriah?"

The Grandmaster's hands were clenched about the ivory canister. He held the answer, everyone knew, within his straining hands. His expression was hesitant. *He remains undecided. He despises the Emperor, distrusts him, but he fears that Proyas's solution is too radical.* Very soon, Kellhus realized, he would be forced to intercede.

"I would ask the Scylvendi," Gotian said, clearing his voice, "why he has come."

Cnaiür looked hard at the Shrial Knight, at the Tusk embroidered in gold across his white vestment. *The words are in you, Scylvendi. Speak them.*

"I have come," Cnaiür said at length, "for the promise of war."

"But this is something that Scylvendi simply don't do," Gotian responded, his suspicion tempered by hope. "There are no Scylvendi mercenaries. At least none I've ever heard of."

"I do not *sell* myself, if that is what you mean. The People do not sell—anything. What we need, we seize."

"Yes. He would *seize* us," Conphas interjected.

"Let the man speak!" Gothyelk cried, his patience waning.

"After Kiyuth," Cnaiür continued, "the Utemot were undone. The Steppe is not how you think. The People war always, if not against the Sranc, Nansur, or Kianene, then against themselves. Our pastures were overrun by our competitors of old. Our herds slaughtered. Our camps burned. I became a chieftain of nothing."

Cnaiür looked over their intent faces. Stories, if fitting, Kellhus had learned, commanded respect.

"From this man," he continued, gesturing to Kellhus, "I learned that outlanders could have honour. As a slave he fought at our side against the Kuöti. Through him, through his God-sent dreams, I learned of your war. I was without my tribe, so I accepted his wager."

Many eyes, Kellhus noted, were now fixed upon him. Should he seize this moment? Or allow the Scylvendi to continue?

"Wager?" Gotian asked, both puzzled and slightly awed.

"That this war would be unlike any other. That it would be a revelation . . ."

"I see," Gotian replied, his eyes suddenly bright with faith remembered.

"Do you?" Cnaiür asked. "I do not think so. I *remain* a Scylvendi." The plainsman looked to Proyas, then swept his eyes across the illustrious assembly. "Do not mistake me, Inrithi. In this much Conphas is right. You are *all* staggering drunks to me. Boys who would play at war when you should kennel with your mothers. You know nothing of war. War is dark. Black as pitch. It is not a God. It does not laugh or weep. It rewards neither skill nor daring. It is not a trial of souls, not the measure of wills. Even less is it a tool, a means to some womanish end. It is merely the place where the iron bones of the earth meet the hollow bones of men and break them.

"You have offered me war, and I have accepted. Nothing more. I will not regret your losses. I will not bow my head before your funeral pyres. I will not rejoice at your triumphs. But I *have* taken the wager. I *will* suffer with you. I will put Fanim to the sword, and drive their wives and children to the slaughter. And when I sleep, I will dream of their lamentations and be glad of heart."

There was a moment of stunned silence. Then Gothyelk, the old Earl of Agansanor, said, "I've ridden on many campaigns. My bones are old, but they're my bones still, not the fire's. And I've learned to trust the man who hates openly, and to fear only those who hate in secret. I'm satisfied with this man's answer—though I like it little." He turned to Conphas, his eyes narrow with distrust. "It's a sad thing when a heathen schools us in honesty."

Slowly, this assent was echoed by others.

"There's wisdom in the heathen's words," Saubon shouted over the rumble. "We'd do well to listen!"

But Gotian remained troubled. Unlike the others, he was Nansur, and Kellhus could see that he shared many of the misapprehensions of the Emperor and the Exalt-General. News of Scylvendi atrocities were a daily fact of life for the Nansur.

Without warning, the Grandmaster sought his eyes through the crowd. Kellhus could see the catastrophic scenarios wheel through the man's soul: the Holy War ruined, and all because of a decision made by *him* in the name of Maithanet.

"I have *dreamed* of this war," Kellhus said suddenly. As the Inrithi yielded to his as yet unheard voice, he gathered them in his watery gaze. "I wouldn't pretend to tell you the meaning of those dreams, for I don't know." He stood within the hallow circle of their God, he had said, but he possessed no presumption. He doubted the way upright men doubted and would brook no pretence in the search for truth. "But I do know this: the decision before you is clear." A declaration of certainty fortified by the admission of uncertainty that prefaced it. *Those few things I do know,* he had said, *I know.*

"Two men have asked you to make a concession. Prince Nersei Proyas has asked that you accept the stewardship of a Scylvendi heathen, while Ikurei Xerius has asked that you bind yourselves to the interests of the Empire. The question is simple: Which concession is greater?" The demonstration of wisdom and insight through clarification. Their recognition of this would cement their respect, prepare them for further recognitions, and convince them that his voice belonged to *reason* and not to his own mercenary concerns.

"On the one hand, we have an Emperor who willingly provisioned the Vulgar Holy War, even though he knew it was almost certain to be destroyed. On the other hand, we have a Chieftain who has spent the entirety of his life plundering and murdering the faithful." He paused, smiling ruefully. "In my homeland, we call this a dilemma."

Warm laughter rumbled through the garden. Only Xerius and Conphas did not smile. Kellhus had circumvented the prestige of the Exalt-General by fastening upon the Emperor, and he had depicted the problem of the Emperor's credibility as equal to that of the Scylvendi's—as only a just and equitable man would do. He had then sealed this equation with gentle wit, further securing their esteem and blurring comedic insight into the insight of truth.

"Now, I can vouch for the honour of Cnaiür urs Skiötha, but then who would vouch for me? So let's assume that both men, Emperor and Chieftain, are equally untrustworthy. Given this, the answer lies in something you already know: we undertake the God's work, but it's dark and bloody *work* nonetheless. There is no fiercer labour than war." He studied their faces, glancing at each as though he stood with him alone. They stood upon the brink, he could see, on the cusp of the conclusion reason itself had compelled. Even Xerius.

"Whether we accept the stewardship of the Emperor or the Chieftain," he continued, "we concede the same trust, and we concede the same labour . . ."

Kellhus paused, looked to Gotian. He could see the inferences move of their own volition through the man's soul.

"But with the Emperor," Gotian said, nodding slowly, "we concede the *wages* of our labour as well."

A murmur of profound agreement passed through the Men of the Tusk.

"What say you, Grandmaster?" Prince Saubon called. "Is the *Shriah* satisfied?"

"But this is more nonsense!" Ikurei Conphas cried. "How could the Emperor of an Inrithi nation be *as* untrustworthy as a heathen savage?!"

The Exalt-General had immediately seized upon the hinge of Kellhus's argument. But his protest was too late.

Without speaking, Gotian opened the canister, revealing two small scrolls within. He hesitated, his stern face pale. He held the future of the Three Seas in his palms, and he knew it. Gingerly, as though he handled some holy relic, he opened the scroll with the black wax seal.

Turning to the silent Emperor, the Grandmaster of the Shrial Knights began reading, his voice resonant like a priest's. "Ikurei Xerius III, Emperor of Nansur, by authority of the Tusk and the *Tractate*, and according to the ancient constitution of Temple and State, you are ordered to provision the instrument of our great—" The roar of the assembly reverberated through the Emperor's garden. Gotian's voice rumbled on, about Inri Sejenus, about faith, about misplaced intentions, but already the joyous Men of the Tusk had begun abandoning the garden, so eager were they to prepare for the march. Conphas stood dumbstruck on the step below the Emperor's stool, glaring at the Scylvendi King-of-Tribes at his feet. Nearby, Proyas accepted the congratulations of his peers with dignified words and jubilant eyes.

But Kellhus studied the Emperor through the flurry of figures. He was spitting orders to one of his resplendent guards, orders that, Kellhus knew, had nothing to do with the Holy War. "Take Skeaös," his lips hissed, "and then summon the others. The old wretch hides some *treason!*"

Kellhus watched the Eothic Guardsman motion to his comrades, then close on the faceless Counsel. They led him roughly away.

What would they discover?

There had been two contests in the Emperor's garden.

The handsome face of Ikurei Xerius III then turned to him, as terrified as it was enraged.

He thinks I'm party to his Counsel's treachery. He wishes to seize me but can think of no pretext.

Kellhus turned to Cnaiür, who stood stoically, studying the naked form of his kinsman chained beneath the Emperor's feet. "We must leave quickly," Kellhus said. "There has been too much truth here."

CHAPTER EIGHTEEN

THE ANDIAMINE HEIGHTS

. . . and that revelation murdered all that I once did know.
Where once I asked of the God, "Who are you?" now I ask,
"Who am I?"

—ANKHARLUS, LETTER TO THE WHITE TEMPLE

The Emperor, the consensus seems to be, was an excessively
suspicious man. Fear has many forms, but it is never so danger-
ous as when it is combined with power and perpetual uncertainty.

—DRUSAS ACHAMIAN, COMPENDIUM OF THE FIRST HOLY WAR

Late Spring, 4111 Year-of-the-Tusk, Momemn

Emperor Ikurei Xerius III paced, wringing his hands. After the debacle in the garden he'd begun shaking uncontrollably. He could go no farther than his imperial apartments. Conphas and Gaenkelti, the Captain of his Eothic Guard, stood silently in the room's centre, watching him. Xerius paused by a lacquered table, swallowed a deep draught of liquored anpoi. He smacked his lips and gasped.

"You have him?"

"Yes," Gaenkelti replied. "He's been taken to the galleries."

"I must see him."

"I advise against this, God-of-Men," Gaenkelti replied carefully.

Xerius paused, stared hard at the massive Norsirai Captain. "Against? Is there sorcery here?"

"The Imperial Saik say no. But this man has been . . . trained."

"What do you mean 'trained'? Spare me your riddles, Gaenkelti! The Empire has been humiliated this day. *I've* been humiliated!"

"He was . . . hard to take. Three of my men are dead. Four more have broken limbs—"

"Surely you jest!" Conphas cried. "Was he armed?"

"No. I've never seen the like. If we hadn't had extra guards assigned for the audience . . . As I said, he's been trained."

"You mean," Xerius said, his face stricken by terror, "that during all this time, all these years, he could have *killed* . . . killed *me?*"

"But *how old* is Skeaös, Uncle?" Conphas asked. "How could this be? It *must* be sorcery."

"The Saik swear it's not," Gaenkelti repeated.

"The *Saik!*" Xerius spat, turning for more anpoi. "Blasphemous rats. Scuttling around the palace. Plotting, always plotting against me. We need independent confirmation." He took another deep drink, coughed. "Send for one of the other Schools . . . The Mysunsai," he continued, his voice pinched.

"I've already done so, God-of-Men. But I believe the Saik in this instance." Gaenkelti grasped the small, rune-covered sphere that rested against his breastplate—a Chorae, the bane of sorcerers. "I hung this before his face after he'd been subdued. There was no fear. There was nothing in that face."

"*Skeaös!*" Xerius cried to the engraved ceilings, reaching again for the anpoi. "Slavish, damnable, shuffling Skeaös! A spy? A trained assassin? He trembled whenever I addressed him directly—did you know this? Trembled like a fawn. And I'd say to myself: 'The others call me a God, but Skeaös, ah *good* Skeaös, he *knows* I'm divine. Skeaös alone has submitted . . .' And all the while he dripped poison in my ear. Whetted my appetite with his tongue. *Gods of damnation!* I'll see him skinned! I'll wring truth from his broken frame! Blast him with agony!" With a roar Xerius heaved and overturned the table. Glass and gold crashed and clattered across the marble.

He stood silently, his chest heaving. The world buzzed around him, impenetrable, mocking. Everywhere the shadows clamoured. Great designs were afoot. The Gods themselves moved—*against him*.

"What of the other, God-of-Men?" Gaenkelti dared ask. "The Atrithau Prince who led you to suspect Skeaös?"

Xerius turned to his Captain, his eyes still wild. "The Atrithau Prince," he repeated, shuddering at the recollection of the man's composed expression. A spy . . . and with a face that bespoke utter ease. Such confidence! And why not, when the Emperor's own Prime Counsel was one of his own? But no more. He would visit him with terror soon enough.

"Watch him. Scrutinize him like no other."

He turned to Conphas, studied him briefly. For once it seemed as though his godlike nephew was perturbed. The small satisfactions—he had to cling to these through the night to follow.

"Leave us for now, Captain," he said, recovering himself. "I'm pleased by your conduct. See to it that Grandmaster Cememketri and Tokush are summoned to me immediately. I would speak to my sorcerers and my spies. And my augurs . . . Send Arithmeas as well."

Gaenkelti knelt, touched his forehead to the carpeted floor, and withdrew.

Alone with his nephew, Xerius turned his back to him and walked to the open portico on the far side of the chamber. Outside it was dusk, and the Meneanor Sea heaved darkly against the grey horizon.

"I know your question," he said to the figure behind him. "You wonder how much I've told to Skeaös. You wonder if he knows all that *you* know."

"He was with you always, Uncle. Was he not?"

"I may be fooled, Nephew, but I am not a fool . . . But this is moot. We'll know all that Skeaös knows soon enough. We will know whom to punish."

"And the Holy War?" Conphas asked cautiously. "What of our Indenture?"

"Our own house, Nephew. First, our own house . . ."

Or so your grandmother would say.

Xerius turned his profile to Conphas, paused in thought. "Cememketri has told me that a Mandate sorcerer has joined the Holy War. Summon him . . . yourself."

"Why? Mandate Schoolmen are fools."

"Fools can be trusted precisely because they *are* fools. Their agendas rarely intersect with your own. These are great matters, Conphas. We must be certain."

Conphas left him alone with the dark sea. One could see far from the summit of the Andiamine Heights, but never, it seemed, far enough. He would ply Cememketri, Grandmaster of the Imperial Saik, and Tokush, his Master of Spies. He would listen to them squabble with each other, learn nothing from them. And then he would go down to the galleries. See "good" Skeaös himself. Dole out the first wages of his transgression.

The journey from the encampment to the Andiamine Heights held something of a nightmarish quality for Achamian. But such was Momemn after dark—something of a nightmare. The air was so pungent it had taste. Several times he glimpsed a tall finger of stone—the Tower of Ziek, he supposed—and for a short time, as they passed near the temple-complex of Cmiral, he could see the great domes of Xothei arched like black bellies beneath the sky. But otherwise he found himself submerged in a chaotic warren of avenues hedged by ancient tenements and punctuated by abandoned bazaars, canals, and cultic temples. Complex by daylight, Momemn was labyrinthine by night.

The troop of torch-bearing Kidruhil formed a glittering thread through the darkness. Iron-shod hoofs clattered against the stone and muck, drawing frightened, pasty faces to nearby windows. In full ceremonial armour, Ikurei Conphas himself rode beside him—aloof.

Achamian found himself glancing periodically at the Exalt-General. There was something unnerving about the man's physical perfection, something that made Achamian acutely self-conscious of his own portly frame, almost as though through Conphas, the Gods had revealed the cruel humour behind the accumulated flaws of more common men. But it was more than his appearance that unsettled. There was an air about the man—something too self-assured to qualify as arrogance. Ikurei Conphas, Achamian decided, was possessed either of a terrible strength or a frightening lack.

Conphas! It still beggared belief. What could the Ikureis want of him? Achamian had given up asking the Imperial Nephew. "I have been sent to fetch," the man had said blankly, "not to banter."

Whatever the Emperor wanted, it was important enough to make an errand boy of the Imperial Nephew.

From the first, the summons had filled Achamian with a sense of tight-lipped foreboding. The heavily armoured Kidruhil had spilled through the avenues of the Conriyan camp as though executing an assault. Several moments of jostling and angry words by firelight passed before it became clear that the Nansur had come for him.

"Why would an Emperor summon me?" he'd asked Conphas.

"Why summon any sorcerer?" the man had replied impatiently.

This response had angered him, had reminded him of the officials from the Thousand Temples whom he'd plied for details of Inrau's death. And for an instant, Achamian had understood just how insignificant the Mandate had become in the great scheme of the Three Seas. Of the Schools, the Mandate was the besotted fool whose bloated claims became more and more desperate as the night waxed. And like any other embarrassment, the powerful religiously avoided desperation.

Which was why this request was so unsettling. What could an Emperor want with a desperate fool like Drusas Achamian?

As far as he could tell, only one of two things could induce a Great Faction such as the Ikureis to call on him. Either they had encountered something beyond the abilities of their own School, the Imperial Saik, or the mercenary Mysunsai to resolve, or they wished to speak of the Consult. Since no one save the Mandate believed in the Consult any more, it had to be the former. And perhaps this wasn't as implausible as it seemed. If the Great Factions commonly laughed at their mission, they still respected their skills.

The Gnosis made them rich fools.

Eventually, they passed beneath a looming gate, rode through the outer gardens of the Imperial Precincts, and came to the base of the Andiamine Heights. The relief Achamian had anticipated, however, was nowhere to be found.

"We've arrived, sorcerer," Ikurei Conphas said curtly, dismounting with the ease of a man bred to horses. "Follow me."

Conphas ushered him to a set of iron-bound doors that seemed ancillary to the rest of the immediate structure. The palace, its marble columns shimmering in the countless torches that ringed its perimeter, climbed the rambling heights above them. Conphas hammered on the doors, and they were pried open by two Eothic Guardsmen, revealing a long passageway illuminated by candles. Rather than climbing the Heights, however, it led to their buried heart.

Conphas strode through, but he paused when Achamian hesitated.

"If you're wondering," he said with a small, wicked smile, "whether this passage leads to the Emperor's dungeons, it does . . ." The candlelight glossed the intricate reliefs stamped into his breastplate—the many suns of Nansur. Underneath the breastplate, Achamian knew, lay a Chorae. Most nobles of rank wore them, their totems against sorcery. But Achamian did not need to infer its presence—he could feel it.

"I'd surmised as much," he replied, standing at the threshold. "The time has come, I think, for you to explain my purpose here."

"Mandate sorcerers," Conphas said ruefully. "Like all misers, you assume that everyone is after your hoard. What do you think, sorcerer? That I'm so stupid as to publicly barrel through Proyas's camp just to *abduct* you?"

"You belong to the House Ikurei. That's cause for apprehension enough, don't you think?"

Conphas studied him for a moment—a tax-farmer's look—and apparently understood that Achamian could not be bullied by mockery or rank. "So be it, then," he said abruptly. "We've discovered a spy in our midst. The Emperor needs you to verify that sorcery was not involved."

"You don't trust the Imperial Saik?"

"*No one* trusts the Imperial Saik."

"I see. And the mercenaries—the Mysunsai—why not use them?"

Again the man smiled condescendingly—much more than condescendingly. Achamian had seen many such smiles before, but they had always seemed shrill somehow, polluted by small despairs. There was nothing shrill about this smile. His perfect teeth flashed in the candlelight. Predatory teeth. "This spy, sorcerer, is most uncanny. Perhaps beyond their limited talents."

Achamian nodded. The Mysunsai were "limited." Mercenary souls were rarely gifted ones. But for the Emperor to send for a *Mandate* sorcerer, to distrust not only his own magi but the mercenaries as well . . . *They're terrified*, Achamian realized. *The Ikureis are terrified.* Achamian scrutinized the Imperial Nephew, searching for any sign of deception. Satisfied, he crossed the threshold. He winced when he heard the doors grate shut behind him.

The hallway rushed by them, swallowed by Conphas's long martial strides. Achamian could almost feel the Andiamine Heights pile above them. How many people, he wondered, had walked this hall never to return?

Without warning Conphas spoke: "You're a friend of Nersei Proyas, no? Tell me: What do you know of Anasûrimbor Kellhus? The one who claims to be a Prince of Atrithau."

A physical jolt accompanied this question, and for a heartbeat Achamian had to struggle to maintain their brisk pace.

Is Kellhus somehow involved in this?

What should he tell him? That he feared the man might be a harbinger of the Second Apocalypse? *Tell him nothing.*

"Why do you ask?"

"No doubt you've heard the outcome of the Emperor's meeting with the Great Names. In no small measure, it was a result of the cunning of that man."

"His wisdom, you mean."

Momentary wrath disfigured the Exalt-General's expression. He tapped his breastplate twice below his neck, precisely where, Achamian knew, his Chorae lay hidden. The gesture calmed the man somehow, as though reminding him of all the ways that Achamian could die.

"I asked you a simple question."

The question was anything but simple, Achamian thought. What did he know of Kellhus? Precious little, save that he was perhaps as awed by who the man was as he was terrified by who the man might be. An Anasûrimbor had returned.

"Does this," Achamian asked, "have anything to do with your 'uncanny spy'?"

Conphas came to an abrupt halt and scrutinized him. Either he was astounded by some hidden idiocy in this question or he was making a decision.

They truly are terrified.

The Exalt-General snorted, as though amazed he could worry about what a Mandate Schoolman might make of the Empire's secrets. "Nothing whatsoever." He smirked. "You should comb your beard, sorcerer," he added as they continued down the passage. "You're about to meet the Emperor himself."

Xerius left Cememketri's side and looked hard into the face of Skeaös. Blood clotted one ear. Long wisps of white hair framed his veined forehead and sunken cheeks, made him look wild.

The old man was naked and chained, his body bowed outwards along a wooden table curved like half of a broken wheel. The wood was smooth—polished by many such chainings—and dark against the Counsel's pale skin. The chamber had low vaulted ceilings and was illuminated by shining braziers scattered randomly through its recesses. They stood in the heart of the Andiamine Heights, in what had through the ages come to be called the Truth Room. Along the walls, in iron racks, stood the implements of Truth.

Skeaös watched him without fear, blinked the way a child, awakened in the dead of night, might blink. His eyes glittered from his wizened face, turned to the figures that accompanied his Emperor: Cememketri and two other senior magi, wearing the black-and-gold robes of the Imperial Saik, the Sorcerers of the Sun; Gaenkelti and Tokush, still dressed in their ceremonial armour, their faces rigid with fear that their Emperor, inevitably, would hold them responsible for this outrageous treachery; Kimish, the Interrogator, who saw points of pain instead of people; Skaleteas, the blue-robed Mysunsai summoned by Gaenkelti, his middle-aged face openly perplexed; and of course, two blue-tattooed crossbowmen of the Eothic Guard, their Chorae aimed at the Prime Counsel's sunken chest.

"Such a different Skeaös," the Emperor whispered, clasping his trembling hands.

A soft chuckle escaped the Prime Counsel.

Xerius beat down the terror that moved him, felt his heart harden. Fury. He would need fury here.

"What say you, Kimish?" he asked.

"He's already been plied, briefly, God-of-Men," Kimish answered plainly. "According to protocol." Was there excitement in his tone? Kimish, alone out of those gathered, would care nothing for the fact that it was an Imperial Counsel on the table. He cared only for his trade. The politics of this outrage, the dizzying implications, would, Xerius was certain, mean nothing to him. Xerius liked this about Kimish, even if it irritated him at times. It was a becoming trait for an Interrogator.

"*And?*" Xerius asked, his voice almost cracking. His every passion seemed amplified, hinged upon the possibility of precipitous transformations. Annoyance to fury. Small hurt to agony.

"He's unlike any man I've seen, God-of-Men."

What did *not* become Kimish, Xerius had decided, was his penchant for drama. Like a storyteller, he spoke in gaps, as though the world was his chorus. The heart of the matter was something Kimish jealously guarded, something provided according to the rules of narrative suspense, not necessity.

"Finding *answers* is your trade, Kimish," Xerius snapped. "Why must I interrogate the Interrogator?"

Kimish shrugged. "Sometimes it's better to show than to say," he said, grasping a small set of pliers from the rack of tools beside the Counsel. "Watch."

He knelt and grasped one of the Counsel's feet in his left hand. Slowly, with the boredom of a craftsman, he wrenched out a toenail.

There was nothing. No shriek. Not even a shudder from the old frame.

"*Inhuman,*" Xerius gasped, backing away.

The others stood dumbstruck. He turned to Cememketri, who shook his head, and then to Skaleteas, who said, blankly, "There's no sorcery, here, God-of-Men."

Xerius whirled to face his Counsel. "What *are* you?" he cried.

The old face grinned. "*More, Xerius. I am more.*" It was not Skeaös's voice but something broken, like many voices.

The ground wheeled beneath Xerius's feet. He steadied himself by clutching Cememketri, who involuntarily shrank from the Chorae swinging about his neck. Xerius looked into the sorcerer's sneering face. The *Imperial Saik!* His thoughts howled. Convoluted. Arcane in deed and desire. Only *they* had the resources. Only they had the *means* . . .

"You lie!" he cried to the Grandmaster. "This must be sorcery! I feel it! I feel its poison in the air! This room *reeks of it!*" He thrust the terrified man to the ground. "You've bought this slave!" he shrieked, gesturing to the ashen-faced Skaleteas. "Eh, Cememketri? Unclean, blasphemous cur! Is this *your* doing? The Saik would be the Scarlet Spires of the West, no? Make a *puppet* of their Emperor!"

Xerius stopped short, yanked from his accusations by the sight of Conphas at the entrance. The Mandate sorcerer stood at his side. Cememketri's attendants hastily pulled the Grandmaster to his feet.

"These charges, Uncle," Conphas said cautiously. "Perhaps they are rash."

"Perhaps," Xerius spat, smoothing his gowns. "But as your grandmother would say, Conphas, fear first the closer knife." Then, glancing at the stocky, squared-bearded man who stood at Conphas's side, he asked, "This is the Mandate Schoolman?"

"Yes. Drusas Achamian."

The man knelt unceremoniously, touched his forehead to the ground and muttered, "God-of-Men."

"Awkward, is it not, Mandati—these meetings of magi and kings?" The keen embarrassment of moments before was forgotten. Perhaps it was good, Xerius thought, that the man understood the stakes of this proceeding. For some reason, he was moved to be gracious.

The sorcerer looked at him quizzically, then remembered himself and turned down his eyes.

"I'm your slave, God-of-Men," he mumbled. "What would you have me do?"

Xerius grasped his arm—a most disarming gesture, he thought, an Emperor holding a low-caste arm—and led him through the others to the prostrate Skeaös.

"You see, Skeaös," Xerius said, "the lengths we've gone to ensure your comfort."

The old face remained passionless, but the eyes glittered with a strange intensity.

"A *Mandati*," it said.

Xerius looked to Achamian. The man's expression was blank. And then Xerius felt it, felt the hatred emanating from Skeaös's pale form, as though the old man *recognized* the Mandate sorcerer. The splayed body tensed. The chains tightened, link biting against link. The wooden table creaked.

The Mandate sorcerer backed away—two steps.

"What do you see?" Xerius hissed. "Is it sorcery? *Is it?*"

"Who is this man?" Drusas Achamian asked, the horror plain in his voice.

"My Prime Counsel . . . of thirty years."

"Have you . . . interrogated him? What has he said?" The man almost shouted. Was there panic in his eyes?

"Answer me, Mandati!" Xerius cried. "Is there *sorcery* here!?"

"No."

"You *lie*, Mandati. I can *see* it! See it in your eyes."

The man looked at him directly, his gaze focusing as though he struggled to comprehend the Emperor's words, to concentrate on something suddenly trivial.

"N-no," he stammered. "You see *fear* . . . There's no sorcery here. Either that or there's sorcery of another sort. One invisible to the Few . . ."

"It's as I told you, God-of-Men," Skalateas interrupted from behind. "The Mysunsai have always been faithful. We would do nothing to—"

"*Silence!*" Xerius shouted.

What was once Skeaös had begun growling . . .

"*Meta ka peruptis sun rangashra, Chigra, Mandati—Chigraa,*" the old Counsel spat, his voice now utterly inhuman. He writhed against his restraints, the old body rippling with thin, greasy muscles. A bolt snapped from the walls.

Xerius backed away with the sorcerer. "What does he say?" he gasped.

But the sorcerer was dumbstruck.

"The chains!" someone cried—Kimish.

"Gaenkelti . . . *Conphas!*" Xerius called numbly, stumbling farther back.

The old body thrashed against the curved wood like starving eels stitched in human skin. Another bolt snapped from the wall . . .

Gaenkelti was the first to die, his neck snapped, so that Xerius could see his slack face loll against his back as he toppled forward. A chain took Conphas in the side of the face, flung him against the far wall. Tokush was broken like a doll. *Skeaös?*

But then there were *words!* Burning words and the room was washed with blinding fires. Xerius shrieked and tripped. A blast of heat rolled over him. Stone cracked. The air shivered.

And he could hear the Mandati roaring, "No, curse you! *NOOO!*" And then a wail, unlike anything he'd ever heard, like a thousand wolves burning alive. The sound of meat slapping against stone.

Xerius scrambled upright against a wall but could see nothing for the Eothic Guardsmen who shielded him. The lights subsided, and it seemed dark, very dark. The Mandate sorcerer still shouted, cursed.

"That is *enough*, Mandati!" Cememketri roared.

"Pompous fucking ingrate! You've no inkling of what you've done!"

"I've *saved* the Emperor!"

And Xerius thought, *I'm saved* . . . He clawed his way from between the Guardsmen, stumbled into the centre of the room. Smoke. The smell of roasting pork.

The Mandate sorcerer knelt over the charred body of Skeaös, gripped the burned shoulders, shook the slack head.

"What are you?" he ranted. "*Answer me!*"

Skeaös's eyes glittered white from black and blasted skin. And they laughed, laughed at the raging sorcerer.

"You are the first, Chigra," Skeaös wheezed—an ambient, horrifying whisper. "And you will be the last . . ."

What followed would haunt Xerius's dreams for the rest of his numbered days. As though gasping for some deeper breath, Skeaös's face *unfolded* like spider's legs clutched tight about a cold torso. Twelve limbs, crowned by small wicked claws, unclenched and opened, revealing lipless teeth and lidless eyes where a face should have been. Like a woman's long fingers, they embraced the astounded Mandate sorcerer about the head and began to squeeze.

The man shrieked in agony.

Xerius stood helpless, transfixed.

But then the hellish head was gone, rolling like a melon across the floor-stones, limbs flailing. Conphas staggered after it, his shortsword bloody. He paused over it, sword at his side, and looked to his uncle with glassy eyes.

"Abomination," he said, wiping at the blood on his face.

Meanwhile, the Mandate sorcerer grunted and recovered his feet. He looked around at the stunned faces. Without a word he walked slowly toward the entrance. Cememketri blocked his way.

Drusas Achamian looked back to Xerius, the old intensity returning to his eyes. Blood trickled down his cheeks.

"I'm leaving," he said bluntly.

"Leave then," Xerius said, and nodded to the Grandmaster.

As the man left the room, Conphas looked to Xerius questioningly. *Is this wise?* his expression asked.

"He would have lectured us about myths, Conphas. About the Ancient North and the return of Mog. They always do."

"After this," Conphas replied, "perhaps we should listen."

"Mad events seldom give credence to madmen, Conphas." He looked to Cememketri and knew from the old man's expression that he had drawn the same conclusion as himself. There *had* been Truth in this room. Horror gave way to exhilaration. *I have survived!*

Intrigue. The Great Game—the benjuka of beating hearts and moving souls. Was there ever a time when he'd not played? Over the years, he'd learned that one could play in ignorance of his opponent's machinations for only so long. The trick was to force all hands. Sooner or later the moment would come, and if you had forced your adversary's hand soon enough, you would survive and be ignorant no longer. The moment had come. He had survived. And he was ignorant no longer.

The Mandati himself had said it: a sorcery of a different sort. One invisible to the Few. Xerius possessed his answer. He knew the source of this mad treachery.

The sorcerer-priests of the Fanim. The Cishaurim.

An old enemy. And in this dark world, old enemies were welcome. But he said nothing to his nephew, so much did he savour those rare moments when the man's insight lagged behind his own.

Xerius walked over to the scene of carnage, looked down at the ridiculous figure of Gaenkelti. Dead.

"The price of knowledge has been paid," he said without passion, "and we have not been beggared."

"Perhaps," Conphas replied, scowling, "but we're debtors still."

So like Mother, Xerius thought.

The thoroughfares and nebulous byways of the Holy War were awash with shouts, firelight, and wild, celebratory cheer. Clutching the strap of her satchel, Esmenet shouldered her way between tall, shadowy warriors. She saw the emperor burned in effigy. She saw two men pummelling a hapless third between tents. Many knelt, alone or in groups, weeping or singing or chanting. Many others danced to the husky call of double oboes or the plaintive twang of Nilnameshi harps. Everyone drank. She watched a towering Thunyeri hack down a bull with his battle-axe, then cast its severed head onto an impromptu altar fire. For some reason, the animal's eyes reminded her of Sarcellus's—dark, long-lashed, and curiously unreal, as though made of glass.

Sarcellus had retired early, claiming they needed their rest before decamping on the morrow. She had lain next to him, feeling the heat of his broad back, waiting for his breath to settle into the shallow rhythm that characterized his slumber. Once convinced he was soundly asleep, she slipped from his bed and as quietly as she could, gathered a handful of things.

The night was sultry, the humid air shivering with both the sense and the sound of nearby festivities. Smiling at the enormity of what lay before her, she had hoisted her belongings and descended into the night.

Now she found herself near the heart of the encampment, dodging through crowds, pausing now again to locate Momemn's Ancilline Gate.

Passing through the thick of the celebrations proved difficult. Several men seized her without warning. Most simply twirled her in the air, laughing, forgetting her the instant they set her down, but the bolder ones, Norsirai mostly, either groped her or bruised her lips with fierce kisses. One, a child-faced Tydonni a full hand taller than even Sarcellus, proved particularly amorous. He lifted her effortlessly, crying *"Tusfera! Tusfera!"* over and over again. She wriggled and glared, but he simply laughed, crushing her against his brigandine. She grimaced, experienced the horror of staring into eyes that looked directly into her own and yet were utterly oblivious to her fury or fear. She pushed against his chest, and he laughed like a father dandying a squealing daughter. "No!" she spat, feeling a clumsy hand fumbling between her thighs. *"Tusfera!"* the man roared in jubilation. When she felt his fingers knead bare skin, she struck him as an old patron had once taught her, where his moustache met his nose.

Crying out, he dropped her. He stumbled back, his eyes wide with horror and confusion, as though he'd just been kicked by a trusted horse. In the firelight, blood blackened his pale fingers. She heard cheers as she fled into the crowded gloom.

Some time passed before she stopped shaking. She found a wedge of solitude and darkness behind a pavilion stitched with innumerable Ainoni pictograms. She clutched her knees and rocked, watching the tip of a nearby bonfire over the surrounding tents. Sparks danced like mosquitoes into the night sky.

She cried for a bit.

I'm coming, Akka.

She resumed her journey, shying from groups where no women or too much drink seemed present. The Ancilline Gate, her towers crowned by torches, soon loomed over the near distance. She dared to approach a more sedate group of revellers and asked them where she might find the pavilion belonging to the Marshal of Attrempus. She took care to conceal her tattooed hand. With the laborious courtesy of smitten drunks, they gave her almost a dozen different ways to her destination. Exasperated, she finally just asked them for a direction.

"That way," one man said, his Sheyic heavily accented, "across the dead canal."

She understood why the canal was called "dead" before she even saw it. The humid air grew dank with the smell of rotting vegetation, offal, and stagnant water. Dwarfed by a band of Conriyan knights, she filed across a narrow wooden bridge. Below, the canal was black and motionless in the torchlight. One of the men leaned over the rail to watch his spit plop into the water; he grinned sheepishly at her.

"*Yashari a'summa poro,*" he said, in Conriyan, perhaps.

Esmenet ignored him.

Unnerved more by the size than by the demeanour of the young noblemen, she struck off the main track, with its shadowy packs of carousers, and threaded her way into the deeper gloom. Most believed the greater stature of caste nobles was a consequence of greater blood, but Achamian had once told her it was more a matter of diet. That was why, he insisted, the Norsirai seemed tall regardless of caste: they ate more red meat. Usually she was attracted to statuesque men, to "muscle trees," as she and her harlot friends had jokingly called them, but not this night, not after her encounter with the Tydonni, anyway. This night they made her feel small, diminished, like a toy—easily broken, easily discarded.

She was fairly skulking between tents by the time she found Xinemus's pavilion. Cutting across silent camps, she had followed the dead canal north. She saw a bonfire and more revellers before her. While pondering how to best circumvent them, she glimpsed the standard of Attrempus hanging limp in the smoke and light: an elongated tower flanked by stylized lions.

For a time she could only stare at it. Though she could see nothing of those congregated beneath, she imagined Achamian sitting cross-legged on a mat, his face animated by drink and his famous mock disdain. Every so often he would draw his fingers through his grey-streaked beard—a meditative gesture, or a nervous one. She would step into the light, smiling her equally famous sly smile, and he'd drop his wine bowl in astonishment. She'd see his lips mouth her name, his eyes glitter with tears . . .

Alone, in the dark, Esmenet smiled.

It would feel so good to feel his beard tickle her ear, to smell his dry, cinnamon smell, to crush herself against his barrel chest . . .

To hear him speak her name.

"*Esmi. Esmenet. Such an old-fashioned name.*"

"*From the Tusk. Esmenet was the wife of the Prophet Angeshraël.*"

"*Ah . . . a harlot's name.*"

She wiped her eyes. That he would rejoice at seeing her, she had no doubt. But he would not understand the time she'd spent with Sarcellus—especially once she told him of that night in Sumna and what it meant for Inrau. He would be cut, outraged even. He might even strike her.

But he would not turn her out. He would wait, as he always did, for the Mandate to call him away.

And he would forgive. As he always did.

She warred with her face.

So useless! Pathetic!

She combed her hair with her fingers, smoothed her hasas with sweaty palms. She cursed the darkness for preventing her from using her cosmetics. Were her eyes still swollen? Was that why those Conriyans had treated her so gently?

Pathetic!

She prowled along the bank of the canal, never pausing to think why she did so. Secrecy seemed crucial, for some reason. Darkness and cover essential. She glimpsed the bonfire through odd angles between tents, saw bright figures standing, drinking, laughing. A large pavilion stood between the festivities and the canal, flanked by a number of smaller tents—slaves' quarters and the like, Esmenet imagined. Breathless, she crept behind a threadbare shelter immediately adjacent to the pavilion. She paused in the darkness, feeling like a misbegotten creature from some nursery tale, one who must hide from lethal light.

Then she dared peek around a corner.

Just more revellers around yet another golden fire.

She searched for Achamian but could see him nowhere. She realized the one, the stocky man dressed in a grey silk tunic with slashed sleeves, had to be Xinemus himself. He acted the host, barking commands to the slaves, and he looked a lot like Achamian, as though an older brother. Achamian had once complained that Proyas teased him for looking like Xinemus's weaker twin.

So you're his friend, she thought, both watching and silently thanking him.

Most everyone around the fire was unknown to her, but the man whose corded arms were ribbed by scars, she realized, had to be the Scylvendi everyone was talking about. Did that mean the blond-bearded man, the one who sat next to the breathtaking Norsirai girl, was his companion? The Prince of Atrithau who claimed to dream of the Holy War? Esmenet wondered who else she might be watching. Was Prince Proyas himself among them?

She watched wide-eyed, a sense of awe squeezing the breath from her lungs. She stood, she realized, at the very heart of the Holy War, fiery with passion, promise, and sacred purpose. These men were more than human, they were *Kahiht*, World Souls, locked in the great wheel of great events. The thought of striding into their midst beckoned hot tears to her eyes. How could she? Awkwardly concealing the back of her hand, instantly branded for what she was by their far-seeing eyes . . .

What's this? A whore? Here? You must be joking . . .

What had she been thinking? Even if Achamian had been here, she would only have shamed him.

Where are you?

"Everyone!" a tall, dark-haired man cried, causing Esmenet to jump. He sported a trim beard and a sumptuous robe with an intricate floral brocade. When the last voices trailed, he raised his bowl to the night sky.

"Tomorrow," he said, "we march!"

His eyes shining with fervour, he continued, speaking of trials endured and nations conquered, of heathen struck down and iniquities set aright. Then he spoke of Holy Shimeh, the sacred heart of all places. "We war for ground," he said, "but we do not war for dust or earth. We war for *the* ground. The ground of all our hopes, of all our convictions . . ." His voice cracked with passion.

"We war for *Shimeh*."

A moment of silence passed, then Xinemus intoned the High Temple Prayer:

Sweet God of Gods,
who walk among us,
innumerable are your holy names.
May your bread silence our daily hunger,
may your rains quicken our undying land,
may our submission be answered with dominion,
so we may prosper in your name.
Judge us not according to our trespasses
but according to our temptations,

and deliver unto others
what others have delivered unto us,
for your name is Power,
and your name is Glory,
for your name is Truth,
which endures and endures,
for ever and ever.

"Glory to the God," a dozen voices rumbled, resonating as though a temple congregation.

The sombre air lingered for a heartbeat, then the voices swelled once again. More toasts were raised. More steaming portions were cut from the spit. Esmenet watched, her breath tight, her blood slack in her veins. What she witnessed seemed impossibly beautiful. Bright. Bold. Regal. Even hallow. Part of her itched with the suspicion that if she called out and confronted them with the secret of her presence, they would all be whisked away, and she would be left standing before a cold firepit, mourning her impertinence.

This was the *world*, she realized. *Here.* Before her.

She watched the Prince of Atrithau speak into Xinemus's ear, saw Xinemus smile then gesture in her direction. They began walking toward her. She shrank into the blackness behind the small tent, huddled as though cold. She glimpsed their shadows, side by side, ghostlike across the packed earth and grasses, then the two men passed her, following a wavering lane of light toward the stagnant canal. She held her breath.

"There's always," the tall Prince remarked, "such peace in the darkness beyond a fire."

The two men halted at the edge of the canal, hiked their tunics, then fumbled with their loincloths. Soon two arcs were gurgling across the filmy surface.

"Hmm," Xinemus said. "The water's warm." Even terrified, Esmenet rolled her eyes, smiled.

"And deep," the Prince replied.

Xinemus cackled in a manner at once wicked and endearing. After securing himself, he slapped the other man on the back. "I'm going to use that," he said merrily, "the next time I piss back here with Akka. If I know him, he'll damn near fall in."

"You'll have a rope to throw him at least," the taller man replied.

More laughter, at once hale and warm. A friendship, Esmenet realized, had just been sealed.

She caught her breath as they retraced their path. The Prince of Atrithau, it seemed, stared directly at her.

But if he saw anything, he did not betray it. The two men rejoined the others by the fire.

Her heart pounding, her soul buzzing with recriminations, she crept around the far side of the pavilion to a vantage where she need not fear discovery by pissing men. She leaned up against the stump of some kind of tree, crooked her head against her shoulder, and closed her eyes, letting the voices about the nearby fire carry her away.

"You gave me a fright there, Scylvendi. I thought for sure . . ."

"Serwë, is it? Ah, I should've known the beauty of the name would . . ."

They seemed good people, Esmenet thought, the kind of people Akka would prize as friends. There was . . . *room* between these people, she decided. Room to fail. Room to hurt.

Alone in the darkness, she suddenly felt safe, as she had with Sarcellus. These were Achamian's friends, and though she did not exist for them, somehow they would keep her safe. A sense of drowsiness embalmed her. The voices lilted and rumbled, shining with honest good cheer. *Just a snooze,* she thought. Then she heard someone mention Akka's name.

". . . so Conphas *himself* came for Achamian? Conphas?"

"He was none too pleased. Smarmy bastard."

"But why would the Emperor want Achamian?"

"You actually sound worried about him."

"About who? The Emperor or Achamian?"

But this fragment was submerged by the tide of other voices. Esmenet felt herself drift.

She dreamed the stump she slept against was a whole tree but dead, stripped of leaves, twigs, bark, and branches, its trunk a phallic shaft ringed by winding limbs that hissed through the wind like switches. She dreamed that she could not awaken, that somehow the tree had rooted her to the suffocating earth.

Esmi . . .

She stirred. Felt something tickle her cheek.

"Esmi."

A warm voice. A familiar voice.

"Esmi, what are you doing?"

Her eyes fluttered open. For an instant, she was too horrified to scream.

Then his hand was over her mouth.

"Shhhhh," Sarcellus admonished. "This might be hard to explain," he added, nodding in the direction of Xinemus's campfire.

Or what was left of it. Only a few small licks of flame remained. With the exception of a lone figure curled across mats near the fire, everyone was gone. A pall had unfolded across the distances, as cool and as barren as the night sky.

Esmenet sucked air through her nose. Sarcellus removed his hand, then pulled her to her feet so he could draw her behind the pavilion. It was dark.

"You followed me?" she asked, pulling her forearm from his clasp. She was still too disoriented for anger.

"I awoke, and you were gone. I knew I'd find you here."

She swallowed. Her hands felt light, as though they were preparing of their own volition to shield her face. "I'm not going back with you, Sarcellus."

Something Esmenet could not decipher flashed in his eyes. Triumph? Then he shrugged. The ease of the gesture terrified her.

"That's good," he said absently. "I've had my fill of you, Esmi."

She stared at him. Tears traced hot lines across her cheeks. Why was she crying? She didn't love him . . . Did she?

But *he* had loved her. Of this she was certain . . . Wasn't she?

He nodded in the direction of the abandoned camp. "Go to him. I no longer care."

She felt desperation cramp the back of her throat. What could have happened? Perhaps Gotian had at last commanded him to turn her out. Knight-Commanders, Sarcellus had once told her, were largely forgiven indulgences such as she. But surely keeping a whore in the midst of a Holy War had caused tongues to wag. She had certainly endured enough lurid glares and crude laughs. His subordinates and peers alike knew what she was. And if she'd learned anything about the world of caste nobles, it was that rank and prestige could carry a man only so far.

That was it. Wasn't it?

She thought of the stranger in the Kamposea Agora, of the alleyway, the sweat . . .

What was I doing?

She thought of the cool kiss of silk against her skin, of roasted meat, steaming and peppered, served with velvet wine. She thought of that winter in Sumna four years ago, the one following the summer droughts, when she could not even afford flour halved with chalk. She had grown so skinny that no one would buy her . . . She had come close. Very close.

An inner whisper, small, snivelling, and infinitely reasonable: *Beg his forgiveness. Don't be a fool! Beg . . .*

Beg!

But she could only stare. Sarcellus seemed an apparition, something beyond any excuse, any appeal. Wholly man. When she said nothing, he snorted with impatience, then turned on his heel. She watched until the gloom swallowed his striding figure.

Sarcellus?

She had almost cried this aloud, but something cruel brought her up short.

You wanted this, a voice not quite her own grated.

To the east, the sky brightened beyond the far-away silhouette of the Andiamine Heights. The Emperor would soon be waking, she thought inanely. She studied the lone man lying next to the firepit. He did not move. Unconcerned, she wandered across the packed earth thinking of where she had seen the Scylvendi and where she had seen the Prince of Atrithau. She poured wine into a sticky bowl, sipped. She chewed on a discarded crust. She felt like a child who had awakened long before her parents, or a furtive scavenger nosing about in the absence of stomping men. She stood for a while above the sleeping form. It was Xinemus. She smiled, remembering his joke from earlier in the night, while he pissed with the Norsirai Prince. The coals tinkled and popped, their baleful orange sinking lower into the heap as dawn gathered grey on the horizon.

Where are you, Akka?

She began backing away, as though searching for something too large to be seen in a single look.

Footsteps startled her. She whirled . . .

And saw Achamian trudging toward her.

She couldn't see his face, but she knew it was him. How many times had she spotted his portly shape from her window in Sumna? Spotted and smiled.

As he neared, she glimpsed the five stripes of his beard, then the first contours of his face, cadaverous in the gloom. She stood before him, smiling, crying, her wrists held out.

It's me.

He looked through her, beyond her, and continued walking.

At first she simply stood, a pillar of salt. She had not realized how much time she'd spent both dreading and yearning for this moment. Endless days, it now seemed. How would he look? What would he say? Would he be proud of what she had discovered? Would he weep when she told him of Inrau? Would he rant as she told him of the stranger? Would he forgive her for straying? For hiding in Sarcellus's bed?

So many worries. So many hopes. And now?

What had happened?

He pretended not to see me. Acted as though . . . as though . . .

She trembled. Brought a hand to her mouth.

Then she ran, a shadow among shadows, loping through sodden air, hurtling across slumbering camps, tripping through guy ropes, falling . . .

Her chest heaving, she clambered to her knees. She scooped dust into her hands, began tearing at her hair. Sobs overcame her. Fury.

"Why, Akka? *Why?* I c-came to s-s-save you, to t-tell you . . ."

He hates you! You're nothing more than a dirty whore! A stain on his breeches!

"No! He loves me! H-he's th-the only one who's ever tr-truly loved me!"

No one loves you. No one.

"M-m-my d-daughter . . . Sh-she loved me!"

Would that she had hated! . . . Hated and lived!

"Shut up! Shut up!"

The tormentor became the tormented, and she curled into a ball, too anguished to think, to breathe, to scream. She rolled her face and mouth across the earth. A low, keening wail trembled across the night air . . .

Then she began coughing uncontrollably, convulsing in the dust. Spit.

For a long time she lay very still.

Tears dried. The burn became a sting encircled by an ache, as though her entire face had been bruised.

Akka . . .

She drifted through many thoughts, all of them curiously disconnected from the roaring in her ears. She remembered Pirasha, the old harlot she had befriended and lost years ago. Between the tyranny of many and the tyranny of one, Pirasha used to say, harlots chose the many. "That's why we're more," she would spit. "More than concubines, more than priestesses, more than wives, more even than some queens. We may be oppressed, Esmi, but remember, always remember, sweet girl, we're never *owned*." Her bleary eyes would grow sharp with a savagery that seemed too violent for her ancient frame. "We spit their seed back at them! We never, *never* bear its weight!"

Esmenet rolled onto her back, drew a forearm across her eyes. Tears still burned in their corners.

No one owns me. Not Sarcellus. Not Achamian.

As though rising from a stupor, she pushed herself from the ground. Stiff. Slow.

Oh, Esmi, you're getting old.

Not good for a whore.

She began walking.

CHAPTER NINETEEN

MOMEMN

. . . even though the skin-spies were exposed relatively early in the course of the Holy War, most believed the Cishaurim rather than the Consult to be responsible. This is the problem of all great revelations: their significance so often exceeds the frame of our comprehension. We understand only after, always after. Not simply when it is too late, but precisely because it is too late.

—DRUSAS ACHAMIAN, COMPENDIUM OF THE FIRST HOLY WAR

Late Spring, 4111 Year-of-the-Tusk, Momemn

The Scylvendi wracked her with his hunger, his countenance fierce and famished. Serwë felt his shudder as though through stone, then watched dully as he abandoned his appetite and rolled back into the tented darkness.

She turned away, toward the far side of the cavernous tent Proyas had given them. Wearing a simple grey smock, Kellhus sat cross-legged next to a candle, hunched over a great tome—also given to them by Proyas.

Why do you let him use me like this? I belong to you!

She ached to cry this aloud, but she could not. She could feel the Scylvendi's eyes upon her back, and if she turned, she was certain she would see them glow like a wolf's in torchlight.

Serwë had recovered quickly over the past two weeks. The incessant ringing in her ears had disappeared and the bruises had faded yellow-green. Deep breaths still pained her, and she could walk only with a limp, but these had become more an inconvenience than a debility.

And she still carried his baby . . . Kellhus's baby. That was the important thing.

Proyas's physician, a tattooed priest of Akkeägni, had marvelled over this fact, giving her a small prayer chime with which to sound thanks to the God. "To show your gratitude," he had said, "for the strength of your womb." But she had no need of chimes to be heard in the Outside, she knew. The Outside had entered the world, had taken her, Serwë, as his lover.

The day before she'd felt well enough to carry their laundry down to the river. She perched the woven basket upon her head, as she had when still owned by her father, and simply limped through camp until she found someone she could follow to the appropriate place along the river. Everywhere she walked, Men of the Tusk laid bold eyes upon her. Though she was accustomed to such looks, she found herself at once thrilled, angered, and frightened. So many warlike men! Some even dared call out to her, often in tongues she couldn't understand, and always in crude terms that drew braying laughter from their companions—"You think you limp now, eh, wench?" Those times she dared meet their eyes, she'd think, *I'm the vessel of another, one far mightier and far holier than you!* Most of them would be chastened by her fierce look, as though they could somehow sense the truth of her thought, but a few would glare until she looked away, their lust fanned rather than snuffed by her defiance—like the Scylvendi. None dared molest her, however. She was too beautiful, she realized, not to belong to someone of consequence. If only they knew!

The encampment's dimensions had astonished her from the very first, but only when she joined the masses congregated along the bouldered banks of the River Phayus did she truly understand the Holy War's immensity. Women and slaves, thousands of them, clotted the hazy distances, rinsing, scrubbing, adding to the endless staccato of wet cloth slapping against rocks. Pot-bellied wives waded into the brown river, scooping water to scrub at their armpits. Small groups of women and men laughed, gossiped, or sang simple hymns. Naked children darted through the confusion about her, crying, "No, you! *You!*"

I belong to this, she had thought.

And now, tomorrow, they were going to march into Fanim lands. Serwë, daughter of a tributary Nymbricani chieftain, would be part of a Holy War against the Kianene!

For Serwë, the Kianene had always been one among many mysterious, threatening names—not unlike "Scylvendi." As a concubine she'd overheard the Gaunum sons speak of them now and again, their voices thick with contempt but also hedged by admiration. They would discuss abortive embassies to the Padirajah in Nenciphon, diplomatic feints, trivial successes and troubling setbacks. They would complain of the Emperor's flawed "heathen policy." And the people and places they mentioned would all seem curiously unreal to her, as though a vicious and gritty extension of some child's fairy tale. Gossip with the slaves and other concubines—this was real. The fact that old Griasa had been caned the day before for spilling lemon sauce on the Patridomos's lap. That Eppaltros, the beautiful groom, had stolen into the dormitory and made love to Aälsa, only to be betrayed by someone unknown and put to death.

But that world was gone, snuffed out forever by Panteruth and his Munuäti. The unreal people and places had swept in cataracts through the narrow circle of her life, and now she walked with men who conferred with Princes, Emperors—even Gods. Soon, very soon, she would see the magnificent Grandees of Kian arrayed for battle, watch the fluttering banners of the Tusk storm the field. She could almost see Kellhus in the midst of the fracas, glorious and unconquerable, striking down the shadowy Padirajah.

Kellhus would be the violent hero of this unwritten scripture. She knew this. With inexplicable certainty, she knew this.

But now he looked so peaceful, bent by candlelight over an ancient text.

Her heart racing, she crawled next to him, gathering her blanket tight around her shoulders and against her breasts.

"What do you read?" she asked hoarsely. Then she began to weep, the memory of the Scylvendi still thick between her legs.

I'm too weak! Too weak to suffer him . . .

The gentle face looked up from the manuscript, somehow cold in the pale light.

"I'm sorry for interrupting," she hissed through tears, her face pinched by a child's anguish, by submission, awful and uncomprehending.

Where will I go?

But Kellhus said, "Don't run, Serwë."

He spoke to her in Nymbricani, the language of her father. This was part of the dark shelter they had built between them—the place where the wrathful eyes of the Scylvendi could not see. But at the sound of her native tongue, she was wracked by sobs.

"Often," he continued, touching her cheek and brushing her tears into her hair, "when the world denies us over and over, when it punishes us as it's punished you, Serwë, it becomes difficult to understand the meaning. All our pleas go unanswered. Our every trust is betrayed. Our hopes are all crushed. It seems we mean nothing to the world. And when we think we mean nothing, we begin to think we *are* nothing."

A soft, crooning wail escaped her. She wanted to fall forward, to curl herself tighter and tighter until nothing remained . . .

But I don't see it.

"The absence of understanding," Kellhus replied, "is not the same as absence. You *mean* something, Serwë. You *are* something. This whole world is steeped in meaning. Everything, even your suffering, has sacred meaning. Even your suffering has a crucial role to play."

She touched slack fingers to her neck. Her face crumpled.

I mean something?

"More than you can imagine," he whispered.

She collapsed into his chest, and he held her as she soundlessly screamed. Then she howled her anguish, bawled as she had as a child, her body shuddering, her hands crushed between them. He rocked her in his arms. Rolled his cheek against her scalp.

After a time, he pressed her back, and she lowered her face for shame. So weak! So pathetic!

With soft strokes he dabbed the tears from her eyes, watched her for a long while. She didn't entirely calm until she saw the tears streaming from his own eyes.

He cries for me . . . for me . . .

"You belong to him," he said at last. "You are his prize."

"No," she croaked defiantly. "My body's his prize. My *heart* belongs to you."

How had this happened? How had she been pried in two? She had endured much. Why this agony now? Now that she loved? But for a moment she almost felt whole, speaking their secret language, saying tender things . . .

I mean something.

His tears slowed in his trim beard, gathered and then plummeted onto the open book—stained the ancient ink.

"Your *book!*" she gasped, finding relief in a sense of guilt for an object of his concern. She leaned from her blanket, naked and ivory in the light, and ran her fingers across the open pages. "Is it ruined?"

"Many others have wept over this text," Kellhus replied softly.

The distance between their faces was close, humid—suddenly tense.

She grasped his right hand, guided it to her perfect breasts.

"Kellhus," she whispered tremulously, "I would have you come in . . . into me."

And at last, he relented.

Gasping beneath him, she looked into the dark corner where the Scylvendi lay, knowing that he could see the rapture on her face . . . on *their* faces.

And she cried out as she climaxed—a cry of hatred.

<hr />

Cnaiür lay still, his breath hissing between clenched teeth. The image of her perfect face, turning to him in anguished rapture, crowded the light wavering across the canvas slopes above.

Serwë giggled girlishly, and Kellhus murmured several things to her in that accursed tongue of hers. Linen and wool whisked over smooth skin, then the candle was snuffed. Pitch black. They pressed through the flap and the scent of fresh air wound through the pavilion's interior.

"*Jiruschi dan klepet sa gesauba dana,*" she said, her voice thinned by open space and dulled by canvas.

The rasp of charcoal as someone threw wood onto the fire.

"*Ejiruschina? Baussa kalwë,*" Kellhus replied.

Serwë laughed some more, but in a husky, oddly mature way he'd never heard before.

Something more the bitch hides from me . . .

He groped in the darkness; his fingertips found the leather of his pommel. It was both cool and warm, like human skin bare to the chill of night.

He lay still for several more moments, listening to the hushed counterpoint of their voices through the pop and rush of building flames. He could see the firelight now, a faint orange smear through the black canvas. A lithe shadow passed across it. Serwë.

He raised the broadsword. It rasped from its sheath. A dull orange glimmer.

Dressed only in his loincloth, he rolled from his blankets and padded across the mats to the pavilion entrance. He breathed heavily.

Images from the previous afternoon flitted through his thoughts: the Dûnyain and his bottomless scrutiny of the Inrithi nobles.

The thought of leading the Men of the Tusk into battle stirred something within him—pride, perhaps—but he was under no illusion as to his true station. He was a heathen to these men, even to Nersei Proyas. And as time passed, that fact would come home to them. He would be no general. An adviser on the cunning ways of the Kianene, perhaps, but nothing more.

Holy War. The thought still yanked a snort of breath from his nose. As though all war were not holy.

But the question, he now knew, was not what he would be but what the *Dûnyain* would be. What terror had he delivered to these outland princes?

What will he make of the Holy War?

Would he make it his whore? Like Serwë?

But this was the plan. "Thirty years," Kellhus had said shortly after their arrival. "Moënghus has dwelt among these men for thirty years. He will have great power. More than either of us could hope to overcome. I need more than sorcery, Cnaiür. I need a nation. A nation." Somehow they would exploit circumstance, knot the harness about the Holy War, and use it to destroy Anasûrimbor Moënghus. How could he fear for these Inrithi, repent bringing the Dûnyain to them, when this was their plan?

But was this the plan? Or was it simply another Dûnyain lie, another way to pacify, to gull, to enslave?

What if Kellhus was not an assassin sent to murder his father, as he claimed, but a spy sent to do his father's bidding? Was it simply a coincidence that Kellhus travelled to Shimeh just as the Holy War embarked on a campaign to conquer it?

Cnaiür was no fool. If Moënghus was Cishaurim, he would fear the Holy War, and he would seek ways to destroy it. Could this be why he had summoned his son? Kellhus's obscure origins would allow him to infiltrate it, as he already had, while his breeding or training or witchery or whatever it was would allow him to seize it, capsize it, perhaps even turn it against its maker. Against Maithanet.

But if Kellhus served rather than hunted his father, then why had he spared him in the mountains? Cnaiür could still feel the impossible iron hand about his throat, the pitching depths beneath his feet.

"But I spoke true, Cnaiür. I do need you."

Could he have known, even then, of Proyas's contest with the Emperor? Or did it just so happen that the Inrithi needed a Scylvendi?

Unlikely, to say the least. But then how could Kellhus have known?

Cnaiür swallowed, tasted Serwë.

Could it be that Moënghus *still* communicated with him?

The thought sucked all air from his lungs. He saw Xunnurit, blinded, chained beneath the Emperor's heel . . .

Am I the same?

Still speaking that accursed tongue, Kellhus teased Serwë some more. Cnaiür could tell because of Serwë's laugh, a sound like water rushing among the Dûnyain's smooth stone words.

In the blackness Cnaiür extended his broadsword, pressed its tip through the flap, which he drew aside the width of a palm. He watched breathlessly.

Their faces firelight orange, their backs in shadow, the two of them reclined side by side on the barked olive trunk they used for a seat. Like lovers. Cnaiür studied their reflections across the smeared polish of his sword.

By the Dead-God, she was beautiful. So like—

The Dûnyain turned and looked at him, his eyes shining. He blinked.

Cnaiür felt his lips curl involuntarily, a pounding rush in his chest, throat, and ears.

She's my prize! he cried voicelessly.

Kellhus looked to the fire. He had heard. Somehow.

Cnaiür let the flap fall shut, pinch golden light into blackness. Desolate blackness.

My prize . . .

Achamian would never remember what he'd thought or the route he'd taken on his long walk from the Imperial Precincts to the encamped Holy War. He suddenly found himself sitting in the dust amid the litter of celebration. He saw his tent, small and alone, mottled and weathered by many seasons, many journeys, and cast in the silent shadow of Xinemus's pavilion. The Holy War swept beyond it, a great canvas city, matting the distances with the confusion of flaps, guy ropes, pennants, and awnings.

He saw Xinemus slumbering next to the gutted fire, his thick frame curled against the chill. The Marshal had been concerned by the Emperor's peremptory summons, he supposed, and had waited all night by the fire—waited for Achamian to come home.

Home.

Tears brimmed at that thought. He'd never had a home, a place that he could call "mine." There was no refuge, no sanctuary, for a man such as he. Only friends, scattered here and there, who for some unaccountable reason loved him and worried about him.

He left Xinemus to his slumber—today would be a demanding day. The great encampment of the Holy War would disassemble itself from within, the tents felled and rolled tight about poles, the baggage trains drawn up and heaped with gear and supplies, then it would begin the arduous yet exultant march south, toward the land of the heathen, toward desperation and bloodshed—and perhaps even truth.

In the gloom of his tent, he once again withdrew his parchment map, ignoring the tears that tapped against the sheet. He stared at

THE CONSULT

for some time, as though struggling to remember what the name meant, what it portended. Then, wetting his quill, he drew an unsteady diagonal line from it to

THE EMPEROR

Connected at last. For so long it had simply floated in its corner, more the wreckage of ink than a name, touching nothing, meaning nothing, like the threats muttered by a coward after his tormentor had gone. No longer. The bitter apparition had bared its knuckled flesh, and the horror of what was and what might be had become the horror of *now*.

This horror. His horror.

Why? Why would Fate inflict this revelation upon him? Was she a fool? Didn't she know how weak, how hollow, he'd become?

Why me?

A selfish question. Perhaps the most selfish of questions. All burdens, even those as demented as the Apocalypse, must fall upon the shoulders of someone. Why *not* him?

Because I'm a broken man. Because I long for a love I cannot have. Because . . .

But that road was far too easy. To be frail, to be afflicted with unrequited longing, was simply what it meant to be man. When had he acquired this penchant to wallow in self-pity? Where in life's slow accumulation had he come to see himself as the world's victim? How had he become such a fool?

After three hundred years, he, *Drusas Achamian*, had rediscovered the Consult. After two thousand years, he, *Drusas Achamian*, had witnessed the return of an Anasûrimbor. Anagkë, the Whore of Fate, had chosen *him* for these burdens! It wasn't his place to ask why. Nor could such questions relieve him of his burden.

He had to *act*, choose his moment and overcome—*overwhelm*. He was Drusas Achamian! His song could char legions, tear the earth asunder, pull dragons shrieking from the sky.

But even as he returned his scrutiny to the parchment, a great hollow opened in the heart of his momentary resolution, like the stillness that chased ripples across the surface of a pool, drawing them thinner and thinner. And in the wake of this hollow, voices from his dreams, nagging half-remembered fears, the fog of inarticulate regret . . .

He had rediscovered the Consult, but he knew nothing of their plans, nor of any way to discover them again. He didn't even know how they'd been discovered by the Emperor in the first place. They concealed themselves in a way that could not be *seen*. The single, tremulous line joining "The Consult" to "The Emperor" was devoid of any significance, save that they were somehow connected. And if the Consult had infiltrated the Imperial Court with this . . . this *skin-spy*, he could only assume that they had likewise infiltrated all the Great Factions, the entire Three Seas—perhaps even the Mandate itself.

A face opening like palsied fingers from a skinless palm. How *many* were there?

Suddenly the name, "The Consult," which had been so isolated from the others, seemed spliced to them in a terrifying intimacy. The Consult hadn't just infiltrated factions, Achamian realized, they had infiltrated *individuals*, to the point of becoming them. How does one war against such a foe without warring against what they've become? Without warring against all the Great Factions? For all Achamian knew, the Consult *already ruled* the Three Seas and merely tolerated the Mandate as an impotent foe, a laughingstock, in order to further fortify the bulwark of ignorance that shielded them.

How long have they been laughing? How far has their corruption gone?

Could it have reached as far as the Shriah? Could the Holy War, at its pith, be an artifact of the Consult?

A cascade of heart-pounding implications flushed through him, beading his skin with the cold sweat of dread. Disconnected events found themselves woven into a narrative far darker than ignorance, the way disjoint ruins might be bound by the intuition of some lost bastion or temple. Geshrunni's missing face. Did the Consult murder him? Take his face to consummate some obscene rite of substitution, only to be thwarted when the Scarlet Spires discovered his body shortly after? And if the Consult knew of Geshrunni, would that not also mean they knew of the secret war between the Scarlet Spires and the Cishaurim? And wouldn't that explain how Maithanet also knew of the war? Explain Inrau's death? If the Shriah of the Thousand Temples was a Consult spy . . . If the prophecy of the Anasûrimbor—

He looked to the parchment once again, to

ANASÛRIMBOR KELLHUS

still disconnected, though in troubling proximity to "The Consult." He raised his quill, about to scratch a line between the two names, but hesitated. He set the quill down.

The man, Kellhus, who would be his student and his friend, was so . . . unlike other men.

The Anasûrimbor's return *was* a harbinger of the Second Apocalypse—the truth of this ached in Achamian's bones. And the Holy War would simply be the first great shedding of blood.

His head swimming, Achamian pulled a stunned hand over his face, through his hair. Images of his former life—teaching Proyas algebra by scratching figures into the earth of a garden path, reading Ajencis in the fretted morning sunlight of Zin's portico—brawled through his thoughts, hopelessly innocent, poignantly wan and naive and utterly wrecked.

The Second Apocalypse is here. It has already begun . . .

And he stood in the very heart of the tempest. The Holy War.

Deranged shadows frolicked and cavorted along the canvas walls of his tent, and Achamian knew with appalling certainty that they plumbed the horizon, that some measureless frame had stolen unawares upon the world and fixed its dreadful course.

Another Apocalypse . . . And it's happening.

But this was mad! It couldn't be!

It is.

Breathe in. Now exhale—slowly. You're a match for this, Akka.
You must be a match for this!
He swallowed.
Ask yourself, What is the question?
Why would the Consult want this Holy War? Why would they want
to destroy the Fanim? Does it have something to do with the Cishaurim?

But in the relief of posing this question, a second stole into his
thoughts, one whose terminus was too painful for him to deny. A
thought like a winter knife.

They murdered Geshrunni immediately after I left Carythusal.

He thought of the man in the Kamposea Agora, the one who
he'd thought had been following him. The one who had seemed to
change his face.

Does that mean they're following me?

Had he *led them* to Inrau?

Achamian paused, breathless in the diffuse light, the parchment
numb and tingling in his left hand.

Had he also led them . . .

He brought two fingers to his mouth, drew them slowly to and
fro along his lower lip.

"*Esmi . . .*" he whispered.

Lashed together, the pleasure galleys swelled gently on the
Meneanor outside of Momemn's fortified harbour. It was a tradition, centuries old, to gather thus at the Feast of Kussapokari, which
marked the summer solstice. Most of those on the galleys were of
the two high castes: the kjineta of the Houses of the Congregate
and the priestly nahat. Men from House Gaunum, House Daskas,
House Ligesseras, and many others gauged one another and tailored
their gossip according to the murky webs of loyalty and enmity that
bound the Houses together. Even within the castes there were a
thousand increments of rank and reputation. The official criteria
for such rank were clear, more or less—nearness to the Emperor,

which was easily measured by the hierarchy of stations within his labyrinthine ministries, or, at the opposite pole, affiliation with House Biaxi, the traditional rival of House Ikurei. But the Houses themselves had long histories, and rank between men was inextricably bound to history. So concubines and children would be told, "That man, Trimus Charcharius, defer to him, child. His ancestors were once Emperors," even though House Trimus was out of favour with the Emperor and had been despised by the Biaxi since time immemorial. Add to this the measures of wealth, of learning, and of wit, and the jnanic codes that braced all their intercourse became as indecipherable from the outside as they were bewildering from within—a shrouded bog that quickly devoured the stupid.

But this welter of hidden concerns and instant calculation did not constrain them. It was simply the way, as natural as the cycle of constellations. The fluid things of life were no less necessary for being fluid. So the revellers laughed and talked as though careless, leaning against polished rails, basking in the perfection of the late-afternoon sun, shivering when they fell into shadows. Bowls rang. Wine was poured and spilled, making sticky-ringed fingers even stickier. The first swallow was spat into the sea—propitiation to Momas, the God who provided the ground of these proceedings. The conversations were a wash of humour and gravity, like a promenade of voices, each vying for attention, each hinged on the opportunity to impress, to inform, to entertain. The concubines, dressed in their silk *culati*, had been driven away by the harsh talk of the men, as was proper, and wallowed in those subjects they found endlessly amusing: fashion, jealous wives, and wilful slaves. The men, carefully holding their Ainoni sleeves so they fell into the sun, spoke of serious things, and regarded with amused disdain anything that fell outside the realm of war, prices, and politics. Those few breaches of jnan risked were tolerated, even encouraged, depending on who made them. It was part of jnan to know precisely when to transgress it. The men laughed hard at the sounds of obligatory shock that passed through the women within earshot.

Around them, the waters of the bay were hard blue and flat. Looking like toys in the distance, Galeoth grain ships, immense Cironji carracks, and others moored outside the mouth of the River Phayus. The after-storm sky felt deep with clarity. Toward land, the shallow hills surrounding Momemn were brown, and the city itself looked old, like the ashes of a fire. Through the perpetual haze of smoke, the great monuments of the city could be discerned, like darker shadows hunching over the grey smudge of tenements and chaotic alleyways. As always, the Tower of Ziek oppressed the northeast. And in the city's heart, the Great Domes of Xothei rose above the confused temple-complex of Cmiral. The keen-sighted among the Biaxi faction swore that in the midst of the temples, they could see the Emperor's Cock, as Xerius's latest monument had come to be called. Controversy ensued. There were some, the more religious, who balked at this bawdy joke. But they were swayed by more argument and more wine. They were forced to concede that the obelisk, after all, possessed a wrinkled "head." One of the drunkards among them even drew his knife—the first real breach of etiquette—when it was recalled that he'd kissed the obelisk the previous week.

It was outside the walls of Momemn where things had changed. The surrounding fields were dust, trampled grey by countless feet and textured by sun-baked ruts. The land had broken beneath the weight of the Holy War. The groves were dead. Cesspits festered. Flies.

The Holy War had marched, and the men of the Houses discussed it endlessly, recounted the Emperor's humiliation—no, the *Empire's* humiliation—at the hands of Proyas and his mercenary Scylvendi. A Scylvendi! Would the fiends now hound them on the field of politics as well? The Great Names had called the Emperor's bluff, and though Ikurei Xerius had threatened not to march with the Holy War, he had in the end conceded defeat and sent Conphas with them. The attempt to bend the Holy War to Nansur interests had been a daring gambit, they all agreed, but so long as the brilliant Conphas marched with them, the Emperor might still succeed. *Conphas*. A man like a God. A true child of Kyraneas, or even Cenei—of the old blood. How could he fail to make the Holy War his own? "Think of it!" they cried. "The Old Empire restored!" And they raised yet another toast to their ancient nation.

Most had spent the pestilence months of spring and summer at their provincial estates and had seen little of the Men of the Tusk. Some had grown wealthy supplying the Holy War, and even more had precious sons under Conphas. They had few practical reasons to celebrate the march of the Holy War south. But perhaps their considerations were deeper. When the locusts descended, they grew rich emptying their granaries, but they still burned offerings when the famines ended. The Gods detested nothing so much as arrogance. The world was painted glass—shadows of ancient, unimaginable power shifted beneath.

Somewhere distant, the Holy War travelled the roads between ancient capitals, a great migration of sturdy Men and sun-glittering arms. Even now, some claimed they could hear its horns faint through laughing voices and the stationary sea, the way the peal of trumpets might linger in ringing ears. Others paused and listened, and though they heard nothing, they shivered and rationed their words with care. If glories witnessed moved men to awe, glories asserted but not seen moved them to piety.

And judgement.

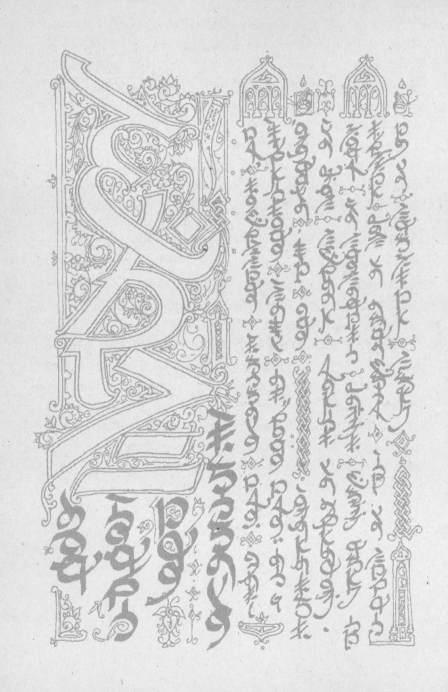

Appendices

Character and Faction Glossary

Anasûrimbor Kellhus (*Ah-nas-soor-imb-or Kell-huss*), a thirty-three-year-old Dûnyain monk

Drusas Achamian (*Droo-sass Ah-kay-me-on*), a forty-seven-year-old Mandate sorcerer

Cnaiür (*Nay-yur*), a forty-four-year-old Scylvendi barbarian, Chieftain of the Utemot

Esmenet (*Ez-men-net*), a thirty-one-year-old Sumni prostitute

Serwë (*Sair-way*), a nineteen-year-old Nymbricani concubine

Anasûrimbor Moënghus (*Ah-nas-soor-imb-or Moe-eng-huss*), Kellhus's father

Skiötha (*Skee-oath-ah*), Cnaiür's deceased father

The Dûnyain

A hidden monastic sect whose members have repudiated history and animal appetite in the hope of finding absolute enlightenment through the control of all desire and circumstance. For two thousand years they have bred their members for both motor reflexes and intellectual acuity.

The Consult

A cabal of magi and generals that survived the death of the No-God in 2155 and has laboured ever since to bring about his return in the so-called Second Apocalypse. Very few in the Three Seas believe the Consult still exists.

The Schools

A collective name given to the various academies of sorcerers. The first Schools, both in the Ancient North and in the Three Seas, arose as a response to the Tusk's condemnation of sorcery. The Schools are among the oldest institutions in the Three Seas, and they survive, by and large, because of the terror they inspire and their detachment from the secular and religious powers of the Three Seas.

The Mandate—Gnostic School founded by Seswatha in 2156 to continue the war against the Consult and to protect the Three Seas from the return of the No-God, Mog-Pharau.

    Nautzera, senior member of the Quorum

    Simas, member of the Quorum and Achamian's former teacher

    Seswatha, survivor of the Old Wars and ancient founder of the Mandate

The Scarlet Spires—Anagogic School that is the most powerful in the Three Seas and has been de facto ruler of High Ainon since 3818.

    Eleäzaras, Grandmaster of the Scarlet Spires

    Iyokus, Eleäzaras's Master of Spies

    Geshrunni, slave-soldier and momentary Mandate spy

The Imperial Saik—Anagogic School indentured to the Emperor of Nansur.

    Cememketri, Grandmaster of the Imperial Saik

The Mysunsai—Self-proclaimed Mercenary School that sells its sorcerous services across the Three Seas.

    Skalateas, mercenary sorcerer

The Inrithi Factions

Synthesizing monotheistic and polytheistic elements, Inrithism, the dominant faith of the Three Seas, is founded on the revelations of Inri Sejenus (c. 2159–2202), the Latter Prophet. The central tenets of Inrithism deal with the immanence of the God in historical events, the unity of the individual deities of the Cults as Aspects of the God as revealed by the Latter Prophet, and the infallibility of the Tusk as scripture.

The Thousand Temples—An institution that provides the ecclesiastical framework of Inrithism. Though based in Sumna, the Thousand Temples is omnipresent throughout the Northwestern and Eastern Three Seas.

    Maithanet, Shriah of the Thousand Temples

    Paro Inrau, Shrial Priest and former student of Achamian

The Shrial Knights—A monastic military order under the direct command of the Shriah, created by Ekyannus III, "the Golden," in 2511.

> **Incheiri Gotian,** Grandmaster of the Shrial Knights
> **Cutias Sarcellus,** First Knight-Commander of the Shrial Knights

The Conriyans—Conriya is a Ketyai nation of the Eastern Three Seas. Founded after the collapse of the Eastern Ceneian Empire in 3372, it is based around Aöknyssus, the ancient capital of Shir.

> **Nersei Proyas,** Prince of Conriya and former student of Achamian
> **Krijates Xinemus,** Achamian's friend and Marshal of Attrempus
> **Nersei Calmemunis,** leader of the Vulgar Holy War

The Nansur—The Nansur Empire is a Ketyai nation of the Western Three Seas and the self-proclaimed inheritor of the Ceneian Empire. At the height of its power, the Nansur Empire extended from Galeoth to Nilnamesh, but it has been much reduced by centuries of warfare against the Fanim of Kian.

> **Ikurei Xerius III,** Emperor of Nansur
> **Ikurei Conphas,** Exalt-General of Nansur and nephew to the Emperor
> **Ikurei Istriya,** Empress of Nansur and mother of the Emperor
> **Martemus,** General and Aide-de-Camp to Conphas
> **Skeaös,** the Emperor's Prime Counsel

The Galeoth—Galeoth is a Norsirai nation of the Three Seas, the so-called Middle-North, founded around 3683 by the descendants of refugees from the Old Wars.

> **Coithus Saubon,** Prince of Galeoth and leader of the Galeoth contingent
> **Kussalt,** Saubon's groom
> **Coithus Athjeäri,** Saubon's nephew

The Tydonni—Ce Tydonn is a Norsirai nation of the Eastern Three Seas. It was founded after the collapse of the Ketyai nation of Cengemis in 3742.

> **Hoga Gothyelk,** the Earl of Agansanor and leader of the Tydonni contingent

The Ainoni—High Ainon is the pre-eminent Ketyai nation of the Eastern Three Seas. It was founded after the collapse of the Eastern

Ceneian Empire in 3372 and has been ruled by the Scarlet Spires since the end of the Scholastic Wars in 3818.

Chepheramunni, King-Regent of High Ainon and leader of the Ainoni contingent

The Thunyeri—Thunyerus is a Norsirai nation of the Three Seas. It was founded through the federation of the Thunyeri tribes around 3987, and it only recently converted to Inrithism.

Skaiyelt, Prince of Thunyerus and leader of the Thunyeri contingent
Yalgrota, Skaiyelt's giant bondsman

The Fanim Factions

Strictly monotheistic, Fanimry is an upstart faith founded on the revelations of the Prophet Fane (3669–3742) and restricted to the Southwestern Three Seas. The central tenets of Fanimry deal with the singularity and transcendence of the God, the falseness of the Gods (who are considered demons by the Fanim), the repudiation of the Tusk as unholy, and the prohibition of all representations of the God.

The Kianene—Kian is the most powerful Ketyai nation of the Three Seas. Extending from the southern frontier of the Nansur Empire to Nilnamesh, it was founded in the wake of the White Jihad, the holy war waged by the first Fanim against the Nansur Empire from 3743 to 3771.

Kascamandri, Padirajah of Kian
Skauras, Sapatishah-Governor of Shigek

The Cishaurim—Priest-sorcerers of the Fanim, based in Shimeh. Little is known about the metaphysics of Cishaurim sorcery, or the Psûkhe, as the Cishaurim refer to it, beyond the fact that it cannot be perceived by the Few, and that it is in many ways as formidable as the Anagogic sorcery of the Schools.

Seökti, Heresiarch of the Cishaurim
Mallahet, powerful member of the Cishaurim

The Major Languages and Dialects of Eärwa

MEN

Until the Breaking of the Gates and the migration of the Four Nations from Eänna, the Men of Eärwa, called the Emwama in *The Chronicle of the Tusk*, were enslaved by the Nonmen and spoke debased versions of their masters' tongues. No trace of these languages remain. Nor does any trace of their original, pre-bondage language remain. The great Nonman history, the *Isûphiryas*, or the "Great Pit of Years," suggests the Emwama originally spoke the same tongue as their kin across the Great Kayarsus. This has led many to believe that Thoti-Eännorean is indeed the primeval language of all men.

THOTI-EÄNNOREAN—Mother tongue of all Men, and the language of *The Chronicle of the Tusk*

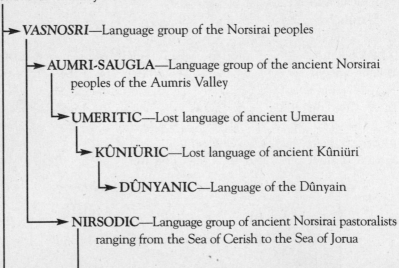

➤ **VASNOSRI**—Language group of the Norsirai peoples

➤ **AUMRI-SAUGLA**—Language group of the ancient Norsirai peoples of the Aumris Valley

➤ **UMERITIC**—Lost language of ancient Umerau

➤ **KÛNIÜRIC**—Lost language of ancient Kûniüri

➤ **DÛNYANIC**—Language of the Dûnyain

➤ **NIRSODIC**—Language group of ancient Norsirai pastoralists ranging from the Sea of Cerish to the Sea of Jorua

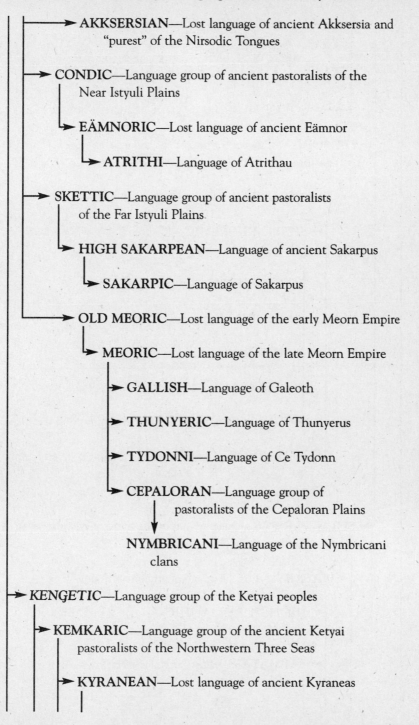

AKKSERSIAN—Lost language of ancient Akksersia and "purest" of the Nirsodic Tongues

CONDIC—Language group of ancient pastoralists of the Near Istyuli Plains

EÄMNORIC—Lost language of ancient Eämnor

ATRITHI—Language of Atrithau

SKETTIC—Language group of ancient pastoralists of the Far Istyuli Plains

HIGH SAKARPEAN—Language of ancient Sakarpus

SAKARPIC—Language of Sakarpus

OLD MEORIC—Lost language of the early Meorn Empire

MEORIC—Lost language of the late Meorn Empire

GALLISH—Language of Galeoth

THUNYERIC—Language of Thunyerus

TYDONNI—Language of Ce Tydonn

CEPALORAN—Language group of pastoralists of the Cepaloran Plains

NYMBRICANI—Language of the Nymbricani clans

KENGETIC—Language group of the Ketyai peoples

KEMKARIC—Language group of the ancient Ketyai pastoralists of the Northwestern Three Seas

KYRANEAN—Lost language of ancient Kyraneas

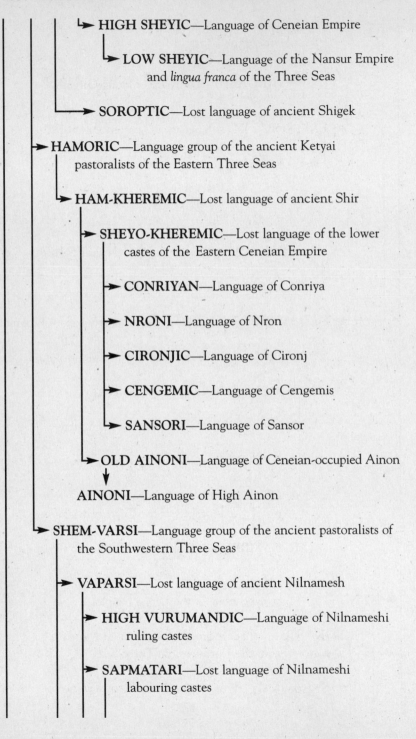

HIGH SHEYIC—Language of Ceneian Empire

LOW SHEYIC—Language of the Nansur Empire and *lingua franca* of the Three Seas

SOROPTIC—Lost language of ancient Shigek

HAMORIC—Language group of the ancient Ketyai pastoralists of the Eastern Three Seas

HAM-KHEREMIC—Lost language of ancient Shir

SHEYO-KHEREMIC—Lost language of the lower castes of the Eastern Ceneian Empire

CONRIYAN—Language of Conriya

NRONI—Language of Nron

CIRONJIC—Language of Cironj

CENGEMIC—Language of Cengemis

SANSORI—Language of Sansor

OLD AINONI—Language of Ceneian-occupied Ainon

AINONI—Language of High Ainon

SHEM-VARSI—Language group of the ancient pastoralists of the Southwestern Three Seas

VAPARSI—Lost language of ancient Nilnamesh

HIGH VURUMANDIC—Language of Nilnameshi ruling castes

SAPMATARI—Lost language of Nilnameshi labouring castes

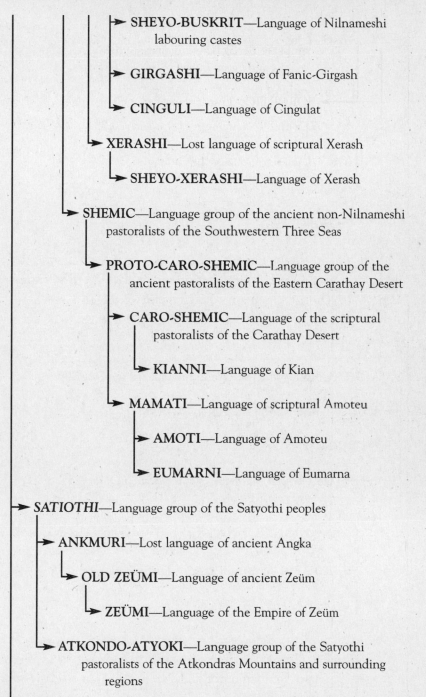

SHEYO-BUSKRIT—Language of Nilnameshi labouring castes

GIRGASHI—Language of Fanic-Girgash

CINGULI—Language of Cingulat

XERASHI—Lost language of scriptural Xerash

SHEYO-XERASHI—Language of Xerash

SHEMIC—Language group of the ancient non-Nilnameshi pastoralists of the Southwestern Three Seas

PROTO-CARO-SHEMIC—Language group of the ancient pastoralists of the Eastern Carathay Desert

CARO-SHEMIC—Language of the scriptural pastoralists of the Carathay Desert

KIANNI—Language of Kian

MAMATI—Language of scriptural Amoteu

AMOTI—Language of Amoteu

EUMARNI—Language of Eumarna

SATIOTHI—Language group of the Satyothi peoples

ANKMURI—Lost language of ancient Angka

OLD ZEÜMI—Language of ancient Zeüm

ZEÜMI—Language of the Empire of Zeüm

ATKONDO-ATYOKI—Language group of the Satyothi pastoralists of the Atkondras Mountains and surrounding regions

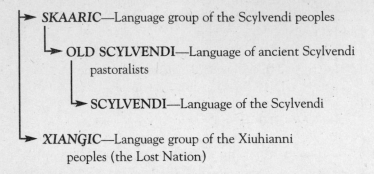

SKAARIC—Language group of the Scylvendi peoples

OLD SCYLVENDI—Language of ancient Scylvendi pastoralists

SCYLVENDI—Language of the Scylvendi

XIANGIC—Language group of the Xiuhianni peoples (the Lost Nation)

NONMEN (CÛNUROI)

Without doubt, the Nonmen, or Cûnuroi, tongues are among the oldest in Eärwa. Some Aujic inscriptions predate the first extant example of Thoti-Eännorean, *The Chronicle of the Tusk*, by more than five thousand years. Auja-Gilcûnni, which has yet to be deciphered, is far older still.

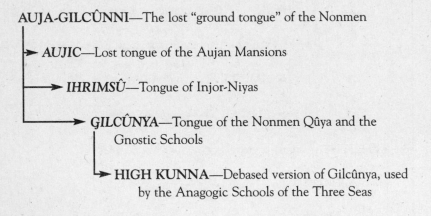

AUJA-GILCÛNNI—The lost "ground tongue" of the Nonmen

AUJIC—Lost tongue of the Aujan Mansions

IHRIMSÛ—Tongue of Injor-Niyas

GILCÛNYA—Tongue of the Nonmen Qûya and the Gnostic Schools

HIGH KUNNA—Debased version of Gilcûnya, used by the Anagogic Schools of the Three Seas

SRANC

In the *Isûphiryas*, the Sranc are first referred to as the Anyasiri, or the "Tongueless Howlers." Through the first books of the *Cûno-Inchoroi Wars*, the Nonmen chroniclers seem reluctant to attribute the power of speech to the Sranc. By the time the first Nonmen scholars studied and recorded their speech, it had fractured into innumerable dialects.

AGHURZOI—Original "Cut Tongue" language of the Sranc

INCHOROI

The Inchoroi tongue, which the Nonmen call Cincûl'hisa, or the "Gasp of Many Reeds," has defeated all attempts to decipher it. According to the *Isûphiryas*, communication between the Cûnuroi and the Inchoroi was impossible until the latter "birthed mouths" and began speaking Cûnuroi tongues.

CINCÛLIC—Undeciphered tongue of the Inchoroi

EÄRWA

4109 Year-of-the-Tusk

THE GREAT OCEAN

YIMALETI MOUNTAINS

Golgotterath

AGONGOREA

RIVER SURSA

Dagliash (A

SEA OF NELEOST

Ishterebinth

Ishuäl

INJOR-NIYAS

Trysë

(KUNIÜRI)

SOBEL

Sauglish

DEMUA MOUNTAINS

Atrithau

IST

(EÄMNOR)

RIVER AUMRIS

Sakar

SUSKARA

UTEMOT

SEA OF JORUA

JIÜNATI STEPPE

THETHA

Mehts

ZEÜM

Domyot

TKONDRAS MOUNTAINS

RIVER SEMPIS

As

CARATHAY DESERT

SHIGEK

Iothia

KIAN

EUMARN

Nenciphon

GIRGASH

Ajowai

Auvangshei

HINAYATI MOUNTAINS

SEA OF

NILNAMESH

Invishi

THE GREAT OCEAN

CINGULAT

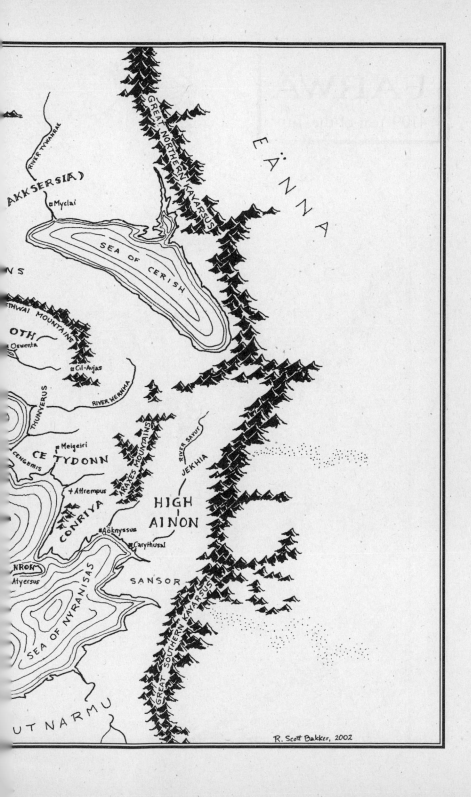

R. Scott Bakker, 2002

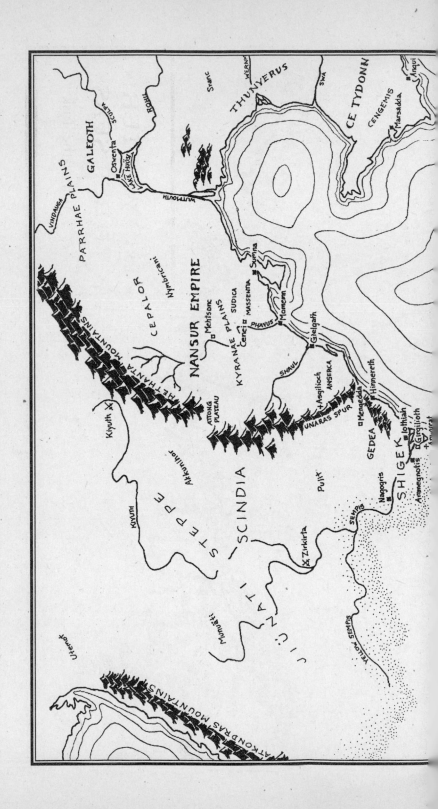